CHERISHED HEARTS

JOSIE RIVIERA

INTRODUCTION

To keep up on newly released ebooks, paperbacks, Large Print Paperbacks, audiobooks, as well as exclusive sales, sign up for Josie's Newsletter today.

As a thank you, I'll send you a Free PDF … The Beauty Of …

Josie's Newsletter

Did you know that according to a Yale University study, people who read books live longer?

"It's always delightful to read a novella by Josie Riviera! Sweet storylines, engaging characters, and enough romance to satisfy any romantic soul."- Amazon Reviewer (*A Love Song To Cherish*)

"Josie Riviera has written this book with the sensitivity of the soul of a genuine musician who also has a deep understanding of God's love and His power of restoration in every area of life. She carefully crafts the personalities of her characters so that each one is unique, and the reader can easily identify with one or all of them. Her attention to detail is remarkable as she allows you to see people and places and to become a citizen of Cherish. You will want to stay there! Thanks Josie Riviera for enriching the Christmas season with this inspiring story." - Amazon Reviewer (*A Christmas To Cherish*)

"Josie Riviera can write the really emotional stories sometimes. This is one that is that way throughout it all and especially a most beautifully written ending. Get your tissues out as you will need them. This is such a beautifully written story of a broken heart that is so hard to mend. It's a story of the one person who is willing to make that stand to not hurt the one he loves. He teaches her to love herself as she is and how to let someone into her heart that won't leave.

The small town of Cherish, South Carolina sounds like the perfect small town I want to live in. Our hero found that in himself as well. He travels and doesn't have a real home to come back to. Now here in Cherish he has found his home and it's much more that this quaint town. I highly recommend this book not just to read on Valentine's Day like I did, but anytime you need to read about a worthy romance full of everything you want in one. There are other books in this series so read them all as I am going to.

Get this book, a cup of your favorite beverage, your tissues and settle into your favorite reading chair and be contented in love that will surround your heart." - Amazon Reviewer (*A Valentine To Cherish*)

"A nice combination of characters....Max, Sarah and also the message of Christmas. Loving nature, the environment was perfect with the birds and the others of the forest. Toss in a harmonica and a puppy....(who doesn't love a little puppy?) and the scene is set.

Truly a wonderful positive story for this upcoming season. Most highly recommended..." - Amazon Reviewer (*A Christmas Puppy To Cherish*)

"Each story in this series is a treasure. I have loved reading each story in this series and the characters are wonderful. I love the faith being openly discussed and how the relationships and romance evolved in each story. Highly recommend these books. Each one gets five stars." - Amazon Reviewer (*A Homecoming To Cherish.*)

"Art made people think. Art made people feel. Art inspired Ashley's students to dance and jump up and down with joy. A page turning summer read set in Cherish, South Carolina with relatable characters (Ashley and David), who enjoyed art, nature, sweets, and a Renaissance Faire. In this stand alone story, previous characters from the Cherish series also make an appearance. Josie Riviera draws the reader into the page turning conflicts and plot, but leaves the reader satisfied with a believable resolution. A touch of humor, an adorable dog named Pickle, Ashley with a fitting nick name, and ALL was RIGHT in a SUMMER to CHERISH. Recipe for Melissa's scrumptious Sweet and Sour Meatballs included." - Amazon Reviewer (*A Summer To Cherish*)

This book is dedicated to all my wonderful readers who have supported me every inch of the way.
THANK YOU!

CONTENTS

COZY UP WITH YOUR FAVORITE
BEVERAGE, AND LOSE
YOURSELF IN THE JOYFUL
SEASONS OF LOVE, WHERE GOD
IS AT THE CENTER.

A LOVE SONG TO CHERISH

A CHRISTMAS TO CHERISH

A VALENTINE TO CHERISH

VOLUME 2

A CHRISTMAS PUPPY TO CHERISH

A HOMECOMING TO CHERISH

A SUMMER TO CHERISH

PRAISE AND AWARDS

USA TODAY bestselling author

DEAR FRIENDS

A heartwarming story is the hallmark of a romantic read. Savor the magic of this collection with six heartwarming, clean and wholesome inspirational romances, brimming with Christian values.

Find out why readers are falling in love with **Cherished Hearts** & staying up all night reading! These stories will warm your heart.

This collection contains 6 books.

Available in ebook and paperback.

Each book and audiobook also sold separately.

A Love Song To Cherish

It's easy to recognize another's pain. The tough part is facing your own.

When Dorothy Thompson returns to Cherish, SC, to play piano for her brother's wedding, memories and fear nearly paralyzes her fingers. If anyone she knew back in high school discovers her secret, the whispers will start. Fake. Fraud. Failure. It's not as if she can blame God for her troubles. No, she did that all by herself. But, remembering His lessons, she's fighting to get back on track. All she can do is pray the wedding vocalist—her brother's friend Ryan, a rising opera star—won't notice the way her hands shake.

When Ryan Edwards sets foot inside a church for the first time in years, he's no longer the pitiable kid from the poor side of town, but someone who's made it on his own. Without God's help—not that He ever cared about misfits like Ryan, anyway. When he lays eyes on Dorothy—all grown up, more beautiful than ever, and clearly hiding something— he almost forgets why he left Cherish. Almost. But while his heart yearns to call the tune, he can't forget his hard-earned career comes first...and his old friend's little sister is off limits. Note: Contains references to opiate addiction and recovery.

A Christmas To Cherish
There's nothing a Christmas kiss won't cure. Except perhaps a shattered heart...

When Emmanuelle Sumter steps off the train in Cherish, South Carolina—a town simply glowing with the promise of Christmas—she finds herself praying God will help her find the broken pieces of her life. Shattered, like her beloved harp. Her dreams. And her trust in men.

Her friend Dorothy told her Cherish is a safe haven. But she never expected Dorothy's brother, Deputy Nicholas Thompson, would relight the one thing she thought she'd lost forever. A spark of hope.

Not long ago, while Nicholas' sister was in rehab, Emmanuelle's voice and smile on his Skype screen held him together. After that, she seemed to disappear, an absence he felt keenly when his ex-fiancée left his faith in God dented but not broken.

Now she's in Cherish, even more stunning in person. Yet she's holding tight to a private pain she refuses to reveal. Nicholas resolves to be patient, vowing that he'll never let anyone hurt her again. Even when her past rears its ugly head to destroy what's left of her heart.

Note: Contains references to verbal and physical abuse.

<u>A Valentine To Cherish</u>

All his life, he's followed a song. Is God showing him it's time to put down roots?

When Scarlett Evans meets Grammy-nominated Christian singer/songwriter Joseph Slater, their attraction dances like the intricate melodies he plays on his guitar. The way he looks at her—like she's perfect, just as she is—is a balm to her recently broken heart.

But who is she kidding? Stars like Joseph pick slim, demure, beautiful blondes, not loud, boisterous redheads with I'm-on-my-thousandth-diet curves. Besides, right after a local Valentine's Day benefit concert, he'll do what men have done to her all her life—hit the road.

Scarlett-with-two-t's is the answer to Joseph's prayer. This exquisite, vivacious woman has reconnected him with his muse. He's writing new songs for the first time in years, with lyrics that make him ache for something his relentless touring schedule never allowed. A home. Family. Love.

But just as Scarlett's hesitation starts to melt, she freezes and pulls away. Now he's praying for the right lyrics to bring her back—and show her that with God's guidance, they can rewrite their future as a duet.

Valentine's Day is all about love. And God has a special plan for a small-town woman and a road-weary singer.

<u>A Christmas Puppy To Cherish</u>

You don't need ears to hear God's plan. All you need is an open heart...

Music of both birds and harmonicas fills Max's life, but it's the near-silent forest guide he meets in Cherish, SC, who captures his attention. Small and slim, pretty Sarah's smiles and graceful hands speak louder than her voice. In fact, she's so quiet, he's not sure he's made much of an impression. But with her, he can imagine making this temporary stopover into something permanent.

Sarah has found a comfortable niche in Cherish, working miracles with plants, arranging flowers for church, and taking in stray animals. In fact, her house is so full, she's not sure she can say yes to the Sheriff's plea to take in one more puppy for Christmas.

Max has definitely captured her interest, and he shares her love of nature. But maybe she should take in that puppy after all, because a ball of fur that needs her will fill the empty space in her heart when Max's research sends him off looking for bluer skies.

A Homecoming To Cherish

All relationships require a commitment, but is she ready to sacrifice her heart again?

Hard-working accountant Nora Lancaster returns to her modest hometown to help manage an inn that her parents once owned. In order to escape small-town living, she'd married young and moved away. Now, as a single mother of a rebellious teenage daughter, she doesn't intend to stay long —only a few weeks at most—or until the current owner of the inn recovers from his heart attack.

World-weary Julian Wilson is a businessman who arrives in town for one reason—to open another restaurant. He's lived life as a bachelor and is at the peak of a rewarding career. Interested in the possibilities of another profitable venture, he views the town as a place to manage an extensive restaurant chain and finally settle down.

Nora never expected to meet a man like Julian—all business, as well as a formidable opponent—or to be instantly attracted to his kind nature and faith in God.

But can Julian convince Nora he's not the rival she fears?

A Summer To Cherish

Faith is fragile. Faith takes time. And the best solutions are always painted with love.

David Fodero followed his artistic vision to a wildly successful career. Now, day by day, that vision is cruelly shrinking, altering his perception, skewing his perspective… and all but destroying his faith.

Alone in a mountain cabin near Cherish, David wrestles with his inner critic as he struggles to put brush to canvas. Until he meets a luminous woman who dispels his crippling fear with her warmth and laughter.

Ashley Madden is a born fixer. So she's sure she can be forgiven for going above and beyond to find out what happened to the artist whose gallery sales support her work with handicapped kids—the artist who disappeared from public life with no warning or explanation.

Ashley's optimism is a balm to David's hurting soul. Yet as their attraction warms, Ashley senses David is holding something back—and that saving her own dream is intimately tied to restoring his faith. But will the truths they finally confess to each other wind up as stumbling blocks too large to overcome?

COZY UP WITH YOUR
FAVORITE BEVERAGE, AND
LOSE YOURSELF IN THE
JOYFUL SEASONS OF LOVE,
WHERE GOD IS AT THE
CENTER.

USA TODAY BESTSELLING AUTHOR
JOSIE RIVIERA
a Love Song to Cherish
A SWEET AND WHOLESOME NOVELLA

Copyright © 2018 by Josie Riviera

All rights reserved.

Author's Note: A Love Song To Cherish was previously published as Love's Sweet Cadence. It has been lightly revised.

No part of this book may be reproduced in any form or by any electronic or mechanical means, including information storage and retrieval systems, without written permission from the author, except for the use of brief quotations in a book review.

PRAISE AND AWARDS

**USA TODAY bestselling author
#1 Bestseller Women's Religious Fiction
#1 Bestseller Contemporary Religious Fiction
#1 Bestseller Inspirational Religious Fiction**

ACKNOWLEDGMENTS

To my patient husband, Dave, and our three wonderful children.

CHAPTER 1

*D*orothy Thompson had vowed to never set foot in Cherish, South Carolina, again. She didn't want to come back here. She couldn't face it.

Sure, she'd lived in the tiny town all her life. And she'd felt alone, despite her popularity, her cheerleader friends, her football player boyfriend. Her mother had orchestrated Dorothy's status, keeping one eye on the stylish girls and the other eye on Dorothy.

"Everything will be perfect once you meet the right man, provided he's rich," her mother had explained. "A poor man does no more good than an eyeless needle."

Nonetheless, everything hadn't been perfect. Dorothy's wealthy boyfriend had cheated on her, and she couldn't compete with the stunning platinum blondes and redheads once she entered high school.

She'd told her mother she didn't care a cow-eatin' cabbage about who liked her and who didn't, although she knew it wasn't true. Her popularity had mattered very much during her tumultuous teens.

All this went through her mind while she parked her Ford

Escort rental in front of Memorial Street Church. She regarded the church's white-painted exterior, the high-arched windows with their beautiful stained glass windows depicting scenes from the Bible and the ornately carved heavy wooden doors. Memories whispered of her singing beloved hymns in the church choir and Sunday school memorizing Bible verses in the church's basement.

So many memories for one little town.

She leaned her head against the driver's seat, no space in her mind for anything except sleep. The previous month, she'd endured the acute stage of opiate withdrawal along with the palpitations and tremors that came with it. And now Dr. Gantori, Dorothy's physician, had said the post-acute withdrawal stage could last two years.

She rubbed a hand over her puffy eyes. She was exhausted, and no wonder. With a sigh, she reached for the bag of chocolate chip cookies she'd purchased at the train station. The bag was surprisingly light. Had she mindlessly eaten the entire contents on the drive?

She rummaged in the bottom of the bag for one last cookie and chewed slowly, vowing to eat healthier tomorrow. The Cherish Hills Inn, the rental she'd booked for the week, boasted a kitchen, so there were no excuses. Besides, she was a good cook.

Dusting her fingers on a napkin in the glove compartment, she grabbed a bottled water and scooped up her leather briefcase stuffed with music.

Her palms were sweaty. She hesitated.

Fear of what might go wrong stopped her from getting out of the car. It had never occurred to her to let Dr. Gantori know she'd be traveling to another corner of the country. What would happen if she ran out of pain medication or experienced a panic attack and her hands froze to the piano keys?

Get back in the game. Keep God as the priority.

She lowered her car window and gazed outside, focusing on deep breaths in and out.

A fold of sleek silver clouds drifted across a robin's egg blue sky—a typical spring day in South Carolina. She knew the weather by heart. The air was mild, blowing a slight breeze against her cheeks. A hound dog lay basking on the sidewalk in the bright noonday sun.

Relax your muscles. Think positively.

She wiped her palms on her tweed skirt. There were pharmacies everywhere, she assured herself, and Dr. Gantori was merely a phone call away. Still, a knot threatened to take up residence in her stomach. What if the doctor didn't answer when she called?

Her brows puckered, her thoughts scattered. *No, no, no.* She bridled her panic. The task of chastising herself was growing thin as frustration poked through her anxiety. Undoubtedly the doctor used a twenty-four-hour answering service.

She was back in Cherish for her brother, not herself. It was high time she rearranged her priorities. There was more to her story than failing to become a concert performer. Through her difficult year of wrist pain when she'd become angry with God, she'd wanted to run away from her problems, disengaging from friends, social media, and to be truthful, from life.

If only her carpal tunnel hadn't been so excruciating, if only she hadn't become addicted to pain relievers ...

If only ... If only ...

But she had, and she'd become an addict.

However, she'd come through the storm intact and had learned to keep her trust in God, because He had her name on something else. But she didn't know what. She only knew it wasn't a concert career.

"Everyone has doubts after a poor performance," Dorothy mumbled, lifting a brief prayer. "What matters is how we react to them."

Holding that thought, she drew her shoulders straight, grabbed her canvas quilted jacket, tasseled purse and briefcase, and stepped from the car.

Her gaze landed on the top step of Memorial Street Church and a rollicking laugh gave her pause.

"Dorothy Thompson, is that really you?" Marge Addyson, the church's associate pastor and the clergy person elected to officiate the wedding ceremony, greeted Dorothy with a flash of a smile that could pass for heat lightning. "Why, you're all grown up. I haven't seen you since your parents went to be with the Lord."

"It's been five years since their funerals." Dorothy gulped air as she replied, that familiar despondency stabbing her heart. Her parent's car accident should never have happened. Her father had always been careful when he drove, mindfully watching the speed limit, and only twenty miles outside of Cherish on the highway near St. Luke's hospital ... no one could have predicted a fatal accident where the other driver was strung-out on drugs.

"When did you arrive in Cherish?" Mrs. Addyson asked.

"Just now." Dorothy gazed heavenward, grateful for the change in subject. "I rented a car at the Cherish Central train station." Her proper black pumps echoed across the pavement as she made her way up the church steps. "Where's Pastor Steven and his wife, Christina?"

"They're taking a well-deserved vacation. You're sure to see them both when they return in two weeks."

She wouldn't be staying in Cherish for two weeks, Dorothy thought, although there was no need to share that information with the kind associate pastor.

When Dorothy reached the church's entryway, Mrs.

Addyson embraced her in a warm hug. "I'm happy as the bluebonnets blooming in spring that you could come back for Nicholas' wedding. I hope it wasn't difficult taking time away from your prominent concert engagements."

Prominent concert engagements? A distant memory. Paying the rent on her expensive apartment in New York City? Not so distant.

"No worries." Dorothy fingered the corners of her worn leather briefcase. "I'd never refuse my big brother anything, nor miss seeing him and Alice get married."

Nicholas and his fiancée, Alice, had insisted that Dorothy play piano for their wedding. They'd requested contemporary music, although Dorothy had also brought along her favorite classical pieces. What wedding guest wouldn't be stirred to stand when they heard J.S. Bach's "Jesu, Joy of Man's Desiring" for the bride's processional march?

Mrs. Addyson stepped back. "And you're still tall and as pretty as a peppermint parfait. You haven't changed a bit."

"Thank you." Dorothy ran a hand down her brown braid. "You haven't changed either."

Kindness beamed from the elderly woman's crystal blue eyes. "I'm ten years older and infinitely wiser." Her salt and pepper hair had grown a little grayer, had been cut a little shorter.

Dorothy shaded her eyes and peered toward the street. "Did the music store close? When I drove by I noticed the building was vacant and a 'For Sale' sign was on the door."

"Yes, Musically Yours went out of business about a year ago."

Dorothy well remembered racing into Musically Yours on Saturday afternoons, fingering the darkening edges of well-loved classical pieces that emitted a scent of paper and leather-bound volumes of first edition music.

All the memories brought a sense of familiarity. In Cherish, people knew your name. She'd missed those things because she'd found city folks indifferent and uncompromising.

The comfortable warmth of the sun hit her face, and her heart felt full for the first time in a long time. She gazed at Memorial Street Church's magnificent steeple with the cross on top, and sadness flickered, disrupting the fullness in her heart. She'd hoped to become so much more than a panic-stricken performer who'd relied on opiates for pain. Despite her brief fame, she'd come back to Cherish with her solitude bigger than ever.

It serves you right, her conscience chattered. *You were a fake in high school, forever seeking approval from your classmates to ensure your popularity. Music became your life, your escape, although you're not great at making music anymore, either.*

"Don't bring your issues to church; bring them directly to God," one of her favorite pastors had once said.

She pushed the steely composure of a seasoned performer into place as Mrs. Addyson hooked an arm around Dorothy's shoulders and led her inside. "I always told your late mother you had an ear for music, honey." She gestured upward to the shiny ebony grand piano in the choir loft. "Is Ryan meeting you here so you two can rehearse?"

Dorothy hesitated. "Ryan who?"

"Ryan Edwards. He and your brother were good friends in high school. He'll be singing the Ave Maria at the wedding ceremony during the offering of the gifts. You're his accompanist."

Dorothy's mouth trembled with surprise.

Ryan Edwards.

She tipped her head back and briefly closed her eyes, visualizing Ryan's skinny build, his quiet demeanor, his booming operatic voice which had prompted his high school classmates to snicker. Often he'd accompanied her to Musically Yours, tendering kind support, encouraging her appreciation of Bach and Beethoven and Mozart. And when he would visit her house, Ryan would bring his precious LP's he'd kept hidden in his room and play Luciano Pavarotti and Placido Domingo recordings for her.

Their friendship had grown, and by the time she'd reached her early teens, she'd had a mad crush on him. He'd never known because she'd kept a cool demeanor around him. He was the high school nerd, and her popularity was at stake. In hindsight, she was glad she'd never let on how she felt about him because by her high school sophomore year, he was gone.

"He's become a well-known opera star in Europe and has flown all the way from Italy at your brother's request. Imagine, two famous musicians in our Lord's house." Mrs. Addyson gave Dorothy's shoulder a slight bump and added a mischievous grin. "When he was younger, that boy got into just enough mischief to make him interesting. Bless his heart considering his family was so poor, his Sunday supper was little more than fried water. We're mighty proud of all he's accomplished. He's a few years older than you."

"He was my best friend," Dorothy murmured. She set her music briefcase on a back pew and rubbed her forehead. "Nicholas mentioned nothing about Ryan singing."

"These days, your brother is busy between getting ready to graduate from the police academy and the wedding plans. It must've slipped his mind." Mrs. Addyson peered up and read the clock in the choir loft. "Ryan was supposed to be here at one o'clock and he's obviously running late, unless he's canceled altogether and sent a replacement singer. I won't detain you any longer."

"Thanks. I'll get started then."

"Don't forget dinner at The Garden Terrace tonight for the pre-wedding celebration." Mrs. Addyson winked and patted Dorothy's arm. "Your brother said he's treating everyone."

"I wouldn't miss *that* first for the world."

Now if she could only get herself to sit down at the piano and play something.

She willed her heart to stop pounding, willed her pulse to stop racing.

Grimacing, she managed a smile. "See you tonight, Mrs. Addyson."

You have nothing to prove to anyone but God, and he's not judging. The thought came quick through Dorothy's mind.

Taking a long swallow, she made her way up the stairs to the choir loft.

CHAPTER 2

Ryan Edwards should've been grinning. The flight from Italy to Atlanta had gone smoothly. The train ride to Cherish was fast and efficient. The Cherish Hills Inn where he was renting a room was well-kept, and he'd managed the short hike from the inn to the church at a brisk pace.

Still, he was late. He knew he was late and there was nothing he could do about it. Returning from a quick jog in town, he'd just had time to shower and change, grab his music bag and come to a short rehearsal. Hopefully the jog would clear his head and help him sleep. He hadn't slept well in months.

Studiously, he kept his head down and ignored the Goodwill Shop and Cherish Sunday Sentinel. Too many difficult memories echoed in these recognizable streets. It was hard enough to enter Memorial Street Church, knowing he hadn't attended a service in years. God had never shown interest in a misfit guy like him.

As a result, he'd made numerous wrong choices. Early on he'd determined what he'd wanted to achieve and had sought the options that suited him best. All people make choices they'd wished they hadn't. Everyone.

And was that God's fault? Guilt nudged.

Perhaps God wanted to help Ryan. Perhaps he should take ownership of his mistakes. Perhaps it was his own fault for resisting.

Nope, he was under too much stress to mull those thoughts around.

He set his jaw and increased his stride, staring straight ahead at the familiar South Carolina landscape—the rolling hills and thick hardwoods and sturdy pine trees. He'd worked hard for his success.

So why was he constantly so fatigued?

He didn't need to prove anything to anyone though he'd secretly relished returning to Cherish to show the towns-people how much he'd accomplished. He was no longer the kid from the poor side of town whose father had killed himself ... a kid to be pitied. Now people looked up to him.

The previous day, he'd received a jolt of surprise when he'd learned that Dorothy, Nicholas' younger sister, was Ryan's accompanist for the wedding ceremony.

Memories of her as a teenage girl brought to mind her spirit, her prettiness, her resolve to be the best at everything she undertook. At fifteen, she'd been gussied up all the time, interested in the latest hairstyles and clothes.

He'd realized that she'd just wanted to fit in.

Didn't we all? At least she'd enjoyed the love of two devoted parents and an older brother. Ryan had no one left except his commode-hugging, knee-walking drunk of a grandfather. His mother had passed away soon after he was born.

He pushed away the disheartening judgments, his thoughts returning to Dorothy. She was an interesting contrast between beauty queen and a homebody, with a streak of tom boyishness thrown in for good measure. His mouth watered just thinking about her homemade pecan pie —sweeter than stolen honey. She was a one-of-a-kind jewel, and acceptance followed her everywhere. And with the dogged way Dorothy went about things, she was most likely a competent pianist, and the entire run-through of the wedding music would take under an hour.

Despite the warmer weather being a month away, Ryan debated about stopping at Whitney's ice cream for frozen yogurt as he hurried by. Glancing at the time on his cell phone, he thought better of it and kept walking. At three o'clock, he'd arranged a conference call with his agent about a coveted opera role.

"Here he is, our opera star," Mrs. Addyson announced to no one except a hound dog sleeping in the sun, when Ryan arrived a few minutes later. "I'm tickled I got to see you before I left. My Chrysler's parked around the corner."

"Afternoon, Mrs. Addyson." With a brief nod, Ryan executed his most charming smile and made his way up the church steps. "How are you?"

"Fine as a summer morning." She tipped her head. "It's been ten years of Sundays since I last saw you and you've become as good-looking as a Hollywood movie star."

"Thanks, and you're still pretty as a supper of cherry pie." He chuckled, leaned forward, and greeted her with a cheek kiss. He almost reached up to tip his baseball cap before real- izing he wasn't wearing it. He grinned. Southern habits die hard. "Ten years goes by fast," he added.

"And you abandoned your hometown for a fine career in Europe."

"Italy is where the opera opportunities are, ma'am."

She tied a royal-blue silk kerchief around her hair and the breeze sent her kerchief fluttering. "Are you joining us for dinner tonight?"

Ryan took in everything—the stately church steeple, the stained-glass windows reflecting Mrs. Addyson's well-taken-care-of Southern features. When his father had died, she'd come to his house bearing kind words and a funeral casserole. When her husband had passed not long afterward, he'd attended the service—the last time he'd set foot in a church. Since then he'd looked for a sign from God, an invitation to return. The more he searched, the quieter God had become.

Ryan returned her gaze. "The Garden Terrace's restaurant at eight. I received the memo and I'm looking forward to seeing Nicholas and Alice."

"We can thank the good Lord for bringing us all back together."

With sublime effort, Ryan forced himself to nod in agreement and entered the church. The scent of incense and candles and musty hymnals made him pause. He exhaled and pressed the heel of his hand to his temple. Yes, too many memories.

Lifting his music bag, he went through the contents and frowned. In his preoccupation to prepare for his agent's phone call, he'd forgotten the "Ave Maria" back at the inn.

No matter. He'd read off Dorothy's music, assuming she'd brought all the pieces her brother and his fiancée had chosen.

As Ryan shrugged off his charcoal-gray pea coat and headed up the stairs to the choir loft, he expected to hear the sound of the piano. Beethoven's "Fur Elise," perhaps, or "Pachelbel's Canon in D." Instead, a beautiful woman sat curled up in a wooden chair with her legs tucked beneath her. Her ear was pressed to a cell phone, her voice sounded strained. She held up a finger to Ryan and mouthed, "One minute."

Dorothy Thompson.

Spirited and lovely as a teen, she'd also been elusive, which was one of the many reasons he'd admired her. He'd watched the way she'd dealt with her friends. She'd listened to their over-the-top compliments with a grin that was part amused skepticism and part gratefulness.

His breath caught. He simply stared.

Nature had partnered with the years. Her lovely face had realized all of its teenage potential. Thick black lashes fringed vivid eyes which changed from emerald-green to deep Scottish thistle depending on her mood. Her figure was still slim and had filled out in all the right places.

She'd abandoned her black high heels, set neatly on the floor beside a quilted jacket. With her hair pulled off her forehead into a gleaming braid cast over one shoulder, and preferring to go barefoot, she presented a captivating contrast between innocence and maturity.

His little Dorothy had grown into a gorgeous woman, breathtaking with shimmers and sparks.

Nope. Don't go there.

He stopped in mid-stride as cold reality slapped his chest.

He was still reeling from an expensive divorce and a cheating ex-spouse, one performance he had no interest in repeating. Involvement with another woman, any woman, wouldn't be happening again, at least not in his lifetime. Women weren't trustworthy, and achieving a successful career was most imperative. He wouldn't be derailed a second time.

He wanted to be successful. He *would* be successful.

Besides, his conscience annoyed, Dorothy was Nicholas' kid sister.

She talked quietly into the phone, and Ryan grew more impatient when one minute turned to two, then three.

"Are you almost finished?" He glanced at his wristwatch and cleared his throat. "Our rehearsal was supposed to begin at one and I have another appointment at three."

She extended a "thank you, Dr. Gantori," into the phone

and clicked off. "And our rehearsal would have started at one o'clock if you were here," she said. "Kindly don't blame me for your tardiness."

He stared into her stormy face, and his lips twitched as her gaze searched his features. "Ryan?" She touched her fingers to her lips. "You've changed."

"For the better, I hope." He leaned back to appraise her shapely form as she came to her feet. "The last time we were together you were doing your best to butcher Mozart's Sonata in C Major."

"And you had perfected an Italian art song, or was it a French mélodie? At any rate, you were preparing to go off to music school on a full scholarship." She cocked her head and smiled. "Oberlin?"

"Juilliard." His gaze flitted over the classical music she'd piled on the piano. "You?"

Her smile wavered. "I'm one of those people who went through high school sporting one image while secretly wanting another."

"Meaning?"

"My mother tried to polish me up to study broadcasting in a prestigious college and marry a rich guy, preferably a billionaire who owned a TV station and several tropical islands. Instead, I practiced my scales and got into a state college. I majored in piano performance."

"You were always so determined. I'm impressed, my love." He'd used that endearment often when they were young, and it just slipped out again, as natural as can be.

Her gaze darted toward the piano. "Was I?" she asked softly.

"I recall you plunking out melodies on Musically Yours' fifty-year-old upright piano."

"You encouraged me … you can say it now … my scales required a lot of work." Her smile was quiet. She waited a fraction, seeming to struggle to find the right words. "I got better and learned to read music."

Good. Wisely, he didn't share that thought aloud, wondering how in the world she'd been able to get into a music college. She hadn't begun formal music training until she'd entered high school. However, she'd exhibited remarkable perseverance and had never given up on anything once she'd set her mind to it.

"Well, we're burning daylight when we should rehearse," he said.

With a firm swallow, she pulled on her black high heels and moved slowly toward the piano.

He set down his music bag. "I brought every piece of music on Nicholas' list except the Ave Maria. In my hurry I forgot it in my room."

Dorothy ran her hand along the curves of the grand piano. "You forgot to bring the only piece you're singing?" She plucked a piece of sheet music from her stockpile and took a seat on the piano bench.

"I'm a busy man." He pulled an empty chair from the corner and came to sit beside her. "Do you know the chords for the Ave Maria?"

"No. Do you?"

In the past, her lovely eyebrows would have arched with a look daring him to dispute her. That look would have been preceded by a list of reasons why he should abandon his practice schedule for an impromptu Frisbee toss in her backyard.

Not this time.

"Can't you improvise?" he countered.

"Perhaps." Rolling her shoulders, she blew out a short breath and looked down at the closed piano lid. "What do you want to rehearse first?"

He massaged his temples. "'The Ave Maria.'"

"Of course." She gave a self-deprecating laugh and seemed to withdraw into herself. "What are we waiting for?"

You, he wanted to say. He glanced at his wristwatch, then at her lovely downturned profile.

"Unless you'd like to begin with another piece," he added.

She placed the music for "The Lord's Prayer" on the piano. "Can you sight-read this?"

"I've learned a lot in ten years, Dorothy. I'm interested in hearing what *you've* learned."

Her lips pressed together, and she didn't reply.

With a decisive snap, he lifted the piano lid and propped it up. "Shall we begin?"

With a slight nod, she placed her hands on the keys.

Now why, he pondered before pulling his gaze toward the music, were her hands shaking?

CHAPTER 3

*R*yan's voice was extraordinary.

Dorothy kept her head down and feigned busyness as she closed the lid of the grand piano. He was a gifted artist, and she was moved by the nuances in his deep bass tone and his incredible vocal range. She'd tried not to glance behind her shoulder and gape while he'd sung the moving lyrics of "The Lord's Prayer." His warm breath had grazed the back of her neck, his rich, dark timbre creating a poignant setting for praising God.

And yes, his virtuoso range had flustered her while she'd played, and she'd halted more than once. Who wouldn't be flustered accompanying a soon-to-be household name in the world of opera? If he'd noticed her hands shaking, he'd politely ignored it.

At eighteen, Ryan had been on the lean side of slim and wiry. Now at over six feet tall, his jaw was firmer, the angles of his cheekbones more pronounced. Gaiety had dimmed from his dark-eyed gaze after his father had died. Afterward, Ryan had become more rebellious, hardly spending any time at the home he'd shared with his drunken grandfather.

She glanced at him, idly wondering if his dark brown hair still took on splashes of gold from the hot South Carolina sun in the summertime.

She'd resisted the impulse to massage her aching right wrist while she'd played and had tried not to grimace whenever she'd reached an octave. Under no condition would she have a panic attack in front of Ryan. She still recalled his admiring glances when they were younger.

His dark eyebrows had lifted whenever she'd held in a moan. She'd controlled her shallow breathing and focused on the impressive vocal range of his bass voice. He made it look so easy.

"Are you sure you're not sick?" he'd asked more than once. "Perhaps you're tired after your long flight from New York."

"I lifted my suitcase in and out of the rental car one too many times." She'd forced a cool dismissal and kept her hands poised on the keys. "Shall we continue?"

His forehead had creased although he said nothing else.

Now that their rehearsal was finished, she grabbed the water bottle from her purse and took a sip, pondering how long it would take to shop for a few groceries at Cherish Country market—beginning with a box of herbal tea, fresh fruit and a bottle of ibuprofen. Probably not enough time, she amended, glancing at the choir loft clock. Check-in at the inn was four o'clock, and then she needed to get ready for the pre-wedding dinner party.

She twisted the cap back on her water bottle and nixed groceries altogether.

With a quick push to her feet, she went to grab her brief-case. She rounded the corner of the piano bench and let out a gasp when she slammed into Ryan's hard chest.

His cell phone was pressed to his ear.

Quickly, he pocketed his phone. His large hands caught

her forearms. "Sorry, Dorothy. I wanted to be sure I hadn't missed a call from my agent." The warmness of his long fingers tingled her skin. She stared back into his intense dark eyes and lowered her lashes. If she were honest, he'd completely disarmed her since he'd walked into the choir loft.

She gave herself a stern reprimand. She was being both imprudent and fanciful, much like when she was a dreamy-eyed teen. A couple years back, Nicholas had mentioned that Ryan had gotten married, although she hadn't noticed a wedding band on Ryan's finger.

"No worries, Ryan. Or should I call you Mr. Edwards?" Her voice lowered a fraction. "You're a celebrated artist now."

"Someday, perhaps, if I continue to work hard." His smile came easy, along with a lazy warmth in his gaze. "Here in Cherish I'm Ryan, your best friend. Remember when you'd race me to the Cupcake Escape for a salted triple-caramel cupcake?"

"And you used to let me win."

"And then we would share a cupcake, my love."

My love. Best friends. A million years ago.

He'd departed for college and never contacted her again. Did he know he'd taken a chunk of her adolescent heart with him?

"You're too fancy for any dare now. Look at you, wearing your well-fit clothes, sporting your Rolex watch." She laughed a little, bantering. "Nicholas told me your wife's father owns a large hotel chain all throughout Europe."

"I've been divorced for over a year." Ryan lifted a palm with a "who cares" attitude. "And if I ever become uber-rich, it'll be because of me and my merit."

Some part of her brain processed his information, and

she lingered, feeling strangely comforted. He was no longer married.

"I didn't mean to rush up from the piano bench," she continued. "I was thinking about going to the market for groceries, then checking into the place I'm staying and taking a quick shower before dinner."

She felt her face heat as she pushed a reasonable explanation into her voice.

Ryan's grip on her forearms tightened. "We're having dinner at The Garden Terrace tonight, right?"

"Yes. I assume you're invited, too." Unable to stop her steps, she moved a little closer and stared up at him.

The air between them stalled, the seconds beating a steady pulsing rhythm.

"I'll walk you outside." He hesitated before releasing his hands. "Where are you staying?"

"The Cherish Hills Inn. You?"

"Me too."

"Really?"

"Really." He threw back his head and laughed, then opened his arms. She collapsed against him with a chuckle, her cheek pressing against the solid thudding of his heart.

He'd worn a gray cotton polo shirt and black fitted jeans to the rehearsal. His dark-brown hair curled to the collar of his shirt, and her fingers were restless, wanting to brush her hands against his hair. He was the most attractive man she'd ever seen.

She pulled out of his arms and stepped back.

What on earth was she thinking?

The last guy she'd dated, an egotistical violinist, was so vain that she'd been surprised he didn't break his arm patting himself on the back after a successful performance.

No more self-centered musicians, she'd vowed. Especially one who was an obvious rising star.

Was that the reason Ryan's marriage had failed? Was his high-profile career worth more to him than his personal life?

She gave herself a strong mental shake. Neither was any of her business and she wouldn't pry. She wasn't waiting for a relationship with a man to feel worthwhile because she'd learned to rely on herself. Besides, her feelings for him in the past were best left in the past.

Deliberately, she pressed any further thoughts of Ryan Edwards from her mind.

CHAPTER 4

The conversation level at The Garden Terrace's restaurant dimmed to a murmur when Ryan and Dorothy strolled in. Ryan was the main draw, the local celebrity, though he seemed oblivious to any commotion he was causing. He looked impossibly good-looking in black pants, a button-down white sport shirt and a gray pea coat that hugged his broad shoulders.

She sniffed appreciatively as he helped her off with her jacket. Scents of grilled chicken and smoky, fall-off-the-bone barbecued ribs smoked over mesquite wood tempted her.

"Smells good, doesn't it?" He drew her hand through the crook of his arm "I'll check our jackets at the coat-check. I assume we'll go back to the inn together." He covered her hand with his warm fingers and winked. "Thanks for giving me a lift to the restaurant tonight, roomie."

"We may be at the same inn, but we're not roomies," she corrected. "I'll drive you back if you promise to treat me to a piece of The Garden Terrace's sugar-free lemon cake."

"You brother is treating tonight. I'll take a raincheck."

She nodded, still shaking her head they'd rented rooms at the same inn, on the same floor. There wasn't an abundance of rentals in Cherish, and despite the fact her brother had offered his apartment, it was small and cramped.

Across the crowded dining room, she noted that Nicholas had pushed from his chair and was starting toward them.

Tears sprang to her eyes when her six foot, blond-haired brother reached her. He was a source of inspiration, a true believer in God, and his faith through their daily phone calls while she'd been ill had empowered her to persevere through the nightmarish days of her withdrawal—the vomiting and insomnia and night sweats.

"Don't worry about your career. Your true calling will show up where you least expect it," he'd reassured her. "Your realizations are within your reach."

She hadn't figured out what those realizations were yet, although she'd checked herself into a residential recovery program in New York City the following day.

"It's been too long," Nicholas was saying. "Dorothy, how's the pain? I was beyond worried and prayed hard for your recovery." She couldn't help noticing the husky emotion in his voice.

Beneath her fingers, she felt the muscles in Ryan's forearm harden.

"What recovery?" he murmured.

Evading Ryan's inquiring gaze, she replied to Nicholas, "Prayers are always appreciated."

She pulled her hand from Ryan's arm and scanned the busy restaurant—the wood-beamed ceiling, the various kinds of deer antlers lining a wall, a South Carolina flag hanging across another wall, the waiters and waitresses carrying heaping plates of brisket and onions. She'd always loved the down-home, rustic interior of The Garden Terrace.

"Nicholas, where's Alice?" she asked.

"An emergency at St. Luke's hospital caused her to work later than expected. That's been happening a lot. We're getting married and I hardly see her. I've been in charge of most of the wedding planning." Nicholas pressed his lips tight, then took Dorothy's fingers in his. "In the meantime, I'll introduce you to the wedding party. The wedding is small —a Best Man and the Maid of Honor. Alice's five-year-old daughter is the flower girl. After the ceremony we're having a small reception in the church's basement."

Dorothy nodded. "I'm sure the wedding will be lovely." She didn't know much about Alice except she'd been married twice before and had one daughter. Nicholas and Alice had only been dating a few months, and Dorothy had been surprised when Nicholas had announced their wedding plans so soon.

Ryan placed a light hand on Dorothy's back while they followed Nicholas to a round wooden table in the corner. Mrs. Addyson sat with a group of smiling men and women whom Dorothy thought she vaguely recognized.

"Have you been sick, Dorothy?" Ryan murmured, slowing his pace to detain her. "Is there something you're not telling me?"

"Nothing of interest." She shrugged and took a small step away from him. "Thanks for asking. I'm handling it."

"I'm here if you need anything."

His words hung amidst a background of dishes clattering and people talking. Unexpectedly, a wave of desolation surged through her for all those lost years between them.

Realizing he was waiting for an answer, she blurted, "Are you? You're here for what—a week—before you disappear again for ten years?"

"What's that supposed to mean?"

"Nothing."

He let out a heavy sigh. "I was offered a full scholarship to one of the most prestigious music colleges in the country. I was eighteen and needed to leave this town. I wanted more, and somehow I sense you're angry at me for my decision."

"You always wanted to be on top and you've achieved your goals."

"Have I? Don't presume what you don't know. You're the one who had the world simpering at her feet."

She arched an eyebrow and added a glare. "Who's presuming now?"

He rubbed the back of his neck and lowered his tone. "Look ... I've missed you, Dorothy, all right? I've thought about you a lot. You were only fifteen when I left and I couldn't allow myself to ..." His gaze drifted over her features, lingering on the top button of her ivory silk shirt before focusing on her lips.

"Dorothy!" Mrs. Addyson waved from a wooden table in the corner of the restaurant. "I've saved you a seat next to me and ordered you and Ryan a glass of sweet tea."

"Thanks, Mrs. Addyson." Dorothy glanced over and beamed a smile. When she turned back to Ryan, he was watching her with undisguised interest. "Ryan, I—"

"Go." He directed a meaningful glance toward Mrs. Addyson. "I'll check our jackets and then join you."

When Dorothy reached the table, Mrs. Addyson drew her down to sit beside her. Their table faced a large window with a wide frame.

"This is such a pretty night for a pre-wedding party, it's a shame the bride isn't able to attend," Mrs. Addyson said.

"Nicholas mentioned that Alice is working at the hospital and would be late."

Mrs. Addyson's gaze flicked upward. "The girl's got more

twisted excuses than a pretzel factory." Her tapered, polished pink nail finger-tapped her iced-tea glass. "I'm so pleased to see you and Ryan together again. You two always got along so well, and I know how much you missed him when he went off to college. For weeks afterward you looked like you were eating sadness by the tablespoon."

Dorothy took a sip of her sweet tea, then placed her napkin on her lap. "A lot has happened since we were teenagers."

He'd become successful with a flourishing career and knew where he was headed. She'd gotten sandpapered by wrist pain that had ended her profession before it had begun.

"The Bible says 'For everything there is a season.'" Mrs. Addyson's freckled hand came down to rest on Dorothy's arm. "This is the season for you and Ryan to become reacquainted."

Perhaps, though a week went by extremely fast, Dorothy mused, toying with her delicious sugar-free lemon cake two hours later. By ten o'clock, the long day coupled with nagging wrist pain was taking its toll. Despite Ryan's relaxed posture and light-hearted conversation, she could think of nothing else except returning to the inn for another dose of pain medication, followed by a long soak in the luxurious tub, then lounging in the king-size bed.

She pondered logging onto her laptop and checking the asking price of Musically Yours, the vacant music store. Mrs. Addyson had mentioned the former owners had lowered the price and were actively looking for offers.

Contemplating the possibilities of opening her own music store, Dorothy stared out the restaurant's window at the full moon lighting a starlit sky.

She didn't have more than a hundred dollars in her savings account and she doubted any bank would give an out-of-work pianist a business loan.

Murmuring to Ryan that they should leave, she placed her fork on her dessert plate. She should rest for the two-hour practice the following morning with the rugged, dark-haired man who'd sat beside her all evening, teasing her in his deep voice, his muscled leg casually brushing against hers.

CHAPTER 5

At nine o'clock the following morning, Ryan strode down the carpeted hallway of the Cherish Hills Inn and tapped on Dorothy's door. "Ready?" he prompted, when she opened the door and invited him into her room.

"I'll get my jacket." She was dressed in a pair of rich-navy twill ankle pants, a slouchy burgundy sweater and brown suede ankle boots. Her room was feminine, an understated floral scent lingering in the air. He smiled, finding comfort in the fragrance he remembered from long ago.

"I need to be finished by noon," he said. "I'm expecting a call from my agent."

"Again?" She favored him with a smile and an exaggerated, knowing nod. "Don't tell me—let me guess. Another important phone call."

Affectionately, he rumpled her shiny hair that hung loose and wavy down her shoulders. She'd taken down the twisted braid from the previous day, and he felt the desire to snatch her in his arms and kiss the smiling mischief from her lips.

This was the fun-loving Dorothy he appreciated, and he

was gratified by the knowledge he'd put a chink in the cool wall she'd erected when they'd rehearsed.

"My agent is confirming the audition date in Palermo for Verdi's opera *Don Carlos*." Ryan hoisted his music bag over his shoulder. "The competition is aggressive. Jack Youngston, an upperclassman of mine when I attended Juilliard, is also interested in the role."

"With a voice like yours, you'll get the part."

"Jack is very, very good." Ryan twisted the top button of his pea coat. "I'm only thirty and considered young in the competitive opera world. My voice is still maturing and the role of Philip is challenging. Jack is a few years older and his experience is broader than mine."

She grabbed her jacket and Ryan draped it around her shoulders. "I'm not familiar with the opera, *Don Carlos*."

"I played the recording for you a long time ago," Ryan said, insisting on carrying her briefcase. "In the role, Philip evolves from a tyrant to a long-suffering husband."

They advanced to the lobby and nodded to the white-haired innkeeper behind the reception desk who looked up from his newspaper and extended a greeting.

The hum of a television in the parlor brought back images of Ryan's father sitting night after night staring blankly at the same black and white sitcoms. Years before that, his father had invited Ryan to watch Westerns with him.

John Wayne. Memories of popping popcorn with his father on their old gas stove.

A person missed the oddest things after losing someone. Little things.

He gazed at the heartwarming stacked rock fireplace in the parlor and pulled in a breath, ambushed by remembrances of his father's struggles with the demons in his head before he'd taken his own life. He'd hanged himself from a bed sheet noose tied to a wooden rafter right in the middle of their living room while a cheerful fire had burned in the grate and canned laughter had come from the television. Ryan had been the one to find him.

Afterward had been a blur. When Ryan emerged from the deep fog of grief and disbelief, he'd realized he had no choice. He had to get away from Cherish and somehow, some way, climb to the top. He needed a fresh start and looked toward the day when he'd turned eighteen.

Repeatedly shaking his head, he twisted the lion signet ring on the pinky finger of his right hand, the only keepsake he'd kept from his father's possessions.

"That ring was your dad's." Dorothy regarded him. "You've worn it every day since his death?"

"Yes."

She offered a quivery smile and lightly placed her fingers on his sleeve. "I know how much he meant to you. He was a good father."

"Yes."

In the beginning, perhaps.

Ryan wiped at the tears prickling his eyes, aware of the familiar knot settling in his gut. Bleakly, he continued to stare at the enormous fireplace.

She stared at the fire with him, offering silence and her presence.

After several beats, she asked, "And what happens next in *Don Carlos?*"

He didn't answer for a moment, silently thanking her for changing the subject. Taking a long breath to control his voice, he guided her to the entry door and opened it. "Near the end of the opera, Philip laments his loveless marriage and loneliness."

He could empathize with the sorrow, the resignation, the emptiness of a man like Philip. No matter where Ryan searched, he never felt fulfilled.

He swallowed and dragged his thoughts away from that fateful night and all the fears it had brought.

"You'll have to fake the loneliness part," Dorothy said, a tiny smile emerging. "When you're popular you're never lonely, and from what I read about you last night on the internet, you're a household name in Europe."

The knowledge she'd been checking up on him made him grin. "So your philosophy is if you're popular, you're never lonely?"

She avoided his gaze. "My mother's saying."

"Was she right?"

"When I was a teen, I grew resentful of my mother, although I've learned to look at situations differently and now have a different perspective." Dorothy slowed her steps. "I've prayed about our relationship and believe she was getting my life confused with her own."

"So God gave you an answer and your problems and reservations were fixed?"

"Nothing changed." Dorothy tapped her fingertips together. "My faith gave me the sight to understand. God's response gave me a new way to see my situation. My mother wasn't overbearing; she was simply being a mom and therefore engrossed in what she believed was in my best interests."

"For example, doing all she could to ensure you were prom queen in your senior year?"

"You heard?" She smiled. "You were well gone by then."

"Thanks to your brother," Ryan amended, "I kept up with more news about you than you'll ever know."

Her gaze narrowed into a pensive frown. He'd noted she'd asked for clarification while she played in their rehearsal, seeming to look at him for assurances. He offered a smile.

Inwardly, he was concerned.

"Please continue. We were talking about your mother," he reminded.

She looked toward the street. "When I complained to Nicholas about our mother, he would say 'look again.' So I did. And then I'd complain, and he'd say 'keep looking.' His faith in God is tremendous."

"Your brother's an awesome guy. I hope Alice is the right person for him."

"I haven't met her yet."

"Neither have I." Ryan chuckled. "Does she exist?"

"With any luck we'll get to meet her before the wedding." With a wry grin, Dorothy regarded her rental car parked at the curb. "Why don't we walk to the church? The weather is gorgeous."

He supported her suggestion with a chuckle and clasped her hand. One block later, they went by Whitney's Ice Cream. The posted sign in the window stated an eleven o'clock opening time.

Despite their quick stroll, Dorothy stopped to peer at the purple and yellow pansies blooming in wooden planters outside Cherish Styles and Clips. "I love flowers, especially bluebonnets." She bent her head, sniffed, then grinned up at him. "Often I think about the times when we'd skip stones across the open stream near the abandoned railway line. The bluebonnets grew so cheerful along the train tracks and always made me happy."

His lips twitched. "From what I recall, we shared a slingshot to snap petals off those cheerful bluebonnets." They started forward and their laughing gazes merged.

The air smelled fresh and clean, and the morning sky blurred from dusky rose to a clear blue. Soon a glowing sun would raise the humidity level. This particularly perfect day sent a stab of homesickness right through him. Nothing beat a spring day in South Carolina.

"Last night at dinner while you were talking with your brother, Mrs. Addyson told me you're a concert pianist in New York City." Ryan tightened his fingers around hers. "Where have you performed?"

"Here and there," Dorothy said dismissively. "You won't be seeing my name on the Carnegie Hall marquee any time soon."

"Why not? Your piano ability at rehearsal was excellent."

She didn't answer and kept her gaze fixed on the sidewalk.

"Will you be returning to New York after the wedding?" he prompted.

She glanced down at their linked hands. "You ask a lot of questions."

"I have undisputed rights to ask all the questions I please because I'm your best friend." They rounded the corner to a local coffee shop. "Coffee?"

"Sure."

"I'll be right back." He placed her briefcase and his music bag near the entrance to the shop and emerged five minutes later carrying a bag with two cups of steaming black coffee poking out of it.

She smiled as he handed her a cup. "Thank you."

"My pleasure."

She gazed up at him, her soft brown hair cascading about her shoulders—so lovely against her flawless complexion and pale pink lips. He studied her for a long silent beat. The summer she'd turned fourteen, she'd cut her long hair into a short bob to copy the latest hairstyle in a popular teen magazine. Predictably, the other girls in her class had soon followed her example. *Dorothy, the trendsetter.* It had been all he could do to rein in his tongue that summer because he preferred her hair loose and long.

"You remembered I like my coffee black?" she asked.

He grinned. "Yes, because I once admonished you for drinking coffee at such a young age."

"My weakness." She returned his grin and tasted.

"Do you have any other weaknesses?" he asked.

"More than I can count." She slanted him a glance. "You?"

His gaze lowered to her face. She was blushing.

Silently, he pondered the edges of the corner he'd effectively pushed them into, took her coffee from her, and set both their cups and the bag they came in on the sidewalk.

"Only one weakness, my love, and she's standing beside me." He inspected her slender form, the way the color in her face intensified as he continued to stare at her. She looked like a tender delicate flower, framed by the wholesomeness of their charming hometown.

"You're beautiful," he breathed.

Her shimmering eyes widened, enormous in her heart-shaped face, adding to the effect of her sweet beauty. And right there on Memorial Street across from the fountain in the town square, he caught her in his arms. He tipped her chin up, his mouth moving closer to hers.

Slowly bending his head, he kissed her. She hesitated, then kissed him back while his hands shifted protectively around her back.

"You're a stunning, desirable woman and I've never stopped thinking about you," he whispered.

"Ryan, I—" She stirred and his arms tightened.

The kiss ended as abruptly as it had begun, and for a lingering second, they gazed at each other. The soft yielding in her eyes, a vivid emerald-green, was as if she had spoken aloud.

She'd felt the same attraction pulling them together.

A breeze rustled the pink and purple blooms of a redbud tree, and overhead a male mockingbird sang the song of every bird except his own.

Despite the exquisite feeling of Dorothy's slim body pressed to his, loneliness invaded Ryan's thoughts. Perhaps if he kissed her again, if they stayed where they were, she'd be able to drive away the aching desolation, the ceaseless tension that had become a part of him.

How could the life he'd chosen cause such a strain? Soon he would have everything he'd dreamed about, and there was no reason for him to feel such sadness. Plenty of people were stressed like tightly coiled springs because of overwork, he rationalized. It was the price a person paid to become a winner.

A red-haired customer balancing two trays of coffee dashed out of the shop, jostling them out of the way. Her sunglasses slipped down her nose and she slid them back up. "Sorry!" she called as she rushed past.

Dorothy blinked up at Ryan. "What was that about?"

"The woman was obviously in a hurry."

"You know that's not what I meant." With a fragile smile, Dorothy pulled from his embrace.

He brushed a kiss on her temple and studied her exquisite face before retrieving their coffee cups. "Shall we continue our walk?" he asked.

She drew an unsteady breath, then considered him before refusing the coffee he extended.

"Do what?"

"Shall we continue our—"

Drawing her delicate eyebrows up, she grinned before racing off. "Last one to the church treats the other person to an ice cream!" she called behind her shoulder.

Hurriedly, he stuffed the coffees into the bag. He seized his music and her briefcase, then bounded after her.

He let out a laugh. She was winning, and that was okay. More important, his old Dorothy was returning, and he liked it.

CHAPTER 6

The music rehearsal at the church proved smooth and uneventful, moving along much quicker than Ryan had expected. Occasionally he noticed Dorothy's face contort with obvious pain, or her fingers tremble on the piano keys. When he asked, she qualified any discomfort behind a forced laugh and lame excuses.

"I owe you an ice cream." He nudged her shoulder when they were finished, then helped her on with her quilted jacket. "May I remind you the race to the church was unfair?"

"May I remind *you* I won?"

"You left me to dash after you carrying two hot coffees and two heavy bags stuffed with music." He checked his wristwatch. "If you can spare the time, let's stop at Whitney's Ice Cream on our way back to the inn."

She laughed impenitently. "Are you sure you're able to squeeze me in? Your life seems full of important appointments these days."

"Nothing is as important as spending time with you." It was the easy, gentlemanly thing to say, and he said the words aloud. Because it was true. It had always been true. Spending time with her had been one of the most cherished aspects of his life.

She smiled with shy hesitation. "Ryan Edwards, are you trying to charm me?"

He had to fight down the impulse to take her in his arms and kiss her again.

Grabbing their music bags, he placed his fingers beneath the elbow of her jacket and guided her down the choir loft stairs. "I've wanted an ice cream and coke at Whitney's Ice Cream ever since I arrived in Cherish."

In the spirit of relaxed camaraderie, they retraced their path toward the inn, then stood in line behind a steady stream of customers at Whitney's before finding two chairs at an outdoor wrought iron table.

After Dorothy was seated, and she'd slung her purse over her chair, he handed her the ice cream cone and a napkin.

"Strawberry is the only ice cream flavor you've ever chosen." He occupied a chair across from her and bent his head to whisper in her ear. "And you've always shared a bite with me."

"Go ahead." A tantalizing smile curved her lips as she extended her cone and he took a lick. "And you've always ordered peppermint chocolate chip."

"I know you, you know me," he said softly.

She pulled in a sharp breath and cut away her gaze.

They ate in silence, interrupted only by the chittering of two squirrels and the jumbled conversations of chattering customers.

"The pain your brother mentioned last night at the restaurant? How often he'd worried and prayed for you?" Ryan set his napkin down. "You asked me earlier and now I'll ask you. What was that about?"

She concentrated on the last licks of her ice cream cone, dabbed her lips with a napkin, and placed it on her lap. "Typical musician injuries. Carpal tunnel problems … you know." She glanced up at him. "What about you? Have you experienced any injuries from all that singing?"

Good deflection, he thought. Going along with her, he finished his cone and downed a swig of coke. "I've had my share. When I was at Juilliard, I attempted a repertoire well beyond me, and my voice wasn't ready."

"You? The master singer?"

"My voice was maturing. Still is, as I mentioned earlier. That's why the opera in Italy is important, because it's a tipping point for my career. I know I'm ready for the challenge."

"You need not prove yourself, Ryan. Not to anyone."

"Perhaps I need to prove something to myself." Meticulously, he squeezed his napkin into a small ball. "Perhaps I'm impatient for my dreams to become a reality."

The familiar prod of guilt prompted him to lean back in his chair and reflect. Perhaps his father wouldn't have committed suicide if Ryan had been a good son. Perhaps Ryan should have sought help from a mental health professional when he'd first sensed his father was ill.

Instead, he'd acted out. Even at an early age, Ryan had gotten into trouble at school. Nothing major, just childhood pranks. Still … was he the reason his father had ended his own life?

"I'm impatient, too," she said. "And I've always been a bit headstrong."

"A bit?" He sent her a teasing wink. "You possess an uncanny ability to fit into any social situation."

"Thanks to my mother."

"Thanks to you. You're fun to be around and your outlook is always positive. However, I've watched you these past two days and I know you're in constant pain. Please, Dorothy. I want to know why."

*D*orothy wrung the napkin in her lap.

Ryan sat across from her. Her Ryan. Her good friend. Her confidante.

Not anymore, she reminded herself. Once upon a time, and only then in her daydreams.

They'd had a silent communication when they were childhood comrades sitting for hours on her back porch on sultry summer nights, watching the sun set into a giant red ball, listening to the cicadas chirp their familiar chorus.

"Dorothy?" Ryan's astute brown eyes assessed her. "We used to tell each other everything."

"Sure, when I was fifteen and the world's ultimate chatterbox. 'Everyone should be quick to listen, slow to speak.'" She recited the Bible verse from James 1:19.

"So you have no interest in talking the legs off a chair anymore?" he teased.

She smiled, then drew her jacket tighter around her.

Around them, the loud drone of customers' conversations seemed to grow unnaturally quiet. Drop by precious drop, she felt her confidence draining away.

Ryan was curious and concerned. He wouldn't rest until he knew the truth, and there was no point in evading his questions any longer.

He was from South Carolina, she assured herself. He had a big heart.

Taking a deep breath, she lifted her chin and met his steady gaze.

"Ryan, you should know ..." Her voice shook and there was nothing she could do to control her trembling. "I'm a drug addict, or rather, the appropriate term is 'opiate use disorder.'"

If he was surprised, he didn't show it. His features remained calm and neutral. He clasped her chilly hands in his sturdy ones. "Are you all right?"

"I'm under a doctor's care."

"What happened?"

"I should have told you sooner ... I know I should have." She glanced at him, but there was no judgment, only concern.

"What happened?" he repeated.

"I was over-practicing and sprained my wrist. The doctor advised rest. I argued there wasn't time because I was preparing for a piano recital at a small college in New York. I begged her for something to get me through the performance." Dorothy pulled from his hold and fiddled with the tassel on her purse. "She prescribed opiates for my chronic pain. I felt light-headed after I took them, but I was so grateful for the relief that side effects didn't matter. I could perform without a glitch."

"You're describing opiates as a miracle drug."

"For me they were, until I became addicted to them." She shifted in the cold chair and brushed at her eyes, wet with tears, then quickly looked away.

"Sounds like the opiates were a nightmare instead of a miracle."

She corrected him with a shake of her head. "In fairness, the drugs weren't the problem. I was. I became addicted because I'm weak. I was never the successful girl you admired ... I'm a sham ... and I've failed as a competent musician."

He opened his mouth to speak, then seemed to think better of it. He grabbed hold of her fidgeting hands and gently brushed a kiss on each palm. He'd given her strength when they were younger by his compliments and encouragement. He was doing the same now.

She licked her lips, and her fingers tightened around his. "I tried to stop several times and felt sick and depressed. Somewhere in my mixed-up thoughts I knew I couldn't quit on my own. That's when I reached out to my brother, and his faith in God guided me on the right path. God spoke, and I listened."

"I'd like to share your faith, Dorothy. I really would." Ryan's lips pressed together. "The God you describe is silent for me."

Shaken by the desolate tone in his voice, her gaze fixed on his prominent cheekbones the slight dark stubble on his jaw, the stubborn turn of his mouth.

"Nicholas reminded me I was too busy and preoccupied in myself to hear God." She lifted her face to the late morning sunlight, then met Ryan's unfaltering gaze. "If you listen, God is everywhere. He was there for me."

"I've sung *piano*, I've sung *forte*." Ryan hesitated, deliberating. "I thought if I searched hard enough I'd find God in Europe while I performed in world-renowned concert halls. I believed I'd found my purpose on century-old stages."

"And did you find your purpose?"

Carefully, he studied her. "People say opera is an emotional, expressive art form about what matters most."

What matters most.

She gazed at this strikingly handsome man whom she'd had a mad crush on as a young girl. Her love for him had never died. He was a part of her life. He mattered.

And he hadn't answered her question about finding his purpose. This was obviously a subject he didn't plan to pursue.

"I see," she replied.

"This conversation is about you, not me." He flicked a dark eyebrow upward. "How are you being treated for your addiction?"

"My doctor, Dr. Gantori, and a nurse case manager are providing medication and check-in phone calls. My cravings for the drug are better now."

"Good. You're on the right road." His smile was slow, his fingers still around hers. "When will you be heading back to New York City?"

"Sunday. You?"

"Me too. I've booked a flight from Atlanta to Italy. The audition in Palermo is slated for early next week."

They had less than a few days together left, and the thought filled her with despondency. She turned, withdrew her hands from his, and feigned interest in the stone pavers lining the patio so he wouldn't know her sadness.

"We should head back." He glanced at his wristwatch and pushed back his chair. As they stood, he took her bag as well as his, then slipped an arm around her shoulders. "Another practice at nine o'clock tomorrow morning, then?"

"Let's rehearse a while longer because Nicholas changed the recessional song to 'Signed, Sealed and Delivered' by Stevie Wonder." She buttoned her jacket and indicated that Ryan follow her around the outdoor tables. "Nicholas' music choices are a perfect balance between classical and contemporary."

"That's one way to put it." Ryan gave a bark of laughter. "Signed and Sealed and I'm Yours—a meaningful ending after Nicholas and his elusive fiancée sign the wedding registry."

Dorothy laughed and started for the sidewalk. "I'd like to take a peek in the window of Musically Yours, or rather, what used to be Musically Yours. I understand if you want to go ahead because of your appointment."

He hesitated. "The music store on the corner of Myrtle and Magnolia? Has the store been renamed?"

"Musically Yours went out of business." Her voice grew quiet. "And somehow I can't bear the thought."

"Neither can I." Ryan greeted the news by placing his palm against his heart, then claimed her hand.

When they rounded the corner to the abandoned store front, his face blanched. Although the bushes were trimmed, and the lawn mowed, the store didn't blend in with the other tidy businesses lining the street. The display window, which in the past had showcased popular sheet music as well as guitars, ukuleles, and violins, appeared sadly desolate.

He stared through the grimy window. "There's nothing left?"

"Everything was sold at an auction. The owners are asking $100,000 for the abandoned building."

"Renovations on a place this size will run into thousands of dollars. Then there's music inventory, lots of it, which is only the beginning."

"Don't forget shelving and monthly heat and electricity bills." She shaded her eyes and peered inside. "The listing stated the space is one thousand square feet. For the customer who would patronize this type of store, the square footage seems adequate."

Ryan set down the music bags and tried the doorjamb. It swung open. Dust and months of disuse spilled out at them.

With a roguish grin, he stood back to survey the badly fractured door frame. "Shall we look inside?"

She perused the empty sidewalks. "We can't enter a property without a realtor. Suppose someone sees us and accuses us of stealing."

He added a wink to his grin. "There's nothing in here except an old ukulele missing all its strings." He nodded toward the broken instrument sitting sideways in the corner. "If anyone asks, we're prospective buyers."

"That excuse wouldn't float for a minute. I can't afford this property and you're not looking. You live in Europe."

He nudged their bags inside. "I used to live in Cherish. This is my hometown as well as yours."

She stepped over the store's threshold with him, fingering the well-loved brick on the interior of one wall while studying the numerous nail holes on the others.

"The music was arranged in rows alphabetically by composers," she said. "Remember?"

He indicated the front window. "The gigantic composer of the month statue always made me pause."

Her gaze automatically surveyed every inch of the space she had once spent so much time in. "And the composer's music was piped as background throughout the store."

"When I used to walk by and hear Mozart, it drew me in like a siren."

She nodded and continued toward the rear. "I always thought the owners should offer music lessons. There's a separate entrance so students wouldn't be traipsing in and out, especially if lessons were held after store hours."

"The owners were elderly. They didn't want the hassle."

"There should be more cultural opportunities in Cherish." An unexpected elation built inside her along with a conviction taking root. "There's Memorial Street Church choir and the high school band. However, a music conservatory would fit perfectly into this community and it could begin right here." She gestured toward the back room which the previous owners had used for storage.

"This is a small community," Ryan reminded. "A conservatory and retail store is a large undertaking, and don't forget there's another music store over in Stanley."

"That store is in the next town."

His phone buzzed. He pulled it out of his jacket, glanced at the message and frowned before pocketing it.

"Anything important?"

He smiled into her eyes. "It can wait."

She drank in the mustiness of the air along with the remembrances. "A music store and lessons would feed off of each other, and monthly recitals and concerts could be scheduled." She wiggled her shoulders and faced him. "I'd have an excuse to get all dressed up again."

"The sight of you in a fancy dress would make me want to fly back to Cherish every weekend." He laughed. The deep throaty sound had always made her heart beat double time. Then he sobered, and the amusement was replaced by a languid gaze, keeping her rooted where she stood.

He moved forward. Bending his head, he brushed his lips against hers, the bristle of his stubble sweeping against her cheeks. "You would light up any concert hall," he whispered.

"Me? Hardly." She waved a hand dismissively, stepped back, and kept her voice steady. "Ryan, I know our community would support a music store and conservatory."

He lifted a dark eyebrow. "*Our* community?"

"Yes. You just said this was your hometown as well as mine." She felt her spine get straighter. "You spent your entire childhood here."

He shrugged nonchalantly. "I suppose if one thousand

square feet was a good enough space for Musically Yours, then it's good enough for us."

Somewhere in the empty space, she allowed herself a small intake of breath. Swallowing, she stared up at him. "Us?"

"Yes, ma'am." He reached for her, and his lips parted hers for a deep kiss. "Are you looking for a silent partner, my love?"

CHAPTER 8

*D*orothy rubbed her eyes and blinked at the early morning sunlight streaming through her window. Lying in the Cherish Hills Inn's luxurious king-sized bed, she flicked a glance at the time on her cell phone, grateful she could rest another half hour.

She rolled over onto her side and faced the window. Although she courted sleep, her mind was active, and she lifted a prayer to God.

"Christ is with me. His plan for me will come to pass. I believe it will happen because You are in complete control and whatever comes my way, I can handle it. Amen."

As she watched the sun rise, her thoughts turned to Ryan —his recklessly rugged face, his arresting gaze, his admiring smile. A cosmopolitan aura surrounded him, his long strides strong with authority. She'd watched videos of his performances on the internet, and it was clear the audiences loved him. During interviews he'd offered a firm handshake, laughing while he'd accepted lavish compliments from his fans with humility and grace.

A star. A talent to be reckoned with.

She could hardly believe this sophisticated man was the same man who'd raced her to church and shared an ice cream cone with her. Or the young boy who'd held back tears after his father's funeral. He'd tried to push the grief away, push her away. He'd been in crisis and had attempted to close himself off from her.

She knew the feeling well. She hadn't wanted to open up to him because she'd felt inept and unworthy, as if she'd just fallen off a turnip truck whereas he was all bland urbaneness. She was a far cry from the popular girl he'd once admired.

Yet she'd ended up telling him everything about her addiction, including her defeat.

Despite his easy smiles, she sensed he was in crisis too, an internal one which couldn't be assuaged by recognition and wealth. He wasn't being honest with himself. More important, he wasn't being honest with God.

She sighed, knowing that in a few days he would be leaving. On the other hand, she'd decided to begin a new chapter in Cherish where life felt safe and friendly and comfortable.

The previous evening she'd notified her landlord in New York City, who'd graciously agreed to let Dorothy out of her lease at the end of the month. Her handful of friends had offered to pack up her apartment and ship her belongings to Cherish as soon as Dorothy sent a forwarding address. She promised to keep in touch, realizing in hindsight that several friends had negatively enabled her by lending her money when she'd fallen short of funds. She'd needed a greater quantity of the drug as her tolerance increased and her addiction had progressed at a frightening rate. Consequently, she'd exhausted her savings.

However, Emmanuelle, a woman of great faith and Dorothy's closest friend, had offered what the doctor termed "positive enabling." Emmanuelle had encouraged Dorothy to seek therapy and check into rehab. She'd also spoken to

Nicholas in nightly phone conversations throughout Dorothy's recovery.

Dorothy had appreciated her friend's concern. Despite Emmanuelle's brilliant musical career as principal harpist for a prestigious symphony, she was dealing with her own issues. She'd been dating a wealthy man that Dorothy considered controlling, yet Emmanuelle refused to recognize his manipulation. She'd moved in with him and had since fallen off the earth.

Dorothy lifted a prayer to give Emmanuelle the wisdom to end her unhealthy relationship. Then she added praise, knowing He had placed numerous good people in her path. Nicholas, Emmanuelle, Mrs. Addyson and Ryan.

Ryan.

She whispered a 'thank you' for bringing him back into her life. In their few remaining days together, she intended to memorize everything about him—his striking face, his charismatic smile, his good-natured teasing—until his return. Because surely he'd come back to Cherish to confirm that his business investment was sound.

"I won't be able to see the day-to-day operations," he'd said before kissing her good night, "so I'll leave all the decisions in your capable hands."

Then, before she'd retired, he'd texted, 'Sleep tight, I'll be dreaming about you. If anyone can ease my insomnia, thoughts of you can.'

She lifted her left hand and stared at her slim fingers. Perhaps as time went by, she and Ryan would become even closer. Perhaps someday she'd be wearing his engagement ring, followed by a wedding band. Perhaps Ryan had been in her future all along, even when they were teenagers.

She smiled, pushed back the covers and scrambled out of bed. It was time to dress for a picture-perfect day and another exhilarating rehearsal with Ryan.

* * *

"I've been thinking about your pecan pie for a month of Sundays," Ryan said, looking up from the music he'd been studying. Looking disgracefully handsome wearing a pair of worn denims and a navy T-shirt, he sat on a high stool at Cherish Hills Inn's large center island, his dark eyebrows drawing together as he sipped a glass of sweet tea. Now and then, he'd softly sing the music from Verdi's opera. Then he'd banter with Dorothy as she'd rolled flour and shortening for pie crust, rousing her into reminiscing about their teen antics. He'd laughed with her, his tense expression easing, his features almost boyish.

The inn's owner had explained that the kitchen had recently been renovated, painted in light gray and white, offset by black countertops, stainless steel appliances and copper fixtures. The effect was a striking combination between beauty and functionality.

"Dorothy." Ryan slid his index finger around the rim of his iced tea glass. "When you asked me to join you this afternoon in the kitchen …"

"You said you'd be here with bells on," Dorothy finished.

He chuckled. "And here I am."

"You could've used the time to prepare for your upcoming audition."

"I'd much rather watch you." He studied her as she sprinkled flour onto the dough, kneaded, then picked up the rolling pin. When she was satisfied, she arranged the single-crust dough into the pie plate, then crimped and placed tin foil around the edges.

"It was nice of the owner to let me use his kitchen and oven and utensils," she said.

Ryan reached across the island and gently wiped a flour

smudge from her cheek. "You realize he'll want a piece of pecan pie as payment? If there's any left."

"You can't eat an entire pie by yourself." With an exasperated sidewise glance, she placed her hands on her hips, smearing flour on her denims. "And I'll want to put slices aside for Mrs. Addyson and Nicholas and Alice."

"Speaking of Nicholas and Alice, will they make their home in Cherish?" Ryan asked.

She set the oven to pre-heat. "The wedding is in three days, and I haven't talked to Nicholas since dinner. You?"

"No, not a word." Ryan fanned through several pages of music. Rubbing a hand down his face, he sighed and closed the music score.

"Done?" She flashed him a smile while she resumed setting out the rest of the ingredients for the pie.

"More than done. It's a challenging role and my voice is pushed from high to low extremes." He ran a hand through his hair. "My audition is slated for next Wednesday, which will give me two days to recover from jet lag after I arrive in Italy. You're staying in Cherish, correct?"

"Yes. I've canceled my flight to New York City and will live here at the inn until I find my own place. Ryan ... you'll ...you'll let me know how your audition goes?"

She kept her tone light. She wanted to add, when will I see you again? We have so little time left together.

She said neither.

"You'll be the first person I contact." He checked his phone, then placed it on the island. "I noticed the 'sale pending' sign on the store and received an email from the bank. The closing is in a couple weeks. That's quick."

"It's quick because we're offering a cash deal. Or rather, *you* are. Thank you for your generous offer. Remember, this is a loan and I intend to pay you back."

He stood, poured her a glass of sweet tea from a pitcher

in the refrigerator and set it on the island for her. "I consider Musically Yours a good investment, and I know the store will be a success with you at the helm."

"And you."

"I'm a silent partner. I won't be able to travel to the states often after *Don Carlos* begins production. That is, if I get the role. My agent informed me that Jack Youngston is already in Palermo."

"I'm certain the role will be yours."

"Thanks." He settled on the stool. "Your confidence in my abilities means a great deal."

She whisked together sugar, corn syrup, the rest of the ingredients and chopped pecans. With a flourish, she placed the pie in the preheated oven, set the timer and piled the mixing bowls in the white ceramic farmhouse sink.

"I've written out a business plan for our store." Ryan reached into his jeans pocket and handed her a list as she took a stool across from him. "Purchasing music and supplies is the first step. Eventually, you may want to sell musical instruments. If kids take music lessons at school, they can rent or purchase instruments at the store, which is added revenue."

Perusing the list, she nodded thoughtfully.

"Then choose your specialism," he continued. "Are you planning to teach piano lessons?"

"Absolutely." She raised the glass of sweet tea to her lips. "I believe God was leading me back to Cherish. He had a purpose, and this is my season to do something I was meant to do all along."

"Your purpose ..." Ryan's gaze was probing, his words careful.

"In every situation, there is a purpose. Every struggle, every setback, every incident. God decided my purpose before I had even glimpsed it."

His gaze flitted around the enormous kitchen. "God is here?"

"God is everywhere. You're always standing at a new opportunity if you give it a purpose." She paused, forming the same question on her tongue, the same question she'd asked the other day. "What is your purpose, Ryan?"

He shrugged indifferently. "Success, I suppose."

"Wealth?"

"The money part never interested me." He folded his arms across his chest and leaned back. "After my divorce, my new wealthy friends didn't offer the support system I thought they would. I was finally part of the 'in' crowd after being an outsider for so long. And you know what? I found I didn't like them—their mentalities, their 'never enough' lifestyles."

She nodded and went to the sink, picked up a clean kitchen towel, and wiped down the shiny black countertops. "So what is your purpose, Ryan?" she asked again.

"I don't know anymore, except that I want what you and your brother have—an unshakeable faith, the strength to forge ahead no matter how disappointing the circumstances."

She studied him and reformed her question. "So what has taken all your attention these past ten years? Your driving ambition, or God?"

"I no longer ask God for anything. I've given up because He's never responded."

"How can you expect God to respond if you don't uphold His standards?" she asked softly. "Those so-called friends were pulling you in the wrong direction."

"In hindsight, you're absolutely correct." He stood, then sat, then stood again, striding to the sink, rinsing mixing bowls, placing wooden spoons on the copper strainer to dry. His gaze shifted to her. "Things have been tough for you and you've pulled through."

She set down the towel. "Thanks to a good support system, I was forced to be honest with myself."

His probing gaze met hers and he offered a smile. Then he turned, seeming to stare at nothing for a long moment. "Honesty isn't easy, especially with yourself."

Despite their gaiety a few minutes earlier, she sensed his smile was strained.

Worried about his upcoming audition? Although she wished there was something she could do to ease the dark circles under his eyes, the lack of sleep was evident in his rugged face if one looked closely.

He rounded the island and drained his glass of sweet tea. He set the glass down and turned to her. "Dorothy?"

"The pie isn't done yet." She attempted to deflect his serious tone with an easygoing remark.

He walked toward her, coming to stand within arm's reach. "Did you know the sweet and gooey scent of pecan pie baking in the oven makes me think about one thing?"

"Calories?" she provided with a tongue-in-cheek smile while taking one wary step back. "You'll want to stay trim for your role as Philip."

A warm gleam softened his eyes. Reaching out, he pulled her toward him. "There's another role I'm much more inter-ested in."

"Ryan, the pie—"

He pressed his finger against her lips. "The pie isn't done yet, so we have lots of time." He drew her to him and touched his mouth to hers, coaxing her lips to part. She placed her hands around his nape, feeling the silky hair curling at the back of his neck.

His cell phone rang. Ignoring it, he deepened the kiss.

When his phone rang the second time, she broke the kiss and glanced toward the island.

His dark gaze lit with amusement. His arms around her tightened. "I'm not expecting any calls. Are you?"

"Obviously not." She rested her forehead against his hard chest, her fingers flattening on the rich woven texture of his shirt.

When his phone pinged for a third time announcing a text message, she indicated that he should answer it. "The caller is obviously being persistent."

With a resigned nod, he strode to the island. He read the text message, his expression changing to one of surprise, then disbelief.

She leaned against the counter and fingered the neckline of her red fleece pullover. "What is it?"

"The calls were from my agent. The opera company has moved up the audition schedule." Ryan looked past her, his gaze unfocused. "I need to be in Italy by Saturday."

"Impossible." She rubbed her arms, her thoughts whirling. "Nicholas' wedding is Saturday."

"I … I'll … Maybe your brother can change the date …"

"Of the wedding? For you? You're joking, right? Even *you* can't believe you're that important."

"I don't." His arms fell to his sides. "But this is a major opera and if I don't audition, I won't get the role."

"What about Nicholas and Alice?"

"I'll explain the situation to Nicholas and I'm sure he'll understand. I can … I can record the Ave Maria ahead of time." Ryan gripped her by the shoulders to face him. "You can play the recording at the church."

She swallowed hard. "What about 'The Lord's Prayer?'"

"Yes … and 'The Lord's Prayer.' I'll sing the solo a cappella, without your accompaniment. I always bring a portable audio recorder with me." He tipped up her chin and pressed a quick kiss on her temple. "All you must do is hit the play button on Saturday. It's easy."

No, no.

"Of course." She offered a false cheerfulness and pressed a hand on the island to steady herself.

The oven timer beeped. She hitched up her shoulders, grabbed two oven mitts from a drawer and lifted the pie from the oven. "What about the Stevie Wonder song we rehearsed for the recessional?"

"Find a good recording. The original is better than anything we put together."

She winced.

"Dorothy, I'm sorry. You know how much this role means." His voice dropped, his eyes tightened. "I'll book a flight out of Atlanta this afternoon, then go pack."

He was talking on his cell phone, busy with travel arrangements, as she quietly set the pie on the stove and shuffled out of the kitchen.

CHAPTER 9

Saturday came in bright with promise. Dorothy showered and washed her hair, then carefully dressed in a simple black sheath with a scalloped neckline. She decided on an elegant dress in a conservative mid-length, critically appraising herself in the full-length mirror in her room. She straightened the black velvet bow securing her hair smoothly at the nape, the rest falling in soft waves around her shoulders. Tiny diamonds sparkled at her ears and she secured a pearl necklace around her throat.

Despite a lump of anticipation in her stomach, she was ready early for the six o'clock candlelight ceremony, allowing herself plenty of time to warm up with scales and arpeggios before the wedding guests arrived.

The previous evening, Nicholas had phoned to cancel the wedding rehearsal, explaining that Alice had said they didn't need one. After all, the wedding was small with only a Maid of Honor and Best Man in attendance.

"No problem," Dorothy had agreed, shifting her attention to Ryan's list of things to do before opening Musically Yours.

By five o'clock, the sun was beginning its descent as

Dorothy made her way from the inn to her car. She secured a parking spot in front of Memorial Street Church a few minutes later.

For several beats, she sat in the car with her eyes closed.

She'd be performing solo. Suppose her fingers refused to play the rapid eighth notes in Pachelbel's Canon in D? Suppose her wrist hurt so badly while she performed Bach's Jesu, Joy of Man's Desiring, that she couldn't continue?

No. She refused to scare herself with negative thoughts and focused on her aim—contributing to her brother's wedding by giving her best performance.

"Thank you, God, for selecting me for this purpose," she whispered.

Taking a confident breath, she double-checked her briefcase containing her piano music and Ryan's solos. Before he'd left, she'd overheard him phone Nicholas to explain why he couldn't perform at the wedding and had ended with a heartfelt apology. As was his character, she knew her brother had wished Ryan only the best.

Ryan had left his recordings on the kitchen island, along with a sealed note addressed to her which she'd found the following morning.

With shaking fingers, she'd opened his note and read:

My love,

I could see it in your eyes you were hurt and disappointed with my choice. I'm sorry. You know how much this role means. I hope you can forgive me and someday give me a chance to make things better between us. You are special and mean so much to me—more than you know.

In his usual bold script he'd signed, *"Love, Ryan."*

She'd installed herself on a stool in the kitchen and stared at the note. Just stared. Tears trickled down her cheeks as she thought of the slim, dark-haired man whom she wouldn't see again for a long, long time. In her dreams she had imagined they might have a future together. Now he was gone, choosing his career over his commitments, his friends, and her.

Without a second thought she knew his success would continue to spiral upward after *Don Carlos* ended, and Ryan's stardom would keep him performing in Europe for years.

They'd never laugh together again. He'd never hold her in his solid arms, never call her "my love" in that tender, affectionate tone he'd used so often.

She'd grasped the note and huddled into herself, whispering a Psalm she knew by heart. "Weeping may last through the night, but joy comes in the morning.'"

When shadows fell to early afternoon, her tears were exhausted. She'd pushed up the sleeves of her plaid blouse and risen to her feet. Once before she'd been held hostage by her disappointment, her hopes dashed. She wouldn't allow it to define her a second time.

Three days had passed since Ryan boarded the plane from Atlanta to Italy. He'd texted her only once, saying he'd arrived safely and was preparing for his audition.

"Good," she'd texted. "Best of luck."

Now, with her posture strong and her breath purposeful, she grabbed her purse and briefcase. She was well-rehearsed to play her best for her brother and his fiancé on one of the most important days of their lives.

Mrs. Addyson, dressed in a lilac wool suit, stood at the top of the church stairs and greeted Dorothy with a nod. Her usually pleasant demeanor was distraught, and she seemed unnaturally quiet.

"Good evening, ma'am." Dorothy paused at the open wooden door leading into the inside vestibule. "I didn't expect you at church this early."

"Haven't you heard?"

Dorothy scoured her thoughts. "Heard what?"

"The wedding is off." Two bright flushes of red heightened Mrs. Addyson's rouged cheeks. "Alice texted your brother a few minutes ago and broke up with him. She's been seeing another fella at the hospital."

Dorothy set down her briefcase and purse and pulled out her phone. "Nicholas will be devastated." She stared down at her hands, then managed to return Mrs. Addyson's gaze. "Where is he?"

"He's still at his apartment. Most likely he's hurt and embarrassed."

"So there's no wedding?" Dorothy gazed into the church. The pews had been simply decorated with white ribbons. Colorful potted plants sat beneath the church's stained-glass windows.

"It's sad. Fortunately, there aren't a lot of vendors to be paid. Nicholas' friends were all contributing a covered dish for the church reception."

"Do they know?" Dorothy absently looked up from her phone. She'd texted her brother and hadn't received a response.

"I've notified everyone." Mrs. Addyson gave Dorothy a penetrating stare. "And I know your Ryan flew to Italy."

"He's not my Ryan," Dorothy said quietly. "With his talent, he belongs to the world."

"I saw the way he looked at you in the restaurant. I remember the way he looked at you when you two were young." She took Dorothy's hand. "He'll always find his way back to you."

Dorothy's gaze flew to Mrs. Addyson, then slid downward. She shook her head, put her phone away and focused on the church steps. A mixture of loneliness and dejection tore through her—gray and dull—but the delicate hope Mrs. Addyson offered bloomed like a bouquet of colorful flowers.

"Can you wait here at the church until the wedding cake

is delivered?" Mrs. Addyson let go of Dorothy's hand and pulled on her proper white gloves. "My Chrysler is parked around the corner and I'd like to get home before dark. The key-holder will lock up the church later this evening."

"What will I do with an entire wedding cake?"

"Take it back to the Cherish Hills Inn, I suppose. The bakery in town hired a talented new baker. He's a bit temperamental, which is why he might be late."

"Another artist," Dorothy murmured.

"Creative people are complex and sensitive." Mrs. Addyson paused, her anxious gaze riveted on Dorothy. "I can come by tomorrow and share a piece of wedding cake with you. The innkeeper told me you've decided to make your home in Cherish. Welcome back."

"Thank you, ma'am. I'm buying Musically Yours."

"That's as fine a bit of news as cream gravy." Mrs. Addyson beamed knowingly. "Nothing stays secret in a town this size for long, you know." With a nod of her elegantly coiffed gray hair, she bade Dorothy a good evening and made her way down the steps. Soon, walking quickly in her sturdy leather pumps, she disappeared around the corner.

Dorothy seated herself on the church's top step and placed her purse and briefcase beside her. She checked her cell phone, noting her brother still hadn't answered her texts. She'd decided to give him room to come to terms with Alice's actions. Tomorrow if he wanted to talk, she'd listen, digest, reflect and pray with him.

Dusk came sooner than expected, and the roads of Cherish, lit by corner streetlights, took on streaks of silver and gray. Tree branches swayed in wafts of cool air, and a flash of a white tail signaled the bob of a shy rabbit searching for cover. Cars hummed the streets, an intermittent flow of red and white lights.

After thirty minutes passed with no sign of a wedding

cake delivery, Dorothy gathered her belongings and stood. In the morning she'd extend her apologies to the bakery and Mrs. Addyson, for there was little use in waiting for a cake no one would be eating, anyway.

A dark sedan pulled to the curb behind her Ford rental.

Dorothy hurried down the church steps. "Perfect timing!" she called as a man emerged.

He didn't carry a wedding cake. And the sedan tore away from the curb and headed down the street.

She hesitated, debating, smiling uncertainly. Surely the temperamental baker hadn't forgotten to bring his own cake.

Except this tall, impressive man wasn't the baker. This man, who was striding toward her clutching a handful of bluebonnets and looking like a broad-shouldered handsome opera singer, was wearing a polo shirt and a beige suit jacket. And he was heartbreakingly familiar.

"Ryan." Her briefcase and purse slid from her grasp. She stopped at the bottom of the steps. "What … what are you doing here?"

"I found my purpose," he said solemnly.

"Purpose?" Her heartbeat raced. A breath wouldn't come. "Where? In Italy?"

"I found my purpose right here in my hometown."

Disoriented by his reply, she avoided eye contact. "Your audition … did you audition for *Don Carlos*?"

"Yes." He closed the distance and stopped within an inch of her. "My agent arranged the audition as soon as I arrived in Italy."

"So why aren't you …" She wasn't easily pacified and tried again. "So when will you hear how you did?"

"I've already heard."

"And?"

He drew a long breath and slowly expelled it. "I got the role."

She should congratulate him. And she would as soon as she had the ability to think coherently. "Ryan, I ... I'll watch your performances if they're televised here in the states. I'll applaud you along with the rest of your—"

"I turned it down."

"You *what?*"

"I turned the role down. After my audition I was offered a contract. I thanked my agent and the casting directors, turned around and booked the next flight back to Atlanta."

Her body tensed. Her eyes widened. "I ... I don't understand."

He handed her the bouquet of the delicate, fragrant bluebonnets, then looked around, momentarily diverted. "Where is everyone?"

"The wedding was called off. Long story." She accepted the flowers and sniffed appreciatively, the fragrance filling the air with a sweet airy scent. "Thank you. Where did you get these?"

"There's an open stream near an abandoned railway line a few blocks from here. You've pointed out frequently that bluebonnets are your favorite, so I picked a bouquet for you."

She fingered the lovely blooms, as delicate as boomtown silk. No store-bought flowers from him. These delicate blue flowers were heartfelt and strong and memorable.

"I didn't expect you to remember that."

"I remember everything about you." The earnestness in Ryan's brown eyes brought a rush of heat to her cheeks. "And now I need to tell you something, Dorothy."

She scanned his face. He was here, but he'd be leaving to go somewhere else, somewhere with brighter and better opportunities.

"What is it?" she asked warily.

"Your faith pushed me toward honesty."

"Ryan, you've always been honest—"

"No, not with myself." His gaze never left hers. They were so close although he made no move to touch her. "Seeing you in a crisis made me take a clear-eyed view of my life. You faced your weaknesses, and your faith in God never wavered. You confronted your failings head-on. I didn't. After my father's suicide I buried my emotions—the anger, the bitterness, the grief—beneath busyness, believing if I could land at the top, I would've achieved my goals."

"You have. You're a—"

"I haven't," he interrupted. "However, on the plane trip to Italy, I dug deeper inside and honestly challenged myself. I'd never done that before."

She considered him, felt the tears standing in her eyes. "And what did you discover?"

Gently, he traced a finger along her cheek. "I found it's much easier to diagnose other people's problems rather than your own. I recognized you were in crisis. What I refused to acknowledge was that I was too."

Puzzled, she looked away. "I don't understand."

"When I saw you again that first day in the choir loft, I almost couldn't breathe. You were barefoot, all curled up on that chair with your legs tucked beneath you, and you were as adorable as a calico kitten."

She leaned back and attempted to speak. No words came.

He placed the flowers on the ground and gazed into her eyes. "You'd grown into the beautiful woman I'd always admired from a distance." He enfolded her into his arms, holding her against his cotton polo shirt. His heart beat solid and reassuring.

"When I was a teenager," she whispered unsteadily against his chest, "I made excuses to be near you. I had butterflies in my stomach every time you were around."

He tipped up her chin. "And now?"

"And now I want to be around you more than ever."

"I thought about you a lot those past ten years." He braced his hands on her shoulders. "Sometimes bits and pieces, along with remembrances of my father—his changes of mood, his agitation. Memories of Cherish, both good and bad, flickered and faded. Seeing you again I realized the good memories had one thing in common."

She attempted a trembly question and swallowed.

"And that one thing was you." His lips moved closer to hers. "Every good memory had you right in the middle of it."

He pressed her closer and her fingers locked around his nape. His lips found hers and he kissed her with a hard, insistent urgency. She returned the kiss with the same earnestness, glorying in the sensation of his mouth, sending spirals of desire clear down to her toes. When the kiss ended, he embraced her face in his hands. Lovingly, his thumbs stroked her cheeks.

Stars twinkled like vibrant crystals in the night sky. The air had turned cooler. Crickets chirped, mingling with a whip-poor-will's chants. Somewhere in the distance, bullfrogs croaked. The sounds of spring, a spiritual promise of renewal, a symbol of new life. Here in Cherish, with Ryan's arms around her, the seeds of growth held promise.

Dorothy leaned her head back and gazed at his full, firm mouth, extending a not-so-subtle invitation to kiss her again.

"If you stare at me like that, I won't be able to finish, and I have more to say." He pressed a kiss on her temple, then murmured against her hair. "I didn't return to Cherish for you. I returned for your brother's wedding."

She gave a rueful sigh and shook her head. "All for naught."

His eyebrows rose. "Was it? Your brother's wedding being canceled makes me realize more than ever that we were both in the right place at the right time." He paused for an interval of several seconds. "Then when I left for Italy, I told myself I had enjoyed our time together and rationalized it was enough."

She stared up at him. "Was it enough?"

"It wasn't enough for me." His gaze was solid and steady. "I love you, Dorothy Thompson. Always have, always will. I'm here because I want you to marry me."

She gaped in speechless joy. She'd racked her brain, trying to think of what she might've done differently to encourage Ryan to stay. Perhaps that day in the inn's kitchen she could have said something, talked with him, implored him. Instead, she'd walked out of the kitchen and left him alone.

And all along, God had planned this reunion. His timing was perfect.

"What about your career?" she asked.

"My career is music. I'll teach vocal lessons and help you open the music conservatory. Together, we'll build Musically Yours back into one of the finest music stores in South Carolina."

"What you're saying ... the store ... the conservatory ... you living in Cherish ... I don't know how to respond."

"I love you back is a good beginning."

"Ryan Edwards, I love you back." She stared up into his earnest expression. "What I have to adjust to is the fact we're really going to get married."

"It's easy. Just say yes."

"Marriage is serious."

He laid both hands on her shoulders. "And I couldn't be more serious."

She shook her head. She needed some place to think. Or did she? Gazing into the face of the man she loved, only one reply formed on her lips.

"Yes."

"Do you mean it?" he persisted.

"I do." Yearning for Ryan's lips on hers, she stood on her toes and slid her arms around his shoulders.

Their hearts now beat in a skillful cadence because God proved that His timing is always perfect.

THE END

A NOTE FROM JOSIE

Thank you for reading *A Love Song To Cherish*. I hope you enjoyed your visit to the scenic town of Cherish, South Carolina, and the new music store, Musically Yours.

If you loved this romance as much as I loved writing Ryan and Dorothy's story, please help other people find *A Love Song To Cherish* by posting your review.

A Love Song To Cherish is available separately in ebook, paperback, Large Print paperback, Hardcover, and audiobook.

My Spotify Play List for A Love Song To Cherish is here.

With sincere appreciation for your support.

Josie Riviera

DOROTHY'S PECAN PIE RECIPE

Prep time: 20 minutes
    Bake 1 hour

Ingredients

- 1/2 cup sugar
- 3 tablespoons flour
- 1 cup light corn syrup
- 1 cup dark corn syrup
- 3 eggs
- 1 teaspoon white vinegar
- 1/2 teaspoon vanilla extract

- 1 cup chopped pecans
- Pastry for a single-crust pie

Directions

- **1.** In small bowl, whisk sugar, flour, corn syrups, eggs, vinegar and vanilla. Stir in pecans. Pour into pastry shell and place foil around edges.
- **2.** Bake at 350° for 35 minutes. Remove foil; bake 25-30 minutes longer.
- Yields 8 servings.
- Enjoy!

USA TODAY BESTSELLING AUTHOR
JOSIE RIVIERA
a Christmas to Cherish
A SWEET AND WHOLESOME HOLIDAY NOVELLA

PRAISE AND AWARDS

**USA TODAY bestselling author
#1 Bestseller Women's Religious Fiction
#1 Bestseller Contemporary Religious Fiction
#1 Bestseller Inspirational Religious Fiction
#2 Bestseller Inspirational Prayer**

Emmanuelle Sumter surveyed the picturesque town of Cherish, South Carolina, brightly lit in crimson and green holiday decor. The town looked as if it had emerged from a Christmas card. Glittering frost framed bare tree branches, and local artists were setting up their canvases for an art walk. The coldness in the air was soundless and serene, comforting in its own way.

She exited the Cherish Central train station, zippered her cobalt-blue puffer coat to her chin, and stepped onto the curb.

Who believed an actual, breathing town could resemble a holiday snow globe?

Evidently, her friend Dorothy did, considering her enthusiasm whenever she described her idyllic South Carolina town.

Emmanuelle stood on the curb and shoved her hands in her pockets. A cold December gust slapped her cheeks, sharp streams of frigid air. She swept a wisp of hair from her cheek and searched for Nicholas, Dorothy's older brother. He was supposed to pick her up. People were shouting greetings, kissing, cooing over babies. A teeming mass of humanity.

But no Nicholas.

A taxi's horn spiked. Emmanuelle jumped, an involuntary nervous reaction.

Take a deep breath. Relax. Dorothy had assured her Cherish was a safe haven, a harbor in a storm.

Repeating her mantra, Emmanuelle hailed the black-bearded taxi driver parked at the curb. She still didn't see any sign of Nicholas, so she'd take the cab.

She handed the driver her suitcase, then slid into the backseat and gave the address of Dorothy's music store, Musically Yours.

They passed charming shops decorated in glittering lights, and a sign advertising a historic home tour. A few minutes later, the driver pointed at the Musically Yours lighted outdoor sign and idled at the corner of Myrtle and Magnolia Streets.

"The store's two hoots and a holler away, ma'am." He hoisted her suitcase from the trunk and set it on the sidewalk. "We've reached your destination."

Destination. Was this where her journey ended after a year filled with pain and abuse? Did hope and encouragement wait for her in this little town?

A new life. With perseverance, she could start fresh.

"Thanks." She climbed from the taxi, paid the driver and grabbed her suitcase.

Daylight faded as dusk crept in, and she tipped her head to take in Evergreen Street. Family-owned businesses had switched on their storefront lights, transforming the town into a fairy-tale sparkle of miniature white lights. The tantalizing scent of honey roasted almonds wafted through the air. Boughs of fragrant holly tied with red velvet bows hung cheerily from tall solitary lampposts. Bright-faced children skipped by, lifting their faces skyward to catch a sprinkling of snow. Their conscientious parents followed close behind.

"Emmanuelle! You arrived right on time!" Dorothy flung open the door of the music store and pressed a welcoming kiss to Emmanuelle's cheek. Dorothy's brown hair was swept up in a French braid, her creamy complexion glowing with an enthusiasm Emmanuelle didn't recall from their days working as struggling musicians in New York.

Dorothy had lived there before moving back to Cherish, her hometown, and marrying her high school crush, Ryan Edwards. He had been an opera star in the making and had given up his touring career to settle in Cherish. They were newlyweds. They were in love.

Love. The beginning was always so alluring. It was the end Emmanuelle feared.

Dorothy regarded the departing taxi. "Apparently Nicholas didn't pick you up?"

"I didn't see him so I took a cab."

Emmanuelle turned from Dorothy and admired Musically Yours' frosty window display, bedecked in an infinite array of treble clef signs. A pine wreath, embellished in antique ornaments—tiny pianos, violins, and harps—adorned the front door.

"It's wonderful," she said. "You've worked so hard to set this up."

"Thanks. Ryan and I are still learning the business, and we're inspired by anything musical."

Emmanuelle smiled, but then shivered. "It's colder here than I expected. At least the blizzard that threatened to shut down New York never came."

"The storm hit after you left," Dorothy replied. "You escaped the worst of it."

Did she? She couldn't answer at first, finally whispering, "Hopefully."

Dorothy raised a delicate eyebrow, but Emmanuelle didn't elaborate. Sure, she'd escaped the snowstorm. An escape from George, her ex, was yet to be determined.

Please God, be with me now in my dark season, when I'm so out of place. The world around me is glowing with the promise of Christmas and I feel dark and empty inside.

She leaned forward to admire two animated polar bears sitting amidst the treble clef signs in the shop's window. Beneath a starry sky, the bears tapped drums to the tune of "Jingle Bells."

"Very clever." She couldn't help a grin. "Thanks for the invite to Cherish."

"We're thrilled you agreed to join us for Christmas." Dorothy grabbed her hands for a reassuring squeeze. She was so pleasant and gracious, Emmanuelle thought. So jovial.

On the other hand, Emmanuelle felt the opposite. All she had become in twenty-five years—a dependable, straightforward woman as well as an esteemed harpist—she'd lost in six months to George.

She'd once been like Dorothy, resilient, independent and a woman of God.

Her ex had taken it all away.

Deep in her coat pocket, her fingers worried an angel ornament she'd purchased at the New York airport. For her, the ornament symbolized the sacred Christmas season, its optimism, dreams, and promise.

She hadn't taken it out of her pocket yet.

"You've been difficult to reach these past few months." Dorothy studiously appraised Emmanuelle. "You hardly ever answered your phone."

"I've been busy with concert engagements." Emmanuelle forced her features to remain blank. "You know, musician stuff." It was a lie, and with the lie came heaviness, a wide band of disapproval. Where had her sense of decency gone?

She tightened her paisley scarf around her neck. Although the violent purple and yellow bruises had faded, she still felt self-conscious.

Dorothy guided her into the music store. "My brother will blame his forgetfulness on his new job, or that gigantic puppy he adopted at the animal shelter. You'd think he'd know better at thirty years old."

"He's a good guy," Emmanuelle said. "Nicholas and I Skyped every night for months when you were in rehab."

"Thanks to you both, I'm better." Dorothy smiled. "And most important, thanks to God."

Once, Emmanuelle would have readily agreed. God was her salvation, her refuge. Now she didn't know how to answer because her faith had wavered.

Truly I tell you, if you have faith as small as a mustard seed, you can say to this mountain, "Move from here to there," and it will move. The verse from Matthew 17:20 came to her mind, a reminder of her strength. All she had to do was reach for it, if she was brave enough.

Inside the store, Dorothy ran a finger along one of the shelves, grinning when she was assured it was dust free. "Ryan and I purchased a cottage-style bungalow four blocks from here and there's an extra bedroom."

"This is your first Christmas as a married couple." Emmanuelle set her suitcase out of the way of a passing customer. "Please celebrate the holiday without me in the middle."

"I insist you stay with us."

"For an entire month?" Emmanuelle shook her head. "Insist all you want. I booked a room at the Cherish Hills Inn. You raved about the inn's accommodations being top-quality when you returned to Cherish for your brother's wedding last year."

"The wedding that didn't happen." Ruefully, Dorothy

sighed. "Nicholas is still healing from the embarrassment and heartbreak."

The ending stages of love. Dreams shattered.

Without warning, the front door burst open. Instinctively, Emmanuelle held up a hand, shielding herself from view.

A heavy-set woman, her hair helmeted in a tight gray bun, ambled inside. She called out a jovial hello to Dorothy.

"Be with you in a minute, Mrs. McManus." Dorothy gave a flap of her hands, and then turned back to Emmanuelle. "Sorry. What were we discussing?"

Emmanuelle blew out a breath. This uneasiness, this fear of being followed, had to stop.

Still shaken, she kept her focus on a Mozart statue topped with a red plush Santa hat sitting on the counter.

"We were discussing the wedding that didn't happen," she replied. "Whenever Nicholas and I talked when you were in rehab, he always reminded me we should place our trust in God."

"Sadly, people change, beliefs change." Worry replaced Dorothy's earlier smile. "Hard knocks can shake the faith of the most devout. I pray he'll go to church again because he's faltered since the breakup."

Suggesting Emmanuelle put her suitcase behind the front counter, Dorothy led her past a display table. As Dorothy paused to rearrange two pairs of oboe earrings so they lined up side by side, she said, "God had other plans for him and for me. I believe things work out for the best."

Emmanuelle frowned and nodded, aborting both actions.

For Dorothy, perhaps. For Ryan. For anyone in this idyllic snow globe town. But not for me. And apparently not for Nicholas.

Her cell phone buzzed. She retrieved it from her tote bag and scanned the screen. *Unknown caller.* Her heart stopped. A telemarketer? A wrong number?

"Who is it?"

Looking up, she saw Dorothy was studying her with keen interest.

"No one." Fumbling, Emmanuelle tucked the phone back into her faux leather tote. "You're right. People change for many reasons." And she'd changed most of all. She'd been a competent, successful woman. Now a chill crept up her spine when a door opened into a harmless music store.

"Are you okay?" Dorothy asked.

"I'm fine, just tired from traveling." Emmanuelle's eyes welled with tears, and she averted her gaze. She'd applied makeup, the first time in months, attempting to conceal her sleep deprivation. The endless worrying and crying had taken a toll.

"We're organizing a concert in the town square the weekend before Christmas," Dorothy was saying. "I meant to ask you to bring your harp—"

"My harp weighs nearly eighty pounds." She picked up a pair of piano earrings and fingered the tiny keyboard. "It's in New York."

Broken. She wouldn't reveal how George had destroyed her harp in one of his lightning-fast rages. The memory caused a block of ice to form in her stomach, a block that she knew would be slow to thaw. She hated the thought of her beloved instrument, splintered into pieces, lying on a New York curb under a pile of snow.

Better the harp than you splintered into pieces.

But his shouted insults and rough slaps had been her fault. She'd provoked him.

No, no, no. Her inner voice took on a sharp edge. That was the old Emmanuelle talking. The new Emmanuelle knew she wasn't a dishtowel to be thrown around on a whim. In hindsight, she should have known George was abusive. The warning signs were there.

She blew out a breath. She'd resolved to find peace and comfort in this holiday … in this town … somewhere … and find her footing again.

"Enough about me." She set down the earrings and dismissed herself with a flutter of her fingers. "Where's Ryan?"

"He's rehearsing in nearby Stanley Valley today and will arrive this evening. He'll be singing 'O Holy Night' for a Christmas Cantata service. He gives so freely of his talent." Dorothy's smile was as radiant as a Merry Christmas bouquet. "He's featured throughout the Carolinas in many guest appearances. Plus, the Atlanta opera house asked him to perform the role of Zoroastro in Handel's opera, *Orlando*. I'm incredibly proud of him."

"You should be." Dorothy's smile was contagious, and Emmanuelle managed a warm grin. "He's famous and extremely talented."

"And you? Any upcoming concerts?"

"None." She answered in a firm tone that she expected would discourage her friend from probing. Judging by the way Dorothy's eyebrows drew together, she'd succeeded.

Fortunately, an acoustic guitar arrangement of "Lo, How a Rose Is Blooming" piped in the background, the ideal holiday music to smooth a lull in the conversation.

"I'm sure you're keen to check in." Dorothy broke the silence. "I'll deal with these last few customers, close the store, and give you a lift. Unless you'd rather walk the three blocks to the inn?"

"No, no. I'll wait for you."

She'd never walk alone again. Not in New York, not in Cherish. Not anywhere, because she'd never feel safe again.

Dorothy gestured toward the front of the store. "If you care to browse, the Christmas music section is on your left. There's a lovely harp arrangement of *The Nutcracker*."

"Thanks. Your store is a music-lover's dream."

Intrigued, Emmanuelle stepped past a buyer laden with music bookmarks and made her way to the sheet music. She thumbed through endless arrangements of Christmas solos, wondering what madness had brought her to this town. She didn't belong here among all this gaiety. Her sadness was a burden refusing to go away.

Disheartened, she stared, trancelike, at the display window. A whimsical model train circled the polar bears, and the sight was enchanting.

Beyond, past the cheery town, past the exuberant children and the enormous Christmas tree illuminating the town square, a darkened sky had followed dusk.

As he entered his apartment, Nicholas Thompson pulled off his deputy badge and set it on a table in the foyer. Except for one traffic violation, a minor fender bender and endless meetings, the day had been relatively calm for a newbie deputy.

He looked forward to relaxing in front of the TV with a good cup of coffee and a chocolate-glazed doughnut. Ever since he'd become a deputy, he'd acquired a taste for both.

All fifty pounds of his six-month-old golden retriever greeted him with an energetic stretch. He'd purchased the dog from an animal shelter in Stanley, two weeks to the day after his fiancée, Alice, had broken up with him. The dog surveyed Nicholas with expectant black eyes and a fiercely wagging tail.

"No, Molly Belle, I'm not taking you for a—"

The dog ran in circles around him and barked.

Nicholas groaned. He'd no sooner walked in and he was forced to turn around and walk out again. "All right, take a tater and wait a sec." He weaved around a mountain of laundry and strode to his bedroom. His bed was unmade, an old sweat-shirt tossed over a side chair. He removed the gun from his holster and locked it in his bedroom closet's safe. Then he loosened his tie and changed out of uniform—white shirt and khaki pants—dragging on jeans, a long-sleeved T-shirt, and work boots. Pausing, he ran a critical survey of his apartment, particularly the coffee table piled with remote controls and junk mail and old catalogues. The large sofa begged for a skilled reupholster, and his sister, Dorothy, had admonished him countless times to hang curtains on his bare windows.

He darted a glance at the motorcycle calendar propped on a shelf. Today was December first, and Christmas was less than a month away. At the very least, the season merited a Christmas tree in the corner and a wreath on his apartment door.

Nope. Not this year.

Despite Molly Belle lightening his days, Nicholas didn't have the heart for celebrations and feasts. What other man in the state of South Carolina had experienced the humiliation of his fiancée leaving him on their wedding day? And by text, no less. Not even in person.

The dog's impertinent barking prompted him to grab the leash, button his navy pea coat and open the front door. With an eager yelp, Molly Belle ran ahead, down his short flight of stairs and onto the sidewalk.

"Slower, girl." The dog, as usual, didn't obey and tugged harder on the leash. Nicholas made a mental note to sign her up for obedience classes.

His cell phone buzzed. He hoped it wasn't a call to drive back to the police station. Relieved to see Dorothy's caller ID, he clicked on.

"Nicholas, are you through with work?" she asked.

"Yes, I just got in." He restrained the dog from sniffing

every blade of glass in a neighbor's garden. "I'm taking Molly Belle for a walk."

"Emmanuelle arrived an hour ago. Did you forget?"

He sighed and slapped a hand to his forehead. He forgot a lot of things lately. "I got sidetracked by last-minute meetings at the police station. Please tell her I'm sorry."

"You can tell her yourself. We're at the Cherish Hills Inn and she's unpacking. Meet us here, then join us at Frank's Pizzeria for a slice. It's your favorite restaurant."

His first response was *no* before he thought better of it. He should extend a polite apology, considering he'd forgotten to pick up the woman. He'd swing by and make his amends and then leave.

As he and Molly Belle neared the inn, it was all he could do not to reverse direction and head back to his apartment.

He could work. He could take care of his spirited dog. But he didn't relish small talk with a woman, especially a woman he'd grown close to during their many phone conversations. What would he say to her after all these months?

"Oh, by the way, Emmanuelle, do you remember me talking nonstop about Alice, my fiancée? She left me the day of our wedding."

Molly Belle ignored his command to walk slower, nearly choking on the leash as she lunged forward.

*B*attling for control of the leash, Nicholas strode into the Cherish Hills Inn's lobby. Briefly, he admired the boxwood wreath hanging on the wooden door, the lighted village scene on a round cherry tabletop in the foyer. He greeted the white-haired innkeeper, Tom Canning, with an apologetic shrug and lifted the dog's leash.

Tom scowled. Crevices grooved the sides of his mouth. "No animals."

"Just this once—for someone you've known your entire life?" Nicholas asked. "For a man who upholds the law in our town?"

Tom sighed, unbending a bit, and peered at Nicholas above the cheaters perched on the bridge of his nose. "Go ahead, deputy." He rewarded Nicholas with a brief nod, but raised his index finger to issue a one-minute warning.

"Thanks." Nicholas strode across the wide plank floors to the parlor where a fire blazed in the stacked rock fireplace, so large an ox could stand upright inside it. On the center of the mantel sat a handsomely carved Nativity set in burnished wood. Artistically arranged seasonal fruit—oranges and apples and pears—were loaded high in a wide pewter bowl on a side table.

He directed his gaze toward Dorothy, who stood near the fireplace, and that was the last thing he remembered.

The undeniably beautiful woman who stood beside Dorothy, clad in a white lace sweater dress, resembled a dainty, sweet confection. Her complexion was pink, her dark lashes slightly lowered, her lips plush and generous. A puffy blue jacket was slung over her shoulders, and she held a tote bag close to her side.

His mind reeled with memories.

Emmanuelle Sumter. They'd Skyped many times, so he'd known she was attractive, but in person she was positively breathtaking. Silky blonde hair rioted around her face in impossibly tight curls, and her huge blue eyes acknowledged a tentative welcome.

"I assume you remember me." He fumbled with Molly Belle's leash as the dog sniffed the rug incessantly. "You look … different in person." *Better,* he amended to himself. *She looked better. More than better.* He extended his free hand. "Please accept my apologies for forgetting you."

"Apology accepted." She placed her small hand in his large one. "How could I forget our nightly conversations? You guided Dorothy through a challenging season in her life."

Emmanuelle's features were so petite, her fingers so fragile. "And you were the friend she counted on." He tightened his grip and vigorously shook her hand.

"You were the person who prayed with her every day." She pulled away, politely, decisively. "You encouraged her."

"Hold on you two, I'm right here!" Dorothy laughingly stepped between them. "Are you competing in a compliment contest I'm not aware of?"

Emmanuelle's dimples winked in a slight smile. "Your brother's the winner."

"Please don't boost his ego, or he'll expect you to treat for pizza." Dorothy chuckled. "Frank's Pizza is within walking distance. They advertise the best pizza in town."

"Because they're the only pizzeria in town." Nicholas helped Emmanuelle on with her coat, then swung Molly Belle's leash up and down. "Unfortunately they don't allow animals and I won't be able to go."

Molly Belle responded with a defiant stare and Emmanuelle leaned down to pet her. "Aww, your dog is so friendly." Soon, the dog was lying on the rug legs up, outstretched in doggy ecstasy while Emmanuelle crouched to rub her stomach.

"You said you'd just gotten home from work," Dorothy said as she encouraged Emmanuelle and the dog to stand, then steered the threesome to the doorway. "Have you eaten dinner, Nicholas?"

"I'll whip up something." He couldn't imagine what although there was a slight possibility a frozen pizza sat in his freezer behind a carton of peanut butter ice cream.

Molly Belle had different ideas, having decided Emmanuelle was her new best friend. With a wiggle of glee, she changed direction and hurled straight into her.

Emmanuelle fell back and Nicholas let go of the leash to stop her fall. Freed from her leash, the dog shot in another direction and knocked over a crystal vase filled with red roses. The vase shattered on the floor.

Tom, eye-glass cheaters in hand, tore into the parlor. His face colored to a beet-red as he tapped his watch. "Your one-minute dog visit was up five minutes ago, Nicholas."

"Sorry. We were just leaving." Nicholas righted Emmanuelle as Dorothy picked up the roses, then he dashed forward to retrieve the leash.

"Shoo, all of you!" Tom said. "I'll clean up the mess."

The women followed Nicholas. They exited to a whip of

icy wind that blew Emmanuelle's curls around her face. Nicholas lifted his hand, an automatic response to protect her from another gust. She flinched, tightened the pink paisley scarf around her neck, and moved a step away.

He tossed an inquiring glance toward her. She ignored him.

As if by mutual agreement to cover up Emmanuelle's skittish behavior, Dorothy began talking about every holiday event scheduled in three counties between Christmas and New Year's.

"Frank's boasts an outdoor enclosed eating area," Dorothy continued, talking in a loud voice to drown out the quiet. She stopped briefly to commend the florist shop's front window decorated in scarlet-red poinsettias and twine wreaths. "I'm sure Frank's will allow Molly Belle inside, Nicholas. She's leashed and we'll take an out-of-the-way table."

Before Nicholas could comment, Dorothy's cell phone pinged. She grabbed it from her tote bag, read the text, then extended an unapologetic grin. "Ryan returned early from Stanley. A few weeks ago, he bought a cookbook called *Southern Charms* at a fundraiser for encouraging women empowerment, and he's been learning to cook gourmet. He's preparing a romantic dinner of rosemary chicken and pasta salad and he wants me to come home now. He has a surprise for me."

"I applaud your husband for buying a cookbook and supporting a beneficial cause." Despite his words, Nicholas sent his sister an exasperated glance. "So, you invited me to join you for dinner and now you're leaving?"

If she was trying to fix him up with Emmanuelle, he refused to go along with it. From what Dorothy had revealed, Emmanuelle had accepted his sister's offer to visit Cherish for the holidays primarily to get away from New York. The result of breaking up with a man. It was always because of a man, he thought, reflecting on his cheating fiancée and her new boyfriend.

He wanted to extend a sympathetic ear, for surely Emmanuelle wanted to talk at length about the break-up, although he wasn't in the proper frame of mind to attend to anyone's problems other than his own.

Yes, he'd gotten along well with her. They had talked nightly for months because of their shared interest in Dorothy's welfare, plus their unshakeable faith in God. But his life was different now. His faith teetered. If he had to define it, he'd say his faith was lukewarm.

He tuned back in when he heard Emmanuelle say, "Don't disappoint Ryan." She put her hand on Dorothy's arm, then flashed a look at Nicholas. "I'll double back and finish unpacking if you don't mind walking me."

This was his out. A polite response and he'd be sitting in his recliner watching television within fifteen minutes flat. Instead, he found himself saying, "We're almost at the restaurant so we might as well enjoy dinner."

Besides pizza, the restaurant had good coffee.

"Perfect! You two go on without me. I'm sure there's a lot to catch up on since you haven't talked in a year." Dorothy tucked her brown hair under the black wool cap she produced from her handbag. With a satisfied wave, she swung in the opposite direction.

"This way." Nicholas touched Emmanuelle's arm. She sidestepped him and ran a hand over the zipper of her jacket. Although she appeared to be an elegant and poised woman, she was as edgy as a newborn fawn.

Perhaps there was nothing left to discuss? Dorothy, their commonality, no longer required their help, and he obviously wasn't interesting enough for pretty and popular Emmanuelle. The thought left him maintaining a chilly and reserved silence as they walked toward the restaurant.

His gaze landed on two tow-headed toddlers running ahead of them. They pointed to the fairyland of Christmas lights in the town square and the sight made Nicholas smile. He loved children, although now he'd never have any. He'd never subject his heart to another battering. He'd successfully barricaded himself behind a solid, protective shell.

Lonely? Sometimes.

Safe? Definitely.

He headed Emmanuelle and Molly Belle toward the next block.

Molly Belle had a mind of her own, though, wanting nothing more than to loll on the sidewalk and hug the ground. He encouraged the dog with an assurance of a treat, and Emmanuelle added a "C'mon girl."

When they resumed walking, he asked, "Are you still the principal harpist for ... I forgot the name of the symphony. It was in a town somewhere outside New York."

"No, I'm not playing the harp anymore. It's gone." Stillness reigned for several beats after her self-deprecating laugh. He recognized the defeat in her shining blue eyes, and sympathy flickered in his hardened heart.

"What about you?" The audible stress in her tone made him hesitate. "I remember you were studying for an important exam."

"The police academy. I passed and I'm a deputy."

Her eyes widened. "A—a deputy ..." She blanched and missed a step.

"And here I thought congratulations were in order," he half joked.

"Yes, of course." She clutched her tote bag and kept her head down. "Umm, congratulations, Deputy Thompson."

Something had happened to her in New York. Something bad, although he couldn't offer any support because he was empty. The woman whom he'd thought had loved him had left him flat. He'd been a blind fool while she'd deceived him for months, but he'd learned a painful lesson and he'd learned it well. Relationships with women were well off his radar, especially when a woman clearly had a hang-up about men.

Bachelorhood was serene. Naught to fear, because nothing—no hearts, no feeling, no plans—would be broken. Besides, a dog was excellent company.

Despite himself, his gaze lingered on Emmanuelle's profile, her slim figure she kept well-hidden beneath her winter jacket and high boots.

Molly Belle barked a little too enthusiastically, prompting Emmanuelle to jump when a black lab trotted past.

"She's high-spirited," Nicholas offered as an explanation.

"Who's in control here?" she asked him. "I used to work around dogs. They were a big part of my life." She patted Molly Belle's head, then smiled when the dog put a wet nose in her hand.

"I'm considering dog obedience classes. Do you think it's a good idea?"

Emmanuelle opened her mouth, closed it again, grinned. "Yes, it's an excellent idea. In the meantime, begin with simple commands like *sit* and *wait*. Can you do that?"

"Certainly. I'm the master."

An irreverent chuckle burst from her lips and he fought the insane impulse to kiss her.

He knew her through those lengthy phone conversations, and every night he'd looked forward to their discussions about God, and their everyday lives, and their pasts. Their comfortable hour-long chats had become easy and familiar. If he hadn't been engaged to his fiancée at the time, he might have admitted the attraction he'd felt for Emmanuelle.

This stiffness between them was foreign. She had frequently sought his advice, the comfort of his faith coinciding with her hard-won beliefs. She'd been orphaned when she was in her teens, but she had persevered, studied hard, and become a virtuoso harpist.

They walked the last block to the restaurant at a quick pace. Her knee-length dress glided along her legs and her suede boots fit high above her knee. Nicholas kept stealing glances at her. The self-sufficient woman he'd known had evaporated. She'd become breakable, her voice soft, her movements hesitant.

They walked up the steps to the pizzeria's entrance, and he reached around to open the door.

"I'm ordering Frank's deluxe-meat lovers special," he said. "Are you the salad type?"

"Salad? Salad is for vegetarians." She walked past him into the restaurant, her expression amused. "I'm the barbecue and corn fritters type."

CHAPTER 4

The next day was Saturday, and Nicholas worked a half day. The morning had started with an arrest for drunk driving and ended in the police station with multiple copies of blank forms to fill out. He loved his job, but he could do without the written procedures and minute details.

When he returned home at noon, he changed out of his uniform and into jeans and a shirt, a white pullover hoodie, and running shoes. He dashed off a reminder note to price affordable curtains over the weekend, then leashed Molly Belle for a quick jog.

Ryan's surprise for Dorothy the previous night had been tickets to a tuba Christmas concert in Stanley, and Dorothy had given Nicholas the not-so-subtle hint that Emmanuelle would be spending the day alone. Despite telling himself a firm *no*, he found himself veering toward the Cherish Hills Inn.

Their dinner at the pizzeria had ended abruptly when Emmanuelle had pleaded tiredness soon after he began telling her about his job as deputy sheriff. He'd started off by regaling her with amusing tales of some of the absurd arrests he'd made. One had been for drunk and disorderly conduct when a spectator ran onto the field of a high school football game declaring he was the sixth offensive lineman. On another occasion, he'd walked an eighteen-year-old home to face his parents after a keg party had gotten out of control, only to have the boy get sick on their front lawn.

As he talked, Emmanuelle's shoulders had tightened and her hand quivered as she'd pushed the barbecue around her plate. Her fear was tangible, stretching across the red-checkered tablecloth, and the pizza set neatly in the center of the table.

He got the hint and stopped talking about his profession altogether, carrying on instead a reasonably normal conversation, albeit one-sided, observing the average winter temperature in South Carolina and New York.

The inn neared, and he closed the distance to the porch steps in five long strides.

He leaned forward to catch his breath and wipe his brow on the sleeve of his hoodie. Wide-slatted rocking chairs were assembled on the expansive front porch and evergreen garland and holly berries were strung across each window.

Although he normally would simply walk into the inn, after the mishap the day before, he thought it best if he knocked first.

Pushing his cheaters down his nose, Tom Canning peered through the entry's side glass, glowered, and flung open the door. "No dogs allowed inside, Deputy Thompson." He tried to sound polite, but there was no mistaking that he was issuing an order. "No exceptions."

"I'm sorry about yesterday, Mr. Canning, and I'll be happy to pay for any damages."

"Good. I'll write up a bill for you."

"No hurry. I mean, please do." Nicholas kept a sneakered

foot in the door as the innkeeper attempted to shut him out. "Will you let Emmanuelle know I'm here?"

Tom took off his cheaters and polished them. "Is she expecting you?"

"Probably not."

"Hi Nicholas." Emmanuelle appeared at the bottom of the curved staircase, looking bewitchingly beautiful. Her blonde hair was piled high at the crown, her ever-present pink scarf around her neck, her puffy blue jacket all zippered.

"I guess she was expecting you." With a conspiratorial half grin toward Nicholas, the owner ushered them outside, then slammed the door, leaving Emmanuelle and Nicholas standing on the porch with Molly Belle.

Annoyed, Nicholas fixed his gaze on the door. "I thought everyone loved animals. Apparently, Tom doesn't like dogs."

"His reasons are excellent." She didn't withhold her chuckle. "That vase of roses spilled water across his rug and cost him thirty minutes of clean-up, not to mention the cost of the vase and flowers."

"I offered to pay for the damages." Nicholas inspected her trim, shapely form. Today, black jeans and high boots accentuated her long legs. A green sweater peeked from beneath her winter jacket. "Were you … expecting me?"

The color on her cheekbones rose to a flattering blush against her creamy complexion. The afternoon sun gilded her blonde hair to streaks of platinum, and he favored her with an unabashed smile. She was stunning.

She stretched on a pair of pink knit gloves that matched her scarf. "Dorothy mentioned you might stop by."

"Several local booths in the town square are selling Christmas items. Are you up for some last-minute shopping?" He was prepared for her to refuse. However, he didn't expect the wariness on her face, the absolutely motionless air between them.

"I have no reason to shop. I'm not buying any Christmas gifts this year." She focused a pained stare on the mixed greenery placed around the white rocking chairs.

An unexpected fury flowed through his veins at whoever had hurt her. When? Where?

"Surely there's something you'd like." He grinned, an attempt to disarm her. "The locals sell handmade jewelry and artwork and leather goods. And I have it on excellent authority that one of my friends, who owns a restaurant called The Grill Room, set up early this morning and is smoking South Carolina barbecue as we speak."

She considered her watch. "It's a little late for lunch."

"It's just shy of two o'clock. We'll call it an early dinner." He hooked his thumbs in the back pockets of his jeans and felt the leash go slack. In an instant, his dog had raced off the porch in a mad chase after a squirrel.

"Molly Belle!"

What happened next occurred in slow motion.

The dog ran into the road. Brakes squealed. A sickening thud.

"No!" Unmindful of traffic, Nicholas dashed for his dog, seeing only Molly Belle's limp body lying helpless in the middle of the road. Blood seeped from her stomach, matting her glossy golden fur. He sank down, right there with his dog, and did something he hadn't done since he was a child.

He cried.

CHAPTER 5

*E*mmanuelle sat in the passenger seat of the innkeeper's lime-green Volkswagen and held the dog in her lap while Nicholas drove. She controlled her voice as she rubbed Molly Belle gently behind her ears. She'd secured a makeshift muzzle using the dog's leash, assuring Nicholas even Molly Belle, a sweet dog, could lash out when she was in pain.

"Looks like a surface wound," she said. Carefully, she lifted the dog's lip, murmuring about capillary refill time. When Nicholas didn't seem to hear her, she added, "Fortunately, the driver stopped in time."

Everything had happened in a blur. Visibly distraught, the driver had burst from his car in a frenzy and groped for the words to apologize. Tom Canning rushed out and offered Nicholas his car, and then dashed to the inn. He was back almost instantly with sterile gauze and a yellow crocheted blanket an instant later. A bystander stopped traffic, which allowed Nicholas and Tom to use the blanket as a sling and carry the dog to the car. Emmanuelle placed gauze over the dog's stomach and applied pressure, murmuring relief when the blood didn't soak through.

Nicholas drove quickly and silently to Cherish Animal Hospital. She took in his granite profile, his short blond hair shoved back from his forehead. He hunched behind the wheel stuffed into a car not made to fit his six-foot frame.

"She doesn't appear to be in shock." She kept her voice quiet and upbeat.

His dog might not be in shock, but Nicholas was. He had taken immediate action, though, and had phoned the animal hospital to tell them they were on their way.

"You don't know that," he finally responded.

"Yes, I do. I've been around plenty of sick dogs."

When they arrived at the hospital, Nicholas parked near the entrance. Once more using the blanket as a sling, they carried the dog past a red-haired receptionist who announced that her name was Scarlett Evans.

Dr. Judson Troutman, the veterinarian, waited for them in the examining room. Nicholas had mentioned to Emmanuelle that Dr. Troutman had been widowed two years earlier.

Slim, serious, and sandy-haired, the vet was casually dressed in khaki pants, a button-down shirt, and a white lab coat. After brief introductions, he checked Molly Belle's lungs with his stethoscope and confirmed Emmanuelle's evaluation. The dog wasn't in shock.

"My father was a veterinarian," Emmanuelle said. Reverently, she ran a hand along the stethoscope after the vet had laid it to one side.

"You learned well, Emmanuelle." His deep-brown eyes were kind, his demeanor innately gentle. He angled toward Nicholas. "I'm going to give Molly Belle all the time she needs, Deputy Thompson. After her fluids are stabilized and the diagnostics run, I'll give you an update. For now, there's nothing else to do except sit and wait."

Scarlett ushered them into the reception area. A nervous-looking woman in her fifties cradling a quivering black dachshund bobbed a brief hello.

Emmanuelle slid onto a thinly padded chair and nudged aside a half-finished cup of coffee set on a corner table. She rubbed her arms and then dropped her head into her open hands. Now that her adrenaline had settled, she felt chilled and kept her jacket and scarf over her shoulders.

Nicholas paced the hallway for several minutes before coming to sit beside her. "I don't know why I wasn't paying attention and didn't hold onto her leash tighter. If only I had …" He stared down at his hands.

She scanned his clenched fists, the skin bunching at his eyes. "Molly Belle is blessed with the ability to love life. You're the most important part and not to blame. She's always on a leash and you do all you can to keep her safe."

Her quiet reassurances seemed to help, for he sat straighter.

"Still, I was lax. Will she ever forgive me?"

"Of course."

She didn't know where to put her hands, so she rested them on her lap.

Scarlett ushered the nervous woman cradling the dachshund down the long hallway. A door banged shut.

"The accident should never have taken place." Nicholas scrubbed his fingers over his face. "I can't make sense of it. Lately, I can't make sense of anything that's happened to me."

"Everything in our lives is a result of God's favor."

"Favor? What favor? My cycle of believing has been broken."

"So was mine. Whenever I think about the person I became these past few months, it makes me sad."

"What happened, Emmanuelle?" He studied her expression. "When we last spoke on the phone you were so upbeat."

She chewed her bottom lip. "A lot happens in a year. Don't ask me about the in-between because I'm not ready to talk about it." Mentally reliving George's abuse, a heavy despair settled in her gut. Whenever he'd banged her body into a wall, he screamed that they belonged together, and he was trying to teach her who was the master. No one had ever hit her before. She'd come from a kind and loving home.

"You were only meant for me, Emmanuelle."

The psychological, and then physical, abuse was always worse after George drank. The sharp smell of whiskey on his breath predicted the flashes of unpredictable anger sure to follow. A familiar sweat of panic slid down her neck. On a jerk, she swung her gaze from Nicholas and locked the terrifying remembrances in a safe compartment in her mind.

"Emmanuelle?"

She faltered, found her axis and drew a fortifying breath. "Dorothy stopped by the inn this morning."

"Why?"

"To talk. And she reminded me I shouldn't rebuke myself for past circumstances. She encouraged me to keep my attention on God and not dwell on myself."

"How can a memory upset you if it already happened?"

"Now there's a question I ask myself. Memories can only upset you if they have your attention. The key is to focus on what really matters." Despite her brave declaration, she couldn't meet his probing stare. Instead, she eyed the white-lighted snowman, accented with sheer purple ribbon, hanging on a far wall.

After breakfasting with Dorothy in the inn's sunny conservatory, Emmanuelle had confessed the beatings she'd suffered while tears had streamed down her cheeks. With every frightening scene she confided, heavy chains had been lifted from her heart.

Dorothy was kindhearted and understanding, a true friend, her intentions always in the right place.

Emmanuelle's rapport with Nicholas was different. He had commended her on her talent and independence, complimenting her on countless occasions. What would his opinion be if he learned she had been foolish enough to allow a man to control her?

She released a sigh and hid her face in her hands. She carried a shame she couldn't describe, not even to herself.

"Care to discuss what happened to you, Emmanuelle?" Nicholas repeated. "You can trust me."

He stared at her. She stared at the snowman.

She could hear a cell phone ringing in the hallway. She could smell the cold, stale coffee on the corner table.

Yes, she trusted Nicholas, even as she feared his admiration would change to disapproval once he understood her situation.

Why hadn't she left George sooner? She'd asked herself the same question more times than she could count.

"Because, Emmanuelle, you were meant only for me."

She shuddered, recalling his bloodshot gray eyes, as he was liquored up more often than not. When had he changed? He'd been so charming at the outset of their relationship, wooing her with lavish dinners and dark chocolate truffles and evenings at the theater.

"Emmanuelle?"

Despite her resolve to start a new life, she pressed her lips tight and didn't acknowledge him.

"You know," Nicholas went on, "I once was a person of great faith." He inclined his head and spoke softly. "This dejection I've felt ever since Alice—"

Emmanuelle's words came quick with no apology. "Your sister said, '"If you despair, you will live in despair."'"

"Dorothy is admirable and Ryan has taken her lead. Together their faith is anchored in God. I want to trust in the Lord again, I really do." He lifted his hand and cupped her chin, raising her face to his, forcing her to meet his gaze.

She didn't flinch, knowing that he needed a fresh start, needed her full attention.

"Begin by reaching out in prayer." She took his hand, holding it as he bowed his head and whispered praises to God. Silently, she joined him.

Scarlett strolled over, stacking used coffee cups and folding morning newspapers. "Do you two want anything? There's coffee in the vending machine."

Nicholas looked up at her. "Is it any good?"

"No. It's instant, and cold, and shuts off sometimes. Often, actually." She grinned. "Anyway, I brought in extra junk food from home. You know, candy and cupcakes, bottles of soda. Want anything?"

Emmanuelle smiled. "We're fine, thanks."

"My motto is to embrace life and indulge yourself."

Scarlett's full-figured form, Emmanuelle noticed, was pleasing and curvaceous. She was empathetic and sunny, a person who saw the bright side, even on a bleak afternoon. Upbeat, she finished cleaning up the waiting room and retreated to her desk.

As afternoon slipped into evening, Dr. Troutman emerged from the hallway. He drew up a chair to sit across from them. "Delightful news, Deputy Thompson. Surgery isn't necessary. There's no internal bleeding, organ damage, or broken limbs."

"She's going to be all right?" The guarded hope in Nicholas's voice prompted Emmanuelle to place her hand on his arm.

"Molly Belle will be fine." The vet came to his feet. "You can take her home tonight. Find a comfortable spot and get her settled with some heating pads. Given time, she'll heal with no scars."

"Thank you, doctor."

"Clean the wound and apply an antibiotic cream. I gave her an injection for her discomfort." Dr. Troutman rooted in his lab coat for a pad and pen. "I'm prescribing an anti-inflammatory and I recommend not leaving her alone for extended periods of time."

Nicholas's face paled. "For how long? A week?"

"Recovery time varies. She's a young bouncy dog, and I predict she'll be fit in a few weeks or less. Incidentally, she might be a mixed breed. Although she's mostly a golden, I'm thinking there's a bit of yellow lab mixed in." He scribbled the prescription and handed it to Nicholas. "I'll ask Scarlett to schedule Molly Belle for a check-up next Saturday."

"Are you sure I can properly care for her at home in the meantime?" Nicholas hesitated before starting for Scarlett's desk. "If it's safer, please keep her overnight for observation."

"Nothing to observe. You and your girlfriend are quite capable," Dr. Troutman said. "She knows her animals."

"I'm not Nicholas's girlfriend," Emmanuelle clarified, quick to get to her feet. "I learned a tremendous amount when I helped my father. We lived in Remsen, a little town outside of New York. For years, I visited his office every day after school."

From the corner of her eye, she saw Nicholas's thick eyebrows raise as he busied himself with paying the bill.

"How far outside of New York is your father's office?" the vet inquired.

The memories flickered, faded, a million miles away. Once, she'd felt safe and happy, living like other people. How easy it had been when she was a child.

"He died ten years ago when I was sixteen." She spoke carefully, not letting her sense of loss, her free and easy childhood, creep into her voice. "He was a highly regarded veterinarian in our little town. Cherish reminds me of Remsen. Without Remsen's snow."

"I've never been to Remsen," Scarlett chirped. "I bet it's pretty there."

Dr. Troutman gave Scarlett an indulgent smile, then turned back to Emmanuelle. "A small town's down-to-earth values and its focus on what matters most in life ... Well, there's not much that can beat that."

"You're absolutely right." Emmanuelle extended her hand. "Thank you."

Over at the reception desk, Nicholas handed Scarlett his credit card, then peered over his shoulder at Emmanuelle. "All those hours we spent on the phone and you never mentioned your animal expertise."

She shrugged. "There were more serious topics to discuss."

Saying he would get Molly Belle, the vet walked down the hallway. He and Nicholas transported a muzzled Molly Belle to the rear seat of the Volkswagen using a large dog crate.

On the drive to Nicholas's apartment, Emmanuelle pondered what to do. Torn between the belief that helping for a week wouldn't matter because she had no other plans, and the fact she'd be immersed in his personal surroundings, she considered how to word her offer before she spoke.

He needed help, especially when he reported to work on Monday. Yet, he hadn't asked for any. A proud, stubborn man, Dorothy had once described her brother when she'd become frustrated at his inability to talk about his hurt after his marriage plans fell apart.

"Once Molly Belle is situated tonight," Emmanuelle began, "I'll stay with her while you fill her prescription."

"I appreciate that."

Guarded, yet so polite.

"Once Monday rolls in, I'll watch her while you're on duty, deputy."

"Wouldn't you rather kill time checking out the Christmas markets and visiting Dorothy and Ryan?"

"I'd rather kill time being of some use."

"All day nursing a sick dog isn't a vacation." His expression indicated his willingness to accept her offer, although he kept his tone carefully noncommittal.

"Who said my visit is about a vacation? Christmas is the season for giving."

What else could she say that was a reasonable justification for offering to help? She simply *wanted* to because Nicholas and Molly Belle had become important to her, but she certainly couldn't say that. "I have experience tending to sick animals."

"I'll pay you." He offered a quick, grateful smile.

"Do you cook?"

"Do frozen pizzas count?"

"You're describing the extent of my cooking skills as well." She grinned. "Fortunately, Ryan is learning gourmet cooking so I'll throw out some hints. Or better yet, I'll borrow his *Southern Charms* cookbook."

CHAPTER 6

ith Molly Belle settled on a blanket near the recliner in the living room, Nicholas went off to get her prescription. Emmanuelle applied a heating pad to the dog's belly, where it seemed she had the most pain. When she was assured the dog rested comfortably, she removed the heating pad and waited for Nicholas to come back with the prescription.

Dr. Troutman's injection had made Molly Belle drowsy. Her brownish-black nose pressed upon the blanket, and her sides rose and fell as she dropped into a deep, sound sleep.

In the solitude of the quiet room, Emmanuelle set to work tidying the coffee table. She boxed up old magazines and catalogues that lay scattered in a mismatched pile beside five remote controls. Why did a man need so many remotes for one television set?

When Nicholas returned, he hung his hoodie by the door and crossed the room. Crouching, he stared at his sleeping dog.

"She's asleep and not in pain," Emmanuelle assured him. "See? Her tail is twitching. She's probably dreaming about chasing purple pigeons or flopping in the grass at the Cherish Hills Inn. When she wakes up, we'll give her the medicine."

Nicholas nodded. "And I have bad news and good news." He rolled to his feet and handed her a white paper bag. "The bad news is the kiosks were closing. The good news is I managed to plead our upsetting afternoon to my friend from The Grill Room. He was smoking a beef brisket and added coleslaw. I figured you were hungry. I also snagged a couple cups of coffee and two honey-glazed donuts."

She gave an appreciative sniff. "My mouth is watering."

He went to the kitchen and pulled a water from the fridge. "What do you want to drink?"

She followed him and put the kettle on the stove to boil. "Hot tea. Thanks."

He folded his shirtsleeves to his elbows and draped a dishtowel over his shoulder. "My place is a mess, although I used to be fairly neat."

"I think I have enough tidying here to keep me occupied."

"Yeah, for at least a year." He grinned, then grew solemn. "Since my failed engagement to a woman who—"

"You didn't fail." She reached for a thick mug in the cupboard. "Your fiancée did."

They dished out the smoked barbecue brisket and coleslaw and brought stoneware, napkins, and utensils into the living room. She placed the stoneware on the coffee table, set her napkin on her lap, and took a neat bite of brisket. Chewing, she nodded toward Molly Belle. "After she sleeps, she may be sore. Follow the directions on the prescription."

"You'll come ... tomorrow?"

She reached for her tea. "I texted Dorothy to let her know what happened. She and Ryan are still in Stanley. She'll stop in tomorrow to see you and the dog."

"And you?"

"I'll be here on Monday morning, as long as you don't mind leaving the dog by herself to come get me."

"The weatherman calls for a pleasant week. Sunny and highs in the fifties. If you'd prefer to walk—"

"I never walk alone anymore, but will walk with Molly Belle." She gulped her tea and set the mug on the coffee table, and then her napkin alongside it. "However, can you drive me to the inn? It's getting late and I'm sure the innkeeper will be worried. Besides, you have his vehicle."

"I phoned Tom, and he knows Molly Belle is fine. He assured me he isn't leaving the inn tonight." He rested his hand lightly on hers. "Please stay a while longer. You haven't finished your brisket, and I could use the company."

Hesitantly, she replaced her napkin in her lap.

Nicholas relished his meal as if he hadn't eaten in a week although she nibbled and pecked at hers. After they finished, he lifted his water for a last pull while she cupped her mug and stared out the narrow window. A splash of light streaked across the black velvet sky.

"You realize we're in full view of your neighbors." She grinned at him over her mug. "One of them is cruising into their driveway."

"Dorothy has reminded me on a weekly basis about buying curtains."

Still holding her mug, she wandered to the window and considered the quiet night covering the sleepy town. The room stilled to a comfortable silence.

"I've been waiting for a beautiful woman to come along who can help me choose the right ones," he said. "Fortunately, I've known her all along."

She pivoted, catching his wicked grin and look of interest as his gaze focused on her face. Her pulse leapt in a disconcerting combination of anticipation and panic.

"Emmanuelle." His voice grew quiet. "I can hardly kiss you when you're standing on the other side of the room."

"Nicholas, we hardly know each other."

"A year ago, we talked regularly. Our bond was strong. Let's be honest. We both know it still is."

She walked to the couch and set down her mug. He set down his water. Their gazes held, the quiet punctuated by the dog's light snores.

Her thoughts scattered. She rearranged them into a semblance of reason. "A year ago we had a common purpose—ensuring your sister made a full recovery."

"Are things so different?" Gently, his fingers curved around her nape, soothing, stroking. "I'll help you make a full recovery from whatever you're struggling with." He bent his head slowly, and his lips met hers with sweet tenderness.

For a moment, she went rigid.

"I'm attracted to you, Emmanuelle," he murmured. "Always have been. I'm here for you."

Her body reacted in a dizzying sensation of emotions she couldn't explain. She didn't want to respond to him. Or perhaps she did because her reaction felt so natural. Trusting a man, feeling safe and cared for in his arms ... She'd thought those feelings happened to other people.

Tentatively, she reached her arms around his neck and returned the kiss.

His mouth deepened as he fit her response to his own. He kissed her fully, insistently, boundlessly, creating a knot of pure awareness in her stomach. The longer his mouth pressed to hers, the more vibrant the sensations became. It was as if a new person had taken the place of the broken Emmanuelle. The new Emmanuelle was sincere and receptive, the former hesitant and uneasy, avoiding any connection with a man.

A sharp woof broke them apart.

Molly Belle lifted her head and regarded them. Before Nicholas could get to her, she laid her head down and went to sleep.

Emmanuelle's lips twitched. "Her injection is wearing off."

He settled on the couch and watched Emmanuelle, his gaze heated. "Shall we continue? We left off at—"

"Your dog may wake up again."

"I'll take my chances." His arms slipped around her, and she reveled in the pleasure of his hard mouth pressed on hers. She kissed him back while his warm hands shifted protectively around her.

Ages later, he lifted his head and cradled her face. Affection smoldered in his hazel eyes. "You came into my life at exactly the right time."

Molly Belle stirred, twitched, woofed to no one in particular, then plunked her nose back on the blanket.

He chuckled. "I think I have a love-hate relationship with that dog." With a sigh, he lowered his hands from Emmanuelle's face. He forked a last bite of coleslaw, leaned against the couch, and stretched out his legs. "Stay a while longer. Please. I'll be sure you make it back to the inn before midnight, Cinderella."

Across the inches of the couch separating them, she met his stare. His striking features were full of hope, almost boyish.

He was an honest man. Genuine and steadfast, his every movement capable, yet easy-going.

"All right, but only because you said 'please,' Prince Charming."

He reached out and gathered her to him. "Remember the night we watched television together when we were Skyping?"

"How did you ever persuade me to stream a documentary

about the Hubble telescope when I had a concert to prepare for the next day?"

He threw back his head and laughed. So good-natured, so familiar. "You should thank me because you learned several new outer-space terms. And all the planets—Mercury, Venus, Earth—"

She laid her hand on his arm. "I'm a musician, not an astronaut."

"Where is your harp, by the way? In New York?"

She kept her features blank and tried to make her voice impassive. "My harp is gone."

His expression was thoughtful as he obviously sensed her bleak mood. A beat passed.

"One of my favorite memories," he said, keeping her in his arms, "is the night you played the harp for me. 'Danny Boy.' Remember? I'd had an argument with Alice, and you said music would soothe me, so you lit candles and darkened your apartment. You had told me your harp was accented in twenty-three karat gold. I remember it shimmered in the candlelight each time you plucked a string. Truly, Emmanuelle, you looked like an angel, and it gave me goosebumps." He traced her cheekbone with his forefinger.

"You sang while I played," Emmanuelle said. She'd clung to the memory of those shared times, although she'd known he was engaged and never pressed him for anything other than friendship.

Not long afterward, Dorothy had gotten out of rehab for opiate addiction, and Emmanuelle had met George, the wealthy hotel magnate.

And George had taken away her harp. Her pride. Her life.

CHAPTER 7

$\mathcal{N}$icholas felt like he danced through the following week, and he wasn't a man who'd ever managed more than a two-step.

Molly Belle improved every day. She had reclaimed her sleeping spot at the foot of his bed, ate regularly, and reveled in her short daily walks with Emmanuelle. She'd even taught the dog to "sit" by holding a treat near the dog's nose. Once Molly Belle was sitting, she'd repeat the command, give the dog the treat, and shower her with affection and praise. She'd repeated the same sequence throughout each day, then demonstrated Molly Belle's progress for Nicholas each evening.

She'd taken Molly Belle to a shop a few doors down from his place and selected a fresh pine wreath, simple and unadorned, that she'd hung on his front door. On another occasion, she purchased curtains in a dazzling shade of lipstick-red and hung them on his bare living room windows. The effect was homey, warm, and Christmassy.

She'd also experimented with cooking new dishes. Thanks to Ryan's *Southern Charms* cookbook, Nicholas never knew quite what to expect for dinner. He only knew an exotic, savory meal waited for him when he got home.

In the evenings, he and Emmanuelle dined in his cozy kitchen, on a wooden table tucked beside a snowy window, polishing off spaghetti carbonara and thick slices of buttery bread accompanied by oven-fried pickles.

"Surprise me," he'd tell her each morning after she'd arrived.

And she did.

He enjoyed her companionship, her considerate nature, the way her dimples flashed whenever she was amused. He hadn't found a word to put to his feelings, especially since he hadn't wanted to become romantically involved with a woman after his breakup with Alice.

With Emmanuelle, though, the word *love* came to mind.

On the last day of the work week, Nicholas issued his customary thank you to her as soon as he strode through his apartment door. Molly Belle wriggled with delight, bounded to his side and greeted him with a continuous train of wet doggy kisses.

He scrubbed a hand along the dog's ears.

Emmanuelle was seated on the couch, intent on studying a page from Ryan's cookbook.

"I've been thinking about dinner all day," he said. He'd been thinking about her too, although he didn't mention that part. For a celebratory end-of-the-week supper, Emmanuelle had declared she was experimenting with a different fix on a traditional Christmas recipe—roasted turkey and sweet potatoes garnished with a fancy topping Nicholas had forgotten the name of.

He slid his gun from his holster, took off his badge. "How was your day?"

"Busy. Despite her size, Molly Belle thinks she's a lap dog." Emmanuelle kept her head down, busy flipping pages.

"And Dorothy and Ryan invited us for Christmas dinner so I tried a new dessert recipe tonight too."

He breathed in a lungful of smoky air just as the smoke alarm went off. "Is something burning?"

"Oh, no!" The cookbook fell from her lap as she jumped to her feet. "I forgot to set the timer."

They sprinted toward the kitchen. The dog whined and raced in the opposite direction, scratching at the door to be let out.

"I was testing a fruitcake recipe," Emmanuelle said as he opened a kitchen window to let out the smoke, and then turned off the alarm.

Not a dreaded fruitcake. Since Nicholas was fairly intelligent, he kept the comment to himself as he retrieved the burnt cake from the oven and set it on the counter. He commiserated with Emmanuelle, sighed, and tried to look regretful. He wanted to joke about the fruitcake making a good doorstop and wisely changed his mind.

"The cake can't be salvaged, so I'll phone for pizza delivery," he said. "Sound good?"

"If you stopped to look around, you'd see I cooked a twelve-pound turkey and sweet potatoes. Is pizza your fix for whatever comes your way?"

"There's no such thing as bad pizza. So …yes." He lifted the foil off the potatoes and pointed accusingly. "What's this white stuff on top?"

"Goat cheese and scallions."

"Sounds awful …" He caught her scowl. … "fancy." He congratulated himself for thinking so quickly on his feet. "Sounds awful fancy. Do you think I'll like it?"

"Fifty-fifty."

He suppressed a chuckle. She looked positively intoxicating, even with her heart-shaped mouth twisted into a grimace as she beheld the burnt cake.

He left the kitchen to check on the dog, who'd resumed her place at the foot of his bed.

When he returned to the kitchen, he drew off the hairband she'd used to secure her hair when she cooked, brought her closer, and embraced her for a lengthy kiss. "We're beginning to sound as if we're a couple, and I like the sound of it."

She drew an unsteady breath and dropped her gaze, but not before he noticed the warmth kindling in her vivid blue eyes, the flush of heat tinting her creamy complexion a soft pink.

"We can't be a couple."

"Why not?"

She kept her gaze rooted on his bare wood floor. "Because I won't be a burden to you." She placed her arm between them, an effective wedge.

He'd half expected her reaction.

Anything to do with Molly Belle's care prompted an easy conversation. So did the latest recipe in the cookbook. Or classical music, especially her favorite composer, Beethoven. She responded to his kisses, molding herself to him. But any talk of a serious relationship put her off-balance.

He drew her to the couch and took a seat beside her. In an attempt to lighten the mood, he teasingly bumped her shoulder with his. "Tomorrow is Molly Belle's vet appointment. I'm hoping you'll go with me."

"Absolutely."

He smiled, relieved. He'd come to rely on her for emotional support.

"Afterward," he went on, "I'd like to buy a Christmas tree. My apartment is begging for a dose of holiday cheer, so are you up for a stop at a tree farm outside of town? In the past I've cut my own tree." He gestured to the dog. "Because she's still recovering, we'll buy a precut tree."

"Perfect." Her smile was luminous and lit his small apartment with merriment.

The attraction sizzled between them. Soon, he thought, when she was ready, she'd tell him her trepidation, and he'd assure her she was safe. Mutually, they'd dismiss her worries. She was in Cherish where life was secure. He'd keep her out of harm's way—whether real or imagined.

Trying to tamp down his eagerness, he reached into his shirt pocket and withdrew a small box wrapped in gold paper with a red satin ribbon. "Thank you, Emmanuelle, for everything you've done for me this week. On my lunch hour today, I stopped at Musically Yours and bought you something." He held the box out to her.

Lightly, she touched her hand to his. "Nicholas, you didn't have to buy me anything. I wanted to take care of Molly Belle."

His senses buzzed, alive to the brush of her fingertips, the thickened skin where calluses had formed. Once she had told him she was proud of those calluses, a badge for practicing long hours to pursue her dream of becoming a professional harpist.

And she had.

He'd taken her suggestion to give God his attention and had begun praying every night. Lately, he'd lifted a plea that she'd make Cherish her permanent home.

She could build a life here. *They* could build a future together.

He slipped an arm around her waist, delighting in her nearness, staring at her for a long moment. "I wanted to buy you a gift. It was my pleasure."

"Nicholas ..." She ran a hand through her unruly blonde curls. Her chin trembled. Although they'd known each other for over a year, she grew unexpectedly shy.

"Please open it." He stilled her hand and kissed her

temple. He was giving her what he could. He wanted to give her so much more.

Nodding brightly, she rapidly undid the paper and unlatched a plain gray box. A tiny harp dangling from a solid-gold chain shot emerald green and diamond prisms across his plain white ceiling.

"The harp charm is from Ireland, from Dublin. I wanted an Irish harp fit for the most gifted woman I've ever known." He brushed his knuckles over her flawless cheek, brushed away a stray tear.

"Happy tears," she said.

He nodded. "Our conversation from the other day about the night you played 'Danny Boy' brought back good memories. I want this necklace to do the same."

"It brought back good memories for me too." She fingered the necklace. Her eyes shimmered a soft blue velvet. "I haven't bought a piece of clothing or jewelry for myself in months. Thank you."

"I looked for a twenty-three-karat necklace to match your harp, but this was the best I could afford. My salary as a deputy sheriff isn't much, though I plan to work my way up to a position of management." He drew her to him and she rested her cheek against his chest. "Someday I'll buy you a real harp."

He spoke above her, breathing in her floral perfume, citrus and violets and expectation.

"Money isn't important," she said. "I know this gift is from your heart."

She was splendid. She made him feel alive again, brought him out of his sadness. After his fiancée had left him, he'd grieved, focusing on his scars. But a new emotion was rising over the scars, allowing him to become again the man he once was—one of faith, free from cynicism, free to open his heart once more.

They avoided eye contact. The moment held too much emotion for her, for him.

"I know how much your harp meant to you," he murmured. "You once let me in on a secret, that your parents surprised you with a harp for your twelfth birthday. They'd saved money for years to buy the best. A Lyon and Healy harp, correct?"

"You remembered." Her tears came hard, sudden, and she let them.

He soothed her, crooning, rocking her. "You're not alone anymore, Emmanuelle."

Any further conversation was forgotten as she wept. When she withdrew, she wiped at her eyes with the handkerchief he provided. "I'm sorry. I mean, crying was uncalled for and I put you in an awkward—"

"Don't apologize. You're the best thing that's ever happened to me." He swept wisps of hair from her nape and secured the delicate gold chain around her throat, then ushered her to the bathroom mirror. "Dorothy assured me you'd fall in love with this necklace."

At first, Emmanuelle kept her gaze downcast before staring at herself. Carefully, she slid a finger along the fine chain and then found the exquisite detailing of the harp. "I haven't worn anything this pretty in many months. Thanks to you, I'm beginning to feel like a woman again. Someone who matters." Her smile sparkled in the mirror reflection.

He stood behind her and rested his hands on her shoulders. "You matter very, very much. More than you can ever imagine."

He stared at her, a vision of beauty with the heirloom-quality necklace shimmering against her creamy skin above her navy-blue cashmere sweater. At that moment he knew. It had returned, his love for a woman.

Only this time it was real.

CHAPTER 8

After Dr. Troutman's nod of approval, Nicholas and Emmanuelle set off for the Christmas tree farm. Molly Belle waited in Nicholas's car while they chose the last fir tree on the lot. The tree wasn't perfectly shaped; in fact, it wasn't shaped at all. Nicholas named the tree Charlie Brown since the branches jutted out in random angles.

"Every underdog needs a loving home," he declared, and Emmanuelle wholeheartedly agreed.

One of the employees at the farm shook the tree to remove any loose needles, then wrapped it for transport. A short drive later, Emmanuelle and Nicholas hoisted the scraggly tree up his flight of stairs and into his apartment.

"The tree looks better already," she said as Nicholas secured the tree in a sturdy metal stand. "It's just begging for lots of care and plenty of water. And we'll trim your whole apartment to resemble an old-fashioned Christmas. Ryan's book features all sorts of inspiring ideas."

Nicholas pushed himself to his feet after pouring water into the base of the tree stand. "I thought it was a cookbook focused on recipes."

"Recipes and decorating tips. And there's a thought-provoking article on empowering women that provides tips on how to keep safe in dangerous circumstances. The entire book is highly motivating."

"Quite the cookbook," he observed.

They referenced a "traditional Christmas" article as a guide and spent the afternoon decorating. Using heavy embroidery floss, they strung popcorn and cranberries. Nicholas found a set of multicolored lights stuffed in his hall closet. He began at the tree trunk and moved upward, wrapping the lights taut by weaving them from side to side.

"There isn't much of a tree to light," he said with a laugh. "The branches are beyond sparse!"

"I'm always drawn to these types of trees." She stepped back to assess the tree. "In the end, it's all about hope, isn't it?"

"True. And few people are as hopeful as Charlie Brown."

"Multicolored lights remind me of happy times with my family in Remsen. Call me nostalgic and old-fashioned."

"Then I'm old-fashioned too. Nothing is better than colored lights on a green pine tree to get you in the mood for Christmas."

"Last year, my ex wanted white lights and neon-blue bulbs on the tree he'd purchased for his swanky condo in a high-rise. I argued for colored lights. He didn't agree, of course, saying white lights were chic and modern. I like modern." She hesitated, combed nervous fingers through her hair. "No that's wrong. I just told him that."

"You lied?"

"I had no choice. He had two switches, calm or angry. I knew better than to disagree and kept my opinion to myself. He'd trained me like we're training Molly Belle—to obey commands." She watched the dog, resting on a blanket in the corner. The dog returned her stare with steady, shining eyes.

"I understand my former situation now," she went on. "It's easier at a distance."

"What's your ex's name?"

She took a moment to adjust her fire-red tunic, fussing and fidgeting, as if the tunic didn't fit correctly over her jeans. "George."

"That's it? George? George who?"

"Just George." She shrugged, shivered. Slight, but he saw it.

"Where's George now?"

Another shrug. She looked around, rubbed her hands together. "I assume he's in New York."

Her ex had evidently hurt her, and the realization brought anger bubbling to Nicholas's throat. When he found him, *and he would,* he'd silence George with a good stiff jab and a command of his own. *Stay away from Emmanuelle.*

He wrapped an arm around her shoulders and she leaned into him. Each time they were with each other, his need to protect her grew stronger.

He turned to the next page in the book to change the subject. She might get too upset if they continued discussing her ex. "The next round of decorating is to find red and green bulbs for our quirky tree. Do you prefer glass bulbs or—"

"I prefer family vintage bulbs and pinecones and silver tinsel. But …" She dug in her tote bag and drew out a tiny angel ornament, brandishing it in the air. "I've carried this with me ever since I left New York. The clerk at the airport told me it was a good luck charm. It belongs on your tree."

"*Our* tree," he corrected her, and hung the ornament on a thin lower branch. "All this decorating warrants a celebration, so let's call out for pizza."

"Again? Is pizza your remedy for everything?"

With a laugh, he pulled his phone from his jeans pocket

and placed an order for a large cheese and pepperoni pizza, with a side of barbecue for Emmanuelle.

After pocketing his phone, he took her hands. "Let's wait for the delivery on the porch steps. The weather is mild, so we can go outside without jackets." He glanced at Molly Belle, sleeping soundly, then eased open the door.

They sat on the stoop. It was one of those inviting South Carolina evenings, when the sun had warmed everything in its path, including his front porch.

The view of his charming cul-de-sac lit with strings of festive lights, the nearby clip-clop of a horse-drawn carriage, filled him with gratitude. He imagined the residents inside their homes, savoring steaming cups of hot cocoa, sitting beside their cozy fireplaces.

From a few streets away came the last strains of "We Three Kings." Sung, he surmised, by the Cherish Church ladies' caroling group. He grinned, envisioning the women, young and elderly, dressed in their traditional Victorian costumes, complete with big bonnets and hand muffs.

The day had been perfect. Ending the evening with Emmanuelle by his side brought a quiet, joyous peace, and he whispered a prayer of thanksgiving. Tenderly, he pressed a kiss on her palms. "Two weeks from today is the Musically Yours holiday concert," he said. "Ryan is leading the elementary school chorus in a Christmas carol singalong and then singing a couple solos."

She rested her cheek on his shoulder. "Cherish is like a picture out of a Christmas card."

He chuckled and went back to appreciating the street decorations. Several neighbors had run animated light displays in a scalloped pattern along their fences.

Yes, this was the ideal town to live, to work, to raise a family.

He put an arm around her and she snuggled nearer, the

warmth of her body reaching out to his. He could get used to this. A delightful woman, her breathing soft and even, whose slight body had grown heavier because she was … sleeping?

He grinned. She'd fallen asleep quickly, even quicker than he usually did. Between taking care of his dog and creating nightly meals fit for a food connoisseur, she was clearly exhausted. He considered her profile, her small turned-up nose, the light sprinkling of freckles on her cheeks. Several times during the past week, he'd caught her staring at her cell phone as it rang. She never answered a call, and a few times her face had turned bone-white when she'd glimpsed the screen.

"Unknown caller," she always said, dropping the phone back into her tote bag. Whenever he pressed for details, she just chewed her bottom lip and stubbornly stayed silent.

He reached into his pocket for his phone and canceled the pizza. No sense in waking her when the delivery person arrived. Surely that frozen pizza was sitting somewhere in his freezer.

From inside the apartment, Molly Belle barked.

Emmanuelle woke with a start and rubbed her eyes. She peered at him, darted a peek at her watch. "Sorry, I didn't realize I dozed. I haven't rested well in several months."

"Because of George?"

A noticeable gap hung in the air as she scanned the street and its bright decorations. Distractedly, she nodded.

He went to brush pine needles from her shoulder and she flinched. He let out a whistled sigh and pulled back his hand. "Don't. You insult me when you do that."

"Do what?"

"Treat me as if I'm your ex. Just because I raise my hand doesn't mean I'm going to hit you." He deliberated, but only for a second. "What's really going on with you?"

"Too much." She eased up, then sat back down. "Nicholas,

I can't give you the relationship you want. I'm not the right woman for you."

"How do you know?"

She closed her eyes. Tears escaped. "Because you're a good man and my life is complicated."

"I like complicated."

"No, no, you don't." She opened her eyes, a deep shimmery blue. They stared at each other.

"It's odd," he mused.

"What?"

"The fact you're a harpist and you don't have a harp. Did you sell it?"

"My harp was smashed to pieces." She didn't pause for his sympathy, didn't bury her face in her hands. "George destroyed it."

"Why?"

He hadn't meant to ask the question because he knew the answer. As a law enforcement officer, he'd come across men like George. Domestic violence was the leading cause of injury to women. He'd read the statistics, recognized an abuser's behaviors and characteristics. After the honeymoon phase, they became controlling and jealous, and oftentimes sought to isolate their partner.

"Why?" Emmanuelle repeated. "Why would a man who supposedly cared for me take away something I loved, something so meaningful? To break me, I suppose." She shook her head; she'd answered her own question. "He knew precisely which buttons to press. He was exceptionally charming and people were attracted to him. Me included."

Nicholas's anger was sharp. He pulled it in. "How did you meet him?"

"His secretary booked me to play the harp for one of his office functions, the grand opening of his tenth boutique hotel in the New York area." Her voice caught. "After we became a couple, he always reminded me I was beneath him and how thankful I should be an important man like him was interested in someone like me … someone who was little more than a street performer."

"You know that's not true. You're a skilled professional."

She trailed her fingers along the edge of the porch railing and let out a sigh.

"When are you deserting me for New York?" he asked.

"I'm not deserting you. I happen to live there." She smiled and broke off, apparently waiting for his rejoinder. When he didn't offer one, she added, "I don't have a definite date in mind. Dorothy offered me a job at her music conservatory. I've considered finding a place in town and teaching harp lessons." She shrugged and blew out a breath. "Although I know it's better if I keep moving."

The last part of her answer didn't register because he'd fixated on the first part. His heart had leapt when she'd mentioned living in Cherish.

"Is he the reason you came here? Is he the reason you choose to keep running?"

"I have no choice and I'm not running." Her fingers nervously worked the hem of her tunic before she propped her chin in her hands. "Okay, yes, maybe I am. If George O'Donnell finds me, I don't know what he'll do."

George O'Donnell. Piercing rage sliced Nicholas like a knife. "He won't do anything to harm you. I'll make sure of it."

"You don't know him. He's well-off and powerful."

He joined her cold hands with his warm ones. "And I'm in law enforcement."

"That's why I'm afraid. If you go after him, you'll get hurt. He operates in influential circles with big-city types."

"In our quiet town, you'll be safe. You must know I'll always protect you."

"Our town," she repeated.

"Yes. And our life."

"Nicholas?" A smile ghosted her lips as an errant tear streamed down her cheek. "Will you do something for me?"

He gazed at her enchanting face, her over-bright eyes. He would protect her with his life.

"Anything," he said.

"Will you hold me for a minute?"

CHAPTER 9

In the ensuing two weeks Emmanuelle slept poorly, despite the inn's exquisitely appointed room and her luxurious queen-sized bed. Nightmares chased her and were always the same: the dim outline of a man with flat black eyebrows above dull gray eyes, trailing her every move.

George O'Donnell.

She'd scramble through unnamed woods while the flash of something vicious, and corrupt, and overpowering, followed her. The nightmare always ended the same, with her weeping and running farther and farther away from Cherish.

She'd wake beneath her cozy coverlet, her heart hammering, searching the room for something recognizable. Country-green walls, the hand-stitched quilt draped over a rocking chair, the braided rug covering the wide-plank pine floor, helped steady her breathing.

"Only a nightmare," she'd murmur, wiping her sweaty brow. "Vivid, horrible, and not real."

She'd focus out the window at the sprinkling of stars

against the black velvet sky. Then she'd close her eyes and think about Nicholas—his kindness, his easy-going manner, his self-assured confidence. Efficient and calm, whether tidying his home or ministering to Molly Belle, dealing with dangerous circumstances on duty or holding her as if she were a china doll. He was all man, all kindness, all compassion.

"In our quiet town, you'll be safe. You must know I'll always protect you," he'd said.

Only then, imagining his capable arms around her, could she seek the peace of slumber.

* * *

BY THE THIRD week of December, Cherish had become a jubilant fairyland, a kaleidoscope of Yuletide hues. Parades were held every weekend, and quaint mom-and-pop stores were decked out in magical window dressings. Children and adults alike stopped and gaped, mesmerized in child-like fascination.

Illuminated by tiny white lights, Emmanuelle's comfy inn, with its snow-covered roof and wisps of smoke billowing from the chimney, looked like a postcard image of Christmas town, USA.

Tom had taken a liking to Molly Belle and allowed her inside, provided she stayed in the foyer and didn't jump on any of the patrons. Unfortunately, the third day she was allowed in, Molly Belle knocked a teenage boy over when she'd leapt on the boy's legs. Despite Nicholas's explanations that the dog was still a puppy with a playful, silly personality, Tom banished Molly Belle to the porch. Both hands braced on his polished wood desk, he'd leaned forward until his cheaters slid down his nose and declared she wasn't allowed inside until she graduated from dog obedience school.

Considering Nicholas had abandoned the idea of obedience school until Molly Belle was fully recovered, Emmanuelle was certain the dog wouldn't be entering the inn anytime soon.

A cold front had brought snow to Cherish, a white dusting that topped off the winter-wonderland. As the snow fell softly, day after day, Emmanuelle's mood became more hopeful. She spent her time at Nicholas's apartment caring for Molly Belle and cooking delectable meals—a flaky crusted chicken pot pie brimming with roasted chicken and baby carrots one night, a sweet winter corn-bread with a splash of jalapeno the next. Oftentimes, she'd bake a tray of Christmas cookies, oozing chocolate chips, warm from the oven. As she cooked, she'd tune the radio to a Christian holiday station and hum along to every Christmas carol.

In the middle of the afternoon, she'd leash Molly Belle for a walk. Few things outshone walking a devoted dog who loved going outside for a squirrel-chasing adventure, especially when sunlight warmed Emmanuelle's cheeks and bracing air brought remembrances of Christmas in Remsen.

At Dorothy's prodding, the two women spent an evening shopping. Emmanuelle purchased a pair of shiny gold earrings to complement her harp necklace, plus a rose-tinted lip gloss. There was something so feminine about earrings and lip gloss, Dorothy said, that made a woman feel attractive. Regarding her reflection in the shop's mirror, Emmanuelle agreed. She'd caught her hair at the nape and secured it with a lace bow, the result a messy bun highlighted by escaping corkscrews of blonde hair.

She'd also painted two opposite walls of Nicholas's living room in a golden-yellow and convinced him to reupholster his couch in a deep-chocolate brown. He'd grinned his approval, and she too was pleased with the result. After

Christmas, she aimed to tackle his kitchen and paint those walls a cool mint-green.

After Christmas.

Yes, because she'd decided to live in Cherish. She hadn't told Nicholas, not yet. She'd decided to surprise him on Christmas, after they attended a church service with Dorothy and Ryan. She'd accepted Dorothy's offer to give harp lessons at the Musically Yours music conservatory and had begun formulating a plan to buy a new harp. Ryan told her that the nearby city of Stanley boasted an excellent symphony that was actively looking for a principal harpist, and encouraged her to audition. She'd agreed, the idea prompting recollections of how much she enjoyed performing.

On the Saturday of the holiday concert in Cherish, Emmanuelle spent the morning peeling potatoes and carrots for a hearty beef stew she simmered on Nicholas's stove. The weatherman had predicted snow, which had rapidly accumulated to several inches.

Nicholas had had to respond to a domestic-dispute call, and she'd gladly volunteered to stay with Molly Belle. He'd added that one of the other officers, Joseph Hannaford, would be on duty at the concert that evening. Large crowds were expected because of Ryan Edwards's performance.

Done with the stew, she surveyed the living room from the kitchen doorway. The Charlie Brown Christmas tree was delightful, brightly lit and brimming with cheer. Her angel ornament hung from one of the branches, and she laughed out loud, inhaling the scents of pine and promise.

Life was good. Very good. On an even more optimistic note, there'd been no sign of George. After she'd begun watching Molly Belle, every morning she'd received a phone call precisely at eight o'clock, a few minutes after Nicholas left for work.

Whenever she answered, no one spoke.

Once, she'd sworn she'd heard breathing on the other end. Bad connection? Most likely. She rejected her suspicions that it might be George. Merely an over-zealous telemarketer, she'd tell herself.

Still, she told Nicholas, admitting to her uneasiness. He listened thoughtfully before assuring her she was right—a telemarketer had programmed her phone number on speed-dial. After a long, thorough kiss, he assured her there was nothing to worry about.

And then, without warning, the mysterious phone calls had stopped.

As the next few days passed, the realization she was finally free from George renewed her confidence. With a strong handsome deputy by her side, friends who loved her, and a spirited dog ever near, what was there to fear? Truly, Christmas in Cherish promised a happiness she'd never dreamed.

CHAPTER 10

*A*fter they'd eaten stew for an early dinner, Nicholas drove Emmanuelle back to the inn to get ready for the evening concert. They passed tree limbs heavy with snow, bushes dusted with a fine white powder.

At the inn, she gifted Tom with a loaf of her crusty bread, prompting him to taste it. He'd chewed with his eyes closed and exclaimed, "Will you marry me, Emmanuelle?"

Before she could reply, Nicholas draped an arm on her shoulders and assured the innkeeper she was spoken for.

She floated to her room where she ran a warm shower, refreshing herself under a stream of multiple jets. The scents of her soap and shampoo—brown sugar and vanilla— reminded her of hot cinnamon rolls slathered in butter cream frosting.

Her anticipation of the evening rising, she grabbed a fluffy towel for her hair, and wrapped herself in a luxurious white robe. She padded across the wood floor of her room and deliberated on her outfit, ultimately choosing a comfortable pair of colored denims and a red cashmere sweater.

Despite his numerous concert engagements, she'd never

heard Ryan perform live, and she was looking forward to the evening.

At 7:00, a light tap on her door signaled Nicholas's arrival.

When she opened the door, he lifted her to her toes and held her. "Emmanuelle Sumter, you look gorgeous and smell like a cinnamon roll." He frequently remarked on her appearance, always complimentary, always causing her to melt, just melt.

She saw the seductive-green passion in his hazel eyes as their lips met.

"And every time I see you," he went on, "I fall more in love with you." He stated his feelings simply, without preamble or fanfare, his mouth brushing against her ear, his warm breath heating her insides.

She ran her fingers over his nape. His blond hair was thick and curled over his collared parka. His lips were smooth, his mouth perfectly shaped. His well-defined jaw and sharp cheekbones brought a chiseled handsomeness to his cover model features.

It's too soon to talk of love, she wanted to say. But it wasn't too soon, because she was falling in love with him too.

She hugged the realization close. This good-looking, conscientious man loved her, and with each heartfelt embrace, each heady kiss, her defenses were thawing. Slowly, she was shaking off her fears and yielding to him.

"Ready for an amazing concert?" he asked.

"I can't wait." She went to her closet and tugged a pink tasseled hat over her hair. "Dorothy said she'd accompany Ryan on keyboard if they can figure out how to run electrical power on stage."

"So far, they haven't," Nicholas said. As she rummaged through the closet, he added that the afternoon sun had melted much of the morning's snow, so the streets were messy tonight.

"Just let me grab my boots. Where's Molly Belle?"

"She's near the porch."

She swiveled. "Alone?"

"She's on her leash. Tom is playing with her in the snow." Nicholas struggled to keep a straight face. "He won't admit he's got a soft spot for dogs, although you and I know he does." He helped her on with her jacket and exaggeratedly hefted her tote bag from the bureau. "What do you carry in this? Lead?"

"Necessities. You know, my cell phone, wallet, loose change …"

"I wouldn't want to tote this heavy bag around."

"You would if you were a sensible woman." She laughed. "I can't be deprived of my pink lip gloss."

Still bantering, they made their way down the carpeted staircase.

As soon as they strolled onto the porch, Molly Belle scampered around them, feathery tail wagging, as if she hadn't seen them in a month. Nicholas thanked Tom and reached for the leash. Hand in hand, Emmanuelle and Nicholas stepped from the porch.

Although the morning snow had blown in quick and heavy, as Nicholas had said, most had melted under sun-kissed daytime skies. As the evening thermometer plunged, what was left had frozen, causing thin sheets of ice to gloss over the surface of the remaining snow. Tom had shoveled a generous path and covered the steps and sidewalk with rock salt.

"I've never listened to opera," Nicholas said, tucking her hand in the crook of his arm as they started for the town square. "I expect—"

"You've never heard Ryan sing?" Her lips twitched with

amusement. "Your sister is married to one of the most famous opera singers in the world!"

"Once, maybe, when we were teenagers, I overheard him singing an operatic version of Dorothy's favorite top-forty hit. I assumed he was trying to impress her. They used to sit for hours on the side porch of our house." Nicholas's deep voice vibrated with laughter. "But I'm all for the idea of a bonfire and roasting s'mores after the concert."

When they reached the square, Ryan and Dorothy gave an absent-minded wave as they arranged chairs beneath a white canvas tent. A stage had been set up alongside the ten-foot decorated Christmas tree. Various kiosks serving refreshments lined the outer edges of the square, and Nicholas briefly introduced her to his coworker, Joseph Hannaford, the officer on duty. As the crowds thickened, a fine, snowy mist began to fall.

A halcyon town awaiting Christmas, Emmanuelle mused. The entire scene was a miniature version of New York's festive theater district. Cheery memories, she thought, … until … until …

She brought a jittery hand to her forehead.

A few months after she began dating George, she wore her favorite sweater to a theater event, and had left her jacket in the restroom at intermission. When he noticed, he demanded they leave before the show was over. She assumed he was angry because she had been foolish enough to have forgotten her jacket. He was concerned, as the theater was cold, she reasoned.

She was way off the mark. He shouted at her and called her a tramp for strutting around in a clingy sweater that he deemed too provocative.

He was jealous. She got that, and even felt flattered.

At first.

The relationship deepened. She believed she was in love

with him, and he was in love with her. However, he began to erupt when she least expected, no matter how fine a line she walked. Scary remembrances of George's viciousness, his narcissistic behavior, his insincere repentance, brought a quake down her spine.

She forced the chilling memories away and glanced at the rugged man standing beside her.

She was being foolish. She was safe, the town was real, this man was real. And this was the picture she needed to carry in order to move forward in her life. The uncommonly large crowd had simply dredged up memories from her uneasy mind.

As if he'd read her thoughts, Nicholas protectively tightened his arm around her waist. "Are you all right?" His hazel gaze locked on hers.

"Yes, I was thinking about how grateful I am to be here. And I'm happy, truly happy."

"So am I." He spoke quietly, tenderly. "I love you, Emmanuelle."

She beamed up at him, this man of faith whom she'd enjoyed endless conversations with, a man who spoke plainly what was on his heart.

"I love you too, Nicholas."

He smiled at her as if she were incredibly beloved.

She sighed with contentment. Finally, her world was coming together, and she whispered a thank you to God for giving her a promising future alongside the man she loved.

As they wove through the tent to find a good seat, she scanned the tent to see where Dorothy and Ryan had gone.

An exuberant Dorothy was arranging the last row of folding chairs. Her simple, classic black sweater dress showed off every curve of her lithe figure. She'd pinned her dark hair into an understated twist at the back of her head, drawing attention to her emerald-green eyes and pearl stud earrings.

Ryan strode over to her, impressively tall with dark, compelling features, his broad shoulders filling out his navy jacket to perfection. He draped a tweed coat around Dorothy. Something she said made him laugh out loud, and he gathered her in his arms and kissed her.

Their delight in each other was so infectious that Nicholas and Emmanuelle shared a grin.

"Well?" he prompted.

"Well what?"

"Well, if everyone is kissing, then where's my kiss?"

"You're impossible. We're not performing in a concert tonight."

"I plan to sing along to every Christmas carol. Does that count?"

She chuckled. "No. Besides, we're not newlyweds."

"Not yet." A slow, roguish smile moved across his face.

She felt her blood heat from her toes to her temple. "You're thinking to kiss me here, with all these people around?" Coyly, she shook her head, teasingly discouraging him. Then with a mischievous smile, she tilted her head back, inviting a kiss.

Dr. Troutman and Scarlett entered the tent carrying two cups of coffee and a bag of chips. They spotted them, waved, and jostled through the crowd. Molly Belle yipped and tugged on her leash in her attempt at a greeting.

Her red hair springy beneath her leopard ear muffs, Scarlett offered a sparkling smile and opened her chips. She offered them to the group, then began munching.

"How's one of my favorite dogs?" Dr. Troutman rubbed Molly Belle's head as she scrabbled her front paws up his legs. He bent and examined her feet. "Just making sure there's no snow trapped in the pads."

"I've been checking," Emmanuelle said.

He sipped his coffee. "Are you two here for the concert?"

"*I* am," Emmanuelle said and then pointed to Nicholas. "He's here for the s'mores."

Dr. Troutman made a dramatic show of choking on his coffee. "Glad to see you're still in Cherish, Emmanuelle. Don't you live in New York?"

Nicholas pressed a light kiss on her forehead. "I'm trying to talk her into moving permanently to Cherish."

"Well, I could use a knowledgeable person in my office. Scarlett is a wonderful receptionist although she's going to be a little busy, now that we're engaged." His hand reached out to cover Scarlett's, but not before Emmanuelle noticed a three-stone diamond ring in a rose-gold setting on Scarlett's ring finger.

"Congratulations," Emmanuelle and Nicholas said simultaneously.

"Thank you." Scarlett's shimmery, ruby earrings swung sideways as she nodded. Enthusiasm glowing in her face, she turned to Dr. Troutman. "I love animals, but I love you more."

Emmanuelle saw the elation in the veterinarian's smile as he swung his attention back toward her. "If you're looking for a job, Emmanuelle, you can work for me anytime."

"My sister beat you to it." Nicholas said, nodding toward Dorothy. "She asked Emmanuelle to teach music lessons at her conservatory. Did you know Emmanuelle is a professional harpist?"

"I'd like to hear you play," Scarlett said.

"Someday." Emmanuelle grimaced. How's that for evasive? she upbraided herself. She was a professional harpist with no harp.

"I'm sorry. I can see from the expression on your face that

I troubled you." Scarlett swallowed a chip and snapped up another. "Dorothy mentioned you don't have a harp."

Emmanuelle stopped her grimace and turned it into a smile. "Don't apologize. Look what Nicholas bought me. Isn't it beautiful?" She drew out the harp necklace from beneath her jacket for Scarlett to admire.

"Yes, very beautiful, and very thoughtful." Scarlett eyed the necklace. "An early Christmas gift, Nicholas?"

"Nope." He laughed. "It's my gift to Emmanuelle for coming to Cherish. She's a blessing to me."

Emmanuelle's heart gave a funny lurch. Nicholas offered safety and security and he was more considerate than anyone she'd ever known. Not every man was cruel and intimidating, she reminded herself yet again. Healing from abuse was a slow road, and it took time and infinite perseverance. And she'd walk that road with the man she loved.

New beginnings.

"You make a very striking couple," Scarlett was saying. "Two good-looking blonds."

"I agree with one of your observations." With a mile-wide beam toward Emmanuelle, Nicholas said, "We'd better claim a seat, my good-looking blonde."

As people converged, aromas of chocolate fudge and honey roasted almonds lifted into the air.

"The staid doctor and his perky receptionist are engaged?" Emmanuelle asked.

"Apparently." He grinned. "He must be twice her age."

"They're charming together and I'm delighted for them.

"The vet has lived alone on his alpaca farm since his wife's passing. He's a moral Christian man and I'm glad he met someone he can share his life with."

"I hope Scarlett likes alpacas." Emmanuelle laughed. "Do they bite?"

"Not normally. And she can eat her junk food while Dr. Troutman's alpaca herd munches on green plants and grass."

They settled on seats in the last row, just in case Molly Belle spotted another dog and attempted to dash off for an impromptu romp in the snow.

When the audience quieted, the first half of the concert began with the elementary school's children's chorus. The music teacher conducted, and everyone joined in a heart-lifting rendition of "Silent Night." Before intermission, Ryan led the crowd in the "Hallelujah" chorus from Handel's *Messiah*. As tradition dictated, everyone stood.

"I've always wondered," Nicholas said under his breath, "why are we supposed to stand?"

"There are many theories, the principal one being that King George II was so overwhelmed by the 'Hallelujah' chorus that he stood up. And whenever the king stood, so did everyone else."

After a brief intermission, Ryan came on stage for the second half. His bass voice, rich and finely textured, was exactly as Dorothy had described, and Emmanuelle felt as if she couldn't breathe during his entire a cappella rendition of "Away in a Manger."

When the concert finished to thunderous clapping, whistles, and cheers, Ryan held up a hand to quell the applause and extended congratulations to the children's chorus. The children scampered back on stage, bowed low, and then grinned and waved at the audience.

Emmanuelle rose along with Nicholas and announced she'd ferret out the booths serving roasted almonds and fudge. Her nose could only take so much temptation.

He circled an arm around her shoulders. "What about our s'mores? The mayor is building the bonfire and we'll eat in a few minutes."

"I'm adopting Scarlett's motto—to embrace life and

indulge yourself. No worries. I promise I'll eat the fudge and almonds and s'mores." She sighed. "Although I won't be able to fit into the holiday skirt I brought if I keep eating at this rate. Fortunately, I also own a pair of slacks with an elastic waist."

Nicholas didn't appease her with a chuckle. Instead, his fingers tightened on her shoulders. "I'll go with you."

"Why?"

"Those suspicious phone calls you were getting …" He looked around and nodded at a busload of fans swarming around Ryan. "There're too many people here tonight."

"I'm twenty-five, not five, and I lived in New York, one of the busiest cities in the world. I can certainly navigate a crowd and get my own snacks without an escort. I've gotten over my fear of walking alone." She shook off his arm and grabbed her tote bag. "Besides, Dorothy's headed our way. Please congratulate her for me. I'll shoot ahead of this next horde and catch up with all of you in a few minutes."

He hesitated. "Are you certain you'll be okay?"

"Enough time has passed. I'm better. Really." She walked purposefully toward the food kiosks. Out from under the tent, she saw the night was black—no moon or stars, and the shimmer of snow was now a gray mist.

She wound past the busy fudge and caramel-corn stands. The stand that advertised roasted almonds was farther down, and there was no line. Actually, the stand looked deserted. Had they sold out of almonds already and closed shop?

She paused, debating what to do, and sensed someone walking up behind her. "Emmanuelle," a man said, "can you give me directions to the stage?"

She was so sure she'd imagined the familiar voice, she started walking toward the stand.

"Emmanuelle."

She froze. Her shoulders tightened, her breathing stopped. *Move,* she commanded her feet.

"Turn around, Emmanuelle."

Obediently, she did. George had always had a hold over her.

The sight of him standing so near was enough to unfreeze her. She shifted, one foot stepping back, but his gaze immediately sharpened on her. If only she could make him believe she was standing stock-still while she slowly moved backward.

"How … how did you find me?" She licked her lips and expelled a quick breath. He couldn't be here. He was locked away in a hidden compartment in her mind, in New York, at a theater festival.

"Didn't take long." He grabbed her arm. "A couple of your so-called friends mentioned you'd gone off to some back-water town in South Carolina for the holidays." He laughed derisively. "'Cherish.' I couldn't even find it on a map."

"You don't know any of my friends." She braced her body against a cold wind and tried not to inhale. He smelled of vodka and anger and day-old sweat.

Despite herself, she couldn't control the shiver that rippled through her. He noticed. She saw the satisfaction in his bloodshot gray eyes. He had foreseen this, her cowering, her clumsiness, as she fingered the straps of her tote bag.

"I hired a few musicians for my office party," he said. His fingers tightened on her arm and she flinched. "They were more than willing to help once I offered a large bonus. You starving performers are always looking for handouts."

She swallowed a terrified scream and eyed her isolated surroundings. Several long sprints lay between her and the roasted-almond stand. She could outrun him.

No, argued her practical self. He was a large man. His pace outmatched hers, and he'd overtake her. All he'd have to do was drag her into the nearby woods, and she'd be alone with him.

Adrenaline consumed her, shaping her terror into a soundless rage. She wasn't a weak, passive victim, shrinking into herself just because he spoke.

This was her town, not his.

Mentally, she reviewed the article from the *Southern Charms* cookbook. If a woman was confronted by an attacker, one of her first lines of defense was her handbag.

She lifted her chin, straightened her spine. "Well, now that you've seen for yourself I'm here, go slither back to your swanky place in New York."

Momentarily, his composure slipped, his fingers loosened. "Every day, I think about when your broken harp was hauled away. I felt so bad, I decided to buy you a new one. We'll call it my Christmas gift to you. It's expensive. You'll like it."

"Keep it. I don't want it."

His eyebrows lifted in distracted mockery. "What—"

She couldn't be afraid. She couldn't allow herself to cringe and plead, but needed to prevent her fright from taking over.

Don't back away. Use the element of surprise. He won't expect you to fight.

"I said keep it." She lifted her heavy tote bag as a club and swung directly for his face.

She was too slow. He saw the blow coming and shoved her to the ground. A dull roar filled her ears, pain firing through her body as she hit solid ice. He fell on top of her, and she fought him, biting and kicking, jabbing at his eyes, focusing all her energy on getting away.

A shiny, silver knife sliced the air and came at her throat. "I heard you've been seeing an officer in town, Emmanuelle. Did you forget? You were meant only for me."

She shut her eyes to keep out the light-headedness, seeking the safety of somewhere dark and safe and silent.

Heavy, racing footsteps cut through her dizzying thoughts.

"Drop the knife and keep your hands over your head."

"George O'Donnell, you're under arrest for aggravated assault."

Two men's voices. Nicholas. And another man. Officer Joseph Hannaford.

"Emmanuelle? Are you okay?" Nicholas's steady tone reached through her fogged thoughts. She squinted. The color had drained from his face, and even in the darkness she could see his distress.

Tears welled. "Yes, yes. I'm—I'm fine. He didn't hurt …"

Her brave declaration was diminished by her sobbing. She couldn't contain her tears and reached out to Nicholas for comfort. She wanted to be held, wanted her apprehension quieted, wanted only him. Her legs wobbled as he helped her to her feet, and she sagged against his strong body. His gaze stayed focused on her.

George sneered at her as Officer Hannaford snapped handcuffs on him. "You won't get away with this, Emmanuelle."

She noted that he showed no remorse.

"I already did," she said flatly. "Quit following me and go back to New York. I never want to see you again."

"This one stop-light town is no fun. I was leaving anyway." He didn't look tough or threatening now, not with his hands cuffed behind his back. "Just remember, Emmanuelle. You're an insignificant nobody."

Nicholas tightened his fists. "What did you say, O'Donnell?"

"Nothing, Nicholas," she said quickly. "He can't hurt me anymore."

The slow dance of George's belittlement, his cruelty, had ended. His hurtful comments would no longer snake through her dreams because she refused to carry her resentment anymore. She'd acted with courage, and someday, with God's grace, she'd forgive George. Just not today.

"Mr. O'Donnell," Officer Hannaford said, "we've been monitoring your activities. Lots of illegal narcotics are being siphoned through your hotel deliveries into other states besides New York. Drug trafficking is a felony, a federal one when it's across state lines. And then there's the evidence of money laundering, illegal weapons, and other crimes." His gaze flicked to Emmanuelle, then zeroed in on Nicholas's clenched fists. "Why don't you bring your girl back to your apartment and cool off? I guarantee this guy will be locked away for a good many years."

CHAPTER 11

*E*mmanuelle looked like a dream and cooked like a gourmet chef, Nicholas decided, taking a whiff of something heavenly as he strode into his apartment. He was greeted by Molly Belle's hopeful eyes and madly flapping tail.

He hung his pea coat by the door, took off his deputy badge, and slid the gun from his holster. With the dog on his heels, he locked the gun in his safe.

"No walks, Molly Belle," he said. "Emmanuelle texted me and I know you've been outside twice already."

Molly Belle cocked her silky ears, then followed him into the kitchen.

Nicholas feasted his gaze on Emmanuelle as she blended ingredients for a holiday fruitcake. She was dressed for Christmas Eve in a red velvet top and black pencil skirt that showed off her perfectly toned legs. She'd tied a plaid apron featuring a gingerbread man over her outfit. Her blonde hair tumbled in ringlets around her shoulders.

"Merry Christmas, angel," he said. "You're stunning." He tried not to stare, but she sure had shapely legs. He'd brought home a bouquet of red and white carnations, a festive beginning to the Christmas season, the florist had declared, when she'd snatched his credit card and rung up the sale.

No matter how hard he tried to budget, money seemed to slip out of his fingers faster than water.

"Well, thank you, Deputy Thompson," Emmanuelle said. "You're quite handsome yourself in your deputy uniform." She wiped a hand on her apron and twirled. "I was able to squeeze into this skirt after all, despite the endless barbecue sandwiches I've eaten lately. How do I look?"

"Gorgeous." He grinned approvingly, then held up the flowers.

Her face lit. "For me?"

"For Ryan and Dorothy's house," he amended. "The carnations are a Christmas dinner centerpiece, a thank you gift to them along with your … fruitcake." He gave himself a silent pat on the back for not grimacing.

He blamed his fruitcake dislike on the media, for the cake was fodder for endless jokes. His favorite was one by Johnny Carson, "There is only one fruitcake in the entire world, and people keep sending it to each other."

He didn't share that quote with Emmanuelle.

"I'm trying a new recipe," she said. "This one was passed down to Ryan by his nana."

"Yes, you'd mentioned it this morning. No *Southern Charms* recipe?"

"This one is better." Emmanuelle grinned and pressed the mixture into a baking pan. "It's so generous of your sister and Ryan to welcome us into their new home for the holidays."

The air smelled subtly of candied cherries and walnuts and dates, and Nicholas sniffed enthusiastically. Should he give fruitcake another chance? Most likely, Emmanuelle's cake would prove as tasty as all the other delicacies she'd prepared the past few weeks.

He set the bouquet on the table and brought her into his arms for a hello kiss.

"I missed you today." He nuzzled her neck. The splendidness of her, her sweet lips pressed to his, her sylphlike form leaning into him, brought him such happiness.

She wiped her hands on her apron and twined her arms around him. When he didn't release her, she shifted. "The fruitcake," she reminded him.

"Fruitcakes are invincible." He kept her close and rested his chin on her shiny blonde curls.

"Nicholas …" She extracted herself to pop the cake into the oven. "The recipe says the cake takes forty-five minutes to bake, which gives us plenty of time to arrive at Dorothy and Ryan's house by seven for dinner. The church service starts at midnight." She glanced at her watch. "It's five now."

Absently, he rubbed Molly Belle's head and eyeballed Emmanuelle as she pulled off her apron and put the flowers in a vase with water.

"Nicholas, did you hear me?"

"I think so."

"What did I say?"

"Something about Christmas dinner." He'd heard the dinner part and little else. He'd been preoccupied with her gorgeous legs.

"I brewed a pot of coffee. Do you want a cup?"

Before he answered, she brought out two mugs from his glass-front cabinet and poured.

"No donuts?" he teased, rousing her into a smile.

"On Christmas we eat fruitcake for dessert."

He sighed and scratched his head. *How could he forget?* He'd just have to keep hoping for the best.

"Emmanuelle …" From his shirt pocket, he withdrew a

neatly wrapped present tied with a white satin bow. "This is a little gift I bought for you."

She looked surprised. "You're very generous, but my wonderful harp necklace is more than enough."

Which, he'd noticed, she wore every day.

"This is another gift because it's Christmas. And because I appreciate you."

Ever since she'd arrived, his apartment had been transformed. Maybe he hadn't paid attention to the dog hair accumulating on his unswept floors before, but he'd sure appreciated it when his wooden floors gleamed.

She smiled. "I bought gifts for you too. They're wrapped and under our Charlie Brown tree. Let's open them now."

With the dog at their side and coffee cups in hand, they wandered into the living room. She clicked on her favorite Christian radio station, then brought a gold-foil-wrapped box from beneath the tree and handed it to him. "Merry Christmas, Nicholas."

They sat together on the floor, backs against the wall, and stretched out their legs. She was barefoot, free from the restrictions of her former lifestyle—one of control and fear. Now, her smile came easy, her movements unrestrained. The subdued colors of the Christmas tree lights warmed her complexion to a healthy rose hue.

Molly Belle settled beside them, patient, good, eyeing them thoughtfully with shiny black eyes.

Nicholas chuckled. He felt like a kid again, filled with the magic of the season. He felt like singing out loud when a new artist's rendition of "O Come All Ye Faithful" lilted from the radio.

"Well? Why are you waiting?" she teased. Expectantly, she watched him open her gift, an electric travel mug. "Do you like it?"

"I love it. Thank you." He shouted with laughter. "This is perfect."

She grinned. "Now that you're a deputy, you're always focused on getting a good cup of coffee. If duty calls and pulls you away from the office, your coffee won't be left cold anymore."

"Thank you. I've become attached to my coffee. And I've become even more attached to you." He pressed a kiss to her temple.

Still grinning, she reached behind the tree and produced another box, this one lighter and wrapped in the same metallic-gold foil paper.

"Two gifts?" he asked. "Why?"

"You bought me two, so now we're even." She placed the box on his lap, her expression growing serious.

He unwrapped the foil paper slowly, revealing a large jeweler's box. Then he paused, regarding her for a long moment, wondering why she'd lowered her head and seemed suddenly self-conscious. He unhooked the lid, and a silver pendant hanging from a heavy chain shone back at him.

"Read the words on the front," she encouraged. "It's a prayer."

"All right." He read aloud. "'Lord, keep my deputy safe from morning till night, give him strength in your precious light.'" He turned the pendant over. She'd personalized the back with an engraved script: "'I'm proud of you.'"

He wiped at his eyes as the emotion swept over him. He swallowed and held the pendant up to the light to admire it. "Thank you, Emmanuelle."

"You're very welcome."

He nodded toward his gift. "Now it's your turn."

Her fingers moved more slowly. She set the wrapping paper on the floor and gazed at the silver case she'd revealed.

Carefully, she unsnapped the lid. A black velvet bed held a solitaire diamond ring in a twist of fourteen-karat white gold.

She drew an unsteady breath. "It's … it's beautiful." Tears welled, falling down her cheeks. She wiped at them, laughed as she brushed the wetness away. "These are happy tears," she clarified, laughing and crying at the same time before she sank her head into his chest and gave in to the weeping.

"I know." He held her until her cry had passed. The same joy had gripped him.

Taking her left hand, he slid the diamond engagement ring onto her finger. "Will you marry me, Emmanuelle?"

She stared at her finger, stared at him. "Read the explanation on the box that came with your pendant first."

He gazed at her and pondered her reply. How had the conversation shifted to *her* gift when she wore *his* gift on her finger? If his feelings weren't in such a tangle because she was sitting so close to him, because it was Christmas, because it was so easy to love life again, he would have noticed how her bright eyes shone with anticipation.

He lifted the box and read the inside flap. "'A deputy's wife's prayer.'" He set the box down. Paused. Reflected. "Wait a minute. A *wife's* prayer?"

"I planned on making my home in Cherish, and wanted to tell you on Christmas Eve." She looked almost sheepish. "Then I decided that if you didn't ask me to marry you, I'd ask you."

"Well, my answer is yes." He smothered a laugh and tipped up her face. "What's your answer?"

"Yes, yes, yes. I love you, Nicholas Thompson."

His mouth descended on hers as she pressed closer. "I love you so much," he murmured, and then his mouth captured hers again for a breathtakingly long kiss.

When the kiss ended, she stayed in his arms.

"I've been thinking," she began, snuggling closer.

He brushed a kiss against her hair. "About what?"

"About the past few days, going over and over what happened the night of the concert. You obviously knew my relationship with George wasn't over. I didn't. And then I fought back when he attacked me. I shouldn't have."

"He's a dangerous man. You didn't realize how dangerous."

She blew out a breath. "Afterward, when I thought about how deserted it was back there, I chastised myself. I reacted foolishly for edging him on, and then trying to fight him."

"It was a knee-jerk reaction. You were threatened. You didn't realize how serious the situation would become, and so quickly. Officer Hannaford and I had been running a long background check on George O'Donnell ever since you told me his last name, so I was at fault. I knew how dangerous he was and I should never have let you go off alone."

"I only walked across the square to buy almonds." She sighed. "Although I've been blaming myself. I'm good at that."

"Don't." He kissed her again. "If anyone is responsible, it's me. I knew that George was involved in illegal activities."

She nodded. "And then I thought, through the bad came the good. Because of you—because of me—because of us, I've taken my power back. I didn't deserve his violence, and I felt so bitter and resentful when I arrived in Cherish. I've prayed a lot, and I finally realized if I kept feeling that way, that meant he still controlled me. So, I've let go of it. New beginnings, thanks to the grace of God."

Nicholas knuckled a tear from the corner of her eye.

She'd confronted her shame, her anger at herself, and realized God had helped her through the storm.

Love was here, love was now. Love was the magic of the

season. They were standing on the edge of Christmas, waiting for the new year and their new life to begin.

For an eternity, they sat together on the floor, his arms enveloping her and holding her close.

* * *

NICHOLAS AWOKE to the sound of Molly Belle's whining as she darted across the living room. The shriek of the smoke alarm had him staring blindly ahead. Smoke rolled out of the kitchen.

"Emmanuelle." He shook her awake. "Are you keeping tabs on the time?"

"Yes, it's—" She gaped at her watch. "It's nearly seven o'clock!"

They raced to the kitchen just in time to extract a burnt fruitcake from the oven.

He shut off the smoke alarm. She winced at the cake.

"Oh no." She blew out a breath. "I hope I have enough ingredients left over to bake another one."

"You mean you're going to try to bake another fruitcake?"

She scanned the counter. "Unfortunately, it's too late tonight."

"Well, there's always tomorrow, although none of the stores will be open on Christmas, so we'll just have to wait."

He tried to sound regretful and knew he didn't.

He opened a kitchen window to let out the smoke and inhaled crisp winter air. A neighbor was inching his car into the driveway, wheels spinning, windshield wipers flapping like a wild bird's wings. Fresh snow was falling to the ground, hugging the landscape in a burst of white potential.

"We may not be going anywhere tonight," Emmanuelle murmured. She stood beside him, peering outside the window.

"What will we eat for Christmas dinner?" he asked.

"Burnt fruitcake and coffee?"

"I'll call Dorothy. Once the roads are plowed, we should be able to get to their house and then attend the midnight church service."

He hugged her. The exquisite feeling of her warm body next to his, made his heart beat stronger. He'd been bitter, just like her. In his bitterness, he hadn't wanted to change. He'd preferred to feed on his own loneliness and feel sorry for himself. And then, God had blessed him with Emmanuelle. He'd brought her into his life at the perfect time.

She was his family now, along with Dorothy and Ryan. And Molly Belle, who'd trotted into the kitchen, plopped beneath the kitchen table and curiously eyed the burnt fruitcake.

By the window, Nicholas kissed Emmanuelle, a kiss full of love and promise. "I love you, Emmanuelle."

Her eyes were wet with tears. "I love you too."

"And I'll take a lifetime to prove it to you, right here in Cherish," he said.

"You don't have to prove anything. I know the man you are, and that's why I love you."

Truly, whatever came their way, they could handle it. His faith had been tested, but these were lessons. He'd bounced back from sadness and adversity. They'd both bounced back.

Because God had them covered. Together and always.

With Emmanuelle in his arms, they were ready to face life's challenges.

And this was a Christmas to cherish.

THE END

A NOTE FROM JOSIE

Dear Friends,

Thank you for reading, *A Christmas To Cherish,* set in the charming fictional town of Cherish, South Carolina.

I've always enjoyed writing about small town life, and Christmas is a special time of year.

Because I am a musician and even played the harp for a while, my heroine, Emmanuelle, is a professional harpist.

The hero, Nicholas, is the heroine's brother in *A Love Song To Cherish,* and I wanted him to have his own happily ever after.

If you loved this romance as much as I loved writing it, please help other people find *A Christmas To Cherish* by posting your review.

A Christmas To Cherish is available in ebook, paperback, Large Print paperback, Hardcover, and audiobook.

Next is Scarlett and Joseph's story in A Valentine To Cherish.

Enjoy and Happy Reading!

My Spotify Play List for A Christmas To Cherish is here.

NANA'S FRUITCAKE RECIPE

Ingredients:

4 eggs
    1 cup flour
    2 teaspoons baking powder
    1 pound candied pineapple
    1 pound pitted dates
    1 pound candied cherries
    8 cups walnuts

Instructions:

Pour flour and baking powder into a large paper bag, shake to mix, then add fruits and nuts. Shake well to coat all pieces with flour.

In a large bowl, beat eggs. Pour the fruits and nuts mixture into the egg mixture and use your hand to mix well. Coat all pieces. Grease a small baking pan and press the mixture firmly into the pan. Bake approximately 45 minutes at 350 degrees or until golden brown.

Enjoy!

USA TODAY BESTSELLING AUTHOR
JOSIE RIVIERA
a
Valentine
to
Cherish
A SWEET AND WHOLESOME NOVELLA

PRAISE AND AWARDS

**USA TODAY bestselling author
#1 Bestseller Women's Religious Fiction
#1 Bestseller Contemporary Religious Fiction
#1 Bestseller Inspirational Religious Fiction
Top 100 Christian Short Stories**

CHAPTER 1

Scarlett Evans eyed Joanna, the skinny girl sitting beside her on the wooden park bench. The girl's legs were drawn up to her chest, her limp brown hair parted to the side and pulled into a ponytail. As always, her hair was tangled, as if she'd forgotten about the process of grooming in the middle of the activity.

Scarlett gathered her face into a sunny smile. "Good thing the rain stopped, Joanna."

"Are we going to Dr. Troutman's alpaca farm?" the girl asked.

"He put his farm up for sale last month, remember? There's someone else taking care of the property now, one of his former employees." Scarlett sighed, preferring to forget the slim sandy-haired man who had stolen her heart and then moved away. They'd been in love, or so she'd assumed. Sure, he'd been twice her age and she'd been warned about having a boyfriend twenty years her senior. But he was self-assured and successful, a noteworthy departure from the insecure twenty-something men she had previously dated.

In the end, though, Judson Troutman didn't want to get

married again after losing his first wife, nor did he want to be raising a child in his sixties. At least, that's what he'd divulged the day before his departure when he'd broken their engagement.

Children. A family. That resounding black hole between them.

And, he'd admitted, he'd grown tired of Scarlett's loud, boisterous manner.

Since then, she'd attempted to be quieter, more subdued. Messy and spontaneous? These were fixable traits. Disorganized and overweight? Well, she was working on it.

"I thought you liked alpacas," Joanna said.

"The farm wasn't mine, and it was his choice. I love animals, but truthfully, an entire pasture full of alpacas was more than I could handle by myself. My new job learning how to train service dogs at Canine Helpers is wonderfully rewarding, so at least I'm still working with animals." Scarlett heard the hollow emptiness eddying between her excuses. The alpaca farm would have been perfect and she'd counted on it.

Restlessly, she fiddled with her bright-red shoulder bag.

How foolish to believe that a well-educated veterinarian could fall for a woman like her. A woman who wasn't polished. A woman who was too brash and flamboyant for his refined taste.

Joanna worried the sleeves of her worn pink hoodie. No matter the weather, rain or shine, the hoodie was a staple in her limited wardrobe. "Is he coming back to Cherish?"

"No." Scarlett shook her head as the familiar desolation crept in. All these years she'd dreamed of a man who would truly love her, a man who wanted to share her life.

How had she missed the most important part? She couldn't have a real relationship, because she was afraid to trust and had put up a protective shield.

With good reason. People always left, oftentimes without saying goodbye. She couldn't count on anyone except herself. In the end, she had probably pushed Judson away with her brash manner—an attempt to hide her insecurities.

"Dr. Troutman moved back to his family home in Arizona," she said. "His father fell ill, so he's helping his elderly mother. His parents also own a vet business, and he felt obligated to take it over. That's why he sold his practice here in Cherish."

There it was. More reasons why she had not only lost her fiancé, but also her job as his receptionist when the practice closed.

Quiet enveloped Scarlett and Joanna for a beat, broken by the chirping of a cherry-red cardinal frequenting a bird feeder, designed for the birds as well as the bird watchers. Not far away, a forgotten Christmas ornament hung on a branch of a tall pine tree, the shiny silver bulb catching the sunlight.

Joanna reached for her dog-eared copy of *Fifteen* by Beverly Cleary. At ten years old, the girl was already an incurable romantic. "What about you? Dr. Troutman should've asked you to go with him."

Scarlett hung an arm around Joanna's thin shoulders. "He did. I refused."

He'd asked half-heartedly, but she didn't insert that part. Besides, she was too loyal to Joanna, her Little Sister, to leave her. For Joanna's sake, Scarlett needed to be dependable. The girl had experienced constant disappointment in her young life when her father had abandoned her and her family, and her childhood reminded Scarlett of her own unhappy past.

"Long ago," Scarlett said, "I made a decision to stay rooted in one spot for the rest of my life. I just didn't know where that spot was."

"So you decided on Cherish, South Carolina?" Joanna

gave a horrified burst of laughter. "This town is way too small for me. I want to have an apartment in a big city when I'm eighteen."

"I lived in Chicago my entire childhood and tried to establish roots there as an adult. All I found were flashing neon signs, traffic lights at every corner, and car horns forever honking." Scarlett scooted closer to Joanna. "I landed here after I applied for the job as a receptionist for Dr. Troutman. And now I intend to stay because I love southern towns."

Certainly, people described Cherish as an *if you blink when you pass through, you'll miss it kind of place*, but the picturesque charm appealed to her. As soon as she'd arrived, she'd known she had finally found a hometown.

She reached into the pocket of her bright-yellow raincoat and pulled out a slim chocolate candy bar. With a snap, she offered Joanna half, then glanced at her watch. "Hey, it's almost three o'clock. Wouldn't you rather hang out with your friends on the weekend than with me? It's not too late to text them."

"What friends?" The girl pushed out a dramatic sigh. "You know what I would give to have a real friend right now? Besides you, of course." With those wisely chosen last words, Joanna added an impish chuckle.

"Thanks," Scarlett joked sarcastically before her tone sobered. "Just remember I'm always here for you."

"I know." Pausing, Joanna took a breath. "Although it's just that … as usual, I'm the new girl in town."

"You came to Cherish in September, and it's January."

Before Scarlett could say more, Joanna frowned. Lately, she smiled often, so the frown was unexpected. "I'm uncomfortable when all the students in my class stare at me."

"Then stare back at them."

"I can't." The girl studied her hands. "I'm not friendly and loud like you."

Friendly was a good thing. Loud—not so good. Demure, polite, and ladylike were never traits Scarlett had mastered, but this was a new year. January, the season for fresh beginnings and resolutions.

Soothingly, she tucked a strand of Joanna's brown hair behind her ear. "Remember you're not the new girl anymore, although you're definitely the sweetest."

Scarlett had been matched with Joanna to be her mentor and Big Sister after she'd attended a recruitment asking for volunteers to give of their time. The Big Brothers Big Sisters program was community based, and it focused on low-income families.

Joanna's homelife consisted of her mother, Tania, a slight, ebony-haired woman who incessantly smoked; a scattering of younger siblings; and never enough money to get the family through the month.

"No, you're the sweetest," Joanna said, looking up at Scarlett. "And the prettiest. I wish I had red hair and green eyes and a gigantic smile."

Scarlett grinned, positioning herself so that she and Joanna could hold hands. Here in this park bordered by a hill, they could breathe in trees and fresh air and solitude. The past few months, the park bench had become their place to sit quietly together. Lately, the air smelled of spring—damp soil and grass and new birth.

God promised new beginnings in the normal trappings of daily life. He gave purpose to common situations. Surely, He would help Scarlett not only survive her heartbreak, but be strengthened by enjoying nature and this precious little girl.

Joanna eyed a clump of low-growing pansies, the deep-violet and eye-catching yellow adding vibrancy to the glistening green grass. "Not that I don't appreciate your candy, but I'd love for a boy to give me chocolate for Valentine's Day."

A boy? Stiffly, Scarlett drew back her head. Joanna was certainly growing up fast. She was only in fifth grade, although with today's social media and television programs, kids grew up faster than when Scarlett was young. Still, the idea was disconcerting. Shouldn't Joanna be more interested in roller skating or board games?

Still, she was tempted to say, *Me too*. She kept the contemplation to herself because a candy delivery wasn't coming her way anytime soon. She squeezed Joanna's hand. "But we have each other, right?"

"Right."

That morning had brought rain, a quick storm rattling trees and sweeping across tidy lawns in Scarlett's working-class neighborhood. Now the clouds had parted, and an afternoon sun emerged in a brilliant blue sky, a typical winter day in the Carolinas, where the weather changed from cold to warm within hours. Nearby, dogs barked and teenagers tossed Frisbees to each other.

Scarlett sat against the park bench while Joanna munched her chocolate bar.

"Aren't you going to eat your candy?" Joanna asked between mouthfuls.

"No. You can have mine too." Scarlett handed Joanna her half. She loved candy and crunchy peanut butter ice cream and all kinds of junk food, and deliberated for a half second before giving the candy bar up.

No, no, no. She pushed out a breath. She couldn't count the number of times she'd attempted to diet unsuccessfully. The lead balloon feeling of failure never left, nor its silent counterpart, shame.

Solid looking, people described her. Or, *She has such a pretty face*. Or her favorite, *She's big-boned*. All subtle reminders she should shed thirty pounds.

This time she would lose the weight, she vowed.

She'd heard the cabbage diet worked well, although she'd never liked cabbage.

Tomorrow. She'd begin a new diet tomorrow.

"C'mon, let's head back into town." Scarlett came to her feet and took Joanna's sticky hand in hers. "We can stop for a slice of pizza at Frank's Pizzeria."

At the end of the street, guitar music wafted toward them. People in the park reacted, drifting toward the music, bobbing their heads to the beat of a Christian contemporary song.

"'And we sing, you are our God …'" The tenor male voice resonated through the air.

"Look, Scarlett." Joanna slowed and pointed to a poster mounted to a streetlamp. The poster advertised a Valentine-themed benefit concert sponsored by Musically Yours, the local music store and conservatory. The event would be held outdoors in the park, rain or shine.

The concert was being held to raise money for Cherish Elementary School's music program. Accompanying the poster was a picture of a good-looking man with dark wavy hair, stubble on his chin, and piercing blue eyes.

Joseph Slater, a Christian recording artist, was headlining the event.

"Isn't he handsome?" Joanna had eaten the entire candy bar, evidenced by smears of chocolate on her chin.

"Yes, but he's a musician," Scarlett said.

"Is that good?"

"It means he's busy recording and performing, so handsome doesn't count because he's unavailable." Scarlett read the poster listing his recent tours and managed a *wow*. Was he ever successful.

"A few months ago, I listened to one of his hits on the Christian station," Scarlett continued. "The DJ went on for five minutes about Joseph Slater because he writes all his own music, as well as songs for various Christian artists. And he was nominated for a Grammy award."

"I knew he was famous." Joanna tented her hands over her eyes and read aloud, "'An international recording phenomenon who recently returned from Australia and is touring the U.S.'" She had a breathless, excited look about her. "We should totally go to the show and meet him. Then you can fall in love again."

At the idea of it—love, dreaming new dreams—a shiver of longing quickened Scarlett's pulse. She believed in the possibility of happily ever after. Just not for her, and certainly not with a touring musician who was here today and gone tomorrow.

"They're selling tickets to the concert at Musically Yours." Joanna tugged on Scarlett's hand. "Don't you know the people who own that music store?"

"Ryan and Dorothy Edwards are dear friends."

"Then you wouldn't want to disappoint your friends, right?"

The joy on Joanna's pale, freckled face had Scarlett fishing for her wallet and hoping she had enough money to cover the ticket prices.

"No disappointments allowed," she declared, counting out a wad of one-dollar bills.

"C'mon." Joanna was off like a rocket, her thin legs moving rapidly toward the music store.

Scarlett couldn't help her smile and quickened her pace. She wanted to attend the concert anyway because she appreciated all kinds of music.

As they rounded the corner, Joanna skidded to a stop.

"That's him! I recognize his picture! Joseph Slater. Playing the guitar."

He sat on a stool in front of Musically Yours, his sharp profile outlined against a sunlit sky. In person, he was even more handsome than his photo. His wavy hair curled at the nape, framing a strong face, straight nose and chiseled jawline. Thoughtfully, he strummed his guitar and sang an inspirational melody to a small enchanted audience. They stood around him and listened intently.

He looked up after he sang his final number, the lyrics about love and peace particularly moving, the deep, rich timbre of his voice striking an unexpected chord in Scarlett's chest.

His clear blue eyes met her gaze.

She sucked in a breath, attempted to wave or applaud, but shelved the idea. Instead, she murmured, "I love that song," to no one in particular. For once, she'd really stopped and listened. The melody was beautiful, and the heartfelt lyrics about trusting God hit her emotionally.

Tears rose in her eyes and she brushed a hand across her lashes.

Silly. She was being silly. Usually, she didn't listen to Christian music, preferring top 40 hits. Besides, she didn't feel comfortable around men who were too good-looking, and this guy lifted drop-dead gorgeous to a whole new level. Attractive guys made her self-conscious about her weight. Besides, in her slick yellow raincoat, she probably resembled a chubby lemon.

She had no idea how many albums Joseph Slater had recorded, but made a mental note to Google him as soon as she returned to her apartment. He'd just topped the number-one spot on her hit list, edging out her favorite rock singer.

"He's staring at you," Joanna whispered.

No. Scarlett was staring at *him* like a gape-mouthed schoolgirl.

He set down his guitar, thanked the audience, and placed the guitar into its case. Smiling an acknowledgement to the cluster of fans, he shrugged on his worn leather jacket, picked up the case, and strode toward her.

Oh my. Now? She was coming face-to-face with him? Now? She must look the size of a house with her wrinkled cotton pants and red boots. And her sweater. She indulged in good cashmere sweaters, although this fitted charcoal-gray one sported a hot fudge sundae graphic on the front. Not exactly a motivation, but the idea of wearing a piece of celery made her inwardly chuckle.

A crisp breeze snapped through the air, and a loose strand of her curly hair fluttered across her forehead. The dampness of the earlier rain had caused her hair to frizz, and she probably looked like she'd been electrified.

As he approached, she felt a jolt of expectation. She and Joanna exchanged glances, and Joanna gave a thumbs up. That is, until he angled past them with a polite smile and entered the music store.

A few minutes later, Scarlett and Joanna greeted Dorothy Edwards inside Musically Yours.

"You're just in time." Dorothy crossed to them and gave Scarlett a teasing, wicked grin. "Joseph Slater is one of Ryan's former classmates. Isn't he all that? And he's a bachelor."

Scarlett paused, at a loss for words. Joseph Slater was well-known for his Christian music, as was Ryan Edwards for his operatic voice.

"I didn't realize Ryan knew him," Scarlett said.

Ryan Edwards, Dorothy's husband, had settled in Cherish when he married Dorothy. They were high school sweethearts, although ten years had passed before they'd met again.

"This way to meet Joseph." Dorothy tugged on the sleeve of Scarlett's raincoat.

Dorothy always looked so polished, her dark hair pinned into a classic chignon, her perfect figure accentuated by a black pencil skirt and burgundy silk blouse.

"There's no need." Scarlett stayed where she was, at the

entry of the music store. She hadn't started her diet yet. Maybe in a year or so.

"Of course there is, because we're all good friends," Dorothy said.

Scarlett twisted her fingers together and eyed the exit. "Joanna and I are here to buy tickets for the Valentine show, but we can come back tomorrow."

"And miss meeting him? You're here now." Ignoring Scarlett's hesitation, Dorothy gaily recited Joseph's numerous awards.

"So your husband went to college with Mr. Slater?" Scarlett asked.

"Mr. Slater?" Dorothy giggled. "That sounds so formal for a casual guy like him. They both received music scholarships to Juilliard. Joseph was only there for a year, though. Then he went on to study worship music in Australia." Dorothy promptly brought Scarlett to the end of a long line. She chuckled at Scarlett's protesting head shake and strolled away with Joanna, showing the girl a stack of musical bracelets—pianos, flutes, and a harp—and encouraging her to pick a favorite.

"I don't play any instrument," Scarlett overheard Joanna saying. "It's hard to choose."

"I think harp lessons will suit you perfectly, so pick a harp bracelet," came Dorothy's reply. "And I know the ideal teacher. Her name is Emmanuelle Thompson and she teaches on Monday evenings. I'll tell Scarlett to bring you back to the store then."

Emmanuelle was Dorothy's sister-in-law who had married Dorothy's brother, Nicholas.

Harp lessons? Scarlett mouthed as Dorothy caught Scarlett's gaze. Dorothy nodded. Obviously, the lessons would be free of charge, and a generous opportunity for Joanna to explore the arts.

Scarlett shifted in line. Mr. Slater sat in a corner behind a desk, autographing CDs.

His leather jacket was slung over a chair. He looked exactly how she imagined a recording artist—the black leather jacket, faded jeans, a white T-shirt that hugged his wide shoulders. The shirt read *Just Have Faith*, and was embellished with a tiny cross.

Have faith? She'd tried that, attempting to lean on her father, praying he'd reciprocate her love for him. She believed in God and attended church. It was just that God had been absent from her life lately.

"Credit your father for doing the best that he can," her mother had encouraged. "Beneath his bad temper, he's a good man."

So Scarlett had tried, while seeking his attention. When she'd been in elementary school her father had propped her up, complimenting her fiery red hair and lively manner. Later in life, when she was an overweight teen, he'd paralyzed her with his indifference.

She blamed her low self-esteem on her upbringing. Beneath her bravado she was almost shy, especially when the man she stood in line to meet was male-model perfect.

Self-consciously, she took a slight step backward when it was her turn.

"Hello, Mr. Slater," she said softly.

There went that handsome-man effect again.

"Hello. Did you purchase one of my CDs that you want me to sign?" Glancing up, he smiled at her guarded retreat, although he didn't remark on it.

"I don't own any. Are they for sale?" Brilliant. Of course they were, which was the main reason he was here. An artist, even an inspirational artist, was probably contracted by his agent to promote, promote, promote.

He nodded toward a stack of CDs placed on a shelf

nearby. "Indeed they are. This CD is a few years old, but the single was nominated for a Grammy."

"Indeed," she echoed blankly. Coupled with her low self-confidence, she was actually starstruck. She began to chuckle at the absurdity of her nervousness. She was a grown woman, not a starry-eyed adolescent.

Surprisingly, his laugh joined hers. "So … did you want to purchase one?" His gaze drifted over her, his astute blue eyes warmly affirming.

"A CD?"

"Yup."

"No. Well, rather, yes." Her hands stilled as she reached inside her shoulder bag. "Unfortunately, I don't have the money. You see, I'm buying two tickets to the Valentine concert, and I only stuck one-dollar bills in my wallet. We had planned on going out for pizza tonight, and then—"

"We? Is that an invitation?"

"No. I mean … Joanna and I." Scarlett could feel the flush of heat on her cheeks. "The little girl—" She was babbling and closed her mouth.

He regarded her for a beat, then reached for a CD on the shelf. He had to duck when he stood. He was tall—probably six feet—and the music store's ceiling sloped at the corners.

"Here." He handed the CD to her. "My treat."

"Your treat for what?"

"For standing in line to meet me. For your preferences. Pizza should always come first, although music and pizza together are perfection. And thanks for the un-invitation."

She laughed.

He grinned, settled in the chair, and uncapped his Sharpie. "What would you like me to write on your CD?"

"Whatever you want," she said. "Best of luck … warm wishes …"

His face lightened with humor. "Do you want me to personalize the message?"

"Sure."

"Should I sign this to you?"

She noted the line lengthening behind her. "Sure. My name is Scarlett. Scarlett Evans."

She peered down while he autographed and recognized her name, although his handwriting was so poor she could hardly decipher it. "That's two *t*'s in Scarlett," she instructed.

"Here you go, two *t*'s Scarlett." He wrote his name and then slid the CD across the table. "My pleasure."

Across the space, their gazes held.

"Thank you." She tucked the CD inside her shoulder bag. "Well, I'm off to buy those tickets."

"I thought you were buying pizza?"

"Oh, right." She was surprised he'd remembered her offhand remark. She shrugged. "Guess not."

"I'll take care of your tickets and leave them with Dorothy. I'm staying at the Cherish Hills Inn for the next few weeks until the concert, so I'll be out and about." He gestured toward the cash register where Joanna sat with Dorothy, swinging her legs on a stool. "Do you need two?"

"Yes, one for me, and one for my—"

"Daughter?"

She cast aside a couple responses. "I don't have any children. I'm Joanna's Big Sister."

The little girl waved gaily at Scarlett and shook her wrist to show off her new harp bracelet.

"Although, wait, please don't buy tickets for us," Scarlett said. "I know the owners and I'll come back to purchase them."

"I know the owners too, and I insist. There's only one catch."

Her head cocked to the side. Was he one of those musicians who assumed no woman could resist him? Would he possibly want to ask her out?

No. She was fairly certain a man of his status wouldn't be interested in a heavy-set small-town woman like her. Unless he was looking for … a fling?

Umm, she wasn't good at flings. And she certainly wasn't about to get hurt again.

"What's the catch?" She tried to keep the wariness from her voice.

He was quiet for several beats. She felt awkward, fingering her shoulder bag.

"Do you sing?" he finally asked. His voice was quiet, deep, velvety.

Taken aback, she chuckled. "Why? Do you need backup singers for your next CD?"

He shook his head. "I'm a soloist."

"Well, then, yes, I sing. That is, if singing in the shower counts?"

"Absolutely." He pressed his hands together. His hands looked strong, his fingertips callused, most likely from endless hours strumming his guitar.

"Should I add the verbs *barely tolerable* to my singing in the shower?" she asked.

"Barely is an adverb."

"Thanks for the English lesson, Mr. Musician." She burst into a wide smile. "What about a tolerable singer?"

"Tolerable is an adjective."

She kept her smile. For a guy who didn't write legibly, he certainly knew his grammar.

Behind her, a man cleared his throat impatiently, which startled her and seemed to visibly annoy Mr. Slater.

"So we've established I'm not a singer," she said.

He rested his hands on the desk and studied her. "You're a good person, being a Big Sister. That's what counts."

She was so disconcerted at the quiet caress in his tone, she blurted, "Although I don't sing well, I love to listen to music."

"Then I'll award you bonus points."

More customers filed into the store. He didn't seem to notice, keeping his gaze fixed on her. It seemed as if he didn't want their conversation to end. Neither did she.

She knew the flush on her cheeks had heightened to a bright pink.

"As long as you love music and promise to attend the concert," he continued, "then the tickets are yours."

No, she thought. He'd done enough, given her a free CD.

"I can't," she said.

"Please, it would mean a lot to me. I pray that my songs will continue to spread God's good word, so I need an audience."

"You're a modern-day writer of hymns, you know that?" She flashed him a smile.

"I used to be." It showed in his eyes, the quick glimpse of frustration before it vanished. He scanned the crowded store, the line behind her. "Not so much anymore."

She didn't know how to answer, eventually murmuring, "I've heard some of the songs you've written and they're amazing."

"Thanks." He signaled to the throat-clearing man to move forward. "I guess some people have been more than patient."

"Guess they are. Sorry," she mumbled to the impatient man as she curved around him.

"Don't forget to come back for your tickets," Joseph Slater said. "I'll leave them at the counter."

She glimpsed Dorothy's attentive expression as she avidly

watched the exchange. Dorothy's interest would soon become an inquisition, then slide into a matchmaking frenzy. She'd been bent on finding Scarlett a man ever since Judson Troutman had left town.

Scarlett couldn't help an inward grin before turning to smile brilliantly at Mr. Slater.

By now, she knew Cherish was different from Chicago, and a person couldn't go far without seeing someone you knew. He'd be in town for several weeks, and she was almost certain to run into him. The thought filled her with unexpected delight.

"Thanks. I won't forget," she said. "Joanna and I will look forward to the concert, Mr. Slater."

"Joseph." He extended his hand, their fingers touching as they shook. A warmth surged through her. She didn't want to let go. His strength was sure and solid.

She sent him an audacious smile and let go of his hand. She began walking away, then called over her shoulder. "Thanks again for your generosity, Joseph."

"That's Joseph with a J," he said.

Beaming, Scarlett expressed her gratitude to Dorothy, and told her friend she'd visit the following day to pick up her tickets. She took Joanna's hand, and the two left the music store and headed for the pizzeria, with Joanna chatting happily about her upcoming harp lesson.

* * *

AN HOUR AFTERWARD, Joseph shrugged on his leather jacket and collected his music as he prepared to leave Musically Yours. The trickle of last-minute customers had cleared out after Dorothy's announcement that the store closed at six o'clock.

"Owning this place is both my business and my passion,"

Dorothy said. She stood behind the counter and clicked her tablet screen while she balanced the money in the cash register. Every inch of space in the store looked inviting, a music lover's haven. Glancing over her shoulder, she added, "But I wouldn't have it any other way."

Joseph looked up. "What did you say?"

"Sorry to interrupt your dreamy-eyed musings." Dorothy's teasing voice roused him from his reflections. "Are you smitten by someone?"

"I'm sure I don't know what you mean." Vaguely, he was aware that Dorothy was watching him. He'd been thinking about Scarlett.

My singing is barely tolerable.

He'd accepted her pleasant jibe at herself with a chuckle. She was quick-witted and good-natured and he'd felt an unexpected pull. He knew it was crazy because of his footloose lifestyle. He was never in one city long enough for more than a casual dinner date. He'd nearly forgotten the names of all of them.

The cities. And the women.

Nevertheless, there'd been a spin of warmth, a raw attraction between them. She was enchanting, with lovely sea-green eyes and creamy fair skin. Unconsciously, she'd swayed back and forth while they'd spoken. She didn't seem the type to sit still for long.

Although other fans had been milling impatiently behind her, he'd wanted their conversation to continue, to get to know her a little better. It was unlike him. After finishing the gig in Cherish, he'd head to Raleigh and then New York City. Scarlett obviously lived in Cherish and their paths wouldn't cross again.

He gathered his Sharpies, song list, and business cards and packed them into his duffel bag. His outdoor concert had gone well. Judging by the enthusiastic crowd, promotion for the Valentine event was a success.

He'd arrived in Cherish that morning lethargic and slightly disoriented, jet lagged because of the long flight from Australia. His noise-canceling headphones, combined with the low whirring of the airplane engine, had lulled him into a deep sleep for much of the flight.

In the midst of a dream he couldn't remember, he'd woken at the airport feeling groggy, and the feeling had continued on the train ride from Atlanta to Cherish. After he'd called a taxi at the train station, he'd ridden through the center of town. He'd let down the window and smelled pine trees and greenery and a whiff of spring. A magical morning light enveloped the neighborhood park.

For a moment, he'd been enchanted—until reality and his hectic concert schedule crowded his enchantment.

He shook his head. Admittedly, it would take more hours than he'd anticipated for his body clock to adjust to East Coast time. For the past few years, being on the road brought a weariness he couldn't explain. There was no silence, no peace in his life anymore. He hadn't felt at home anywhere in the world, not even his beloved Australia.

"On the contrary, Joseph, I'm sure you know exactly what I mean." Dorothy went to the door and posted a *We're Closed* sign. "And it's a wonderful idea."

He forced himself to listen to what she was saying. "What is?"

"Dating Scarlett while you're in Cherish." Dorothy walked over to him, pausing to organize some misplaced items on a shelf. "I saw how you looked at her, how you watched her leave the store. You didn't hear the next fan in line speak to you for a solid minute."

"You're right, but there's another word for smitten. It's called jet lag."

Dorothy grinned and handed him a box of CDs. "These are yours."

"Keep them in the store for giveaways. Or better yet, donate them."

"Happily." Chuckling, she arranged them on a display rack. He regarded his photo on the front of the CD, a black and white sketch of him improvising in a recording studio. He'd sat on a stool wearing headphones, playing his guitar, and singing into a microphone.

He hadn't worked in a recording studio for several years, because he had nothing new to record. Sheets of blank manuscript paper crowded his suitcase, waiting like expectant fans.

The last rays of daylight filtered through the shop's front window. How long had he been awake? Australia was sixteen hours ahead of South Carolina time. Did dozing on the plane count?

"In case you're wondering," Dorothy said, "Scarlett and Joanna went to Frank's Pizzeria for dinner. It's a short walk from here."

"She mentioned they were going for pizza." Briefly, Joseph toyed with the idea of joining them. Perhaps after they shared a pizza and chatted for a while, he could walk Scarlett and the little girl home.

"I'm not used to all this walking," he said. "In a big city, I'm either driving on a freeway or in a taxi."

"Living in a small town with sidewalks is better than any fitness center membership."

He chuckled. "Point taken." He made certain to find a gym everyplace he'd visited, knowing exercise kept him fit mentally and physically.

Dorothy went to the counter and shut her tablet. "Cherish is a town of warmth and light."

"You're a poet now?" he teased. "Or am I dreaming about Oscar Wilde because I'm so jet lagged?"

"You're the one who writes beautiful worship music."

"Once upon a time," he said quietly.

"I'd be happy to help you write the lyrics to your next song. That is, if you need any help."

He managed a smile. "I'll keep that in mind."

She went over to a drawer of sheet music and began to file the pieces alphabetically. "Cherish boasts a number of churches too. Ryan and I attend Memorial Street Church," she said. "Pastor Steven and his wife Christina welcome everyone. And Mrs. Marge Addyson, the associate pastor, was speaking just the other day about adding a contemporary worship service to Saturday evening."

He'd wondered where this was leading. Now he knew.

"And this contemporary worship service would be led by … your husband, Ryan?" he asked.

"Unfortunately, he's too busy. He's turned down at least a half-dozen opera roles, and refuses to travel farther than a few hours away from Cherish. Consequently, you're a good first choice." She passed her hand over the music almost lovingly before closing the drawer. "And don't forget, Cherish boasts an equally fine music store and conservatory run by yours truly. Ta-da!"

He grinned and applauded. He couldn't help surveying the tidy store in awe. Every square foot of space had been carefully planned and painstakingly categorized by instrument—piano, harp, guitar, as well as a host of others.

He gazed at a sign prominently hung at the entrance: *Proverbs 19:21: Many are the plans in the mind of a man, but it is the purpose of the Lord that will stand.*

Ryan and Dorothy had built their business on faith, and their diligence and hard work equaled success. Plus, they'd opened a professional music school.

"You and your husband have created a welcoming environment for music lovers of all ages," he said.

"Thanks." Dorothy took an exaggerated bow. "Therefore, you'll get the best of both worlds here. Music and a close-knit, faith-filled town. People in this community are proud to serve the Lord."

"Are you trying to get me to move here?" he half joked.

She grinned. "Maybe."

A track from one of his CDs supplied background music. "My God Is an Awesome God." He'd been inspired to write the song when flying over the ocean, high in a sea of white clouds. For him, every piece of music started with the melody.

"You know my lifestyle," he said. "I don't stay in one place long. Traveling to different locations, hearing my music played at a variety of churches, keeps my muse creative."

He frowned. Did it? Certainly not lately. He hadn't written a new piece in over two years.

He shifted, focused on the stack of unsold CDs.

"Maybe traveling is a season of your life that's over, Joseph," Dorothy said. "Maybe it's time to settle down. Haven't you been on the road at least five years?"

"Ten."

"Is that what you want?"

"It's all I know. Performing music. And writing …" He focused on the floor, then her. "*Attempting* to write."

She paused, examining his expression. He attempted an easygoing smile, hoping she didn't catch the frustration beneath.

"Care to talk about it?" she asked.

"No."

"What if God is withholding what you want to direct you to what you need?"

He didn't answer, scarcely noticing the concern in her

voice. She was echoing a question that continuously nagged at him.

Resting for a week or two in one place between gigs wasn't enough anymore. For a while now, he'd been disheartened when he picked up his pencil to write music that wouldn't come. The door of his first love seemed to have been locked to him. Now it was the door of disappointment.

He believed in being honest. And he was, with everyone but himself. He just couldn't believe God wouldn't let him through that door anymore.

Is that asking too much, God—unlocking my creative muse so that I can compose worship songs again?

An image of Scarlett sparked through his mind. Why did his attention keep drifting to her?

"Do you want me to give you directions to the pizzeria?" Dorothy asked. Before he answered, she grabbed paper and a pen, and jotted down the address. "Scarlett and Joanna should still be there. Besides, you haven't eaten, correct?"

He stuffed the paper into his jacket pocket. "I'll grab something at the inn."

"I know Tom, the innkeeper, and he doesn't do dinner for his patrons. It's a bed and breakfast." Dorothy shut off the music and the lights, a clear sign she was ready to leave. "I'd invite you to our house, but I'm eating leftovers. Ryan is performing in Atlanta tonight, and I don't expect him home until much later. He's taken quite an interest in cooking and I'm encouraging him—mostly because my claim to fame is only pecan pies."

"You can't eat pie every day."

"A sad fact." She grinned. "Although Ryan could and would never gain a pound."

A loving expression came over her face. She and Ryan were so much in love. Joseph had been traveling when they'd married, but he'd spoken to Ryan a number of times and knew the guy was enamored by all things Dorothy.

When Joseph didn't reply, Dorothy asked, "So, you'll be off to Frank's for pizza?"

He hesitated. He shouldn't go. He should rest and listen to what his body was demanding. Get some sleep.

But he was hungry, he rationalized.

And when had weariness ever stopped him before?

CHAPTER 3

*I*n his beautifully appointed room at the inn, Joseph unpacked and showered.

Although dog-tired, he'd then walked to Frank's Pizzeria. There, he'd been informed by the waitress that Scarlett and her young friend, Joanna, had ordered takeout pizza and left shortly before he'd arrived.

That's what he got for waiting so long.

He ordered a slice of pizza and a soft drink, brought both back to the inn, and then got a decent night's sleep in a luxurious king-sized bed. The linens were top-quality, and the wood plank floor and fireplace exuded homeyness and comfort.

The following morning, Tom, the white-haired innkeeper, prepared a mouth-watering breakfast, setting up tables by a stacked-rock fireplace. After a prayer of thanks, Joseph ate heartily—fresh fruit, homemade corn muffins, a cheese omelet with thick slices of bacon, and hot coffee with heaping teaspoons of sugar.

So now it was noon. Well-rested, overfed, and alert, Joseph zipped up his leather jacket and ventured outdoors.

The weather was brisk and bright, with not so much of a whisper of snow. Ryan had mentioned that Cherish's weather was mild, which proved true on this January day.

After a short walk, Joseph came to Memorial Street Church.

He paused, admiring the picturesque white church, its splendid steeple topped by a cross. He bounded up the church stairs and strode through the open double doors. Kneeling, he clasped his hands and bowed his head.

When would a breakthrough occur so he'd be able to write music again? he asked a silent God. Where was the Lord's blessing on Joseph's life?

True, Joseph had enjoyed the accolades when his songs were well received, the social media explosion of compliments. But he didn't write worship songs for awards and compliments. Did he?

Sometimes he felt like he was fighting a war with the outside world. If he wrote beautiful songs, then people would respect his writing abilities and subsequently, him. And they'd like him. Because it was important to be liked? Wasn't it?

But it was more important to be honorable, to do the right thing for the right reasons. And there was the battle—not with the world and social media. He was fighting a battle within himself.

He shifted on the kneeler. This was his prayer? *This?* Whining and demanding?

He shook his head, closed his eyes, tightened his clasped hands.

None of his failures were God's fault. God wasn't to blame. Any lack of creativity was Joseph's fault. If he got right with God, with himself, then things would fall into place.

As a Christian, he knew this. And if he was more honest,

he'd recognize that his immeasurable pride was in the way of his own blessing. The Lord knew Joseph was far from perfect, yet loved him anyway. Couldn't Joseph do the same, love and respect himself whether or not he was a successful songwriter?

"Through your grace, I will be healed," he prayed.

When he finished and stood, he couldn't determine if his problem had been solved. But he certainly felt more peaceful within himself.

He left the church, retracing his steps, then stopped at a sign mounted on a street corner.

Cherish—one of the most charming towns in the Carolinas.

They'd been spot-on with that description. His breath caught as he crossed to the sun-drenched park and strode around the village green. The town was more peaceful than any he'd seen. Surrounded by budding trees and homespun warmth, Cherish was a special, tranquil place.

He crossed Evergreen Street and discovered a gurgling stream behind an old railway line. Sunbeams glinted off the water's surface, and a scent of moss permeated the air.

"You should see the bluebonnets growing here in the spring," came a familiar voice.

Joseph turned as Ryan Edwards slapped him on the back.

"How are you, my friend?" Ryan asked as the men shook hands. They were the same height. In college, they'd borrowed each other's clothes, which often lay in a dirty heap on their dorm room's floor. None of that mattered then. They were young and carefree.

"Very well," Joseph replied. "You?"

"Couldn't be better." Ryan looked fit and happy, his dark gaze gleaming with contentment. He nodded toward the stream. "When we were teens, Dorothy and I held slingshot contests to see who could snap the most petals off the flowers."

"Who won?"

"Who do you think?' Ryan pulled a hand through his dark-brown hair. "She did."

Joseph chuckled. "Marrying the love of your life obviously agrees with you."

"That's because I married the most beautiful woman in the world."

Tiny specks of snow swirled around them. Here and there, tree branches swayed in a cool breeze. Ryan stuck his hands into his wool jacket and circled toward town. Joseph followed.

"Where are you headed?" Ryan asked.

"Nowhere in particular. Merely exploring the town," Joseph said. "And from what I've experienced in other areas, this weather is almost balmy for winter."

"It's typical South Carolina," Ryan said.

The men fell in step together.

"How was your concert last night?" Joseph asked.

"I sang the role of Gurnemanz in Wagner's *Parsifal* to a sold-out crowd. Are you familiar with the opera?"

"I am. Impressive."

"Thanks. I'm still able to perform in big cities like Atlanta, come home to my lovely wife at the end of the day, and join her at church services on Sunday."

"*Therefore, you'll get the best of both your worlds here,*" Dorothy had said, voicing her not-so-subtle opinion. "*Music, and a close-knit, faith-filled town.*"

"Is your life as easy as all that?" Joseph asked.

"No one said it was easy," Ryan said. "But I'm discovering a joy I once believed was elusive."

"Traveling is hard, though?"

"Yes. Although it's worth it when you're doing something you love." Ryan blew out a breath. "Admittedly, Atlanta is a long drive and I didn't arrive home until well after midnight.

Fortunately, Dorothy insisted on hiring an Uber for me, so I slept in the car all the way back."

When they reached the middle of town, Ryan gestured to a restaurant across the street from them. "Hey, if you haven't eaten lunch yet, I highly recommend The Garden Terrace."

Joseph patted his stomach. "I'm still full from breakfast, although I'd love a glass of something cold."

"We're in the south, so order sweet iced tea and a slice of sugar-free lemon cake. You'll never taste anything better." Ryan glanced at his watch. "I'd join you, but I promised Dorothy I'd take over at the music store this afternoon so she can have a break. We'll catch up later, okay?"

Joseph could think of nothing more inviting than finding a discreet corner in the restaurant where he could unwind. "Sounds good. Although my sweet tooth will demand regular lemon cake, not sugar free."

"The restaurant serves both. Enjoy." With a quick *later,* Ryan spun toward the music store.

The wooden door to the restaurant creaked as Joseph opened it. He slid into a booth at the rear and glanced around. Dimly lit, the place had a sense of timelessness, boasting thick wooden beams on the ceiling and deer antlers mounted on the walls. An appetizing array of grilled meats and homemade barbecue wafted in the mesquite-filled air.

Intending to peruse a menu for a light appetizer to go along with the lemon cake and iced tea, he noticed Scarlett sitting at a booth near the front. She dined with an older man who faced her. Although her back was to Joseph, he'd recognize her anywhere. Her red hair fell in curls over her shoulders. Deep in conversation, she bobbed back and forth. Her shoulder bag was set beside her.

Joseph studied the man, who resembled Scarlett in so many ways, he assumed he was her father. The man had the same strong facial features and wisps of red hair as Scarlett, although he was as thin as a popsicle stick, and his eyes, even from a distance, were watery and bloodshot.

Joseph ordered a sweet iced tea, then thanked the young waitress with spiked black hair as she set the glass in front of him. He grabbed three sugar packets to doctor up his tea to a sugar max.

"It's already sweet," the waitress reminded him.

"Not sweet enough."

She shrugged. "Anything else? We're known for our sugar-free lemon cake."

"So I've heard. I was going to order an appetizer too, but tea is good for now." He shut the menu and handed it to her. He'd changed his mind, preferring to watch Scarlett and her father. "Maybe next time."

"Thanks." She smiled and left the bill on the table.

He took in every detail of the bustling restaurant and soaked in the ambiance—the older couple to his left, sitting side by side, silently concentrating on their meals. The collapse of giggles from two teenage girls.

Joseph took out a notebook and pen he always carried in his pocket and swung his gaze toward Scarlett's table. As a songwriter, he liked to watch people and considered himself intuitive for analyzing what went on with them.

He waited for lyrics to come. Closed his eyes. Waited some more. Nothing flowed. Pinching his lips together, he stuffed the notebook back into his pocket.

As he glanced up, he noticed that the conversation at Scarlett's table had quieted.

She pushed her plate full of salad to the side. Shaking her head, she toyed with a straw in her tall glass of lemonade.

The older man's face reddened. Unexpectedly, he slapped his hand on the table.

Scarlett jumped and the patrons around them paused to stare, then averted their gazes.

Immediately, Joseph sensed the constraint between father and daughter. Although Scarlett froze in place, she attempted conversation again. In response, the man's gaze wandered, and he answered in monosyllables.

On his feet five minutes later, the older man briefly clenched his fingers, followed by words that Joseph couldn't make out.

Another beat, and Scarlett and her father left the restaurant. Outside, the man kept his hands in his pockets while she gave him a quick, awkward hug. As the two departed, they walked in opposite directions. He climbed into a big rig parked to the side.

On impulse, Joseph bolted up, threw money on the table for his iced tea plus a tip, and rushed through the exit.

"Scarlett!" he hailed as he sprinted toward her.

She paused, then whirled. "Mr. Slater?"

"Joseph with a J, remember?"

"Of course." Her voice was strained. She lifted her chin, a sheen of tears in her glorious green eyes. She wore a pink paisley scarf that complemented her peaches-and-cream complexion. Her wool coat was forest-green with a high shawl collar. A navy sweater peeked from beneath, offering a glimpse of a sequin-embossed butterfly. He liked her colorful style and openly admired her shapely figure.

"Umm." She pulled at the front of her coat. "Why are you staring at me?"

Whoops. He swung his gaze to the sidewalk, although it drifted appreciatively back to her face. "I noticed you and that man in the restaurant."

Who was he? Joseph wanted to ask, but stopped himself. He waited to see if she would explain.

She didn't.

"Was he your father?" he couldn't help asking.

"Yes."

"And?"

Ignoring the question entirely, she hooked her shoulder bag on her arm and looked around the street.

Alrighty then.

"A coincidence we were both leaving at the same time," he said into the silence. "I was wondering if you could recommend …" He thought fast, pulling a hand through his hair. "Recommend a good place for a haircut. I wasn't able to schedule a trim before I left Australia."

"Cherish Styles and Clips is a short walk from here. They offer a full-service hair salon for both men and women, and I know the owner, Phyllis. I helped her move into her new place a few months ago." Scarlett pointed to an intersection diagonally from them. "Take a left on that corner, then a right. A couple more blocks and you're there."

"Can you walk with me? I've been known to get lost on a one-way dead-end street."

Not at all true, but he couldn't make himself be concerned with details. He wanted to spend time with her. His conscience tapped him on the shoulder. He'd just seen her the day before, remember?

He stiffened. And? Couldn't he see a woman twice in two days? Nevertheless, his excuse to spend time with her was anything but brilliant. A haircut. Really? So much for being a well-known lyricist. No wonder he couldn't write a noteworthy song anymore.

"Sure," she agreed. "I'll walk with you."

He could scarcely take his eyes off her as she guided him to the corner. They kept their pace slow as she pointed out local landmarks, then gestured to the streetlamps.

"Soon, the town will hang baskets of yellow petunias all along the main streets," she said. "On a sunny afternoon in May, the colors are amazing."

He wouldn't be here in May. For the first time, he understood what that meant and felt a twinge of regret. He'd seen streetlamps and flowers before, but with Scarlett, everything took on a fresh perspective. The whisper of snow, the comfortable strolling, the rays of a wintry sun, felt different.

"Cherish is even prettier than a postcard," he said.

They lingered to admire a shop window featuring a male and female mannequin dressed in red, standing in front of a white background. *Follow Your Heart*, the exhibit stated in bold red letters, with a string of rosy Valentine hearts taped to the window.

"Cherish celebrates every holiday," Scarlett said. "Some are more important than others." A softness came over her expression, making her look younger and somehow vulnerable.

"Where does Valentine's Day rank in holiday importance?"

"For the town?"

"For you."

"Near the top," she said quietly. A gust of wind ruffled her shiny hair. He wanted to stroke his hands through her curls. He wanted to hold her, right here in the middle of this appealing town. He wanted—

No. What was he thinking?

He cleared his throat. "Anything else?"

"Anything else about what? The town?"

"About you." He knew the difference between talking and listening, so he steered the conversation toward her. He wanted to listen. "For example, tell me about your Little Sister. You mentioned her name was Joanna."

"Where do I start?"

"How about at the beginning?"

"Well, I enrolled at the Big Brothers Big Sisters organization, then went through an extensive interview process to become a mentor."

"What are the requirements?" he asked.

"Applicants need to be eighteen years old. At the age of thirty, I was welcomed."

He laughed. "I'm thirty-five."

"You'd be approved too. You seem stable and would probably be a positive role model."

He couldn't contain his grin. "Probably?"

"Dorothy and Ryan speak highly of you, so I'll amend that probably to a definitely." She shared his grin. "The goal of mentoring is faith, and for the child to have confidence in you. They need to know you won't let them down."

Faith again.

"A mentor doesn't need to be rich or famous," she added, throwing him a meaningful look.

He was certainly not wealthy, as he donated half of the proceeds from his CD sales to charities. Famous? He shook his head. Hardly, although Scarlett might refute him.

Farther along the sidewalk, she stopped to study the ice-cream flavors on a sign posted outside Whitney's Ice Cream. Wistfully, she sighed and pointed to peanut butter crunch ice cream, describing it as creamy, decadent, and, well, crunchy.

"The crunch is the rice cereal," she explained. "And it's delicious."

The outdoor dining space beside the restaurant hosted an array of tangerine-colored, wrought-iron tables.

"Want to buy a cone?" Joseph stepped forward, examining the long list of flavors. "Do they carry candy?"

He could get a haircut anytime, he rationalized.

"Candy? Ice cream? You're joking, right?" With her corkscrew curls bouncing around her shoulders and a mischievous gleam in her eyes, Scarlett presented a delightful picture. "I'm staying far away from peanut butter crunch ice cream. It's one of my red-light foods."

"Which means?"

"If I have it around, I'll eat the entire container."

He was torn between drawing her closer for a kiss, or the similarly pleasant notion of feasting his gaze on her. For now, he decided to gaze at her.

"You'll need to go down the street to Charlie's Chocolatiers for your candy," she said. "Just don't ask me to taste anything because I'm on my ten-thousandth diet." A strand of hair fell across her eyes. She didn't push it away. "Which started today."

"Why?"

"Really?" She gave a small smile. "Look at me."

She was beautiful and full of life, and his heart skipped several beats as he studied her from head to foot.

"You don't need to diet. You look great."

"You've been traveling too long," she said. "Particularly in Western culture, women are encouraged to be as skinny as possible."

"I don't agree." He couldn't get his compliments out fast enough. "Truly, you're absolutely lovely."

A rosy flush crept across her high cheekbones, and her chin trembled.

"Hardly," she said, so quietly, he barely heard her.

So there were definite chinks in the armor beneath her smile.

And he wanted to get past the armor.

Nope, don't go there. No long-distance romances. He was leaving Cherish in a few weeks. Moreover, he'd closed himself off from emotional attachments and his barricade was firm. Two disastrous relationships in two different cities had been enough.

But the way Scarlett had brightened when he'd asked about Joanna, her cupid-shaped mouth and her eyes shining like polished emeralds, chiseled away at his barricade's unguarded cracks.

They resumed their walk.

"You were asking me about the Big Brothers Big Sisters program," Scarlett said. "Still interested?"

He gazed at her. "More than ever."

"The organization matched Joanna and me up. She comes from a single-parent home and faces difficult obstacles. This particular transition has been tough. The poor kid moved five times in three years, and she hasn't seen her father in ages." Scarlett took a handkerchief from her shoulder bag and dabbed at her eyes. "As she matures, it's my job to steer her away from risky behaviors."

"You fix things for her. You protect her. Bravo."

"As best I can, although that's not my role." Reaching into her bag again, she lifted out a small album with photos of Joanna—at the library, at the park, at the movies. Through the progression of time, Joanna's transformation from a sullen girl to a young lady bearing a proud posture was remarkable. In the last photo, dressed in a pink polka-dotted sweater dress, Joanna smiled broadly and gave a thumbs-up. She stood outside Memorial Street Church with an older woman and looked directly into the camera.

He nodded approvingly. "Who's the lady with the bright-red rouge?"

"Mrs. Marge Addyson, the associate pastor. A lovely woman, widowed, and she views everything in a Christian, down-home way. If you get a chance to meet her, you'll know what I mean. She's wonderful to Joanna, and is a mentor too."

"Every minute I'm in Cherish, I find more people to admire. You all follow the Lord's example of giving. Dorothy, Ryan, Mrs. Addyson, you …"

"We try our best. I'm here for Joanna to lean on and to share opportunities," Scarlett said. "Such as the Valentine tickets you bought for us, and the harp lessons Dorothy graciously offered."

"I bet you're a remarkable influence."

"I hope so." She indicated the harp bracelet on her wrist. "Joanna insisted that she and I wear matching bracelets, although I'm no harpist. It was a surprise and so considerate, along with Dorothy's big-heartedness, of course." Scarlett puffed a deep breath. "Soon Joanna will enter middle school. She'll face difficult choices—drugs, alcohol, peer pressure. I'll be there to steer her on a positive, Godly path."

"Joanna got lucky when her family moved to Cherish."

"Millions of kids need an adult role model. And I'm the lucky one. Joanna is smart and funny and has a heart of gold. I'm in and fully committed."

"How long is the program?"

"The organization asks mentors for a yearly commitment, which is no problem." Scarlett's entire face lit up. "It's under-standable, because it takes time for a child to build up trust."

"Are you involved in any other worthy causes?" In the spirit of their comfortable rapport, he took her hand as they rounded the last corner to the hair salon.

She didn't pull away.

"Well, I love animals, although that's not really a cause. It's more like my passion. I was the receptionist at a veterinarian practice in town before it shut down." Her expression closed, briefly unreadable. "Currently, I'm learning how to train service dogs at Canine Helpers. It's part-time, Monday through Friday, and Thursday I work a half day."

"Service dogs for …"

"Any person with a disability who can benefit from the service. These dogs help disabled people lead a more inde-pendent life."

"Define disability."

"Any physical or mental impairment that limits a person."

"Fascinating." He squeezed her hand, and they continued in silence. It seemed like they could have a conversation without ever having to say anything. That was how in tune he felt with her. "I'd like to hear more about it."

A tap on the shoulder again from his annoying conscience.

In tune with her? How? You've only known her a short time.

"Anytime," Scarlett said. "Oh, and did you know dogs are the only species recognized as service animals?"

"Not horses?"

"Good question." Approvingly, she nodded. "No, not horses. Although miniature horses are regulated and some-times used."

He smiled as they reached the entrance to Cherish Style and Clips. Purple pansies accented the shop's window boxes. "Any other worthy causes you'd like to share with me, Scarlett?"

"I like to call them passions, remember?"

"Passions, then. Even better." They were still holding hands. Beneath his fingertips, her skin was smooth and delicate.

"Cooking is my specialty," she said. "No shock there, I'm sure." Another deprecating laugh. She did that often, and there was no need. Didn't she realize how perfect she was?

"Any special recipe?" he asked.

"I've prepared a tasty meatloaf and mashed potatoes recipe my friend, Cathie, gave me. She works with me at Canine Helpers. The meatloaf is comfort-food delicious, and uses a homemade barbecue sauce with brown sugar and spicy brown mustard and tomato sauce."

"I'd like to try that sometime." Yes, dinner at her place sounded just the thing.

He knew he was staring at her mouth, and forced himself to look away.

Overhead, the sun was high. An abrupt gust of cold wind reminded that spring was still a couple months away. Notwithstanding, a young couple strolled past arm and arm, swinging a picnic basket.

Probably on route to the park, Joseph surmised. Already, he was getting to know the layout of the town.

Scarlett's gaze flicked to the hair salon, then back to him. "Are you asking me to cook dinner for you?"

"Is that too bold?" He took a step closer. He couldn't help himself. Everything about her intrigued him.

"No. I love to cook."

Lightly, his fingers grazed her cheekbone. "And I won't need dessert," he said softly. "You're sweet enough."

She retreated a step and pulled her hand from his. "This isn't a good idea."

"What? Cooking meatloaf?"

"This." She moistened her lips. "Us."

"Why?"

"Because you're in Cherish for a few short weeks. And I'm here ..."

"For the long haul." He finished her sentence. His gaze focused on her mouth again. Without thinking, he bent down and his lips brushed against hers. She tasted like fresh-squeezed lemonade—refreshingly tart, yet sweet.

She didn't stir, although she inhaled slightly. He hoped it was a sigh of pleasure.

"So we can date while I'm in Cherish," he murmured against her lips.

"You are so not listening." She shifted another step back. "You're a world traveler who has undoubtedly dated scores of women and then gone on to the next big city. I will not be one of those women." She pivoted, then seemed to change her mind as she curved back to him. "Thank you for the tickets, though."

He was still reeling from her refusal. He covered his disappointment with the lazy grin he'd adapted over the years. "You're welcome, Scarlett. Enjoy the concert. Thanks for showing me the way to my first haircut in weeks."

"Anytime. And say hi to Phyllis." A hint of a smile crossed her face. "Don't let her talk you into dyeing your hair purple or anything like that."

His gaze slid meaningfully to her hair. "I won't, as long as you stay a redhead."

"You never know." Her smile widened. "I always liked green."

"In your hair?"

"A few green highlights will complement the red. And the color green symbolizes nature."

"And red symbolizes a fiery personality."

"But not everybody can pull off both colors at once."

"You can, because you're amazing." He grinned, admiring her spirit, and said good-bye.

Goodbye for now, he amended.

As he entered the busy hair salon and took a seat, he was informed that Phyllis had the day off. Furthermore, as a walk-in customer, he would need to wait at least thirty minutes before a hairdresser could fit him in.

"No worries," he replied. The half hour gave him the opportunity to think about Scarlett. Her laughter, her optimism, her obvious passion about the things she cared about were utterly appealing. And they all revolved around three themes.

Faith. Service to others. Home.

Faith. He got that. He prayed that he could harness her faith, as his was elusive lately, and he was fast becoming a sorry excuse for a worship songwriter. How could he feel good about himself when he wanted God's guidance, but wasn't willing to make any sacrifices that went along with it?

Lately, his songwriting attempts had been half-hearted, and many times he'd given up before he began.

Service to others. Sorely lacking on that front too, he reflected. He'd visit the Big Brothers Big Sisters organization in Cherish to see if he could mentor in some way while he was here.

Home. For him, that was wherever he happened to be. He was on a never-ending trek to see the world.

With Scarlett, however, things were different. She was an obvious homebody.

Usually, he'd be looking right about now for the fastest way out of town if he had so much of an inkling that he was attracted to a woman like her.

But he couldn't, because he couldn't deny her desirability. Everything about her intrigued him. However, his reluctance to settle down in one place weighed equally as strong.

CHAPTER 4

The next morning, Scarlett awoke to the incessant ringing of her cell phone. Blinking in bewilderment, she checked the time and glanced at the caller ID.

"Hi, Dorothy," she answered groggily.

"I didn't wake you, did I?" came Dorothy's reply.

Sluggishly, Scarlett opened her eyes to a peek of morning sun filtering through her bedroom's sheer white draperies.

"Nope. I'm always awake by seven a.m."

"Joseph came by our house last night with an idea," Dorothy said. "In fact, he and Ryan talked about it for hours. We wanted to run it by you."

"What is it?"

"Joseph wants a kids chorus from the Big Brothers Big Sisters organization to sing back-up for two of his songs at the Valentine concert, and he's hoping you'll help."

Well, whoa. Scarlett placed the phone in her lap and regarded her freckled hands, her clenched fingers. He hadn't mentioned anything of the sort the day before. And why was her stomach doing a somersault at the thought of seeing him again?

She had to think, reviewing the facts she'd gathered about him. She shouldn't be nervous. He'd been kind and pleasant the entire time they'd been together. And he was extraordinarily well-liked, evidenced by the excitement at the music store when she'd waited in line. That radio DJ had carried on and on about him too. And her dear friends, Ryan and Dorothy, spoke well of him.

So what was Joseph's motive? More advertising?

Unlikely. She couldn't imagine he'd seek more publicity, especially for a benefit concert. He seemed like he wanted to spread the word of the Gospel, a genuinely good Christian man.

And a handsome one at that.

Her heart fluttered at the image of his chiseled features and sparkling blue eyes. Did he know how good-looking he was? Did he know those good looks were intensified by his quiet charm, his apparent unawareness of his appeal?

Scarlett brought the phone to her ear. "What about my ticket? And Joanna's?"

"Joseph said to donate them. Perhaps a couple people from Canine Helpers might want to go."

Scarlett's mind scrambled for another excuse. "But Joseph is a professional solo artist. He wouldn't want a kids' chorus accompanying him."

"He's requesting something different. His pieces are beautiful and timely and the audience can sing along too," Dorothy said. "Did you know his songs are sung all over the world?"

"Yes. I checked his biography on the internet last night." Scarlett's cheeks warmed at her admission. The previous evening, she'd spent hours indulging her interest in him while she watched him sing and perform on YouTube. No matter how many times she'd scolded herself not to, she'd been too enthralled by his concerts to do anything except watch in admiration. He'd also been interviewed by a famous Christian pastor in Australia, and had responded to the pastor's questions with effortless grace. The clip had received numerous hits on YouTube.

"His biography stated that he hasn't written a new single in a while," Scarlett noted.

"He said he's been inspired to write a couple new songs. We'll record at least one at the concert, and it will get first-hand coverage by the local TV and radio stations."

"Record it where?"

"Ryan installed a recording studio in the conservatory's rehearsal room, complete with a computer, microphones, headphones, studio monitors—you name it. Now when he's recording music for opera auditions, he won't need to leave home."

"Your expansion efforts are nothing short of remarkable."

"Thanks. The Lord has truly blessed us." Dorothy hesitated. "So you will help us, won't you?"

Hauling herself up to a sitting position, Scarlett fluffed the pillows behind her and then collapsed against them. With more curiosity than enthusiasm, she asked, "How?"

"Well, you're involved in Big Brothers Big Sisters. Joseph suggested you be in charge of enlisting five kids to sing with him."

"I don't sing, so I'm no expert. Will I need to audition the children?"

"Of course not. He doesn't want perfection. And I assume you'll include Joanna because she'll love it."

Scarlett took a sip from the water bottle on her nightstand. Dorothy was right, of course. The kids would be thrilled. Joanna would be thrilled. The community would be thrilled.

But what about Scarlett? Her heartbeat accelerated at just

the thought of seeing Joseph again, working side by side with him.

Be rational, she told herself. This wasn't about her.

Okay.

Then she could admit she was ridiculously nervous about the entire undertaking. Joseph made her feel like a girl with her first crush, and she couldn't tamp down her attraction to him.

"Scarlett?" Dorothy asked. "Are you still there?"

"Of course." Scarlett studied the beams of sunlight creeping across her beige carpet.

"Without your assistance, his idea might not fly," Dorothy said. "He said you'll need to be at every rehearsal."

"Okay."

"What does that mean? Is that all you can say?"

Scarlett shoved a hand through her hair. "What do you want me to say? Somehow, I think this was all decided without me."

Dorothy laughed. "Just say *yes* with an exclamation point. What's stopping you?"

Joseph, she thought. Being close to Joseph.

But how could she share these reservations with Dorothy, or the fact that Scarlett had been thinking of little else but him since they'd walked to the hair salon the day before?

"Nothing's stopping me," she replied, tempering her voice. She didn't want to sound too enthusiastic. She didn't want Dorothy's matchmaking antenna to go up any higher than it already had.

"Consequently, you're good with this then, right?" Dorothy pressed. "We all assumed you would jump at the chance."

Aha. "Really? You all assumed?"

"Well, yes."

"Even Joseph?"

"It was his idea. He said you can be his assistant director."

Scarlett gave an exasperated shake of her head. She had informed him she didn't want to get personal while he was in Cherish. Apparently, he followed his own agenda.

Once more, she set the phone in her lap. With a sigh, she looked around the empty bedroom. So why would he assume she'd jump at the chance?

Reason one: Because he suspected she was already interested in him. She hoped her feelings weren't that obvious.

Reason two: He knew she'd never disappoint Joanna. A practical explanation.

Her heart, however, chose a different reason. Perhaps *he* wanted to spend time with *her*, thus using her involvement with Big Brothers Big Sisters as an excuse.

She couldn't contain her smile. She couldn't contain her hope, either. That is, until she quickly shoved aside that notion.

She refused to live in a fantasy world. He was a famous musician who had visited more countries than she could count on two hands. She was an overweight woman living in a small town. A woman whose fiancé had left her flat. A woman who, beneath her bright outward appearance, was self-doubting.

"You can't control your emotions," she'd once heard a pastor say, "but you can control your focus." And her focus should be about others, not herself.

"Scarlett? Where did you go now?" Dorothy asked through the muffled phone receiver.

"I'm here." Quickly, Scarlett pushed out a breath and drew the phone to her ear. "And I'd love to help."

"Great. I assume you'll stop at Big Brothers after work? I'll drop Joseph's music off there, so the kids can take a peek."

"As soon as my shift at the service-dog facility is over at

three o'clock," Scarlett replied. "And Dorothy, thank you. The idea sounds beneficial for the entire community."

"Yay! I agree."

The happiness and relief in her friend's voice almost reduced Scarlett to tears.

Sternly, she reminded herself she hadn't agreed because she'd have the opportunity to work with Joseph. She'd agreed because it was an amazing break for the children. Plus, not only would the concert provide delightful worship music for the town, but it also supported things that mattered—money for the elementary school's music program, and a one-of-a-kind experience.

A few minutes later, Scarlett sat at her chrome kitchen table eating a healthy breakfast—fat-free Greek yogurt, a banana, and black coffee. Today was the first day of her diet, and she felt excited and motivated. As she sipped her coffee, she went about convincing herself that this new undertaking with Joseph could also be healthy for her in a personal way.

Often in the past, she'd run away from anything that scared her.

In this case, working with a man who made her heart go into overdrive would be good therapy. This time, she wouldn't avoid the situation. She'd have to get over the fact that this tall, handsome musician brought up unresolved sadness from her childhood just by standing next to her.

These were feelings she preferred to keep under a protective bubble, but she wouldn't disappoint her friends and Joanna for anything in the world.

Would she?

Drop by drop, she felt her self-assurance draining away and swallowed hard.

Wasn't this how difficult things worked? A person faced challenges directly in order to move on.

She leaned back in her chair, placed her hands behind her

head, and glanced out the window. Already, the sky promised a gloriously sunny day.

She relaxed her muscles and stood. Her steps to her bedroom were swift and purposeful.

* * *

AT THREE THIRTY in the afternoon, Scarlett arrived at the brick building on Main Street that housed Big Brothers Big Sisters. She'd successfully finished her work at the service-dog facility, training a German Shepherd to switch on the lights inside a home for a man suffering from PTSD. The man, Mark, had recently returned from combat duty overseas and was feeling wary about his safety. The dog gave Mark a sense of security and also served as a physical barrier between him and the outside environment. Plus, the shepherd forced Mark to exercise—going outdoors to walk the dog. A win-win on all counts.

Pausing at the entrance to Big Brothers with her hand on the brass door handle, Scarlett cleared her thoughts and swept inside.

Isaac Albertson, the director, was in his office. He stood with his back to her, studying the large bulletin board that listed the week's activities for the children and their mentors. He stepped out of his office to greet her with an enthusiastic hand slap.

"Are you here to see Joanna and your new chorus?" He reached for a leather briefcase and handed it to her. "Dorothy dropped this off for you." He grinned, and his silver-white mustache lifted. His balding head shone in the overhead fluorescent lights.

"Thanks. You heard about the children's chorus, then?" Scarlett unzipped the briefcase and peered inside. Five copies of Joseph Slater's sheet music entitled, "And We Sing,

You Are Our God" were neatly filed, the lyrics clearly typed.

"Dorothy briefed me, and the idea is excellent," Isaac said. "I asked all the elementary kids. Five are ready and willing. One is Joanna, and there are two other girls and two boys. I've checked with their parents, and permission slips are all signed."

"Wow, you are efficient."

"Shh." He pressed a finger to his lips. "Don't let word get out. Someone at the state level may want to cut my hours."

Scarlett grinned and couldn't help thinking that without Isaac's tireless work and enthusiasm, the organization in their little town would never have grown to the proportions it had. This brick building was just one small haven in a big, dangerous world, but it meant so much to these precious children.

Isaac followed her to a large gymnasium full of noise and confusion and laughter. Some children read books aloud with their mentors, others played board games, while a group of middle-school boys shot baskets.

"Here's your charges." Isaac gestured to a group of children sitting at one table. "Two are third-grade girls, and the other two are fourth-grade boys."

"And me," Joanna reminded as she stood. "I'm in fifth grade."

Scarlett grinned at the youngsters as they gathered around her.

"You're a great bunch," she said. "Can anyone sing?"

They all raised their hands. That is, every child except one of the fourth-grade boys. With a defeated slump of his shoulders, he said, "I don't want to be in the concert after all."

"Why not?" she asked.

"My older brother will call me a sissy." He jutted out his chin. "Besides, I can't sing."

"Do you want to be in the concert"

He shuffled his feet and looked down. "Yes," he mumbled.

"Remember, different people are good at different things. And I know if you work hard, you'll do great." She offered her most encouraging smile. "It will be fun, and I promise lots of great men are artists."

"Promise?"

"Promise. So will you sing with the other children?"

He peered up at her through a curtain of black bangs and nodded.

Isaac led the children into a rousing rendition of "Row, Row, Row Your Boat," then handed out the music to Joseph's song and read through the lyrics with them. When they finished, Scarlett applauded and shouted, "Bravo!"

The dark-haired fourth-grade boy peered up at her. "I'm Russell."

"I'm Scarlett."

He held a half-eaten chocolate cupcake in his hand and offered it to her.

She scooped him up. "Thank you, but I'm on a—" She was cut short when the boy threw his arms around her neck and gave her a chocolate-frosting-laden kiss.

"I really want to be in the concert," he whispered.

"Hurray!" She took a bite of his cupcake and smiled while her heart melted. What would she do without these kids? They'd enriched her life in more ways than she'd ever imagined.

After using the restroom, the children retrieved their coats, then Scarlett and Isaac herded them out of the building. They had so much energy, passersby chuckled at their boisterousness. They walked two blocks and took a right down Evergreen Street to Musically Yours. Isaac marched the children in single file through the music store, reminding them to be on their best behavior. As always, the store looked bright and hospitable, welcoming musicians and music lovers alike.

Emmanuelle Thompson, a lovely woman with silky blond hair, huge blue eyes, and a face that seemed carved out of bone china, smiled a greeting at Scarlett while assisting a customer. Scarlett paused to stop and say hello.

Emmanuelle was Dorothy's sister-in-law, having married Dorothy's brother Nicholas, the deputy in town.

"No children yet," Emmanuelle had once said to Scarlett with a laugh. "Nicholas and I are content with our dog, Molly Belle. Believe me, she keeps us extremely busy."

Emmanuelle had once been principal harpist in a prestigious orchestra. Nowadays, she taught harp lessons, performed locally, and worked in Musically Yours.

When Scarlett reached the large rehearsal room at the back of the store, she stopped to talk with Ryan, who was setting up a row of five chairs. While they chatted, the children bounded for the chairs like a shot.

After Isaac seated everyone, he took the opportunity to leave, explaining he needed to stop back at Big Brothers Big Sisters. He'd been asked to expand the mentoring program to a neighboring county, was meeting with a group of interested volunteers, and was sorry he couldn't stay. He didn't look the least bit sorry, Scarlett thought with an inner smile. Isaac was dedicated to the organization, but preferred his quiet office rather than a group of rambunctious children.

Dorothy sat at the upright piano, her fingers poised on the keys, ready to accompany the songs in a supporting role for the rehearsals. Joseph had claimed one of the two empty stools beside her. Despite Dorothy's pointed stares, he ignored her. He plucked the strings of his guitar with his long fingers, sang softly, and then hastily scribbled notes on a sheet of manuscript paper. The melody was lovely and one that Scarlett didn't recognize.

Even in this concentrated pose, with his brow furrowed in utter concentration and his full lips pressed together, she needed to assure herself that he was real. This handsome, famous man, wearing worn jeans and a long-sleeved navy T-shirt, was rehearsing for a concert in a town so small, it had only one elementary school.

He didn't belong here. He belonged on a concert stage performing for thousands of avid fans, as he'd performed at the Grammy awards on national television.

No, she corrected herself. He looked completely comfortable and in his element—singing in an environment with other professional musicians.

She was the one who didn't belong. She didn't know anything about music. She only knew about children and animals, cooking and volunteer work. She couldn't even sing on pitch in the shower.

She glanced down at her clothing, hastily picking the dog hairs off the sleeves of her green coat. Beneath the coat, she'd worn a color-block sweater in a flashy pink and purple, fitted blue jeans that were admittedly a tad too tight, and gray leather ankle boots. Any stylish effect was ruined by her unkempt hair piled in a side bun, and the chocolate frosting stain on the sleeve of her coat. The makeup she'd applied that morning had faded, and she hadn't had time to reapply lipstick.

Keeping her position in the doorway and feeling utterly self-conscious, she watched Ryan walk away and grab a bottled water from a cooler. While her insecurities tumbled in her mind and she considered retreating, she stole another surreptitious glance at Joseph.

She had vowed not to run from the situation, she reminded herself. She would be here for the rehearsals leading up to the Valentine concert. She was a Big Sister, a mentor. A woman Joanna could depend on. Without Scarlett's friendship, Joanna's precarious security and self-worth issues could be turned inside out.

Managing to look a million more times confident than she felt, Scarlett stepped into the room.

A couple of employees from the music store conversed amiably with Ryan. She overheard Ryan telling them that the audio interface connected to the computer was an integral piece of recording equipment.

From what she could hear above their conversation and the children's playful giggling, Joseph continued to pick out notes on his guitar while half-singing lyrics that were hard to make out. She paused, listening, counting the number of times he used the word *love*.

Yes, he loved the Lord. But this song seemed different. The lyrics sounded like a love song between a man and a woman. The melody was slow, reminding her of a long-ago ballad by Elvis Presley, "Can't Help Falling In Love."

As if sensing her presence, Joseph looked up, and his blue eyes caught her stare. Setting down his guitar, he strode to her.

"Hello, Scarlett." He studied her for a long moment. So long that the familiar flush of hot pink crossed her cheeks.

"Hi, Joseph."

"I'm happy to see you again."

She studied his face for a sign that he was teasing her.

"Not for my singing ability, I assume," she replied. "I don't want to ruin your concerts."

"I bet your voice is lovely." He stepped closer. "As are you."

She glanced down at her disheveled clothes. This close to him, she inhaled his scent of fresh air and a hint of leather.

"Hardly." Self-conscious again, she looked away. "Although I haven't dyed my hair green yet." Her gaze traveled to the ever-present dark stubble on his chin, his thick, wavy hair. Despite the haircut, his hair still curled at the nape.

"I've been reading up on hair dyeing," he said, "and a drastic hair change sometimes means a woman is looking for a transformation in her life."

She lifted her eyebrows. "All that? Can't it just be for a fun change?"

He turned her to face him squarely, placing his hands on her shoulders. "You look great either way."

"Suppose I dyed my hair blue?"

He grinned. "Surprise me." Taking her hand, he led her to the stool next to his.

CHAPTER 5

The next two weeks stretched in front of Joseph in a delightful routine.

Scarlett's part-time schedule at Canine Helpers allowed her to rehearse with him and the children after school. Because Valentine's Day was fast approaching, they spent an hour every weekday practicing.

On Thursday, he met Scarlett at noon and walked with her to the Goodwill store. Winter had tightened its hold on the town, and she was diligent in her efforts to keep every child warmly dressed.

Once inside Goodwill, he insisted on footing the bill for children's coats, scarves, and an array of woolen mittens. He knew Scarlett struggled with finances, as she'd recently lost her full-time job as the receptionist at a veterinary clinic in town.

As they exited the store, he took her gloved hand in his.

Notwithstanding the cold, a pale sun shone overhead, prodding jewel-colored violets to bloom. He snatched a delicate bunch from the ground and handed the flowers to her.

"An early Valentine's gift," he said.

She paused in midstep and sniffed them. "Thank you. They're beautiful." A radiant smile lit her expression.

Her green coat hugged her voluptuous curves, and leopard ear muffs partially covered her lustrous hair. She looked gorgeous, with the brisk air adding a healthy tint to her cheeks.

As he continued to gaze at her lively eyes, her pert nose, her cupid lips, he felt an unexpected melancholy. He would be leaving soon. And he would miss her.

She had such a likable personality, animated and earnest, especially when she smiled. He liked the optimism surrounding her and her patient love for the children.

She exhibited, he thought with an inward sigh of sadness, all the traits he'd been looking for in a woman.

"No one has ever given me flowers before," she said.

"Really? I'm surprised."

She dismissed his comments with a wave. "Your compliments are far too generous."

"On the contrary," he started to say, before she bit her bottom lip and turned away.

He'd pondered what to get her for Valentine's Day, the final day of his concerts. Flowers? Candy? A parting gift? He drew a long, ragged breath. His chest tightened. He couldn't imagine never seeing her again.

"When violets begin to bud," she said, "spring can't be far behind."

Her words carried the realization that a new season was upon them. Spring—rebirth and light, the promise that God's will in nature, and in life, would be done.

Shoulder to shoulder, they continued walking through the park carrying two bags of children's clothing.

"Why did the veterinarian practice close?" he asked.

She kept her gaze straight ahead. Nearby, a young family flew a kite, their toddler racing across the grass and giggling.

"The vet moved away," she finally said.

"And consequently, you were out of a job."

She flinched, but he wasn't sorry for bringing up the subject. "Dorothy mentioned that you and the vet were dating." Actually, Dorothy had told him about Scarlett's broken engagement, but he wanted Scarlett to explain.

She gazed at the kite billowing in the air. "I don't want to burden you with my problems."

"Try me." He beckoned her to sit on a park bench, then slid beside her.

"Judson and I were engaged." With a sigh, she tucked the bags beneath the bench, then fanned the violets carefully beside her. "And then Judson broke the engagement."

"He's a foolish man to let you go," Joseph said.

"He didn't like my personality." She blinked, then shaded her eyes, watching the toddler tumble in the grass. "Rest assured, I'm well over the good doctor," she hastily added.

"Good."

"Why?"

"Because I really like your personality." Joseph slid an arm around her. "And I like *you* a lot."

"Don't go there." Her shoulders stiffened. "My heart is out of reach."

"That's not what I see when we're together." He tipped her face up to him. She was so attractive, although her expression was full of wariness.

"Joseph, I—"

He lowered his head. "Kiss me," he murmured against her lips.

She didn't fight him. Instead, she pressed nearer to him, her mouth meeting his for a long sweet kiss.

When the kiss ended, he rested his chin on her head. She stirred, and his arms tightened. "Don't move yet," he whispered. "Let's stay like this for a while."

He longed to kiss her again, to have her drive away the ache that filled his chest. As the days had passed, he'd come to realize that his life was now fuller than it had ever been. And his muse had been restored, inspiring him to compose again.

She shifted. "We don't want to be late for your rehearsal."

"I have it on good authority that the rehearsal is being run by an extremely good-natured musician."

She laughed. "Do you happen to know his name?"

They gathered their bags and continued their walk to the Big Brothers building hand in hand. A light dusting of snow began to fall, a wintry reminder, transforming the landscape to a powdery white.

"There go the violets," he said.

"The flowers are hardier than you think. And, besides, this snow won't last. By tomorrow, the sun will come out and melt everything."

SHE'D BEEN CORRECT. The following day, the icicles on the eaves of the shops had melted and the sidewalks were clear.

Daily practices were even better than their walks, Joseph decided. He'd earmarked the stool beside him for Scarlett, encouraging her and the children to belt out the chorus of his worship song in their loudest voices. Admittedly, throughout the rehearsals, he only had eyes for Scarlett.

The following week, Joseph didn't know what to expect when he sprinted into the rehearsal room at exactly 4:00. Normally, he'd meet Scarlett beforehand at Canine Helpers, but he'd accepted a long-distance call from Australia and had texted her to go ahead without him. He hoped she'd managed okay—walking the children to rehearsal, getting them settled and handing out lyrics took a great deal of effort, and she'd admitted to him that she was disorganized.

He rushed into the rehearsal room with his guitar in hand. He'd made record time, dashing from The Cherish Hills Inn to Musically Yours in under fifteen minutes. He'd been in a hurry to finish the phone call so he could see Scarlett. "A pastor in Australia is requesting a new worship song for the grand opening of their church," he explained. He didn't add that he'd ended the conversation by saying he couldn't commit.

Joseph glanced around the rehearsal room at the children. "Hi everyone."

They giggled, waved, and held up their music.

"We're ready!" Joanna said.

"Joseph, you're out of breath," Scarlett said. "I'll get you a bottle of water."

She had been sitting on a chair next to Joanna and fixing the girl's ponytail. When she got up, he did a double take. Oh, boy. He could gaze at her forever. Her luxurious mane spilled over her shoulders, and her hips swayed as she walked over to the cooler for a water bottle and then brought it to him. She wore a magnificent peach-colored sweater, embellished with a sparkling daisy pin, and a pair of black slacks that outlined her stunning, curvy figure.

He met her halfway. Defying propriety, he placed an arm around her shoulders.

"You look gorgeous," he said.

That figure. Those sea-green eyes. He'd be thinking about her the rest of the evening.

"We are being closely watched by five children," she murmured.

"And I'm merely leading my lovely assistant director to her rightful place beside me." He kissed her lightly on the forehead, prompting cheers from the children.

Thirty minutes later, they'd reviewed the chorus of his song, "And We Sing, You Are Our God," several times.

"Can I show you something new I've been composing?" he asked.

Encouraged by the chorus of yeses, he plucked the melody on his guitar and then handed the lyrics to Scarlett.

"'The Kingdom Of Heaven Never Stops.'" She glanced at him. "Will you sing it for us?"

He obliged, playing the opening chords. "'No fear. The kingdom of heaven never stops.'" He sang straight through to the final chorus: "'We sing your praise on earth as in heaven.'"

He looked up. The room had stilled and Ryan and Dorothy stood in the doorway. Silently, they applauded before returning to the music store.

"My new favorite song," Scarlett breathed as the children clapped.

"Do you like it?" He grinned.

"I love it."

"Thanks. We'll sing this, and 'You Are Our God' for the concert finale," Joseph said. "Okay?"

"You're only giving us a few days to learn a new song."

"I just finished the melody last night. But I bet if the kids rehearse a few more times, they'll get it. They're professionals. They don't even need musical directors."

"Alright." Scarlett paused. "Dorothy mentioned you were writing two songs. Are you finished with the second one?"

"We won't need that one for the concert. It's ... personal." He took a long drink from his water bottle. The song meant too much to him. He wanted to sing it to Scarlett when it was finished. When it was flawless. Like her. "So let's call this rehearsal a wrap and play cards."

"Cards? Play cards? During a children's music rehearsal when you've just given us a new song?"

"A couple more practices and they'll be top-notch." With that, he sat on the floor. Extracting a deck of cards from his duffel bag, he beckoned the children and Scarlett to sit around him.

"Who wants to play Crazy Eights?" he asked, laughing as Joanna raised her hand. He dealt out cards to each child and indicated a brightly wrapped box in his duffel bag to Scarlett. "I found Charlie's Chocolatiers," he whispered.

"Do you just follow around your sweet tooth?"

He winked. "Mostly I just follow around you like it's my profession."

A half hour later, he'd purposely allowed a different child to win each card game, and indulged them by giving out chocolates as prizes.

Scarlett chuckled. "Remember, we are the adults in the room."

"Adults play cards," he replied.

"That's not what I meant. Adults don't make funny faces after each play, or sing silly songs, or stuff three pieces of chocolate in their mouth every five minutes. The kids need to respect you so they'll cooperate with your requests."

"Aren't they cooperating?" he asked.

She shook her head. "Not if you keep acting like a kid."

"Lately, I'd forgotten the sheer joy of just having fun. Some of these children have serious home matters," Joseph said quietly. "Let's keep laughter in their lives."

He'd spoken with Isaac about becoming a mentor, and Isaac had explained that it was a commitment to one child for a year. Joseph's heart grappled with what that meant—a promise, staying in one place. And he'd prayed, waiting for God's answer.

Although what if his prayers weren't about God's response, but more about his own convictions?

"Time's up, kids," Scarlett announced, nudging Joseph and tapping at her watch.

As they stood, Russell raised his hand. "Mr. Slater, where are you from?" he asked.

"A small town in Pennsylvania," Joseph replied.

"Do your mom and dad still live there?"

"No, but my sister does." Joseph held the deck by its sides, and with a light touch, shuffled the cards before stowing them into the case.

"I didn't know you had siblings," Scarlett said.

"Yes. My sister Samantha." Joseph was silent for a moment. "She's a couple years older than me. She's not married, either."

"Where are you parents?" Joanna spoke up, twisting and untwisting the ties of her pink hoodie.

"They're in heaven." Briefly, Joseph smiled. "They passed away when I was a teen."

"Where do you live now?" Joanna again.

"Nowhere." He hesitated, reflecting. "Everywhere."

"You mean you don't have a house?" Russell asked.

"Nope."

With a defeated slump of his shoulders, Russell muttered, "Neither do I." He refused to join Joanna and the other children, now cavorting around the room.

"See what I mean?" Scarlett murmured to Joseph. "No discipline and we'll have chaos on our hands."

Joseph hardly heard her. He was paying particular attention to Russell. Striding over, he took a seat beside him and they chatted quietly for a while.

When Joseph rejoined Scarlett a few minutes later, she asked, "What was that about?"

"Russell is a good kid. I wanted to see if I could help in any way. It's obvious he's been wounded. I don't know if something happened at home, or at school …"

"That's a roadblock you'll encounter many times," she

said. "Home life, lack of two stable parental figures, limited finances. These kids have experienced many hard knocks."

Joseph drew in a quiet breath. Between him and Scarlett, the silence was broken only by the sounds of giggling children, and the heartbreaking sight of one small boy with slumped shoulders and straight black hair sitting alone.

Music blared from the music store, as Dorothy apparently had switched the background recording to a Mozart piano sonata.

"You don't have a home, then?" Scarlett asked.

"I haven't found a place to settle down."

Until now. The thought came to the fore, unbidden.

But didn't he consider himself a Nowhere Man? The name from one of his favorite songs by the Beatles. *He was a real nowhere man.* He glanced at Scarlett, who openly stared at him. As usual, she was in tune with him, although she hadn't said a word.

But was "he making all his nowhere plans for nobody"?

"I want to travel and see the world like you," Joanna declared as she raced by, with the other children happily in pursuit. "I want an exciting, fun life and I want to meet lots of cool people."

Cool people.

Joseph grinned. Scarlett grinned. "She's growing up too fast," they said in unison.

"I never met a stranger," he said to Joanna as she raced past him again. "Just remember no matter how far you travel, keep your family and friends close. And God is most important."

Joanna put her hands on her knees and leaned over to catch her breath. "You say that because you write worship music."

"God is the center of my heart, and my experiences figure

into my songs. What I see, what's occurred in my life, is all part of the song."

As Joanna scampered away, Scarlett asked, "Do you think she got any of that?"

"I hope so."

"Your songs bring tears to my eyes, you know that?" Scarlett said.

"Thank you. That means a great deal coming from you."

"Why? I'm no music critic."

"You're a million times better than any critic because you speak from the heart." He sealed his words with a light kiss on her lips.

At exactly five thirty, Isaac and another mentor arrived to escort the children back to Big Brothers. Scarlett helped with their coats and boots, then bid them goodbye.

"Can I walk you home?" Joseph asked as Scarlett grabbed her coat.

"Sure." She shook back her hair and tied her paisley scarf into a graceful knot at her throat. "I'd like that."

THEY STROLLED HAND IN HAND, covering the easy walk in thirty minutes. At the doorway to her apartment, she wavered. "Would you like to come in?"

"You said you cooked, right?"

"Yes."

"And it's dinnertime."

She regarded her watch. "Yes, it is."

"Then do you remember telling me about a meatloaf recipe your friend, Cathie, gave you, using homemade barbecue sauce?"

"You have an impressive memory." Quickly, Scarlett went over in her mind the food in her refrigerator and pantry.

Ground beef and potatoes, lettuce for a salad. "Are you up for mashed potatoes, as long as you peel?"

"Comfort food on a cold February night? Are you kidding? I'll peel a five pound bag."

"You'll only need to peel two pounds for us." She tried to tamp down the little thrill of elation that ran up her spine. After all these days, they'd be sharing their first meal together. Anxiety battled with elation.

They entered her apartment, and she switched on the lamps in the living room. She'd decorated the interior with care, opting for sunny yellow and turquoise throw pillows to offset her orange-checkered sofa and side chair. The coffee table was a miniature wine barrel she'd found at a flea market, and a fluted bowl of fresh oranges sat on the table.

"I love orange," she explained.

"And green hair," he reminded.

"Did you know orange is the color of enthusiasm and joy?"

"I do now," he said with a grin. "And the color fits your personality perfectly."

Her curtains were a pressed gray silk. She'd painted the walls greige, a combination of beige and gray, and a cream-colored carpet completed the airy design.

"Nice place." He took her coat, then shrugged off his own and hung them in her foyer closet. "Your creativity and sense of design is amazing."

It showed in his gaze, his sincere admiration and interest in her, and she smiled as she led him to her tidy, efficient kitchen.

He washed his hands at the sink, then pulled up a stool at the island. "Bring it on. I'm ready to peel."

"After the potatoes are cooked and drained, the recipe calls for sour cream."

He rolled up his sleeves. "I'm liking this dinner better and better."

After handing him a peeler, knife, and empty pan, she set to work making the meatloaf—washing her hands, dicing an onion, and including a loaf of Italian bread to the mix.

"Can I add something for Valentine's Day?" He rose to stand beside her as she spooned the meat into a baking pan.

"Valentine's Day isn't for a while yet," she reminded.

"But we're together now." He shaped the meat mixture into a heart and stepped back.

"Where did you learn how to cook?" she asked.

"Here and there. I've lived alone ever since I went on the road. A guy can't eat take-out every night of the week." He offered a devastating smile.

He was all male. His shoulders seemed strong enough to carry the heaviest burden. He was witty, talented, and generous. And his scent—sweat and brisk air—made her wish he would always be near, that this evening would last forever.

She knew it couldn't. He'd be leaving the day after the concert.

"Plus," he said, "my father always made meatloaf on Valentine's Day for my mother. I remember them laughing in the kitchen while he cooked. My sister and I would peek around the corner of the living room and watch them."

Scarlett set the timer on the oven for one hour. "Your father must have been very romantic. Most men think of just buying flowers and chocolates, or taking a woman to a fancy restaurant."

"Looking back, my father was a romantic. And do you know what happened next?"

She chuckled. "What? Your father burned the meatloaf?"

"Nope. It came out perfect every time."

Joseph brought her into his arms and pressed his lips to hers. "This happened." His hands slid across her shoulders and down her back, pressing her to him. Helpless, she surrendered as he kissed her thoroughly and repeatedly.

Please, don't ever stop, she thought, as she wound her hands around his neck.

Sixty minutes passed, and the meatloaf came out of the oven. She allowed it to cool, then set it on a white stoneware platter.

"Watch this." Grinning, Joseph carefully arranged mashed potatoes around the heart-shaped meatloaf.

They sat at her chrome table in her tiny kitchen, and he offered a prayer of thanks.

One hour later, they'd eaten dinner and cleared the table. Joseph insisted on helping her load the dishwasher, pausing between dishes to nuzzle her neck with a kiss.

She couldn't think beyond the gentle touch of his lips. The sweet tone of his voice as he sang—the Beatles, traditional hymns, a recent pop hit. His tenor voice filled her with optimism. She wanted this, wanted him, every day of her life.

Afterwards, in her cozy living room, he sat beside her on the sofa, legs touching, his arm circled around her.

"I was surprised this afternoon at rehearsal," she began.

"About how well the kids sang?" He pressed a kiss on her temple. He did that often. "Thanks to my excellent assistant director, they're well-rehearsed."

"It's not me. It's you. You have a way with them—a rapport that's innate. They worship you."

"I don't want them to worship me. I want them to worship God."

"I didn't mean it in that way. They look up to you. You're a good role model."

"As are you."

"Joseph." Unwilling to let anything dampen the marvelous evening, she gave him a reassuring smile before she spoke. "I learned something new about you today. Your tours take you far and wide, but you've managed to keep the relationships that really matter—with your sister Samantha, and with Ryan and Dorothy—close."

"Isn't that the way it's supposed to be?"

"I've always believed that relationships are more grounded if a person stays in one place." She sighed. "I suppose it's because of my father. He's a roamer. And still, after all these years, I can't accept that."

"Are you an only child?"

"Yes." She closed her eyes for an instant. "Unlike you, my father can't be depended on to stay in touch, especially after my mother passed a few years ago. Sometimes it's a few days, sometimes weeks or months go by without a word from him. I get so angry, so frustrated, when he goes dark and won't return my calls."

"You can't change him, Scarlett."

"I know, and I'm sorry."

A puzzled smile touched Joseph's lips. "For what?"

"When I first met you, I compared you to my father."

He frowned. "And that isn't a compliment."

"Sadly, no." She replayed the scenes of her childhood in her mind. "When I was young, I lived in Chicago with my parents. Every time my father was ready to leave, I would tug at his coat and beg him to stay. And then, after he left, I'd count the days until his homecoming." She closed her eyes, could hardly inhale. "The fat girl, staring out the window waiting for her father's return. Pathetic." She glanced at Joseph for his reaction, but his face remained impassive. Still, fearful he might feel sorry for her, she waved her hand airily. "It doesn't matter, of course."

"Did he travel on business?"

"He was a salesman, but he gambled his money. We always struggled financially. Now he drives a rig."

Joseph's arm around her tightened. "And your mother?"

"She never reacted, just always agreed with him." Scarlett's smile was grim. "My mom and I were exact opposites. I questioned him, whereas she stayed silent. 'Why couldn't he stay in one place?' I'd ask her. In my opinion, that's what made a person dependable and trustworthy."

"Strong roots. Staying in one place."

She nodded. "Yes."

"And you shared your opinions with him, also?"

Her gaze clouded as she recalled the distressing scenes—her crying, him walking out the door. "Many, many times."

"So when I saw you with him in the restaurant, he was just passing through Cherish?"

"My father's patented remark—*Just passing through*. He managed to have lunch with me, but when I asked him to stay longer … Well, he just couldn't, I guess." She blew out a breath. "What causes people to wander?"

"Travel sometimes ignites a hunger for more."

"More what?"

"I'm not sure. Maybe God placed wanderlust in some of us to carry the Gospel." He paused, silently reflective. "Many times at the end of a concert, I'd walk outside and find a quiet place, preferably at the top of a hill. I'd look out over the city, sparkling with lights, and sing a favorite psalm. I'd praise Him. I refused to allow myself to forget that God created everything."

"Joseph, your faith is truly inspiring." She realized she was staring at him with love in her eyes. This exquisite Christian man.

He looked down at her, and his expression of interest, of sincere caring, touched every nerve in her pulse. "Or sometimes," he said, "we wander because we haven't arrived yet."

"Arrived where?"

"Home." He traced his finger along the curve of her cheekbone. "Home at last."

Softly, she laughed, feeling outrageously elated. With him, she felt safe and loved. Sharing his faith, he'd explained that his sights were set on heaven, but his feet were firmly planted on the ground.

"Cherish is my home," she said.

"And as each day passes, I believe that God brought me here for a reason." He tipped up her chin, looked deeply into her eyes. "I'm a man who strives to tell the truth."

"And the truth is?"

"I believe I am falling in love with you."

Her heart felt like it was beating in triple-time. "It's too soon," she murmured. Her words said one thing, the right thing, but her emotions felt another.

"Not if it's meant to be. I'm hoping you're feeling what I'm feeling."

She was, but she couldn't tell him, for soon he'd be gone. She stroked her fingers against the ever-present stubble on his chin. "I care for you, but we don't know each other well."

He smiled. "So you've said." He seemed to accept her explanation, although he cocked a dark eyebrow as he spoke.

How could he believe her protests, when she didn't believe them herself?

His lips brushed against hers. "Can you admit you're as happy as I am?"

"Yes. Extremely happy." She attempted to smile, but tears blurred her vision.

Gently, he cupped her face between his fingers, and his thumb stroked an errant tear from her cheek. "So why are you crying?"

"Because you're a good man and—"

She left it at that as he kissed her.

He was a man who deserved a confident, slim woman by his side. And she deserved someone who would be there for her, not on some Skype screen halfway around the world.

Still, she snuggled into his embrace as she dashed the tears from her eyes and pondered his words.

Effectively, he had spun a new meaning to the term *wanderlust*. He'd proved there could be positive aspects to a life lived lightly rather than deeply grounded.

His path had taken him one way, hers another.

And perhaps either way was good.

As she did every morning, Scarlett walked to her job at Canine Helpers. The days with Joseph had delightfully blended together, and there was a decided spring to her step.

Her cell phone chirped, and she recognized the caller ID.

"Good morning, Dorothy," she answered.

"All three Valentine performances are sellouts," Dorothy said. "Friday and Saturday nights, and the Sunday matinee. Isn't that remarkable for such a small town? Ryan and I discussed a Sunday evening performance, but it is Valentine's Day and all."

"And all what?" Scarlett asked. "You and Ryan want to celebrate the holiday?"

"Not us. We're newlyweds and know we'll be together."

"Uh-huh." Scarlett expelled a long breath. "And?"

"And, well, you might want to spend the evening with a certain famous musician. Maybe dinner at a fancy restaurant, discussing your future, holding hands ... Whatever two people in love might do."

"Two people in love?" Scarlett parroted. She blinked, massaged her temple.

Dorothy sniffed, an all-knowing sniff. "Your attraction to Joseph is written all over your face. On his too."

"Is it that obvious?" Scarlett blurted, and then quickly closed her mouth. But really, what did Dorothy see?

Love.

"The entire town is buzzing about how you two are so good together. In church this past Sunday, you held hands during most of the service. And word is that Joseph met with Isaac about becoming a mentor."

"He did?" Scarlett had reached the center of town. She paused to eye the shop windows, the traditional red and white Valentine designs festive and eye-catching.

"Didn't he tell you?" Dorothy asked. "I assumed that by now you two were sharing everything."

"No, as a matter of fact, he didn't mention meeting with Isaac."

This was completely new territory, and Scarlett wondered why Joseph hadn't spoken about it, especially because mentoring meant so much to her. But then, since he'd arrived, everything had happened so rapidly, coupled with the powerful feelings he ignited in her, that she'd barely had time to comprehend their chemistry. She just reveled in it.

"You're reading too many romance novels," she said. "Life doesn't work that way and Joseph is committed to perform in several major cities. He's leaving on Monday for Raleigh, and I'm sure he'll have a list of things to do before he checks out of the inn."

And he was checking out of her life. Any hope she'd clung to that he might stay had promptly disappeared with the passing days when he hadn't mentioned a future they might have together.

"You know him, but I know him too," Dorothy said. With that, she clicked off before Scarlett could ask, "What's that supposed to mean?"

Before she could harbor any false expectations, she dismissed fanciful dreams from her mind. There were Big Brothers Big Sisters organizations in numerous major cities, and Joseph could mentor a different child in each.

No. No he couldn't. The organization wanted a one-year commitment. So there went that idea.

Still, Joseph had hinted that he'd like their relationship to continue, although he hadn't come out and made a specific plan. Sure, they talked constantly—about nothing and everything, like what time of year bluebonnets were in full bloom, their favorite ice cream flavors at Whitney's, (hers was peanut butter crunch, his butter pecan although he preferred the candy store), and the benefits of eating dark chocolate versus milk chocolate.

And always the conversation swerved to encompass his music and songs, her passion for animals, her love for Joanna and how proud she was of her accomplishments. Much to everyone's delight, Joanna was excelling in her harp lessons —already reading music and practicing a measure at a time (as Emmanuelle had instructed) on a small harp Dorothy had lent her for home use.

In the evenings after rehearsals, Scarlett and Joseph would walk to her apartment, stopping at the grocer to buy fresh, nutritional ingredients for dinner. He'd insist on buying a bouquet of flowers—cheerful daisies with a button center, or rainbow-colored carnations, or an array of large golden sunflowers—and he'd arrange them in a large glass vase in the middle of her kitchen table.

After dinner, their non-stop talks went on until late in the evening. For a midnight snack, she'd brew a pot of herbal tea, along with toasted slices of whole grain bread topped with local honey.

He spoke of his travels, embellishing his descriptions about the lush greenery of Ireland, or the high-rises in New York City, or the natural beauty of an Australian beach. And his stories of those places made her yearn to travel, which surprised her.

Her. The homebody, who had vowed she'd never leave the safe, stable confines of Cherish.

This is risky, I'm endangering my heart, she'd think, as he thrummed melodies on his guitar—some old, some new, some happy, some sad. She knew that no matter where he journeyed, after he left he would take a piece of her heart with him.

On his cell phone, he'd shot various selfies of them at Musically Yours, in front of Canine Helpers, and loads of photos with Joanna. He had developed many of the shots into large colorful photos and hung them on Scarlett's living room walls. In one particular photo of Joseph and Russell, taken in front of Isaac's office, Russell held a blue balloon proclaiming "Happy Birthday," as it had been Isaac's birthday that day. Joseph, dressed as usual in jeans and a T-shirt that proclaimed *God is Love*, had his arm firmly around Russell's shoulders. Both smiled into the camera.

"I care so much about these kids," Joseph had said when he'd hung that picture. He took Scarlett into his arms. "Almost as much as I care about you."

A shiver went through her as he held her close. She tried to make light of his remark by giving her standard answer: "We don't know each other well enough yet."

"I know all I need to know about you," he refuted.

"It's necessary to date a person a certain length of time before anything serious can develop," she said.

"How long?"

"Obviously, longer than a few weeks. There are certain rules, Joseph."

He shrugged. "I've never been a follower of rules."

She smiled, liking the sound of that. She'd wanted to press her cheek against the soft cotton of his shirt and declare that she'd never cared for rules, either.

Please stay. But she said nothing.

Hopefulness was a funny thing. It could break your heart quicker than anything else. Tear a person apart. And she couldn't hinge her dreams on a man who was here today, gone tomorrow.

He'd also made sizable donations to both Canine Helpers and Big Brothers, and word had spread quickly throughout the town of Joseph's generosity.

Therefore, the weeks since he'd first set foot in Cherish had been the best weeks of Scarlett's life. So much, that on the Thursday morning before the concert weekend, she grappled with surges of despondency and the stark realization that time was passing much too quickly.

At noon, Joseph met her on the steps of Canine Helpers. Neatly dressed in his favorite pair of dark-washed jeans, a graphic T-shirt that said *God Is with Us*, and his black leather jacket, he was impossibly handsome. She felt exhilarated, and smiled at the utter delight of seeing him.

He set down his duffel bag and enveloped her in his arms. "Today," he said, "we are going out to lunch."

"We can't." She patted her waistline. "I'm on a—"

He put a finger to her lips, opened his duffel, and extracted a brown bag. "I figured you'd say that. So I bought a salad at The Garden Terrace for you, and two slices of lemon cake for me."

"Two slices? Do you know how many calories are in a slice of lemon cake? If the second piece is for me—"

"The choice is yours. If you don't eat it, I will." He shook the bag. "The restaurant gave us plastic forks and bottles of water too."

"We were going back to the Goodwill store this afternoon, remember?"

He made a show of shading his eyes and staring at the vibrant Carolina sky. "You predicted the snow would melt. It did. And the kids now own so many gloves and hats that they could trek across the Arctic Circle and never be cold."

"It's February. More snow could easily be coming."

"We'll take our chances." With a flash of white teeth, he favored her with a charming grin. "At the restaurant I asked which salad is your favorite, and the waitress with spiked hair said that last time you ordered a Cobb salad and didn't finish it."

Scarlett laughed. "Now why would you go through all that trouble?"

He gazed at her for a long moment, drew her into his arms, and said in a velvety voice, "Surely you know why."

Her heart hammered wildly while caution screamed in her ears. *Don't risk it. A few more days and he'll be gone.*

She stepped away and whispered frantically, "Please don't look at me like that."

He stepped an inch forward and kept his hands at his side. "Also, I wanted to thank you for your help," he said softly. "Without you, I never would have been able to pull this concert off."

"I highly doubt it, but I'll accept your compliment." Considering, she stared at Canine Helpers—the covered walkway, the squat wooden exterior, the small forested area in the back. "The waitress remembered I didn't finish the salad?" she asked.

"Small towns. Everybody knows everything about everyone."

She burst out laughing. "You're 100 percent correct."

"I'm starting to like small-town life." He kissed her hair. "So we can play hooky today."

"What does liking a small town have to do with playing hooky?"

"Absolutely nothing." He stated it with such conviction, she didn't know how to dispute his reasoning. Shaking the bag again, he asked, "Lunch it is?"

"We can't." So much for not disputing him. "The kids will be disappointed."

"They won't arrive at Big Brothers until after school." This close, the warmth of his body made her feel like nothing could ever go wrong in their world. The faint scent of his leather jacket tingled her nostrils, causing her pulse to quicken. "And just in case, I phoned Isaac and informed him we might be a little late."

"As usual, you took care of everything."

He gestured toward a hill past the park. "You look gorgeous in that fuchsia blouse, by the way. I like you in the red family."

"Red family?"

"You know, red, pink, rose."

"The colors are a family?"

He grinned boyishly. "Why not?"

She laughed at his logic and studied him as they walked.

When the time comes, accept that he'll leave and don't cling to him. Be grateful for the affection you've received.

In the midst of sunshine and breezes full of expectation, he took her hand. His grip was strong and reassuring, bringing her comfort.

She tossed him a light-hearted smile. "Did you know I've lost five pounds?"

"I do, because you've mentioned it a half dozen times. And I always respond the same way— you don't need to diet. You're perfect."

"Skinny is considered the epitome of attractiveness."

"That's ridiculous."

"You're being very kind. But thanks." Despite her shrug, she smiled, his compliment warming her insides.

* * *

As they kept walking, Joseph couldn't stop himself from openly admiring Scarlett. The vivacious smile he'd come to appreciate, the freckles on her cheeks, the bright colors she wore—which today was that fuchsia blouse and matching slacks beneath her green coat. Shimmery green earrings dangled from her delicate ears, the color of emeralds, faultlessly matching her glorious eyes.

Everything about her was exceptional. Her appearance always eye-catching and somewhat outrageous, his Scarlett.

His Scarlett?

He couldn't help grinning as they walked hand in hand.

He opened his mouth to begin a conversation, then closed it. The Lord had taught him that it mattered where he started a conversation and where he ended it. Although he'd positioned his life around God, he'd also targeted his life around, well, himself. And *self* was a small focus to center on in such a big world. The realization that he needed more, needed her, was beginning to make absolute sense.

And so he'd planned this excursion for several reasons. Of course he wanted to spend as much time as possible with her before he departed. But there was another reason. He wanted to test his feelings about bringing their relationship to a deeper level—without the babble of pudgy-faced children, or in the midst of peeling potatoes, or within the confines of a noisy rehearsal room.

Wind plucked at the ever-present paisley scarf tucked around her throat. A flame of red hair, the whisper of her laughter, a jangle of shiny silver bangles on her wrist. Everything reminded him of Scarlett, because she had pervaded his senses until he could think of little else.

Did he want to develop their relationship on a deeper level?

Most definitely.

Because lately he could only focus on one thing. He wanted her. He wanted to spend every day, every night, with her.

In this scenic town, they'd embrace a simpler lifestyle, joining close friends at church, as they had every Sunday since he'd arrived. He'd grown to love the pastors, particularly Marge Addyson. Marge was also a mentor at Big Brothers and spent several days a week with Savannah, a troubled teenage girl from a broken family.

Marge was a knowledgeable woman with a rollicking laugh, often showering Joseph and Scarlett with shrewd observations.

"Seeing you two holding hands makes me as happy as a bouquet of bluebonnets in the spring," she had teased them after church last Sunday. "You belong together." As Scarlett had blushed gorgeously, Marge had fixed him with a laser-sharp gaze. "If you don't stay in Cherish, you'll never forgive yourself."

He'd laughed. On the church steps, they had all laughed.

But Marge Addyson had known.

He was in love with Scarlett. And he had told her in a thousand subtle ways, hadn't he?

He squeezed his eyes shut, sending up a silent prayer. *God, what should I do when second thoughts invade my happiness?*

Would he truly be content in a town this size? He knew Scarlett wouldn't be happy moving from one city to another. She wanted permanency and sameness, the security of building a family and living in one place.

They strolled through town, remarking on the shop windows exquisitely decorated for Valentine's Day. He guided her into the local florist and admired the artfully arranged designs—pink azaleas and long-stemmed roses in crystal vases, lavender daisies and white lilies with intense, fragrant blooms.

"Do you have a favorite flower?" he asked. He planned on surprising her with a festive bouquet after the final concert on Sunday.

"The roses are beautiful," she replied, complimenting the shop owner, who was dressed in jeans and a white blouse, an embossed apron draped over her slim body. "But I prefer handpicked flowers, and gifts that come from the heart."

He got it and knew better than to say anything, fearful he would spoil the Valentine surprise he had in store for her.

They exited and continued their stroll.

They discovered a broad winding path and wandered to a sun-dappled gazebo. Setting down his duffel bag, he steered her inside. The gazebo allowed them a limited amount of privacy.

He braced his hands on her shoulders and turned her to face him. Slowly, his head descended, his lips brushing against hers.

"Joseph—" Her voice was unsteady. "Here?"

"Kissing you on this beautiful day is perfectly acceptable. I have it on good authority the townspeople would approve."

Softly, she laughed. "Which townspeople, exactly?"

"Dorothy and Ryan," he said agreeably. "And Isaac and Marge Addyson. And Joanna. You mentioned she was a romantic."

Scarlett chuckled. "That awesome memory of yours again."

He drew her into his arms, and she tipped her head up for

a kiss. Moments later, without warning, she broke the kiss and stepped back.

He took her hands in his and regarded her. "Anything the matter?"

She glanced at the hill beyond, her expression solemn. "We should get going."

Quietness punctuated a lengthy moment.

"Okay." He tried to reply as impersonally as she had. He picked up his duffel bag and they continued at a quicker pace.

However odd her response, it was heaven to clasp his hand around hers, to be in a comfortable, Godly place without the barriers of travel and suitcases and exhaustion.

So what if she was quieter than normal? Women were quiet sometimes, weren't they?

When they arrived at the top of the hill, the view provided a picturesque expanse of the town. The sky provided a celebration of brilliant sunshine, and birdsong drifted from the trees. Beside him, Scarlett amiably responded to his questions about becoming a mentor.

He was surprised she didn't pry him for more details, but she didn't. Instead, she inserted stories about Joanna and Joanna's mother and siblings.

As Scarlett spoke with animation, he pictured her as a little girl growing up in big-city Chicago, her hair in red pigtails, carrying a pink lunchbox, skipping to school. And then going home, filled with confidence and its counterpart, uncertainty, wondering if her father would be there.

"I've packed everything for our picnic," he said. "Right down to ..." He pulled out a blanket he'd stuffed in his duffel bag and spread it on the cool grass. They sat and ate the feast he'd provided, her salad and his lemon cake, and washed the food down with bottles of water.

When they'd finished, he pulled his gaze from the familiar scene of the town park.

"Let's go behind the railroad tracks," he suggested.

She sent him a wry look. "Excuse me?"

"Ryan showed me where he and Dorothy used to sling-shot when they were kids. Apparently, Dorothy was excep-tionally good."

Scarlett laughed. "If you're gauging my abilities with a slingshot against Dorothy's, you'll be sorely disappointed."

"I don't carry one myself, so you're in luck. And I doubt I could ever beat Ryan, anyway."

She smiled, then eyed her wristwatch and stood. "High time we get to Big Brothers. It's almost three o'clock."

"I told Isaac—"

"Yes, but we don't want to be late. This afternoon is the final rehearsal before the concert tomorrow evening."

"Don't you want to spend our last hours alone together?" He attempted to keep his feelings in check—annoyance, disappointment, wanting her to explain why she didn't want to prolong the moment of being alone in this exquisite place.

"Joseph, we've spent the past three hours together. Isn't that enough?" She pursed her lips. The sharp tang of her remark cut through him.

He stiffened. "Sorry to waste your time."

She grabbed their belongings and began walking. "Don't be ridiculous."

"I'm leaving Monday morning." He hastened to keep up with her. "Shouldn't we talk about it?"

She slowed and gazed at him. Her beautiful eyes darkened with an emotion he couldn't read.

"Why? What is there to say?" she asked softly. He was surprised when the shrug she offered seemed somewhat indifferent. He'd expected a warmer response—a fervent *Yes, how can we arrange a long-distance relationship?* Or, *Have you considered staying in Cherish?*

"I'm thinking about becoming a mentor," he said.

"So I heard. I wondered why you didn't say anything when I was going on and on about Joanna."

It took a Herculean effort not to ask her why she hadn't mentioned anything to him. Of course, he hadn't mentioned anything to her, either, but that was because it was an idea—one based on prayer and faith and love—but still only an idea.

He shot her a quizzical glance. "I assumed you would be excited."

"I am. Good luck with it. I'm sure you'll find mentoring rewarding."

He waited for her to ask where he planned to mentor—in Cherish, in New York, in Atlanta …

"That's it?" he asked.

"I wished you luck. Should I add *safe travels*?"

"I'm not flying off to the moon." Slowly, he reached for her hand.

She pulled back. "Australia is almost as far."

"Our time together has just begun, Scarlett."

He wanted her to agree. *Assumed* she would agree.

She hesitated, tightening her green coat around her. "You and I must be on a different time frame. Our time together is ending."

Right.

Wrong.

His mind stopped working. He couldn't counter with a snappy comeback. He could feel her withdrawing further and further away and he didn't know how to bring her back.

"Is that what you want?" He stopped short. "We've continuously had fun together."

"Yes, it's been fun."

It's been fun but ... The word hung silently in the air between them.

And she hadn't answered his question.

"I think it's better," she said slowly, "if I don't join you for tonight's rehearsal."

"Why? What about the concert?"

"You said yourself the kids are so good they don't need a musical director, so they certainly don't need an assistant musical director."

"Now you're the one being ridiculous because you refuse to talk about it."

She winced and met his gaze straight on. "Talk about what?"

"You don't get what I've been trying to tell you all afternoon?"

"Apparently I don't." She took a deep breath and swung her gaze to the florist shop's window. All this time, they'd been walking toward town. He'd hardly noticed.

"And you know what else?" he challenged. "Perhaps that's what you've wanted all along. Me to leave. Perhaps that's what has made me so appealing to you."

"Well, you should know, because you've become such an expert about me in a short amount of time," she lashed out.

"Scarlett." He put his hands on her forearms. "Let's face it. This isn't about me, or even us. It's about you and your absentee father. And your absurd notion that a home has to be in one place or else it doesn't count."

He was spot on. He could see it from the wounded expression on her face—just before she spun from him and stormed away.

On Friday afternoon, Scarlett phoned Dorothy to explain that she wouldn't be able to help with the concerts after all. She added a sincere apology.

"Are you sick?" Dorothy questioned.

Frantically attempting to think of an excuse, Scarlett mumbled through a *not exactly*.

"Okay. Hope you feel better soon."

Dorothy was so caught up in the concert preparations, eager to discuss erecting a tent at the park in case of rain, the chair set-up for the audience, the recording gear and portable outdoor heaters, that their conversation was brief.

"Ryan is saying the sound equipment just arrived," Dorothy said. "And we hired two catering vans to serve refreshments. And security. I'd better tell Nicholas to get on that."

"It's good to have connections with the town deputy," Scarlett murmured. With a final *Good luck*, she clicked off.

Next, she reviewed her conversation with Joanna before she telephoned. As Scarlett expected, Joanna's mother answered. When Joanna insisted on talking, Scarlett offered up a brief apology, saying she wasn't able to attend the Valentine concerts.

Nonetheless, she told Joanna she and the other children would be great. "Break a leg," she added.

"Huh?" Joanna asked.

"That's show-biz talk for good luck."

"Breaking a leg is good luck?"

"It's a theater superstition. If you wish a person good luck, it really means bad luck."

"Huh?" Joanna asked again.

"Don't worry about it. Just have fun."

"Then you aren't coming to any of the concerts?"

Scarlett swallowed, knowing her voice was heavy with unshed tears. "No."

"Why not? Are you sick?"

"I'm okay."

"Are you faking because you're avoiding Mr. Slater? He was great at rehearsal yesterday, but seemed, I don't know, kinda sad somehow. Did you guys have an argument?" In her usual straightforward way, Joanna had zeroed in on the fact.

"Some things are better a certain way, and I know the concerts will be a huge success." Scarlett struggled for composure—to be the adult Joanna knew and respected. But as hard as she tried, she'd let the girl down this time and there was no hope for it. "I'll see you after school on Monday at Big Brothers, okay? I love you."

"I love you too. And Mr. and Mrs. Edwards are taping the concert to make into DVDs, so don't forget to buy one, okay?"

"I won't." Scarlett fidgeted with the tie on her terry cloth robe. "Sing well."

"Sure." With a resigned huff, Joanna clicked off.

Scarlett reassured herself that there were other people to

help with the children—Dorothy and Ryan, Emmanuelle and Nicholas. And of course, Isaac.

Now it was Saturday. Forty-four hours had passed since her argument with Joseph, and those days had been a blur. Her life had lingered in another place, another time, and refused to move forward. Every thought led back to one man.

Joseph. The first time he sang about love and peace in front of Musically Yours, expertly thrumming his guitar. And signing his autograph. *Here you go, two t's, Scarlett.*

Joseph, after finishing his new song, boyishly, expectantly watching for her reaction.

Joseph, waiting patiently for her in front of Canine Helpers. *Today, we are going out to lunch.* He'd respected her diet, asking the waitress which salad Scarlett preferred.

He'd phoned several times in those forty-four hours. He'd texted too. And she hadn't responded because, really, what would she say?

Goodbye? They'd already traveled that road.

Come Friday he'd repeated his calls and texts. She'd vacillated, staring at her cell phone and asking herself: Should I answer?

On the one hand, she knew she should. She wasn't the type of person to leave someone hanging. An argument could only be settled when two people talked openly and agreed to disagree.

On the other hand, what good would it do? He traveled all over the globe and she wouldn't accompany him, although his descriptions of exciting locales had called up a sense of adventure in her.

All good, although the truth was she couldn't handle living on the road. Her life in Cherish had been carefully built, and she wouldn't tear it down to follow a musician who never settled in one place longer than a few weeks. Of course, he also hadn't asked her to come with him. Nor had he said that he would stay.

Don't think about his handsome face, his kind eyes, his full lips.

Sadly, that was all she wanted to do.

Twice, she had reached for her cell phone to call him. Then she reminded herself that she couldn't endanger her heart again. Not even for him. If they did continue their relationship and she chose not to accompany him, she'd share her life with a man who was hardly ever around.

Never again would she be forced to stare out an apartment window, waiting for a man's return.

I yearn for you like crazy, although I refuse to wear rose-colored glasses. You're here, there, and everywhere. I'm in one place, where I intend to stay.

Still, she missed him more than anything, and compulsively replayed all the good things that had occurred between them.

In many ways, her weeks with him had been transformative. He'd forced her to face her feelings about loneliness and loss, about people leaving her life for purely selfish reasons and through no fault of her own, and to accept and forgive them anyway for being who they were. She'd been upset and incensed at Joseph's parting remark, but his words had niggled at her.

This isn't about me, or even us. It's about you and your absentee father. And your absurd notion that a home has to be in one place or else it doesn't count.

Blowing out a sharp sigh, she opened the living room window and let in a waft of air scented with evergreens. The February weather had been undecided, but today was a lovely spring-like day. The sunshine brought a glow, the grass a sparkling green, and new warmth promised wildflowers and tiny buds appearing on the trees.

She padded into her small kitchen and set a kettle on the stove for tea.

A cardinal hopped onto her windowsill, its feathers the color of crimson.

"Hi, little fella," she cooed.

The cardinal nervously flicked its eyes toward her and flew away.

Not once in the last two days had she cried, knowing that crying about a successful musician whom she'd never see again would turn her into an emotional faucet. However, in doing so, she had stored up a horrendous weight of emotion. A sweet bird who preferred to fly away rather than look at her was the final straw.

Tears welled, and she dabbed at her eyes. "Joseph Slater, don't you dare turn me into a blubbering fool." As tears streamed down her cheeks anyway, she poured her tea and went into the living room. Settling on the sofa, she drew her knees up to her chest and wept.

When there were no tears left, she wiped her eyes, perched her chin on her hands, and glanced at her watch. The hours had dragged; showing only midafternoon. Would it always be like this without him? The days long and desolate?

She did what any fat girl would do. She got dressed, went to town, and purchased a quart of peanut butter crunch ice cream at Whitney's, adding a slice of chocolate fudge from Charlie's Chocolatiers. Swinging the bags, she went back to her apartment.

Since Joseph had arrived in Cherish, she'd lost several pounds and was at a weight she hadn't seen since high school. Their nightly dinners included healthy entrées and nutritious appetizers. She'd stuck to her diet and eaten no desserts, save for local honey on toasted bread at midnight.

That was then. This was now.

She'd always used food to tide her over when she'd had a particularly trying day—after the breakup with her fiancé, when she'd felt anxious about her new job at Canine Helpers, pretty much whenever she needed comfort. Stress eating. Emotional eating. Because comfort food, which unfortunately was mostly sugary and processed, made her feel better.

She sat on the sofa and opened the ice cream container.

With the first spoonful halfway to her mouth, she caught the glimmer of sunshine outside her window, the sky dotted with fluffy white clouds.

She paused.

What was she doing, about to gorge on ice cream on this fine Saturday afternoon? After all the weeks of dieting, did she really want to sabotage her weight loss with ice cream and candy?

She fell back against the sofa and closed her eyes.

No, not this time. Making smart, daily choices was the way to wellness. She could banish the word *diet* from her vocabulary, because no magic diet would help her reach her goals. The entire process was solely up to her.

It was big, this change in her mindset, and she realized it. Had she always looked to food for consolation?

Certainly.

But no more.

She placed the ice cream container back in the freezer, the spoon in the dishwasher, the candy in the cupboard, and decided to check out the Saturday service at Memorial Street Church. Normally, she attended on Sunday morning, but there were two excellent reasons why Saturday evening was better.

First, Joseph, Dorothy and Ryan wouldn't be there, as they would be preparing for the concert. So there'd be no awkwardness, no avoiding people, no uncomfortable questions.

Second, Saturday offered a new contemporary service. Chances were good she wouldn't run into anyone except groups of teenagers.

When early evening approached, dusk washed across the sidewalks as Scarlett walked to church. The service proved inspiring and energetic, the pastor's words adding layers of meaning about forgiveness and obedience to God.

When it ended at seven, she slipped from the pew and headed to the exit at the back of the church.

"Scarlett? Is that you?" Marge Addyson's cultured southern voice stopped her. "What are you doing in church tonight?"

Scarlett swiveled, "Hi, Mrs. Addyson. Umm, right. I usually attend on Sunday morning."

Marge's proper pumps clattered across the aisle. For an older woman, she was spry and well-kept. As usual, her gray hair was perfectly coiffed. "What I mean is, I heard you weren't present for last night's concert because you were so sick you needed three beds."

"Is that what you heard?" Scarlett grinned and pressed a greeting kiss to Marge's rouged cheek.

The woman smiled back and tugged on the jacket of her powder-blue wool suit. "I missed you. We all did."

"I'm sure the music was lovely," Scarlett said, congratulating herself on how well she had sidestepped Marge's questions.

"The children were delightful. And that musician of yours has a dreamy, raspy voice that could melt butter. The last worship song—that new one—had everyone on their feet weeping during the finale."

"Yes, I've heard it and it's beautiful." The remembrance brought a well of emotion bubbling to the surface, and Scarlett dashed tears from her eyes, hoping Marge wouldn't notice. "We're not together anymore."

"You were the ideal couple. What happened?" Marge extended her arms, and Scarlett moved into the bear-hug embrace. Something within her wanted to burst open, to tell the elderly woman everything.

"It's a long story."

"The church is empty." Marge gestured to a pew in the back.

They sat in silence for several beats. Scarlett focused on an arched stained-glass window highlighting a full-length angel, the muted colors glowing as pure silver.

Never quiet for long, Marge nudged Scarlett's shoulder. "I'm a good listener, as well as a good talker, you know. Give me a try."

Scarlett wiped her hands on her pencil skirt. Firmly, determinedly, she fought to control the thickness in her throat as she explained Joseph's kindness, how good he was to her, his rolling-stone lifestyle. All the highs, all the lows. She spoke until there was nothing left to say.

"Dorothy's told me and half the town that you and Joseph are in love," Marge said.

"Has she now?" Scarlett felt a warm blush stain her cheeks as she recalled Joseph's lips moving tenderly on hers.

Don't move yet, he'd whispered. *Let's stay like this for a while.*

"And cute little Joanna told me the same thing when I mentored Savannah a few days ago."

"Joanna is a romantic." Scarlett shook her head. "And Dorothy. Well, Dorothy—"

"Knows you and Joseph well. So your stories about how kind Joseph is, how he opens doors for you and stands when you enter a room, leave out the most important part." Marge took Scarlett's cold hands in her own. "He loves you, and you love him. Everyone else realizes it. Now it's time for you to realize and do something about it."

Scarlett's stomach gave a funny lurch. "Like what?"

"Show up at the concert. There's still an hour left before it starts at eight." Marge tapped at her watch. For the first time, Scarlett noticed the dirt beneath Marge's fingernails. She'd taken up indoor gardening, planting a few tender seedlings. Knowing Marge, she would have the most beautiful garden in Cherish come summer.

"I can't. Not tonight," Scarlett said. "There's something I … Well, I'm making an appointment to go somewhere tomorrow morning."

"After your appointment, then. I'll be there because Ryan invited me to say the blessing before the concert." Marge placed an age-spotted hand on Scarlett's cheek. "You're a vivacious beautiful woman and full of life. Joseph is lucky to have you."

"Hardly." Self-doubt poked through. "He can have anyone. A sweet skinny woman would be able to—"

"He wants you just the way you are. You're foolish if you let a good Christian man leave your life without fighting for him. Go. And be sure to sit in the first row where he can see you. Be a blessing and an encouragement."

And there was the challenge. Hastily, Scarlett nodded, promising Marge before she lost courage. Only her hurt pride had prevented her from making the first move. And if she didn't reach out, Joseph would leave Cherish believing she didn't care about him, and nothing was further from the truth.

"Scarlett, one more thing, and it's the most important." Marge stood and pulled on a pair of tan leather gloves. "Ask God to lead your heart and mind. The Lord wants you to be happy."

A smile touched Scarlett's lips. She had come to church.

She had met Marge. Surely the Lord's hand was in this. With His blessing and her friends' support, she could do this. Besides, she couldn't imagine her future without Joseph.

On Sunday morning, Scarlett rose early although she hadn't fallen asleep until dawn. When the alarm rang, she sprang to a sitting position, hurtling from a bottomless dream to full wakefulness in five seconds.

"I can't do it," she whispered to the empty room. Marge had given the worst advice ever.

Of course you can. Just swing your legs over the side of the bed, shower, and get dressed.

Bundled in her terry cloth robe, she deliberated on her wardrobe choices. Cute clothes had always been a problem because of her size, although Joseph had complimented her on everything she'd worn.

She dressed with great care in a pink silk blouse that tied at the waist, black slacks, and animal print pumps sporting a kitten heel. It was Valentine's Day, after all. A bright rosy lipstick, red crystal drop earrings, and Joanna's harp bracelet completed the ensemble. Although the weather promised temperatures in the high fifties, she donned her green wool coat for extra warmth.

Then she texted her hairdresser, Phyllis, convincing her friend to pay back the favor from when Scarlett had helped her move into her new apartment. She made an appointment for eleven o'clock.

With a fluttery feeling in her stomach, she pushed back her shoulders and began a fast-paced stride to Cherish Styles and Clips. First the hairdresser, then the concert. The important thing was that she and Joseph would meet again, face to face. It was so simple, and all she had to do was look him in the eye and tell him how much she loved him.

At one o'clock, Scarlett emerged from the hair salon. The sky was a soft blue, the clouds drifting across it in slow motion. Chirping birds circled in languid arcs, while Scarlett joined the throngs of people headed for the 2:00 matinee. Outside the white canvas tent where the concert would be held, Emmanuelle chatted with Nicholas, holding their golden retriever, Molly Belle, by her leash.

The couple waved gaily to Scarlett and she grinned a hello. She'd reached the park in record time.

She went straight for the back-stage area and placed her coat on a chair.

"You made it!" Joanna exclaimed. "My mom came to the performance last night, and now you're here." She wore a pleated black skirt and white shirt, her hair pulled back in a neat ponytail, and her almond-shaped eyes shone with excitement. "And I love your hair! And your bracelet is awesome, just like mine." She jingled her harp bracelet, prompting Scarlett to do the same, and then nudged Russell. "I told you she wouldn't disappoint us. You owe me a dollar."

The boy elbowed her back. "No, I don't. Anyway, I don't have a dollar." He looked young and vulnerable, an oversized pair of black dress pants and freshly pressed white shirt overpowering his slight frame.

The moment Dorothy came around the corner, her gaze riveted on Scarlett. "Thank goodness you're here. Isaac is running late—some crisis at Big Brothers—and Ryan needs my help with the microphones. Can you watch the children backstage?" She indicated a row of chairs.

"I'm more than happy to help," Scarlett replied.

"Oh, and for the finale, the children are singing twice, the final number being Joseph's new worship song. Do you remember it?"

Scarlett drew a quiet sigh. How could she forget? "His lyrics are so inspirational, I hardly took a breath while he sang."

Ryan came backstage with Marge Addyson. "Are we

ready to begin?" he asked Dorothy, giving her a quick hug. "Thanks for organizing all this, my love."

Dorothy grinned. "Happy Valentine's Day."

What would it be like to have a man love a woman so much that he put her before any other goals in his life? Scarlett wondered. Seeing their interaction caused a flash of longing in her heart. She was truly happy for them, as their romance hadn't come about without trials. At the same time, their joy only expanded her own aloneness.

Marge patted Scarlett's arm. "I'm glad you're here."

Scarlett took a deep breath. "Me too." She paused, then turned. Joseph's voice came from the stage as he spoke with one of the sound technicians, followed by the familiar strum of his guitar as he warmed up. Tenderness flooded her heart. She couldn't wait to talk with him again.

She waded into the middle of another disagreement between Joanna and Russell, separated them, and sat them in a row with the other children. Then she peeked around the curtain to catch a glimpse of Joseph.

At 2:00, Marge and Ryan took the stage. Joseph stood in one corner as Ryan invited Marge to offer the opening prayer.

"Thank you, Ryan, for the privilege of praying with all of you." The epitome of poise and elegance, Marge bowed her head and clasped her hands together, requesting the audience to do the same. "Dear Lord, thank you for this fine February day. We are grateful that every seat for this concert has been filled. Bless all those present, and may the uplifting music fill our hearts and ears as we worship you in song. Amen."

After Dorothy seated Marge in the front row, Ryan continued. Engaging and relaxed, he spoke to the crowd with enthusiasm, wished everyone a happy Valentine's Day and thanked them for their support. He then expounded on the benefits of expanding the elementary school's music program.

"Music allows children to build self-confidence, as well as listening and math skills," he explained. "Studies conclude that music fosters creativity and relieves stress." He ended when Marge shouted from the front row, "Ryan, there's so much music and so little time. Let's get on with the concert."

With a broad grin, Ryan introduced Joseph to a deafening round of applause.

Scarlett watched as Joseph claimed his stool and took command of the stage. He studied the audience, his gaze drifting up and down the rows as if he were searching for someone. He looked breathtakingly handsome in his concert attire—black pants and a white dress shirt, and his broad shoulders filled out the shirt to perfection. He acknowledged Dorothy in the front row next to Marge with a tip of his head.

He played the instantly recognizable chord from his Grammy-award-nominated hit, "Sing Glory Forever." When the audience cheered, he smiled and encouraged everyone to sing along.

As she peeked from the curtain, tears blurred Scarlett's view of him. She'd listened to his songs countless times on his CD, and she loved them all.

As the one hour concert sped to its finale, Joanna whispered to Russell, "Are you nervous?" The children would go on stage for the final numbers.

When it was time, Scarlett encouraged each child with a quick hug, and sent them in single file on stage. As Joanna passed Joseph, she beckoned him to bend down and whispered something in his ear.

He looked around, expressions of hope, surprise, and happiness dancing across his handsome face.

Then he smiled at the children. "Ready?" he asked.

"'And we sing, you are our God …'" His familiar tenor voice resonated throughout the crowd, throughout the tent, and Joanna and the others joined him on the refrain.

After his second song ended, silence reigned for a beat. Then Joseph and the children bowed to a standing ovation.

Scarlett high-fived each child as they marched offstage, congratulating them on an outstanding performance.

"I'll take you all out for ice cream." She laughed. "Or salad."

"Ice cream!" they shouted in unison.

Isaac appeared. "I got here just in time. And I'll take you up on your offer for ice cream."

"You're on." She pulled back the curtain in time to see Dorothy gesture to the audience.

"Ladies and gentlemen," Dorothy said, "let's thank Joseph Slater and the children from Big Brothers and Big Sisters once more." Amidst another standing ovation, she started for the stage, but stopped as Joseph held up a hand.

"I have one more song I'd like to sing," he said. "I've been writing it ever since I came to Cherish." He cleared his throat, seeming nervous as he thumbed his guitar strings. "She's someone I think about all the time, and I want to wish her a happy Valentine's Day. And to tell her that she's the love of my life."

He hesitated, strummed a chord. "The name of the song is, 'I Need to Learn.'"

Scarlett stepped back, her hand pressed to her mouth. Was she breathing?

At first, he sang the lyrics softly. "'I need to learn that I don't got to travel anymore. / You're small town, I'm big city / but we both look at the same sky, both love the same God. / Oh, Scarlett, Scarlett, you've taught me how to dream.'"

Somewhere behind her, Scarlett heard Isaac ask in a whisper, "Scarlett, should I get your coat?"

She couldn't answer. She forgot about her coat. She forgot about everything in the world around her.

When Joseph sang her name again, sang about love, she touched her hand to her heart, the tears flowing freely. Everything around her seemed to quiet.

Somehow, Dorothy's hand had linked to her arm.

"He wants you to come on stage," Dorothy said.

"How?" Scarlett asked.

"By walking with me."

On legs like rubber, she followed as Dorothy guided her. "He's been writing this song for weeks," Dorothy went on, whispering in Scarlett's ear. "At first, I asked if he wanted my help with the lyrics. He said he didn't need my help, because the lyrics just flowed. He asked me to give the song to you this evening, but then Joanna told him you were here when she went out to sing."

Now they were on stage. Scarlett stepped into the spotlight, and Dorothy moved to the side.

Joseph set down his guitar, pushed back the microphone. He stood and came to her.

Her heart took a leap. He stood straight and tall, aching tenderness in his blue eyes. Up close, he looked a bit scruffy, hardly put together, like a man who had been pacing for days. His wavy hair was tousled, as if he'd incessantly run a hand through it. And he'd skipped a button on his shirt.

Still reeling, she gazed up at him as he fingered the highlighted strands of green hair around her face. He grinned and whispered, "No blue?"

"Just green."

He took her hands in his. "'I don't got to travel anymore," he sang softly, "'because I'm home.'" Certainty shone in his eyes. "'And we're both going to love each other right here in Cherish.'" The softness of his breath brushed against her cheek as he bent to kiss her.

He was professing his love in front of the entire town, hundreds of people. And wasn't all this being recorded?

She swallowed. "You're flying to Raleigh tomorrow." The risk of tears had passed, the lump in her throat disappearing. A stubble covered his jaw, shadows beneath his eyes, but his gaze radiated expectation and hope.

"I canceled it."

"Joseph, you shouldn't. Not for me."

He pressed his finger to her lips. "I did it for us. I'd much rather be here with you."

The moment Scarlett stirred, Dorothy and Ryan rushed over, and Dorothy jostled Scarlett and Joseph away from the spotlight.

"Quite the encore, you two lovebirds." Dorothy's lips trembled with laughter.

"How's that for a real Valentine's Day surprise?" Ryan joked to the audience with a wry smile. "A true happily ever after." He thanked everyone as murmurings grew to a fever-pitch, then asked the technicians to play one of Joseph's songs and turn up the volume.

* * *

Two hours later, as a light gentle wind teased the air, Scarlett and Joseph walked to the inn holding hands.

"The children enjoyed their ice cream," he said.

"Originally, Joanna had wanted candy for Valentine's Day, but she was okay with ice cream after all."

"And you ordered low-fat frozen yogurt."

She smiled. "My new favorite dessert."

"And now they're safely back at Big Brothers with Isaac."

"They deserved the applause, the ice cream, everything," Scarlett said. "They were awesome."

"And I'm going to be mentoring Russell personally."

Personally. A commitment. She laid her hand against his cheek. "You're a good man."

"I try."

They settled on the inn's porch on an old-fashioned love seat, until only a sliver of moonlight lit the sky. Once again, they held hands.

"I'm going to spend the next few weeks here at the inn. The owner, Tom, okayed it," Joseph said. "I told him my booking was temporary, just until we got married."

"You and Tom?"

He laughed softly. "You and I." He brushed a strand of hair from her temple. "Will you marry me?"

The flutter in her heart went straight to her belly. "Joseph, are you sure you've thought this through? Your fans are waiting for you all across the country."

"Other excellent worship artists will cover for me. While you were sorting ice cream flavors, I made a few phone calls."

"What about Australia?"

"I guess you'll have to come with me."

"I'm not sure. I might …"

"If and when the time comes, we'll discuss it." He kissed her forehead, her nose, her cheeks.

She chuckled. "Do you need glasses?"

"I don't think so. Why?"

"Because your aim needs to improve." She lifted her lips for a kiss.

After the kiss, he held her. "In the meantime, I'm a concert artist without a concert. Guess I'll be settling in Cherish with a certain green-haired redhead."

In the flicker of moonlight, she leaned back and gazed up at him. "Are you sure you like it here?"

"I love it. I'm even planning to lead the contemporary worship service at church. That is, if they'll have me."

"Suppose all this doesn't work out? What about your

wanderlust?"

"Together, we'll pray." He threaded his fingers through her hair. The curls were well beyond unmanageable by now. "God will show us the way."

"Us?"

"You and me. Husband and wife. Trust me, we can do it all."

She stared at him. "I didn't expect this."

"What *did* you expect?"

Truly, it was all a wonderful dream, with his arms securely around her.

"I assumed we would talk after the concert and hoped we would reconcile," she said.

"We did."

Absurdly happy, she laughed.

He framed her face between his fingers. "So, will you marry me?"

"Yes, yes." She nodded, nestled closer.

"I want children. I want a family." He brushed kisses on her cheeks.

"So do I." He wanted the same things she did—love and family—the things that mattered.

"I have something for you for Valentine's Day," he said.

"You wrote me a love song." She pressed her face against his broad chest, heard the solid beating of his heart. "Isn't that romantic enough?"

"Not on Valentine's Day." He stood and strode into the inn's lobby, emerging with a bouquet of hand-picked violets, a nearly illegibly written card attached to them.

She read the note aloud. "'Scarlett with two t's, you taught me that dreams can come true. Don't give up on me.'"

"I never did," she said quietly.

"Thank you." Joseph swallowed, always in tune with her, knowing the moment was poignant for both of them. "Tom's a good guy, keeping these flowers in water since I picked them this morning."

"He's the best."

Tenderly, Joseph stared at her. "Scarlett Evans, I love you. And when I didn't see you for a couple days, I realized if I left, I would have missed the most important person in my life. God brought me to Cherish for a reason."

"God's plan is perfect." She held the flowers close as Joseph's lips captured hers.

His kisses were sweet, his closeness warm and inviting. She planned to stay with him, here in Cherish, or wherever he traveled, forever.

As evening air touched her cheeks, she watched the twinkle of stars overhead, the landscape of Cherish ever changing, yet eternally the same. Like life itself. Strong, faithful, and always good.

What a perfect Valentine's Day. A wonderful sweet journey.

"I will always love you, Joseph Slater. Always." For the rest of her life when she remembered this special day, she knew she would cry tears of joy.

For God had given her a Valentine's Day to cherish.

The End

A NOTE FROM JOSIE

Thank you for reading *A Valentine To Cherish*. I hope you enjoyed your visit to the scenic town of Cherish, South Carolina, the music store, Musically Yours, and all of the wonderful characters, including Scarlett and Joseph.

If you loved this inspirational romance as much as I loved writing it, please help other people find *A Valentine To Cherish* by posting your review.

A Valentine To Cherish is available in ebook, paperback, Large Print paperback, Hardcover, and audiobook.

My Spotify Play List for A Valentine To Cherish is here.

VALENTINE-SHAPED MEATLOAF RECIPE

Meatloaf (preheat oven to 350 degrees F)

2 pounds meatloaf mix (beef/pork/veal)
   1 medium onion, diced fine
   1 loaf of Italian bread or French baguette, stale
   1/4 cup of milk
   2 eggs
   1/2 cup Parmesan cheese
   1 tablespoon garlic powder
   1 teaspoon salt
   1/4 teaspoon pepper
   1 teaspoon Italian seasoning

1. Cut loaf of bread in half the night before you are going to make the meatloaf and cover it with paper towels.

2. When you are ready to start your meatloaf, remove all of the bread from the crust. Use the crust for something else.

3. Put the bread in a large bowl, and add the milk. Stir it to get the bread saturated.

4. Once the bread is saturated, squeeze out some of the milk. You want it wet, but not dripping. Pour out the excess milk and put the bread back into the large bowl. Add the onion, eggs, cheese, garlic powder, salt, pepper, and Italian seasoning. Mix well.

5. Add the meat to the bowl and with your hands mix everything thoroughly. Shape the meatloaf into a heart shape.

6. Place the meatloaf into a 1-inch deep pan.

7. Place in oven and cook for about 1 hour. Check to make sure the internal temperature is 165 degrees F.

Barbecue Sauce
1 can tomato sauce
1 tablespoon spicy brown mustard
1/4 to 1/2 cup brown sugar (to taste)

1. Mix in bowl and set aside until the meatloaf has cooked for 1 hour. Carefully drain fat from the meatloaf pan. Pour barbecue sauce over meatloaf and put it back in the oven for 15 minutes. Remove from oven. Tent with foil until ready to assemble.

Mashed Potatoes:
2 pounds russet potatoes
4 tablespoons butter (I prefer unsalted butter)
1/2 cup sour cream
Salt & pepper to taste

Milk for thinning out the potatoes, as necessary

1. Peel potatoes, cut into 1-inch cubes, then rinse. Place in a 2-quart saucepan with enough water to cover the potatoes and add 1 teaspoon of salt to the water. Bring the potatoes to a boil and after 20 minutes, check them for tenderness. If not quite done, check every 2 minutes until done.
2. Drain potatoes in a colander, and put back in the pot. Put the pot back on the stove on high. Shake the pan to dry the potatoes. When dry, move the potatoes to a bowl, add the butter, and using a mixer mix the potatoes until there are no lumps. (Using a potato masher will not add air to the potatoes to make them fluffy.) Mix in the sour cream. Add milk to lighten the potatoes, but still allow them to stay in peaks when you pull the mixer out. Add salt and pepper to taste.

How to assemble:

1. Place meatloaf onto a platter with at least 3 inches of room around the meatloaf.
2. Spoon potatoes around the heart shaped meatloaf to look lacy. Using a teaspoon put little depressions in the potatoes.
3. You can pour some more of the BBQ sauce from the pan onto the meatloaf, but not a lot. Serve the BBQ sauce in a gravy boat.
4. Add a favorite vegetable and enjoy!

VOLUME TWO

JOSIE RIVIERA

A Christmas Puppy to Cherish

PRAISE AND AWARDS

USA TODAY bestselling author

Top 35 Amazon Bestseller Animal Fiction

Maxwell Archer gave up. The harmonica wasn't there.

He might as well walk the short distance from his rental home in Cherish, South Carolina, to Musically Yours, the local music store. The store was reputed to be the finest in town. Likewise, it was also the only music store in the small town.

Open suitcases lay on the floor in the compact, plain living room of his rental. Further cluttering the room was a confusion of chirping budgies, oversized birdcages, and a stack of research notes piled beside his computer. He definitely needed some air.

Momentarily diverted by Angel, a silvery green budgie who chattered, "God bless us, every one," over and over, Max shrugged on his olive-green twill jacket, uttered a brief good-bye, and headed out the door.

He'd recited numerous words to his parakeets. The key to teaching a parakeet to talk was repetition, but "God bless us, every one," was the only phrase Angel repeated. She was a rescue bird, and her previous owner had been an elderly woman who apparently had watched Charles Dickens's, *A Christmas Carol*, on television many times.

The other two parakeets—one timid, the other bolder—squawked, chirped, and carried on between themselves.

As Max strolled, a brisk December breeze invigorated him, and he paused to regard the poignantly familiar mom and pop shops. Whitney's, the ice cream store, and Big Brothers Big Sisters, where he'd spent many afternoons after school finishing his homework. The brick building looked the same.

At twelve years old, Max had delivered the *Sunday Sentinel* to all the businesses along Main Street, accompanied by a racing dog his foster family, the Monroes, had owned. He remembered that dog. He loved that dog. A Labrador husky named Tinsel.

He couldn't contain his smile as he reminisced.

The calendar showed December fifth, and downtown was in the process of being transformed into a Yuletide fairyland. Numerous workers scurried past him, draping tiny white lights on bushes and sprinkling artificial snow over miniature pine trees.

Through the years, he'd indulged in visions of settling here in Cherish. He had envisioned a prestigious house on the prosperous outskirts and living out his days wealthy and respected.

Three decades had passed, and he hadn't accumulated wealth in any sense of the word. In fact, his last year's research project had been stalled because of insufficient funding.

And respected? In academic circles, perhaps. He fingered the bow tie beneath his chin—his acknowledgement to the realm of academic nerds, in which he was a charter member.

In any event, his appointment to the ornithology department of a large university in Jacksonville, Florida, began January first.

As he stepped inside the music store, a slim woman with dark hair and striking green eyes greeted him.

"May I help you?" she asked.

He nodded toward the frosted-glass front window decorated with treble clef signs, animated polar bears, and a model train weaving around an ice-covered mountain scene. "Nice." He made a comical face. "The motifs enhance the window with a …"

She raised an eyebrow. "Festive touch?"

"Complete with tiny icicles." He moved inside, toward a shelf crammed with key holders and picked up a key holder shaped like an amplifier. Clever. However, he doubted he was allowed to hammer nails into his temporary rental house.

He sighed and surveyed the tidy store. "Do you sell harmonicas?" he asked.

"Yes. A wide assortment." The woman nodded toward a side wall. "Is this for a Christmas gift?"

"For myself. I lost my harmonica during my move." He rubbed his shoulders and unzipped his jacket. Though his rental was furnished, his limbs ached from lifting heavy bird cages and suitcases. He was an academic, not a body-builder.

In addition, his brain was flooded with information. He'd been embedded in research the entire morning when he should have been unpacking. The hours flew by whenever he examined data and he frequently lost track of time.

"Any particular brand or style?" she was asking.

"Fenders. Key of C."

"I'll show you our bestseller, which comes with a vented plastic case." She wended around numerous aisles, located a gold-edged case on a display shelf, and handed it to him.

"Here's our most popular model. A twenty-tone diatonic harmonica in the key of C."

"An exact replacement for the one I lost." He ran his fingers along the case. "Thanks."

A sudden, booming symphony burst through the speakers, and they both jumped.

"Sorry," the woman said. "The background music in the store constantly needs adjustment." With a self-conscious grin, she dashed to the counter and lowered the volume. "Beethoven will do that."

"Do what?

"Startle customers with crashing chords." She darted him a sideways glance. "I haven't seen you before, by the way."

Well, that didn't take long, he thought. A stranger in a small town called for questions from the local shop owner.

"I lived here for a brief spell when I attended junior high school," he said. "I arrived yesterday after an almost three-decade absence."

She didn't press for additional information, and he didn't elaborate.

"Are you here permanently?" she asked.

"Only for December. Then I'm off to my dream job in Florida." Again, he massaged his nape. Was it from the move or stress? "My name is Max, by the way. Maxwell Archer."

"Hi, Max. I'm Dorothy Edwards. My husband, Ryan, and I own this store and we sell music, instruments, and fun novelties. We also offer lessons if you're ever interested."

"Which instruments?"

"Harp, voice, guitar and piano." She hailed an entering customer with a warm smile. "Joanna, are you here for your harp lesson with Ms. Emmanuelle?"

The little girl nodded.

"She's waiting in her studio."

"Thanks. Is the puppy here? Ms. Emmanuelle mentioned that he might be."

"He's in the back."

"Yay!" The girl's face brightened. "Sorry, I'm late." She clutched her music to her chest and hurried past them.

"Joanna attends Big Brothers Big Sisters," Dorothy said. "Are you familiar with the organization?"

"Yes."

Uncertain where the conversation might be leading, Max looked away. The last subject he cared to discuss was the Big Brothers program. He remembered it well. Fond memories surfaced. Some not so fond as well, but those weren't because of the excellent program.

"Scarlett, who is married to Joseph Slater, is heavily involved," Dorothy went on. "Emmanuelle is providing Joanna with free instruction and a harp. Joseph is a well-known worship singer and songwriter. He's also on our staff when he isn't touring."

"I've never heard of him," Max said.

"Do you listen to contemporary Christian music?"

"Never." Max dismissed her inquiry with a wave. "Does anyone teach harmonica? I play for fun, not professionally, but always appreciate any tips."

"Sorry, we don't. Try YouTube," she joked.

He had. He did. On a shoe-string academic budget, self-taught lessons suited Max perfectly. Learning had little to do with musicality, and more to do with determination, goal-setting, and an appreciation for music.

Dorothy set the harmonica on the counter. "What brings you here, Max?"

"I study budgies and how they mimic birdsongs and music." He smiled and handed her his credit card.

She rang up the order. "The two are related?"

"Absolutely. To quote a noted philosopher, 'birds vocalize conventional scales.'"

"Interesting."

Interesting? The fact was more than interesting.

"You studied birds in college?" she asked.

"Yes. I earned a master's degree from a New York City university affiliated with the Audubon Society."

"Is New York City home for you?"

"I don't have a permanent home. I drove down from New York to Cherish yesterday."

"A ten-hour trip," she commiserated. "My husband travels to Atlanta for opera rehearsals, and the four hours back and forth is exhausting."

"My trip was quite an adventure—to put it mildly, especially with three parakeets, all my possessions stuffed into two suitcases and a canvas backpack." He grimaced as he recalled the harrowing journey through the icy Virginia mountains.

"The birds stayed in their cages?"

"I can't imagine them flying around my van while I drive. I secured their cages with seat belts." Max leaned forward, warming to the conversation. "For safety reasons, I always remove the mirrors, bells, and swings, and placed their wooden perches close to the bottom of their cages. And I keep bottled water handy for refilling their cups."

"Good to know." Dorothy shot him a tongue-in-cheek smile. "Not that I ever plan on purchasing a pet. My brother, Nicholas, owns Molly Belle, an overgrown pup who gets into everything. That dog cured me of owning any animals."

Max chuckled. "In some respects, birds are easier than dogs."

"Nicholas is trying to find a home for a puppy that showed up at the sheriff's station a couple days ago. Are you interested?"

"What type of dog?"

"He's guessing a mixed breed—a toy poodle and York-shire Terrier."

"A Yorkipoo."

"Maybe. He's a real cutie, brown with silvery-white mark-ings." She paused. "Wait. I'll be right back."

Dorothy emerged two minutes later clasping a puppy to her chest. She set him down and the puppy bound forward in little jumps, then stuck his nose under the counter. Furiously, he tugged on a pencil that had fallen.

"No, no. He loves to chew." At the sound of Dorothy's voice, the little ball of fur rushed headlong down an aisle, apparently unheeding of her calls. He turned a corner and almost lost his balance. Dorothy scooped him up and brought him over to Max. He licked Max's outstretched fingers as he petted him.

"He's a cute pup, isn't he?" Dorothy asked.

"He's also a bundle of charming, unrestrained energy."

"Any chance—"

"Sorry." Max shook his head. "I'm only in town for a month." Plus, he'd vowed never to own a dog again. He'd missed Tinsel too much after he'd been placed with another foster family.

Dorothy returned the puppy to the back room, then placed Max's harmonica and a complimentary candy cane in a bag. "I'm sorry it's such a short stay, but this town is welcoming, especially during the Christmas season."

Max expected he'd enjoy spending December in Cherish. The lease on his apartment in New York had ended, and he'd preferred to travel in early December rather than January.

"Are you a musician?" she asked, offering an irrepressible grin. "Naturally you are—considering you're in a music store purchasing a harmonica. Ryan and I are—"

"Concert artists."

She handed the bag to him. "I'm a pianist."

"And Ryan is an opera singer."

She tipped her head. "How did you know?"

"My friend Gerry Adams lives in Perrytown. He often shops in your store."

Unlike many of the undergraduate students Max taught his online Joy of Birdwatching class to, Gerry had been interested and engaged. Most of Max's students selected his course as an easy elective.

Not Gerry. In his fifties, he'd developed an increasing appreciation for Max's expertise that had led to a friendly rapport between the two men. Gerry had become a sort of guru, offering guidance and awareness on another subject that interested Max: music.

"I know him." A smile dawned on Dorothy's face. "Gerry sings in the choir at Memorial Street Church."

No comment on the church part, though Max had recognized the wooden sign mounted above the store's entrance.

Proverbs 19:21.

He once knew the proverb, but could no longer recall the words.

Dorothy cast her gaze heavenward. "'Many are the plans in a person's heart, but it is the Lord's purpose that prevails,'" she recited.

Max kept silent.

Memories of sitting in a stiff pew during Sunday services came back in a blink. He'd tried, but he'd never pleased God as a child. He never pleased God as an adult, either. Where was the path to peace God promised? It remained elusive.

The successes Max had achieved hadn't been enough. Thus, at the age of twenty-five, he'd given up on religion.

As far as his career, he sometimes wondered if he was on the right path. Was his research nothing more than a "fluffy" elective for uninterested college freshmen? Society seemed to think along those lines, and reports through the academic grapevine whispered that ornithology programs were soon to be scrapped.

Sure, Max was appreciated—which was the reason why he was in hamster-wheel performance mode—to continue proving himself to his colleagues.

"Gerry and I are in a band," he replied, when he realized Dorothy waited for him to say something. "We rehearse online."

"Online?" Her brow furrowed.

"You're a professional, so you expect frequent in-person rehearsals. But our band rehearses virtually every week. Technology is marvelous, isn't it?"

"Not as rewarding as live rehearsals, though."

Max had to agree. "There's a likelihood Gerry and I will perform this month, if we can find a venue."

"Inquire at The Garden Terrace restaurant. The owners book entertainment on Friday evenings. In addition, I'd be delighted to host you here at the store. Do you have any CDs for sale?"

"You're kidding, right?"

"What's the name of your band?"

"The Bearded Elves."

"Hmm. Neither of you sports a beard."

"We change our name with the season."

She grinned. "When February hits, you'll become …"

"The Bearded Valentines. But I won't be here in February. My work takes me all over the US, and I'm headed to Florida in January."

"Well, I look forward to hearing you perform this month."

"Thanks. Gerry encouraged me to rent a place in Cherish. He believes all this down-home goodness is beneficial for me."

"You're on a vacation the entire month?"

"I'm rarely on vacation."

"No wife or children?" Pointedly, she peered at his left hand.

"Neither. You're looking at a forty-year-old bachelor."

She granted a conspiratorial smile. "The right woman will come along and change your mind."

"I doubt it. Women can be … exasperating."

She chuckled. "Will you travel to New York for Christmas?"

"I'll spend Christmas day with Gerry, his wife, Melissa, and their newborn colicky son. They're first-time parents."

Dorothy rolled her eyes. "So I've heard."

Besides Gerry, there was no one else, Max thought. Unless Max's foster brother, John, who resided in a faraway Portuguese village, counted.

It didn't matter. The season had lost its meaning eons ago. December twenty-fifth was just another day that passed in the flicker of an eye.

Dorothy's fixed smile didn't vacillate. She seemed the sort who put immense emphasis on the holidays.

He shifted. "I'm grateful for the opportunity to hunker down with my research this month."

At Dorothy's quizzical glance, he added, "On birds."

"Along with performing a live gig or two."

"Gerry and I aren't expert musicians like you and your husband, or that Slater worship singer guy. Our specialty is performing at roadside diners for a free meal."

"I well remember those days." She shook her head. "Since you'll be working here for the month, do you need any assistance with your research?"

"Can you recommend someone who could go birding with me tomorrow morning? I'd appreciate a guide."

Dorothy studied him. "I picture you in a forest, somewhere more suited to your rugged looks, rather than writing papers. You must spend a great deal of time outdoors."

"I try." He pushed a hand through his thick hair. When had he last gotten it cut? "The Carolinas have various bird species I'd like to listen to."

"Your parakeets will truly mimic other birds?"

"Optimistically, although I haven't had much luck with them imitating anything."

Except "God bless us, every one."

"I know the ideal woman," Dorothy said.

"She likes nature?"

"Absolutely, and she's passionate about hiking." A gleam of mischief shone in Dorothy's eyes. "She works at Thumbs Up, a local florist, but might be off tomorrow. I'll text her."

"What's her name?"

"Sarah Hartman." Dorothy snatched a cell phone from beneath the counter. "She dropped out of college to care for her elderly aunt, then went on to pursue a degree in floral design."

"How old is she?"

"Sarah turned thirty last month. She's the type who juggles a half dozen projects, numerous details, and never gets frustrated. And ..." Dorothy paused to accentuate the words. "Her flower arrangements are exquisite."

He'd never purchased store-bought flowers in his life. The most magnificent blossoms—miniature red roses, deep violets, and pale blue ivy—spilled alongside brooks or grew wild in a field.

A response flew across Dorothy's phone screen. "Sarah confirmed she's not working until tomorrow afternoon," Dorothy read. "She had plans but is happy to change them. What's your address, Max?"

"I rented a house a couple blocks from here. It's 8 Poplar Lane. Tell her I'll bring the hiking essentials."

Dorothy typed into her phone, then delivered the response. "She'll pick you up in the morning."

"A hiker and a florist is an attractive combination."

"Oh, and she's plenty more. Animals love her. The cat at the greenhouse that handles mice won't let anyone near her except Sarah. Likewise, dogs practically grovel at her feet." Dorothy glanced up. "Remember Molly Belle?"

"Your brother's unruly dog?"

Dorothy choked a giggle. "She adores everyone and is beyond energetic, although remarkably calm and obedient around Sarah."

"Does Sarah own any pets?"

"Are you giving away birds?"

"I'd never part with my parakeets. Angel is the oldest, and she's been with me for several years." He lifted a quizzical brow. "What about Sarah?"

"She owns a few animals."

"Is she married?" He didn't want an irate husband or boyfriend on his tail for going birdwatching with Sarah.

"She's coming off a sorry relationship, but you'll discover she's a stunner."

Another word for mantrap. He understood the type well after dating a flirtatious woman who'd been beautiful enough to be on the cover of *Vogue* but who abruptly ended their month of dating with a cursory text.

From that point forward, he'd avoided any romantic overtures from beautiful women. They were interested in a guy's money and power. As soon as they realized Max had neither, they hightailed it out of his life.

"You'll learn all about her tomorrow." Dorothy peered at the phone screen, grinned, then snapped it shut. "She drives a yellow pickup truck and said she'll see you at eight."

CHAPTER 2

The following day, Max rose before dawn to wash and dry the parakeets' food bowls and water bottles, then placed a slice of kiwi in their cages. Angel, a female, occupied her own cage, while the two males shared a cage.

"God bless us, every one," Angel chirped.

Max covered three sides of the wrought-iron cage and faced her on the open side. Over and over, he enunciated, "Angel. Angel. Angel."

"God bless us, every one," Angel repeated.

"You can say that entire sentence, but you can't pronounce your own name?" He threw his hands up and surveyed the other two parakeets. The blue-winged roommates perched on their respective swings, then burst into a flurry of activity for no apparent reason, effectively distracting Angel.

And thus, the lesson was over.

Max choked on a laugh. Some things never changed.

Regardless, he was in jovial spirits. Although his new bed was lumpy and the bedspread a musty chenille, he had slept well and left his window open a crack. The whisper of a floral-scented breeze had provided him with a comfortable, peaceful slumber.

He flicked a fatigued glance at his handwritten notes, twenty pages and counting, spread out on the computer desk. His suitcases still sat on the floor, waiting to be unpacked. He'd rummaged through them for a clean pair of jeans, a blue button-down shirt, boots, and his favorite bow tie.

A half hour after he'd showered and passed on shaving because he couldn't find his razor, he heard an engine and peered out the window.

A yellow pickup idled in the driveway. The truck boasted reindeer antlers attached to the windows and a red nose on the front grill.

The woman in the driver's seat caught his stare and waved, her smile bright and pleasant.

Sarah Hartman, he assumed. Punctual at eight o'clock in the morning.

Admirable. They were off to a promising start.

He had filled a thermos with fresh coffee and stuffed thermal cups, peanut-butter banana sandwiches, and his favorite brand of frosted sugar cookies in a bag. Hoisting a backpack over his shoulders, he headed out the door.

He opened the passenger door, smiling in at her. "Sarah, right?" he said. He put the food bag and his backpack in the back seat, then slid onto the passenger seat.

"Correct." She nodded to him. "And you're Max?"

"Indeed. Max Archer." He set his thermos in the truck's oversized cup holder. "And you're driving Rudolph."

She laughed, gentle and musical. "I love Christmas."

"Let me guess, you're a sentimental movie junkie too." He gestured to her glittery pine tree earrings and the white snowflake steering wheel cover.

"Sentimental movies are the best." She tilted her head, studying him with sea-green eyes. "You look exactly the way Dorothy described."

"Not a reindeer covered in snowflakes, I hope?"

She swallowed a chuckle. "No."

"How did Dorothy describe me?"

Sarah stared at his lips. "She said you had dark hair, silvery-gray eyes, wore a bow tie and would probably have a backpack."

"A battered and weathered one." He twisted and motioned to his backpack, its ripped seam fixed with duct tape. "Today, it's filled with necessities—bottles of water, a first-aid kit, binoculars, and my fully charged phone."

She nodded. "Sounds like you've got everything you need."

"Yes. I've brought my microphone and recorder too. To record birdsongs, I'll demonstrate the setup when we arrive at the mountain."

"Okay."

"Are you carrying a cellphone?" he asked.

"I always carry one for emergencies, but I also use my phone camera to take photos."

"Photos of wildlife?"

"Mostly deer, although I can never get closer than fifteen feet before they bolt."

"Deer aren't always the sweet, docile animals you may imagine. Be careful around them."

"I am."

Those green eyes fringed with thick russet lashes, and her creamy complexion, enhanced by light freckles across her nose, stopped him from responding with anything other than "Good."

She continued to watch him, and he returned her stare.

This beautiful, intelligent woman hadn't been scooped up by a guy?

Wearing a hooded red jacket, gloves, and brown hiking boots, she was small and slim. He estimated no taller than five feet. He found himself staring at her delicate lips before his gaze wandered down to the silver cross necklace around her slender neck.

Preoccupied with an attraction he hadn't expected, he picked up his thermos. "Another requirement for a morning outing is caffeine. Do you like black coffee?"

She nodded.

"Then we share commonalities—coffee and hiking. I also brought a package of cookies. They're store-bought because I'm not a baker. The cookies, not the coffee." He returned his thermos to the holder. "Juniper Mountain is our first stop."

"There's another?"

"Crandall's Mountain, depending on our time frame."

"Okay. My morning is free," she replied.

"Mine too."

With a quick bob of her head, she backed out of the driveway.

He stretched out his legs. "It will be good to go for a long hike. I arrived in town yesterday, driving down from New York. I'm here for the month, then heading for a job in Florida."

Another nod. She probably already knew that because of chatty Dorothy.

Because he liked to have music playing, he asked her if he could switch on the radio. She hesitated and then said yes, and he scanned the stations, on a quest for something other than a holiday tune. He settled on Jon Bon Jovi singing "Please Come Home For Christmas." Not typically merry, but more of an expressive classic.

Satisfied, Max drew out his cellphone. "Do you need directions to the mountain?"

She twisted. "Say that again?"

"Directions?" He spoke louder.

"No. I've hiked Juniper for years. It's part of the Carolina state park systems."

"I mapped the distance to Crandall's, because the mountains are within a few miles of each other."

Another glance. He repeated that Juniper and Crandall were near each other.

Each time he talked, she swiveled to look at him. At one point, he almost advised her to watch the road, not him.

He lowered the volume on the radio. Possibly, music distracted her when she drove.

"I brought a knapsack," she said after a few silent minutes. "It's on the back seat."

Don't turn around to show me, Max silently implored.

He didn't initiate any further dialogue, spending the time glancing sideways at her appealing profile.

After they arrived at Juniper Mountain and she parked, they got out of the truck and he poured two cups of coffee, handing her one. He grabbed a swallow, pleased the coffee was still hot, and scanned their surroundings.

Today might provide a breakthrough in his research, an ultimate realization of success. That is, if his parakeets cooperated and actually repeated the birdsongs.

He gazed at the gorgeous woman beside him, leaning against her truck, and smiled. Surely, Sarah would bring good fortune.

When they finished their coffees, they detoured to the visitor center and procured a map. Sarah lingered at a Christmas ornament display, sputtering in disbelief when the park ranger stated that the store was sold out of a particular ornament featuring a bear, hiker boots and the inscription, "Take a hike."

She pointed to an exhibit on the wall. "The ornament is hanging right there and will go perfect on my holiday tree."

"Those are display items only and can't be sold," the ranger responded. "More should arrive by the end of the month. Check back."

She stuffed her gloves in her pockets and tapped her fingers on the counter. "By then, Christmas will be over."

Eager to lighten the mood, Max steered her out the exit to a wooden bench. "Let's study the map. There are eleven trails." He beckoned her to sit and settled beside her, indicating a twisty pathway. "The Maple Tree route is strenuous with rocky terrain and unsuitable for beginners."

"Fortunately, I'm not a beginner," she replied matter-of-factly.

"Neither am I."

"Maple Tree isn't difficult, but I recommend …" She ran her finger along a trail marked Oak. "This one passes through Walnut Forest, down to the Nanchee River's edge, up through a meadow, and finishes on a grassy path leading back to the visitor center."

She peered at him for a deciding opinion.

Based on the fact she'd resided in Cherish for many years, Max readily approved.

With her so close, her scent reminded him of an elusive flowery fragrance, similar to the breeze floating through his window last night. Rosewood, perhaps. Peaceful and serene.

He liked that. He liked *her*.

Their gazes merged, and he couldn't stop staring. She was stunning—high cheekbones and a flawless complexion—the type of beauty that prompted people to gape.

"You're the expert in these parts, Sarah." Max thought he spoke, but he wasn't certain, because the world had become unfocused, and she was at the center. He moved his index finger alongside hers, along the map, a light brush of fingertips.

And the attraction. His heart did a backflip.

He forced himself to concentrate on the map and swallowed. Surely, she felt it too.

An easy smile worked its way across her features.

Was she interested in him?

With any luck, she was.

At the same instant his brain shouted no, no, no. He was here for research purposes, and Sarah Hartman was a romantic complication he could ill afford. He had enough conflicts in his life—a stressful job, and no relationship at all with religion. Her necklace signified she was a Christian, and before he knew it, she might be declaring, "'This is the day that the Lord has made.'"

He'd believed that psalm once upon a time. Not anymore.

He pulled his extra pair of binoculars from his backpack and handed them to her, then hung his own around his neck. Next, he retrieved his recording device, a pocket-sized digital recorder and the microphone.

She rose. He automatically stood too.

"Your gear is more sophisticated than I envisioned."

"After years of trial and error, I finally realized my equipment had to be top of the line." He plugged the module into a mini jack cable. "The shotgun microphone has a powering module containing a battery."

She gazed at him with wide eyes and a wider smile. "I'm impressed with you and your work, Max."

"I'm impressed by you too," he replied.

"I haven't done anything remarkable."

He pressed his fingers on her forearm, lightly, to make his point. "There aren't many women who'd change their plans to assist a newcomer in town."

"I'm always happy to help."

He told himself to finish readying the equipment rather than gaze at her lovely, upturned face. He covered the microphone with a wind sock. "This reduces the noise created by the wind."

She acknowledged his description with a nod.

He scanned the sky, checking the angle of the sun. The haze was beginning to clear, gray clouds giving way to shades of pink and lavender. "Sunny days are ideal, but overcast is also fine," he said.

In the wash of the morning light, her complexion glowed. "Birding is a first for me."

"I was under the impression you're an animal lover."

"I am. Usually, I bring my dogs here."

"How many?"

"I have two dogs."

He noted her smile. "Is something amusing, Sarah?"

"I was thinking you're remarkably efficient and obviously an expert in your profession. I admire a man who makes things look easy and effortless."

Her compliment caught him off balance. He uttered a heartfelt, "Birds are my life and my career."

A December breeze rustled the trees and blew her shiny hair across her face. He smoothed an auburn lock from her cheek, and she stepped back out of his range.

"In any case ..." He cleared his throat and passed her a protein bar.

"Is this lunch?"

"I packed sandwiches. This is a snack."

Before he could say anything else, she whispered a prayer, asking God to bless their food, Max's career, and the picturesque day.

Max scratched his neck. Nothing made him feel more like

a fraud than thanking an imagined God. For what? A protein bar? A clear day?

God had never granted any of Max's requests.

Nevertheless, he bent his head and studied the protein bar's wrapper while Sarah prayed.

After finishing with an amen, she said, "I love animals too," as if their conversation hadn't been stalled by prayer.

His response was a dull nod.

She nodded to the knapsack on her shoulders. "Are you interested in what's inside?"

He took a bite of the protein bar. "Sure."

"I have sunscreen and used tea bags."

At his questioning look, she clarified, "Tea bags are a natural alternative to commercial products and will ease the sting of bug bites. Or, for instance, if you walk into a poison ivy plant."

"A person doesn't walk into a poison ivy plant."

"Sure they do. At least, I have."

He grinned. "We're both protected and covered." He surveyed her hooded jacket and jeans. For a petite woman, her legs were long and shapely.

"A slight brush of poison ivy leaves on your skin is all it takes for a rash," she said.

"I'll protect you."

She wrinkled her nose. "From poison ivy?"

"From anything." Protectiveness for her stirred inside him, an unforeseen response. He'd blurted the words aloud before forming the thought in his mind.

Her dubious gaze leveled on him.

"You don't believe me?" he asked.

"We hardly know each other, and I certainly don't need protecting. In addition, I packed bear repellent."

"I doubt we'll come across any bears."

"Let's hope not, but just in case." She withdrew a soup can

from her knapsack and shook it. "It's full of pebbles and makes a handy noisemaker."

"A bear weighs a lot more than we do, and we can't outrun one. Bear that in mind." He chuckled. "Pun intended."

The joke seemed to slide past her. "I've read about bear encounters," she answered. "There are certain rules to remember, such as to speak calmly, not make direct eye contact, and never run."

"If your handy deterrent doesn't scare away a bear, the loud noise will no doubt encourage any birds in the area to take flight."

"That's not a good thing if you're trying to record bird-songs," she replied with a grin.

They burst out laughing, then started down a gravel trail.

He stood on the forest's edge and watched for motion. "Look. Listen. There's a golden-winged warbler in the trees." He raised his binoculars and encouraged Sarah to do the same.

She regarded him blankly.

He held up his microphone and began recording. "The warbler has suffered the steepest decline of any songbird."

"Why?"

"Loss of habitat for breeding."

A sharp *chip* and a melodic *warble* diverted him. He signaled toward a metal-gray and yellow bird hopping between bushes in a cluster of thick ferns.

"You're hearing an adult male Canada warbler," he said.

"Oh."

Oh? *Oh?*

"Some people pish to encourage birdsong." He imitated the sound. "I don't. I've found birds will come out no matter what and I wait for their natural behavior."

As they continued along the path, he was absorbed in recording and figuring out what birds he heard, and Sarah offered no help in identifying any of them. Every few minutes, the hushed air was fragmented by a high-pitched cry, and Max stopped to record.

Well into their walk, an outbreak of wings sounded louder than the crunch of leaves beneath their feet. Before he raised his binoculars, a bird flew out of range and into the brush. Max skimmed the shorter branches to find the bird, disregarding a group of energetic high school students breezing by with their teacher guide.

A second stir of motion in his peripheral vision had Max rushing to record.

Each clue necessitated an intermission, an awaiting, a heeding.

The appeal of ornithology. Search and find.

Max had become engrossed in the study of birds when Mr. Lenny, a foster parent, had brought him birding. He was a kind man with wavy gray hair and tortoise-rimmed eyeglasses. He was the only adult who'd shown a true interest in Max, and they started a tradition of birding every Saturday morning. For a child with precious few traditions, the man was a father figure. Lenny had made a lasting impression, inspiring a young boy who had no real home.

A woodpecker ripping through the brush, accompanied by three cardinals singing *cheer, cheer, cheer,* snapped Max out of his reminiscing. He spun and monitored their calls, tiptoeing through the undergrowth, peering above and below.

Sarah, on the other hand, seemed anxious to move on. She pointed her binoculars skyward and rarely spoke.

That is until they reached the Nanchee River's edge.

"An ideal spot for a picnic." Max nodded to the waterfall beyond and fished in his bag for sandwiches.

The weather had changed, and clouds covered the sky.

"I'll keep my cellphone handy," Sarah remarked, "in case I see a deer."

A crash came from somewhere he couldn't pinpoint. Max whirled around, searching for the source, and glimpsed a large animal emerging from the river.

"I can finally take a close-up photo of a deer," Sarah declared. She stepped toward the river, but slipped on a patch of wet grass and clung to his hand.

It wasn't a deer, Max thought. A deer would shy away.

It was a bear. A wandering yearling male by Max's estimate.

The bear started for them on all fours.

Sarah's breath burst—an inhale, an exhale.

Seconds froze.

"Where's your deterrent?" Max abandoned his equipment and drew her close. She grabbed her knapsack and pulled out the soup can.

The bear came up on hind legs, almost eye to eye with them, and with one hand, Max flung his peanut butter sandwiches, the cookies, and the protein bars as far as he could. Sarah shook the can, yelled, and tossed it near the bear.

The bear backed away, then turned and ran.

Sarah licked her trembling lips, her eyes damp. "Thank you, God."

Max kept his arm around her tight shoulders and provided a reassuring squeeze. His heartbeat raced, his mouth dry. "We're safe."

"These things happen in books and movies. Not to real people." She attempted a feeble stab at humor.

Despite her ashen complexion, he was impressed she'd lost none of her composure and had reacted quickly. Still, her rounded green eyes shone luminous beneath her russet, delicate eyebrows.

Max didn't have a boatload of experience with women, but he'd lived with enough foster sisters to know when a female was on the brink of tears. Sarah bravely tried to hold them at bay, blinking ferociously.

He wavered between his male instinct to sidestep any prospect of a sobbing woman—or the reasonable desire to offer support.

Her lips parted, her smile sluggish. "Countless questions are running through my mind," she said quietly.

"Let's begin with the most important. Are you okay?"

"Yes." He heard the quiver in her tone. "We've established we're both fine."

He lifted her chin. "Let's celebrate how grateful we are."

"By prayer?"

"A consideration for a Christian, I assume, but I thought of something more like this." He brought her closer. Unhurried, he kissed her.

Her expressive eyes gazed into his. When she veered, his hands tightened, and his mouth moved more firmly.

"Max."

"Hmm?" he murmured.

The air was hushed, the only sound the babbling river.

She slid her fingers up the collar of his jacket. "Nothing." Hesitant, she returned his kiss.

Max got so caught up in kissing Sarah, a moment went by before boisterous talking penetrated his brain. He lifted his head and glimpsed the same high schoolers from earlier.

With a self-conscious shift, Sarah pulled from his grasp. "I see we have company," she said.

"Right." *And at a most inopportune moment.*

He darted a glance at his watch, retrieved his equipment, and pushed out a sigh. "I suppose we should head back."

As they retraced their steps, Sarah glanced up at him. "Max, I can't believe…"

"I wanted to kiss you as soon as I saw you this morning," he said.

She bit her lip. "Did we do everything right?"

"The kiss was perfect."

A rosy blush tinted her cheeks. "I'm referring to the bear."

He chuckled. "All I remember is throwing food at him."

"Thank you for protecting me."

He hadn't, really. If anything, *she* had protected *him*, protected them *both*, with her bear deterrent.

"Thank *you*." He reached for her hand, soft and delicate, and a rush of emotion made him smile.

In silence, they returned to her truck.

Still dazed by the whirl of emotions between their fear and the resulting kiss, they spoke little on the drive back to Cherish. Max didn't bring up hiking Crandall's Mountain, and he kept the radio off.

When she pulled into the driveway of his home, he didn't encourage her to join him birding again. Nor did he invite her inside—something he had considered along the entire route.

"The sandwiches are gone," he said. "Sorry. No lunch."

"We could have been lunch for the bear."

"Thankfully, we weren't. Besides, he was young and not very aggressive."

"Even when he charged straight for us?"

"He's undoubtedly partying right now, devouring cookies and sandwiches and protein bars with his friends." Max tried a laugh, then sobered. "Sorry you didn't get a picture of a deer."

"I took a rapid sequence of photos with my cellphone."

"Did they come out?"

"I haven't had the opportunity to check yet."

"You had time. I knew we were safe all along," Max declared.

"Uh, huh." She became absorbed in tracing the pattern of

snowflakes on her steering wheel. "As long as the bear didn't swat the ground with his front paw."

"Or snort," Max countered.

"Or lunge."

He answered with a smile. She was lovely, amiable, and attractive, and his instinctive reaction was to lean over and kiss her again.

However, other instincts warned to keep his distance. A short-term romance didn't benefit anyone, and Sarah deserved more. With his relentless studies, travel, and limited financial resources, he had little to offer her.

He told himself he was wed to his profession, as a girlfriend from long ago had once accused him.

The mood in the truck became quieter.

Let's face it, he reasoned. Sarah wasn't excited about his profession, anyway. She'd responded to his interest with little more than a few nods. Birding was his passion, and he wanted someone to share his enthusiasm.

Satisfied with his decision, he grabbed his backpack and opened the passenger door. "Thanks for the ride and for being my guide. Have a marvelous afternoon."

Their experience would be remembered as a memorable exploration. A couple hikers who scored a birding, or rather, a bear adventure.

And their kiss? Yes, there was that. Delightful, tender, and exquisite.

Like Sarah.

CHAPTER 3

After dropping Max off, Sarah stopped by her home to tend to her animals before continuing on to Thumbs Up, the nursery/garden center where she worked.

To her intense relief, the garden center's parking lot was nearly empty. Many customers, particularly older gardeners, preferred to shop for plants in the morning. She blew out a thankful breath. She needed the quiet to revisit her moments with Max.

She'd admired his home when she drove up to the neat and tidy rental, encouraged that he didn't have a bird perched on his shoulder as she'd half imagined.

Dorothy had texted Sarah the previous evening, detailing Max's plans. He didn't intend to stay in Cherish forever— only a month to explore the area for information supporting his research.

December is an unusual month for research, Sarah had texted, *considering the holidays.*

Apparently, any close family is nonexistent, Dorothy replied. *Plus, I asked if he was married and he isn't.*

Sarah could scarcely believe that the brilliant, handsome

man, his muscular physique filling out his twill jacket, was so approachable.

On closer range, his eyes, brimming with kindness, shone light silver beneath dark, straight eyebrows. His hair was thick and longish, and she was tempted to brush back the waves that constantly fell across his forehead.

Of course, she didn't. They hardly knew each other.

Besides his intellect (she'd looked up his profile on an ornithology university website), he was amicable, humorous and thoughtful. She made the blunder of staring at him often to hear his words more clearly, and her gaze had been drawn to his firm mouth.

Then the kiss had happened.

Oh my, such a kiss! At first, she'd been tentative and self-conscious at their closeness. His mouth had sought hers with cool expertise, then persistence, then increasing claim. Her heart had responded in rapid, thudding beats.

If the teenagers hadn't entered the scene, would she still be kissing him?

Her cheeks warmed. They must have seen her and Max together.

Almost unwillingly, Max had lifted his head to end the kiss.

A kiss she never should have allowed. What an imprudent, impulsive thing for her to do—in the middle of a public state park.

Yet, his lips had been persuasive and tender.

A part of her insisted she should have ended the kiss first. The other part maintained that she and Max had shared a distressing incident. Subsequently, their mutual fright had drawn them closer.

When the bear came upon them, Max had held her. He'd kept his promise, prepared to protect her.

Once they had begun the hike, Max had been fixated on

his work. For her, the birdcalls that excited him had been faint and distant.

Why?

Why couldn't she hear the birds Max was obviously eager to record? He was so in tune with them.

Lately, she'd found that if she didn't watch people's lips while they spoke, she sometimes missed what they said.

Regardless, she appreciated Max's spontaneity, fairly bouncing on his toes as he dashed through the brush. She was accustomed to sitting on the sidelines. Her loud, raucous, older brothers had consistently stolen the spotlight, and her parents often overlooked her.

She fingered the silver cross on her neck.

Max gave the impression of being uncomfortable when she offered a prayer before eating, whereas she was a Christian and faith was important to her. By his quick exit when she'd taken him home, he obviously wasn't interested in her, anyway.

As she always did in moments of confusion, she turned to God to set her course.

The psalmist in Proverbs 4:23 had written, "Above all else, guard your heart, for everything you do flows from it."

She'd had her heart broken by a budding architect. Their relationship had ended quickly, although she'd wept for days. Since then, her emotions were precarious at best.

Nonetheless, she'd vowed to reset her path after that painful experience. Her heart wouldn't be broken a second time. Not even by Max.

Her eyes squeezed shut, and she uttered a prayer. "God, set me free from my reservations and uncertainty. Please show me the way." She always felt better after praying. Her God was a big God, bigger than her hurts and disappointments.

Taking an easy breath, she exited her truck and pushed

opened the nursery's heavy steel doors.

"Good afternoon, Sarah." Bonnie Ellerman, a coworker, tapped Sarah on the shoulder. "You're fifteen minutes early. I'm on register today, and you're working the floor. The amaryllis flowers are thriving, and timing the bulbs to bloom for Christmas worked like a charm. No wonder the garden center relies on your expertise. You have a magical green thumb."

"Hardly magical." Sarah tied a blue employee apron around her waist. "If the rest period for the amaryllis begins in late summer, the bulbs will respond. Customers appreciate the extensive blooms, thus it's worth all the planning."

Sarah picked up a warehouse broom to sweep soil off the concrete floor. She tackled the chores she disliked first, before arranging the pink, white, and red poinsettia plants for Memorial Street Church.

An unexpected thickness formed in her throat as she gazed at the tastefully decorated Christmas trees lining an entire side wall. The prospect of returning home to spend another night by herself during the Christmas season … during any season … Well, she yearned for more.

To cheer herself up, she organized a Christmas gift list in her mind. Uncle Gerry, her great-uncle in Perrytown, played guitar. Accordingly, a gift from Musically Yours would be ideal.

An insistent voice in Sarah's ear interrupted her thoughts as Dorothy Edwards came into view.

"Hello," Dorothy said. "I stopped by to purchase a pink poinsettia plant for Musically Yours." Dorothy grinned mischievously, and Sarah knew at once that Dorothy had come into the nursery for more than a poinsettia.

"Who's minding your music store?" Sarah asked with a chuckle.

"Emmanuelle." Dorothy changed the poinsettia from one

arm to the other. "So, how was your hike together?"

Sarah quirked an eyebrow. "With …"

"Maxwell Archer."

"Enjoyable."

"That's it?"

"That's it." A wry smile touched Sarah's lips as she navigated the subject back to Dorothy. "Is Ryan in Atlanta?"

"He's preparing for a classical concert there. He's the lead in a chamber choir and singing a sacred text in Latin. The concert will be live-streamed next weekend." Dorothy paused. "You know I love gushing about my husband's accomplishments, but now I want to find out about your date details."

"Hiking a mountain is hardly a date." Sarah attempted to compose her features and disguise her attraction to Max. He was so different from the architect she'd dated, who'd had arrogant qualities and a slight build. Max, on the other hand, exuded strong masculinity. He was also smart, passionate about his work and gentlemanly.

And the kiss.

The sigh-worthy kiss.

Animated chatter from customers swirled nearer, blending with the clink of a clay pot as Bonnie handed Sarah a paperwhite narcissus and requested a price check.

Dorothy trailed Sarah to the stand of blossoming paperwhites. "What are your thoughts regarding Max?"

Sarah focused on Dorothy's mouth in order to lip-read.

She'd been ignoring the polite remarks from friends about having her hearing checked. A woman of thirty was *not* hard of hearing. For the time being, she'd employ all the tools at her disposal, and one was lipreading.

"He seems nice," she replied.

"Nice. Nice?' Dorothy flung a hand to her hip. "What sort of description is *nice* for a handsome, well-versed man?"

"He's well-versed on birds." Sarah gave Dorothy a good-natured shove. "Period."

Well, no, that should probably be a comma. He was also well-versed on kindness. Similarly, he's sweet and understanding, with a romantic nature she hadn't anticipated.

"I can tell by your reddened cheeks there's more to the story." Dorothy smothered a laugh. "You're attracted to him."

"He's polite and humorous." Sarah's gaze veered to Bonnie, who was frantically signaling another employee over to the narcissus plants.

Sarah's attention swung back to Dorothy.

"Am I right?" Dorothy asked, grinning.

"Maybe."

"I knew it!" Dorothy's expression went from happy to happier.

"My reactions are mixed. He's brilliant, yes—"

"Plus, he's an animal lover, just like you."

"Let's not forget he's taking a position at a Florida university in January."

"Yes, yes." Dorothy moved to the side to allow the employee to pass. "You actually start working here at one, right?"

Sarah nodded.

"So, we have a couple more minutes. Have you considered adopting the adorable dog that Nicholas and the Cherish sheriff department are caring for? An officer is complaining they are on call 24/7. The dog has a tremendous appetite and eats a lot of puppy chow."

"Have they named him yet?"

"They're waiting for the right person to adopt him. We all agree you are the perfect new owner."

"Who are we?"

"Me, Nicholas, and Emmanuelle."

"I adopted two abandoned dogs, two cats, a goldfish and a

hamster," Sarah said. "Plus, my house is a one-story bungalow."

"You'll adore him when you see him."

"I'm touched, and would love to help … but I can't."

Dorothy sighed. "Notify Nicholas if you change your mind. Deal?"

"Deal."

"One more thing." Dorothy glanced at her watch at the same time Sarah did.

"Go on."

Dorothy pulled in a breath. "One of the reasons Max decided to stay in Cherish this month is because he's friends with Gerry."

Sarah stumbled back a step. "My great-uncle Gerry?"

"The men play in a band together. Max told me when he was in my store yesterday to buy a harmonica."

"Uncle Gerry never discussed Max before. How long have they been friends?"

Dorothy winked. "Ask Max."

With that, Dorothy waltzed to the cash register with her blooming pink poinsettia.

Sarah was left staring at the paperwhite in her hand, trying to remember Bonnie's request. Was the flower supposed to be restocked or bedecked with a ribbon?

No, no. A price check. But another worker had taken care of it.

Sarah stifled a quiet moan. Her focus was fractured. And all because of a man named Maxwell Archer. A sensitive, fascinating and accomplished man.

And then another thought formed.

Perhaps, just perhaps, she could enlist her great-uncle's help to meet Max again.

With a radiant smile and a lively step, Sarah clocked into work at exactly one o'clock.

CHAPTER 4

A week later, Max strode into his living room and ducked as Angel flew by. He allowed the parakeets to fly at least an hour a day and kept the doors and windows closed for their safety. The routine kept them healthy and happy because they needed to explore. He'd limited their time the first week, in order for them to get used to the unfamiliar environment of the rental.

For now, the roommates were back in their cages, which left only Angel perching on a curtain rod. He'd trained the budgies to return to their cages, but Angel sometimes preferred not to.

Earlier, Max had compiled his notes and organized the pages in a computer file. He'd worked eighteen-hour days all week, although emailing his file to the ornithology department in Florida hadn't produced the desired accolades. The university had demanded additional bird recordings—particularly of his budgies repeating the birdsongs.

Except his birds hadn't responded or repeated any of the songs.

After Max received the university's reply, he didn't trust

himself to respond. His ideal job. How could the department question him?

Perhaps he was in the wrong profession after all. Published studies demanded reliable facts, and budgies, as well as birds in general, were unpredictable.

Budgies mimicked humans and the sounds of their mates. However, their response to his recordings had brought distress and frustration. They peered around, attempting to establish where the birdsongs came from. When they failed to locate their perceived new friends whom they suspected were close by, they became anxious.

Max contemplated his options.

He wouldn't return to New York City, and the Florida university position didn't seem as appealing anymore, considering the head of the ornithology group wanted Max to work round the clock for little pay.

At any rate, another hike to Juniper Mountain was in Max's forecast. He considered contacting Sarah and asking her to accompany him.

During the past seven days, he'd given the morning they'd spent together deeper consideration. He remembered her face going pale when the bear charged. He also recalled how sweet she was, and how fearless. He admired her beauty, but was more intrigued by her modest and steady presence. She'd bravely held back frightened tears after scaring off the bear.

Society sometimes displayed a cynical indifference to the wonders of nature, but Sarah appreciated the unspoiled forest. He had recognized the romantic interest whenever she gazed at him, and it melted him with surprising tenderness as he recalled their affectionate kiss.

And how did he repay her kindness after she'd given up her morning to hike with him?

Why, he'd departed with a quick, "Thanks for the ride and for being my guide. Have a marvelous afternoon."

Who said such words after sharing a morning with a beautiful woman?

Apparently, he did.

He rubbed a hand over his face. After their tender kiss, what must she think of him? Their hours shouldn't have ended with such finality. He blamed his cool farewell on the fact that he was weary after the lengthy drive, his move, and endless unpacking.

Nevertheless, he needed to rectify any misunderstanding because she fascinated him.

But how?

He lifted a cup of wassail to his lips and swallowed, and a familiar comfort surged through him. Years earlier, Mr. Lenny's wife, Amanda, had mixed homemade wassail using ingredients on hand—apple, orange, and cranberry juice.

Ultimately, Max had come to realize those long-ago times of assembling in Lenny's cheery kitchen drinking wassail with him, his wife, and their son, John, had resulted in Max's fantasy of heart-warming holidays surrounded by loved ones.

That fantasy never materialized. Still, he felt a sense of allegiance and gratitude to Lenny that exceeded every other emotion. Which was why, he supposed, he drank wassail.

A few short months after Max's placement with Lenny and his family, Max had been returned to his birth mother's care until she was hospitalized with liver disease. By then, the water and electricity in their apartment had been shut off. He never learned what happened to his father, who had never been a part of Max's life.

A loud knock on the front door sounded, and Gerry's voice bellowed, "Anyone home?"

"Just me and a bird flying around the living room."

A snicker. "You've been around birds so long you learned to fly?"

"Hang on while I catch Angel."

"Will it take a while?"

"Anywhere from five minutes to an hour, depending on if she cooperates."

A loud guffaw. "The weather is comfortable and I'll wait on the porch. I brought you a housewarming gift. A bottle of blackberry brandy."

"Really? I don't normally drink brandy … but thanks."

From experience, Max knew coaxing Angel to her cage was no easy task. Parakeets were flock animals, and keenly aware of a person's body language. They were, after all, low man on the food chain and had learned to be cautious.

Max chatted quietly and walked nonchalantly, coaxing her down from the curtain rod. After he picked her up, he held his hand lightly over her wings and carried her to her cage.

A half hour later, he and Gerry sat in Max's tiny kitchen drinking cups of wassail. Gerry poured a shot of blackberry brandy into his cup, claiming he needed something to calm his nerves, being a spanking new father and all.

Max declined the brandy. He wanted to keep his wits about him while he engaged with the birds. Tonight, he planned on playing the harmonica—perhaps a scale followed by a soulful ballade. Maybe they would mimic the musical sounds.

He leaned back in his stool as Gerry brought him up to date on living with a newborn and how he embraced fatherhood in his fifties. Then Gerry poured himself another shot.

Max's initial thought upon seeing his friend in person for the first time in years was that Gerry's hair had turned a bushy stark-white—whiter than it appeared on screen—framing a robust, pink-cheeked face. His glacial-blue eyes were piercing, yet friendly. His once crusty exterior had softened.

By day, Gerry worked in a pet store in Perrytown. By night, his passion was music. Over the course of their Internet jam sessions, Max discovered that Gerry had a powerful bass voice, and his guitar skills were disciplined and focused.

Gerry raised his cup for a toast. "To the Bearded Elves. Forever may we sing."

"Forever may we sing … anywhere?" Max clinked cups.

"An opportunity will present itself."

"Dorothy Edwards suggested The Garden Terrace."

"We'll check it out." Gerry ran his tongue over his lips. "Hey, this is tasty wassail for a bachelor."

"Wassail is my holiday indulgence. I learned how to make it from my foster mother and father."

Max tapped a relaxed fist against his heart. "They were the epitome of kindness."

"I've known you many years, my bird singing comrade. You don't celebrate Christmas. Wassail is Christmas."

Amused, Max drank a final gulp. He too appreciated the irony of savoring wassail, rather than, say, a cold beer. Avoiding answering Gerry, he looked into the living room. The parakeets were busy quibbling with their toys and preening.

Gerry took the hint. "Any luck with the birds repeating your recorded songs?" he asked.

"None, even though I play different tracks for them every day."

"Maybe your birds would respond well if there was another animal around. I hear there is an adorable puppy in need of a home."

"A puppy galloping through my legs every morning, and keeping me up half the night?" Max shook his head. "This house is a rental, and a puppy is known to chew everything in sight. I already bumped up the place when I lugged my suitcases inside."

"My wife and I have discussed pet ownership, but newbie parenting is enough for now." Gerry commiserated with a nod, then gestured to the parakeets. "What do they mimic?"

Max shrugged. "Nothing."

As if on cue, Angel blurted loud and clear, "God bless us, every one."

Gerry swiveled on his stool. "Is that your bird?"

"You're hearing Angel's favorite, and only, sentence."

"Ho, ho, ho. You own a budgie who celebrates the holidays." Gerry chuckled. "Have you seen the Cherish town square transformation?"

"Too busy."

"Those little wooden houses lined up around the ten-foot Christmas tree resemble a Norman Rockwell village when lit at night. There's also a craft fair selling local wares. My wife prefers cranberry-scented candles and pine-smelling soaps."

"It's going to be challenging to shop with a newborn."

Gerry linked his hands behind his head. "Barring the matter that neither of us has slept more than three hours since little Freddie's birth, my answer is yes, it will be. Are you up for any babysitting?"

"Perhaps when he's a little older. He cries a lot?"

"He's colicky." Gerry stared into his cup, then at Max. "I thought you always wanted children."

"Someday. In the meantime, call me when he turns five."

As Gerry rambled about the egalitarian share of chores in his marriage, Max's thoughts gravitated to his research. Should he expand his study to include cardinals? A recent article by a colleague had supported a claim to include natural-history habitats, and cardinals were the state bird in neighboring North Carolina. Perhaps the Jacksonville university would be more attentive if Max's study included additional birds.

He massaged his nape. Shouldn't the ache be gone? He'd moved in a while ago.

Stress, a little voice nudged.

No. An adamant no. Stress is a motivator.

In the meantime, didn't the department head realize Max couldn't *force* his budges to talk?

"Seen the live reindeer at the children's petting zoo?" Gerry asked.

Max's musings gravitated to Sarah. She loved taking photos of deer.

Aware his friend regarded him, Max shook his head. "No time." With a weary sigh, Max picked up their cups and rinsed them in the sink. Then he led Gerry into the living room. "I'll let the birds fly around if that's okay."

"Suits me. I let my cat roam throughout my house."

"Just don't bring your cat to my house when the birds are out."

"You'll meet my new baby before you ever see my cat. I can bring little Freddie over anytime."

"Looking forward to it," Max murmured.

At the far end of the room, beyond a scarred wooden coffee table, stood a cushioned sofa and a side chair. Two large cages were hung at chest level on the opposite wall, situated near the window so the birds could see outside.

Gerry pushed his hands into his jean pockets. "I identified the recordings you sent—a golden-winged warbler and a Canada warbler."

"You're correct. You were always a top-notch student."

Gerry knew his birds. He could have found the information using birding apps, but a conscientious and deliberate Gerry most likely had done his research.

"All the birds were recorded at Juniper Mountain?" he asked.

"Yes. And the setting is superb." With an airy wave of his hand, Max gestured toward the threadbare sofa for his buddy to get comfortable, then opened the doors to the bird cages. "I enlisted the help of a local guide."

"Who?" Gerry took a seat, shooing away a bird that quickly decided to roost there. "A park ranger?"

"A woman named Sarah Hartman. She lives in Cherish and—"

"Sarah Hartman? Sarah is my great-niece."

Max stared in surprise. "You never mentioned that."

"Why would I? Our conversations center on birds and music. So, what's the consensus?" He sounded so matter-of-fact that Max grinned.

"About Sarah?"

"Who else?"

"She's lovely. Absolutely lovely." *Okay, yes, that was an understatement.* His vision of her lustrous hair cascading over her shoulders, the red highlights glistening in the sun, served as a reminder of her beauty. "And plucky. We had a close encounter with a bear and she was magnificent."

"A real live bear?"

"Big and breathing, but Sarah's quick thinking came to our rescue. She's marvelous under pressure."

"Sounds like her. She's a wunderkind with animals."

"I've heard."

Gerry leaned in. "Can I tell you something about her I've noticed lately?"

"Should you betray her confidence?"

"It's more of a speculation shared by me and a number of her friends. We believe she has a hearing deficiency she's denying."

Thoughtfully, Max nodded. That would explain her

occasional hesitancy to speak and the way she kept looking at him when she was driving, as if she had trouble hearing him.

He felt a clutching in his heart. He, more than anyone, should understand. Not exactly the same, but Mr. Lenny had worn a hearing aid, saying it helped him listen and communicate—mainly in noisy situations.

Max waited while Gerry went into the kitchen and refilled a fresh cup—all brandy and no wassail.

When he returned, he stopped short and regarded Max for a suspiciously long time. "Well?" he prodded.

"Well, what?"

Gerry took a quick swallow of brandy. "Did you and my divine niece get along?"

Max cleared his throat. "Of course." He turned, a clear sign he wasn't willing to make any small talk when it came to his feelings toward Sarah. Some subjects were personal, and she was special.

"Alrighty then." Gerry's laughter rippled through the room. "Next topic. Church."

"Let's close that topic before you begin." Max flipped open his computer, scanning the files, calculating how successfully he could change the church subject without Gerry asking a thousand questions.

"Let me reword. Not church, necessarily, but the Cherish church *choir*." Gerry hesitated for emphasis, his tone growing insistent as he touched on the real issue. "A strong baritone voice is needed for our cantata. The choir is performing at the six o'clock service on Christmas Eve."

"If you're hinting for me to join, I haven't set foot in a church in years."

He'd attended as a child, since Mr. Lenny had served at the local church as an associate pastor, but Max had gotten away from anything religious once he heard of Mr. Lenny's death. None of his other foster families, nor his birth mother, had favored religion.

"Come once to rehearsal, Max, and see if you're a decent fit. I think you are, though it's your call. The choir members are good people and—"

"No one's refuting their goodness."

"Then help us out." Gerry extended a sheepish smile.

"Isn't Ryan Edwards your main singer?"

"Normally, although he's conducting the choir on Christmas Eve. And right now, he's in Atlanta rehearsing. Another member is stepping in for the next couple of weeks."

Max hesitated, ready to cut off any additional arguments from Gerry with a shake of his head.

"You're here for Christmas, correct?" Gerry asked. "And staying through New Year's."

"I am. However—"

"You'll recognize the traditional hymns: 'Away in a Manger,' etc. You'll catch on quick. You're a fine note-reader."

Max's eyebrows furrowed. His friend knew he wasn't a churchgoer, yet he was asking him to sing in a church choir. He considered Gerry's earnest expression as his mind scrambled for an excuse. At a loss for how to decline, he returned to the computer files.

"Did I mention Sarah is usually at the church when we rehearse?" Gerry added. "She designs and arranges the altar flowers. Sure looks pretty all decked out in red with green velvet ribbons."

"The church or your great-niece?"

Gerry winked. "Both."

Max sprang to his feet. "When are the rehearsals?"

"Thursday evenings at seven o'clock."

"Sarah is usually there?"

"Usually."

"I'll give the choir a try."

"I thought so." Gerry sent Max a knowing grin. "Oh, and bring your harmonica."

"Why?"

"The finale is a rousing rendition of 'We Wish You A Merry Christmas.' I'm playing guitar and a harmonica would be a nice touch."

"What about Joseph Slater? He's a professional guitarist."

"He and his wife, Scarlett, are flying to Australia next week for a worship conference. They asked me to step in."

"No one else plays harmonica in this town?"

"None that I know of. Consider it an honor to be asked. I wanted to add a sixteen-measure solo at the end."

Max digested this and considered reverting to his earlier decision. Singing in the choir was one thing. Playing the harmonica in front of Ryan Edwards, a world-renowned opera singer, was quite another. He opened his mouth, but Gerry interrupted.

"The other day, Sarah mentioned hanging wreaths on all the church windows on Thursday night."

Max chuckled. "I'll bring my harmonica."

Gerry drained his cup. "I knew you wouldn't let the baritone section down."

CHAPTER 5

Harmonica tucked in his pocket, and his favorite bow tie in place, Max arrived at the white-painted Memorial Street Church on Thursday evening. Night had darkened the winter sky, forming a blanket of black velvet, and the steeple soared proud and magnificent against it.

An outdoor nativity scene took center stage. The life-size creche included the Holy Family, two white lambs, kings and shepherds, and a wooden stable.

Gas street lamps were wrapped in fragrant pine boughs, and a trembling wind rustled the tree branches.

Inside, an assemblage of youthful and older men and women were taking their places on the risers, and a small group of women hung wreaths on the arched church windows.

Looking around, he spotted Sarah balanced on the third rung of a stepladder.

He strode over to her and tapped her on the back. "Good evening, Sarah."

She whirled and almost fell into his arms. A burst of

delight lit her face, and everything around him—the stained glass depicting Bible scenes, the whiffs of incense and candles, the other people's voices—faded away. The intensity of her gaze did funny things to his insides. Regardless of the way their last time together had ended, she looked pleased to see him.

"Max!" She clung to the sides of the ladder for support. "I chatted with my uncle Gerry this week and he claimed you're singing in the church choir."

"Temporarily," Max corrected.

"You're also in a band with him?"

"The Bearded Elves." Max steadied the ladder as she climbed down.

"The Bearded Elves? That's … different."

"Don't get hung up on the name. It will change soon."

She tilted her head to the side.

"When you're *not* a number one hit band, you're granted some flexibility." He grinned. "Wait until February. You'll see."

But then, he wouldn't be here in February, which left him with a sense of sadness.

She didn't reply, accepting his explanation without question, not even with the prompt of "What happens in February?"

Then again, maybe she hadn't heard him.

"Uncle Gerry raved about your superb baritone voice and perfect pitch," she said instead.

"He's biased since he was an undergrad student in my bird-watching class." Max removed his jacket and placed it on a pew. "Besides, doesn't every choir member sing in tune?"

"I'm not certain. Based on my great-uncle's comments, some don't." Sarah stepped to a side table and gathered red spray roses and luxuriant ivy, creating an elegant bouquet in a green glass vase. "The choir is all volunteer. These folks aren't professional except for Ryan Edwards and a few of the others."

Max turned her to face him. "Are you brave, Sarah?"

She looked startled by his unexpected question. "I try."

"You're the most courageous woman I've ever known."

Her cheeks pinkened. "Thanks."

"I intend to explore Crandall's Mountain next weekend. Will you join me? I hesitated inviting you, considering our adventure last week."

"You mean, because of the bear?"

"Because of me. I apologize for my rudeness. We didn't part on the finest note."

"You're here now. The present is all that matters."

"Is that a yes?"

Her nod of affirmation was accompanied by a smile of delight. "Let me check my work schedule, but it sounds like fun."

She was full of life. Eager. Forgiving. And stunning. The hiking gear she'd worn the previous weekend hadn't done her justice. She'd looked anything but glamorous in a hooded jacket, snowflake gloves and boots. The woman gazing at him now was entrancing. By the light of numerous church candles, the jeweled sparkle of her emerald eyes mesmerized him.

"For the record, I like hiking more than ever," she said.

Her statement thrilled him, sending a rush of gladness straight to his heart.

Before he could reply, Gerry called him to the choir to begin the warm-up.

Max nodded at Gerry over his shoulder, then curved back to Sarah. "The rehearsal runs an hour. Will you be here when it's finished?"

"Most likely. There are thirty windows in the church."

"I'll see you after rehearsal then?"

She chewed her lip. Glanced away.

He stared at her in eager silence. "Well?"

"Sure. If I'm done beforehand, I'll wait."

The recognizable first notes of 'Joy To The World' led by the sopranos, announced the beginning of choir practice.

Max hurried to the risers and took his appointed place between Gerry and a gray-bearded man. He retrieved a hymnal and thumbed through the selections until he located the correct piece.

The uplifting lyrics and melody, published by Handel in the 1700s, plucked him backward to a tiny church, sitting on a hard wooden pew as he listened to Mr. Lenny's heartfelt sermon.

Max focused on the associate conductor for the most part during the rehearsal.

However, he often stole glances at Sarah. She wore black slacks and a shimmery candy-red sweater, and her slim figure kept drawing his attention.

Whenever she caught his gaze, she quickly looked away. However, she smiled first, and he reciprocated with a responsive grin.

The final selection called for a guitar and harmonica. The "honor" of playing a harmonica solo in front of the other musicians was one that Max would've happily forgone, but when he was done, he was satisfied with his performance.

"What's your decision?" Gerry asked once the rehearsal ended.

Max slid the harmonica into his pocket. "I'll join."

"What was the deciding factor? The beloved hymns, my brilliant persuasion, or my great-niece's presence?"

"The latter," Max assured him.

In a refined southern drawl, an elderly woman introduced herself as Mrs. Marge Addyson. Her gray hair was neatly coiffed, and her rouged cheeks plumped with her smile as she held out a freckled hand. "Your baritone voice is as fine as a sunny winter's day. Welcome to Cherish. I'm the associate pastor."

"Thank you, ma'am. I'm Maxwell Archer." He shook her hand, frail yet sturdy. He was surprised at the callouses.

In a deafening stage whisper that garnered the notice of the remaining choir members, Marge announced, "You're the professor birdman who went hiking with our Sarah."

Our Sarah?

Intent on sidestepping a discussion involving Sarah that might be overheard, Max replied, "I'm affiliated with an ornithology department at a university."

"Birds."

"Ornithology is a branch of zoology," he clarified, "and is a discipline involving the study of birds."

"Impressive, and a distinctive description."

"Animals are important in my life and profession."

He expected Marge to rhapsodize about the significance of pets. She did just that, but offered a particular recommendation.

"Nicholas, the town sheriff, is looking for someone to adopt a cuddly homeless puppy," Marge said. "Considering your animal expertise, you're ideal."

Although both startled and pleased by her consideration of him as a candidate, he replied, "I've already been asked by the woman who owns the music store."

"Dorothy Edwards?"

"Yes, and I declined."

"Aren't you a fan of stray mongrels?"

"I should be, because I'm one myself." He regarded her with an ironic grin. "I used to live in Cherish."

"When?"

"Three decades ago, and for a brief spell. My foster family's last name was Monroe."

"I don't recall a Monroe family, although oftentimes my memory fails me." She pursed her lips. "I'll remember something that happened a decade earlier and forget something that happened a minute ago."

By the looks of Marge Addyson's well-heeled style and demeanor, Max assumed she resided in the wealthy outskirts of town. The Monroe family had occupied the impoverished fringes.

"I'm in no position to take on the responsibility of a dog," he said. "I move around a lot and my three parakeets are a literal handful. In January, I begin my dream job in Florida. I've struggled for ages to be on the faculty of a prestigious university."

"I express the feelings of the entire town when I say I'm overjoyed you're in Cherish." Marge reached for her handbag and tugged on a pair of flowered red gloves. "Regardless of your job, I hope you're here a long, long time."

"I appreciate your hospitality."

It warmed him—this undeniable sense of community, a welcome transition from big city living.

"Our church holds services on Saturday afternoons and Sunday mornings. On Christmas Eve day and evening, we offer several services." She studied him with an astute gaze. "Christmas is an opportune season to honor our Lord."

For a split second, their exchange grew awkward. Max wasn't about to divulge his lack of faith to the elderly associate pastor in the middle of a church.

He opted not to reply, although he recognized the wisdom flowing from her heart.

"You need honest and caring people in your life," she said.

He managed a grim smile.

"Do you serve God?"

Surprised at her bluntness, he answered truthfully. "I tried the religion route when I was younger. It didn't go well. The people in my circle …" He shrugged.

"Perhaps the season has come for a different circle." She squeezed his hand, her intelligent eyes exuding care and friendship. "Press on, Max. We're all here for you in your journey."

Journey to where?

"'Thanks be to God for his indescribable gift,'" she proclaimed.

"Second Corinthians 9:15." At her lifted eyebrows and inquisitive gaze, he avoided eye contact. "My special foster father was a pastor," he said.

"Special?"

"Yes."

"Was?" She grasped her blue tweed coat draped over a music stand.

"Mr. Lenny died many years ago."

She fiddled with the silver bell brooch on her coat's lapel as she studied him. "You miss him."

"Very much." Max glanced toward Gerry, who was collecting choral music.

Gerry picked up his guitar, slicked back his white hair, and approached them. "Hi, Mrs. Addyson."

"Hello, Gerry." Marge smiled up at him. "I just asked our newest choir member if he was interested in adopting the stray pup that wandered into Nicholas's office."

"What was his answer?"

"I'm right here, Gerry." Because they were close friends, Max caught the drollness in Gerry's tone. "As much as I'd love a puppy, I can't commit."

"I refused as well because my plate is full. Sorry." Gerry flashed a guilt-ridden smile. "However, let's all go out for a celebratory drink at The Garden Terrace."

"What are we celebrating?" Max inquired.

"You joined the church choir."

"Don't you have to rush home to your new baby?" Caught between amusement and confusion, Max and Marge inquired in unison.

Gerry shot them a look filled with emotions—including self-reproach and longing. "My mother-in-law is visiting and insisted on rocking the baby to sleep. She holds the magic touch."

Max grinned. "Therefore, your and your wife's roles aren't egalitarian tonight?"

"Little Freddie giggles from head to toe whenever I make faces at him," Gerry replied. "Or raspberry kisses. I'll do both in the morning."

Mrs. Addyson left shortly afterwards, pleading tiredness, and shaking her head in refusal at the invitation. She reminded them that she was past retirement age and went to bed early.

A bang of the ornately carved doors signaled the last of the choir members filing out.

Max peered around. Sarah was hanging a final wreath on a window.

"Go ahead to the restaurant," he instructed Gerry. "We'll be along shortly."

"We?"

"I'm hoping Sarah will join us."

Gerry clapped a hand on Max's back. "I'm rooting for you, my friend. I'll inquire about a gig at the restaurant while I'm waiting."

"Do you think the management will agree?"

"Simple logic. We order a meal and they'll hire our band."

"Just because we eat there doesn't mean they'll want us to *play* there," Max countered. "Hundreds of customers dine at the restaurant every day."

"It's a start."

"Will we get paid?"

"I was thinking more along the lines of free drinks."

Max bit back a grin at the logic he didn't see at all, pulled on his jacket and hurried to Sarah.

"Perfect timing," he declared.

"For what?"

"You're finished, and I am too."

"I'm *nearly* done." She swerved around him to a table and secured buckthorn berry branches into florist foam, then arranged the branches with a trail of ivy in a copper vase.

He followed her as she set the vase near the altar. "Will you join us?" he asked.

"Where?"

"The Garden Terrace."

"It's after eight o'clock."

"Hardly late."

"There's cleanup here. In addition, I'm scheduled for a double shift tomorrow."

"I'll finish." To Max's relief, a short, heavyset woman spoke up. "Sarah, you go on and enjoy yourself with this handsome newcomer."

Max turned to her. "How do you know I'm a newcomer?"

"Cherish is a small community." The woman reached for the last two poinsettias. "Word travels fast."

"Thank you, Rosemary." Sarah's shoulders lifted as she turned to Max. "I'd like to, but—"

"Do you have any noteworthy plans on a Thursday night?"

"After I tend to my pets, I planned to catch up on some reading."

He persevered. "Did you drive here?"

"I walked. I don't live far."

"There's a chill in the air, Cinderella. Ride with me, and I guarantee you'll arrive home before midnight. Besides, I don't know where the restaurant is."

She laughed. "I'm certain you can find it without my help." In the flick of a few seconds, her mood had switched from indecision to humor, and it struck him that no matter her disposition, he appreciated her companionship.

"I have it on excellent authority you're the ideal guide," he said.

She gathered a half dozen stemmed red roses and placed them in a bucket filled with water. "From whom?"

"Me."

With a sideways smile, Sarah retrieved her jacket, then tucked her hand through his arm.

He couldn't help grinning as he escorted her out the wooden doors and down the church steps.

CHAPTER 6

The Garden Terrace wasn't the restaurant Max imagined. Certainly, the Monroes hadn't been able to afford such luxuries as dining out.

He'd pictured a genteel garden, a sparkling fountain, and an abundance of plants. After all, the restaurant's name alluded to a *garden*.

Instead, he and Sarah were welcomed by lively waitresses, a boisterous clatter of dishes, and heavenly whiffs of mesquite smoked chicken. An oversized sign at the entrance stated in bold letters, "The holidays are for barbecue." Multi-colored lights were strung from the ceiling and pine cones and faux red berries wound around rustic poles, accentuated by tan burlap. A keyboardist provided a background performance of "Carol of the Bells."

"This restaurant doesn't subscribe to minimalism," he joked.

"They're renowned for sugar-free lemon cake and sweet tea," Sarah told Max as he led her through the crowd and ushered her to a booth Gerry had claimed.

Somehow, Max remembered that about this restaurant.

He'd eaten a slice of the cake in his youth and had savored every bite. Another aspect of this appealing town were that things stayed the same. A time machine rewound to an era without the push and shove of big-city living.

"Sugar and sugar-free." Max helped her off with her jacket, tugged off his, and hung both on a coat hanger. "Isn't that a juxtaposition?"

"An oxymoron." Sarah teased him with a nudge. He noticed that she had watched his lips as he spoke. The restaurant was noisy and even he strained to hear their conversation. "Or rather, one cancels out the other. The calories in sugary tea—"

"Is a paradox," Gerry interrupted, indicating the guitar on his seat. He motioned them to sit across from him.

"Wrong," they contradicted him, which produced lots of laughter.

In the minutes between ordering and waiting for their meals—hot chocolate topped with marshmallows for Sarah, a slice of the sugar-free lemon cake and tea for Max, and a draft beer and two platters of French fries for Gerry—Max arrived at several important deductions.

First, Gerry wasn't, as Max earlier had presumed, merely a first-rate student, a talented musician, and a newbie father. Gerry was also candid and clever. While he inquired about Max's and Sarah's hiking adventure, he closely observed the way Max draped an arm around her shoulders.

And Sarah, with her delicate features and lilting voice, had a remarkable gift. She was charismatic, and she gave an enthusiastic account of the bear adventure, flavoring it with enough elements to engage Gerry. By doing so, she successfully avoided any reference to the kiss she and Max had shared.

Smiling at her wide-eyed gaze as she described the

babbling river, he felt inside him the stirring of a sentiment so remote, so foreign, he gasped in denial.

He was falling for her.

Not in the cards, he told himself. He was leaving in January.

Even so, the sentiment prompted him to curve a lock of shiny hair behind her ear. Her glittery gold star earrings winked back at him.

"You forgot our interruption by the teenagers," he said.

Her eyes glistened with laughter. "If they hadn't approached, we would still be ..."

"Kissing," he whispered in her ear and squeezed her shoulders, a gentle reminder in case she'd forgotten.

Oblivious to the direction of the conversation, Gerry pulled out his cellphone, concentrated on a text and frowned. "My wife," he muttered.

"Is little Freddie sleeping?" Max inquired.

"Almost." Gerry tried for a smile that said all was well, although he didn't entirely convince Max.

After their drinks and food were served, Gerry took a deep pull from his beer and set it down. "Incidentally, my friend, management agreed."

"To what?" Max handed him a bottle of ketchup and watched him smother the fries, then slid the platter to the middle of the table for all to share.

"To us performing here a couple Fridays from now." Gerry broke off a fry and chewed. "The Bearded Elves are back in business."

Max helped himself to an ample portion of fries after scarfing down his cake. He'd forgotten how much he liked lemon. "We weren't ever *in* business. Nonetheless, your news is exciting. Are they paying us?"

"Our gig is doubling as a debut audition and management is requesting familiar holiday tunes." A smile quirked Gerry's mouth. "I'll organize a playlist. We can rehearse separately, then together before our unveiling."

Sarah joined in with a chuckle. "Am I invited?"

"Absolutely. We'll perform in that far corner. There's even a dance floor." With his half-eaten fry, Gerry gestured to where the keyboardist played on a small stage.

Once their table was cleared, Gerry insisted on paying the bill, then peered at his phone and announced, "I'm heading home before my wife and her mother murder me."

"Did the baby wake up?" Max asked.

"The baby never went to sleep."

"No magic touch from your mother-in-law?"

"Our next option is to phone Merlin the Magician. Evidently, little Freddie is offended by the idea of sleeping."

Sarah surged up as quickly as Gerry did. "I should leave too." She peered at the restaurant's rustic wall clock, which showed after nine o'clock.

"Don't rush on my account." Gerry waved toward the dance floor. The keyboardist had begun a jazzy rendition of Ray Charles's "That Spirit of Christmas," and a handful of couples swirled to the rhythm.

Max slid his arm around Sarah and led her to the intimate dance floor. She was so petite, scarcely five feet tall, her head hardly reached his shoulder.

She gazed up at him with a jesting smile. "Are you the type who steps on your dance partner's feet?"

"Exactly." He chuckled, tempted to kiss the edges of her smile. "You?"

"The same, so watch out." Her laughter was mellow and melodic. He loved her ability to laugh at herself, as well as with him.

"Has anyone ever described you as a wonderful, caring man?" she asked.

"I dislike labels."

"I do too, but my intuition tells me you're a good person."

"Never tell a man he's good. Strong, maybe, or marvelous—"

She rested her head against his chest, and he whirled them around and around. Her steps were agile, gliding to the rhythm. Above them, the multi-colored lights sparkled, creating a wondrous, otherworldly effect. Her hair spun with each pivot and twist, and he kissed her forehead, her cheeks, her lips.

"What a wonderful feeling," he sang, adlibbing the lyrics, "to waltz with a precious, vivacious woman who is as sweet as a sugarplum."

As they danced, he reviewed the plan he'd conceived within the past half hour. While he lived in Cherish, he'd see her as often as possible.

Her descriptions of him—good and caring—were poignantly familiar. Mr. Lenny's wife had often called him a "caring little boy." Once, his outlook on life had shone optimistic.

His timeworn thoughts now were shadowed with the awareness that a future with a loving wife hadn't come to pass.

He blew out a labored breath.

He'd gotten over the injustice of being born to birth parents who couldn't focus on anyone except themselves.

Some children were born lucky. Other weren't.

But now he'd met Sarah.

How wonderful they could spend a few weeks together.

How awful they could only spend a few weeks together.

Seeming to sense the dipping of his mood, Sarah muttered she was sorry for stepping on his foot—she hadn't —but her comical expression portrayed her attempt to cheer him and her refreshing humor. But then she added, "I should get home."

With a nod, he maneuvered her off the dance floor and retrieved their jackets. Outside, the streets were dark and quiet. Gas lamps flickered, forming pools of warm light.

"How far do you live from the restaurant?" he asked.

"Three blocks." She turned right. "My house is in the center of town."

"I'll escort you. It'll give me a chance to walk off my fried-food coma."

Plus, it would take longer than a quick drive in his car, and he wanted to enjoy every precious minute with her. He pointed toward the town square as he heard voices rise in harmony. He recognized the "Silent Night" refrain.

"What's going on?" he asked.

Sarah hesitated. "Going on?"

"The singing."

"Oh, singing. It's carol singing," she replied. "The town's Christmas committee sponsors caroling three nights a week in December. Anyone can join. Afterwards, they serve hot apple cider and roasted chestnuts."

Now that she had mentioned it, he recognized the scorching charcoal aroma, rich and nutty, permeating the air, along with the hint of woodsy fireplaces.

Beams of silver fell around them. A full moon graced the sky, and a smattering of stars twinkled in shimmering beauty.

A chilly burst of wind tugged at their jackets.

Sarah bowed her head and closed her eyes to avoid the sting.

His gaze fell to her long, thick eyelashes, an unmistakable reddish-blond. Her copper-colored hair, as smooth as the finest silk, fell loose around her face.

"I recalled Carolina weather being warm all year round," he said, "but my remembrances are from a youngster's perspective."

"How long were you here?"

"Briefly." He shifted the subject, in no mood to upset the fine balance of a pleasant evening by being reminded of his tumultuous upbringing. "I assumed the climate was comparable to Florida."

"Do you like hot weather?"

"In all honesty, no." His reflective pause initiated a jab from his conscience. *Dream job, remember? You're moving.* "How about you?"

"I've lived here my entire life. I know everyone and am comfortable here. Still, I sometimes wish to see other places."

"Like Florida?"

"Are there more palm trees than the Carolinas?"

"Probably."

"You'll receive a pay raise with your new job?"

"Not necessarily, although I'm optimistic my research will resonate with people avid about ornithology. That is, unless my appointment is cancelled. Universities are tightening their proverbial belts, and bird study isn't at the top of their budgets." He shrugged, sighed. "If it happens, it happens."

"You work a lot of hours. It's a considerable workload." She seemed to choose her words carefully.

"Which will become heavier once I take on more responsibility."

"I'm sorry you're not a hot-weather fan."

"I don't particularly like cold weather, either. Nor do I care for synthetic snow, the kind the outdoor fairs manufacture for gala events."

"The Carolinas enjoy four distinct seasons," she replied. "I eagerly wait for snow on Christmas Day. No assurances, though. The weather here is unpredictable."

"I lived up north for years. If it doesn't snow, we're surprised."

She grinned. "In Cherish, if it *does* snow, we're amazed."

Several of the shops' single-paned windows had frosted over, and they peered through the glass, admiring one-of-a-kind gifts—a man's handmade striped red tie, a vintage green and gold pinecone necklace, and jars touting themselves as a "One-Stop Spa." An innovative store advertised a pet-friendly dog bakery, and Sarah commented on the unique toys, ranging from whimsical Merry Christmas bandanas to tail-wagging elf sweaters.

While they strolled, she was more outgoing than the day of their hike, regaling him with hilarious stories of her pets, beginning with what happened when she returned from work each day to a houseful of welcoming animals.

"My two dogs and two cats wait by the door until I arrive," she described. "Even if I leave for ten minutes to get the mail at the post office, they're under the impression I've been gone for hours, and the greeting parade begins anew."

She grew more gorgeous by the second. Her cheeks had grown rosy from the cold, her wide-set eyes sparkling a deep emerald. When she chuckled, tiny puffs of her breathing filled the air. He couldn't look away.

"My budgies are happy," he said. "They spend their days singing or talking."

"Uncle Gerry told me they haven't mimicked the birdsongs you recorded."

"Nothing yet."

Max went over the endless hours he'd spent with his birds. Why wouldn't they mimic other birdsongs or harmonica music? He reined in his frustration and focused on Sarah. "My budgies have individual temperaments. One male is timid, the other bolder, and the third, a female, speaks her mind."

"Hurray for the female. What does she say?"

Max pushed out an exasperated breath. "'God bless us, every one.'"

"From *A Christmas Carol*? Tiny Tim?"

"Exactly. She's a rescue bird. An elderly woman owned her."

"What's her name?"

"Angel." He resisted the urge to laugh. "Don't be fooled. She's the most unangelic bird of the three."

"Is unangelic a word?"

"It is now."

"We all have distinctive personalities, because God created variety and uniqueness."

"You're saying He knew what to do."

"Exactly."

"But how, Sarah? I'm not at peace with all this religious jargon."

"Don't search for peace." Her tone softened, and he felt his expression grow less rigid. "You already are at peace. God is inside you."

She expressed herself with her body, gestures, and expressions rather than a deluge of words.

He had appreciated her artistic flower arrangements at church and he knew she was hard working and industrious. Her faith in God was clear, and he sensed she possessed what Mr. Lenny had called "a new creature in Christ." Combined, these attributes contributed to her magnetic personality.

In the sparkle of twinkling lights dancing from nearby homes, the sadness in his heart diminished. Sarah carried the same unique gift—to enhance the world around her merely by her presence. She was an extraordinary, special woman.

Soon, they reached the gaily decorated Musically Yours. Although the music store was closed, they paused to admire the window display of the polar bears, treble clef signs, and model train.

How many hours, Sarah mused aloud, had it taken Dorothy and Ryan to dress up the window with such flair?

"Maybe they had help," Max said.

"From who? A polar bear?"

"Maybe Beethoven himself." Max curled his fingers around hers. Happiness lifted his spirits, and, judging by Sarah's contented sigh, the holiday atmosphere of the winsome town affected them both.

"Cherish Hills Inn also has particularly noticeable decorations. The inn is located farther up the street." Sarah gestured with her chin. "The innkeeper, Tom Canning, is a long-time resident, and strict about who he rents to."

"I tried to get a room there, but Tom wasn't keen on renting to me and my birds for the entire month of December."

"Not surprising. The inn is posh and unconducive for pets."

"Ah. That explains Tom's half-hearted response."

"What did he say?"

Max grabbed a mouthful of air and shouted, "No."

"That's why Tom doesn't have anyone currently staying at his inn. He's choosey and a stickler for elegance."

"Thank you." Max picked her up and twirled her around.

"What for?" She giggled. Wriggled.

"For sticking up for me."

"I did?"

"Yes. You stuck up for me instead of Tom."

"I'm getting dizzy. Put me down."

He continued to spin, but slower this time, holding her close. "Not until you guarantee me something."

"You expect an assurance after that?"

"Promise me you'll never change." He gazed at her amazing face, trying to ignore the flip in his pulse.

She met his stare. "Our lives, our paths, take many forms, Max."

He spoke clearly and deliberately, as he had done all evening. "Not with us."

He set her down and reached for her hand, whistling the entire last block to her house. It was set back from the road and surrounded by bare-branched trees. The front door was painted gray and bedecked with shiny pink ornaments and a garland heavy with silver tinsel.

"You're a true holiday-lover," he remarked. "I hope the porch doesn't collapse under the sheer mass of the decorations."

At her doorstep, with barking dogs and loud meows in the background, he slipped his arms around her. So close their foreheads touched, he tipped up her chin and kissed her.

She stood on her tiptoes and yielded to his hungry mouth. Her lips were plump and inviting, fitting together with his, two pieces of an intricate puzzle matching perfectly. Her hands reached up and her slim fingers tangled behind his neck.

Her enticing sweetness obliterated his concerns—an uncertain job market, his research, his turbulent past—and he savored every second of their kiss. The promise of December, creamy hot chocolate and tart lemon cake—he'd hit the jackpot when he met Sarah.

He was filled with anticipation and gladness.

And a spark that completely surprised him.

A spark of love.

CHAPTER 7

The following day, Sarah clocked in at the greenhouse at ten o'clock in the morning. Fragrant whiffs of lush evergreens never failed to bring thoughts of sparkly white lights and an array of gaily wrapped gifts.

That morning, she'd secured her flyaway hair with a green headband because it always frizzed after shampooing, even when she used her favorite rosewood shampoo. Then, she'd tugged on a cream-colored cable-knit sweater, jeans, and snowman dangle earrings.

After a wave at Bonnie, who had positioned herself at the cash register, Sarah sorted Christmas cactus. She lavished care on each showy red and white flower. Many had been overwatered, which led to root and stem rot.

While she tended to the first plant, she tried to ignore the butterflies in her chest as memories of her previous evening with Max kept surfacing.

His animated features when he chatted about his birds, his quick-witted banter, his musicality, were all part of his personality. He was bold yet vulnerable; humorous yet sensitive.

And she loved every minute she spent with him.

He'd dismissed his upcoming Florida job with a casual "if it happens, it happens" as he rubbed the dark stubble of his beard. Nonetheless, his dismissal had only confirmed that he cared about the prestigious position more than he let on.

The plants, she reminded herself. The plants.

She tended to the next one and again, her mind meandered.

The mouth-watering food and drink at The Garden Terrace, her intimate dance with Max, their leisurely stroll ending in an earth-shattering kiss—all those memories came back in a rush. Rational thought had a way of abandoning her whenever she was within two feet of him.

She pressed a finger to her lips. Was last night a first date? After all, he'd invited her to a restaurant. Or was it a second if she counted their hike on Juniper Mountain?

"Do you have any noteworthy plans on a Thursday night?" he'd asked her.

Um, no, unless scrubbing the kitchen floor and vacuuming were considered noteworthy. In any event, she was glad she'd accepted his invitation.

At the end of the evening, he'd requested her phone number and had promised to text, phone, and see her often.

He was a man, he assured her, who never reneged on his promises. True to his word, he'd texted a few minutes later, telling her how much he'd enjoyed their hours together. That text had resulted in an hour's worth of conversation.

Was his kiss the beginning of something extraordinary, something lasting?

As quickly as it came, she released the thought.

He was in Cherish for one month. He'd made that fact abundantly clear.

Nevertheless, his affectionate words and tender actions were sincere.

Weren't they? What if he didn't call or text again?

A favorite passage from the Bible, Matthew 6:34, reassured her: "Do not be anxious for tomorrow, for tomorrow will be anxious for itself."

She wondered about Max's past, because Marge Addyson had left a voice mail for Sarah that morning when Sarah was in the shower.

"I scoured the Big Brothers Big Sisters files," Marge said. "I believe I've found a photo of your Max, probably taken close to thirty years ago when he lived in Cherish with his foster family. You'll want to see it, I'm sure. I'll stop by your home … I'm assuming after six o'clock? Call me if that's not okay."

Her Max.

Sarah's heartbeat had drummed at Marge's reference, and she scarcely paid attention to the rest of Marge's words.

Wait.

Big Brothers Big Sisters.

Despite Max's brilliant mind and academic demeanor, his background apparently wasn't silver-spoon. She considered him handsome, but there was a blunt masculinity to his square jaw and muscled physique. Had he been the type of boy who'd been in many brawls?

She knew he wasn't afraid of anything.

Not even a charging bear.

By the river, his strong, chiseled arms had held her tight.

Images of a Christmas spent with him brought comfort to her lonely world, a breathlessness whenever she recalled the glimmer of interest in his gray eyes. His dark hair, a tad too long, curled at the nape, and she'd wanted to smooth the adorable cleft on his chin.

By far, he was the handsomest man to set foot in Cherish.

He's leaving, her sensible side was quick to remind. *Do you honestly want to get hurt again?*

A jarring announcement over the store's loudspeaker called for a price check. Quickly yanked back to the present, Sarah surveyed the rows of cacti, trying to recall which plants she'd tended. White blooms or red?

The nursery door opened, and a blast of wintry air hit her.

Nicholas, the town sheriff, accompanied by Molly Belle, his rambunctious golden retriever, strode toward her. Molly Belle's leash didn't prevent her from romping away from him. She knocked over a bunch of plants in her hurry to chase … nothing.

"Stop." Nicholas tugged on the leash and peered at the spilled soil on the concrete floor. "Sorry, Sarah."

"It's a fast clean-up." Sarah grinned at Molly Belle. "Are those doggy obedience classes helping?"

Nicholas shoved a hand through his blond hair. "The instructor recommended she get lots of exercise. What an understatement." His moan was part sigh, part frustration. "We take her out often, although she's easily distracted."

The dog beamed up at them with expectant black eyes, then went back to lapping the water spilled from the plants.

"Here, Molly Belle." Sarah grabbed a water bottle, foraged for an empty container, and poured water into it. "You'll find this is tastier."

Nicholas crossed his arms and turned to face her. "You're one of only a handful of people Molly Belle will listen to."

Sarah appreciated that aspect of living in a small community. Folks were now using strong, clear voices when talking to her. Needless to say, it wasn't because she had a hearing impairment, despite what her friends hinted. They merely needed to speak louder, especially when she was in a crowded place with many voices.

Perhaps another reason why Dorothy had recommended Sarah as Max's hiking companion was because she knew that Sarah preferred the quiet solitude of nature.

"Molly Belle isn't obeying your commands?" she teasingly asked Nicholas.

"Once in a while. Once in a *great* while."

Sarah laughed, wiped her hands on her employee apron, and grabbed a broom. "Are you purchasing anything in particular today?"

"I'm here for two reasons. First, my wife wants a live wreath for the front door, rather than the fake one I purchased at the grocery store."

"The wreaths are all hung outside. You passed them when you entered." Sarah swept the soil into the dustpan and discarded it. "What's the second reason?"

"I hoped to discuss the puppy who wandered into the sheriff's office—"

"We discussed the subject. My answer is no."

"Sarah, you're the ideal choice."

"I can't, Nicholas. My house is overrun with pets."

He kneaded the back of his neck. "You have two cats and a hamster."

"Plus two dogs."

"Your dogs are friendly."

"You didn't remember I owned dogs until a second ago. My Shih Tzu is ten years old and set in her ways, and the other dog is a cocker spaniel who thinks she owns me rather than the other way around. I'm confident someone will welcome the puppy as the perfect addition to their family."

"Who?" Nicholas muttered, half to himself. He tugged his phone from his pocket, scrolled through it, then drew her attention to a tiny puppy with fuzzy silver-colored fur. "Do you agree he needs a loving home for Christmas?"

"Absolutely." She scrutinized the photo. "He?"

"Yup." Nicholas eyed Molly Belle, who had secured a place on the concrete floor in a spot of sunshine. "He lacks a safe, loving environment. Here's some videos. Doesn't he look like he's ready to take on the world?"

A bouncy puppy filled the screen, a roll of fat evident under his chin. In the second video, he chased Nicholas and nipped at his pant legs. This was followed by a short bark as the puppy rolled onto his back and stared into the camera with sweet doggy eyes.

"We've had him vet checked and he's healthy. Plus, he's handled daily and exhibits a devoted personality." Nicholas pointed to the screen. "Look at that shiny coat."

"That puppy is in constant motion. Wagging his tail and wriggling all over the place."

"He's a gem, right? The vet estimated he's eight weeks old, and vaccinated him for the first series of shots."

Sarah smiled and leaned in. "Nicholas, you're persuasive, but—"

A tap on the shoulder caused her to whirl.

"Hi, Sarah." Max stepped within a foot of her. He smiled at her and scowled at Nicholas. "Am I interrupting something?"

"Max." She touched her fingers to her throat. "I didn't expect to see you today."

He shoved his hands in his pockets. His lips pressed together. "I wanted to say hello and—"

He looked sinfully handsome, and the thought crossed her mind that Nicholas might book Max, because it had to be illegal to be that good-looking. He wore black jeans that accented his toned legs and a chambray shirt. His familiar bow tie peeked beneath the olive-green twill jacket.

The time showed mid-morning—the hours when Max normally pored over research.

Yet, he was here, and her heart did a slow flip.

Max's scowl stayed on Nicholas.

"You're not interrupting a thing." Nicholas clicked his phone shut and shoved it back in his pocket.

Sarah flinched, sensing an unmistakable hostility between the two men.

"I'm glad you stopped by the store, Max." She gave an uneasy laugh and swallowed. "Let me introduce you to the Cherish town sheriff. Nicholas Thompson, meet Maxwell Archer."

At the same height, six feet tall, both men's features were similar—sharp and athletic and wary.

They shook hands, although Max treated Nicholas with chilly courtesy. He bent to pet Molly Belle. She responded with a gleeful tail wag.

"I'm Dorothy Edwards's brother," Nicholas clarified as Max straightened. "My wife, Emmanuelle, teaches harp lessons at Dorothy's store."

Max's expression eased. "You're off duty today, sheriff?" He sized up Nicholas' casual attire of khakis and a sweater, then positioned himself between Sarah and Nicholas, bracing a hand on a pole above her head. Although the men's verbal volley might have ended, Max was sending Nicholas a clear message.

He was interested in Sarah.

Because he was jealous. Jealous of *her*. The knowledge brought a wry smile.

"Nice bow tie," Nicholas said flatly.

"Thanks."

Okay, so it was unusual to wear a bow tie into a garden center, but Max was unique. The tie made him unforgettable, offering an air of distinguished academia. Although, considering his disheveled hair, he reminded her of an absent-minded professor.

"Today is my day off." Nicholas offered a scarcely

disguised smirk. "You don't, by any wild chance, break the law, Max, do you?"

"Never, sheriff. I'm new in town, and my rental is begging for a little holiday cheer." His gaze rested on Sarah. "I'm here to purchase flowers. Can you help me, Sarah?"

"Definitely."

"Dorothy mentioned our little town had acquired another fine musician," Nicholas said. "The other day, a man stopped by her store to buy a harmonica. I assume that was you?"

"I'm an average musician and a temporary resident," Max corrected.

Nicholas narrowed his gaze. "So, you're here *temporarily*."

"Yes."

Nicholas glanced at the pole where Max still braced his arm. "You won't want to get too familiar with folks, then, if you're leaving them soon." With a crisp nod, he turned toward the entrance. "Well, I'm off to grab a wreath. C'mon, Molly Belle."

The dog didn't move and stared up at Nicholas with a kindly expression.

"Come." Gently, Nicholas pulled the leash.

Again, no response.

"Up, Molly Belle." Sarah ducked beneath Max's arm and stepped over to the sunny spot where the dog sat. "Up Molly Belle. Obey your master."

Molly Belle immediately stood. Her tail wagged with so much enthusiasm her entire body shook.

"You do have a way with animals, Sarah." Nicholas extended a rueful laugh, then regarded Max. "Don't forget that she's an exceptional woman, and well-loved by everyone in this town."

Max gave Sarah a teasing wink. "I've already discovered she's extraordinary, and she's hands down the bravest woman I've ever known."

Sarah felt her cheeks flush pink. She blamed it on the heat and sun in the garden center.

As Nicholas and Molly Belle headed out the door, she set down the broom she hadn't realized she still held. "What types of plants are you looking for, Max?"

"My birds are happiest around dazzling flowers."

"The poinsettias this year are brilliant." She signaled for him to follow her. "Any particular shade?"

After he selected two vibrant red poinsettias and a purple cyclamen with upswept flowers and silver foliage, he said, "A bike was left in my rental and I rode it here. Any chance you can bring the plants by my house when you get off work?"

"I'm done at six o'clock."

He nodded. "Excellent. I'll prepare dinner for us."

"I can't." She bent to pick up Molly Belle's water dish. "I haven't decorated the inside of my house for Christmas and I planned to start hauling decorations down from the attic tonight. Although I don't know why I do both inside and outside decorating. The cats think the artificial tree is a scratching post, and the dogs chew the ornaments. And don't get me started on holiday baking. Why, the dogs will eat everything in sight and ..."

She was babbling, and Max was grinning.

"Can decorating wait one more day?" he asked.

Something in his tone prompted her to study him.

A couple of customers wandered over, asking how to care for a Christmas cactus.

"My specialty," Sarah exclaimed. She cut her conversation with Max short and bustled over to show them the array of cacti. When they had chosen one and carried it to the register, Max was standing exactly where she'd left him.

She intended to refuse his invitation, but an entirely different answer emerged from her lips. "I need to stop home first."

"No problem. Say, seven o'clock?" His expression had softened. He looked pleased.

"You cook?"

"No. Fortunately, The Garden Terrace offers a delicious barbecue takeout."

"If you drive to the restaurant, you can easily swing to the nursery for your plants."

"Hmm." He shuffled his feet.

"Hmm?"

His gaze leveled on hers, the teasing evident. "I'll grant that your idea makes sense, although it ruins my excuse."

"Which is?"

"To see you tonight."

A giggle escaped her. "It would be a true calamity if your excuse was ruined."

"Is your answer a yes?"

"I'd love to have dinner with you."

Her spirits soared madly beneath the brilliance of his ready smile.

CHAPTER 8

$\mathcal{A}$nother December night had fallen in the Carolinas, and stars emerged in the sky one by one.

When Max ushered Sarah inside his slightly messy bungalow, she immediately noticed the three colorful blue, white and green budgies near the window—two sharing one cage, the other alone in a separate cage. Mounds of scientific and bird magazines were stacked on a desk, the floor, and various shelves.

He kissed her tenderly on the cheek, thanked her for delivering the flowers, and rushed to take her coat. "Come. Sit on the sofa. It's comfortable. I made chip and dip."

Although he set the poinsettias and cyclamen on a tall pedestal table, she felt his probing silver gaze drift over her.

"I bought sandwiches, slaw, and a gingerbread cake for dessert." He gestured to the kitchen beyond. "Homemade wassail is simmering in the crock pot."

The cinnamon and apple aroma of the wassail made her mouth water. She grabbed a chip.

"I assumed you didn't cook," she said.

"I don't, but this is an easy family recipe."

Ah, so he had a family. When the subject had come up while they'd texted the night before, he'd veered to other topics—the weather, his research, his birds.

"Well, it smells delicious." She skimmed her fingers across her brown leather tote bag, which contained a precious manila envelope. When she'd stopped home after work to feed her animals and change into dark-wash jeans and a red striped sweater, Marge Addyson had met her at the door.

"Here is the photo from Big Brothers Big Sisters. Max looks young." Marge pressed the sealed manila envelope into Sarah's hands with excessive care. "He's very sweet and that worries me."

"Then or now?"

"Both. That sweet boy has become a charming, caring man."

"Why are you worried?"

"At choir rehearsal I stood across from him, and he could hardly keep his eyes off you. I wasn't sure the interest was mutual, but then I saw your return smiles. He cares for you a great deal."

"We've been friends only a short time," Sarah reminded Marge.

"But long enough. I know you, Sarah, and there's not a mean bone in your body. Do you believe in love at first sight?"

"Is there such a thing?"

"Certainly." Marge paused. "Max tries to hide it, but he's wearing his heart on his sleeve. I was at The Garden Terrace this afternoon for a bit of tea and cake, and he was there, ordering dinner for the two of you. He drove everyone crazy, asking about your favorite foods, obsessing about creating a splendid meal. It was almost as if the queen of England was coming to dine. He insisted on an exceptional holiday dessert."

"Lemon cake?"

"Gingerbread."

"He is very sweet." Sarah offered an affable grin, the kind that pacified fussy customers. Nonetheless, Marge wasn't easily placated.

"And?" Marge asked.

"I care for him a great deal too," Sarah replied. "However, he's leaving in January."

"Is he?"

"A promising career opportunity awaits him in Jacksonville. He's looking forward to it."

"Uh huh." Marge nodded perceptively. "Remember the Bible verse from Corinthians? 13:13?"

Sarah recited along with Marge. "And now these three remain: faith, hope, and love. But the greatest of these is love."

Now, standing in Max's living room, Sarah adjusted her leather tote bag.

"I finished another page of my research paper a few minutes ago," he was saying "This timing worked out well. Dinner at seven is an ideal fit for me."

"Me too."

"Do you often eat alone?" he asked.

"More often than not. You?"

"It depends." He exhaled. "Who am I kidding? I always eat alone." He ran his thumb and forefinger along the edge of a laptop computer, then firmly closed it. "Would you like to meet my uncooperative birds?"

She chuckled. "Sure."

"I want to tell you, Sarah, I'm thrilled you're here."

The question in his persuasive gray eyes was well-defined. *Do you feel the same?*

Slightly, she bobbed her head, a silent response he immediately understood.

He took her in his arms and kissed her. Long and sweet. Her eyes closed, and her breath came in a sigh. He kissed her again and again. Deeply, exquisitely, and soundly.

After the kisses, with her head against his chest, Sarah smiled. Things were so good.

But only for now.

She lived in Cherish, worked at a job she enjoyed, and embraced her church, family and friends. He was off to a promising career opportunity in Jacksonville.

She was a Christian.

He was not.

She loved Christmas.

He tolerated Christmas.

Therefore, she must steel herself for their imminent separation.

She pulled out of his arms, brushed a hand over her hair, which she'd secured in a French braid, and approached the bird cages.

The parakeets squawked as she peered inside.

"Hello, pretty birds," she said.

All three began chirping at once. Vibrant birdsongs flooded the room.

Max came beside her, looping an arm around her. "Fascinating," he said, staring at the birds.

"What's fascinating?"

"The birds. Their reaction to you. I've never seen such behavior from them before."

LATER, they dined in his tiny kitchen on scrumptious barbecue served on his finest white ceramic plates, drinking bottled water. When dinner was finished, he ushered her into the living room and switched on the overhead pendant light.

"Would you like a mug of my homemade wassail with our dessert?" he asked. "The gingerbread is from the restaurant."

"You didn't make the gingerbread too?" she joked.

"My contribution to a festive meal is wassail." He retreated to the kitchen, then returned with two steaming mugs of wassail and slices of gingerbread on a tray. The consummate host. He set the tray on the coffee table, handed her a mug, and took the other for himself. He tapped a seat beside him on the sofa, waited for her to sit, then settled so close their legs touched.

She sniffed appreciatively. Fruity, spicy aromas rising from the mug conjured images of Christmas. The perfect warm drink for a brisk winter night.

She happily sipped and nibbled. The gingerbread tasted fresh out of the oven—sugary, buttery, and delectable. She expressed her compliments aloud, then added, "You touched on the fact that wassail is a family recipe."

Max smiled, but it was distant and distracted. His forehead tensed, and he gave the impression of wrestling with her statement.

Into the beat of an uncomfortable silence, she said, "I have a surprise for you from Big Brothers Big Sisters. Marge Addyson came by my house." Sarah drew the envelope from her tote bag. "She brought this."

Max frowned and pushed his plate of half-eaten gingerbread to the side. "Which is?"

She noted the hesitation in his voice and dipped her head toward the envelope. "A photo of you when you lived in Cherish. You were … maybe twelve years old?"

He faltered. "Close enough."

"You attended Big Brothers, correct?"

"Every afternoon after school when the Monroes worked

late." He managed a sardonic laugh. "Or rather, when they forgot about me, which was often."

Knowing she might be placing him in an awkward situation, she handed him the envelope with the same care as Marge had handed it to her.

"You don't have to open it if you don't want to," Sarah said.

"I'd like to." Yet he flinched, as if gearing for a disappointment.

He shoved out a breath, then withdrew a black-and-white glossy photograph.

Sarah peered over his shoulder. "Is that you?"

He nodded. The dark-haired boy staring back at them held a stoic expression. His fingers grasped the collar of an enormous dog who stood by his side.

Her heart turned over at the boy's brave demeanor, despite the uncertainty in his eyes. She wanted to hug the photo to her chest, hug the young boy and never let him go.

"Your features haven't changed." Emotions welled inside her, although she managed to keep her tone even. "I'd recognize you anywhere with that determined expression. It's been what, over thirty years?"

Max sipped his wassail, a deceptively casual gesture. "I remember when this was taken, right around Christmas."

"Is that your dog?"

"Not mine. The Monroes." His gaze swung to the parakeets, who perched silently on their swings. "I missed that dog more than anything when I was moved to another foster family. More than I missed the Monroes. Much more."

Sarah swallowed the lump in her throat. "What type of breed was the dog?"

"A Labrador husky." Max rubbed his eyes with his forefinger.

She waited for him to continue, but he showed every sign

of being lost in troubled reflections. He stared at the photo, then looked away.

"What was the dog's name?"

"Tinsel."

She studied the photo. A young Max stood outside Big Brothers Big Sisters. His jeans were five inches too short for his long legs. He looked thin, almost undernourished. But his eyes were warm. Max's eyes.

"Want me to refresh your wassail?" he asked.

"I'm good, thanks." She held a hand over her mug. "Did you want to discuss the photo?"

"Nope. I'm a foster kid, Sarah. I moved around a lot. I had some good foster parents, and some not so good." He choked on the words. "The Monroes were not so good."

"And the family where you learned to make wassail?"

"Mr. Lenny's family."

"Where are they now?"

"He and his wife died. My foster brother, John, lives in Portugal. A few years ago, I gave up trying to stay in touch with him."

"Why?"

"What's the point? He lives so far away." Max didn't move a muscle. He cleared his throat. "Do you suppose it's in a man's best interest to suppress unhappy events, to keep them hidden from the woman he's falling in love with?"

Sarah's cheeks warmed. *Max was talking about her.* "The question is, how can that woman help a man repair those inner hurts?"

"I don't know. Sometimes I want relief from all the past pain." His face was expressionless. "My heritage, or rather, lack of heritage."

Now she understood where his resolve to make something of himself had been formed. It had started with the photo.

Or perhaps years earlier. Perhaps in other photos, in different towns with different families. Perhaps with different pets. And every single heartbreaking situation had strengthened Max with the fortitude to break free and make something of himself.

"Try prayer," she said softly.

"Been there." He linked his hands behind his head and peered at the ceiling pendant. "Done that."

"Try again."

His memories, unwelcome and agonizing, would continue to haunt him until he released them.

He dragged in a breath. "Years ago, I prayed to God to grant my foster brother a successful surgery."

"Go on."

"John only got one shot at a basketball scholarship. I knew how much it meant to Mr. Lenny."

She measured her words. "What happened?"

"God didn't listen. A week before Christmas, John's last surgery left him with a distinct limp and one leg shorter than the other."

"A physical disability." Sarah slid her fingers through Max's. The appeal, the warmth of his hand … this attraction only grew stronger each time they were together. "A handicap."

"Handicap? Ask John how much of a handicap. He didn't attend college. Now he lives in a faraway village, and I haven't seen him in years."

"How did Mr. Lenny react after the failed surgery? You obviously hold him in high esteem."

"He didn't share my anger and frustration at God. He was a pastor—a virtuous and noble man. After listening to my ranting, he reminded me that John was alive and healthy, which was all that mattered."

"Lenny was right."

"At what cost?" Max tore his hand from hers. "Why were the other athletes on John's team strong and whole? He had a promising pro basketball future."

"Lenny was a man of faith."

Max stared straight ahead. He didn't seem aware any longer that she sat beside him. "Lenny declared that John had God on his side and God was all he needed."

"You don't agree?"

"I can't shake my resentment toward a God who plays favorites."

"Try again. Try prayer," she repeated.

"Prayer will make the hurt go away?"

"God will. Reflect on the healing truths of His words every day."

Max lifted his arms and surveyed the room. "I don't see God anywhere."

"Just because you don't see Him, doesn't mean He isn't here."

His expression gradually relaxed, and her chest still ached for him. He had erected a barrier around his heart. A barrier that was impossible to breach until he put aside his resentment and anger.

Pushing up from the sofa, he carried himself stiffly as he walked to the computer.

A moment later, birdsongs floated through the room, the same songs he'd recorded during their hike.

She came to stand close and motioned to the parakeets. "They aren't repeating anything?"

"Nothing. Not even when I play my harmonica."

The single green and white budgie in a wrought iron cage flapped her elegant feathers. In a clear, bell-like voice, she said, "God bless us, everyone."

CHAPTER 9

A few hours later, Sarah headed home.

Max sat on his living room's threadbare carpet and leaned against the sofa.

She was exceptional, fascinating, and extraordinary. More than extraordinary.

The Big Brothers photo had transported him back to the land of unfulfilled dreams. Life with the Monroes had been intolerable, specifically during Max's difficult adolescence.

He wasn't certain why Marge Addyson had gone to the trouble to find that photo and then give it to Sarah. A woman of well-meaning honesty, she may have wanted him to confront past issues in order to move forward.

But he'd done that already, hadn't he? He was accomplished. He'd succeeded in establishing a noteworthy career. Besides, life-altering injustices could never be forgiven.

He shook his head, a rueful smile. His thoughts harbored the very bitterness he thought he'd overcome.

Days ago, Sarah had encouraged him to reflect on the truths of God's word.

"Start with Psalms," she had advised. "The verses will promote healing, comfort and well-being."

"All that?" he questioned.

"All that," she echoed an assurance.

He'd heeded her advice about reading the Bible, although he hadn't told her. It wasn't a subject that came up in daily conversation. Although he could have told her tonight …

Sarah. Sarah. Sarah. They were friends, and there were times when she kept him at arms-length. But there were other times when an electrical current, a snap of lightning, flowed between them. Even when they were a few feet apart, it seemed as if they touched.

He unfolded himself and straightened. He embraced the tranquility he felt when he was with her, and their evening had passed in a blur of laughs and kisses and a hint of rose-wood perfume from her fragrant hair.

Peace was indeed a part of her, a serenity and content-ment he attributed to more than her excitement for the upcoming Christmas season. It was her Christian faith. This woman, this town, was a shift for him, when his daily life was filled with more duties than he could accomplish.

He mentioned as much to Gerry when they met a few days later for an impromptu jam session at Musically Yours. Dorothy had afforded them an after-hours studio, and the men had gratefully accepted.

A grin on his weather-beaten features, his fuzzy eyebrows raised in a tickled question, Gerry responded by saying, "So, you're in love?"

Max pulled back, disconcerted. "Who said that?"

"You did."

"When?"

"By your eyes, words and actions."

Max navigated to safer ground. "You sure you don't mind

meeting here to rehearse? The drive from Perrytown is a haul for you."

"You and I share a passion for music, and rehearsing in person is a blessing."

Max tugged out his harmonica. "I assume your wife is understanding about the hours away from little Freddie?"

"Totally. As long as I'm home by ten o'clock." Gerry set an amp on the floor, then searched for an outlet. He plugged one end of a cable into the amp, the other into the guitar. Snaps and shrill bangs followed, and Gerry switched the volume down.

Because Max lived a few blocks from the store, he had walked, admiring the decorations on the way over, likening them to a Christmas postcard.

The temperature had dropped in the past few days, and blades of grass peeked through a frost of white. Holly bushes were in vibrant red-berry bloom, and blinking red, green, and white lights were everywhere.

He passed a busy coffee shop with folks bustling in and emerging with large cups of hot chocolate topped with creamy whipped cream. Aromas of fresh brewed coffee and toasty chocolate brought scents of the season to mind. A vendor on the corner peddled roasted chestnuts in paper cones. Giggling youngsters ran by him, their laughter high-spirited over the chatter of adults. On side streets, flickering candles gleamed from residences, and vibrant lights from their evergreen trees shone from the windows.

Max never remembered decorating a pine tree, except for the year with Lenny and his family. The snapshot of that one perfect tree, the one perfect Christmas, lived forever in his mind.

When he reached Musically Yours, he was immediately immersed in the harmonies of guitar music sounding from the speakers, the cozy overhead lights, and the warmth of an excellent heating system. After greeting Gerry, who was already there, he asked what they were listening to.

"Joseph Slater's newest worship song, a contemporary Christian arrangement," Gerry noted. "He slowed the tempo, kept the instrumentals simple, and let his voice do the heavy lifting. He's an awesome vocalist."

"Awesome, indeed." Max tilted his head, and allowed the poignant lyrics to wash over him.

"'Mary Did You Know?' is one of my favorite pieces," Gerry said. "Are you aware that the composer took seven years to complete it?"

"Good things are worth the wait, time, and effort," Max replied. "And when you find something good?"

"Never let her go."

Max regarded Gerry. "I'm assuming you mean Sarah?" he asked, and then went on to talk about her in such a way that Gerry told him he was in love.

Gerry brought on a grin and didn't reply.

Focus on the music, Max told himself as Gerry finished tuning his guitar.

They decided on a playlist for their upcoming performance—a medley of carols that included, "O Christmas Tree," "Santa Claus Is Coming To Town," and the finale, "The Twelve Days of Christmas."

"A fun holiday singalong," Gerry said. "For the encore, we'll perform "All Is Well," which is uplifting and inspirational."

"You're certain we'll get enough applause for an encore?"

"Stranger things have happened," Gerry mused while he plucked his guitar. "On another note, my wife and baby are attending. My mother-in-law too."

"How's little Freddie lately?"

"I anticipate my wife's hasty exit after our first song."

"Hopefully, we won't sound that bad."

"We're fairly decent. Besides, my wife deserves a night out."

"With little Freddie," Max reminded with a grin. He pointed to an autographed album hanging on a wall, the cover depicting Joseph Slater and an acoustic guitar. "Musically Yours sure promotes this guy."

"He's a big-name artist who lives in Cherish."

"Joseph settled here," Max mused, arching a single eyebrow.

"Same goes for Ryan Edwards. Love is like a fairy-tale, at least that's what my wife parrots. Joseph met Scarlett when he was here for a music promotion. He decided to put down roots after all those years of touring and married her last year."

"Because of Scarlett, he gave up his career?"

"Hardly. Life is a compromise, my friend, and you're clearly smitten too. Are you still coming to my house on Christmas Day for dinner?"

"Unless you're having second thoughts."

"On the contrary, I'm thinking about inviting my great-niece to join us."

Max beamed. "A tremendous idea."

"I suspected you'd be receptive." Gerry smirked, then leaned back in a wooden chair he'd snagged from the student waiting area. "Now let's rock-and-roll to some favorite Christmas carols."

On the Friday evening of The Bearded Elves' debut, Sarah grabbed a seat at a round table near the band, along with Dorothy, Ryan, Gerry's wife and son and mother-in-law, Nicholas, and Emmanuelle.

She'd dressed with care for the evening—a fit and flare lace dress, strappy-leopard print heels she already wanted to kick off, and sparkly gumdrop-red earrings. She'd topped her outfit with the fine royal blue wool coat she wore on special occasions.

During the past two weeks, lighthearted conversations and dinners with Max at The Garden Terrace, their stolen kisses, their bantering texts, had become routine. Max invited her on another hike, and she'd happily accepted.

Each time they parted, he promised to see or text her the following day.

And he always did.

She should have been joyful. She was. But a heaviness weighed on her spirit because the days flew too quickly. Soon, January would arrive.

Refreshed by endless glasses of sugar-free lemonade, she sang along to the familiar carols with the others, especially during Ryan's sidesplitting rendition of "The Twelve Days Of Christmas."

As he reached the final, "And a partridge in a pear tree," his operatic voice swelled through the restaurant.

Max confirmed his ability as an excellent harmonica player. He'd been too modest, she thought. Whenever he hit an imagined wrong note, he glanced at her with a chagrined smile. The keen, honed bite of blues he produced on such an inexpensive instrument proved him a man of many talents, and pride flowed through her.

Can you believe the tunes a person can produce from such a modest instrument? he had texted a few days earlier. *Wood, two pieces of metal and minute brass reeds.*

The only thing I can play is the radio, she'd texted back in jest, despite his assurances that he would teach her how to read music.

When? she'd wanted to ask. However, she remained silent.

Wait till you hear our encore, he'd responded.

What's the name of the song?

It's an inspirational piece. It'll bring tears to your eyes.

She was seeing a side of him she hadn't envisioned beneath his polka-dotted tie, chambray shirt, and jeans—a look she'd catalogued as distinctly Max.

During each fifteen-minute break between sets, he'd made it a point to sit next to her. He drew her close, his arm draped around her shoulders in a gesture that seemed possessive, but delighted Sarah immeasurably.

After the band's first set, Melissa, the baby, and her mother left. Little Freddie had been fairly well-behaved, and Melissa and her mother had taken turns walking around the restaurant to soothe the baby.

Sarah surprised herself by offering to help. She'd never been an active participant in group situations, and had felt increasingly uncomfortable in even small crowds now—reticent to speak in case she'd misheard someone, and hesitant to ask people to repeat themselves.

In any case, she wasn't used to these feelings—the attention from Max, the joy of being among a welcoming, friendly group. This was camaraderie, sharing jubilant hours with friends and family who cared.

After the rousing rendition of "The Twelve Days of Christmas," Gerry and Max grinned and bowed to enthusiastic applause. As calls for an encore rose, Max stepped down from the small stage. Dorothy stopped him, saying something to him. Sarah couldn't see Dorothy's face, but she could see Max's, and she couldn't resist eavesdropping by reading his lips.

"January first," he seemed to be saying, "I'm eager to leave for Florida and head up an ornithology department."

January. Leave. Eager.

Sarah's stomach tightened.

She half rose in her seat. But no, she shouldn't be

surprised. He'd repeatedly cited his new Jacksonville job. His time in Cherish was temporary.

Unexpectedly weak, she braced her hands on the arms of her chair. She'd been a fool for falling for him. Hoping against hope, while knowing the romance would come to an end in January.

Questions surfaced with no answers. He was a man of his word and had accepted the university position months ago.

Nevertheless, confronting the pain of his departure brought unexpected heartache. They'd never actually discussed him leaving. It was a point in the future neither had chosen to broach.

No matter. She'd slip into the background again, a pattern she'd honed over the years. Loneliness encroached so swiftly she couldn't react, save for tugging on her shoes and scouting out the quickest path to the exit.

She'd been unmoored by the attentions of a stranger. She'd only known him a few weeks. *A few enchanted weeks.*

She swallowed hard and stood to leave as soon as Max and Gerry returned to the stage to more applause. The diners had awarded the men a standing ovation, and the enthusiastic applause soon quieted.

Max angled a glance at her with a broad smile. *Success*, he seemed to say. *Thank you for supporting me and my music.*

She grabbed her coat and turned away, then rounded to glimpse him one last time. His chin drew in, perplexed, as he lifted the harmonica to his lips.

Dorothy caught her hand. "You're leaving? What about the last song?"

"It's later than I thought." Sarah made a show of peering at her watch, aware of how quiet everyone at her table had become. However, she couldn't face another conversation with Max.

From the onset, he'd spoken the truth. Nonetheless, truth

was difficult to confront, especially when it waylaid you at the happiest moment of your life.

Nicholas stood and excused himself from the others. "Sarah, I'll walk you to the door."

"Thanks. I can manage." She veered left, away from him, struggling to keep her emotions in check.

"It's no bother. I have an ulterior motive."

They passed straggling diners, plates of food being cleared from empty tables by tired-looking waitresses, while Max's bluesy harmonica accompanied Gerry's vocals.

"'All is well all is well, … Sing Alleluia.'"

"It'll bring tears to your eyes," Max had said.

And it did.

The lyrics were hopeful and encouraging, and Max harmonized with Gerry, his baritone voice complementing the uplifting words.

A Christian song. Max was singing a Christian song.

"What's your motive?" she asked Nicholas when they reached the entry. "The abandoned puppy?"

"Yep. And if I don't find a home for him, he'll end up in an animal shelter. It's a no-kill shelter, but still …" His words trailed off.

She opened her mouth. Closed it. She was about to refuse when she paused. A darling puppy would be the ideal distraction for her hurt heart.

"I'll take him," she burst out.

"Sarah, thank you! Why did you change your mind?"

"I can't let a lovable puppy spend the holidays in a shelter."

"I'll bring him over to your house in a couple days." Clearly, Nicholas was uncertain whether he'd understood her. "I realize Christmas Eve is almost here …"

"No worries. The puppy has spent too many nights alone already."

CHAPTER 10

On Christmas Eve, Sarah sat alone.

Only for tonight. Tomorrow, she would drive to Perrytown to dine with her great-uncle, his wife, and little Freddie. He'd phoned her, and she'd gratefully accepted the invitation. In years past, she'd spent Christmas Day with her parents and brothers, traveling to their homes in the Carolina mountains. They'd moved away from Cherish, and she was the only one who had remained.

This year, she'd elected to stay home with her growing number of animals.

She had already attended the three o'clock church service. She'd done so purposely, in order not to run into Max, who would be singing in the choir at the six o'clock service. Right about now, he would be entering the church to get ready.

She'd returned from the service invigorated and encouraged. The sermon had touched on how God didn't free people from traumatic situations, but rather, He was there walking with them every step of the way.

Yes, she'd experienced troubles and challenges. However,

any expectations fixed on the Messiah to grant a person's peace came from within. God didn't promise an easy life, and Sarah couldn't experience peace when she had been anticipating a textbook Christmas with the man she loved.

Her mind traveled back to the loving way Max had regarded her—by the river, at the restaurant, in his home. His tenderness when he kissed her.

No. She couldn't allow him into her thoughts anymore. He belonged to the huge, widespread world of birds and his research, not the microscopic town of Cherish.

Yet she'd felt loved and protected when his lips pressed against hers—his strong arms shielding her when they'd encountered that bear.

She hadn't wanted to lose that, the sense of being cherished and safeguarded.

But Max's love was never hers to begin with.

She peered at the roly-poly puppy nestled in his crate. Already, he'd created a wealth of joy in a short period of time.

He was beginning to eat solids, and she'd continued the transition of soaking the food in warm water, then blending it to the texture of gruel. A fresh supply of water was ever present.

The past couple days, she'd brought his toys into her home first for the other animals to sniff. When the puppy arrived, the dogs ignored him except for an occasional sniff. She'd rewarded their unaggressive behavior with upbeat praise, and had placed the resident dogs' toys and food bowls in a separate location.

Likewise, the cats wandered over for a sniff, then dismissed the puppy.

Sarah's goal was to allow the animals to learn to trust each other. So far, so good.

She switched on a holiday radio station, and The Mormon Tabernacle choir sang "Adeste Fideles" in Latin.

Max would've appreciated the arrangement. He was so musical.

Sighing, she looked at the framed photo on her side table. When she had finally scrolled through the photos she'd taken with her cell phone the day of their hike, she found a wonderful one of Max. It was a profile picture. His face had been near the camera, and every handsome quality was evident—the dark stubble of his beard, his silver-gray eyes, his determined demeanor.

She'd also gotten a surprisingly good photo of the bear. She'd auto-merged them into a silly collage, the bear and Max staring at each other, eye to eye.

She'd planned to gift him the photo and had bought a wooden frame depicting the great outdoors with the words Into the Woods on it. She'd captioned the photo, "I knew we were safe all along."

Max's words.

She would never hear his voice again. She squeezed her eyes shut and took a deep breath. "I love you, Max," she murmured, vowing to rely on time and faith to heal her broken heart.

She slid the photo into a bag and placed it in a drawer in the side table.

As MAX LOOKED around the church on Christmas Eve from his vantage point on the top riser, his heart dropped. He scanned the pews—the exquisitely appointed windows and altars bedecked with the brilliant display of flowers that Sarah had arranged. But Sarah was not there.

"Surely, she'll attend church," he muttered to Gerry, as the men took their places in the baritone section.

Marge Addyson, standing near the altar, turned. "She attended the earlier service," she said.

She did? Why?

Two days ago, Sarah had left The Garden Terrace before The Bearded Elves' performance was over and without a farewell. Thereafter, Max's phone calls and voice mails had gone unanswered.

The previous morning, he'd stopped by the nursery. Her coworker, Bonnie, declared that Sarah was in the greenhouse dealing with seedlings and couldn't be disturbed.

The service ended with the cantata and Max's harmonica solo. When the service was over, he exited the church with his heart touched and his spirits lifted. The sermon had delivered a message of optimistic goodwill.

"God's son appeared in the least likely situation and to humble people," the pastor had addressed the congregation. "Forgive and let your resentments go. What will prevent your happiness is to strive for perfection in yourself and others."

Hadn't Max always sought excellence? Blame it on his upbringing, but he'd endeavored to become top-notch in his profession. But what good was that perfection without someone to love?

Unwilling to accept the end of their relationship, he strode from the church to Sarah's house. In a short time, he'd become accustomed to small-town living, where most places were within a few blocks' walking distance. He'd purchased a special present for her and held the package securely under his arm.

When he reached her house, he stood silently on her front porch. Although he didn't move, wild barking sounded from inside before he could even knock.

Then the barking ceased.

He knocked, hesitant to ring her doorbell. Okay, maybe

he shouldn't have dropped by unannounced, but what else could he do when she kept slipping away from him?

Suppose she was sleeping?

At eight o'clock on a clear and cold Christmas Eve? Sarah? Unless she wasn't home … But where …

Tiny yelps sounded. A yipping.

The door opened a crack, and a wobbly puppy shoved his nose through the opening, wagging a fluffy white tail.

Sarah scooped up the puppy, then gasped as she stood in the doorway. "Max?"

"Merry Christmas."

"How long were you standing on the porch?"

He shrugged. "A while."

"What were you doing?"

"Praying."

"Praying? What are you praying for? An extraordinary gift on Christmas Eve?"

"I'm praying for the most extraordinary of gifts. You."

Her striking green eyes glistened with tears, her features a flood of emotions. "Merry Christmas."

"May I come in?" She couldn't just stand at the door holding a puppy.

"Yes. Please."

He stepped inside and brushed a kiss across her temple. She cuddled the tiny Yorkipoo to her chest. He grinned at the pom-pom tail, the paws reminding him of a hedgehog, and the molten-brown eyes peeking beneath half-closed lids. Perhaps he wasn't a Yorkipoo …

"Apparently, Sheriff Nicholas convinced you?" Max asked as he stroked the puppy's velvety fur.

"Careful," she warned. "His teeth are like little needles." She set the puppy inside a blanketed crate. The two older dogs settled. The cats walked away.

And Sarah walked into Max's embrace.

He drew her closer, pressing his lips to hers, fearful to break the hold for fear she might disappear.

When the kiss ended, she rubbed her cheek against his jacket. "I'm glad you're here."

Her home wasn't decorated for the holidays, which surprised him, considering her festive porch.

"My fake tree and ornaments are in the attic." She seemed to read his mind. "I haven't had time."

Or rather, had she felt like him, and didn't have the heart to decorate?

She was gorgeous in a crimson cashmere sweater and form-fitting black pants. Her figure was trim with curves, a wreath of dark russet curls framed her perfect face.

"I do have appropriate holiday cookies and eggnog, if you're interested," she said. "And both were bought from the grocery store."

They shared another commonality besides coffee and hiking and a love for animals. They appreciated store-bought items when homemade wasn't an option. Or, he supposed, even if it was.

He smiled, removed his jacket, and adjusted his bow tie. For the Christmas Eve service, he'd elected to wear black dress pants and a crisp white shirt.

"Can I be direct?" he asked, after she'd taken a jug out of the refrigerator, poured him a glass of eggnog, and set out a platter of frosted vanilla sugar cookies in the shape of snowmen.

"I wouldn't expect anything else."

He placed his gift on the coffee table. He'd wrapped it in plain brown paper tied with twine, topped with a green and white parakeet ornament.

"Why did you leave the restaurant without saying good-bye?" His hand slid up her arm in a caress. "Furthermore, why were you avoiding me? Is my singing that bad?"

She smiled. "No."

"I'd like to continue seeing you."

She fixed her gaze on a point beyond him. "I can't deal with a long-distance relationship and you're leaving for Jacksonville in a week."

He heard the hurt in her tone. His gaze stayed on her.

He invited her to sit on the sofa in the living room and he settled beside her. "Who said I was moving to Jacksonville?"

"You've mentioned little else since you arrived in Cherish. The other night at The Garden Terrace when you spoke with Dorothy, you declared your eagerness to leave for Florida in January and head an ornithology department."

And then it hit him. Sarah cared about him. Deeply. So deeply, she couldn't face him leaving.

And he was delighted.

He pulled her nearer. "I said I was eager to greet the new head of the ornithology department in Florida in January."

She blinked. "I don't understand."

"I declined the position. The latest candidate is a colleague from my New York university days who's done amazing research on zebra finches. She's a workaholic and will be an excellent fit."

"So much for my lip-reading abilities. And eavesdropping." Sarah sat straighter. "You didn't accept the position?"

"No."

"I made an appointment with an audiologist to test my hearing. I've read that I won't be as fatigued at the end of the day if I haven't had to struggle with the effort of listening."

"If you indeed have a hearing loss, it should be addressed." Max smoothed his lips over her hair. "I should've been clearer about my feelings. I would've been if you hadn't vanished."

"I haven't gone anywhere."

"This project has involved numerous researchers working

around the world. My bit with budgies is only a small part of the larger study on birdsongs."

"And?"

"The paper will take a couple years to complete, especially as current research sends scientists in different directions. Which means I'm not going anywhere. I can continue my research here and will receive a full-time salary."

"You're staying in Cherish?"

"I renewed my lease on 8 Poplar Lane."

"Does this mean more hiking adventures?"

"Weekly." He grinned. "This place, and you, have allowed me to slow down and reflect. However, I will have to travel to Jacksonville twice a semester to meet with other members of the department. I'm hoping you'll accompany me."

"I'd love to."

"I'd also like to visit the university I attended in New York."

"I've never seen a big city."

"New York is filled with diversity, culture, and excitement. I'll take you to see the famous landmarks."

"I'd like that," she said softly.

"And I have a brother in Portugal."

"Yes."

"I need to reach out to him again. If he invites us to travel to Portugal to visit him, will you accompany me?"

She nodded. "Happily."

"Good." He peered upward. "Where's your attic?"

"You're looking in the right direction."

"I've only decorated a Christmas tree once in my life—with Lenny and his family."

"Is that a hint?"

"A broad hint. But first." He nodded to his gift.

Glancing at him, she unraveled the twine. In the box was

an ornament—a bear, hiker boots and the inscription, "Take a hike."

She smiled, smoothed her fingers over the words, then curled near him. "You remembered?"

"Of course. After numerous phone requests to the ranger, a shipment finally arrived."

"Thank you." She slid open a drawer in the table beside her and handed him a bag. "I'm sorry it isn't wrapped. By the time the order arrived, I assumed I'd never see you again."

"Yet here I am." He pulled the frame out of the bag and read aloud her caption. "I knew we were safe all along."

"Because we'll do life together."

For a long while, he held her. "I missed you at church tonight. Mrs. Addyson remarked on the preacher's outstanding sermon."

"Yes. I thought so too."

"I played the harmonica. The choir was beautiful."

"I'm sure they were. I'm sure you were awesome."

"You'll hear me play and sing again because I joined the choir." He tipped back his head, as if he were gazing toward heaven. "I was distracted—by my bitterness, and by life. I'm starting to realize that God is for me, not against me. My perspective was messed up, but finally, at forty, I'm seeing more clearly."

"God has always been your champion. He is never against you."

She whispered a word of praise, and Max joined in.

"Gerry declared that dinner tomorrow is at two o'clock, give or take a few hours," she said.

He returned her smile. "He told me the same. I guess it depends on little Freddie's schedule."

She hesitated. "I didn't realize you were dining there too."

"He didn't mention it?" Max chuckled. "He must've forgotten when he phoned you."

"You knew he called?"

"I stood next to him when he made the phone call."

"So, you figured between tonight and tomorrow, we'd see each other?"

"That's one of the things I love about Christmas. All this togetherness." He reached for his jacket and pulled out a handful of wildflowers from his pocket—intense violets and pale blue ivy. "These grow at the edge of town. I'm impressed that plants bloom here in the winter. I'd forgotten. In any event, I picked them for you. Sorry they're wilted."

"They're not. They're beautiful."

He muffled her protest with a deep kiss and drew her into his arms. "I can't give you much, but I'll give you my love."

"I love you too."

The puppy whimpered, and Sarah freed him from his crate and nestled him in her arms. When Max extended his hands, she placed the tiny bundle in his lap.

"What's his name?" he asked.

"Tiny Tim."

Max swallowed the thickness in his throat, the emotions overcoming him.

He drew Sarah near. She was all he needed, all he'd been searching for. The woman he loved by his side, a reverence for a God who was no longer elusive, and a significant, heartwarming Christmas.

"Merry Christmas, Max," Sarah whispered. "And God bless us, every one."

The End

AMANDA'S EASY WASSAIL

Ingredients:

2 cups apple juice
  2 cups orange juice
  2 cups cranberry juice
  2 cinnamon sticks

Add everything to a crockpot, mix, and warm until the desired temperature is reached.

For a larger batch: (almost a gallon)

5 cups apple juice
  5 cups orange juice
  5 cups cranberry juice
  3 or 4 cinnamon sticks, as desired
  Enjoy!

A NOTE FROM JOSIE

Thank you for reading my holiday romance, A Christmas Puppy To Cherish. I hope you enjoyed this heartwarming, inspirational story. This is the fourth book in my contemporary "Cherish" series.

You don't need ears to hear God's plan. All you need is an open heart...

This story is set in the charming fictional small town of Cherish, South Carolina. The book follows A Love Song To Cherish, A Christmas To Cherish, and A Valentine To Cherish.

In A Christmas Puppy To Cherish, I introduce two new characters to our beloved mix of familiar heroes and heroines. Many of you may know that music is an important part of my life, and many of the characters are musicians.

I also researched the hero, Maxwell's, fascinating profession of ornithology. (The study of birds.)

And the heroine, Sarah, with her kind heart, is the perfect match for him.

If you loved this story as much as I loved writing it, please help other people find it by posting your review.

A Christmas Puppy To Cherish is available in ebook, Paperback, Hardcover, Large Print Paperback, and Audiobook.

My Spotify List for A Christmas Puppy To Cherish is here.

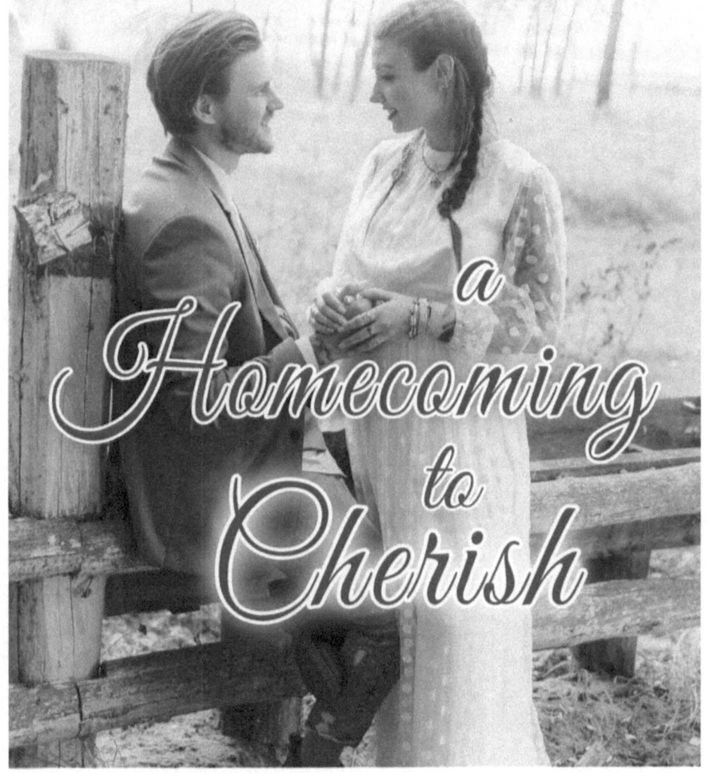

USA TODAY BEST-SELLING AUTHOR
JOSIE RIVIERA
a Homecoming to Cherish

PRAISE AND AWARDS

USA TODAY bestselling author

#25 Amazon Bestseller Religious Romance
#38 Amazon Bestseller Contemporary Religious Fiction

CHAPTER 1

"You expect us to live here, in this stuffy little town with one traffic light?" Samantha, Nora Lancaster's fifteen-year-old daughter, stood on the steps of the Cherish Hills Inn, arms crossed, wearing her infamous, *I'm bored,* pout. The hot-pink beanie that she wore no matter the weather, sat askew on her head, a whimsical contrast to her black curly hair.

"Why? What's wrong with Cherish?" With an encouraging smile, Nora surveyed the inn. "Wow. The exterior is still painted white."

"Actually, the paint is peeling, Mom, though I wasn't talking about the inn. I was referring to the town."

"We're only here for a month," Nora replied.

"An entire month without seeing my boyfriend! Four whole weeks."

"What's his name again? Eric?"

"Edison."

"I can't keep track. Your boyfriends change regularly."

"Edison is awesome."

"Edison. Like the lightbulb?"

"Yeah, Mom, he's a lightbulb." Samantha breezed past her mother's comment. "He's the cutest boy in the senior class, and his parents are allowing him to drive to Cherish so we can study together. They're buying him a car for his eighteenth birthday."

"Because he invented the lightbulb?"

"Not funny, Mom." Nora had learned to ignore her daughter's eye rolls, though it was still difficult. "I'll turn sixteen soon, and then I'll be able to get my license too."

"Whoa. Backpedal. Study for what? You completed your school term early."

Samantha and a boy alone in a car, plus the idea of Samantha driving set off heart palpitations.

However, Nora had felt the same way when she was only a few years older than Samantha was now. She'd wanted her independence. Once she became a teen, she'd counted the days until she could hightail it out of Cherish. Lifting heavy linens, changing beds in the inn's guestrooms, and fatigue had taken its toll. Along with school, no opportunity remained for fun, extracurricular activities.

She'd appreciated the supportive encouragement from her parents, and the camaraderie with the inn's handful of workers had resulted in friendships. However, at the end of the day, friendship hadn't been enough. Nora had slaved at the inn all those hours … for what? An inn repeatedly on the brink of bankruptcy?

Luckily, she'd never been a boy-crazy teenager.

Or had she?

Nora's gaze strayed to Samantha's precocious smile, and her heart swelled. Oversized hoop earrings and a silver-studded belt were expressions of Samantha's personality, but didn't take away from her fresh-faced beauty. People remarked that mother and daughter were mirror images, although Samantha was slim, whereas Nora carried twenty extra pounds on her five-foot-eight-inch frame.

"This little town isn't how I remembered." She grinned at her fond childhood memories—skipping in the park, playing hopscotch with friends after school, and eating Dutch chocolate ice cream at the local ice cream parlor.

Truth be told, her younger days had been filled with happiness. This self-contained community of Cherish, which she'd termed claustrophobic once she hit her teens, embraced respectability and decency. What was wrong with that?

However, to sustain the anger toward her parents, Nora had zeroed in on the disagreeable moments. She'd shut the door on the pleasant times and locked her heart, simpler than confronting her weariness and frustration.

"How do you remember the town?" Samantha seemed suddenly talkative.

"Short-sighted." Nora searched for a better answer, though none came.

"Which was what, thirty years ago, Mom?"

"More like fifteen, honey. I'm not that ancient." Nora pinned on a smile, grabbed Samantha's hand, and mounted the expansive porch stairs to the front door of the inn. As expected, Samantha tugged free from her grip.

I could use some help with this young woman, Nora thought. Similar to most teens, Samantha wanted to fit in while asserting her individuality. On a good day, Nora glimpsed her daughter's former sweet self, though she'd quickly close up, perhaps for fear of sharing too much. An image of a giggling, pudgy-cheeked toddler surfaced. Where had her pleasant little girl gone?

"Look at it this way." Nora kept her smile. "You completed the semester early, so now you'll enjoy a longer summer recess."

"Enjoy? Here? I didn't mind getting out of dull, boring school, but living in Cherish for a month isn't a vacation."

"I didn't say it was. I suggested it was an opportunity." Nora turned to take in the picturesque street—the rows of flowering trees, the orange daylilies lining the sidewalk, the cheerful *Good mornings* from folks passing by. Why hadn't she appreciated the joy of ordinary life in this quaint town? Lately, her accounting job in Richmond had carried more and more responsibility and later evenings.

It was wrong, she knew it was wrong, to agree to overtime instead of spending the evenings with her daughter. Even so, Nora was the lone parent who paid the bills.

"An opportunity to work with no salary?" Samantha challenged her.

"Volunteer work is the best kind." Nora turned to her daughter. "Besides, where else would you rather be?"

"Back home in Virginia." A frown from Samantha. "Or sunny Florida, or an exotic island in the Pacific."

"I'll keep it in mind," Nora replied with a teasing laugh.

They both knew that wouldn't happen. Nora was fortunate to have an excellent paying job, a lucrative career. Nevertheless, she still struggled financially.

The door of the inn opened, revealing a skinny, elderly man with stark-white hair. A scowl took over his vein-reddened features.

Nora shouldered her purse and came forward. "Hi. Mr. Canning?"

He shoved up his cheater eyeglasses. "Call me Tom."

Scarcely the greeting Nora had hoped for. Her shoulder muscles tightened as she approached. "Hello, Tom. I'm Nora Lancaster. We spoke several times on the phone." She twisted, revealing her daughter standing behind her. "And this is Samantha."

"Hi." Samantha gave a half-hearted wave.

"I figured." Tom rolled up the sleeves of his tan-colored shirt, exposing thin, pointy elbows. "You're the woman who wants to take my inn away from me."

"Hardly," Nora said. "I'm … I mean *we're* here to help with any work required around the inn until you're fully recovered."

She didn't dare make eye contact with her daughter, assuming Samantha's over-tweezed eyebrows were raised. Lately, the words *help* and *work* weren't in her daughter's vocabulary.

"I'm standing here," Tom was saying. "I am recovered, and I told you not to come."

"And I told you I was coming, regardless. Heart attacks require rest and recuperation, and you spent only three days in the hospital."

"Are you spying on me?"

"On the contrary, I'm concerned."

He scowled. "Nowadays, hospitals don't keep patients any longer than necessary."

"True." Nora regarded his pale features, the stoop of his shoulders. "Nonetheless, you can neither rest nor recuperate if you're operating this place by yourself."

"My employee, Louise, has been with me a decade," Tom replied. "I can't run the inn without her."

"I'm certain she's a hard worker, notwithstanding the fact that your large inn requires more help."

"Are you a doctor?"

"I'm an accountant." Nora shifted. "However, I can visualize every corner of the inn because I worked here nonstop when I was younger. I'm also familiar with the community mindset, and from what I've observed so far, nothing has changed."

"Precisely how the townsfolk like it."

"I remember when my parents wrote to tell me they'd

sold the inn to you. I want to make certain you don't lose it as they did."

The warm June air stilled. Nora chastised herself for speaking her fears aloud.

"Are you saying I'm not capable of running my own inn?" Tom asked. "I bought this place from them, fair and square."

Nora breathed in. She should be patient and tactful. She had had enough conversations with Tom to know he was hard on himself for not being able to do what he used to in his younger days.

"My offer comes with no obligation," she said. "You know, it's okay to accept help from someone who cares."

He raised his milk-white eyebrows at Samantha. "There won't be much for a young person to do."

Samantha grunted her assent.

"She's ambitious," Nora put in. "She's able."

"Right." His tone reflected precisely the opposite. "Decades have passed. Doesn't mean you have a legal claim to the inn now."

"I never suggested that."

He blew out a loud breath. "I was surprised when you contacted me."

"I understand. I've simply kept an eye on it all these years."

"Why?"

"Because it was a part of my every waking hour while I was growing up. Besides ..."

She shifted.

Nope. Not going there. Some subjects were too personal. Guilt rose—brought on by the urgency to fix what she'd come to regret.

He inspected her from head to toe. "I don't remember the likes of you when I bought the place."

"I'd left by then." She curled her fingers around the strap of her handbag. "Moved out of town and got married."

"Your parents were nice people."

Were being the operative word.

She swallowed. "They died in a car accident not long after they sold the inn to you."

"I'm sorry."

"Me too."

"Where's your husband?" He peered here and there, as if a husband might miraculously appear.

"We've been divorced for many years." Nora shoved past the troublesome thoughts whenever a conversation alluded to her ex. Samantha didn't seem to care that she'd never known her father. He'd left when she was an infant.

"Uh, huh," Tom said.

Somehow, Nora felt like her lack of a partner was a strike against her.

Please Lord, don't let Tom turn me aside.

Why was a prayer coming to mind? She'd avoided religion for years.

"I … we can pretty much handle any chores and duties." Nora concentrated on Tom. "My accounting background and experience can't hurt either."

"I'll admit your timing is excellent." He closed his mouth, then opened it again. "Mondays are slow, and only a few guests are here."

She patted her daughter's shoulder. "We're ready to assist and can start immediately."

"Tomorrow, eight more guests are arriving." Tom tilted his head to the side. "Three are an advance team from Fresh 'n' Good, a high-end chain that might open a new restaurant in town."

"I've heard of them. One of their restaurants is near us in Virginia."

"Probably several." Tom snorted. "One guy from the chain has already arrived."

"You offer dining here too. I saw that on your website, clicked on all the photos."

"I should update the website." Tom scratched his head. "I usually rely on one of the busboys to do it. Teenagers can do these things in a snap."

Nora nodded. "Nowadays, guests expect up-to-date information." She didn't add that the website was outmoded.

"My restaurant has been a success up till now," Tom went on. "We're little, though, and Fresh 'n' Good is big." He tugged on the hem of his crewneck sweater. "C'mon inside. Photos are fine, but showing you the inn is better. Besides, I ought to sit down."

"Our luggage is in my car."

"No one will steal it. I figured you were hard-headed and would come anyway, so I asked Louise to prepare rooms for you upstairs."

Nora and Samantha followed him through the carpeted hallway to an expansive parlor, and the fragrant traces of flowers filled the space. A glass vase of crimson roses was set on a cherry wood table, and sunlight gleamed through the front window. Defining the seating area, a cornflower-blue tapestry rug covered a portion of the oak wood floor.

He waited while Nora and Samantha settled on an overstuffed sofa. With a slight groan, he sagged into the chair across from them. Life-sized ceramic roosters faced each other on the mantel of the stacked rock fireplace.

The interior was a bit dusty and messy, and countless knickknacks added a colonial-flavored clutter to the space. In fact, both the interior and exterior screamed for a thorough cleaning and update. Old-fashioned dark paneling covered two walls, and the plaid patterned wallpaper on the other ones created a folksy flavor that might not appeal to the current market.

Nora folded her hands on her lap. "Will the new restaurant threaten the livelihood of existing local eateries like yours?"

"Maybe. Maybe not. We pride ourselves on our signature desserts, all prepared in house." He hesitated, though not for long. "You mentioned you could begin immediately."

"Immediately?" Samantha, who had been busy scrolling through her cellphone, came to full attention.

Tom stared out the window, away from them. "The doctor advised me not to do anything too physical this month," he mumbled.

"Sound advice." Nora stood. "We'll grab our luggage, freshen up, and start in an hour."

She ignored the gasp from her daughter. Instead, she signaled Samantha to follow her to the car to help carry the luggage.

CHAPTER 2

An hour later, Nora and Samantha had unpacked, showered and changed. Tom had allotted each of them their own bedroom and bathroom, with an adjoining door between. Nora's room, with forest-green walls, an oval braided rug, and a hand-stitched quilt draped over a rocking chair, was pleasant. However, she mentally removed the rooster painting over the bed as well as the farmhouse pillows. She envisioned the heavy draperies replaced with sheer window coverings to allow more natural light, and provide a sleeker, more modern design.

She wasn't here to redecorate; she reminded herself, only to help Tom.

She'd made the offer ahead of time that no money would be exchanged, and she and Samantha would work in payment for rent and food. Now, Tom had accepted the agreement.

When she and Samantha returned to the lobby, Tom introduced them to Louise, a plump, pear-shaped woman. She was in charge of cleaning and kept the inn running behind the scenes.

Lightly, he touched Louise's shoulder. "She's my peach cake."

She reciprocated with a playful punch to his arm. "You're the kindest man in the world."

He smiled, a huge smile earmarked only for Louise, then excused himself to retire to his suite.

"You're both angels and an answer to my prayers." Louise said. She secured a wiry strand of silver hair into her bun while surveying Nora and Samantha. Her demeanor was kind, her hazel eyes thoughtful. She ran her palm along the stairwell's dusty bannister. "Maintaining this place is becoming more and more difficult. It used to be easy, though not so much anymore."

"We're hardly angels," Nora murmured. She'd forgotten so many of the town's residents regarded Christian faith as paramount. Her brain ushered recollections of Sunday services at Memorial Street Church. She wondered if Marge Addyson was still the associate pastor.

Whatever the case, Nora wasn't venturing down the religion road again, save for a quick need-filled prayer now and then. God hadn't been happy with her decision to desert her parents.

She pushed out a breath and focused on what Louise was saying.

"We're in fine shape for the evening, except for some last-minute tidying and wiping down the furniture." Louise's Southern accent was thick as molasses. "We're state-of-the-art and clean with microfiber cloths."

Hardly state-of-the-art, though Nora wasn't about to correct the pleasant woman.

"Tom employs a kitchen staff," Louise continued. "They can use help in the dining room tonight because a server is out sick, and I bet your daughter would be perfect for waitressing."

Samantha nearly melted into the elderly woman's encouraging hug, and a whiff of powder and orange blossoms filled Nora's nostrils. Louise was the epitome of the grandmother Samantha had never known, and they seemed to form an instant connection.

"I haven't waitressed in years," Nora replied. "My daughter never has."

"There are only a couple of guests along with one of the restaurant people who arrived earlier today."

"Tom mentioned someone was already here from the team," Nora said, as they followed Louise to the entrance of the dining rom.

"His name is Julian Wilson." Louise flicked her gaze to a corner table, and Nora regarded the man.

He wore khaki pants and a dressy button-down shirt. His frame was solid and well-built.

He seemed to realize she was looking, because he turned. He smiled as their gazes met, a smile so genuine it brought heat to her cheeks and a skip to her heartbeat.

Oh my. A pleasing yet bewildering rush stirred her pulse.

He was masculine and utterly in control. She wasn't sure how she knew that. Perhaps because of his well-defined jaw, thick, reddish-brown hair, and handsome features.

"Mr. Wilson is a bigwig," Louise pronounced.

Nora shifted. "An owner?"

"A top manager. He oversees and manages Fresh 'n' Good's new restaurants, which are always successful."

Nora fastened a smile on her face. "I can help with the serving, but let me warn you waitressing isn't my strong suit." She had a tendency toward clumsiness. Nevertheless, surely she could balance a tray and take food orders with only a handful of patrons.

"I'll observe tonight," Samantha put in.

Nora couldn't immediately disagree. "Okay, although be

prepared to roll up your sleeves tomorrow." With a half-hearted nod, she steered Samantha into the dining room. "And remove your beanie."

Nora's sensible tan loafers sank into the plush, silver-gray carpet. Splashes of color on the walls—from dove gray to dusty coral—enhanced the décor.

Tom had built on the restaurant after he'd purchased the inn from her parents. Considering the flickering candles, the mouth-watering aroma of rib roasts from the nearby kitchen, and the polished wooden floors, he'd created a remarkably appealing ambiance. She wondered if he'd used an interior decorator.

Samantha headed to the nearest empty table, slunk into a chair, and shrugged off her hoodie. With her inky-black hair and fair complexion, she was an attractive young woman, although she hid her beauty beneath oversized clothes.

Nora donned a red-checkered apron over her dark slacks and yellow blouse. Encouraged by Louise, she approached Julian's table.

"Good evening." Nora fixed a smile and extracted a notepad and pencil from her apron. "I'm Nora, and I'll be your server. May I start you with a glass of wine?"

He peered up from his menu. "Water is fine, thanks."

Time stopped.

Up close, he was even more attractive. Surely it wasn't legal for a man to be this good-looking. His close-shaven jawline proved even stronger than from a distance. His full lips had tugged into a smile, but it was his startling gray eyes that interrupted her breathing.

His gaze appraised her. "What do you suggest for a main course?"

She paused, giving her nerves a chance to calm and her brain a second to stop racing. "The entire cuisine is delicious and Chef George is agreeable."

She hadn't met the chef, though surely he was … agreeable. She hadn't heard him bark orders or throw pots at the cooks. Was he proficient or was he a chef who couldn't tell the difference between butter and margarine?

Julian blinked. "So he's … agreeable?"

"Oh, I'm certain. What's more, all our desserts are prepared in-house. Plus this dining room—the candles, the subtle gray color—is delightful."

She sounded like a Realtor trying to sell him the dining room.

"So far, everything is charming." He studied her face. "The rooster stoneware, though, is surely from another era."

"They're still in style."

"Roosters?" He grinned. "Maybe, if you're aiming for a family-friendly and more feminine appeal."

"What's wrong with feminine?"

He caught her stare and held it. "Absolutely nothing."

Was he flirting with her? No, he couldn't be. She leaned away, attempting to make herself look smaller. Not easy in her case.

She skirted a glance toward her daughter, who mouthed, "You're embarrassing me."

Nora drew herself up straighter. "In truth, sir, I haven't eaten here yet. Perhaps try the Cherish Inn special?" She'd noted the entrée on the sideboard. "Rib roast simmered in brown gravy, served with garden vegetables."

He perused the menu again. A grin twitched at the corner of his mouth. "Suppose I told you I was a vegetarian?"

"Oh."

Really? A vegetarian? She mentally ran through a list of options. "Then I'd recommend the … garden vegetables."

"I'll take the rib roast special."

"Wait. What? Aren't you a vegetarian?"

"Not tonight." He chuckled. "Actually, not any night."

"Neither am I. I love BLTs."

Her face heated. Now why had she blurted such a thing? He'd probably realize bacon was the reason why she couldn't shed her extra weight.

"Are you doubling as a comedian?" she asked.

"Evidently not a funny one," he said. "I flew into Atlanta early this morning, then boarded a train here. Will pleading travel fatigue dignify my remark?"

"I arrived this afternoon too."

"May I apologize, then?"

"Apology accepted, although you weren't rude." She didn't know how else to respond. "Where were you before Atlanta?"

He gazed toward the ceiling. "Mars."

Her eyes widened and she smiled. She could joke. She could make small talk. "Anywhere a little closer?"

"I rent an apartment in Pennsylvania." He cocked his head. "You?"

"Virginia. I drove here."

"You rent?"

"All I can afford," she replied.

"I'm Julian Wilson."

"Nora Lancaster."

She returned to refill his water glass. When dinner arrived and she'd placed it in front of him, he closed his eyes, clasped his hands together, and whispered a prayer of grace.

She tried to remember when she'd last expressed thanks to God for a meal. It had been a long, long time. Why wasn't her faith as effortless as Julian's apparently was?

Thirty minutes earlier, Nora had been congratulating herself that she'd managed not to spill food on any of the guests, although she had mixed up some orders, including Julian's. And there was the glass of water that had slid off her tray when she half-tripped over the carpet. Water splattered in all directions, barely missing Julian, and she'd fastened her fingers to his table to steady herself.

"No worries," he'd murmured when she knelt on the floor to clean up the mess, saying sorry. He bent to assist her, blotting water and ice with his napkin. "I've spilled food and beverages too numerous to mention. Most haven't been easy clean-ups."

They were nearly nose to nose, and their hands touched. This close, his aftershave, a spicy-woodsy combo, sent a tingling sensation through her. Now why on earth would aftershave have such an effect? Or was it his fingers?

Abruptly, she drew in a breath.

Perhaps it wasn't the aftershave. Perhaps it was the man wearing the aftershave. Hastily, she grabbed several more cloth napkins and kept blotting. Even though they were now crouched several inches apart, that slight brush of his fingers still lingered.

You're his waitress cleaning a spill that could've left him drenched. He didn't invite you to spend a week in Hawaii with him, thus there's no reason to be flustered.

She glanced up.

He didn't attempt to hide his grin. "Did you hear me?"

"Of course." *Of course she hadn't.*

"Want to know what else I've spilled?"

"Sure."

"A full mug of coffee on a porcelain white countertop that is now eternally stained."

"Weren't your countertops sealed when they were installed?"

"I assumed so."

She dropped the sodden napkins on her tray. "Try making a paste. Combine dishwashing liquid with a cup of flour and water. Mix it together, then apply it to the stain and cover it with plastic wrap. Scrape off the paste and rinse with water."

"Thanks." He quirked a rueful eyebrow. "Did the same thing happen to one of your countertops?"

"Yes. The stain was from grape juice."

Brilliant, Nora. This is not the occasion to have a conversation about cleaning methods, while mopping up water on the carpet in a public restaurant—especially with a man you're supposed to be impressing.

She peered at her daughter. She was tipped forward in her chair, fixated on her phone, undoubtedly playing video games and texting. Why had she consented to Samantha's constant requests to have her ears pierced? One earring, okay, but three in each ear?

Well aware that Samantha still managed to keep a critical eye on her, Nora wasn't surprised when Samantha cut her gaze to hers and pressed out a long sigh.

"Your daughter?" Julian extended his hand to assist Nora as they stood. She was a tall woman, but he was taller. She estimated he stood at six foot two. His crisply pressed shirt, open at the throat, emphasized the breadth of his shoulders.

Her heartbeat again picked up speed. She let go of his hand, breathed in, and flattened her apron. "How can you tell?"

Samantha had plucked a slice of bread from the basket Nora had set on her table and began buttering it. She was examining the menu.

"Three reasons." Julian's gray eyes danced with humor. "To begin with, her features are the spitting image of yours. Is your husband with you?"

"I'm not married."

"What's your daughter's name?"

"Samantha."

He nodded. "Nice name."

"And the second reason?" Nora asked.

"You're both beautiful."

"Wow. A pickup line I haven't heard in years."

He didn't miss a beat. "I thought it was ingenious."

Quietly, she laughed. "Another word for smart?"

"Another word for it's the truth."

"That's three words."

He grinned. He was definitely likable. "Plus, your cleaning tip was spoken like a mother with experience."

Though motherly experience might be the death of her.

"Third, you and your daughter have a silent communication."

"You noted our exasperated glares at each other?"

He chuckled. "Is she strong-willed?"

"Let's say she's bordering on persistent when she wants her way."

"She's a blessing," he said. "Her tenaciousness will lead to confidence. Our troubled world needs resilient young leaders."

"In the meantime, the season she's in is challenging." From the corner of her eye, Nora glimpsed Samantha glowering at her, as if warning her mother not to utter another word to this strange man.

But he wasn't a stranger. Nora knew his name, knew where he was from.

He laughed, displaying white teeth and a dimple on his chin. "I didn't mean to stare at you both. I confess it's my pastime."

"What is?"

"Studying people. Their actions and interactions. All folks are fascinating, and I find it essential to gauge people's likes and dislikes when running a restaurant."

"Nothing much exciting goes on here, I assure you."

He brought his measured gaze to hers. "I beg to differ."

She peeked at his left hand, relieved he didn't wear a wedding band.

"I'm not married." Apparently, he read her mind. Or caught her not-so-subtle glance at his hand. "Nor am I a creep who hits on women."

Okay, so he was honest. And good-looking. Thoughts surfaced about spending time with a guy that hadn't surfaced in decades.

"Do you?" she asked with a tease in her voice.

"Do I what?"

"Beg to differ. Are you usually argumentative?"

"No, though I'm known to pursue what I want."

Another pickup line. Was he referring to the new restaurant? Or to her?

No. Nope. Nay.

He was obviously a man who'd honed his charisma. Most likely, numerous females in … where was he from again? Pennsylvania? … seized any opportunity to swoon over his charms.

Nora spun to wait on another table.

"Medium rare," Julian called after her.

She shifted back. He was still standing. "Sorry?"

"The roast. I'd prefer the meat cooked medium rare. In addition, I have a choice of two sides."

"You do?"

"They're listed on the menu."

"The roast is served with garden vegetables."

"So you've stated. What are the garden vegetables this evening?"

She tried to read the notes she'd scribbled on her pad, but he was already saying, "I'm assuming zucchini and corn, which are fine."

She jotted down his order. "Sorry."

"Please don't be sorry," he replied. "I'm quite impressed."

"Because I'm botching up a simple menu request?"

"That sounds like an apology, which I won't accept. You're the best waitress I've ever had."

She smiled. "Which is, sir, a fabulous lie."

"Well-intentioned."

"I'll give you that."

He laughed, which made him that much more attractive. His white shirt was in sharp contrast to his tanned features.

She shuffled backward, then hurried to the kitchen to place his order.

Despite their pleasant bantering, Nora maintained her distance for the rest of the evening, save for serving his meal. She added his dinner tab to his room bill.

"Thank you, Mr. Wilson," she said as she attempted to scurry away.

"You can call me Julian, if I may call you Nora. By the way, aren't you going to recite the dessert options?"

"Absolutely." She touched a hand to her forehead. "Would you prefer our—"

"I'm a vegetarian, remember?" He winked. "I'll pass. Black coffee is fine."

She burst out laughing. Only later, when he'd slid back his chair and left, did she realize his joking response made no sense. Desserts, as a rule, didn't have meat in them.

Too bad she hadn't thought quickly enough to counter.

The name of the game in waitressing was concentrating on details. Obviously, being a waitress wasn't her forte, and Tom and Louise were better representatives of Cherish than she could ever be. However, she'd accomplished her first task at the inn since her teens, and an innate sense of satisfaction ran through her—despite having done nothing extraordinary.

She leaned against the wall. If there was anyone she wanted to tell, it was her parents. Perhaps her mother would've smiled and said, "Fine job, Nora." Her father would've glanced up from reviewing their profits and losses and offered a thumbs-up.

If only they were still here.

Nora's chin trembled, her chest ached. Nothing diminished the sorrow, and deep inside, forgiving herself for deserting them seemed continually out of reach. Working at the inn was payback in her own humble way.

The air skirted out of her lungs. Years ago, she had resolved to ground herself in the here and now, with her gaze firmly fixed toward the future. She'd been curious how the inn had evolved in her absence. Yet in the present, all that curiosity circled back to a certain man named Julian.

He was staying here. She might run into him repeatedly.

The idea brought a flutter to her chest.

In under two hours, he'd had quite an influence. Yes, he was undeniably appealing. When he'd gazed at her, he'd made her feel special—like the doe-eyed woman she'd once been.

Was that a good thing or a bad thing? She'd been reckless and foolish in her teens, though she'd loved the feeling of being in love. However, she'd carried hurt for many years and couldn't lift such a heavy burden again. It would only weigh her down.

CHAPTER 3

The next morning, Julian, dressed in jeans and a short-sleeved navy T-shirt embossed with his employer's logo, decided to take a stroll through the town. He was satisfied with his room at the inn, its luxurious bathroom, a sitting area with a soft chair and computer desk, a king-sized bed, and an inviting fireplace.

As he entered the downstairs lobby, he noticed Tom behind his desk and they chatted. During their conversation, Julian learned only a little about the community. Tom did mention that a farmer's market was held in the town square every weekday morning.

Julian's team members of the Fresh 'n' Good chain were scheduled to arrive by midday, and dinner was set for six o'clock, allowing Julian ample time to wander. If the company elected to open a restaurant in Cherish, he was slated to be the person to run it. Therefore, he intended to peruse the place he'd be living in for a few months.

Once he'd breakfasted on thick slices of French toast, bacon, and buttery scrambled eggs, he managed only a sip of coffee, because it was again tasteless and bitter. He'd wanted to inform Nora, the beautiful waitress. He'd hoped she'd serve the morning meal, but he hadn't seen her anywhere.

The night before, he hadn't been able to catch her gaze after his dinner.

He'd flirted with her when she'd served him, something he rarely did. More often than not, women responded to him by flipping back their hair and tittering an encouraging response. In contrast, Nora had challenged him for using a pickup line.

She'd caught his interest, his attraction. Good nature radiated on her lovely features, and she made him feel happy in a way he hardly understood. Once he'd entered his thirties, he'd found he was no longer intrigued by giggling females who were all too available. Every relationship he'd had recently had become history after a few months.

"Six months at tops," he affirmed as he exited the inn. Following Tom's directions, he found a gravel path and a sign directing him to the square.

An ideal South Carolina morning beckoned—the sun radiant and enveloping his arms in warmth. The sky boasted a blazing blue, and graceful flowers bloomed a buttery-yellow.

He paused at Memorial Street Church, noting its central location, its high-arched windows and ornate wooden doors. He typed the hours of the services into his phone. He dodged a boy on a bicycle and followed the sights and sounds to the farmer's market.

Hope quickened his steps. Nora might be there. As a further bonus, if she was buying fresh produce, there would be superb meals in store at the inn.

A half dozen strides brought him to rows and rows of booths, and whiffs of recently picked peaches, fragrant ground spices, and touches of citrus swirled around him.

Somewhere a dog barked, shadowed by the distinguishable yelp of a puppy.

Julian froze. His chest tightened. It wasn't the large dog that stopped him. It was the small dog.

Completely irrational, he reminded himself. The chance of encountering a dog in this people-loving, presumably dog-loving community was high and he should prepare himself.

He dismissed his fear and noticed Nora weaving in and out of the aisles, toting a wicker basket overflowing with juicy peaches and blueberries.

Julian paused, pleased with his good fortune.

She was a natural beauty, tall and shapely, wearing a pair of figure-hugging capris and a flowered blue blouse. God had certainly placed favor on her because she was a classy Rubenesque woman, and Julian couldn't contain his grin.

People, young and elderly, bustled past, their genial banter punctuated by laughter. Everyone seemed to know each other by their first name.

He liked that. He liked the special feeling of community. So far, Cherish appealed to him. At a stand, he purchased a homemade pretzel dipped in melted cinnamon and sugar, and quickly polished it off.

Nora had wandered to a booth teaming with wildflowers. She scooped up a hand-tied bunch of dried lavender and placed it in her basket. Sidelined by a cordial shopkeeper, she bought a slice of thick vanilla cake frosted with strawberry icing.

Watching her relaxed and chatting with the townsfolk was as pleasant for Julian as when she'd waited on him. In both instances, her sweet smile captivated him.

He debated striding up to her when a sturdy, muscular golden retriever followed by a gangly puppy raced through the crowd. Both dogs trailed their leashes, both obviously excited by an escape from their owners. Intent on chasing a squirrel, they dashed past him.

"Tiny Tim! Molly Belle!" A man wearing casual pants, a shirt and a bow tie clapped his hands and sprinted after them. The retriever veered toward an empty aisle, then snatched up a pastry. "Give the cinnamon roll back!"

"Sorry," the man muttered as he bumped past Julian. "That mischievous golden is teaching my innocent Yorkipoo some bad habits."

Julian tried to ignore his rapid heartbeat as his gaze strayed to the small dog. "Are they … partners in crime?" he inquired.

"Unfortunately." Max quickened his pace. "Molly Belle, she's the retriever, will steal any pastry she can reach."

"Watch out!" someone cried out. The dogs had circled and were bounding straight toward Nora.

Juggling the slice of cake and her full basket, Nora tried to dodge the dogs as they dashed past. The retriever sideswiped her. She barely managed to keep from falling, but her cake and basket went flying.

"Nora!" Julian hurried to her. "Nora. Are you all right?"

She whirled to face him. "Yes. I was only startled."

Julian realized how alarmed he'd sounded, and tried for a joking tone. "I'm here to rescue you."

"From what?"

"I was afraid you were hurt."

"I'm fine, and the dogs are harmless."

Harmless? Julian didn't reply.

She smoothed her blouse and then crouched down to pick up the cake and basket.

He bent near, grabbing errant fruit before it rolled out of reach. "We should stop meeting like this," he joked.

"Tidying up messes, you mean?"

"We were made for each other." *Now why had his disloyal tongue blurted out such a romantic declaration?*

"Perhaps if we were opening a cleaning service." Their gazes met, and she grinned. At least *she* appreciated his sense of humor. "By the way, you're not obliged to help me."

"I insist." Quickly, he placed the fruit in the basket, stood and helped her to her feet.

"Thank you."

"You're welcome." He inspected a couple of bruised peaches. "Is this fruit ruined? I hope you weren't intending to serve peach puffs for the specialty dessert this evening."

"What are peach puffs?"

"A puffy peach, I would imagine." He shrugged. "I saw the recipe in a magazine once, and the photo was picture-perfect."

"Heaven forbid I was in charge of the inn's menu. I purchased the fruit for me and my daughter to snack in our room. I'm hoping it will encourage her to eat more than junk food."

"Young people. They'd rather eat potato chips and drink soda."

"Right."

"Like us."

She laughed. "Truer words were never spoken."

Her slightly wild hair tumbled around her shoulders, framing her angelic face and fair complexion. Her flowered blouse reflected the color of her huge blue eyes.

She was a gorgeous woman, especially when she laughed.

He cleared his throat. "Are you staying at a place here?" He wasn't sure he could speak, but apparently he could.

"I am. Temporarily."

"I'll walk you back."

She started toward a vegetable booth and he trailed behind.

"You don't know where I'm staying," she said.

"Guide me." Next, he planned to request her phone number.

She rested the basket on her hip, emphasizing her generous curves. A dab of strawberry frosting was smudged on her cheek. He reached up and gently smoothed it away.

She lifted her dark eyebrows.

"Sorry. You had …" He held up the frosting on his fingers as evidence.

You're staring at her. He dropped his hand.

"My daughter and I are renting rooms at the Cherish Hills Inn," she replied.

"Me too."

"Yes, I know."

He beamed. More good news. They were staying in the same place. His mood grew brighter by the minute.

"Obviously, our walk doesn't put you out of your way," she was saying.

"The inn is only three blocks over."

As if she didn't already know the location of the inn.

"I can find it by myself."

"It's no bother," he said. "I was heading back there myself."

He wasn't. He'd contemplated stopping at the local Big Brothers Big Sisters center. He hoped to sign up for volunteer opportunities if he was going to stay in Cherish for a few months. The program was community based and directed toward low-income families. Julian had never had children of his own and took delight in mentoring them, especially the older kids. Writing donation checks was easy. He was more of a hands-on man.

He kept their pace sedate. "How long are you in town?"

A smile lit her face. "Samantha and I are here for the entire month of June."

"If my bosses decide to open a restaurant here, I'll be in

charge and staying for a few months. I'll probably rent an apartment."

She studied his T-shirt. "Fresh 'n' Good."

"The food you love—prepared fresh." He parroted the chain's motto.

"I've heard that jingle on the radio more times than I can count."

"Advertising is a sizable part of our budget."

"You're not the owner, correct?" she asked.

"I'm a manager."

"Right. Well, I lived in Cherish for eighteen years," she said. "A chain might not fit into the community."

"Why not?"

"Too … large. From what I recall, the city council was never keen on expansion."

"Stifling growth isn't beneficial for any place," he countered. "To survive, a town should welcome industry."

"A quiet environment is preferred by the folks here." Her argument was interrupted by a woman wheeling a baby in a carriage. The woman smiled an acknowledgement as she zipped by.

"The owners are sensitive and adhere to regulations," Julian responded. "A bonus is that the new restaurant will create good-paying jobs."

She deliberated in front of Whitney's Ice Cream Shop, eyeing the listings and the sign touting butter pecan as the flavor of the day.

"Therefore, the chain won't put independent places out of business?" she asked.

"Of course not."

"At least, not on purpose," she murmured in a quiet undertone.

Fresh 'n' Good had shuttered lesser establishments. Julian knew that. Larger, well-capitalized chains were positioned for growth and withstood economic downturns and competition. Little businesses? Not so much. He didn't share his musings, sorry that reality had intruded on their pleasant stroll.

For reasons he couldn't explain, he wanted to gather Nora close and reassure her, though he wouldn't overstep his bounds. They'd only known each other a short while. Instead, he provided a heartening smile. "I'll do my best to ensure no one goes out of business here."

"Promise?"

"I'll try." He guided her across the street. "I don't make the final assessments, I just work out the kinks once the restaurant opens."

They changed direction and drew near the Memorial Street Church.

"This church has been here for fifty years. Still painted white." She smiled. "I remember it well."

"Did you attend? They offer services on Sunday mornings and Wednesday evenings."

"As a child, I went happily and willingly. However, when I reached my teens, I dug in my heels and refused, though my parents were strict and tried to force me. I wanted to hang out with my friends instead."

"On a Sunday morning?"

"More accurately, I preferred to sleep late."

"Evidently your friends weren't churchgoers, either."

"I longed to fit in with the popular girls, and peer pressure is powerful," she replied. "Church wasn't on their list of Sunday morning priorities."

"Did you?"

"Did I what?"

"Fit in?"

She expelled a breath. "No. In truth, never."

"I'm surprised." He studied her exquisite features. "Surely, all the high school guys were jostling for a position to ask you out on a date."

"I was too busy working. I didn't have time for cheer-leading or any fun activities."

"Cinderella, someone should've taken you to the ball."

She smiled and didn't elaborate, and he didn't press for details. Her gaze fixed on a window box brimming with greenery and silver petunias across the way.

"If this is any consolation, we both can agree that dynamics in middle and high school are brutal." His cell-phone vibrated in his pocket and he ignored it. "I was athletic, but hung out with the wrong crowd too."

"I didn't hang out with the wrong crowd. No one was interested in me because I was never available. Thus, my social status was nonexistent."

"Well, I played basketball, the key to popularity. Only difference was I was dirt-poor compared to the other kids."

"Care to tell me about it?"

He grinned. "Only if we can get ice cream."

"We passed Whitney's already. I'm on a—"

"Let's double back." He captured her hand, and she didn't shake him off. His heart skipped a beat. Holding her slim fingers in his felt right.

Once they reached the shop, he turned to Nora with an expectant smile.

"I don't usually indulge and eat ice cream in the morning," she objected. "Besides, I'm dieting."

"Ridiculous. You? Why?" He sighed. *Women and their outlandish ideas about their bodies.* "Nonetheless, I'll try to convince you of the wisdom of the idea because ice cream is nutritious." He led her to an outdoor table beneath a striped canopy.

"Ice cream isn't nutritious," she replied.

"Some may argue ice cream is part of a healthy, well-balanced diet."

"Uh, huh."

"How about this?" He assumed a tone that brooked no more debate. "I'm treating."

"Okay, then." She grinned. "Dutch chocolate is my favorite, except Whitney's seldom used to serve it."

He squinted toward the sign. "Chocolate is listed. What's the difference?"

"Dutch chocolate is more mellow than regular chocolate."

"I'm not seeing Dutch chocolate on the menu." He drew bright-yellow chairs into place around a wrought-iron table. "Is soft-serve regular chocolate okay?"

"Sure, although I shouldn't."

Her smile was a bit self-depreciating.

He opened his mouth to protest, but asked instead, "Cone or cup?"

"Surprise me."

"One scoop or two?"

"One."

While waiting for their orders inside the shop, he stepped to a quiet spot and yanked out his cellphone. He'd received numerous text messages from his teammates: they might get stranded at the Atlanta train station because the trains were running late.

Keep me posted, he texted, then shoved the phone back into his pocket.

He returned to Nora carrying two cones—a scoop of chocolate in one and three scoops of butter pecan in the other. He handed her the chocolate cone and settled across from her.

She took a bite, rolled it around her tongue, and smiled. "The ice cream is delicious and exactly how I remembered.

This entire town is stuck in time. I can't get over how slow the pace is compared to Virginia."

"Where do you live in Virginia?"

"Richmond."

"Richmond has, what, a couple hundred thousand people?"

"Even higher at last count," she said with a breezy smile. "Where are you in Pennsylvania?"

"I live in Scranton, though I don't call it home because I'm on the road so often. I go wherever the job sends me."

"A company man."

He shrugged. "I suppose, although the company has been fair and very generous."

She studied him over her cone. "What's the length of time you stay in a city?"

"Never more than six months," he replied. "I'm used to moving around a lot. My mother never had us stay in one place for long, either."

Now why bring up his mother? Inwardly, he shook his head.

"Why not?" Nora was asking.

"My mother was invariably chased by creditors." There, he'd said it aloud. He well remembered middle-of-the-night exits from dingy apartments, and the familiar embarrassment and shame washed over him.

"I'm sorry," she said. "Getting acclimated to different schools must have been difficult."

"I was taught never to complain, never to display emotion." Avoidance and running was the fabric of his existence. He'd moved around to establish a distance between himself and his mother, his brother. But now? What was he running from now that he never stayed in one place longer than a few months?

He ate in record time, then waited for Nora.

"Do you attend a church in Richmond?" he asked.

"No."

"That's it? Just no?"

She contemplated the rest of her cone, then finished it. "I wrestled with doubts about Christianity during my teen years. I still do. You?"

"As I've alluded, my high school crowd was … shall we say misguided?"

"That's your whole story?"

"Only the beginning." He fixed his gaze on a point beyond her. He'd tried to add status, add alcohol, to ensure his popularity as a teen. Always the new kid in a new school. His efforts had been successful, although the emotional expense had left him exhausted.

"And?" Nora's steady voice roused him from unhappy remembrances, the weight of decisions he was sorry for.

"When I was a senior, the guys on my basketball team drank beer on weekends. I figured I'd join them." Julian examined his palms. "I grappled with my choices, I knew they were wrong, but alcohol became an addiction for me. I also confronted my conscience, or rather, it confronted me."

Nora studied the inked rose and cross tattoo on his upper left arm. A sign of his commitment to God. "Go on," she encouraged.

"Toward the end of the year, a counselor urged my mother to admit me to a treatment program. I resisted at first. In hindsight, the therapy was exceptional, although guess who helped me the most in the end?"

Nora propped her chin on her fists. "Who?"

"God. He gave me hope when I was in a dark place. He comforted me through my challenging hours. On the flip side, my conviction is a constant struggle."

"Regardless, my watery faith doesn't compare with yours. Yours is steadfast." Her voice grew heavy. "My days are filled with busyness, and I'm no saint. I married young and—"

"It doesn't matter to God. Don't look back. Look forward. God loves us for who we are."

She fidgeted with the slim silver band on the index finger of her right hand. He hadn't noticed the ring the previous evening.

"What about Samantha?" He took Nora's restless hands in his. "What are her views regarding religion?"

"She says little. My parents' insistence has reaffirmed my belief that Samantha is her own person who must form her own opinions. If she wants to attend church, she'll tell me."

"Everyone's path is different," he replied. "Guide her to find worth in what is true."

"Which is?"

"All the right stuff. Our creator lives within us. Stay the course and believe. Our God is a faithful God."

He didn't normally speak about his faith so openly. What was it about this woman that brought out his need to connect—both as a friend and spiritually?

"I try to lead a good life and often make mistakes. Samantha isn't an easy child to raise. She's frequently will-ful." Nora didn't meet his gaze. When she did, he saw defenselessness in her eyes. He wanted to envelope her in his arms and assure her she never needed to bear her worries alone.

He was here for her.

However, he didn't reply, didn't react further.

They were sitting outside an ice cream shop, and their relationship wasn't at the point where he could hold her close and murmur agreeable assurances. He'd said enough.

He ran his thumbs soothingly over her palms. And why did Nora bring out such a protective instinct in him? She was certainly accomplished and capable.

His cellphone vibrated again. In fact, it had been vibrating for the past several minutes.

He sighed. "If you're ready, we should head back."

"All right." She grabbed her basket. "In any event, you gave me a lot to process."

His mouth grew dry. Had he said too much? He'd merely wished to share his religious principles with her. He broke the silence when they reached the gravel path leading to the inn.

"You're fond of Cherish," he said.

"It goes without saying." She lifted her shoulders in a swift shrug. "But then again, I moved away."

"Why? This area is delightful."

"Delightful?" Her lips curved into a crooked smile.

Actually, she was the one who was delightful.

"I took off with my boyfriend when we turned eighteen," she murmured. "We married a short while later and divorced before our first wedding anniversary."

"You and your ex have been apart since …"

"Since Samantha was a baby." Nora replied in a manner more emotional than dismissive. "Colic and late-night feedings weren't his thing."

So Nora was a long-time single, just as he was. Although, in Julian's case, he'd never married.

He debated how best to respond.

"Will you have dinner with me?" He shoved his hands in his pockets. "Not necessarily at the inn—I realize you work there. I assume waitressing is a part-time gig for you."

"Very part-time." Her eyes twinkled. "Couldn't you tell last night?"

"Not in the least." He opted for politeness. "You were speedy and competent."

"Speedy, thanks to the kitchen's efficiency."

"And your agreeable chef?" he teased.

She flashed him a jaunty grin. "Not so agreeable, it turns out."

"May I ask why you're in Cherish if not to work in the restaurant?"

"I have other business at the inn."

"What type of business?"

"Unfinished business."

Okay, that was vague.

He leaned over. His breath whispered against her fragrant hair. She smelled of lilacs and brightness and everything valuable in life. "Again, will you have dinner with me?"

"I can't."

"Because?"

"Because I have a daughter."

"Plenty of single women with children date."

"When Samantha gets older, perhaps." Nora briefly closed her eyes, her silky black lashes sweeping down her cheeks. "At present, she's going through a tough time. I intend to be supportive and available for her."

"Are you a helicopter parent?"

They'd reached the inn and she paused in midstep. "Julian, do you have children?"

"I've never married. And no, no children."

Dark red stained Nora's cheeks. "Then wait to give advice when you can speak from experience."

"I've obviously put my foot in my mouth and you're right. However, I still want to take you out to dinner. If we don't click, we'll say we tried."

"Why wouldn't we click?"

"I've thrown around bad jokes and given parenting advice when I shouldn't."

They ducked under a majestic oak tree and climbed the front steps of the inn, settling on two wide-slatted rocking chairs on the porch. He allowed the charm of this modest town, the mild June breeze, to sweep over him. Chubby squirrels chattered, leaping from branch to branch.

"It's lovely here," he mused, rocking back and forth.

"The town is idyllic." She set the basket beside her and ran her fingers along the peaches. "I never dreamed I'd say those words when I was a belligerent teen, but I'm beginning to think I'm a small-town girl at heart."

"Yet you created a different life in a provincial capital."

"I craved a cosmopolitan existence—the concrete jungle and all that."

"Now?"

"Now I'm unsure."

"Me too," he admitted. "I'm warming up to the idea of settling permanently in a modest, serene community."

"I've been thinking along the same lines."

There was a connection between them, weightless at first, growing ever stronger. His heartbeat increased, and his gaze drifted to the beauty rocking slowly beside him. His enthusiasm for travel and exciting new places was fast losing its allure.

"Are you free on Friday night?" His voice came out louder than he'd expected.

She hesitated, twisting the silver ring.

"Pretty," he observed.

"Thanks." She smiled. "The ring was my mother's."

"Is she in your life?"

A lengthy pause followed. Nora sobered, the smile gone from her features. "I wish I could say yes. The truth is, my mother and father died in a car accident not long after I left Cherish. The ring was her gift to me on my eighteenth birthday."

He studied Nora's classic profile, her high cheekbones and flawless skin. "When did you last speak to your mother?"

"We talked on the phone after I left, but not often. The conversations were brief and stilted. I never told them I was pregnant." Tears brimmed in her glorious eyes. "They never met their granddaughter."

"They never saw Samantha before they died?"

She flinched. "No."

"It must be hard. Sorrow and mourning. I wish I had the right words, though I'm truly sorry for your loss."

"Thank you." She nodded and didn't say more.

This was a discussion she obviously didn't want to broach.

Direct me, Lord, he prayed. *I won't dwell on a distressing topic that brings her pain.*

An emptiness settled in the pit of his stomach. If she felt comfortable, they could talk again. For now, he steered the conversation toward a lightheartedness while respecting her sadness.

As they exchanged pleasantries, he reached over and tucked a rebellious strand of her hair behind her ear. "We'll dine at a local establishment," he said. "Any suggestions?"

"I indulged in many BLTs at The Garden Terrace when I lived here. Plus, they serve the best mesquite barbecued ribs and sugar-free lemon cake. I drove by yesterday, and they're still open after all these years." Her gaze brightened. "They sponsor a local band every weekend."

"Ideal. A good meal and music. Shall we plan for seven o'clock on Friday evening?"

Her upturned gaze met his. "I'll check with Tom to be sure I'm not scheduled to work. If he gives the okay, then yes."

"Call me old-fashioned, but I insist on treating. Deal?"

"I call it chivalrous and generous."

"Deal, then?"

"Deal."

Immensely cheered by her response, Julian perked up.

She'd accepted his invitation. He waited for his pulse to

level off and considered his next words. He'd dated women in many cities and wasn't known for wearing his heart on his sleeve. However, with Nora the stakes were higher.

His fingers grazed her graceful chin. "I'd love to spend more time with you." He'd never made such a heartfelt declaration to any woman.

"Me too," she replied.

The moment was special. If he didn't reach out and take hold, it would disappear.

He leaned forward and brushed his lips on hers. It was all the encouragement she needed, because the kiss deepened. Soft, delicate, and delicious. For a few seconds, the squirrels stopped chattering, the wispy breeze paused, the snippets of conversation from a couple strolling by ceased. All that mattered was Nora and the delectable wave of emotion heading straight for his heart.

She placed her hands on his chest. "Julian, we're sitting outside on a porch."

"Yes, and the kiss was amazing."

"You're leaving. I'm leaving."

Truth prodded the recesses of his brain.

She was right. This was correct. He was going to lose her, lose *this*.

His chest pinched. He managed a smile. "Then let's treasure the days we have together and not analyze anything."

Her sweet smile reminded him that every moment in Cherish was special. Especially if the beautiful Nora was by his side.

CHAPTER 4

The other members of Julian's team—a man and two women—were able to catch their train, and a measured commotion heralded their arrival.

Perched behind the front desk in the lobby, Nora checked them in. Amidst a round of laughter, they regaled Julian with hilarious stories about their travel mishaps. All three had taken the train into Cherish Central station directly from Atlanta.

Julian introduced them to Nora, and she welcomed them with a radiant smile.

Already, he missed their rapport from a few hours earlier. He ran their conversation through his mind and grinned, recalling her crooked smile when he'd referred to the Cherish area as delightful.

He noted her competence and courtesy. She remembered everyone's names and offered to carry their bags to their rooms. Julian quickly intervened, despite Nora's protests.

No bellboy, he mused as he lugged a third set of designer suitcases up two flights of stairs. No elevator, either. Wasn't Tom aware they were living in the twenty-first century?

Moreover, where *was* Tom? Julian had overheard Louise, who divided her time between housekeeping duties and keeping a watch on the staff, complain to Nora before lunch that despite his recent heart attack, Tom refused to follow his doctor's orders to rest. Apparently, Tom insisted on a hands-on approach, and Julian had already seen how Louise fussed over him, overly protective of his welfare.

When Julian finished carrying suitcases and escorting his team to their respective rooms, they all agreed to meet at the restaurant at six for dinner. Back downstairs, he looked around for Nora, finding her in the dining room setting the tables. His smile was enormous and completely over-the-top whenever he looked at her, yet he couldn't help himself.

He settled in the parlor with his laptop, pretending to work when he was really watching for any glimpse of Nora. She seemed in constant motion, tending to other guests as they arrived, answering the phone, running the vacuum over the carpet in the hall.

She worked too hard. She worked too much.

And the same question arose. Why? Were Tom and Nora related? If not, what was the connection? Judging by her frowns, her daughter didn't want to be there.

An image of the pretty teen, her mischievous smile when she thought no one was watching, her large ice-blue eyes and abundance of earrings, came to mind. Surely there was more to her than her outward, moody appearance. Was this typical adolescent rebellion?

He'd acted out in his teens. His mother hadn't taken an interest in him until his battle with alcohol surfaced.

Her neglect had fostered an outsized longing in Julian to be accepted, which ultimately had contributed to his alcohol abuse. It wasn't his mother's fault. He loved her, she'd made an effort, and he accepted full responsibility for his actions. His father had died when Julian and his brother were young, and he had no real recollection of him. Only his mother, who'd hung on to her resentment of being a young widow for years.

Nora had become a single mother too soon as well.

Nora again. She was a treasure, comparable to a spray of sunflowers, spreading sunshine wherever she went. From what he'd observed, Samantha was foremost in Nora's heart.

Behind Samantha's petulant expression lay a promise of the beauty God had bequeathed to Nora. Surely, she had hidden talents and interests, and her spirit could be influenced by kindness. That is, if he could reach her, because she was as approachable as a prickly pear.

In his remaining days in Cherish, he wanted to get to know her better. After all, he was taking Nora out to dinner, so he was also interested in Samantha and how she might feel about him dating her mother.

One dinner is not a date, he repeated to himself.

Because his job required him to travel from city to city, he'd concluded long ago that he should remain single. He'd tried long-distance relationships, though the last break-up had been so hurtful for him and the woman, he'd never even returned to the city where she lived. Who would want a husband who was never around?

Indeed, he loved children and mentoring.

Was it enough? He'd been content. A bachelor's life with no strings …

But still …

Earlier, before his team arrived, Julian had run into Nora after he'd eaten a delectable lunch in the restaurant. Trying to get to knew her better, he had asked if she liked music.

"Very much," she answered.

"There's a music store a ten-minute walking distance from here called Musically Yours," he said, watching as she arranged fragrant pink roses in a vase in the front hall. "I understand that thanks to the owner, Cherish boasts more world-renowned musicians and performers per square mile than any place south of Manhattan. Her husband is Ryan Edwards. I don't listen to opera, but even *I've* heard of Ryan Edwards."

"Opera singers' voices are so elegant," Nora replied. "My father tuned in to the Metropolitan Opera broadcast on the radio every Saturday. But I've already been to Musically Yours. I stopped on my way to the farmer's market this morning and met Dorothy Edwards, the owner, and she is lovely. Then I went back an hour ago and bought a guitar."

Julian stared at her. "You bought a guitar?"

She smiled. "Yes, for Samantha."

"She'll be taking lessons while she's here?"

"She prefers online instruction. Everything seems to be virtual nowadays, so I didn't object."

"You can't learn guitar in an afternoon."

"I'm sure Samantha realizes that."

"Can she read music?"

"No." Nora turned away from the vase, massaging her temples. "I'm encouraging her. Otherwise, she's glued to her phone."

A computer isn't much better, Julian wanted to say.

He kept silent. He recalled Nora's sharp rebuttal about judging another person's parenting skills when he had no children of his own.

Perhaps music could become common ground for him and Samantha. Though Julian wasn't a musician, he'd heard that Joseph Slater, a renowned worship artist and musician, lived in Cherish, and participated in the worship music ministry at the church.

Julian had made peace by welcoming God into his life, and he prayed for the same peace for Samantha and Nora. A love of music might spark Samantha's interest to listen to worship songs and thus lead her and her mother on a church-attending path.

One could only hope, he thought. One could only pray.

HOURS LATER, Julian gave up on pretending to work and headed to the lounge to wait for his team. He noticed Tom sitting alone, nursing a glass of wine. Julian asked for a glass of soda water and then weaved around the tables to join him. He intended to ask Tom about Nora. Who knew better about her stay than Tom?

With a genial smile, he gripped the back of an empty stool and greeted him. "We briefly chatted yesterday. You may remember I'm Julian Wilson."

Tom's gaze narrowed. "Course I remember. You're from the Fresh 'n' Good chain."

"I trust you've read our five-star reviews."

"I've read the criticisms."

"If I can be of any help, let me know," Julian said. "I have a lot of experience running restaurants."

"So do I. Your company lacks a certain something."

Julian suppressed a smile at Tom's outward distaste of the chain. "Such as?"

"Personal interest in the patrons. I know everyone who eats at my restaurant. I understand their lives, their interests, and even their pets. Can you say the same?"

"No. I can't." Julian was used to giving orders. Perhaps he should listen more to people like Tom—an entrepreneur with a boatload of wisdom and experience.

The men exchanged a brief handshake.

"You have a fine place here," Julian said.

"Yep." Tom cast a critical eye at the bartender engaged in a heated conversation with a customer while another unsuccessfully tried to signal him. Then Tom's gaze traveled to

Louise, who had entered the lounge. She caught his attention, and he grinned, giving her a head-to-toe stare.

"May I join you?" Julian held onto his glass, not positive he should set it on the table.

"For a while." Tom peered at his watch, then acknowledged the stool across from him. "I'm due to duck into the dining room soon."

"I won't keep you." Julian slipped onto the vacant stool. "I wished to compliment you on the well-prepared dinner I enjoyed last evening. Your chef is outstanding."

"Yep."

"Nora was my waitress."

"Yep."

"She's efficient," Julian confirmed. *And wonderful.*

"Uh, huh." Tom came straight and rigid on his stool.

Rifling in his mind for how he'd given offense, Julian came to the assumption that his praises were too feeble.

"She's excellent and efficient." He hastily sifted through his declaration. "Outstanding."

Tom slid the stool back. "Nora is an old hand at innkeeping."

"How fortunate." Julian intended to fasten onto Tom's every word. "Is she your relative?"

No answer.

"I'm needed in the dining room." With a grunt, Tom rose, threw Julian an abrupt nod, and turned on his heels. Louise also headed to the dining room as Julian's party started toward him. He took a last gulp of his drink and hailed them.

Tom ushered the foursome into the restaurant, where mouthwatering scents of chicken and dumplings tempted Julian's nostrils. It was dinner hour and conversation bubbled.

Each table was covered with a paisley tablecloth, a pink rosebud in a golden-flecked vase placed at the center. Tiny tea lights and tapered candles burned with welcoming flickers, and Julian took note of the steps taken to create a hospitable atmosphere. He imagined savoring numerous meals in this friendly community, shopping the farmer's market with Nora and Samantha, and attending church services together.

A fantasy, not a reality.

The admonition brought a clench to his chest. He might be staying in Cherish for a few months. Nora wasn't. And he certainly wouldn't have time to learn any of his restaurant's patrons by name.

"Julian. Hello! We meet again."

Julian swiveled at the sound of a familiar male voice, and a man sporting a bow tie waved. He sat at a table with two women and another man.

"Hi." Julian strode over as Tom seated Julian's team nearby.

"Maxwell Archer. Call me Max." Max rose and performed formal introductions. "The resident bird-watcher, at your service."

"You're joking."

"About my name?"

"About being the resident bird-watcher."

"I never joke about my birds." Max drummed his fingers on his legs. "Those colorful creatures bring a sparkle to my days. Besides my wife, obviously."

The woman next to him smiled and ducked her head. The others laughed.

"Did I miss something?" Julian asked.

"Join us on a bird-watching hike sometime," the woman said. "The hike will explain an hour's worth of conversation."

"I'm Julian Wilson." Julian shook hands with Max. "I don't own birds or dogs. I run restaurants."

Max adjusted his bow tie. "We were wondering why you were in Cherish."

"My coworkers and I work for Fresh 'n' Good." Julian gestured to the table where they sat. "We're scouting the area because the chain may open a restaurant here." A stab of guilt reminded him of his assurance to Nora—that the eatery he oversaw wouldn't drive any local place out of business. He touched the base of his neck and prayed for guidance to steer the owners toward becoming an asset to the community, not a hindrance.

"By the way, Max," Julian asked, shuffling backward, "did you catch your dogs?"

Max patted his shirt pocket. "There's invariably a mishap when those dogs run loose. Happily, bacon treats are the key." He beamed at the woman beside him. "Allow me to introduce my beautiful wife, Sarah. Across from us is Sheriff Nicholas Thompson and his wife, Emmanuelle."

A tall blond-haired man was already on his feet. "If I can be of assistance, Julian, please holler."

"Nicholas is an integral part of our local law enforcement," Max put in. "He spends his days enforcing the law, and his dog, Molly Belle, spends her days racing up and down every block and breaking the law."

A collective sigh of agreement came from both wives.

"Molly Belle is a handful," Nicholas admitted. "But many golden retrievers are energetic."

"Energetic?" Tom approached the table. "Why, I still remember when you brought her into the inn and she knocked over a crystal vase filled with roses. There was water and broken glass everywhere."

"You banned Molly Belle from ever entering your establishment again," Nicholas reminded.

"With excellent reason." Tom scratched his whiskered

chin. "Take Molly Belle to Frank's Pizza, instead. They offer outdoor accommodations there."

"Anywhere except here," Nicholas muttered. "Is that what you're saying?"

"You got that right." Tom turned to Max. "My ban also includes Tiny Tim."

Julian let the relief sink in. He wouldn't be forced to encounter a small dog.

Max waved Tom's reference aside. "Why? He's only a puppy and eager to please." Max's obvious bewilderment at how anyone could doubt his dog's character brought a glimmer of amusement to Tom's eyes.

Laughter filled the silence after a few seconds, then everyone talked at once.

Special friends, Julian thought. Citizens creating experiences, building each other up in a tight-knit community. He wished for a close connection with people, yet he'd pushed his wishes into the background while a successful career propelled him ever forward. He told himself moving from place to place suited him. It was the way he'd grown up, and the only life he'd ever known.

He said good-bye to the friends and joined his team members. As he sat, he scanned the dining area for Nora.

A while later, she entered and didn't notice him.

His mouth opened in surprise as Samantha followed her, wearing an apron over a pair of slim-fitting jeans and a peach-colored blouse. Cheerily, he waved, and she reciprocated with a tentative smile.

Much to his dismay, neither Samantha nor her mother waitressed his table. When coffee was served bitter once again, he frowned into its contents.

. . .

Dusk had fallen by the time Nora finished computing bills, collecting payments, and checking room availability.

As the dining room had filled, she'd noticed several locals had reserved tables. Soon, Louise and Tom approached her in the lobby.

"Can you and Samantha waitress?" Louise asked. "We're short-staffed again."

Excuses poured out of Nora—her presence was required at the reception desk, the parlor cried out for a tidying, the laundry attendant complained it was impossible to keep up with the demand for clean linens.

"A job will keep Samantha busy." Louise softened her tone and tapped a finger to her temple. "She's a smart girl."

"She's only fifteen. Isn't she too young for waitressing?" Nora refuted. "I presumed Tom wouldn't hire her."

"I'm not hiring her," Tom reminded her. "She's working for free in exchange for room and board. Besides, you insisted on offering your tips to the Boys and Girls center, and I assume Samantha will do the same."

Her parents had continuously donated extra linens and supplies to the various shelters in the community. It was the least Nora could do.

"Perhaps several hours of training for Samantha first ..." she began.

"On-the-job experience is the greatest kind." He and Louise gave identical nods.

"Tom is brilliant." Louise touched his upper arm and smiled.

Tom wrapped up the discussion by blowing out a labored breath. He sagged against the doorway, which unwittingly prompted Nora into action. Louise fixed his shirt collar and volunteered to walk him to his suite as Nora hurried off.

She climbed the stairs to her room and quickly showered. Then she cast an appraisal in the mirror over her clean turquoise blouse, tailored honey-colored slacks, and leather loafers. A quick swipe of mascara and pink lip gloss completed her makeup routine. She styled her hair in an orderly bun.

Mentally, she rehearsed her approach as she knocked on Samantha's bedroom door, sending a plea to the heavens for serenity. She wasn't prepared for an argument.

"Come in. The door's unlocked," Samantha called out.

A guitar was balanced on her lap, and her computer screen displayed an instructional YouTube video featuring a soft-spoken teen playing a guitar. Her phone was open beside her.

Nora stepped farther into the room. "Did you learn a lot today?"

"I'm reading tablature. Basic chords are next and then strumming patterns."

"You're off to a fine start." Nora tilted her head toward Samantha's cellphone. "Who are you texting?"

"My boyfriend."

"Edison is learning guitar too?"

Samantha sighed as if Nora had just asked if her boyfriend had three heads. "He's interested in music and is a proficient guitarist. He's forming a band and asked me to join."

"Tell him good luck and good-bye, honey. We're needed downstairs. The restaurant is full to the rafters with diners."

Samantha's complexion turned colorless. "Now?"

"Now."

Samantha's thumbs flew across her phone's keyboard, then she snapped it shut. "There's a weak internet signal here, anyway."

"Oh well," Nora countered cheerfully.

"I really want to learn how to play the guitar."

"I applaud your efforts, Samantha, but Rome wasn't built in a day."

"What does that mean?"

"It means patience is a virtue, and time is required to accomplish greatness."

"Can I ask you a question, Mom?"

"Certainly."

"Why are we really here in Cherish?" Samantha set the guitar beside her.

"Your grandparents once owned this inn."

"You've told me that a hundred times."

"I owe them this—a tribute to all their effort. When I learned Tom was ill, I reached out to him."

"How were they—Grandma and Grandpa? I mean, I've seen pictures."

"They were wonderful and moral people." Tears pricked Nora's eyes. "Reliable, conscientious and loving."

"I never met them."

"Sadly, no."

"I think about them a lot." Samantha drew a wobbly breath. "I've prayed to God, but He hasn't given me any answers."

"Prayed about what?"

"What I can really do in my life to make a difference, so Grandma and Grandpa would be proud of me."

"You're at the in-between stage. It's not up to you to figure the world out at fifteen." Nora placed an encouraging hand on her daughter's shoulder. "I'm in my thirties and I'm still not sure. I can only try my best."

Nora had never understood a God who didn't respond to prayers. How could He take her parents, Samantha's grandparents, away from them?

Correction. Nora had deserted her parents when they needed her most. Not God.

She'd listened to sermons about a person's days already being written in God's book. Her heartache ran deep because of her faulty resolutions.

She offered an inward prayer—*Help me, Lord, to advise Samantha to follow the right path*—and felt lighter for the asking, as if a boulder had been heaved from her chest.

She wasn't forced to raise her daughter alone. God would assist her, and she shouldn't drive Him from the picture. His blessings were significant and meant to be embraced.

How? She prided herself on being a self-sufficient, independent woman. Or was she stalled in a version that wasn't truly her? Independence was noble, but wasn't it still okay to rely on someone else? To have a partner to share life with?

"*Guide Samantha to find worth in what is true,*" Julian had advised. "*Stay the course and believe.*"

Her heart gravitated toward him. He was a decent, honest man who truly loved God. His words brought hope.

"Perhaps," she said to her daughter, "we'll go to services at Memorial Street Church. I attended every Sunday when I was in elementary school."

Samantha smiled, dimples prominent, despite the apprehension shadowing her features.

Nora drew in a breath. "Did you wish to discuss your prayers?"

"Some other time." Samantha surged to her feet. "Give me a moment to change."

"Okay," Nora said. "I'm here whenever you want to talk."

Ten minutes later, mother and daughter descended the stairs to the lobby.

"Last night the dining room was almost empty, except for the guy you kept smiling at," Samantha observed. "You drenched him with a jug of water. Remember?"

"A glass of water, not a jug, and he didn't get wet," Nora corrected.

They reported to the kitchen, and Nora donned the inn's trademark red apron.

Samantha did the same, then clutched her hands together. "I've never waitressed before. Louise and Tom know that, right?"

"They have complete faith in you, as do I. An exemplary waitress is cordial, attentive to the customer, and quick," Nora explained. "A thorough knowledge of the menu is helpful, so let's review tonight's offerings."

"I studied the menu last night," Samantha said. "Has anything changed?"

"This evening's special is roasted chicken with dumplings. The recipe was given to Louise by a young woman named Crissy and is a favorite dish here."

Samantha zipped over to a cook and plied him with questions, then inspected the plated entrees ready to be delivered to the dining room. The cook forked a serving of chicken onto a plate, and Samantha took a bite. She chewed for several seconds, then swallowed.

"Flavorful and moist," she declared. "I can taste the rosemary."

"Flavorful? Rosemary?" Nora blankly echoed. She didn't think her daughter even knew what rosemary was.

"Mom, can't you taste it?" Samantha asked.

"I haven't had time to eat." Nora realized she must still be grinning like a court jester. Her daughter was displaying an interest in food other than pizza and potato chips.

"Always sample the specials," another server said, pausing in the doorway. "Then you can honestly recommend the dishes."

"I watch the food channel on my phone sometimes." Samantha piled dumplings onto her plate. "Though I'm not sure if I'll be a good waitress."

Nora patted her daughter's arm. "If you ever finish eating, you'll be sure to wow all the diners."

Moments later, the twosome emerged from the kitchen. Nora's posture was strong, her gait wide. Samantha's shoulders slumped as she walked to her first assigned table.

And then an amazing thing happened.

To Nora's astonishment, Samantha proved skillful at waitressing. Her chest filled with pride at her daughter's charm and grace as she chatted up the diners and recommended Crissy's chicken and dumplings. She'd shed her sulkiness and wasn't clumsy at all.

With a silent chuckle, Nora applauded this small step forward in her daughter's growth.

As she refilled wine glasses for an elderly couple, she identified Julian's voice before she saw him.

She turned.

He'd been watching her, and his gaze drifted appreciatively to her face.

Her cheeks burned—embarrassed he'd seen her again out of her element. He looked drop-dead gorgeous in a pristine white pressed shirt that emphasized his broad shoulders. Black dress pants fit his long legs to perfection. He grinned his approval toward Samantha, then returned his gaze to Nora.

"You're enchanting," he mouthed.

"Another pickup line," she mouthed back. "But thank you."

When he turned to his team members, she lingered to listen in awe as he carried off a clear description of the area, then noted his keen attention when one of the others spoke. He was so at ease around people, so poised. He knew just what to say and when to say it. She'd always been quiet and a bit shy.

A harried server approached, reminding that the elderly

couple had inquired about their meal. Another server brushed by, whispering that they were running low on chicken, and thus the night's special would soon run out. Nora hurried to the kitchen for the couple's dinner, then apologized to them for the wait and promised free desserts of their choice.

The pressures of the long day and evening soon left their mark, and Nora dreamed of soaking in an inviting bubble bath and reading a riveting romance novel when she finally was able to relax in her room. By the time most of the diners had left, save for some stragglers, she felt like she'd switched to autopilot.

She didn't permit herself to look directly at Julian, not wanting the distraction.

Several times, though, she couldn't resist, and he caught her gaze and smiled.

My, that did odd things to her insides. Quickly she focused elsewhere. When she couldn't help herself, she chanced another glance in his direction. His gaze was always on her.

The meaning in his eyes—desire, a magnetic attraction beyond rationalization, caused her pulse to speed to an alarming rate.

Stop acting as if you're a besotted schoolgirl, she reprimanded herself as she replenished drinks. She should be grateful he'd only be in Cherish a while. When she passed his table a final time, she hid a yawn with her fingers. Her knees wobbled, and she braced a hand on the wall to steady herself.

"Nora?"

His concerned voice came from behind her. She spun. He was only within a few inches from her.

"You're exhausted, Cinderella," he said. "Your day has been filled with work, work, work."

"I've been on my feet a long while tonight." She extended

a trivializing wave, fearful he might feel sorry for her. "I should've changed my shoes and worn sneakers instead of loafers."

He fetched a chair. "Please sit down."

"I can't. There are tables to clear and—"

"Please." He gently placed his hands on her shoulders.

With a resigned smile, she sank into the chair. She longed to kick off her shoes and soak her aching feet.

"You and your daughter were brilliant tonight," he said.

"Thanks." She looked around the near-empty dining room. "Where is she?"

"In the kitchen."

"She's probably scouring the counters for leftover dumplings."

"More nutritious than potato chips?" He brought on his devastating smile.

She grinned. "Absolutely."

"Are you all right?"

"Certainly."

"You look tired."

"That's not a very complimentary thing to say to a woman."

"I'm sorry. You're gorgeous, though slightly pale."

"In truth, I'm exhausted." She blew a stray strand of hair from her face. She must look a sight with her bun coming undone and the little makeup she'd applied long faded.

"I'll finish for you."

"By waitressing?"

"I'm a restaurant man. I've served in every capacity from busboy to concierge."

"You've assisted in the kitchen too?"

"I try. I'm not much of a cook, though."

"What's your specialty?"

"Toast."

She chuckled. She enjoyed his witty sense of humor. He thought quick, whereas it took her forever to think of a humorous response.

"Now you're a top manager who calls all the shots," she said.

"Touché." He tipped his head back and laughed, a rich throaty chuckle. But then his laughter was replaced by a burning intensity in his eyes. "I'm looking forward to seeing you on Friday evening."

"You're seeing me right now." She stretched out her legs. "We're both staying here, so I assume we'll bump into each other often."

"Your assumption suits me perfectly."

She peeked over at the table where he and his team had dined. The others were gone. When had they left? All her concentration had been focused on Julian.

He cupped her chin. "Please promise me you'll get some rest." His deep velvety tone wrapped around her.

"I promise."

"Have you eaten?"

Her forehead throbbed. She rubbed her temples. "No."

"Will Tom and Louise mind if I sneak into the kitchen?"

"They left earlier. Together, naturally." Nora wiggled her eyebrows. "I'm certain it's okay."

"I'll fix you a plate to bring to your room." He strode to the kitchen and returned with a closed container and plastic utensils. Samantha trotted beside him, amiable yet reserved.

Julian was kind and considerate, all traits Nora admired in a man. He also harbored a profound religious faith, which he openly shared.

She recalled a Psalm, 37:23, which she'd memorized as a child. "The steps of a good man are ordered by the Lord."

Plus, Samantha seemed to like Julian, at least a little.

"Your waitressing was outstanding tonight," Nora congratulated her daughter.

"Thanks, Mom." Samantha shrugged indifferently, trying to act as if the praise didn't affect her. "I think Grandma and Grandpa would be proud."

Nora's heart melted. "Very proud, indeed. Both of your grandparents had high expectations and were sticklers for excellence. You were utter perfection."

Samantha's forehead creased. "Is perfection an admirable trait?"

"Definitely," Julian said. "Reach for the stars and never underestimate yourself."

"Well, I'm off to my room." With a wide grin, Samantha yanked off her apron, snatched up her takeout container, and left with the easy, breezy gait of youth. Her hips and delicate waist were filling out more each day.

Outwardly, Nora smiled. Inwardly, she questioned herself.

She swung in the opposite direction from her parents when it came to rearing her daughter. She wanted to allow Samantha the freedom to express herself. But perhaps there was a middle ground. Mistakes. Corrections. Dust yourself off and try again.

Wasn't that the definition of life's cycle? Compromises. In Nora's case, she incessantly confronted the same challenges and insecurities in different seasons of her life.

She wasn't worthy to receive God's grace at eighteen. She wasn't worthy at thirty-three.

"Your daughter is enchanting," Julian was saying.

"I agree. Thanks."

It seemed as if all Nora did was thank him.

The jaded side of her interrupted. Was Julian's thoughtfulness one-sided? Was he putting on a show for his team by acting interested in Nora's welfare?

No. It couldn't be.

Her ex had professed undying love and vowed to care for her and their daughter. Alas, both were fleeting traits of a teenage boy who'd married her on a whim—the exhilaration of juvenile infatuation. Love was more than that. It had to be.

Julian was mature. His actions were sincere and heartfelt.

He settled on a chair beside her. His gray eyes, soft as a pencil drawing, drew her to him. The woodsy scent of his aftershave sent her senses into turmoil.

She couldn't remember afterward if she'd stopped breathing.

His lips grazed her ear. "I didn't see you nearly as much as I'd hoped this evening."

"Clearly you observed the dining room was filled to capacity."

He leaned closer.

Her lips parted and her heart did a double flip. Surely he wouldn't kiss her in the restaurant. Pleasure swept through her at the thought of him wrapping his arms around her. Kissing her as she clung to his muscular frame.

Could she be falling for him despite her misgivings?

Certainly not. She wouldn't jeopardize her heart with a long-distance romance. She was years past being a foolish adolescent.

The romantic, fancy-free half of her brain was thrilled he'd arranged their Friday night date. Nevertheless, the reasonable and sensible half chattered on about their two different lives and two different universes.

She should've told him her days were too hectic. She should've refused his offer.

She hadn't.

Looking back at her life as the pounds had piled on, she'd harbored resentment and hurt until they had almost broke her. But in the end, those same conflicts had brought her strength.

A win, to be sure.

However, her anguish over her dissolved marriage had led to wariness, and one of the hardest things to shake off was distrust. Her goal was to make it on her own. She didn't depend on anyone.

Still, was Julian the man she'd been searching for her entire life?

CHAPTER 5

Several days passed quickly.

Despite the fact that Nora recommended that Tom recuperate in his upstairs suite, he was invariably within a few feet of her. Today, on the first Saturday of her month-long stay in Cherish, he'd finally agreed to rest.

Pencil in hand, Nora sat at a rosewood writing desk in his private office. He preferred handwritten documents rather than a computer because pencil and paper were convenient and readily accessible. She tugged open a drawer and rummaged through stacks of billing, seeking the current month's invoices. Unable to locate anything, she set down the pencil. Her mind immediately gravitated to her date with Julian the previous evening.

He'd been polite, gentlemanly, and oh-so-considerate.

He'd met her in the Cherish Hills Inn lobby promptly at six thirty, allowing them ample time to get to the restaurant. Earlier in the week he'd requested her cellphone number, texting each evening to inquire about her day and wishing her sweet dreams. Each time his name crossed her phone screen, her spirits soared.

He was attentive and thoughtful. She'd never been with a man who held such consideration for her, and she appreciated his attention.

For their date, she'd chosen a flirty, pale-green chiffon dress, strappy sandals, and a chocolate-brown leather clutch rather than her everyday handbag. She gathered a silky, sea-green scarf around her shoulders in case the night was chilly.

As she descended the stairs to the lobby, her pulse fluttered in excitement when she saw him. He closed the distance between them in two long strides.

"Good evening, Nora. You are gorgeous." He greeted her with his customary warm smile and admiring appraisal.

Nora bit back a smile. He'd complimented her more in a few days than her ex had during their entire relationship. Julian was amazing.

"Thanks." Her fingers welcomed his soothing grip. "Though you always say that."

"Because I tell the truth." He held her gaze. His eyes were a deep, smoky gray. Purposeful, earnest, and comforting.

Instinctively, she held in her stomach. She'd forgotten to pack shapewear for the trip. And then she thought, *No worries*. This was Julian, and he seemed to appreciate her no matter her size.

He captured her hands in his. "The opportunity to go out with you tonight is a special gift."

"We've seen each other all week," she reminded.

"With constant interruptions. This night is ours and ours alone."

As guests passed, they stood in the lobby holding hands.

He didn't let go. Neither did she.

His almond-brown polo shirt and tan pants emphasized his magnificent, all-male physique, and her heart lurched. Oh, and his wonderful smile.

"Is Samantha taking a virtual guitar lesson tonight?" he asked.

"Tom bulldozed her into waitressing again." Nora inclined her head toward the dining room. "For me, a win-win. I won't worry about her. Bonus—she'll eat a hearty, nutritious meal."

"Good on both counts." Julian placed a casual arm around her shoulders. "The Garden Terrace is only a couple streets over. Shall we walk?"

"I was going to suggest the same."

He ushered her to the doorway. "See?"

"See what?"

"We're already clicking because we're reading each other's minds."

She laughed, the chiffon swirling around her as they descended the stairway. Her limbs were light, her soul carefree. The fragrance of spicy-sweet summer blossoms, the promise of gladness, nurtured every thread of her being.

A breeze grabbed a lock of Julian's hair, and she stilled the impulse to push it back with her fingers. The setting sun highlighted the natural mahogany hue, reminding her of the finest, shiny wood. Her heartbeat thudded louder, and it took a great deal of effort not to stare at him.

When they arrived at The Garden Terrace, he escorted her inside. Mesquite barbecued ribs beckoned. She sniffed, savoring the scrumptious smells.

He'd made reservations, though she'd assured him it wasn't necessary.

She was wrong. The place was packed. Waitresses scurried by with dish after dish of brisket and fried onions, and the chatter of diners pervaded every inch of the space. Yet it all faded into the background as Julian kept his fingers laced through hers.

"This place may lack sophistication, but the down-home food is delicious," she said.

His lips curved into a playful grin while he regarded the wood-beamed ceiling. "I'd hoped for a more romantic atmosphere."

Romantic. Julian was a romantic. He probably was the sort of man to send flowers and pick out distinctive gold foil cards. Blank cards so he could handwrite a message.

Besides his chivalrous manner, there was no mistaking the expression on his face when he looked at her. A deep affection was growing and more than a passing interest.

The feeling was mutual. She grinned back at the man she was beginning to fall for.

Julian flashed a smile to a couple sitting at a table near the stage. Their curious gazes had swiveled to him and Nora.

"Who are they?" Nora asked.

"Nicholas, the town sheriff, and his wife, Emmanuelle."

"You've been here less than a week," Nora said, "yet you know more folks than me."

"And Max is the guy who chased after the two dogs at the farmer's market."

"The big dog and the cute tiny dog?"

"Right." Visibly, Julian shivered.

"What's wrong?"

He shrugged. "Not a thing."

"Don't you like dogs?"

"Big dogs, sure." His eyebrows drew together. "Little dogs, not so much. Someday I'll explain my phobia."

Julian had a phobia? And when would he tell her? He was leaving soon.

"Who is Max?" she asked instead.

"He's the fellow on stage wearing a bow tie and playing the harmonica. That's his wife, Sarah, standing over there, and her uncle Gerry is half of this band. Max is the other half, and I understand their band's name is"—Julian peered at the sign by the stage—"The Bearded June Bugs. I overheard someone saying they change their name with the seasons."

"I can hardly keep track of my own name, let alone change it," Nora said.

"Likewise." Julian nodded agreement. "Initially, I had Cherish pegged as a sleepy little town."

"If I remember correctly, you described the area as delightful."

He offered a lopsided grin.

"Other observations?" she asked.

"Two more words. Flawless and special." His gray eyes shimmered. "Like you."

Flawless. Special.

She focused on his words, and her heartbeat sounded in her ears.

He drew her hand through his arm and led her to Nicholas' table to exchange introductions. Nicholas and Emmanuelle were both strikingly attractive. Each had blond hair, and they extended generous, welcoming smiles.

Nicholas' eyes sparkled with perceptiveness as he remarked to Julian, "And this lovely woman is …?" He winked, and they all chuckled. Apparently, the rumor windmill was already spinning. "Didn't she waitress at the Cherish Hills Inn the other night?"

Nora extended a hand. "I'm Nora Lancaster. Tom has been sick and I'm here from Virginia to help him."

"You are friends?"

"A fair description. My parents once owned the inn."

Julian's sharp gaze landed on her. She avoided it.

"A pleasure to meet you." Nicholas shook her hand. "Welcome back to Cherish."

"Such a great town. My daughter agrees."

At least Nora hoped Samantha agreed. It was too soon to tell since the teen changed her moods with the wind.

"Nora's daughter is the competent young woman who also waitressed tables when you dined at the inn," Julian clarified. "Cheers to her lovely mother. Anyone can see she's doing a fine job raising her daughter."

Nora glanced up, surprised to see the expression of pride on Julian's face.

"Samantha was our waitress," Emmanuelle chimed in. "She told me she's learning how to play the guitar online, and I congratulated her. I'm a harpist and teach lessons at Musically Yours. I told her if she ever wanted formal instruction to read music, I'm available."

"This is a wonderfully artistic community," Nora said.

"We wouldn't live anywhere else." Nicholas drew an arm around his wife. "Tight-knit and caring, our Christian fellowship will support you through life's rough patches."

Emmanuelle's observant gaze lingered on Nora. "Can we expect to see you both in church on Sunday morning? Ryan and Dorothy, the owners of Musically Yours, direct the worship music, and our illustrious duo"—Emmanuelle gestured to the stage—"sing in the choir."

"Not everyone in town is musical," Nicholas piped in. "We sit in our favorite pew in the front row, listen to an outstanding sermon, and I sing my heart out, albeit out of tune, to all the hymns."

"You're describing me," Julian agreed.

There was a lull in the conversation and Nora stared at the deer antlers mounted above Nicholas. This was the part where these decent faith-filled people expected her to declare that she would attend church.

She grappled with a suitable reply before opting for the truth. "Neither Samantha nor I have attended services in years."

I'm not sure why God wants someone like me, she thought. *I've been married, divorced, and my mistakes are too numerous to count.*

Aloud, she managed, "I suppose I'm a work in progress."

Julian tightened his grip on her hand. "God will meet you wherever you are." With that, he bade Emmanuelle and Nicholas to enjoy their meal.

Nora and Julian followed a server to a cozy booth in a secluded corner.

Nora loved it all. Their bantering while they dined on bacon-wrapped mushrooms—one of her favorites, she told him. The chaotic clattering of dishes, the laughter that went on for hours.

They'd each finished a plate of sticky barbecued ribs, twisting the bone apart and feasting on both sides, then wiping their hands on numerous napkins while downing glasses of cold, sweet tea. Max's band played a classic 80s rock song, and she and Julian sang along with the chorus.

"My favorite music era," Julian declared. "Who doesn't love 'Free Fallin'?"

"Or 'Born in the USA,'" Nora agreed with a laugh.

When she declined the specialty sugar-free lemon cake, Julian offered an indulgent smile. "There's always room for dessert," he encouraged.

She patted her stomach. "I eat my fair share, believe me."

"What do you mean?"

"Julian, I'm not exactly a toothpick. I should lose a few pounds."

"You're kidding, right? I like a woman with curves."

"Uh, huh. Perhaps if there was a little less of a curve around my waist."

"Women are so ill-advised." He shook his head, his gaze warming as he smiled at her. "I assume you lived here for many years."

"Right."

"What's your favorite remembrance of Cherish?"

"Hmm." She paused at the unexpected question, admiring the way he'd deftly navigated the conversation away from her perceived faults. "I suppose when I was little, my remembrances were the same as any child. Carefree summers racing through a sprinkler on a sweltering day and pedaling to a bee farm on the edge of town with my friends."

"A bee farm?"

"The owner harvested and sold the honey, and his nephew baked homemade sourdough bread. In fact, my parents bought the honey and mixed it in tea for sore throats."

"I've done the same and drizzled honey on toast."

"And pancakes."

"What else?

"Well." She rested her elbows on the table and leaned her chin in her hands. "I once had a winter adventure I'll never forget."

"Indeed?" The question was light, his tone cautious.

"I was ten years old." She settled in her seat. "It was a snow day, my parents were working at the inn, and my friends and I were swinging on a playground set in my backyard. We were all bundled in hats and gloves and heavy coats."

She blew out a sigh.

"And then?"

"I got off the swing and accepted a dare."

He quirked an eyebrow.

"One friend dared me to touch the metal part of the swing with my tongue."

"Oh, no."

"Exactly."

"What did you do?"

"I brought the swing into my house with my tongue attached."

"What?" He laughed, the bottomless, throaty laugh she loved, and raised his hands in mock horror. They enjoyed the same sense of humor. A bit wry but always fun.

"So what did you do?" he asked.

She took a swallow of iced tea. "Do you want to know what was I *expected* to do or what actually happened?"

"I've heard you're supposed to be patient and your tongue will unfreeze itself."

"Correct."

"But …?"

"I tried to pull my tongue off, and it hurt." She concealed the fact she'd been near hysteria. "Fortunately, my friends ran to get a neighbor and she used warm water to thaw my tongue."

"You're mentioning friends and neighbors." He grabbed her hands, his thumbs massaging her palms. "No siblings?"

"I'm an only child. You?"

"My brother and his wife and kids live in Pennsylvania. We're a few hours from each other. I see him and my twin nieces whenever I can."

"I assume not often, considering your constant travel."

Julian gave a curt nod.

She closed her fingers around her glass of tea. She still felt the warmth of his thumbs on her skin. "Now that you've heard my story, what's your best childhood recollection?"

"The first day of school," he replied. "No matter what state we lived in, my mother always took a photo of my brother and me holding our bookbags and waiting for the school bus. She'd buy the bookbags at a local thrift store, and they weren't always in the best shape. Ripped, zippers wouldn't work, that sort of thing."

"Oh. I'm sorry."

He shrugged. "It's okay."

"Did you like school?" Nora asked.

"Some subjects, like English, and sports. Little League games on mild summer nights were fun."

"Lots of memories, both happy and sad," she mused. Few happy ones for her once she'd reached the difficult teen years, when she rebelled and questioned why she was constantly knee-deep in chores.

Even when they were done eating, they hung out at the restaurant for another two hours, chatting with townspeople as they passed, sharing their keenness for lyrics as Max's two-man band belted out familiar tunes.

When servers pointedly began clearing tables, Nora surveyed the near-empty restaurant. Most of the patrons were gone, and even the band had packed up.

She stood. "We'd better leave."

Julian paid the check and dropped a generous tip. "I'll walk you back to the inn."

"How chivalrous, considering you're going to the same place," she teased.

His hand lightly touched her back. "My pleasure, my lady."

Together, they exited. A restful June breeze washed over her, and Julian tucked her silk shawl closer around her shoulders. The moon flashed a sliver of silver, and a twinkle of stars blanketed the dark sky.

Dinner had been delectable, the iced tea refreshing.

The moonlight stroll with Julian, however, was exquisite.

In a matter of days, he'd become a good friend who happened to be staying in the same town. A happy coincidence. Serendipity. Nothing more.

Nevertheless, they'd become more than friends since they'd gotten to know each other.

No, no, no.

But then he smiled at her and slid his strong fingers through hers.

Okay, he was definitely more than a friend.

A lump formed in her throat at the realization that everything in this tranquil town—including spending time with Julian—would soon end. Her real-time existence in a crowded city, the exorbitant cost of living, cramped spaces and rush-hour traffic jams, tightened an anxious knot in her stomach.

"I'm getting tired of the rat race," she admitted softly.

"Which is?" he asked, his gaze expressive.

"Running myself ragged. My job in Richmond is satisfying, although the deadlines are taking a toll on my relationship with Samantha. She's left alone after school too often. She's responsible and an exemplary student, though I still worry."

"At my wise age of thirty-five, I've concluded that people make time for what's important to them. Perhaps electing to take shorter hours at your job might help?"

She bristled. "My boss depends on me. I'm not an entrepreneur who has the luxury of creating my own schedule."

"You're free to choose where, how, and when. Sometimes solid principles are shoved to the side by our will to succeed." He sighed. "I'm philosophizing, and my explanation is meant more for me than for you."

It was a quiet statement, and she accepted it in the manner in which it was intended—as an honest assessment of their lifestyles.

"What's important to you?" she asked.

"God and church, my mother, my brother and his family. Oftentimes my priorities are out of whack because of my hectic calendar, though I've made certain my mother lives in her own home and is financially secure."

Nora nodded. This was Julian, always looking out for others. Kind and caring to his mother.

And he was right. She knew she shouldn't choose her job over spending time with her daughter. Guilt encompassed her like a veil of sadness, and her eyes misted.

"You're an amazing woman, Nora."

She blinked back tears. "I'm a single parent carrying all the expenses. Nonetheless, it's not a fair excuse."

"Fair to whom?"

"Fair to Samantha."

He stroked her cheek. No one had done that in such a long time, and she'd missed the closeness.

"I wish I could make your days easier," he said.

He did, by strolling with her, talking with her. Comforting her.

"Thank you." It was a relief to voice her feelings, realizing innately he'd never judge her. She reached up and touched his cheek before she realized the action was too familiar, too intimate. Hastily, she dropped her hand.

They neared the inn, and he stopped at the corner. Ever so gently, he snuggled her against his sturdy chest.

"I'm beginning to love this little town and everything in it." A glimmer of happiness lit his expression. "In addition, I have news."

Her breath caught. "Good or bad?"

"Good. I'm staying in Cherish a while longer. I told the owner of the chain I needed more days to scope out this area. Tom checked the registry and there's a room available for me for at least another week."

Julian had prolonged his stay because of her. He didn't say it. He didn't have to.

"Best of all, I can spend more hours with you, Nora." He bent his head and claimed her lips.

Her heart filled with three realizations as she weaved her fingers around his neck and kissed him back.

First, he was a man who liked kissing.

Second, they were definitely clicking.

And third, she wanted the kiss to never end.

CHAPTER 6

On Monday morning, Nora reported to the lobby at eight a.m, blinking at the glittering sunlight streaming through the front window. The day promised a brightness that filled her to the core, though she suspected her optimism was based on something more than the weather.

Julian was still in Cherish. Therefore, she was sure to see him.

Today she'd chosen to wear a watercolor-print midi dress and leopard flats, and had snagged her rebellious hair into a semblance of a ponytail.

Samantha had begged to sleep in, promising to appear downstairs by ten. Her pre-lunch job required washing, drying, and folding laundry linens. Her afternoon chores necessitated waitressing in the dining room.

Humming, Nora stepped into Tom's office and scanned the pile of correspondence. The effort involved in running an inn of this size, of any size, never ceased.

She pushed a dusty ceramic rooster to the side of the

desk. What was it with Tom and roosters? And who was in charge of dusting? Surely they needed more than microfiber cloths. She glanced at the heavy draperies. They certainly needed a good whack with a towel.

Of course, a greater concern reared, having nothing to do with roosters or drapes.

Nora had come to the realization she'd never be able to help Tom in all the areas of innkeeping as she'd originally intended. There was simply too much to do. Outwardly, things ran efficiently. Behind the scenes proved the opposite.

In the days she'd been there, the air-conditioning and heating system had broken down with frightening regularity, and pricing and bookings constantly fluctuated.

Tom had surprised her by requesting that she examine the budget. He'd voiced concern because the numbers didn't add up, though he'd embroidered his statement with a crusty, "Being you're an accountant and all, you might see some extra money left over for repairs."

Her level of expertise was business foundations, she'd explained.

"Good," he'd muttered. "I think."

Nevertheless, he had confided in her, and she'd do her utmost not to let him down.

Seating herself at the desk, she struggled to concentrate on the ledgers. Soon her traitorous mind strayed to a more delightful thought:

Julian.

Julian and their Friday night date. She relived his kisses, their amiable bantering, and the desire in his molten-gray eyes whenever he gazed at her.

With a happy sigh of remembrance, she thrust the ledgers aside, leaned back in her chair, and rested her hands behind her head.

Once Friday evening had been behind them, she hadn't expected to see much of him again. His team members were still in town, and several closed-door meetings had ensued.

When he'd ducked out of a meeting on Saturday morning to spend a few minutes with her, he'd expounded on how he and his team evaluated costs, secured the best locations, applied for the required licenses, and the hours of groundwork all these assessments entailed. He kept appearing all day, finding her in Tom's office, the parlor, the dining room. He forever seemed to know where she was working.

He'd also invited her and Samantha to accompany him to church services on Sunday morning.

"I don't know anyone," he'd explained to Nora. "I'd like you to go with me."

She hung her hands on her hips. "Already, you are friends with more people in town than anyone. Soon, you'll be running for mayor."

He grinned. "If you recall, we were invited to church by the sheriff and his wife."

How could she forget?

In the end, Nora pleaded fatigue, Samantha seemed relieved, and Julian attended the service alone.

A brief knock on the office door yanked her back to the present.

"C'mon in," she called out.

Julian entered carrying a bouquet of pink-petaled daisies, bringing with him the whiff of clean air that was a part of him. He'd rolled up the sleeves of his denim shirt, exposing his muscled arms.

He leaned against the doorframe. "Good morning, gorgeous."

"Hi." She stood. "You've grown taller."

"Must be the flowers." He beamed and crossed the room

to hand her the bouquet—precious and heartening to lift her spirit. "These are for you. Daisies signify happiness, new beginnings, and loyalty."

"Thank you. They're beautiful." She set the flowers on the desk. "I'll go find a vase."

He caught her hand as she rounded the desk. "Flowers can survive for a few minutes without water."

"Is that a fact?"

He pressed a tender kiss to her forehead. "Absolutely."

She sought to maintain a cool, professional demeanor. However, how could she when he was so thoughtful and utterly masculine? *A heady combination.*

"Are your team members gone?" she asked.

"They left late last night for Atlanta. I'm still here, though."

She gazed up at his handsome face. "I see that."

"Aren't you curious about yesterday's church service?"

She shifted. "A little."

He ignored her lack of enthusiasm. "The sermon was inspirational and the worship music divine."

His soft reply made her feel ill-natured and impolite.

"Did you recognize every single person in the congregation?" she asked.

"Well, Max was there, for one."

"The June Bug singer? He and his wife are the puppy owners, right?"

"The very same."

He pulled a ladder-back chair over to the desk and told her to go ahead and sit again. He sat so near their knees touched, and the warmth of his body permeated her clothes.

"The puppy's name is Tiny Tim," she said.

He grimaced. "Right."

"Cute name. Tiny Tim reminds me of a Christmas story."

"True."

"I take it you don't like dogs?"

"I like dogs." He tapped his knuckles to his lips. "I'm just not a fan of small dogs."

"Your phobia?"

"Indeed."

"You mentioned you might tell me about it."

"Did I?"

"Yes, and I'm listening if you're ready to share."

He was unusually hesitant. His eyes reminded her of the color of the sky before a rainstorm.

"You must've had a frightening experience with a dog," she began.

Julian dismissed her statement in an offhand manner she didn't believe for a minute. The upcoming conversation was undoubtedly heavy on his mind.

"Have you heard the term *cynophobia?*" He seemed to have trouble finding his voice.

"Never."

"The definition is a person who is afraid of dogs. My fear persists no matter how hard I try to get over it. I realize it's totally irrational." He seemed annoyed with himself and expelled a breath.

"What prompted your fear?"

"When I was young, I petted a puppy who was chained to a fence outside by his owner." He rubbed his forehead. "I felt sorry for the sweet little dog. The day was hot, and he unexpectedly nipped me."

She winced. "How old were you?"

"Six."

"Were you hurt?"

"No, just frightened. Nonetheless, the memory and resulting panic stayed with me."

"Both children and dogs are inherently curious," she

assured. "The owner was irresponsible and raising an unsafe dog."

"I should be well over it." Julian pumped a foot, restless. "Thank you for listening."

Alrighty then. He'd obviously decided to end the conversation.

"Thank you for trusting me," she replied. Their gazes held, and the frozen band around her heart began to thaw. Behind his potent maleness, he was vulnerable, yet he'd chosen to reveal his emotions and had freely expressed his fears.

She realized vulnerability was the course to deeper human relationships, and he was reaching out to her. He didn't ask for pity. If anything, he acknowledged his worries.

"I'll help you sort it all out," she offered. "Your feelings, your reservations."

"I understand my fear on a cognitive level, though I can't seem to overcome it."

She managed a grin of assurance. "We'll take puppy steps."

"Puppy steps." He smiled, leaned over, and cradled her in his arms. She admired his earnestness, his honesty, and felt valued and cherished for being important enough to him to confess his helpless emotions.

The door was open, and she didn't care how many people saw them.

Tom, Louise, the staff, the guests. She didn't care, because there it was again, the invisible tug drawing her ever nearer to Julian.

No. Wait. He traveled the country, never staying in any area for long.

She pulled out of his arms and sprang to her feet. She fiddled with the daisy petals, a way of busyness to cover her rebellious emotions.

He cleared his throat and stood. "Like I said, the sermon was outstanding."

Right. The church service.

She realized he was watching her. "Oh," she replied.

"Oh?"

"How should I respond?"

"By agreeing to attend services with me this upcoming Sunday." He'd wiped his face clean of weakness. He'd found his way back to his competent self.

"You'll still be in town?" she asked.

"Will you?"

She laughed. "You know I will."

"Then so will I."

The tenderness of his assurance sent a tremor through her body.

"Marge Addyson, the associate pastor, is presenting a series on learning how to trust God's loving guidance," Julian continued. "Yesterday's sermon touched on being in a state of grace. Next Sunday she'll address how God speaks through unbelief."

"Sounds like her sermon was written just for me," Nora replied.

"God's truth communicates to us all, Nora. I suspect I need the pastor's sermon more than you." He shook his head.

He was too hard on himself, she thought.

"I haven't stepped a foot into a church since my divorce."

"Ryan Edwards will be singing *The Lord's Prayer.*"

"The opera singer?"

"He'll be in town."

She narrowed her gaze. "Are you trying to bribe me with an opera singer?"

"Maybe."

She worked her bottom lip. "I told you my father loved

opera. He once said that an opera singer is classically trained to focus on diction and tonality."

"I'm aware."

"You don't like opera, but you know this about opera singers?"

"I know now."

Nora hesitated, noting Julian's wide grin. "Let me think about it. Samantha hasn't entered a church in ages, either."

"There's no time like the present."

"She hasn't indicated any interest."

With a gleam of amusement in his eyes, Julian said, "Encourage her by sharing two words."

"Opera singer?"

"Nope."

He was silent, evidently, waiting for Nora to ask again.

"Which are?" she relented, too inquisitive to stay mute.

"Joseph Slater."

"A name."

"A prominent musician," Julian corrected. "He's a Grammy-nominated recording artist recognized worldwide for his worship songs. He's singing at the Sunday service too."

"Samantha listens to bluesy jazz. She won't have any inkling who Joseph Slater is."

"Ask her." He brought her into his arms for a lengthy kiss. A while afterward, he ran a hand along her back and murmured, "I'm off to scout out an abandoned building near the railroad tracks that might be ideal for Fresh 'n' Good."

"You mean the old shoe shop that went out of business years ago? I remember shopping for shoes there."

"It's located in a timeworn mill, and there's plenty of foot traffic."

She grinned. "Shoe shop? Foot traffic? Clever."

"Right." He smiled. "My boss is pressuring me to come up with a suitable location for the restaurant … and soon."

She rested her head on his chest and drew a long breath. It felt so relaxing to be in his arms.

Remember? Her rational brain intruded. Their time together was short-lived.

Unannounced, an inexplicable sadness settled over her.

Julian pulled back, studying her. He seemed aware of her change in mood and began regaling her with entertaining stories of various potential restaurant sites he'd encountered over the years—caves, train tunnels, and treehouses—and she couldn't help but laugh with him.

"I'll stop by the office later," he said. "Will you still be here?"

"Most likely."

"If you're not, I'll find you."

His answer prompted her wry response. "I'm sure you will."

"We'll go for dinner afterwards. My treat."

"You don't—"

"Sure I do. We'll celebrate."

"Why?"

"Because it's Monday."

"We're celebrating Monday?"

"Every day we're alive is a celebration."

She grinned. Julian, ever the optimist. "Where?"

"You're being picky when I'm treating?" He brushed his lips across her forehead. "Let's try Frank's Pizza. Tom recommended it as the best pizza place in town."

"From my recollection, it's the only pizza place within fifty miles."

"Another reason why I like it here. There are fewer choices." He chuckled at his own observation. "Please ask Samantha to join us."

"All right."

One more kiss, a gentle squeeze of his hand, and he was gone.

Nora stared at the empty doorway, then turned to the daisies on the desk. Daises were all about cheerfulness, fresh starts, and trustworthiness.

An accurate description of the flower. An accurate description of the man.

Julian's presence brought peace to her lonely, aching heart. His upbeat humor and romantic nature filled her with gladness.

However, he was busy with his work, and she was busy with hers.

Which was how her parent's marriage had evolved. Each had claimed their own set of chores and responsibilities. Theirs had been a business partnership rather than a love match.

A reality check of Nora's life emerged.

Perhaps that was the reason she'd been hesitant to find a man she could truly love after her divorce. Love had been elusive, and the youthful dreams of fairy-tale endings had indeed turned out to be make believe. She'd learned that hard lesson the hard way.

Her dating life had been nonexistent. Often, she'd given herself pep talks to sign up for an online dating app, or attend social events on the weekend. All too often, she'd convinced herself that she had enough on her plate with the everyday challenges of raising a child.

She blew out a sigh and reexamined the inn's budget.

By midafternoon, her brain was ready to explode.

Tom was correct. The monthly income hardly covered expenses.

She flipped to another page on his budget sheet. The cost of replacing burnt lightbulbs and broken hair dryers involved a revolving door of corrective upkeep. However, bigger problems emerged, beginning with preventive maintenance, which entailed comprehensive changes to the way things currently were handled.

More capital was required and operating costs needed to be cut. If not, one guarantee for the Cherish Hills Inn loomed.

Bankruptcy.

CHAPTER 7

ora was unable to accompany Julian to church the following Sunday, since Tom needed both her and Samantha to serve brunch. Samantha actually grumbled about not attending, and Nora suspected her discontent was because she wanted to see and hear Joseph Slater, the singer. However, Tom was looking wearier by the day and Nora wouldn't refuse him.

Julian didn't press Nora, and she was grateful for his quiet understanding.

"God will get tired of waiting for me," she declared with a half laugh.

"There's no wrong schedule for God," he said. "The best things from God aren't according to any agenda. He will move you when the timing is right. The highest blessings have no itinerary." As if to reassure her, he reached for her and held her close, and she appreciated his steadfastness and positivity.

Already she was beginning to know him—his faith, his strength, his convictions. Julian listened attentively, provided stability, and his optimism lifted her spirit.

Her conscience reminded she had fled from an intimate relationship with God because she believed she wasn't good enough.

Nothing had changed.

The old insecurity reared its head. Same misgiving, different seasons. She was a woman seeking faith, and looking to inspire her daughter to take the right path.

Trouble was, the world got in the way.

"You're always God's chosen child," Julian had counseled during one of their nightly text messaging sessions.

Her heart focused on finding a church. Her mind wasn't certain she was ready.

"Puppy steps," Julian had also advised, echoing her encouragement regarding his dog phobia. He'd included a smiley face emoji and wished her sweet dreams.

Yearning for a spiritual connection, Nora decided to attend the service on Wednesday evening. Clouds had given way to rain by late afternoon, and the constant drumming of droplets against the inn's windows had been soothing.

After dinner, she donned a bright-red raincoat over her black pencil skirt and printed silk blouse, snagged an umbrella, and marched the few blocks to the church for the seven o'clock service. June was heating up with the intensity of a Southern summer, and a rain-drenched breeze added a thickness to the air. Pansies and tree leaves drooped under the showers, and she splashed through the newly washed shimmer of water on the sidewalks. After church, this was a good night for warm cinnamon tea and cozy socks.

Julian had earmarked the evening to tutor Logan, a teenage boy enrolled in the Big Brothers Big Sisters program, and Samantha was waitressing. Nora hadn't told either of them of her resolution to attend church.

The previous week, Nora, Julian, and Samantha had

grabbed dinner at Frank's Pizza. Casually, Julian had opened his cellphone and introduced Samantha to Joseph Slater's worship songs. The guitar chords were simple, the melody basic, and Samantha was hooked. Julian remarked that Joseph had written the song, "Sing Glory Forever," which had been nominated for a Grammy award, slipping in the fact that Joseph and his wife, Scarlett, lived in Cherish.

"Louise mentioned that Scarlett volunteers at Canine Helpers." Nora glanced meaningfully at Julian while she spoke. "They train service dogs."

"Big dogs or little?" Julian inquired.

"Usually big."

"Piece of cake," he joked. "I like golden retrievers and German shepherds. Where do I sign up to help?"

"Service dogs come in all shapes and sizes," Nora clarified. "Small dogs are often used to warn their owners of changes."

He set down his pizza. "What kind of changes?"

"I'm not sure. Perhaps changes in their owner's mood? See for yourself."

His straight eyebrows drew together. "I'll consider it."

"Bravo." She raised her glass of iced tea and they clinked glasses.

Samantha, a slice of pepperoni pizza halfway to her mouth, paused to consider them, then ignored them in favor of the shaggy-haired teenage boy behind the counter.

As Nora entered Memorial Street Church, memories of past Sunday services rushed to the fore: the year she'd sat with her first grade class praying she wouldn't forget her memory verse, her dark-haired mother dabbing her eyes with a flowered handkerchief when the pastor's message was especially poignant, her tired-looking father wearing his Sunday finest—a navy suit, white shirt and tie.

Nora slid into a rear pew in case she felt compelled to dash out for some reason.

She didn't. In fact, she stayed until the final note of a long-forgotten hymn from her school days, "Amazing Grace," had been sung by the solo soprano.

How sweet the sounds, indeed, Nora reflected. Could it save someone like her?

She tapped her fingers to her heart, finished with a silent prayer, then lingered to sit with God for a while. "Praise you for the love you've given me and my daughter," she whispered. "I'm grateful. Please guide me on the right path."

She reminded herself the Lord sometimes took many days to reply. Often, He never replied at all.

No matter, for she was at a crossroads. The serenity of the peaceful church and the lyrical psalms had restored her balance on the heels of too many hectic days.

She rose, calmed and renewed, and fell into step with the other churchgoers. She exited the church and breathed in a lungful of clean air and wet earth. Post-rainstorm clouds streaked across the sky and a pastel sunset graced the heavens in strokes of gold and purple. The rain had stopped, and she slung her raincoat and handbag over her arm.

"Nora?" The recognizable, deep male voice made her pause. "I'm thrilled you're here."

Her mood soared as she turned to see Julian.

"Weren't you mentoring tonight?" she asked.

He took the stairs two at a time to reach her. "I did. Only Logan has a math test tomorrow and ducked out early to study. Are you headed back to the inn?"

"Where else?"

"Me too."

"What a coincidence."

He laughed and laced his fingers through hers. "We'll pass by Whitney's. Are you up for an ice cream cone?"

"I can't keep eating ice cream and pizza. Correction." She held up a hand. "I'd like to but—"

"Why not, then?"

"I want to continue fitting into the dresses I brought with me. I hoped to go down a size while I was here, rather than up one."

"Women are misguided. Stop reading fashion magazines and watching television and listen to real men." His gaze did a slow perusal of her figure, and he smiled. "A woman who fills out a skirt is sheer perfection."

Their stroll took them to the main street and the quaint shops that defined Cherish.

"There are pros and cons of living in a microscopic community," she observed.

"List the pros first."

"People will pitch in if there's a problem."

"You speak from experience?" he asked.

"My parents often needed assistance at the inn because of the ceaseless responsibilities."

He winked. "And here I assumed owning a successful inn meant sharing blueberry muffin recipes and collecting antiques."

She laughed, then sobered. "Once, a careless guest left a cigarette burning in his room. The fire was extensive and my parents were forced to close the inn for a month. The entire community donated money and furnishings and helped repair the damage. Then the whole town celebrated our reopening."

"God, family, and friends make all the difference." His gaze softened. "Let's list the cons."

"Let's?"

"I may be living here," he reminded her.

"A few months in Cherish is hardly a lifetime."

He shrugged. "Cons?"

"Towns this size can be small-minded and resistant to change. Residents are intent on safeguarding their routines and the manner in which they do business is paramount."

"Do you consider a Fresh 'n' Good restaurant an ostentatious eatery?"

"I never used the term *ostentatious*."

His lips tugged up at the corner. "Because *grandiose* is better."

"Fair warning, most folks here are content with plain and simple."

"There's nothing wrong with glamour. Studies prove that fine dining, an elevated ambiance, and superb service are highlights for diners."

She couldn't refute his rationale and kept silent.

They stopped in front of Whitney's. He stared at the sign listing the flavors as if he was searching for spelling mistakes. "A cone?" he suggested again.

Reluctantly, she shook her head, and they resumed their walk. "By the way, did you approve of the empty building near the train station?" she asked.

"I did, actually." He kept his fingers linked with hers. "Look, instead of discussing business, I'm interested in your thoughts on tonight's service."

"Marge Addyson is an inspirational pastor, and the worship music was beautiful. I recognized the hymns and sang all the lyrics. It's funny how certain memories never leave you."

"We're not navigating life alone," he said, rephrasing Marge's sermon. "God is always with us."

When they reached the inn, he paused. They stood beside a fence, shaded from view beneath a giant oak tree.

In a voice as rich as velvet, he said, "Thank you for another delightful evening."

His tender expression caused her insides to quiver, while a warning screamed in her ears. Proceed with caution. He's leaving. Why sacrifice your heart for a few hours of happiness?

She ignored the warning as his hands glided to her shoulders. He pressed her near and claimed her lips in a sweet, hungry kiss.

A FEW MINUTES LATER, they entered the lobby hand in hand. The clock in the hall chimed nine o'clock, and the restaurant had emptied out. Tom and Louise were nowhere to be seen.

Samantha erupted from the parlor, guitar in hand.

"Hi Mom." She smiled. "Hi Mr. Wilson." She frowned.

"Hi honey," Nora said while Julian extended a cordial hello.

"Guess what? Edison is driving to Cherish next weekend so we can rehearse. That is, if it's okay with you."

"Back up a minute." Nora briefly closed her eyes. "Rehearse for what?"

"His band. When we get back home to Virginia, he wants me to be a member."

"We're not leaving Cherish until the end of June."

"The weeks go by fast, Mom."

Truer words had never been spoken.

Nora glanced at Julian. The expression of disappointment on his face mirrored her own.

Why? They hadn't arranged to see each other once July appeared on the calendar. They were both merely passing through Cherish.

Nevertheless, she thought he might give her hand a slight squeeze, assuring her their relationship would continue.

He didn't.

His phone buzzed. He retrieved it from his pocket and glanced at the caller ID.

"Sorry." He excused himself. "One of the owners of Fresh 'n' Good is calling."

CHAPTER 8

*L*ater the following afternoon, Julian and Fred
Johnson, the Realtor representing Fresh 'n' Good,
met to review the purchasing of the shoe shop
building. Fred looked to be in his fifties, wasn't much taller
than Samantha, and assured Julian he'd do whatever neces-
sary to ensure an effective transaction. He was a long-time
resident of Cherish and proudly elaborated on the town's
history to whoever would listen.

Julian had recommended that Fresh 'n' Good purchase
the building because the location was highly visible and, in
his opinion, a hidden gem. The bustle of pedestrians and
ample street parking were all advantages. He'd checked the
interior of the shop, thickly coated in dust, and discovered
racks and racks of shoes. Many were in their original boxes
and perfectly preserved.

An inspection of the second and third floors exposed
broken glass and vine-covered walls. The men's footsteps
echoed on thick pine floors and splintered doors revealed
worn paint and an upper room taken over by a flock of
pigeons.

"Are the owners renovating everything?" Fred asked.

Julian grinned. "The use of a little elbow grease will convert the upper floors into condos."

After the meeting concluded, they stepped outside.

Clouds skittered across a cobalt sky. Summer had come to the Carolinas, and birdsong warbled from the trees. The breeze carried the candied fragrance of flowering magnolias.

Fred walked to his car and Julian followed.

"One more thing, Fred," he said.

"You want a pair of shoes from the 1970s?" Fred joked. "Help yourself. Many are still in style, and just need some sprucing up and leather polish."

"I'm set, thanks," Julian replied with a quick smile. "However, I'm thinking I want a permanent place to live here in Cherish."

"Permanent?" Fred made an impressive show of trying to keep his features noncommittal. "When we first spoke, you mentioned if the deal was successful, you planned to live in Cherish for six months, tops."

In the brief time Julian had known Fred, he seemed the type who followed his observations with a half-dozen questions. He didn't disappoint.

"Are you planning to rent out your house if you travel?" Fred inquired.

"No," Julian replied.

"Are you aware a town this size can have plenty of loudly expressed opinions, both good and bad?"

"Yes."

"The church is an integral part of many of the residents' lives."

"God comes first in my life too," Julian responded. "A home of my own has become important to me.

"To buy or to rent?"

"Either." Julian summarized his choice under Fred's shrewd gaze. "Whichever is quicker."

Fred's mouth curved in amusement. "The pretty Nora and her daughter are in town."

"I'm well aware."

"Tom bought the inn from Nora's parents many years ago," Fred continued. "They were in tough financial straits, and she was long gone by then."

"Where did she go?"

"Rumor was she eloped with her boyfriend. Some skinny kid from a nearby city who never kept a job."

Julian leaned against a tree. He allowed Fred all the time in the world to offer more details.

"Hmm." Fred's forehead creased. "You and Nora have been seen together on several occasions. In fact, you're the talk of the town."

The rumor mill again. Julian smiled.

"I'll look through the real estate listings and contact you."

As Fred headed for his car, people passing by exchanged friendly good wishes both to him and Julian.

Julian loved the fellowship of this old-fashioned town where children skipped exuberantly, and purple and pink petunias burst forth from decorative window boxes.

The idea of a place of his own opened a floodgate of emotions he'd kept bolted for many years. He'd spent the last several years of his life traveling across the United States, managing restaurants. There hadn't been much sense in purchasing a home he'd live in less than half a month.

Now, he intended to finally settle down. Not for six months. Permanently, although he hadn't figured out how to carry out his decision.

He took a seat on a bench, loosened his tie, and shrugged off his jacket.

It was time to settle down with a wife. A woman like

Nora—with wild black tangled hair, a striking contrast to her creamy complexion, high cheekbones, and amiable demeanor.

Her vivacious smile and quick wit drew him in. She was an intelligent beauty with a tall frame, small waist, and undeniable curves. The first time he'd kissed her, her long dark lashes had fluttered as she'd gazed up at him, and his world had come to a stop.

This was the woman, he'd thought. This was the woman who could change everything.

Undeniably, it would be difficult to start a relationship with someone who lived elsewhere.

So, why couldn't he ignore his attraction to her?

He rose, slung his jacket over his shoulder, and proceeded to the inn. As he passed Whitney's, he scanned the sign for the flavor of the day.

Dutch chocolate. Nora's favorite.

He paused and texted her. *Where are you?* he inquired.

Hawaii, came her reply. *I needed a break.*

He grinned. *Take a return boat to Cherish and meet me at Whitney's.*

I'm preparing a budget report for Tom.

Run it later.

I can't.

I have two words for you.

He visualized Nora's beautiful face, her forehead puckered in a frown.

Are you using the opera singer bait again?

Nope. He grinned, knowing any protest would soon die on her lips. Then he typed in the magical two words.

Dutch chocolate.

I'll be right there, came her quick reply.

Fifteen minutes later, Nora and Samantha headed toward him. Nora wore a lush floral sundress and sandals, and

Samantha had dressed in her pink beanie, jeans, and a balloon sleeve top. Samantha also lugged her guitar case, and her jaw tightened when she sighted him. Their quickening pace matched the quickening of his heart as his gaze refocused on Nora.

She tugged at a snarl in her hair as she and Samantha approached.

"Hi, Nora." He debated brushing a kiss on her cheeks, but opted for placing a hand on the small of her back. An innocent acknowledgment in front of her eagle-eyed daughter.

"Hi, Julian." Nora smiled a greeting.

"Greetings, Samantha," he went on. "Why the guitar?"

"Hello, Mr. Wilson." Samantha focused on his fingers, casually touching her mother. "I tagged along because I have a lesson at Musically Yours."

"With who?" He feigned surprise, although he'd arranged for Joseph Slater to teach her.

"*The* Mr. Joseph Slater."

"Those online lessons weren't cutting it?" Julian asked.

"Not so much."

"We'll walk you there. Then I'll buy you a takeout container of your favorite flavor."

"No thanks. I'm good." He didn't miss the grimace Samantha sent him.

Once they arrived at Musically Yours, Joseph Slater, a tall man with dark wavy hair and piercing blue eyes, hailed them.

Samantha was evidently starstruck, eyes glazed and totally speechless.

"If you care to meet my wife, she's over at Canine Helpers right now," Joseph said to Nora and Julian. "The center isn't far, and I'm sure she'd be delighted if you stopped by. I'll text her."

"Are there dogs there?" Julian's voice raised as he stepped back.

Joseph sent him a silent and quizzical, *You've got to be kidding*. Aloud, he answered, "I'm thinking yes. To begin with, Max dropped off Tiny Tim."

"The little dog?"

"Tiny Tim is a toy poodle and Yorkshire terrier mix," Joseph clarified.

"A Yorkipoo," Nora put in.

"A little dog," Julian repeated.

"We'll visit Canine Helpers." Nora said. "Thanks."

"Puppy steps," she reminded, as she half-dragged Julian and his stiff legs to Canine Helpers.

"A little dog," he reiterated. The wind caught his hair, and he wiped tiny beads of sweat from his forehead.

Scarlett Slater met them at the doorway. Her flamboyant red hair, deep green eyes, and jovial laugh should have put Julian at ease.

Nope.

He froze, rooted near the door, his gaze fixed on the fluffy miniature dog Scarlett held.

"Meet Max and Sarah's dog," she said. "Want to hold him?"

Nora loosened her grip on Julian's arm and cradled the dog. She and the dog shared a mutual, adoring gaze.

"Tiny Tim is friendly," Scarlett was saying. "We aren't training him. I'm watching him while Max and Sarah are working. He's a curious cutie."

Nora stroked his fur, murmuring, "You're also a sweetie." She swiveled to Julian. "Your turn?"

Aware of the women's gazes, he held his arms out straight, and Nora placed Tiny Tim in them. Scarlett politely remarked that Julian looked like he was holding a grenade rather than a dog weighing under ten pounds.

His face heated. At thirty-five years old, he shouldn't have to deal with such a fear. It was absurd. Determined, he peeked at Tiny Tim, then at the sky, pleading with God to deliver courage. When Julian looked back down, the dog's shiny black eyes were staring up at him affectionately.

"He's fond of you," Nora encouraged, depositing the dog back with Scarlett.

As they walked away, Nora found his fingers. "You were wonderful, Julian."

"I held Tiny Tim for all of ten seconds." His voice held a broad dose of uncertainty. "Surprisingly, though, it wasn't so bad."

His biggest lie ever. He'd almost neglected to breathe.

"Briefly is a promising start." Nora's response was soothing and nonjudgmental.

They sauntered past the park, leaving Canine Helpers far behind. He and Nora had analyzed his irrational fear, so rehashing it wasn't something he wanted to do. That settled, he reminded her they were going right past Whitney's.

"I can't resist." She patted her waistline. "I'll start my diet tomorrow."

"Breaking news," he said.

"Are you finally acknowledging I should lose weight?"

"I'm saying the opposite. You're perfect and don't get me started on your weight obsession." He kept her hand in his. "Before I forget, Fresh 'n' Good is slated to open by September or October."

"That's quick, considering how large the abandoned building is."

"They'll renovate a floor at a time." He gave her a wide smile. "What's your shoe size?"

"Huh?" She blinked. "My shoe size? Are you serious?"

"Always."

"Size eight."

"And Samantha's?"

"We wear the same size." She squinted at him. "Why?"

"Merely asking."

"Don't tell me you have a shoe fetish."

"I won't."

She sighed and airily dismissed his comment. "I think I've developed brain fog from analyzing Tom's budget. Or, more concisely, his lack of a budget."

"Did you find anything serious?"

"He's heading down a losing road, just like my parents."

"Is that why you're here? Because of your parents?"

"I should've been here for them when times got tough. I wasn't. Helping Tom is the least I can do."

"Guilty conscience?" he inquired.

"Always." She pushed out a breath and waved away the question. "I'll prepare another report for Tom, though my gut instinct is he'll suffer a substantial income loss after your restaurant opens."

"Disclaimer. Fresh 'n' Good isn't mine." Julian clipped a hand through his hair. "I'm merely the manager."

"Spouting that fact doesn't make you blameless, Julian."

In his opinion it did. Just like Nora shouldn't blame herself for not being there for her parents. He told her as much.

"Let's look at the bright side." He gestured toward Whitney's. "An established chain will attract more visitors, and the additional revenue is a win-win."

"We won't know for sure, and I won't be here." Her gaze volleyed to the wooden planters bedecked with purple pansies beneath Cherish Styles and Clips. "My boss is already asking if it's necessary that I'm gone until early July."

"Everyone is expendable, Nora."

"Thanks for the vote of confidence. When someone is no longer of value, I assume you mean they can be discarded?"

"I didn't mean anything like that."

"Like what? Like you're a control freak, telling me when and where I can and cannot work? Who is important and who is not?"

"You must realize my beliefs by now." He sucked in a sharp breath. "What brought this on?"

In his mind, he answered his own question. Frustration. The same frustration he felt at the realization they would soon be parted.

As they neared the ice cream shop, Nora fixed her gaze on the Whitney's sign. Julian was watching her, so a tree root growing up from the sidewalk caught him off-guard. He tripped and lost his balance. Nora tripped with him, and his arm shot out to prevent her fall. Her ankle bent, awkwardly contorting.

"Ouch!" Her voice held surprise. Her expressive eyes held pain.

Worry, quick and consuming, surged through him. "Are you hurt?"

"I'm okay." She offered a wobbly, reassuring smile. He extended his arm, and she seized it in a death grip. "I think I twisted my ankle."

He supported her the last few feet.

Limp. Limp. Limp.

He steadied her, eased the unruly hair from her forehead, and pulled out a chair in front of Whitney's. Gratefully, she sank down.

He loosened her sandal and ran a hand over her bare ankle. Nothing appeared broken, and he exhaled a relieved breath.

"Rest here." He yanked out his phone. He'd done a fairly competent job maintaining his composure, though his heartbeat hadn't yet returned to normal. "I'll call a cab to drive us."

"Don't be ridiculous, Julian. I can hobble a few blocks."

"Nora—"

"I insist."

"Can you move your ankle?"

She flexed her foot and grimaced. "Yes."

"I'll contact Joseph Slater." Julian fired off a rapid text. "He'll tell Samantha to meet us back at the inn when her lesson is finished."

"Sure."

A waitress appeared. "May I take your order?"

Nora massaged her ankle. "Believe it or not, Dutch chocolate ice cream isn't in my immediate plans anymore."

"We'll take a rain check. Thanks." Julian draped his arm around Nora's shoulders. "If you insist, we'll walk slowly."

She leaned against him all the way back to the inn, which delighted Julian.

Samantha didn't share his enthusiasm when she dashed through the front door.

"I'll find Louise," she volunteered. "She's competent."

Her message to Julian was crystal-clear: We don't need you. Women take care of each other.

Of late, Samantha had spent her off hours with Louise. She'd shown Louise several chords on the guitar, and Louise had taught Samantha how to knit her own beanies. Despite the age difference, both the older woman and the teen seemed to crave the companionship and someone to listen to them.

"Elder hunger," Nora had half joked, when he'd reported his observation.

"They're bonding," he acknowledged. "And Samantha has taken to calling Louise *Auntie*."

"Samantha never knew her grandparents, and I'm reminding myself not to interfere, because then their dynamics will be different," Nora said. "Louise is an admirable and wise influence. Even Tom is warming up to Samantha."

"You're a smart woman and caring parent, Nora," Julian responded. "They're teaching each other to observe the world through each other's perspective."

Nonetheless, Samantha was still possessive of Nora when it came to Julian.

In many ways, she reminded him of himself with his own mother. She'd been a single parent, and as the oldest son, he was protective of her.

He ordered himself to be understanding and validate Samantha's feelings, then closed his eyes and whispered a plea to God for guidance.

CHAPTER 9

$\mathcal{A}$ sprained ankle, Nora soon learned from Louise, demanded four treatments: rest, ice, compression, and elevation.

"RICE," Louise declared. "An easy acronym to remember."

The tenderness and swelling had subsided. Even so, Louise insisted Nora not place any undue stress on her ankle.

Julian heartily approved.

From Louise's sidelong grin, Nora suspected she was relieved Nora wouldn't be waitressing.

"For how long?" Nora asked.

"Three days, possibly less," the doctor advised when Julian had brought her into his office for an examination. "Your ankle seems stable. The pain and stiffness you've described is moderate, and there are no torn ligaments."

And so she rested.

The following day, an early morning dawn cast a rosy hue across the sky, and Nora flopped in a rocker on the porch. Samantha and Louise checked out guests at the front desk, and Julian was on a phone consultation with one of the owners from Fresh 'n' Good.

Nora had nearly closed her eyes when Tom greeted her with a gruff, "Are you awake?"

Her eyes flew open. "I dozed for a second. The air is pleasant and peaceful and—"

"Mind if I join you?"

She swept out her hand. "This is your inn."

Tom collapsed next to her with a grunt. Silently, they rocked back and forth for several beats.

"I remember these same swaying tree branches and summer breezes," she said. "As I grew older, there were many occasions when I would've traded my eyeteeth to hang out with friends and swim at the community pool." She sighed, half to herself. "Alas, those dreams weren't meant to be because of the constant work schedule."

Tom stopped rocking and fixed her with a blunt stare. "May I be frank?"

"Absolutely."

"By the time your parents sold me the inn, I suspected their hearts were no longer in it."

Nora's eyes widened in surprise. "The inn was the center of their universe."

"No, you were, from what I understand," he said. "Perhaps the reason their passion died was because they lost you."

"They didn't 'lose' me. We just … lost touch." Or rather, she broke ties with them. Angry and rebellious, she'd rashly eloped with her boyfriend and moved far away from Cherish to prove she was adult enough to make her own choices. Good or bad. Right or wrong.

"Are you returning to your accounting job soon?" Tom's voice interrupted her thoughts, her misgivings.

"My boss texts every day. Apparently, the firm is finally beginning to appreciate me."

"Huh."

Huh?

She pushed the rocker hard with her toe. "Why bring this up?"

"Maybe you should consider a change of career."

She steeled herself. Tom was parroting Julian's words. Next he would offer a "Nobody is expendable" speech.

"To do what?" She pressed her hands together in her lap.

"You have a knack for innkeeping." His gaze swept the lawn, and the overgrown bushes begging for a pruning. "I'm thinking about eventually slowing down and retiring. Louise has dropped hints and I'm looking for someone competent to take over."

Someone like her?

A myriad of reasons to say no came to the fore. She'd disconnected from the inn years ago. Sure, she'd returned, but only for a short time.

"Are you suggesting me?" she asked.

"It crossed my mind."

She gazed at him. "I prefer a reliable and steady income."

He remained silent for so long, she wondered if he had heard her. She was about to voice more opinions when he said, "Spoken as a responsible and careful accountant."

"From our shared experiences, you can't refute that owning an inn is a 24/7 job with no holidays." She shook a disobedient curl from her face. "A substantial cash reserve is essential to weather the losses. Most inns operate at only 50 percent capacity, not to mention the extra capital required for health and property insurance. I won't live on hope, Tom. Teenagers are expensive, plus there's college for Samantha in a few years."

"At my advanced age, I've learned nothing is 100 percent secure. For example, take your twisted ankle, or my heart attack, or the new restaurant." His lined face sagged heavily with regret. "Our days on Earth are brief and constantly changing."

On Sunday, neither Nora nor Samantha waitressed, and Julian volunteered to walk them to church for the service. The doctor had proclaimed Nora's ankle healed, due to the proper rest and the ice she'd frequently applied.

The previous evening at an impromptu dinner, Julian had mentioned to Samantha that Joseph Slater would be playing guitar at the service. As he no doubt anticipated, she nearly popped out of her pink canvas sneakers at the opportunity to attend church.

"You're incorrigible," Nora had murmured to him.

He widened his eyes. "Me?"

"You have a talent with words. Two words in particular."

"Joseph Slater?"

"Um, no."

His earnest gaze fastened on her. "You're beautiful."

She felt her cheeks pinken as he grabbed her hand under the table, his thumb caressing her palm while Samantha dug into her strawberry shortcake.

"Ready?" he asked when they met in the lobby.

Then he did something Nora never expected. He ignored her and chatted the entire few blocks to church with Samantha about Joseph Slater's music.

After the inspiring service, Nora, Samantha and Julian stood outside and conversed with numerous townspeople they'd come to know.

"Are you both interested in a sneak peek at the vacant building Fresh 'n' Good bought?" Julian gave Nora a gallant bow. "However, only if you feel up to the walk."

"I'm fine," Nora said.

Samantha declined. "I'm going back to my room to practice guitar. Mr. Slater said he'll email me the music for his worship song, and I can't wait to play the chords for Auntie Louise and Uncle Tom."

Nora and Julian exchanged knowing, smiling glances.

"How about we bring you a slice of Frank's pizza when your mother and I return?" Julian asked Samantha.

"Jake is bringing a pepperoni pizza to the inn." Samantha signaled to a shaggy-haired youth standing a few feet away. "We're eating lunch together."

Nora looked from Jake to her daughter. "What happened to Edison?"

"Old news, Mom. Jake saw me in church just now and texted about grabbing a pizza. I texted him back and said sure."

"I didn't see you texting."

"Teenagers text quick. We don't even look at our phones."

Nora squinted at the tall, lanky boy. "How old is he?"

"He's my age."

"Where did Jake get your cellphone number?"

"Auntie Louise."

Nora's lips pursed. "She gave him your number?"

"She's friends with his parents." Samantha smiled. "Everyone is friends with everyone here."

"You make it sound like a reason to stay."

"This town is awesome."

When had Samantha experienced such an abrupt change of heart? The interest of a caring community had had a positive influence, and that realization brought a grateful smile to Nora's face.

Along the way to the vacant building, Nora and Julian peered through the sparkling-clean windows of boutique stores, discussing the unique giftware—mason jars, herbal gardens, flowered tea towels, and vintage postcards. Laughing and conversing with him had taken on an other-worldly quality all its own.

"God's grace is upon us." Julian said, bringing up the sermon. "He is our strength."

"No matter what adversities come onto our path." Nora repeated the pastor's declaration. "Leave the negative behind."

"Imagine the tiny mustard seed. Faith grows sure and steady in our lives."

"And you are planting the seeds."

"God is also, as well as your parents. They took you to church all those years ago. Don't skip that part because the process of faith doesn't happen overnight."

When they reached the building, Julian extracted a key and led her inside.

He pointed to the racks of shoes. "I convinced the owners to distribute these to Big Brothers Big Sisters, and then the rest to the community. However, I found a gift for you, Cinderella. Size eight, correct?" He dusted off a bench and beckoned her to sit, then reached behind the counter for a box.

An objection formed on her lips.

He kissed her, smothering her protest, then prompted her to open the box.

Inside was a tiny crystal slipper.

She held it up to the sunshine pouring through the window, admiring the shoe's rainbow reflection and design. "Julian, this is hardly a size eight."

"Size two is the best I could manage." He slipped her a rueful glance, then kissed her palm. "I don't recommend you wear such a high heel, especially with your recovering ankle. When I began cleaning the store, this discovery was magical.

I researched and learned the slipper was exhibited in the front display case."

She hid a smirk behind the slipper. "Only one?"

"There's more than one?"

His grin was so boyishly appealing that she laughed. "Don't you remember any fairy tales?"

"Hmm. I'll try to find a match." He seemed relaxed as he mangled the story lines of several fairy tales with charming wittiness. He obviously did know his fairy tales—probably better than she. Another quality she appreciated. His humbleness.

She blew him a kiss. "Thank you, Prince Charming. Thank you." Warmth radiated through her chest. This was happiness.

He smiled, his laugh lines evident. She hadn't noticed them before. "I was hoping for more than an air kiss."

"How about shoes in my size?" she teased.

He tugged out a box from a section labeled size eight and presented her with a pair of red Mary Jane shoes, flat, closed toe, and embellished with a strap. "Will these be okay?"

"They were popular in the 1900s."

"You'll wear them?"

"Certainly. They're back in style." She set the box beside her, then rubbed her thumb over the mirror-like glass of the slipper. "I'll treasure your gifts always—mementoes of my stint in Cherish."

"A month isn't nearly long enough." His voice deepened, a throaty murmur.

"A month is all we have." There, she'd said it aloud. The elephant in the room.

"Why? We have so much in common. Our shared humor, how well we get along." His gray eyes welled as he swept a kiss along her brows. His lips traveled, exploring her cheeks, lightly kissing her mouth.

She congratulated herself on doing a fabulous job of maintaining her poise. "Lots of folks share commonalities. My priority is my daughter and livelihood, and an unpaid four-week position in Cherish doesn't count."

He threw her a convincing grin. "Our priorities regarding family and friendships are the same. Our ..."

Love.

He didn't say the word aloud. He didn't have to. She saw the emotion in his eyes, his smile. He was falling in love with her. And she was falling in love with him.

He stared at her, refusing to let go. The dusty shop, the glass slipper, the entire world melted into nothingness. All that mattered was Julian's intense, smoldering gaze.

No, no. Her hours in Cherish were earmarked for Tom, for the memory of her parents. She hadn't come searching for romance.

Though here it was. Or rather, here *he* was. Julian.

Moral and honorable, he truly cared about her and her daughter. A man she valued as a friend. A man she could happily spend a lifetime with.

He leaned close and cuddled her. His strong arms wrapped around her, and her soft body molded to his chest.

She ran a finger across his lips. "Julian, we both know this isn't a good idea. I'm leaving soon and so are you. We shouldn't complicate matters."

"I'm not leaving."

An odd feeling fluttered in her stomach. "You're not?"

"I'm setting down roots in Cherish." Before she could ask any questions, he kissed her again—tender and gentle and passionate, as was his nature. He took his time. The man who loved to kiss. "And I'm not ready for you to leave either," he murmured.

She rested her head on his chest, hearing the quiet thud of his heartbeat.

This was news. He was asking her to stay.

Wasn't he? Or was he demanding?

"Competent help is necessary for the business side of a restaurant," he continued. "The main office has its own accounting branch, though each eatery runs independently."

"All these job offers," she muttered. "From Tom and now you."

"I don't understand."

"Nothing. Nothing. Whom do you normally employ in these instances?"

"Usually locals," he replied.

"There's your answer."

"What was my question?"

"Aren't you offering me a job?"

"Perhaps, if you were a local."

She stiffened. "Which, as you undoubtedly know, I'm not."

"But you *were* once, and could become again."

Beats of silence. Awkward seconds while she debated how to respond.

"Are you asking me to remain in Cherish?" Her voice tripped over the question. She didn't wish to appear needy. A strong dose of embarrassment would surely pour through her if she'd misinterpreted his words.

"Your choice. Whatever your current salary is in Virginia, I'll match it if you relocate here and I'll add a yearly bonus along with sick leave and benefits."

She narrowed her gaze. "Once again, you're trying to tell me how to live my life."

"You already have two jobs between the Cherish Hills Inn and your full-time accounting position. I was musing aloud."

"Musing?" She grabbed hold of the shoes. "Sounds like you were doing more than musing."

"You jumped to a conclusion."

"Did I?"

He eyed the shoes. "Are you planning to throw those at me?"

"It crossed my mind."

"Forget it," he said.

Forget what? His offer or throwing the shoes at him?

They packed up. Their pace scarcely resembled their earlier stroll to church. Now, they didn't speak, their steps quick. She tucked the boxes under her arms, refusing his request to carry them for her. One held the Mary Jane shoes —sensible and practical. The other boasted the glass slipper —a fanciful dream.

She refused to chide herself for their disagreement. Yet later that evening she stared at her bedroom ceiling for hours. Their argument had stemmed largely from her being self-protective. No one could blame her for being anxious about getting too close to someone. Not if they knew her experience, relying on a teenage husband who'd bolted when nights with a newborn got rough.

Julian's offer, if indeed he'd made an offer, was too much, too unexpected. She was strong and independent. She'd established herself as a career woman and created a stable home in Virginia. She and Samantha were content.

Weren't they?

CHAPTER 10

Three days later, Nora decided she was returning to Virginia and taking Samantha with her.

"We're leaving almost a week early?" Samantha displayed the calendar on her phone and put her finger on the date. "Why?"

"Aren't you glad?" Nora laid her folded chiffon dress and silky sea-green scarf in her suitcase. "You preferred not to be in Cherish, anyway."

"I changed my mind. I like everyone here." Samantha slung her hands on her slender hips. "Did you tell Uncle Tom and Auntie Louise?"

"Not yet, honey." Nora rubbed her upper arms, her muscles stiff.

She'd secure an internet setup between Tom's computer and hers because she didn't want to leave him hanging, and intended to work on his budget remotely. Through questioning the staff, she planned to implement cross-training as a means to save money. There was no reason why the woman who handled the laundry couldn't help out at the front desk during the busy hours, or the teenage busboy update Tom's social media on a regular basis. However, Nora was mindful the personnel shouldn't be overburdened, and resolved to share her concerns with Tom.

"I love my guitar lessons with Mr. Slater." Samantha darted her gaze to the guitar propped in the corner. "Besides, I've finally started to make friends. Jake gushed about the fantabulous music program. Music and math are his favorite subjects, exactly like me."

"We have so much in common," Julian had told Nora.

Memories of their afternoon in the shoe shop surged, and her throat clogged

Tears had filled his eyes as he'd swept a kiss along her brows, her cheekbones, before affectionately kissing her mouth. Her stomach had quivered at his gentle touch, so tender despite his compelling masculinity. Julian wasn't ashamed to show his emotions. As a little boy, he'd been taught not to cry, yet, as an adult man, he hadn't hidden his tears.

He'd texted her the previous evening. Then he'd left a voice message. He and his Realtor were viewing homes for sale in Cherish all day.

She never responded, nor did she disclose her resolution to leave. Soon, she told herself. Soon. Just not today, although she didn't know if she could endure living apart from him.

Now that she was in her thirties, she strove to be wiser in a relationship. Nonetheless, she wasn't prepared to sacrifice her heart solely to have it shattered. True love and fairy-tale romances? Not possible, at least not in her life.

Still, she prayed—even though God hadn't answered.

"Nice shoes, Mom." Samantha glared down at Nora's shoes. "Red matches well with our aprons tonight."

"I'm not waitressing anymore. There are other jobs to attend to."

"Another decision?"

"A necessary one."

"You're making too many choices without considering what I want." Samantha stomped from the bedroom, declaring she was heading to Frank's Pizza to share a calzone with Jake and then would report to the restaurant.

Nora sighed, closed her suitcase, and set it on the floor. She couldn't be a coward forever. She was obligated to inform Tom.

Tom first. Then Julian. The idea of leaving Julian brought a leaden hollowness to her chest. She sucked in a healthy whiff of resolve and, emboldened, marched down the stairs.

The angry voices emerging from Tom's office caused her to pause.

"I'm ready to retire, Tom." Louise's distinct Southern drawl held an edge. "We're at an age when we should think more about ourselves and less—"

"Cherish Hills Inn is an institution," Tom cut her off. "I've considered what you're saying regarding retirement."

"How long then?"

"A few months."

"Months?" Louise's voice raised. "I'm not a spring chicken anymore. I can't wait months."

"How about a few weeks?"

"No!"

Nora wasn't sure when Julian appeared beside her. He pushed open the office door to reveal Louise and Tom. They stood, hands clenched at their sides, confronting each other.

Louise's chin was high, her complexion reddened.

Tom made a sweeping motion with his arm. "Julian, can you talk some sense into this woman? I can't up and leave the inn tomorrow."

"Listen, you two lovebirds." Julian said, while Nora held her breath. "No decision needs to be finalized this evening. Tomorrow is soon enough to plan your retirements."

Louise's posture remained stiff. "I've never visited Arizona. I want to see the Grand Canyon."

"You will," Julian assured her.

"Come, my peach cake. I'll treat you to dinner." Tom bent to plant a kiss on her cheek and she swatted him away.

"You own this restaurant, you cheapskate," she blustered. "I better mean more to you than a discount date."

"I'll take you anywhere," he called as she fumed from his office.

She whirled. Her eyes sparked. "Arizona! Our next meal together will be eaten in Arizona."

"What's in Arizona?" Tom asked no one in particular when she slammed the door behind her.

"The Grand Canyon," Nora and Julian replied.

THE NEXT TWO HOURS DRAGGED. Nora had requested Julian allow her space because crunching Tom's budget numbers awaited. He'd sighed resignedly, tipped his head with a reminder he'd text later, then retreated.

In frustrated silence, she sank into the desk chair.

She couldn't carry on a reasonable conversation with Julian after the scene with Tom and Louise. Abruptness wasn't part of her nature, and she'd been ill-mannered for dismissing him so shortly. Nevertheless, her duty to Tom was paramount, and costs should be cut to reduce his bottom line. Negotiating lower vendor rates was a sensible beginning, and she'd suggest Tom schedule in-person meetings with the sellers. Also, guests staying extra nights could reuse towels and request when they'd prefer their rooms cleaned, not necessarily every day, requiring no additional cost to the inn besides a simple note on the door. She grinned at the ceramic rooster, running a finger along its dusty feet. She'd find all the roosters a happy home at the thrift store.

When she was too tired to continue, she climbed the stairs to her room, dropped into the rocking chair, and removed her shoes. As she set the shoes in her lap, a knock sounded at the door.

"Nora?" a familiar male voice called.

She sat up. "Julian?"

"May I come in?"

His tone sounded oddly urgent, and she frowned. "Yes. The door is unlocked."

He quickly stepped inside. "I assume you haven't heard the news because you didn't respond to my texts."

His unintended accusation raised her hackles. "I left my phone in my room. I just returned and haven't checked for messages."

"I'm sorry. I didn't mean—" His appearance was ragged. He looked scruffy, a stubble of beard on his chin. She hadn't noticed it earlier.

"What is it?" Panic gripped her chest. She half stood. The shoes fell to the floor.

"Tom suffered another heart attack. He's in the intensive care unit."

"No." In apprehension and despair, she slumped back into the seat.

"Don't worry." Julian crossed the room to give her shoulder an encouraging squeeze. "His condition is stable."

She pushed herself up. "We need to go."

They leapt into motion.

Nerves battered Nora in the fleeting distance to the hospital. She drove her car, and they avoided the "What if anything happens to Tom?" topic. Quiet dominated the space between them. Where had their relaxed banter gone? The easy chatting she and Julian once shared?

Julian finally spoke, saying he'd texted Samantha. "She's with Jake and she wants us to phone her when we learn anything. Louise is already in the hospital and blaming herself since her and Tom's argument."

"Ridiculous," Nora murmured as she parked.

Soon after they arrived and had consoled Louise, Tom's condition was attributed to indigestion, and the doctor declared he would be released in the morning. Louise insisted on staying the night with him, and Nora phoned Samantha with the heartening message. In the hush of the late June evening, Nora and Julian walked back to her car.

Julian opened the door for her, then went around to the passenger side. These actions defined him forever the gentleman.

They sat together in the parking lot. The hour neared midnight, the lot uncrowded save for a few cars passing now and then.

"There's a subject I wish to discuss," Julian began without preamble.

She started, attempting not to act as interested as she was. "Such as?"

"I was thinking ... hoping ... that we can visit the church tomorrow and schedule an appointment with the pastor to begin preparations for our marriage."

Her breath hitched. Her skin tingled. "Us? Marry?"

"Yes. I love you. And I'm almost certain you love me."

"Almost certain?" Her voice sounded soft and halting to her ears.

He grinned. "I'm fairly certain. Right, okay, I *am* certain. I hope to adopt Samantha and already love her as my own."

"Samantha ... I can take care of her. I've done that all my life."

"I'd like the opportunity to be a father to her. I know what you wish to provide her, and I want the same. A place where she is surrounded by people who care and support her. A town that prays and values church and God." He swallowed. "I made an offer on a brick ranch-style home. I'll put a hoop up over the garage for Samantha."

Nora tried to speak. Elated tears misted her vision. "She's never played basketball."

"Once we're married, I'll teach her how to shoot baskets. The house even has a yard."

"Big enough for a dog?"

"I'm not that brave."

"Wait. You're certain that I love you?"

"Beyond a doubt." His lips twitched. "You've voiced it many times without words. I see it in your eyes. I feel it whenever I kiss you."

Tears streamed down her cheeks, and he cradled her face in his hands. "Why are you crying?"

"An honest Christian community is the only place I want to live."

"Me too. I've asked myself, where are we in our lives, Nora? Where are we headed?" With a touch of his fingertips, he absorbed her tears.

She gazed at the handsome man sitting by her side, and her heart pitched.

They were headed in the same direction. Together. Wherever she traveled would always be in partnership with him.

"The house is located near the high school." He met her stare, his gaze intense, gauging her reaction. "The district is ranked number one in the state."

Nora couldn't contain her smile. "Samantha mentioned the school is top notch."

"And you ... you could ..."

"Please don't suggest running the inn. I'll help Tom, though it's not my dream job."

A million ideas floated through her head.

"Perhaps set up your own accounting business and handle the reports for the Cherish Hills Inn and Fresh 'n' Good."

"True." She didn't want the inn to fail and could work with Tom to keep it solvent.

Julian hugged her, then tipped up her chin. "Nora Lancaster, will you marry me?" His voice was solemn and husky.

She gazed into his pure gray eyes, and a rush of tenderness ran through her. Her husband to be. Thrilled, she nodded her agreement. "Yes. Yes. I'm in love with you, Julian Wilson."

He traced his fingers along her cheekbone. His woodsy male scent flooded her senses. "I knew it," he whispered.

He kissed her like a man who'd fallen head over heels in love.

Happiness filled her spirit. Soon, she and Samantha would carry his name.

Beneath the cotton of his polo shirt, his chest was comforting and solid. Her fingers covered his thumping heart.

He was silent for a long beat. "I fell in love with you the first night in the dining room, when you announced the chef was agreeable."

"He seems pleasant, as long as you don't cross him."

"Good to know."

"And you had me believing you were a vegetarian." She chuckled. "I get your sense of humor."

"Appreciated."

Looking back, she realized she had fallen in love with him at that same moment—when they'd mopped up spills, and spoke of cleaning kitchen counters, and discussed her and her daughter's similarities.

After decades of running away, Nora and Julian had arrived at a place, a home, where they truly belonged. A family to raise her daughter.

Surely, this was a day to remember, and a joyful homecoming to cherish.

EPILOGUE

*D*ear Auntie Louise and Uncle Tom,

How is Arizona? I can't believe it's been two years since you moved there. I loved the pictures of the Grand Canyon you sent. It's so cool, and I'm looking forward to vacationing with you there. Mom and Dad said you're living in an RV and traveling around the country.

I finished my senior year in high school and am counting the days until I attend college. I'm majoring in music and composing worship songs on the guitar. Mr. Slater said they're decent, but he always says nice things.

We attend church every week, and often on Wednesday nights too. Mrs. Addyson is one of my favorite preachers. Her sermons are awesome, and I believe she is speaking directly to me. How does she know? Mom said the sermons always resonate with her too and we discuss prayer a lot. Dad said prayer is a comfort and God will always be there for us.

Mom works at her accounting business during the day, and Dad said buying Cherish Hills Inn from Uncle Tom is the best decision he ever made after he left Fresh 'n' Good. I think adopting me was his best decision. When I told him, he agreed, then asked me to shoot hoops in the driveway. I'm getting fairly decent at basketball, though not as good as him.

It was awkward at first after he and Mom got married. I didn't know what to call him, but he was patient. I decided on Dad, because he is my Dad, and he seemed really happy when I told him.

He buys flowers for no reason. When I asked him why, he said it was to celebrate another day. He also gives Mom and me handwritten cards. His messages always make me smile, and Mom says he's a romantic at heart.

He also volunteers at Big Brothers Big Sisters every week, and I often go along to help. The little kids are so cute and always need assistance with their homework.

Fresh 'n' Good is a popular eatery, and Dad says they're healthy competition for the inn. We'll eat at both places when you come visit Cherish, and you can tell me your opinion. I like the inn's food better. The first thing Dad did when he bought the inn was to install a new coffee machine.

P.S. Did I tell you we got a dog? He's one of Molly Belle's puppies and adorable. Sheriff Nicholas reminded Dad that he'll get big. Dad looked kind of nervous, though Mom assured him small dogs are friendly and that she'd help him. I'm not sure what she was talking about. Then they kissed, as usual. So it's all good.

P.P.S. You asked about my boyfriend, Jake. He's old news. I met a cute boy at Whitney's Ice Cream shop. His name is Sebastian. I hope you get to meet him before I break up with him when I go to college.

Please write soon.

Love,

Samantha Wilson

THE END

CRISSY'S CHICKEN 'N' DUMPLINGS RECIPE

Ingredients:
1 pound uncooked chicken breast chopped
5 cans low-sodium chicken broth
1 family-size can of cream of chicken soup
2 1/2 stalks of celery chopped
1/2 large bag of frozen super-sweet white corn
3 russet potatoes, peeled and diced
1/4 pound baby carrots, chopped
1/4 teaspoon onion powder
1/2 teaspoon black pepper
Fresh rosemary, if desired.

Dumplings:
  1 1/2 cups flour
  1 egg
  1/2 cup milk
  1/2 teaspoon salt
  1 1/2 teaspoons baking powder

Directions:

Place chicken broth, chicken, and potatoes in pot on medium-high heat and bring to a boil.

Cover and boil until chicken is tender, approximately 7-10 minutes, depending on size of chicken pieces.

Reduce heat to medium.

Add cream of chicken soup, seasonings, and remaining vegetables.

Keep covered and boil 15-20 minutes or until vegetables are tender.

For dumplings:

Add all the ingredients to a large bowl and mix to combine. Using your hands or a spoon scoop into dumplings, about the size of an overflowing tablespoon. The dough will be sticky.

Carefully drop dumplings into boiling soup or stew and cook for 15-20 minutes, or until dumplings no longer fall apart. Cover with a tight-fitting lid while cooking.

Enjoy!

Thank you for reading *A Homecoming To Cherish.* I hope you liked my sweet inspirational romance. I've enjoyed creating the fictional, faith-filled community of Cherish, and hope you have come to love the characters as much as I loved writing them.

Sometimes a story and romance just clicks, and this happened when I wrote the heroine, Nora, and the hero, Julian. I found their sweet, inspirational romance irresistible.

I also had fun creating Samantha, Nora's teenage daughter.

Please help other people find *A Homecoming To Cherish* by posting your review.

A Homecoming To Cherish is available in ebook, paperback, Large Print Paperback, hardcover, and Audiobook.

My Spotify Play List for A Homecoming To Cherish is here.

USA TODAY BEST-SELLING AUTHOR
JOSIE RIVIERA
a Summer to Cherish

InD'Tale Magazine Crowned Heart of Excellence 5 Star Review:

"When the main ingredient in David Fodero's artistic career threatened to shut everything that defines him, he withdraws from the rest of his world to a secret place where he hopes no one, from the life he is choosing to exit, can ever locate him. Ashley Madden who solely relies on David's art supplies, though indirectly, to keep her business alive, has to do something when the man holding the keys to her business disappears. Not knowing where to find him, she makes a trip to one of her close friends, Sarah, hoping to get a lead. True to her instincts, her friend gives her the much-needed help to locate the famous artist who has decided to shut the door to the business world. She barely knows the man. How will she even start questioning his disappearance?

What begins as a casual attempt to keep one's livelihood afloat takes a huge spin when the curtain of the artist's cool cabin split open. When the witty character of Ashley and the stoic no-nonsense stature of David mix, a rainbow of humor, hope, joy, and a great romance is born.

What an artistic piece of literary art!
The reader is totally carried away by the sequential waves of storyline that keeps the boat rocking, making it a perfect read for any day, any time. The theme of how to deal with people's disabilities through compassion shines throughout Ashley's role, making "A Summer to Cherish" a perfect mirror for the contemporary society. Undoubtedly, lots of work, thoughts, and amazing talent went into what became this wonderful read."- JM Lareen

"A delightful romance from Josie Riviera, reminding readers to value moments spent with those who fill our hearts with joy."
--SHANNA HATFIELD, USA Today bestselling author

PRAISE AND AWARDS

USA TODAY bestselling author

#43 Amazon Contemporary Christian Romance Books

#75 Amazon Contemporary Christian Romance

CHAPTER 1

*Every child is an artist. The problem is how to remain an artist
once he grows up.*
- Picasso

A famous artist didn't just disappear.

Ashley Madden steered her beat-up Chevy convertible around the final treacherous curve connecting her hometown of Greenwood, South Carolina, to Cherish, South Carolina. Earlier, a storm had kicked up, leaving a debris of tree branches and leaves. Fortunately, the trip took less than two hours to drive by car.

The route led her through the center of the town, which boasted peaceful, immaculate streets, brick-paved sidewalks, and a decided lack of skyscrapers.

She lowered her car window, drew in a breath of a rain-soaked breeze, and snagged the last peanut butter cup from her stash. She took a bite and exhaled a contented sigh.

Unhealthy food was definitely the tastiest.

Her gaze fixed on the road ahead, and she eased up on the gas pedal as she neared her destination. She kept her chin high, her eyes alert. This artist needed to be found, and she intended to find him. She was determined to preserve her free art program for handicapped children and their families low on funds.

Art made people think, made people feel. Art inspired her students to dance and jump up and down with joy.

And art lasted a long time—certainly longer than her relationship with her ex, who'd dumped her with a quick text:

Sorry it didn't work out between us.

And just like that, the relationship was over.

She eased her convertible into the first available parking space near Thumbs Up, a plant retail store and greenhouse. Squinting in the rearview mirror, she patted down her cowlick. Why couldn't it grow in the same direction as the rest of her hair?

It never occurred to her to fuss with her appearance. She didn't consider herself pretty—she was slight, though her feet were too big. People often remarked on her ready smile, though.

Today, she'd dressed in her typical uniform of a plain white T-shirt and chambray shorts. She couldn't imagine styling her honey-blond, shoulder-length hair other than tying it in a haphazard ponytail. Her makeup ritual consisted of sunscreen and a rosy lip gloss.

She shut off the ignition, unbuckled her seatbelt, then walked across the damp grass to the entrance of the greenhouse. Thick summer air hung heavy, the sun appearing through a gauze of humidity.

She shaded her eyes and peered at the sky. God's golden assurance, sunlight, was forever faithful. Regardless of the rain, He repeatedly guaranteed something better was around the corner.

Ashley entered the greenhouse, instantly recognizing the dark-haired woman engrossed in watering a pot of mauve African violets.

"Sarah?" Ashley came up behind her and tapped her on the shoulder.

Sarah whirled. "Ashley! Twinkle!"

Ashley smiled. Her nickname from a precious student. The name had stuck.

Sarah set the watering can to the side and tugged the apron from her slim waist. "How was the drive?"

"The roads are a mess from the windstorm." Ashley spoke slowly to help Sarah read her lips. Sarah had been diagnosed recently with a hearing loss and wore hearing aids.

"Were the roads littered with trees?"

"It could've been worse." Ashley embraced her friend in a hug. "However, I'm here and I'm fine."

"I'm due for my lunch break. Will you help me haul these bags to the storeroom first?" Sarah pointed to several bags of soil and sheepishly smiled.

Ashley returned the smile. "Of course."

Afterward, they headed toward the rear patio. Sarah grabbed a couple of bottles of water, a turkey sandwich on rye bread, chips, and a chocolate bar.

"Want to share?" She handed Ashley a bottle of water.

"Sure." Ashley slid onto a picnic table beneath a pink-flowered crepe myrtle tree. "I'll take the candy."

Sarah sat across from Ashley and whispered a prayer of grace before unwrapping the sandwich.

Ashley opened her candy bar. Chocolate, her favorite. "Any luck locating David Fodero?" she asked.

Sarah unwrapped her sandwich. "You mean, your reclusive painter?"

"He's not *my* painter. He's Nancy Trainor's painter," Ashley corrected between bites.

Sarah frowned. "Why would an artist like David have his work carried in a small gallery in a tiny southern town?"

"He and Nancy studied together in New York City. She decided her talent lay more in finding and promoting artists than in being an artist." Thoughtfully, Ashley chewed. "David is happy to help out her gallery by having her represent him."

Sarah raised an eyebrow. "Doesn't his artwork sell for tens of thousands of dollars?"

"He allows his works to be sold for lower prices in her gallery. The smaller pieces, not his large canvases." Ashley took another bite of her candy bar. "Without his paintings to sell, her gallery may close. The income his works provide allows her showroom to remain open. Luckily, he's prolific."

"Which implies your art studio will also be shuttered if he disappeared for a long haul," Sarah said.

"No one will rent me space as inexpensively as Nancy does. Plus, her showroom is a source of inspiration for my kids."

"So David Fodero isn't *your* painter, but the kids in your program are yours?"

Ashley grinned. "Every child is unique, and I love them all for their special talents and gifts."

She'd worked hard to make ends meet to provide for her students—whether it was brushes, soap, or an artist's table—and it was all worth it. Truly, she was blessed. She adored teaching kids and had shaped a satisfying career for herself.

"Maybe you can persuade David to donate funds for your art supplies." Sarah grabbed a chip. "He's certainly wealthy enough."

"If I can ever find him, I just might."

"Poor unsuspecting fellow." Sarah threw Ashley a smirk.

"He doesn't realize what he's in for. You don't put the brakes on until you achieve your goals."

"Poor unsuspecting, *mysterious* fellow," Ashley amended.

"It's odd no one has been able to reach him." Again, Sarah offered Ashley half her sandwich. At Ashley's refusal, Sarah happily finished it. "I wonder what happened."

"These genius artists are impossible. Nancy said he's very serious and oftentimes difficult. She walks on eggshells when she deals with him."

"I researched him on the internet." Sarah stood, indicating her break was over. "He is celebrated for his avant-garde portrayal of everyday subjects. Have you seen his *Woman by the River*?"

"That painting has been analyzed and torn apart by critics, though it's a fan favorite. When Nancy displayed it in her showroom, a student of mine, a nine-year-old girl with Down syndrome, continuously stared at it and smiled." Ashley's eyes welled. Her emotions, her affection for each precious child, brimmed inside her. "The girl didn't need any language to convey how she felt."

Sarah gave Ashley's hand a squeeze. "You care too much for people. You're eternally optimistic."

"I can't help it."

"That's why you're special. Don't ever change." Sarah retrieved the discarded wrappers and tossed them in the trash, along with their water bottles. Arm in arm, the women revisited the outside garden center before doubling back inside.

"For the record." Sarah's forehead furrowed. "I never figured out where the river actually was in David's painting."

"Neither did I."

"Who is the woman with the chestnut-brown hair in the corner?"

"Art enthusiasts have speculated about that for years. He's

been photographed with every leading actress on the planet. Perhaps the woman is one of them."

Ashley well remembered the day David Fodero had stridden into Nancy's showroom, the one and only time she ever saw him. He'd worn scruffy jeans and a casual navy-blue T-shirt. Yet he looked as handsome as when he'd been photographed wearing a black tuxedo at a glitzy fundraiser. His picture had been splashed on several society pages the following morning.

Nancy had confided he was growing tired of the endless social functions that demanded his attention, and he sought clean air and a calmer lifestyle in Cherish, a small Southern town not far from Greenwood.

Sarah gazed at the ceiling, as if David might miraculously appear. "He's drop-dead gorgeous, and every female on Earth wants to date him."

"Except you."

"I'm happily married to Max. But you're single."

"Yes." Ashley sighed. "Now and forever."

"Never say never." Sarah examined the African violet. Satisfied, she smiled. "Don't lose heart because of one failed relationship."

Don't lose heart.

What woman wouldn't lose heart after being dropped by a guy she'd dated on and off since college? Well-meaning acquaintances speculated she'd set the bar too high. Perhaps her ex couldn't live up to her expectations.

Which were what, exactly?

To show up when he promised her a date at the movies? To phone when he was out of town for long weekends?

Was there a man anywhere who was true to his word, a man who would sincerely care about her, and loved God as much as she did?

She shook off her reflections.

"I'm here on business to help Nancy." Ashley admired a particularly lush plant with cherry-red blossoms and considered buying it. However, she wasn't certain the plant would survive. Unlike her friend, her thumb was the opposite of green. "Nothing more."

"Unfortunate." Sarah sighed dramatically.

"Why?"

"You and David both like art. You couldn't ask for more."

"We're from two different orbits. He lives in New York City with a population of eight and a half million, while Greenwood has, what, five thousand residents?"

"Greenwood and Cherish are similar in size."

"A similarity we don't share with New York City." Ashley couldn't help a giggle. "It'll take more than art appreciation to ignite a spark between David and me. A distinguished painter and a woman who can't draw a stick figure to save her life isn't an ideal match."

"Perhaps." Sarah waggled her eyebrows.

Sarah, the incurable romantic. The women had shared a relaxed candor ever since they'd attended a friend's wedding five years earlier.

Bending, Sarah checked the water level of a particularly dry-looking violet. "David is better looking than your ex."

"Looks aren't everything."

"Looks are something."

"My ex is currently dating a knockout." Uttering the words aloud hurt, and Ashley pressed her lips together. "I saw them together at an upscale restaurant. Luckily, they didn't see me."

"You're a knockout too."

"Thank you." Ashley gnawed her bottom lip. Her ex had stripped away her self-confidence. In fact, he'd been cheating on her the entire time they'd dated. "However, I don't trust men anymore."

"All men?"

"Men in general."

"You enjoy reading romance novels."

"Those men are fictional."

"Never give up. Love will arrive when you least expect it." Sarah's tone was low and steady. "By the way, I discovered why David came to Cherish. Marge Addyson, the pastor of Memorial Street Church, commissioned him to paint a church portrait for their one-hundredth-anniversary celebration."

"And?"

"Last week, he was spotted on the church steps taking photos. Tall man with longish black hair, a trimmed beard, and crystal blue eyes, correct?"

"Yes. Or you could just say *brilliant and gorgeous*."

"Uh, huh. So I've heard."

Ashley belatedly pondered the wisdom of her description, although it was her first thought whenever she pictured him.

Sarah slid her a wise glance. "You know him better than any of the Cherish residents."

"I don't, because we never formally met. I only laid eyes on him for an instant when he appeared in Nancy's showroom to drop off a sketch. I was sitting on the floor of my adjacent studio, stenciling with an eleven-year-old boy. David glanced my way before he chatted with Nancy and gave me his legendary, wry smile."

"What did you do?"

"I smiled back, and we exchanged a friendly wave. His entire conversation with Nancy lasted all of five minutes before he dashed out the door."

She'd estimated he was several inches taller than her, which placed him at over six feet. Muscular and tanned, his physique contrasted sharply with her image of an artist—a thin, whiskered chap sporting a beret and wielding a paintbrush. David's broad shoulders and masculine features were a stark reminder he was light-years beyond her—a teacher who spent her days amidst classes of giggling children, hanging art pieces on austere gray walls while complimenting drawings of princess castles.

Ashley shifted from foot to foot. "Nancy just sold his last oil painting and is adamant about connecting with him."

Much as she wanted to help her friend, Ashley's search for David Fodero was self-serving. Her studio and a café owned by a friend were both connected to Nancy's bustling gallery—a setup that benefitted all three businesses. If any failed, all would be left on rocky financial ground.

Ashley and Sarah reentered the store part of the nursery and were hit with a blast of cold air. The whir of an air conditioner ensured customer comfort from the relentless seasonal heat.

"People say he stays to himself and lives out on the edge of town." Sarah grabbed a metal watering can and filled it with water from a hose. "When my husband went bird-watching at Juniper Mountain yesterday, he saw David standing by his easel near a grove of trees."

"Where is Juniper Mountain?"

Sarah reached in her pocket and pulled out a discarded receipt. Flipping it over, she drew a makeshift map. "The mountain is in the state park. Max hikes the Walnut Forest route."

"Is it difficult?"

"Aren't you an exercise fanatic?"

"Sure. On a treadmill."

"Walnut Forest isn't challenging. David told Max he welcomes the solitude of nature and seemed absorbed in whatever he was painting."

"He is a true artist." Goosebumps rose on Ashley's arms whenever she envisioned his paintings. She speculated about what inspired him to create his pieces—and why he chose certain textures and shades of colors, the scope of the canvases. "I wonder if he finished it."

His landscapes commanded thousands of dollars. It didn't matter what he painted. If patrons discovered his name signed on a canvas, they were willing to pay exorbitant sums.

"Trees, birds, and a pond were in the vicinity. I imagine those were in there somewhere." Sarah set down the watering can and began pruning a flamboyant-fuchsia flowering petunia. "Folks in town say he's polite, but his responses crackle the air like a broad band of heat lightning if someone dares to ask a personal question."

"He's known to be reclusive. Anything else?"

"I imagine Max led a painstaking description of all the birds in the park because he's the resident bird watcher." Sarah grinned. "But we all know how fiercely David guards his privacy, so few will infringe on that—not even talkative Max."

"Which may be why he hasn't answered any of Nancy's phone calls or texts for the past three months."

"He donated an oil landscape to Canine Helpers for their annual fundraiser—the cutest depiction of a dachshund who accompanies him everywhere." Sarah pulled dead leaves off the petunia. "At least, I think it's a dachshund in the painting. The dog's body is sketched in blue, and the ears are purple and red."

"Classic rebellious David." Ashley grinned. "Your information is appreciated."

"One more thing."

Ashley glanced at her watch. Sarah had been due to clock in ten minutes earlier. "I won't keep you any longer."

"No worries. I usually work overtime." Sarah brushed a piece of soil off her dark-green pants. "Max spoke with a park ranger who told him David purchased a dilapidated cabin a few miles outside the state grounds. He's been renovating it these past few months."

"That's where he's living? He bought a—Ashley made quote marks in the air—'dilapidated cabin'? He's not renting?"

"No. The cabin is on ten acres, bordered by state land on all three sides."

"What's the name of the road?"

"Pine Knoll Lane, and it's the only habitable property near the park." A wide smile crossed Sarah's face. "If you touch base with the ranger, he'll provide the general location. Although I warn you, solitude seems paramount to David."

"He's becoming a hermit."

"Right. So don't think you can just appear on his doorstep."

"I'm not here to marry him."

Sarah chuckled. "You're staying for the weekend, correct?"

"Yes. A substitute is teaching my Sunday school class." Ashley raked her hair from her forehead. "What time are the church services in town?"

"Memorial Street Church offers two services at 9:30 and 11:30. The pastors are outstanding, and the worship music is uplifting. I'll introduce you around if you attend."

"Count me in. I rented a room at the Cherish Hills Inn."

"Julian Wilson is the owner, and the church is a short walk from there. David drops by there for takeout meals, so maybe you'll meet him there."

"What are the odds? He may not stop in for another month." Ashley hesitated, then perked up. "Although a happy coincidence may occur."

Sarah frowned. "I've seen that look before. Are you up to something?"

"Have you ever heard the saying, if the mountain will not

come to Muhammad, then Muhammad will go to the mountain?"

"Sure. It means, if things don't go your way, then you change events so that they do."

Ashley tapped her fingers on a shelf stacked with clay pots. "Precisely."

"Are you Muhammad or the mountain?" Sarah tipped her head. "How can you run into someone who is rarely seen in public and doesn't answer his phone or email?"

"I'm whoever I need to be in order to locate him."

A foolproof plan had formulated. Well, perhaps the plan wasn't foolproof, but it was a start.

Her instincts shouted *no*. The plan was filled with the likelihood of failure, although she couldn't think of anything better.

She dismissed her reservations because her brain shouted yes.

Ashley was Muhammed. And Muhammed was going to the mountain.

CHAPTER 2

Art is a lie that makes us realize truth.
- Picasso

*D*avid had spent the entire day painting. Or, more accurately, attempting to paint.

He stood at his easel surrounded by oak trees, a jewel-like river bubbling in the distance. Shadows cast by the branches shielded him and his dog from the sun. He'd brought water for them both, in a thermos and doggie dish respectively, as well as an energy drink for himself.

New Yorkers who were accustomed to snow and temperatures below freezing weren't supposed to be fond of penetrating summer heat. Yet he relished everything about Cherish, including the weather. This quintessential Southern town was proving private and off-the-grid, boasting natural beauty and a sunny climate. In just a few months, he'd met more sincere, down-to-earth folks here than in his entire two decades in a large, impersonal city.

As the afternoon gave way to early evening, the sun glowed with a burning hue.

The golden hour. The hour most flattering. The light was diffused, the silhouettes intense.

"Red and soft and magical. Right Pickle?"

His dog looked up at him with shiny oval eyes and angled his head.

David grinned at his devoted dachshund, consistently in tune with him and his moods. Pickle's long, low body always seemed balanced, his black-and-copper coat smooth, his demeanor curious. Never farther than a few trots from his master, Pickle proved that adopting a dog from a pet rescue center was one of David's finest decisions.

He stood back from the easel to assess his work.

One tree.

Two endless weeks of sweat, countless energy drinks, and one tree.

What was he doing? Anyone could paint a tree. A child could paint a tree.

Just because he'd framed the tree in a garish-orange stained glass window didn't make it any better. Any more unique. There was a fine line between avant-garde and absolute nonsense.

He tossed down the last of his energy drink and regarded the river, the sun's rays glittering along the water's surface. Some days, the anger and sadness at his loss subsided, as he appreciated the splendor of his surroundings.

Not today.

His designs from earlier years had been described as radical and unorthodox, and he'd been acclaimed as a prodigy. Newer pieces were applauded because of his experimental approach to design and color.

When he'd first become recognized, he'd scoured every email and text he received, checked the tweets that mentioned him, holding out hope his older brothers would recognize his contribution to the art world. If they did, they hadn't bothered to inform him. And his father? Hardly a word of praise, even when David used to phone him on weekends. Their relationship had always been strained.

Once, he'd fantasized about moving back to the mid-sized city where he was born and purchasing the original homestead, just to prove he could. He'd amassed enough money with his art sales to buy the entire city. His livelihood was effectively guaranteed and predicted to become even more impressive.

But currently?

Though too soon to determine, he was certain he'd despise his latest piece when it was finished. Inspiring paintings didn't come easily anymore. In retrospect, they never had.

Neither did innovation. All artistry required direction, analysis, and exceptional ideas to execute, with a healthy dose of diligence and confidence.

He wanted to create pieces the artistic community had never seen before. He wanted to rescue his career. The sad truth was he hadn't liked anything he'd painted the past few months. Not since he'd woken up one morning, barely able to see out of his right eye.

He was an artist. This wasn't supposed to happen to an artist.

So what?

He had nothing left to prove. He'd accomplished every artistic milestone at a relatively young age.

The knowledge he could no longer paint anything worthwhile left him humbled and dispirited. He'd considered other art forms—perhaps picking up his oboe again or writing poetry—for fulfillment. Or purchasing another estate, or docking a yacht on an exclusive island, or escorting a starlet to a dazzling social gathering.

He couldn't bring himself to engage in any of those activities anymore. A part of him—ethics, morality, the boy who had once believed in God—was dejected by a shallow, affluent lifestyle.

So much for doctors. So much for irony. So much for God … taking away an artist's eyesight. What sense did that make?

"C'mon, Pickle." David grabbed his easel and paints, and then picked up his ten-pound dog, being sure to retrieve the dog's favorite toy—a plush, striped elephant.

David buckled Pickle into the dog car harness in the back seat of his crew-cab pickup truck. Then he buckled himself in the front seat and drove the short distance to his cabin. He had no trouble driving. Just as his ophthalmologist had predicted, David's brain had adjusted to compensate for the loss of depth perception.

"You'll be fine," the doctor had assured him.

Right. What, exactly, described *fine*?

Claude Monet, the French Impressionist painter, suffered from cataracts, and his eyesight had been impaired as he aged. He'd complained of foggy vision and undergone surgery. His paintings had changed as a result of the deterioration.

David certainly shouldn't compare himself to Monet, but he recognized his work was shifting—and not for the better.

He pulled his truck into the gravel driveway of his home and regarded the remote area and vast acreage. His cabin was concealed from the road by thick woods.

Rustic, yet remarkably well-appointed following David's renovations, the cabin offered an ideal retreat. The timbered ceiling was braced by beams of weathered cedar, and a spiral staircase led to a bedroom loft, which offered a panoramic view of forest and mountains. On a vibrant, sunny day, the scene was magnificent.

He kicked off his shoes as soon as he entered. The hours ahead promised peaceful solitude and reflection. In winter, a crackling fire in the massive stone fireplace would be a requirement. For a June evening in the Carolinas, he'd opt for a riveting adventure thriller audiobook, while he and his dog settled in his favorite chair, a redwood armchair. He prized the exposed rustic tree knots and polished design.

In former years, devotions to God would have highlighted his reflections, as well as Bible study. He especially enjoyed reading from the Old Testament. When despondent, he had absorbed the poetic, inspiring psalms that described God's love and mercy. The words had entered him like an inspirational melody.

Those were days long past.

God had taken too much away. As a result, he maintained a distant relationship with God. His plea for help had never been answered.

David's foundation was gone, his faith unfocused.

The feeble protest of his conscience to utter a prayer, any prayer, fell by the wayside.

With a harsh sigh, he gazed out the living room's front bay window. Flecks of dust danced in the pitch of afternoon sunlight. The windowpanes needed dusting.

Aware of the fleeting minutes, David regarded the plot of land he considered ideal for a garden. He'd never tended soil. Perhaps now he would. A garden offered order to the forest, direction for his thoughts.

He scratched his temple. What vegetables and flowers grew under a fierce summer sun? Was June too late in the season for planting?

His deliberations drifted to work and obligations.

Tomorrow, he'd begin sketching the commissioned

painting of Memorial Street Church he'd agreed to finish by summer's end. He'd taken various photographs of the church's white painted exterior, ornate wooden doors and high-arched windows, from different angles.

He threw an ironic glance at his reflection. How could he complete a project he hadn't begun? Procrastination wasn't his style, though with a few words, the ophthalmologist's diagnosis had altered everything.

David's optic nerve to his right eye wasn't getting enough blood. He was slowly going blind.

AN HOUR LATER, after a quick shower and dressed in his usual T-shirt and jeans, he situated himself on a bench facing the tree painting. He couldn't help himself, couldn't stay away from painting. Pickle sat on a woven wool rug, his striped elephant beside him.

A tap on the door brought David and Pickle to their feet.

No one visited. No one, thankfully, knew exactly where he lived.

With an irritated shake of his head and the dog at his heels, he padded to the entry.

A slight, dainty woman stood on the porch steps, dark glasses covered her eyes, her blond hair swinging from a side part and spilling to her shoulders. Wayward, shiny strands drifted across her cheek. Dappled sunlight shone through towering pine trees, and shadows formed on the ground. Somewhere, the fluttering of unseen wings broke the silence.

Her figure was slender. The thought came to mind that a strong windstorm could blow her off her feet.

"Hi." Her voice was bright and breezy, resembling her appearance.

"May I help you?" He opened the door wider. "If you're selling cookies, I'm not buying."

"Who said I was selling cookies?"

"You don't look any older than a university student."

"Do university students sell cookies?"

"For fundraisers, I suppose."

She paused. "Do you have any?"

"University students?" He glanced over his shoulder. "Nope."

"Funny. Not."

"Oh, you're referring to cookies." He surveyed her from the top of her smooth forehead down to her manicured toes, peeking out from strappy sandals. She wore slim-fitting jeans and a green floral blouse. Her complexion was healthy, a sun-kissed tan along her cheeks and the bridge of her freckled nose.

He grinned. "I stored a couple boxes of cookies in my freezer."

"What kind?"

"Chocolate with a creamy-white filling."

Her generous lips pulled into a smile. "My favorite. I have it on reliable authority most cookies thaw quickly, though I've often eaten them frozen."

He patted his stomach. "I've inhaled half a box in one sitting."

"Frozen?"

"Microwaved."

Inwardly, he shook his head. They were actually discussing cookies. If this was considered lighthearted conversation, it felt foreign. He had forgotten the pleasure of conversing with a lovely, quick-witted woman.

She slid the dark glasses down her nose. Huge, hazel-green eyes flicked him a glance.

A shadow of a smile crossed her lips. He wasn't sure why.

With an about-face, she gestured toward a blue Chevy

convertible parked in front of his cabin. "Unfortunately, I'm stranded."

"I'm sorry. Trouble with your car, ma'am?"

"Miss." She plucked off her glasses and perched them on her head.

They locked gazes.

Time stood still.

He wasn't an overly emotional guy, yet feelings that hardly made sense bombarded him. Attraction, an instant connection, a familiarity he couldn't explain.

"My convertible stalled, and my cell phone battery is dead." Her statement sounded far away, and he dragged his mind to attention.

"I'd offer assistance." He scanned the road. "Regrettably, my skills as a mechanic are sorely lacking." *They were, in fact, nonexistent.*

"May I use your phone to call a friend? I don't intend to drive these deserted roads at night. The curves are difficult to navigate."

He peered outside. The sky was etched in pinks and grays. Dusk set slowly in the Carolinas, and darkness wouldn't occur for another hour. "You're on Pine Knoll Lane. I'm surprised you made it this far without realizing there's no outlet. Loop around, and you'll connect with the state park entrance in a few miles."

"Once my car is running again." Her tone was easygoing, her smile angelic. "My sense of direction is faultless, though I obviously lost my way."

"Obviously." He shifted. Why was he thinking this woman was special? He didn't even know her. "If you're looking for a tree-lined residential street, head to Cherish. There's nothing of interest on this road."

"There are lots of things of interest." She caught his stare, then turned to peer at the deserted road. "I planned to hike Grandfather Mountain today."

"Isn't Grandfather Mountain in North Carolina?"

"Oh."

Oh? She was in the wrong state?

"I'm a mountain climber."

She certainly didn't look like a mountain climber, and she didn't know her mountains very well, either. Where was her backpack, and why wasn't she wearing sturdy shoes caked with mud? Her sandals were white and clean.

No business of his. Perhaps her gear was packed in her car.

Still, why hike at dusk?

He watched her in silence. Soon she'd be on her way. The sensations that raced through him, that instant flare of attraction, would soon disappear.

"May I use your phone?" she repeated.

"Certainly. C'mon inside. I left my phone in the kitchen."

"Thanks." She offered a helpless laugh. "I hope I'm not putting you out."

He glanced at his canvas by the window and reminded himself that people were more important than work. He strove to achieve balance, although it wasn't easy.

"You're not putting me out at all." He led her into the living room. The worn hardwood floors creaked beneath their feet, and he motioned to the L-shaped sofa. He suspected the sofa hailed from the 1960s, judging from the plaid pattern and velvet armrests, but it was clean and homey and comfortable. He hadn't replaced all the furniture yet. Likewise, he hadn't gotten around to a kitchen remodel.

Pickle trotted beside them and sniffed the woman's sandals. Quickly surmising she was a friend, he brought his striped elephant close to her and flopped on his back for a belly rub. She accommodated him while cooing that he was the cutest dog in the county. Judging from the dog's rapturous pose, her compliment delighted him.

"Adorable." She nodded at the elephant.

"His favorite toy."

"I've never owned a dog."

David looked at her as if she'd uttered a statement entirely foreign to him.

"I can't," she explained. "I've fantasized forever about adopting one, but my apartment is tiny, and I spend most of my days and evenings at my studio teaching." She smiled. "I love animals, though."

"Visit your local rescue center, adopt a miniature chihuahua, and bring the dog with you to your studio."

"Helpful advice." Her smile faltered. "Perhaps someday."

"Someday." David glanced from her to Pickle.

"You can't beat a pet to combat loneliness." She went on rubbing Pickle's stomach. "Animals help humans reconnect with nature. Some say dogs are God's messengers because they grant us grace."

"Pickle is a significant part of my life. He's my comrade."

She looked up at him, her gaze sparkling. "Pets are extraordinary."

He nodded in agreement and headed for the kitchen. "Extraordinary, indeed."

He reached in the freezer for a box of cookies and decided on bottled water instead.

Retracing his steps into the living room, he asked, "You're not from around here?"

"No."

He had assumed she'd be sitting on the sofa, rubbing Pickle's belly.

She wasn't.

Pickle was snuggled in his doggie bed by the fireplace. She stood facing David's unfinished tree painting.

She refused his offer of hospitality by shaking her head at the water and gestured to the painting. There hadn't been graffiti on the tree, although he'd added it, enhancing the graffiti in bold purple letters. The blue sky, devoid of clouds, conveyed a curious juxtaposition against the solemn moss-green grass. Carroty stained-glass windows stood out sharply in the background.

She surveyed the canvas. "Is this a happy or sad painting?"

He set the water bottles on the coffee table, noting she hadn't answered his earlier question about where she was from.

"Paintings don't have feelings."

"People do."

He clasped his hands. "I haven't decided."

"About people's feelings or the painting?"

He didn't reply. Instead, he handed her the phone and provided her with the local mechanic's number.

"Thanks." She focused on the canvas. "All your paintings bring up complicated emotions."

"All? How do you—?" She must be an art enthusiast who recognized his work. He was obliged for the support, though lately he couldn't muster any sentiments—gratefulness, productiveness, motivation. Everything he'd taken for granted had evaporated when he'd received his eyesight diagnosis.

She wandered away with his phone to her ear, muttered a few sentences, then disconnected. "I called my friend who can repair anything that goes wrong with a car."

Already feeling useless as an artist as well as a mechanic, David murmured, "Good." If he were one of his brothers, he would've dashed to her car, yanked the appropriate tools from his pickup, and fixed the problem for her.

He wasn't that kind of man, though. He'd never been mechanical.

Left brain, right brain, he theorized. He was the opposite of a methodical thinker. His right-brain dominance made him creative, prone to day-dreaming, intuition, and visualization.

"No tools here beyond a couple screwdrivers and a hammer." He shrugged. "My truck is loaded with canvases, watercolors, and an easel."

"No worries. Everyone can't be a pro at everything."

"Your worldview theory?"

"I look at life through God's perspective."

Noncommittally, he shook his head. "Whatever works for you."

She peered at him. "You sound like you're hard on yourself. Are you?"

"Not enough to be psychoanalyzed in my own living room."

"Right." She chewed her lower lip. "So, my friend will be here soon."

The longer he gazed at her, the more familiarity niggled, though he couldn't place her. Her blond hair was a hundred shades of gold. Those startling hazel eyes seemed to change from green to brown at will. Doe-eyed. Perceptive and luminous.

He cleared his throat. These intense feelings roused recollections of his teenage years over two decades earlier.

He bent to go after a paintbrush lodged under the sofa. "How long?"

"Hmm?" She stepped closer to his canvas.

"How long?" he repeated.

"How long what?"

He stood. "How long before your friend arrives?"

"Not long." She laser-focused on the painting. "This tree really is magnificent."

"You figured out it was a tree?"

"Yes. Is that good news or bad news?"

"For an avant-garde artist, I'd consider it bad news."

She folded her hands behind her back, peering at the landscape. A clear invasion of his privacy. Then she fixated on the rusted coffee can on the fireplace mantel.

"Quite an unusual decoration," she noted.

"Thanks." He searched for an explanation and decided on none.

"And the redwood chair in the corner is … rustic."

"I moved it here from my Manhattan apartment." He set the paintbrush in a bucket. "I helped create the design."

"Is it comfortable to sit on with all that wood jutting out all over the place?"

He smiled. "Chair pads soften the experience."

"The sitting experience."

He chuckled. "Correct." He couldn't stop drinking in the sight of her slim figure. Her jeans hugged her curves to perfection.

What? He gave himself a mental shake. He was seeking a laid-back lifestyle without complications. Perhaps then he'd be inspired to paint something worthwhile.

She concentrated on the coffee can. "Is there an artistic significance in that?"

"Maybe." He crossed his arms, narrowed his gaze.

"Is the living room your studio?"

"This room gets the most favorable light in the house since it faces north."

Canvases slanted against the walls, wrong side out. She gestured to them. "Do you ever show your work?"

"No." True enough since he'd moved to Cherish.

"Why not? You should paint often and sell everything."

To dissuade her from asking any more questions, he flashed her a frown. "Look miss, I don't even know your name."

Not losing a beat, she held out her hand. "Ashley Madden."

He tilted his head to the side. In some way, the name was recognizable too.

He took her hand and shook. Her fingers were fragile and delicate, sending a warm tingle through him.

Indeed? For a woman's hand? He really needed to get out more.

"David Fodero," he replied.

Admiration shone in her gaze. "Hello, David."

"Likewise, Ashley."

She arched her graceful blond eyebrows. "*Likewise?* Quite the introduction."

"I'm not known for flowery words. What I meant was …" His formal upbringing kicked into gear. "My pleasure."

He assumed he'd let go of her hand, but peering down, he realized he hadn't.

"My friend should be here within a half hour." Ashley continued their earlier conversation as if no lapse had occurred, then dropped her hand. "I assume that's okay?"

Did he have a choice? "Of course."

"Why not?"

He took a sip of water. "I'm not following." Clearly, this woman shifted topics with the speed of a tornado.

"Why not show your pieces? Your art is thought provoking."

Respect threaded her tone. He recognized it, appreciated it, but couldn't respond except for a nonchalant, "My work isn't good enough."

"You're joking, right? Surely you don't believe such a thing."

"It's my opinion, which is the only opinion that matters."

He indicated they should sit, and they chose either ends of the sofa. She was silent. He was well aware she had set aside her curiosity and inquiries about his paintings because of his blunt reply.

"I have iced tea in the fridge." His statement broke through the silence. "Care for a glass?"

"No, thank you." She shot him a measured smile across the breadth of the sofa. "I prefer sugary soda."

"I'm an energy-drink guy."

"I noticed." She darted a glance at the empty cans in the wastebasket near his bench.

His brain faltered for something else to say. He wasn't chatty—unless discussing art or photography—and lately even those subjects made him uncomfortable.

He gazed around the room for a way to restore their earlier banter because he regretted the loss. Playfully and without thinking, he tossed a fringed throw pillow at her.

She let out a startled shriek. The dog leaped up, barked, and circled the table. The friendly mood returned as Ashley laughed and threw the pillow back at him.

"Don't you dare!" She held up a hand to fend off another throw.

"Give up?" He stood and swung the pillow back and forth. "What's a little pillow fight to a seasoned mountain climber?"

"You're right. You win." She switched an innocent smile on him before grabbing another pillow from the sofa.

A knock brought their hands to their sides. Ashley tidied the pillows they'd disarranged. With her pink cheeks and a sparkle in her eyes, she created a fetching picture.

"Now who might that be?" He rubbed his chin. "Someone else selling cookies?"

She grinned, peeked out the window, and waved. "I'll get it."

"Be my guest," he mumbled with wry courtesy.

Her laughter rang out as she opened the door. An auburn-haired woman stepped inside.

"David Fodero, meet Sarah Archer," Ashley said. "She's my handy repair person."

A woman.

Sarah offered a hello and took a step back. Reserved and a bit shy, he mused.

"All set, Twinkle," she said to Ashley.

Twinkle? David opened his mouth to inquire about the name, but Ashley ignored him.

Sarah mumbled something about a mysterious engine part, and Ashley responded by using sign language.

Wait. Ashley's friend was deaf?

Sarah offered him an abashed smile. "I'm losing my hearing. I denied it for ages, until my husband, Max, prodded me to confront my fears and visit an audiologist. I believe you met him at the state park."

"The birdwatcher who always wears a bow tie?"

"Yes." Sarah smiled. "Now that I've adjusted, my hearing aid is a blessing, along with signing."

He turned to Ashley. "You know sign language?"

"I run an art studio that's attached to a couple other businesses, one being a café." Ashley reached for her water bottle. "A waitress who works there is deaf."

"You own a business?"

"Yes, for handicapped students. I cared for my dad when I was young and missed a lot of school. I fell behind and the teachers labeled me as a slow learner. After a while, I quit trying. Then I met a wonderful mentor, and he was an inspiration. From then on, I vowed to help others." She waved a dismissive hand. "More information about me than you would ever possibly want."

"No, not at all." He was still reeling from this personal insight about her. "Is your studio in Cherish?"

"No."

More questions came to mind.

Before he could inquire, Ashley gestured to Sarah. "My friend has the greenest thumb on the planet."

He considered congratulating Ashley for another rapid subject change. Instead, he remarked to Sarah, "I've contemplated planting a garden."

"I work at Thumbs Up, the nursery in town." She pulled a business card from the back pocket of her jeans and handed it to him. "Give me a call."

"Thanks." He pocketed the card and glimpsed the two women, a little unnerved at the smile that passed between them.

Sarah eyed his dog, who had permanently attached himself to Ashley. Crouching, she rubbed his stomach. It was amazing what dogs did for a belly rub.

Sarah glanced up at him. "What type of plants are you interested in?"

"Whatever will grow in this hot sun."

"I recommend zucchini and squash and carrots."

"Sugar-coated carrots are delicious," Ashley chimed in.

"All my favorites," he joked, then sobered. "I'm sorry. I'm not sure how to converse with you, Sarah. I never studied sign language."

She stood. "I read lips and understand you perfectly."

"Are you a musician?" He perched his hip on the edge of the redwood chair.

Both women frowned in confusion, and he immediately regretted his words. But Sarah's disability had made him think of his own—although it was constantly on his mind anyway—and he'd wondered if she was an artist too.

"My husband plays harmonica and is in a band with my uncle," Sarah answered. "Why?"

Were they really discussing musicians? Yes, and he had initiated it.

He peeked at Ashley. This woman knew hardly anything about him, yet he sensed her interest in his answer.

His muscles tightened. He was up for the challenge.

"Beethoven suffered from deafness." He picked up his water bottle and rolled it between his hands. "Any theories why that would've happened to him?"

Ashley regarded him with a sideways glance. "I'm not certain."

"I assume you'll lay it on God. That He works in mysterious ways."

"Often, He does." She stood straighter. "Faith is fragile. Faith takes time. Hold on to faith when there's too much of life and too little of you."

"Is that what Beethoven did?"

"I don't know."

He sighed heavily. "Therefore, according to you, I should take a step toward believing in God."

"God is always working on a solution."

How had this become a theological discussion?

"Then tell me this," he challenged. "Is a musician losing his hearing comparable to a painter losing his eyesight?"

He saw the shock in Ashley's eyes, knew when the impact of his words struck her.

She pressed a hand to her lips. "David, is there anything—?"

In the soundless aftershocks, he kept his features bland and didn't answer. He'd revealed too much already and hoped she wouldn't read into his response.

"DAVID FODERO IS GOING BLIND?" Ashley whispered to Sarah as soon as they left David's cabin. The women stepped along a stone path and hastened to their cars. Rather than broaching the subject further, Ashley had opted to remain silent. Sarah had wordlessly agreed. Besides, he'd quickly banished any questions by his cool response. Or rather, lack of response.

"He wasn't necessarily referring to himself," Sarah said.

"Of course he was." Ashley tried not to appear as troubled as she felt. The pride stamped on his face, the jut of his chin, declared that David Fodero wasn't the type of man who resigned himself to his fate. Yet there was a profound sadness in his eyes. "Who else might he be referring to? Van Gogh?"

"I thought Van Gogh was supposed to be color blind."

"Judging from David's voice, he was referring to his own disability. I want to help him find a solution."

"Your infinite optimism is surfacing again." Sarah inclined her head toward the cabin, then at Ashley. "You constantly try to solve other people's problems. Rest and leave it to God."

The air was eerily stagnant, the sun beginning its descent as Ashley and Sarah hugged each other goodbye. As soon as she reached her car, Ashley leaned her head against the door to collect herself. Her chest knotted at the awareness of David's blindness. Despite his attempts to sound casual, his expression and deep voice had revealed raw emotion.

Now she knew the reason why he hadn't responded to Nancy's emails, phone calls or texts. Ashley's heart missed a beat at the image of his troubled, handsome face. The consequences of his disability plagued her long after she'd retired to Cherish Hills Inn for the evening.

She sat on the cozy white comforter on her bed, drew up her legs, and wrapped her arms around her knees.

He wasn't blind *now*. He'd looked at Ashley as if he saw her with no trouble. He didn't seem to encounter any difficulty moving from room to room. And he obviously still painted.

His depiction of the tree was wonderful. Different from

his earlier works, this canvas was darker, more melancholy. According to well-informed art critics, David's talent was phenomenal, an unstoppable force that had shaken up the art world.

She couldn't make that sort of judgment. She simply respected his talent and skill, his distinctive portrayals of nature and everyday life expressed his recognizable style.

In Greenwood, she was on a mission to make a difference, providing an art platform for handicapped children.

In David's case, surely his condition could be treated by a skilled physician.

And prayer.

CHAPTER 3

Art washes away from the soul the dust of everyday life.
- Picasso

Sunday, Ashley rose early and breakfasted in the inn's solarium. The room had been recently added onto the original building, a hostess explained. Benefitting from the natural light, the lavender paint on the window trim and the pops of greenery, along with white wicker tables and chairs, completed the cheery environment.

The breakfast offerings included fluffy French toast drenched in pure maple syrup and black coffee that Ashley doused with sugar and cream. All served by Samantha, a pleasant young waitress with ice-blue eyes and dark hair. She worked during her summer break from college, she explained to Ashley. Her father was the owner.

"No work-out room?" Ashley asked, scanning a colorful pamphlet with descriptions of the inn's services.

"Sure, we do." Samantha gestured toward the hallway. "Complete with a weight machine and treadmills."

Ashley made a mental note to exercise the following day.

As she watched the comings and goings of other diners, she focused on how next to approach David.

The prior evening had gone as planned. She'd found him at his cabin.

Her breath had caught at how good-looking he was—wearing jeans and a white T-shirt that clung to his wide shoulders. His hair was rumpled, his strong jawline appealingly stubbled. He'd padded barefoot through the living room, his strides long and purposeful, and he'd been welcoming, inviting her to make herself comfortable.

She'd felt a strong attraction to him, a pull she couldn't deny.

With a nervous lungful of air, she'd seized the chance to study his one visible painting when he went into the kitchen for his phone. Of course, she hadn't needed to phone Sarah, and a tinge of remorse for her deception tightened her stomach.

Soon, she'd reveal to David the real reason she'd come to Cherish. She'd also acknowledge she was mechanically inclined and could've fixed her own car if something had actually gone wrong.

She attributed her self-reliance to her father. He'd raised her as a single parent and made certain she could take care of herself. He had also been a devoutly religious man, frequently reminding her that God knew her life from beginning to end—and to release any burdens she carried to God.

She'd vowed to pass her father's teachings along and did what she could to minister to other people.

A peaceful determination swept through her, banishing any reservations and leaving her mind sharper. She was here for a reason.

Yes, to help Nancy. But something more.

God's hand was imperceptible, but He was never idle.

That flutter of excitement? The butterflies in her stomach when she and David had locked gazes? She dismissed it as a passing attraction.

Nevertheless, her reaction confused her. She couldn't get him out of her mind.

She drained her coffee and left the restaurant with a fast-paced stride, phoning her two part-time employees and asking them to cover her for the upcoming week.

She stopped at the lobby and extended her stay, then walked the few blocks to Memorial Street Church. Sunday mornings were meant for more than a leisurely breakfast and steaming coffee. Sunday mornings were meant for reverence and allowing God to provide a path. Specific details? They weren't needed. All that was needed was trust.

AFTER BEING SEATED for dinner at the inn's restaurant later that evening, Ashley spotted a painting on the wall. The landscape—wildflowers, trees and water—seemed to be in David Fodero's familiar signature style. The colorful wildflowers were upside down, the bubbling river noticeable only if an observer looked closely. David's brushwork was detailed, his design abstract.

She was so lost in thoughts of him, it took a few seconds for her to realize the owner had approached her table.

"Complex, isn't it?" Julian Wilson, a tall man with gray eyes, held a silver water pitcher. He eyed David's painting as he filled her glass.

"Thanks." Mesmerized, she perched her chin on her hands to continue to stare at the painting, then turned to him.

She'd spoken with Julian on several occasions when she'd

made her reservation. He was always pleasant and helpful and seemed able to accomplish numerous tasks with ease.

"Distinctly David Fodero," they remarked at the same time.

"David doesn't title his artworks." Julian pointed to the top of the canvas.

"He used to, probably for cataloguing and sales purposes." She dismissed Julian's observation with a shrug. "Not anymore, though. His art is so unique people recognize his work immediately."

"Notice the dog." Julian set the pitcher on her table and edged his finger along the strong lines of a tiny dachshund in the upper right-hand corner.

"David inserts minute details a casual observer might miss." Ashley folded the cloth napkin on her lap. "However, the bold yellow and orange tints of the wildflowers stand out."

"He pushes boundaries. When I first saw his work, he was painting everyday objects and enhancing them."

"Such as?"

"The sides of a barn painted lime green. Daffodils were growing out of the roof."

"He still paints the everyday objects, only now his paintings are more intricate."

Julian hesitated. "You're an artist?"

"No." Ashley smiled at his question. "I own an art studio for handicapped children in Greenwood. My studio is connected to a café and an art gallery run by a friend. She has sold quite a few of David's works, including his lithographs."

"He moved to Cherish a few months ago, but I haven't seen much of him. When we talk, I brag about the advantages of living in a close-knit town where faith emboldens the residents."

Ashley grinned. "What's his response?"

"He replies with a noncommittal shrug." Julian brushed an invisible speck off her linen tablecloth. "All we can provide is prayer and trust God to show David the right direction."

"I've perfected worrying, and I worry about David."

"Why?"

"He's remarkably talented. Maybe too talented." She paused, frowning at her reply, conscious it made no sense. She chose not to divulge David's vision loss in case Julian was unaware.

He studied the painting further. "Everyone in the community is thrilled he decided to live here."

"An acclaimed artist who fled the center of the art universe when he reached the pinnacle of his career."

"New York City's loss. Cherish's gain."

Her server set down her appetizer, which had been recommended—sweet and sour meatballs.

Ashley bowed her head to say grace, then helped herself to a meatball. "Delicious." She dabbed a smear of sweet sauce from her chin.

"All the credit goes to Melissa, our magnificent cook. Her secret ingredient is orange marmalade." Julian threw a satisfied glance toward the kitchen. "I understand David hasn't completely cut his ties to New York. He still owns a penthouse on Central Park."

Ashley nodded. "I remember seeing photos. Glasswrapped and two full floors, with a whopping eight thousand square feet of space."

Julian glanced at the New York guidebook Ashley had set on the table. "Have you ever visited Manhattan?"

"Never, though it's on my list of places to see."

"If David felt the need for a change of scenery, I guess it makes sense that he decided to buy a cabin here. I hear he did extensive renovations. Rumor is the place is a stunner."

She nodded. Her lips quirked in a smile. What she'd seen of David's place was stunning, with a distinctly masculine vibe.

"Once in a while," Julian added, "he breezes in for a takeout meal."

"He never dines in the restaurant?"

"No." Julian turned to an unoccupied table, fine-tuning the glassware. "He seems a good guy the few times we've spoken. He's generous to the shopkeepers and an excellent tipper. He donated his artwork to various businesses including a silent auction for Canine Helpers, a volunteer organization that supports veterans, and his piece raised thousands of dollars. When word of his contributions spread, tourism will surely increase."

"Which would be great for Cherish. It's such a quaint and charming town."

"I agree. I first came here a few years ago to supervise the opening of a new restaurant. I expected to stay only a few months, but I ended up meeting the woman of my dreams. Now, we're married and I'm helping raise Samantha, my precocious stepdaughter. She recently turned twenty."

"I met her at breakfast. She is lovely."

"She is musically talented, as well." Julian beamed, then fired a glance at a waitress displaying an assortment of desserts to an older couple who hadn't yet finished their meal.

"What's the name of the new restaurant?" Ashley bit into another meatball, savoring the tasty blend.

"Fresh 'n' Good, and it isn't new anymore. You may have seen the building." Julian's gaze swung to another waitress who attempted to balance too many entrees on a single tray. He stepped over to assist.

"I haven't had time to explore the town," Ashley said when he returned, "although I'm familiar with the chain."

"The restaurant is near the train station and was a former shoe store. I like to think we're friendly competition. Keeps both of our restaurants on our toes." He grinned. "Get it? Toes? Shoes?"

"Clever." Ashley laughed and turned toward the enormous picture window overlooking the street. The night sky glowed with the lights from the town. Traffic was easy—a brown Jeep and an old-fashioned Volkswagen drove by. At the intersection was a gas station attached to a bustling diner. When she had checked in the day before, Julian had told her that men sat there for hours solving the world's troubles, and coffee was poured nonstop.

"The town is growing, yet Cherish remains a faithful community honoring God," Julian said. He gave her an inquisitive glance. "What brings you here, besides the wonderful accommodations, religion, and delicious food?"

She grinned. "Wonderful accommodations?"

He actually puffed out his chest. "Tried, tested, and true."

She smirked. "Sarah Archer and I met at a mutual friend's wedding a few years ago."

"I know her and her husband well."

"We stay in touch through phone calls and emails and wanted to catch up in person."

There was more, a lot more, but Ashley couldn't divulge anything else to this gracious innkeeper.

"Samantha and I play a game." Julian shifted their conversation. "Whenever we see a David Fodero original, we try to describe it in two words."

"You narrow his complicated pieces down to two words?" Ashley considered the idea, staring down at her water glass. "It's not possible."

"Sure it is. My turn first. Radical and imaginative."

"Not fair. You've had loads of practice." She lifted her glass to salute him. "Scenic and surreal."

"Excellent." He reached for the water pitcher and waved down a waitress balancing another dessert tray. "David painted that landscape when he first moved to town and brought it here one afternoon. He insisted I hang it wherever I wished."

"And you wished to hang it on a prominent wall in your restaurant."

"Why not? I'm a businessman and publicity is publicity." Julian grinned, held up a hand to the waitress and mouthed, "I'm coming."

Ashley nodded at the painting. "Where is the place David painted?"

"Close. So close, in fact, you can walk there. When you reach Memorial Street Church, go a little farther and you'll see an abandoned rail line bordered by a river."

"I'll check it out."

"Are you an art lover?"

She contemplated her answer, choosing to be 100 percent honest. "Actually, I'm the planet's most enthusiastic fan."

Especially of David Fodero, she amended to herself.

Inspiration does exist, but it must find you working.
- Picasso

When the sun rose the following morning, Ashley considered checking out the work-out room, but then decided to wait another day. Instead, she showered and washed her hair with lemon-scented shampoo, then chose a pair of cotton tie-dyed shorts and a chambray button-up top. After a quick breakfast to spoon a container of yogurt and drink a cup of sugary coffee, she exited the inn. She couldn't resist pausing on the front porch to rock back and forth on one of the inn's wide-slatted rocking chairs before heading to the town square.

She picked up a basket of ripe peaches from the farmer's market, inhaling whiffs of buttered popcorn and spun sugar, and treated herself to an herbal lavender tea served in a miniature paper cup.

She decided to bring the peaches to David's cabin as a

gesture of gratitude for his hospitality. Sure, it was an excuse to speak with him further, though she couldn't explain away the urge to see him again so soon.

David. She smiled just thinking about him.

Polite but distant, he'd offered to help with her car. She well remembered the quirk of his dark eyebrows when he'd remarked on Grandfather Mountain being located in North Carolina. His chuckle had been deep, holding good-natured amusement.

She must come clean with him, and soon. Still, she hesitated. She suspected David didn't appreciate dishonesty.

Slow. Think it through. Use finesse. And pray.

She tramped back to the inn, then drove to the town's outskirts. Following the exit that led to the state park, she soon sighted Pine Knoll Lane. She parked in front of David's cabin and followed the stepping-stone path to the door.

With a rapid knock, she called out, "Anyone home?"

She peered around. No dog bark from Pickle, and David's green pickup truck wasn't in the driveway. She peeked through the expansive bay window. The living room looked the same—neat and orderly, with assorted canvases, paints, brushes, and a metal tray stacked and sorted.

She tried the handle, surprised when the door opened. Fearful the fruit wouldn't tolerate the heat well, she set the basket on the foyer floor. A glimpse of the distinctive redwood chair prompted her to peek further inside.

The entryway led to the living room. Beyond, a full bathroom and a study. A wooden desk was cluttered with art books, and a laptop computer sat closed. A layer of dust begged for a housekeeper, and she had the sense he must employ someone once in a while. As she doubled back to the living room, a sleek black metal spiral staircase beckoned.

No. Too personal.

Should she? She twisted her hands, then craned her neck

upward. No, she shouldn't, but she couldn't resist. Quickly, she mounted the steps. An upstairs bedroom boasted a double bed with a wood paneled headboard and brown tweed comforter set. The air smelled of him—sandalwood and pine.

The room was neat and clean, the exception being a pair of jeans and a T-shirt draped over the bed. An elaborate sound system took up one corner, and a stack of audiobooks stood on a nearby shelf.

Odd that a man who painted such abstract art chose traditional décor for his personal space. It didn't fit his narrative, although nothing about David surprised her.

She retraced her steps downstairs, and the kitchen proved a shocker. Despite the meticulous renovations throughout the cabin, this room appeared untouched, as if taken straight from her grandmother's era.

She returned to the front door and grabbed a scrap of paper and a pen from her purse.

Sorry I missed you! I stopped by to thank you for the use of your phone. I hope to catch up with you soon.

Ashley Madden

She skimmed the note. Ugh. Had she mentioned her last name when she'd introduced herself? She couldn't remember.

Was the wording too forward? And what about the exclamation mark? She *was* sorry she missed him, but she didn't want him to suspect how much.

Well, she couldn't wipe out her message and begin again, as with an email. The note would have to suffice. She placed it with the peaches, closed the front door, and walked along the gravel driveway back to her car.

In the town center a while later, she wandered through the appealing boutiques, thrilled to discover David Fodero originals—quirky, fun and bold—in nearly every shop.

The owners all recounted the same tale when she inquired about the small canvases. David requested they not sell them but were free to display them. The paintings were gifts because he was pleased to be part of a caring community.

In Musically Yours, a music store in town, Ashley introduced herself to Dorothy Edwards, the owner. She was a spunky woman with emerald-green eyes and a slim figure. Dorothy was a pianist and her husband, Ryan, an opera singer.

"Please attend our outdoor concerts in the village park this summer." Dorothy gestured to a bulletin board tacked with the town's events.

"I'm only in Cherish for the week. I'm visiting."

"What brings you here?"

"A friend. You may know Sarah Archer?"

"Certainly. This is a tiny community. Her husband sings and plays harmonica in our church." Dorothy bobbed toward a mountain of sheet music on the counter. "The latest hymn arrangements just came in."

"I teach art to children, and also teach Sunday school."

"Art and music are closely related." The continuously busy Dorothy moved on to arrange a display of Percy Grainger statues, explaining that the store was celebrating the composer's birthday all month.

"I've never heard of him," Ashley confessed.

"Many people haven't, which is why we're spotlighting him. He was born in Australia and became an American citizen. Listen to his arrangements, especially 'Seventeen Come Sunday,' an English folk song. Or, his piano rendition of 'Country Gardens.' You'll recognize the tune."

Ashley's gaze returned to David's canvas behind the counter. "Outstanding. I can identify his paintings immediately."

"He presented the painting to me as a gift when he first moved here," Dorothy said as she filed a pile of Percy Grainger posters. "I got the impression he was subtly giving a message—he valued friendship but didn't want his privacy breached."

"Fair enough." Ashley's gaze skirted again to David's painting.

Nancy's art gallery displayed his larger canvases and sold them for several thousand dollars. Upon closer inspection, Ashley preferred his 8 x 10 inch, more intimate pieces—always with a hidden, or not-so-hidden dog in the upper right-hand corner.

She might even be able to afford one of his smaller works, and mentally redecorated her apartment, finding blank wall space where she could hang his paintings. However, they weren't for sale anymore, not in Greenwood, not in Cherish. Not anywhere.

She detoured to where David had painted the landscape he'd donated to the inn. She parked at Memorial Street Church and walked a short distance to an abandoned railway. The pavement glittered with the hotness of the midday sun.

After she worked her way through a narrow trail and reached a clearing, she didn't expect to encounter him. But there he was. In the same grove, surrounded by a kaleidoscopic array of wildflowers, with oak trees and a river beyond.

The air was scented with moss and earth, and the hint of summer blossoms.

She stared at him, open-mouthed, thrilled with her good fortune.

His heather gray T-shirt touting a well-known New York tourist attraction and slim-fitting Bermuda shorts enhanced his muscular physique. Again, he didn't fit her image of a reclusive painter.

But then, he wasn't painting. Rather, he was taking photographs, the camera slung around his neck by a strap, a tripod beside him.

She approached him from behind, on his right side, and he didn't seem conscious of her until she stepped in front of him. Or perhaps because his dog raced over with welcoming barks and sturdy tail wagging.

David looked wildly around and raked the dark hair from his forehead. The skin bunched at the corner of his eyes. "Ashley Madden. I didn't see you at first."

"Hello, David." Her heart shouldn't tingle because he'd uttered her name. And why wasn't there a sense of strangeness? They'd only just met.

"Sorry," she went on. "I didn't mean to come up on you so quietly." She stepped back while inwardly reprimanding herself. She'd been inconsiderate for advancing on him without warning.

He ran a thumb across his camera. "When I'm involved in my work, I'm focused and block out everything else."

She couldn't ignore the pride on his handsome face when he'd recovered from being startled by her approach. Surely a man like him never succumbed to weakness or defeat. Clearly, he hadn't seen her, though he'd object to anyone feeling sorry for him. Still, he needed support and morale boosting from someone.

And who might that someone be?

Nope. Not going there.

Sure, he was talented, an animal lover, and definitely generous.

And she'd begun to daydream about him, although she stifled any romantic notions. Nevertheless, she was drawn to him.

"How did you come upon these broken-down railroad tracks?" He grinned. "The running train is located on the opposite side of town."

"I'm not going anywhere." She smiled from ear to ear. "Today, I'm discovering Cherish."

He set the camera on a stool beside him. "You're still looking for Grandfather Mountain?"

"Grandfather Mountain? Why would I—"

"Remember? You're a mountain climber."

A glimpse of his boyish grin, more relaxed now, and she forgot her reasons for anything besides him.

"Grandfather Mountain is a distinctive mountain in the Blue Ridge Range," she informed him. As soon as she'd gone back to her room, the first day she met him, she'd done her research on the internet.

"How tall is it?"

"What is this? *Jeopardy*?"

"Just asking."

"Five thousand, nine hundred, and forty-six feet."

"Excellent." He laced the word with teasing amusement. "What other mountains do you climb?"

She bunched her hands into her pockets. "I stick to the basics."

"Basic mountains?"

"I'm referring to my gear."

"I assume you bring a rope, climbing pack, helmet and a harness."

She fumbled for the right words. "Yes, and a ... a headlamp." Once, she'd watched a television documentary about a mountain climber and he'd used a headlamp.

David feigned absorption in the rushing river behind her. Yet when he met her gaze, she caught a glimpse of unaffected warmth in his blue eyes.

"A climbing headlamp is useful after sundown," he suggested helpfully.

"A super bright lamp is crucial." She stalled, searching her mind for helpful details, counting on someone, anyone, who might appear and come to her rescue. In the end, it was David.

He moved closer. "You don't know all that much about mountain climbing, do you?"

"An understatement to say the least." She scooped up Pickle, who rewarded her with a dozen licks to her chin. "How did you guess my secret?"

"Call me a regular Sherlock Holmes. Or maybe it was the headlamp reference." Lightly, he brushed his knuckles over her cheek, disarming her. "I'm just messing with you. I don't know anything about mountain climbing, either."

"I'm ignorant when it comes to mountain ranges too."

"Well, you could've fooled me." He seemed to try his best not to look surprised. "By the way, someone broke into my house today."

"Huh."

"Huh? Meaning?"

"It was me." She held up a hand. "Although to clarify, I didn't break in because the door was unlocked. Plus, I had an excellent reason."

"I can only imagine." He waited, shifted. "Go on."

"I was worried about … about the peaches."

"I wasn't aware peaches had feelings."

"The heat is excessive, and the peaches were already ripe when I bought them at the farmer's market. I feared they might spoil. Your doorstep gets a lot of sun."

"You're blaming your break-in on my sunny doorstep?"

"It wasn't a break-in," she clarified, straightening her shoulders. "But yes, it's all your fault."

"Well, that explains everything." His laughter rang out,

and the last bit of tension vanished from his face. "Thanks for the treat. They're delicious. I already ate two."

"You're welcome."

"What made you decide on peaches?" He shifted to face her. "They're my favorite fruit."

"Peaches were a wild guess, though they're in season and I assumed everyone likes them." She set Pickle down. He lapped up the water in his dish and found a shady spot in the grass beneath an oak tree. "Thanks again."

"Glad to oblige." David's smile was candid. "Next time we'll devour a box of cookies and drink sugary soda."

Next time? She muffled a self-conscious laugh while her heart skipped a beat.

She stepped over to the tree and crouched to give Pickle a belly rub. The dog rolled onto his back, feet splayed to provide better access to his stomach.

"Did you peek through my house while you were inside today?" he asked.

"Snoop?"

"Peek, snoop …"

"Neither is flattering. I was in and out quickly. *Fairly quickly,* she amended, sending a prayer to God. In retrospect, it had been an intrusion on David's personal space.

God is within me. God is rooting for me. Focus on His word and God, please forgive me.

Now was a suitable time to explain to David why she was really in Cherish. But he was smiling, and the mood was congenial. She didn't want to spoil it.

"You mentioned you're not from around here," he said.

"I live in a town fifty miles away."

"Not far."

"Not far. It's similar in size and population to Cherish, though Cherish has more of a quintessential…"

"Charm?"

"The optimal description."

He waited, apparently, for her to continue.

"I own an art studio for handicapped children. I allow my students the freedom to create art in any form they choose. There's no right or wrong."

"Admirable." He yanked open a portable cooler at his feet and offered her a bottle of root beer and an almond biscuit from a bakery in town, which she gratefully accepted. He grabbed an energy drink for himself.

"The soda isn't sugar free." All the while, his gaze stayed on her. "Neither is the biscuit."

"Best news of the day."

He laughed. "I assume your teaching is challenging?"

"My students are a pleasure, and my studio is a work in progress. I love sharing the beauty and wonder of art."

He transferred his weight from one foot to the other. "Why are you here in Cherish?"

She blinked, caught by his question, scarcely able to breathe because of his closeness. "I'm searching for distinctive art supplies to stock my studio."

Actually, she was in Cherish because of the tall, handsome man eyeing her with undisguised interest.

He reached for another biscuit. "Aaron's Art is an excellent shop in town."

"I'll stop by while I'm here."

"I can show you sometime."

She answered with a surprised smile. "I'll take you up on your offer."

She tried to ignore the leap of her pulse at the sight of David's dazzling grin. He gave a thumbs-up.

"Do you pay for your studio items out of your own pocket?" he asked.

"Of course, although I charge minimal tuition." An abrupt memory of the many months when she'd scarcely been able to pay the heat and electric bills flashed through her mind. "Sometimes, I receive donations from my church, which is a huge help."

"If you ever need anything, I own a warehouse in New York filled with supplies."

"Thank you. I'm always running out of metal buckets and paint brushes and canvases. It's all worth it, though. Art is healing."

"Exactly." He treated her with a mixture of courtesy and sincerity. There was a guarded attentiveness from this urbane, handsome man. She couldn't shake the feeling he sensed their growing attraction, too.

He uncapped his energy drink. "What else do you provide for your students?"

"Unconditional love and support."

"There's nothing better." His gaze, shining with respect, met hers. "You're staying at the Cherish Hills Inn?"

"Yes. I booked a room for the next few days. The owner is accommodating, and the food is fabulous." She paused, the biscuit in her hand temporarily forgotten.

Nerves kicked in. Why was he asking? Was he interested in her? In a sense, he'd asked her out by offering to show her the art shop. And he'd mentioned sharing cookies.

"Julian is a hands-on owner, and his cook, Melissa, produces marvelous dishes."

Thinking of her exquisite meal the night before, she nodded. "The restaurant offers top-notch service. I enjoyed dinner there, and the sweet and sour meatballs are scrumptious."

"You ate alone?" David asked. He finished his second biscuit and drank half his energy drink.

"I'm single and usually eat by myself."

Something stirred in the immeasurable depths of his eyes.

Something warm. "I prefer to dine with a beautiful companion."

Judging from photos she'd seen of him through the years, there was often a glamorous starlet hanging from his arm. Ashley swallowed, torn between awkwardness and self-consciousness. She was neither stunning nor a starlet.

The warmth in his eyes was replaced by an emotion she couldn't pinpoint. And then he became unreadable.

"In all honesty," he said, shoving his hands into his pockets. "I'm surprised."

"Why?"

"A breathtaking woman like you should've been snatched up long ago."

"I'm a seasoned solo diner with no romantic commitments. I'm also a foodie."

"I eat by myself more often than not."

Her eyes widened. She couldn't imagine him dining alone. "Do you prefer it?"

"Not a bit."

She smiled. "When dining in a restaurant, the secret is to take along props."

"A fork and a spoon?"

She choked on a laugh. "A travel book is good. I recommend *The Lonely Planet*."

"Where do you travel?"

"Nowhere, though I've always wanted to tour Italy, particularly the Campania region and Naples."

"I've visited. The word *scenic* doesn't capture Italy's breathtaking coastlines. Traveling is my passion, and that country is a favorite."

"I've read that every meal in Italy is a memorable experience."

"Tuscany resembles something straight out of a picture book."

Now they had Italy in common, besides art and a love of animals.

"When dining alone …" She paused for a dramatic effect. "I pull up the e-reader on my phone."

"How about taking a companion with you to dinner?"

Her eyebrows raised, along with her spirit. She couldn't be certain if he was flirting, but elected to participate. "Do you have anyone in mind?"

"Me, because I haven't eaten there yet."

"I heard you frequently order takeout." She prayed she wasn't initiating a topic too prying, but took the dive, anyway. "Julian Wilson mentioned it last night."

A sparkle lit his eyes as he placed a hand on her shoulder. "I'm the center of a conversation?"

Her mouth went dry. She swallowed. Truth? These days, he was the center of all her conversations. All her thoughts.

She dismissed his teasing query with a chuckle. "You were worth a quick mention."

"Thanks for letting me down gently." He granted her a rueful smile. His hand leisurely massaged her shoulder. "Hence, will you?"

"Hence? Will I …Wait. Are you asking me out to dinner, or am I asking you?"

A softness shone from his blue eyes. His eyes, she decided, were designed to mesmerize. She couldn't look away.

"To clarify, I'm asking you. I hope you'll accept." His hand remained on her shoulder, and the chemistry between them heated. He realized it, too. She heard the evidence from the tenderness in his tone.

"You're splashed on the front page of gossip newspapers with models and actresses—" Ashley stopped herself. Whoa. This chat was becoming overly personal.

"Gossip newspapers don't reveal a factual story. Many of

those women simply craved publicity. I was the man of the hour, though insincerity isn't my thing." The edginess vanished from his voice, replaced with a hint of gratefulness. "The woman of my dreams has a sense of humor and is a delight to be around."

"I've never dated anyone famous."

He rubbed his forehead. "Why bring up that particular word at this precise minute?"

"Because I'm the opposite of your usual choice in women."

His gaze narrowed. "You're an authority on me in the short time we've known each other?"

"You mentioned insincerity wasn't your thing," she continued. "I'd welcome the same consideration."

"You don't believe I'm sincere?"

"I don't know you well enough to determine either way."

"So I'm guilty."

"I didn't say that."

She had, though.

Too late, she noticed his troubled expression, and regretted allowing her emotions to steer her toward such a blunt outburst. She braced herself for a verbal lambasting, but after a blink of silence, he replied, "I value your honesty. You're a refreshing change in my jaded world."

She drew in a breath and didn't meet his gaze.

Her conscience tapped her on the shoulder. Insincerity? She was the one being dishonest. What about the bigger explanation of her sudden appearance in Cherish?

"Ashley?" David's tone was just enough of a caress that she ignored her conscience. Though if he was extending a genuine invitation, she wasn't sure how to respond. She only knew she was pleased and thrilled and welcomed the excitement seeping through her body.

"Yes?"

"I'm sincere." His gaze dropped to her mouth.

In a state of expectation, she waited for him to kiss her. When it proved apparent after awkward seconds passed that he hadn't planned any such thing, she disguised her disappointment beneath a luminous smile.

"I'll accept your dinner invitation under one condition," she replied.

"Which is?"

"Cookies are on the dessert menu."

"Any particular kind? Frozen, I assume?"

She chuckled. "I have an affinity for chocolate. Frozen is incomparable. Thawed is acceptable."

"I'm certain the innkeeper can arrange chocolate cookies to your liking." David burst out laughing, then pressed a fleeting kiss to her forehead.

She tipped up her chin. "What's that for?"

"The laugh or the kiss?"

"The kiss."

His admiring gaze roved over her from head to toe. "My kiss is expressing gratitude for keeping me on track. For granting me the unexpected freedom to laugh out loud. For looking incredibly enchanting in a simple outfit of shorts and a chambray blouse."

That described her to a T. Simple. Not striking. Not glamorous.

Simple.

His compliment was nothing more than lighthearted flattery. She gazed past him at the spectacular scene of mountains and sky far beyond the crystal-clear river.

He chucked her under the chin and the romantic moment, if that was indeed what it had been, eased.

He nodded toward the stool and gestured for her to sit.

She threw him a questioning glance. "But there's only one stool."

"And it's for you." An amused sparkle lit his eyes as he leaned against a tree. "Unless you'd like to share it."

Rather than disagree, she sat as he requested, and set the soda beside her, leaving no space for him. She was certain her cheeks had heated to a flushed pink that had little to do with the warmth of the day, and more to do with the good-looking man standing a few feet away.

"You asked a lot about me," she said, "but why are you in town, David?"

"I'm here on Marge Addyson's invitation. I was commissioned to paint a portrait for the centennial celebration of Memorial Street Church." He grabbed a third biscuit, thoughtfully chewed, then drained his energy drink. "Marge is the associate pastor, my benefactor, and a kind, thoughtful woman. Based on her request, the artwork will be personalized with a then and now quality."

"Two paintings?

"I haven't decided. Perhaps two-sided art, or two renderings of the church, the older version drawn in charcoal."

"On the same canvas?"

"Maybe."

"I'm certain anything you paint will be marvelous."

"Let's settle on acceptable."

Her heart skipped a beat at the uncertainty in his expression. If she hadn't glanced up, she would've missed it, so fleeting had it crossed his face.

She groped for an upbeat topic. "Do you intend to live in Cherish permanently?"

"I signed a contract."

"For the commission or the cabin?"

"The commission, which is to be delivered the final week of August. I purchased the cabin outright."

Mentally, she gauged the price. With David's extensive

renovations, she estimated a cost of at least a half million dollars.

"I'm single with no ties," he went on. "I wanted a discreet out-of-the-way house. When I first visited, this town fit the bill. The right place, the right season in my life."

She hung onto the beginning of his sentence. "Why?"

"Why I'm not married? I'm only thirty-five. There's still time." He rubbed his eyes. "I suppose the first reason is because no woman seemed interested in dating a starving artist."

"You're hardly starving anymore."

"I was dirt-poor for many years." His eyes shuttered, a sharpness carried his tone. "You've heard of overnight successes?"

"Hasn't everyone?"

"Whatever you're inclined to believe, there is no such thing. Almost 100 percent of anyone who has achieved any semblance of success worked hard to get there."

"You mentioned a first reason." Ashley rounded on him. "Is there a second?"

"Second what?"

"Second reason you're not married."

"I never allow a relationship to last over the three-month line." He rubbed his temples. "I found it's easier that way. No one gets hurt."

She fixed her stare on the tranquil scene of wildflowers and water and a sleeping dog. He'd certainly given her something to mull over.

David picked up his camera, slung the strap around his neck, then began taking photos. He used his left eye to focus.

"I'm left-eye dominant too." She stood and stepped to an oak tree near the river. "Most people are right-eye dominant."

No answer, only more camera clicks.

"Gorgeous and natural," he murmured.

She surveyed the base of the tree. "Do you fish?"

"Nope."

"There's certainly access to fishing in this town."

"Yup."

Pickle woke, stretched, then dozed again.

"Will you use these photos as a reference to reproduce on canvas?" She anchored her foot on the lowest branch of the tree.

A fair question, though again, David didn't respond. Instead, he stepped back and muttered something about tight and wide shots.

She squinted up at the sun. "What's the ideal light for outdoor photography?"

"It depends on what I'm shooting."

She curled her fingers around the next tree branch, testing to be certain it would hold her weight, then scrambled to the sturdy upper limb.

He swiveled toward her, open-mouthed. "What are you doing?"

"I'm climbing a tree."

"I'm quite aware." His lips quirked. "May I ask why?"

"So I can sit."

"There are stools for the same purpose."

"I see better up here."

"Isn't that a bit childish?"

"I'm an adult, but it doesn't mean I should give up everything I loved to do when I was young. The view is different up here. Better. I can see beyond the river to the grassy knoll bordering the mountains." At his curious look, she added, "Haven't you ever climbed a tree?"

"When I was ten."

"What was it like?"

He blinked and averted his gaze. "I climbed an old maple tree higher and higher. Then I looked down."

"And?"

"I closed my eyes and gasped for oxygen. When I opened them, I was sweating profusely."

"What happened next?"

"I lost my balance and fell out of the tree."

"Oh, no." She clung tighter to a skinny branch. "I hope you weren't hurt."

"Only my pride." He gazed up at her. "My brothers thought it was the funniest thing they'd seen in a decade. They laughed for days."

"Did you ever try again?"

"Nope. Do I look like a fool?"

"Chicken."

Her prim correction brought a chuckle. Then a sigh. Then another series of clicks as he lifted his camera.

"How many shots do you usually take?" she called down to him.

"Thirty or forty." His manner was preoccupied. "I file my photographs in an image library."

"All part of the creative process." She shifted to a different branch. "I've learned that subject is most important in art and photography."

Again, he placed the camera close to his eye and took aim at the river. "And in life."

His statement, his philosophy, she wasn't sure.

She looped strands of hair slipping loose from her ponytail behind her ear. She repeated to herself that she was in Cherish for a purpose, to discuss if he planned to sell his artwork anymore. Equally important, he should consult an eye doctor.

Perhaps he already had. He certainly had the financial resources.

Should she ask? Wouldn't that be prying into his personal affairs?

And why couldn't she keep her gaze off him for longer than half a second?

By now she had surmised he was losing, or perhaps had lost, total vision in his right eye. He was discernibly uncomfortable discussing the subject, though he'd alluded to the eyesight loss in his cabin. Just as easily, he had shut the discourse down before she'd uttered a word. He had a knack for dictating a conversation.

Another stretch of silence. She climbed down from the tree, reached for her soda and took a sip. The drink was warm, and flat.

When she brought up how summer colds were sometimes worse than winter colds, citing various reasons, David teased her about being a regular Dr. Google.

Then, she focused on the wildflowers.

"They're exquisite, aren't they?" she rhapsodized. "I especially love red and pink. The shades are vibrant."

"Yup," came his reply.

Not much of a response. Artists realized the power of color, and she'd taught her students that color brought out emotions. She recommended vibrant, cool, warm, and complementary paint in every piece her students created.

When she had exhausted any further attempts about uncontroversial subjects—the weather, various dog breeds, favorite television shows—hers was the *Andy Griffith Show*, David packed his camera and tripod in a brown leather messenger bag. He expelled a breath, hoisted the bag over his shoulder, and leashed Pickle.

"Are you headed to the inn, Ashley?" He glanced at his watch and frowned. "I'm giving up for today."

"Giving up what?"

"Work, photographs, art. Nothing is cooperating, including the weather."

"Why? Is it supposed to rain?" She caught his frown, then raised her gaze to the heavens. As if the mention of rain had conjured up the finale of a picture-perfect sky, clouds had begun to form.

"Nothing in the forecast, and the weather is warm but pleasant." He cut off any further questions by stating, "It's getting late."

Four o'clock in the afternoon was hardly late for two grown adults. Tree branches swayed in the breeze, and squirrels scampered from tree to tree.

She scowled at her flat soda. Suddenly, David had become aware of her again.

"As a matter of fact, I am headed to the inn," she said.

"I can walk you there."

Was he sincere or offering out of courtesy?

Around him, her thoughts became increasingly tangled. She felt like she was on a roller coaster—thrilling, adrenaline-filled, and exhilarating when he was near. At other times, the hours slowed, and she could hardly catch a breath.

Both instances had the same common denominator.

Him.

An hour ago, they seemed in perfect accord. Presently, she was trying her best to ignore the blow to her pride by his sudden memory loss. Had he forgotten he'd suggested they have dinner together?

"I'm fully aware of the inn's location," she said. "I don't require an escort to walk a few short blocks." She sought to sound indifferent and knew she didn't when the words trapped in her throat.

Nonetheless, she didn't appreciate the way he'd dismissed her.

Typical difficult artist.

"Besides," she added, "my car is parked a short distance from here." She offered a grim smile. "Thanks anyway. Good day, David."

Later, she'd wonder how she pulled off ending the conversation with such supreme self-confidence. She kept her posture straight, whirled on her heel, and marched away.

CHAPTER 5

*H*ours later, David shook his head. *Wow, had he bungled that badly.*

When he and Ashley had stood near the oak tree, he'd watched her delicate eyebrows knit together in a frown before she'd stomped away. Contrary to his expectation she'd accept his offer to walk her to the inn, she'd done the opposite.

It was his fault.

She'd given such a jaunty declaration that she knew where the inn was, that he'd wanted to take her in his arms and kiss her soft, full lips.

Standing by the window in his cabin, he gazed out at the night sky. The slender leaves of willow oaks flickered under the silver light cast by a quarter moon. He stared blindly at his reflection and raked a hand through his messy shag, begging for a haircut.

He braced an arm on the frame and surveyed the last of the clouds. Despite the forecast, it had rained earlier. He opened the window to allow the breeze to wash a freshness through the room.

He hardly knew how to cope with the range of emotions he was experiencing.

An attractive, charming woman had expressed interest in his paintings, perhaps in him, and he'd been less than enthusiastic. He reprimanded himself over the unfairness of taking his frustration over his lost eyesight out on her, but he hadn't been able to see into the camera as easily as he'd anticipated. He'd been in the zone initially, snapping photos intuitively and envisioning them. Exhilaration and enthusiasm had pressed him to continue. Soon, he'd questioned himself as he realized he couldn't identify subjects as clearly as he liked.

In addition, he'd felt disheartened when Ashley had remarked on his fame.

If anything, he felt like a failure. Sure, he'd spent his entire adulthood beneath the celebrity umbrella, but the mention always made him uncomfortable.

Was that all she saw in him?

He wasn't an award for a woman to parade on her arm. He was a living, breathing man, not a slicked-up magazine cover. Similar to newsworthy men in the public eye—movie stars and prominent sport figures—his tranquility had been invaded by women fascinated not by him nor his art, but by the prospect of enlisting him as their escort for popular media events.

Not the man. Not him.

Rather, how the reclusive, mysterious artist might bolster their career.

The afternoon with Ashley was the first time he believed

a woman was drawn to him solely for himself. He'd learned a little about her and had been captivated by her kind-heartedness and ideals. She was a breath of pure air, and refreshingly uninterested in money and power.

Thus, he was surprised he'd been wrong about her.

But no, no, he wasn't wrong. He'd recognized the interest in her gorgeous hazel eyes whenever she gazed up at him.

Something was happening between them. Something special. Something magnetic.

While he'd taken photos of the landscape and river, he'd caught her staring at him from the corner of his good eye. Involuntarily, he'd begun to memorize her face—all pink-cheeked and beautiful and captivating.

His feelings were utterly illogical. He'd just met her. Nevertheless, the upsetting emotional and physical unbalances he'd faced because of his eyesight, coupled with the hours in her charming company, had merged together.

The result was excitement, a kind of euphoria he'd never experienced before.

The result was chaos. His reaction and judgement weren't functioning clearly.

Part of the time, he had the wildest sensation that she couldn't possibly be as genuine as she seemed. Vivacious and enchanting and embracing life, she brought to mind an eighteen-year-old girl on the verge of becoming a woman.

On the other hand, she made him feel like he was eighteen again, for she remained constantly in his thoughts.

He'd been sincere in his suggestion to walk her to the inn, hoping to prolong their afternoon together. It wasn't a big shock she refused. Why would she want to converse with someone like him, so sulky and self-absorbed?

"Ashley, Ashley." He whispered her name aloud.

Ideal on a marquee, definitely traditional, and beyond compare.

And her other name: *Twinkle.*

Why had her friend called her that?

Ashley had ignored his inquisitive stare at the time, though he intended to ask her the meaning of the nickname. She was an enigma he wanted to get to know better, and so he'd absorbed every word she'd uttered when they were together.

The first day they met, they'd shaken hands. Hers was dainty, like the woman herself, her fingers slim and firm. When she'd slipped off her sunglasses, she'd afforded him a glimpse of her startling eyes. Fascinating. Hazel eyes were set apart from brown or blue eyes because of their combination of green, gold, and brown.

She embodied the ideal subject—great cheekbones, finely arched eyebrows, and rounded, subtle features.

When Sarah and Ashley had readied to leave his cabin, he hadn't anticipated spouting about deaf musicians and blind painters. He'd just blurted it out. Shock and disbelief had flashed across Ashley's face.

She was considerate and compassionate. Her face lit up when she chatted about her students.

He closed the window, nodding quiet approval for her tender spirit.

When they'd stood by the river, her breath had quickened. He had wanted to kiss her, though he'd been uncertain if the timing was right. They were in the earliest stages of a relationship, slowly learning about each other. His heart had skipped a beat at her disappointed expression when he hadn't kissed her.

Taken aback by his next thought, he sighed. Why was he unsure about kissing her when every instinct told him it was right?

Why? Because he wasn't clear about anything anymore.

He glanced at Pickle, sleeping on a rug by the fireplace.

"Can you understand this relationship any better than I can?" he asked.

The living room lamps were on. The dog didn't respond, just continued sleeping with his legs extended. Pickle could sleep just about anywhere.

David closed his eyes and went over their afternoon again.

In addition to all the reasons he was intrigued by Ashley, she also liked his paintings and championed him. Her open praise was a welcome switch from his inner harsh criticism. Perhaps he should lighten up on himself.

THE NEXT DAY, David assessed the photographs he'd taken. Surprised, he sorted numerous shots with Ashley in them. He hadn't realized he'd included her. He hadn't been able to see her clearly whenever she stepped to his right and hadn't noticed her in his viewfinder.

Or had his subconscious known she was there all along? Maybe...

He printed the best photos, assessed them, and chose one with her sitting in the tree, a suggestion of a fairy. She had shifted toward the water, and her profile—small, turned-up nose and lifted chin—created a fetching picture. The sun gilded her blond hair to a honey gold, her shapely legs were long and tanned, her creamy complexion sprinkled with freckles.

She'd glanced at him. He'd caught her expressive gaze, her lips poised in a smile. Rosy-red, her lower lip was fuller than her upper lip. Her chin was smooth, her cheeks velvety and dimpled. Yet he couldn't ignore the strength in her features.

Deprived of rational thinking, he'd captured her in a reflective, relaxed pose. Against the natural backdrop, Ashley Madden proved the ideal focus for a painting. Flawless.

Could he paint her from the photos without her permission?

Meeting her, capturing her exquisiteness…

Circumstances or all a coincidence?

He brought the photos into the kitchen. Well aware the kitchen was the main room to tackle when renovating an old house, he'd spent an afternoon listening to a builder explain traffic patterns, heating, plumbing lines, the latest "must-have's," and had opted to wait. He didn't need glass-fronted cabinets, stainless-steel appliances, or a marble-topped island. He preferred the rustic charm of blue painted cabinets and a stone floor.

He sat at the vintage wooden baking unit he used as a table and laid out the photos.

Surprisingly, Julian's voice rang in his ears. Whenever David stopped at the inn for takeout, Julian extolled the advantages of living in Cherish, sometimes peppering David with questions about his faith. For Julian, it was of utmost importance that the residents remained steadfast in their unwavering belief in God.

Had these last few months been guided by God's divine hand? Or could he attribute it to fate—the unexplainable law of the universe—that had brought him and Ashley together?

He poured himself an energy drink, took a gulp, then slumped back on the antique chair. Ah, the adrenaline of caffeine. Just the ticket to spur his brain's neural activity and quicken his thought process.

The dog trotted over and rested at his feet.

He scooped Pickle onto his lap and stroked the silky fur.

Perhaps Cherish was where he'd find his greatest freedom. Perhaps he should allow former priorities the opportunity to escape. Be inspired by a fresh perspective. Let go.

Let go of what exactly? His painting? His beloved art?

He wasn't certain. He just knew the faint murmur in his

heart whispered the observation that what he needed might be directly in front of him.

Nope, nope, nope. His hand stilled. He gazed at the beamed wooden ceiling. Dating? Women? Faith? Too much struggle. Too much conflict. Too much difficulty.

He well remembered his strict religious upbringing—the drone of Sunday sermons by an aged pastor when his parents had dragged him to church as a boy. His mother's insistence he dress properly in beige pants and a blue polo shirt. Their gasps of horror when he declared the sermons boring. He was an adolescent when doubts about God and Christianity had taken hold.

He gave a sad, small laugh. At himself, at the universe.

Maybe the time had come to accept whatever God had in store for him.

You're joking, right?

He shook off his musings, set the dog down, and shoved to his feet, turning to the refrigerator. He pulled a box of cookies from the freezer.

When he bit into one, still frozen, the way Ashley liked them, reality intruded.

God had been absent for decades. God wasn't interested in a man like David—with faults more numerous than the number of paintings he'd painted through the years. Besides, he was too much of a skeptic to change his religious views.

With a decisive nod, he vowed to be more attentive to his art and less attentive to his thoughts about Ashley. Surely thinking about her shouldn't consume him.

Ashley.

Any artist would clamor to paint an enchanting woman with such expressive eyes. A woman with a lean, breathtaking figure and a face that conveyed tenderness and compassion.

She was fascinating, and he wished to see her again. With

his mind made up, he placed the cookies back in the freezer. It would be better if he and Ashley ate them together. Along with bottles of soda loaded with sugar.

TIME HAD SMOOTHED over Ashley's upset of the previous day over David's not-so-polite dismissal of her. A morning workout crossed her mind, but she quickly dismissed the idea. Instead, she chose to explore the town more. In order to rationalize her morning jaunt, she popped into Aaron's Art, the shop David had mentioned. She invariably needed supplies for her studio.

Aaron, the owner, a hunched-over fellow with a white curly beard that reminded her of sheep's wool, sang David's praises. David had come into his store, learned Aaron struggled to meet his monthly rent payments because business was slow, and paid for the store's new heating and air conditioning unit. He'd made all the arrangements and sent Aaron a check to cover six months' rent as well.

"He's beyond generous. It's a shame he's hidden himself away." Aaron crossed over to her. "He'll appear for a couple hours and is gone by the time anyone realizes he was around."

"He's certainly made his mark in the artistic community." She instantly regretted saying anything, because she could almost see Aaron's ears perk up.

He stepped over to a display of pencil pocket sets. "Haven't you heard? He keeps himself scarce because he's losing his eyesight." Aaron scribbled a sign: *Superb For Traveling.*

"Rumors spread like wildfire, don't they?" Ashley said.

Aaron fixed her with a level look. "Sometimes."

Not everyone knew about David's eyesight loss, she

wanted to tell Aaron. Only those who spent a lengthy amount of time with David would have figured it out.

Like her, for instance. She was fortunate to have shared hours with him. He was complex and charming and … impossible. She hadn't broached the eyesight subject with him because she didn't want to hinder his creativity. And it seemed as if he was always creating. Also, she didn't want to interrupt their time together with upsetting conversation.

She remembered the way his gaze had dropped to her lips, the warmth of his skin. She longed to run her fingers through his messy, disheveled hair. Did he realize his hair curled at the nape?

They'd stared at each other as if they were both waiting for something.

What, exactly?

He wasn't falling in love with her, nor was he about to declare an everlasting declaration of any kind.

Neither was she.

She had resolved to preserve her heart behind a sheltered and safe wall. Love wasn't a part of her future, and any fleeting thoughts of her and David had to be quickly squelched. With him, she'd keep things businesslike. Besides, she wasn't stunning and sophisticated or similar in any way to the women he apparently preferred.

Allow me my privacy was his philosophy, and the reason why he'd attempted to conceal his whereabouts in this idyllic community.

She picked up a framed watercolor of Venice, Italy, and then gazed out the shop's front window. Townsfolk cheerfully greeted each other as they strolled along the sidewalk. Children skipped, the seniors walked slower, arm in arm.

Cherish had a glow all its own.

The simple acts of fellowship should have made her

spirits soar. Instead, they plummeted because all that good cheer effectively took her back to David's suffering.

Hiding his loss under an unbreachable demeanor might be his way. Not hers. God had placed outward limits on David's body, but His inner blessings were greater. She promised to pray and believe and lean on God. She wanted to inspire David to do likewise.

She purchased pocket sets, pens, and pencils for her students and thanked Aaron, suppressing her dismay that she wasn't able to afford more expensive items. She could've used an assortment of mason jars, but would have to wait.

She passed a sign on the corner advertising a Renaissance Faire in a neighboring town. She'd always wanted to attend one, but never had the opportunity.

Perhaps this time?

Her imagination conjured the aroma of pork on a stick, or a steak and mushroom meat pie, and her stomach rumbled. The idea of escaping to a medieval world, outside of modern everyday life, held a sense of adventure and decent, old-fashioned fun.

But no, not this trip. David Fodero absorbed all of her attention.

An hour later, Ashley had showered and changed into a yellow sundress that hugged her slim figure, a bold necklace featuring a golden sunflower and beige leather sandals. Before she forgot Dorothy's recommendation from the music store, she listened to Percy Grainger's performance of 'Country Gardens.' She read about the pianist's fascinating life, spending more time on it than she'd foreseen, as he was praised for his talent.

Another typically difficult artist, she smiled to herself.

By seven o'clock, she was perched on a stool in the inn's

lounge, sipping a tall glass of sweet iced tea, mulling over different ways to help David.

Julian greeted her with a smile as he wended between bistro tables. He held a tumbler overflowing with fresh-squeezed limeade. He'd expounded earlier that limeade was an inn specialty beverage because of the addition of fresh mint leaves.

"I heard you were here." He leaned against the stool opposite her. "I'm the messenger this evening. Someone in the parlor wants to see you."

"Is Sarah here?" She sat forward. "I thought we were having lunch together in a few days. I hope I didn't get the times mixed up."

"I assure you it's not Sarah." Julian chuckled. "I haven't seen her tonight."

Ashley half stood. "Who, then?"

Julian toasted her glass with his. His eyes sparkled with merriment. "I'm fairly certainly you'll recognize him immediately."

CHAPTER 6

Good artists copy, great artists steal.
– Picasso

S eated on an overstuffed sofa in the parlor of the Cherish Hills Inn, David set a bouquet of wild-flowers on the coffee table, and then rifled through a pile of periodicals. Particularly catching his interest was a gardening magazine, reminding him that he planned to start his vegetable garden. He needed to contact Ashley's friend, Sarah.

"Anything I can help you with, sir?" A pleasant woman whom he guessed to be in her sixties, with curly gray hair and red-rouged cheeks, all beams and buoyancy, wheeled a trolley cart stacked with beverages and snacks toward him.

"No thanks. I'm set." He held up the magazine as proof.

Optimism all around seemed to be a prerequisite for living in Cherish, along with its close cousins—positivity and religion.

He smiled at her, then feigned absorption in an article touting the optimum season to plant pumpkins seeds. He assumed it was the fall. He was wrong. In the Carolinas, early July was deemed best. He'd better get on it so he could harvest something he'd be able to swallow. Sarah had mentioned squash and carrots and… What was the last vegetable? Something green he'd certainly not eaten before, and which was probably tasteless.

When he finished the article, he looked around, cheered by the surroundings—a stacked rock fireplace, cornflower-blue tapestry rug, and gleaming oak wood floors. A shaft of late-day sunlight slanted through the front window. Outside, the sky blazed a magnificent tangerine-orange. In the distance, a dog barked.

He'd considered bringing Pickle with him, but was uncertain if dogs were allowed. From comments on the internet, he'd learned the inn's previous owner had banned dogs. He wasn't certain of Julian's stance.

Before he had left his cabin, he'd given Pickle a gnawing toy and his favorite striped elephant. He'd tuned his radio to a country station that would provide, the DJ assured him, easy listening for Pickle. As he'd left, a male singer was crooning about how much better life would be if he only had a boat.

David smiled. Country music was fun and all about emotions. He was fairly certain there were no cleverer lyrics on earth.

The tensions of the day had drained as he stepped outside his cabin and into the sultry June evening. The air was thick and heavy, and a five-minute rain shower hadn't cooled things off.

Shifting to the present, he sat back on the sofa and pulled out his cell phone. He'd invested in a doggie camera he'd stationed in his living room, and streamed to his phone.

Currently, Pickle was participating in his favorite activity: sleeping.

"David?"

Ashley entered the parlor, a surprised smile on her face. He pocketed his phone, picked up the bouquet, and sprang to his feet. Her yellow dress complemented her blond hair, which spilled over her shoulders in delicate waves. She dressed with a casual finesse, perfectly suiting her symmetrical features.

"Hi, Ashley." His admiring gaze glided from the top of her head to the tips of her manicured toes.

"Hello." She set a glass of iced tea on a side table, her movements elegant, yet tentative. She reminded him of a pretty summer posy, feminine and romantic.

"I assume your tea is weighted down with sugar." He groped for the ideal words, stronger words, funnier words, and hoped his humor was contagious.

"I take three teaspoons. What's your preference?"

He matched her cheerful response. "I survive on energy drinks. I work better at night, and they help me stay awake."

"Not very healthy."

"Said the pot calling the kettle black."

"You realize caffeine is addictive?"

His retort was a bark of laughter. "Moderate consumption is okay."

"Now who is Dr. Google?"

He half smiled. Somehow, she'd flipped the conversation, causing him to consider the amount of caffeine he drank each day. Caffeine elevated his mood and kept him more alert. However, there was a major shortcoming. He'd come to rely on the drinks.

She raised her glass. "I assume you're a health nut."

"Me?" He wasn't smiling anymore. He was laughing.

"But you are into vegetables." She gestured to the magazine he'd been reading. "Aren't you planting a garden featuring everyone's favorite vegetable, zucchini?"

Right. The vegetable he couldn't remember.

Animated buzzing of conversation filled the inn's hallway, and the chiming of the pendulum clock had recently sounded the hour.

"I'd prefer to plant coffee beans bursting with caffeine," he replied.

"And I'd plant chocolate candy bars."

He started toward her, stopping within inches.

She stared up at him. "I didn't expect to see you tonight."

"Yet here I am." Captivated, he focused on her amazing smile. "Apparently, I can't stay away from you."

Ashley regarded him and stayed silent.

"The flowers are for you. Sorry, they're wilted. I'll blame it on the humidity." He offered her the bouquet, wrapped in paper towels. He'd stopped by the river and gathered the spray of fiery pinks, cardinal reds, and stems of gray-purple violets.

"Thank you. They're exquisite." Ashley set down her glass, then sniffed the delicate fragrance, a woodsy scent mingling with a hint of fresh strawberries. "David, you remembered."

A declaration, not a question.

He grinned down at her. "I listened to every word you said yesterday."

"I didn't think you heard me. You were preoccupied."

"My work requires me to stay focused. Fortunately, men can do two things at once."

She lifted a skeptical eyebrow. "Can they?"

"Yes. I can listen and work at the same time."

"Really?" She planted a hand on her hip. "What else did I say yesterday?"

"Before or after you climbed the tree?"

"After."

"Well, you enlightened me on every dog breed on the globe and provided next month's weather forecast." He flicked a glance toward the window to emphasize his point. The dark-green leaves of a majestic oak tree bent in the steamy evening breeze. "And your favorite television show is the old *Andy Griffith Show*."

"Because it's the funniest sitcom ever produced," she informed him. "I laugh each time I watch an episode, even though I memorized the lines and know the outcome by heart."

"I prefer to watch documentaries on my computer."

She slanted him a cheeky glance. "Anything special?"

"*Gladiator*."

"That movie is not a documentary or entirely accurate, though it's certainly wonderful. I'd categorize it as a love story."

Slightly mollified because she hadn't disputed his taste in documentaries, he replied, "The movie is inspired by factual events in ancient Rome."

"Uh-huh. Whatever you say. You never told me your favorite show."

"I don't own a television set."

"No way." She peered at a nearby wall, where a wide-screen TV was mounted. "I've never known anyone who doesn't own a TV."

"Now you do."

She met his gaze with disbelief. "Are you some type of minimalist?"

"On the contrary, I love TV." He offered a guilty shrug. "I discovered, though, that it's too distracting and robbed me of my most valuable asset."

"Which is?"

"My time when I could be painting."

"You're here." Her sigh was edgy, as if she was blaming

herself for his presence at the inn. "You could be painting now."

He felt it—a curious tug on his heart, the odd ache whenever he reflected on how she always considered others before herself.

"Time is valuable. People are valuable." He brushed his fingers across her cheek. "Spending time with valuable people is most valuable."

She swallowed. "A lot of valuables in your sentences."

"A lot of meaning too." He smiled into her gorgeous eyes. "May I tell you the truth about something?"

"Always."

"I fantasized about kissing you. Your skin is soft, and your mouth… I'm saying words out loud I've never told another woman."

He stepped closer. Their breaths mingled.

No. He was saying too much. He thought about pulling back. He didn't.

She gazed up at him, her chin tipping ever slightly. "I'm flattered." Her voice vibrated with the same emotion.

He understood.

He kissed her, a gentle brush of his lips on hers. Sparks of adrenaline in his veins didn't match the tenderness of their kiss, he thought.

And then he stopped thinking at all.

That is, until she stepped back and firmly shook her head.

She set the flowers down, her hands flitting like a wild bird. She didn't seem to know where to put them. "You're quite thoughtful for a guy who accomplishes two tasks at once." Her tone was easy, but her mannerisms indicated otherwise. She was shaken, as he was, by their attraction.

He dragged in a long breath. "I owe you an apology."

"For what?"

"Yesterday I wasn't as attentive as I should've been."

"No apology is necessary. You're more observant than I imagined." She picked up her tea and sipped. Her hand was trembling. She glanced at him, apparently wondering if he noticed. He did.

"You're an exceptional artist, David, and need your space." She set down the glass. "I respect you for those traits. Praise God for giving you a unique talent to share with the world."

It wasn't her affirming statements that brought a swift beat to his heart. It was the manner in which she regarded him—with appreciation in her magnificent eyes and subdued marvel in her tone. It was refreshing to be viewed as a man with merit, as if he were heroic and exceptional. A gift more precious than any he'd ever received.

He debated about reaching for her again, more insistently, by circling his arms around her and keeping her close. He wanted to create a magical evening for them—to cancel out his rudeness from the prior day. He wanted to begin the night with kiss after kiss.

Upon gauging her guarded reaction, however, he instructed himself to slow down.

"Are you ready for even more truth?" he asked.

His question elicited a puzzled gaze from her, and she shuffled her feet. "Truth is always welcome, David."

"There is another important reason why I'm here tonight."

She tilted her head, searched his face. "I'm listening."

"I wanted to see you again." He fought down more words, the knowledge of spending enchanting hours with her. Truth was, he *had* to see her again.

A rosy blush crept up her cheeks. "Oh."

Not exactly the response he'd hoped for, but considering their growing relationship, he'd accept it. He assessed her rigid bearing, and his stomach plummeted. He could almost hear her refusal.

He hesitated. "Will you join me for dinner?"

Her mouth lifted at the corners. "I'd love to. Otherwise, I planned on dining alone."

He blew out a relieved breath. "Did you bring any props?"

"You're referring to *The Lonely Planet* guidebook?" She laughed. "Not tonight."

"Excellent. No distractions." *Except him.* "Let's create a celebratory occasion."

Years before, he'd read an entire book about celebrations. A modern-day spirituality book, advising the reader to rejoice in every activity. He'd never done that, embracing precious happiness as it came, and he intended to begin with Ashley.

"By ordering champagne with dinner?" She nodded over her shoulder toward the hallway.

"I don't drink alcohol. You?"

"Me neither. I prefer any beverage with sugar."

"Wow," he noted with a straight face. "You could've fooled me."

Her infectious smile was his reward for following through with his plan. He hadn't been certain she'd be willing to dine with him. He'd taken a gamble, entering the lobby with a bedraggled bouquet and a whisper in his gut that honest joy might be waiting for him around the corner.

And here it was. And here she was.

His mind flashed back to several signs he'd seen on his drive into town.

There'd been one advertising the farmer's market, another for a church bake sale, and a third for a Renaissance Faire in a nearby town.

The farmer's market was a possibility.

The Renaissance Faire? He'd never attended one, although the brochures he'd seen had always seemed to suggest a gigantic costume party. He wouldn't be caught dead in one of those getups people spent months creating.

As for the church bake sale, he hadn't seen the inside of a church in years. He tried to be a good person but harbored too much pain and resentment to pray.

Realizing his presence at the inn might produce a stir of local gossip, he'd parked his pickup truck a half block away and walked to the inn. Not that it made a difference, though perhaps he might slide inside discreetly, wildflower bouquet in hand.

No such luck.

The setting sun cast long shadows on the ground as he approached. Julian greeted him with a hearty hello and a boisterous chuckle.

"I messed up when I was with Ashley yesterday," David began.

"Welcome to the human race." Julian clapped David on the back and ushered him through the hallway. "We all have our faults."

"Some more numerous than others. I'm here to ask her to dinner."

"No objections on my end, and there's nothing like an apology to set things right. I assumed you weren't hankering to dine with me tonight." With a good-natured grin, Julian continued. "Ashley is a unique, giving person. I gathered from a recent chat she highly rates your art."

David scanned the dining room, his gaze landing on his painting. "I debated calling her, but I didn't have her phone number."

"Ask her for it."

"I plan to."

"Go with your gut." Julian attended to a tray of drinks on the sideboard. "Do what's appropriate, for the finest of reasons, and you'll receive your reward."

David looked from the painting to Julian. "Is this some form of religious teaching found in the Bible?"

Julian's smirk was reassuring. "Common sense straight from yours truly."

"Then what is my reward?"

"The hazel-eyed blond sitting alone in the lounge. I'll get her for you." Julian lifted a hand in salute. "You'll learn I have a penchant for meddling in people's lives, especially when they've taken the first step and brought flowers."

With that, Julian had steered David into the parlor.

David watched Ashley now, knowing he couldn't explain, even to himself, how he felt about her. He didn't intend to examine the countless emotions compelling him to spend every minute around her. A spot-on Christian might proclaim it was God.

Maybe God. Maybe.

"David, are you coming?" Ashley had gathered the wild-flowers and started for the hallway. She darted a glance over her shoulder. "I'll ask the hostess for a vase and we can leave the flowers here."

He caught up with her in two strides. "Why don't you bring the flowers into the dining room? Julian will wave his hand and a vase will magically appear."

She offered a plucky grin. "You're probably right."

"You've met Julian. I'm not *probably* right. I'm *definitely* right."

His assertion was rewarded by her bubbling laugh. Without taking his gaze from hers, he asked, "Do we need reservations for dinner?"

"Nope. I know the owner."

As they entered the hallway, he took her hand in his. "Me too."

He was heartened by the fact she didn't pull away. If anything, she nodded her acceptance.

CHAPTER 7

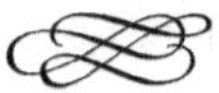

Action is the foundational key to all success.
- Picasso

The Cherish Hills Inn dining room lived up to the accolades David had heard about since his arrival. The walls were salmon-colored, the decorations lush gray, and tiny tea light candles on each table created an inviting ambiance to the elegant, understated atmosphere. Here, subtlety was the key. The artist in David noted these details as well as the table settings—gleaming silverware, sparkling glasses, tapered candles, and gold-rimmed china plateware. He also noted that heads swiveled, and the noise level dropped as he and Ashley walked in.

Ashley handed the flowers to the maître d', who then pulled out a chair and seated her. He assured her the flowers would be sent to her room, a complementary crystal vase provided.

"Perhaps a table closer to the window?" David asked, gesturing toward a particular table.

"Sorry, sir. The town sheriff and his wife sit there." The maître d' wore an apologetic smile as earnestly as he wore his black tuxedo.

Ashley and David scanned the menus, both opting for the signature dish of smoked ham, scalloped potatoes, and green beans topped with almonds.

After they placed their orders, including a carafe of fresh-squeezed limeade and Cobb salads for starters, David gazed at her across the table.

He couldn't get enough of her delightful, heart-shaped face. "Thank you for allowing me to be your dinner companion this evening."

"I never would have refused you." The soft warmth in her eyes and the catch in her lilting tone gave him pause. Absorbed by the feelings expanding inside him, he slid his hand across the table and rested it on hers. In the background, the piped-in harmony of a solo saxophone and bass violin added to the emotional mood.

When their salads were served, she bent her head and whispered a blessing for their food. Although he hadn't prayed in years, David reverently bowed his head. He didn't participate, though he remembered the simple prayer of grace.

When she finished her prayer, she sampled a portion of hard-boiled egg and avocado doused in vinaigrette.

"I've never tasted savory greens." She pinched two fingers together and touched her lips. "In fact, I don't usually like greens."

He agreed the salad was incredible and attributed the delectable taste to the olive-oil-based dressing and bits of bacon. He wasn't a leafy vegetable person, but figured he'd better start getting used to it, given a garden was a part of his future.

His gaze skimmed the room, and fragments of conversation swirled around him. "I'm glad I changed out of my paint-spattered clothes and decided on dress pants and a cotton button-down shirt."

"And sport coat," she reminded.

He'd draped his navy-blue sport coat over the back of his chair.

"This is a fancy place. And well-trained staff."

Their server, wearing the inn's trademark red apron, magically appeared when they were ready to order, brought their food and kept their glasses filled. Otherwise, he was satisfyingly absent.

After they savored a superb dinner and their table was cleared, David became keenly aware they were being watched by the staff.

While their server crumbed the tablecloth and replaced the silverware and water glasses, another waiter brought a fresh carafe of limeade and refilled their glasses. As before, Ashley added more sugar to hers. A cheese plate assortment with bread, crackers, and candied nuts also appeared.

Julian joined them and asked if the meal was prepared to their liking. They assured him the food was exquisite.

"Will you be having coffee or dessert?" Julian inquired. "Our featured special is blackberry sorbet." He snagged a silver water pitcher from a side table and refilled their glasses. "Our desserts are made in-house. The sorbet is refreshing, and the blackberries are local."

"We hoped you served cookies." David smiled at Ashley, noting the laughter in her eyes. "Particularly chocolate cookies."

"I'm certain our pastry chef can create something

extraordinary." Julian snatched a menu from an empty table and flipped to the dessert listings.

"Particularly frozen chocolate cookies." David smeared spicy mustard on a cracker and popped it into his mouth.

If Julian was caught off guard, he didn't show it, except for a widening of his eyes. In the meantime, Ashley's cheeks colored a hot pink.

"Excellent choice." Julian glanced toward the doorway. "I apologize for intruding on your evening, Mr. Fodero, but my wife, Nora, and our daughter, Samantha, are hoping to meet you. Samantha is attending college and keen on her course work."

"What is she studying?"

"Baroque composers—Bach, Handel and Scarlatti."

"The arts, along with novel ideas and challenges, will help her discover where her passion truly lies." David paused. "By the way, Julian, you've called me David ever since we met."

"Of course." Julian said, as though the opposite was true. "In a more formal setting, though, everything is more … formal."

"Please ask them to come over." He had no intention of leaving Ashley out of the conversation and gestured to her. "I'm assuming they haven't met Ashley yet, either."

"I met your daughter already." Ashley scooped a handful of candied nuts.

"And I told both my wife and daughter a little more about Ashley." Julian regarded them with a warm smile.

A short while later, a dark-haired woman and a young lady, who looked to be in her early twenties, hurried to their table.

Julian quickly made the introductions while Ashley and Samantha said hello to each other.

"It's great to meet you, Mr. Fodero," Samantha said. She looped a strand of inky-black hair behind her ear, and David couldn't help but grin at her ear piercings—three in each ear, chunky gold hoops interspersed with miniature crescent moons and stars. The young woman definitely expressed her unique style.

"David," he corrected. He kept his expression pleasant, but her exuberance discomfited him. He didn't deserve it. "Ashley merits the genuine praise. She owns an art studio and gives back to the community by providing classes to handicapped children and adults. Me? I just paint."

"I adore my profession." Ashley looked at the others, then met his approving stare. "Though you are the true artist."

"In the artist-fan relationship, both the artist and admirer are important," Julian put in. "Also, a painter works at his or her own pace. The admirer is a supporter, encourager, and exhibits patience."

Ashley murmured an agreement.

"See why my dad is so smart?" Samantha grinned and turned to Ashley. "I never used to volunteer, but after my parents coaxed me into giving it a try, I discovered that volunteering is fulfilling."

"I'm liking your parents more and more for the values they're instilling in you." David lifted his glass. "What are you studying?"

"Music is my first love." Samantha continued gawking at David whenever she looked his way. "But as much as I loved the Baroque period, I'm also studying avant-garde art, which is much more modern."

"Hurray for avant-garde." He followed her gaze and realized she was staring at his painting. "I commend you. Follow your dream."

"Her major instrument is guitar," Nora said, automatically straightening the cutlery on the table next to theirs.

"What type of music is your favorite?" David asked Samantha. Considering her age, he assumed her interests were countless. "I like all kinds of music, and especially country."

"Worship music is my choice," Julian, Nora, and Samantha announced in unison.

His gaze encompassed all three of them. Yup. He was definitely surrounded by a community that valued God and family. He studied Ashley, this gorgeous woman sitting across from him. He had tasted her mouth and sensed her pleasure in their embrace. More and more, he felt an attraction he couldn't rationalize with a flippant dismissal.

"Worship music is elevating." Ashley surveyed the cheese plate and selected a firm cheese and a slice of bread. "Whenever I listen, I feel calm. The lyrics are soothing and inspirational."

Soothing and inspirational. Like her.

David struggled to arrange his thoughts in order and discovered he already had. With her, he was at peace because she had become his inspiration.

In truth, God had once been his inspiration—to create, to bring out his level best. To enlighten him.

Sure, on occasion, particularly when the going got rough, David considered revisiting prayer. However, he always talked himself out of it, which was easy. He hadn't realized all were excuses until he'd examined his motives.

Which were?

Making justifications for things he didn't want to do. For anything that made him uncomfortable.

Like God?

He presumed God didn't wish to hear from him only during the rough patches. But perhaps there was a chance to reconnect with God. Perhaps Ashley could help him.

Ashley.

He couldn't ignore the gentle tug on his heart whenever

he gazed at her. Change was happening, however subtle. With God. With Ashley.

"When are you going to start painting again, Mr. Fodero?" Samantha asked.

"Hmm?" Absorbed in reflection, he'd drifted away from the exchange.

Ashley shot him a rueful look. "He's a typical artist. Sometimes I've lost him in the middle of a discussion too."

He reached out and squeezed her hand. "In the days since we've met, Ashley is beginning to know me well."

"Uh-huh, Mr. Planter of Gardens." She plunked another sugar cube into her limeade and stirred. She did that a lot. Whenever she was uncomfortable, she craved sugar.

"Samantha," Nora said, "what a rude question." She rested a firm hand on her daughter's shoulder. "The decision is up to Mr. Fodero to decide when to paint, not you. Dad just mentioned how a fan should be patient and respect the artist."

"But the public is waiting." Undeterred, Samantha looked again at David's painting, then back at him. "More important, the entire world is waiting."

"To everything there is a season." Julian quoted the familiar Bible passage and smiled. "C'mon ladies, there's work to be done here."

"Dad, I can't help at the inn tonight." Samantha splayed her hands on her slim hips. "I have to get home and take the dog out."

"Our house is two blocks away, and the dog can wait another half hour," Nora replied, and they all chuckled at Samantha's audible groan.

"You own a dog?" David inquired.

"A golden retriever." Samantha's smile was unrestrained. It was amazing how quickly a young person's mood shifted.

"Canine Helpers is where Dad and I volunteer and it's awesome."

David nodded. "I agree. The place is awesome."

"Do you like dogs, Mr. Fodero?"

"I love dogs. In fact, I own a dachshund named Pickle." He pulled out his phone to show her a photo, then decided to go a step further. "I invested in a doggie camera so I can see Pickle when I'm not home. The camera streams to my phone."

"Pickle is adorable." Ashley favored another scoop of nuts. "Although I can't speak from experience because I don't own a pet, unless my goldfish, Frederick, counts. Fortunately, one of my friends is feeding him while I'm away. My apartment is tiny and—"

"No excuses," David countered.

The mood of pleasantness faltered, and he searched for a way to restore it.

"I'm sorry," he said. "I shouldn't judge."

Ashley frowned. "No, you shouldn't."

"Alrighty then," Julian said. "Now that we've discussed dogs and college and the arts, let's allow David and Ashley the opportunity to get better acquainted, shall we?" He smiled at them. "Your server will bring you cookies and coffee." With an apologetic grin, Julian piloted his wife and daughter from the dining room.

"Is that what we're doing?" Ashley peered at David over her glass. "Getting to know each other better? Do tell."

"First, I'm abandoning the subject of dog ownership, so you'll stop scowling at me."

She coiled a strand of silky hair around her finger and displayed a sunny smile.

"Much better." David leaned back as their waiter returned. With a flourish, the waiter poured piping-hot coffee into their cups, then positioned a crystal creamer, sugar bowl, and a glass-topped plate of fancy-looking choco-late cookies in the center of the table.

Ashley went for the sugar.

David quirked an eyebrow. "Well, my beautiful compan-ion, shall we begin?"

CHAPTER 8

Everything you can imagine is real.
—Picasso

"You first." Ashley used a silver tong to pick up three sugar cubes and plunked them into her coffee. "How about a story from your childhood, David?"

"Anything in particular?"

"How many siblings do you have?"

He eyed her coffee, frothing with sugar. "Two older brothers and a younger sister. I'm a middle child. There was lots of boisterous shouting over the din of flag football tournaments on our front lawn or when fixing cars in our garage."

"You're mechanical?"

"Not even a little. My brothers are excellent mechanics, though."

"Are you athletic?" She gave him the once-over, her gaze lingering on his shoulders.

"I jog and I've got a workout room in my condo in New York. Plus, I played football in high school." He blew out a breath. "Mostly to please my father, who was intent on raising his sons to be jocks. He was a competitive sportsman and almost made it to the pros."

"Were you a jock?"

"Football earned me dates with girls who would never have looked at me otherwise." David laughed. "I concentrated on painting and artwork. Perusing art galleries and sketching were my favorite Saturday afternoon pastimes."

"Tell me more."

His jaw tensed, and he forced himself to relax.

He expected the interest—the "getting to know each other" conversation Julian had endorsed. He just wasn't used to opening up to people. "My father wanted his sons to live up to his legacy as a star athlete."

Ashley provided an unabashed smile. "You're a star painter."

"Believe me, it's not the same." He pushed back his coffee cup.

"Instead, you lived up to the art world's expectations and well beyond."

His nod was quick, though he fell silent. The waiter came by, refilled their coffee cups and pointedly looked at the untouched cookie plate.

"I promise we'll eat all the cookies." Ashley smiled at the waiter, who quickly disappeared, then shifted her gaze to David. "You accomplished your numerous successes in your own style."

Evidently sensitive to his moods and body language, she had realized the significance of their conversation and how much his father's opinion mattered to him. Even now, after all these years. Even now, after all the rotten things his father had done.

He lifted the glass top off the plate and offered her a cookie. "Delicious, fancy chocolate."

She chuckled. "Excellent subject change."

"I try."

"I prefer plain store-bought cookies with a creamy center."

"Are you easy to please?"

"Sometimes."

"You're hedging."

"So are you." She laughed, then bit into the cookie. "These aren't frozen and taste more like fudge."

"They're posher and more expensive."

Thoughtfully, she chewed. "As long as I'm scarfing down chocolate, I'm happy. Any food from the inn's kitchen is awesome."

His mood relaxed, and their banter once again became upbeat.

The flickering candlelight cast a gleam on her thick blond hair, transforming it to silver. Her creamy complexion glowed.

She glided her fingers around the rim of her limeade glass. Her hands were slim and graceful, her fingernails cut short and tapered. She was a natural beauty.

The cozy, romantic atmosphere, along with the melodic background violins, enhanced her loveliness and brought a sparkle to the entire evening.

He wanted her to describe her art students. He enjoyed how her face lit up whenever she mentioned them. When he was about to shift the conversation toward her, she asked, "Do you see your father often?"

"No. He passed away."

"Oh. I'm sorry."

"Thanks."

"Well." She cleared her throat. "Did you used to see your father often?"

"No."

"That was an abrupt answer."

"He was a difficult guy. Like father, like son, I've been told." David sighed. "When I attended elementary school, I learned he was unfaithful to my mother."

"How did you find out?"

"He and a woman I didn't know brought me to a circus. I was confused because the woman wasn't my mother. He made me promise never to tell anyone."

"Did you?"

"I was seven." The memory of his father's stern lectures still resounded in David's brain. "You want the short answer? No. He died over a decade ago and his secret died with him."

"Did you ever wish to snatch back your promise and tell your mother?"

"Oh, I considered it many times. My heart broke for her since she had a good-hearted and trusting nature. But I was a little kid and taught to obey. Invariably, I struggled to please him."

He'd never succeeded.

Ashley snatched another cookie, pulling it apart before dipping it into her coffee. "And your mother?"

"She was my biggest cheerleader."

"So, she never learned of your father's unfaithfulness?"

"If she did, she never let on. I guess she trusted him." Unlike David. He'd learned not to trust his father. He hardly trusted anybody.

Ashley folded her hands and stayed silent.

"My mother's beauty was ageless," David went on. "No plastic surgery for her, though she insisted on dyeing her hair to cover the gray."

"Was her hair brown in her youth?"

"I believe so. Her parents immigrated to the United States from Scotland, although none of her children inherited her coloring. We all favored our Italian father's Mediterranean looks."

"Thus your attractive combination of dark hair and blue eyes."

He grinned. "I'm attractive?"

Ashley swallowed. Her cheeks flushed to her ears. "A little."

"You're attractive too. The difference is, you're attractive a lot."

"Wait, a minute." She fixed him with a stare that wouldn't let go. "Is the mysterious woman in your painting *Woman by the River*, your mother?"

"Very observant." He tugged at the collar of his shirt. "Though the woman isn't mysterious when you analyze my motives."

"Which are?"

"I add whoever is special to me and my life to my paintings."

"Like your dog. Like your mother. Anyone else?"

"Nope. Often, my mother whispered words of praise in my ear. About my art," he clarified. "Every night after prayers, she'd encourage me to continue sketching and painting."

"I like to hear that."

"Hear what?"

"I like to hear about prayers and encouragement."

He shifted. "Right."

Her head crooked to the side. "You have a problem with encouragement?"

"Nope."

"Prayer?"

Despite her reproachful tone, her eyes held kind gentleness.

"Prayer …" He paused and pondered. "Sometimes." He replied cautiously, not wishing to tread on a religious landmine, especially with a devout believer like Ashley. This was territory he hadn't navigated since his teens. "If I'm candid, I have a problem with prayer. Or rather, unanswered prayers."

"Try again. You'll find solace by talking to God."

"To each his own." He grabbed her hand. "Prayer isn't for me. If it's for you, I'm pleased you've found comfort."

"Comfort is only the beginning." She withdrew her hand. "Your mother heartily approved of your art?"

"She motivated me often whenever I wanted to quit."

He was telling Ashley more than he'd ever told anyone about his childhood, but he refused to scrutinize the emotions welling up inside him that urged him to keep speaking.

She was easy to talk to, her gaze focused solely on him.

"Please go on," she urged.

"When I was awarded a generous art scholarship to NYU, my father finally sat up and took notice, though afterward I hardly heard from him. Which is why I settled in New York City instead of moving back home."

"Where is home?"

David wrapped his hands around his cup. "A seacoast town in Georgia."

"I'm sure the area is lovely." Ashley touched his hand, her fingers lingering. Her hand seemed to gravitate back to him of its own accord. "And now?"

He didn't have an answer. Remembrances flashed of his father's final days and how David had stayed by his bedside, although his father hadn't recognized him.

Ashley opened her mouth, closed it, opened it again. "What about your brothers?"

"We don't speak. I've tried to connect, and they seldom reply. They're simply not interested. In this day and age, it's hard to believe guys think anything to do with art is a dreamer's profession reserved for sissies. I suspect they're embarrassed of me."

"You're kidding."

"I wish." He regarded the somber twist of her lips. "Happy finish, though. After undergraduate and graduate studies, New York City started to feel like home."

"Now you've landed in Cherish."

"These days, I'm living the dream."

"Which is?"

"The freedom of answering to no one."

"A confirmed bachelor?"

"Maybe."

For the time being, he added to himself.

Her mannerisms quieted. Was she interested in him, and not thrilled by his "confirmed bachelor" declaration?

No. Not possible. She was an engaging, enterprising woman who devoted her life to helping others. He was a painter who couldn't sketch a tree branch.

She picked up her fork and pressed down the cookie crumbs left on her plate. Her silence spurred him to continue.

"Both of my brothers were varsity athletes. Quinn, my sister, played soccer all through high school and college. In fact, Quinn reminds me of your friend Sarah."

"Sarah is an extremely capable woman. She hasn't allowed deafness to hamper her story. Once she recognized her disability and acknowledged she needed treatment, she embraced it. Beforehand, she waded through stages."

He leaned forward. "Such as?"

"What you might expect. Shame, refusal to accept her body's faults."

He gave himself fair warning. He was inquiring about Sarah and how she coped, though he was also interested in his own disability. "What's the result?"

Ashley bit down on her lower lip. "Sarah exhibits more self-confidence now. She's focused, and she recently declared life's too short not to value every hour. She's pleasant, practical, and I'm proud to call her a wonderful friend."

David pushed out a sigh he didn't realize he was holding.

Perhaps he should come to terms with his own disability instead of ignoring it and expecting it to go away. Perhaps hope beckoned. The prospect brought optimism to his heavy heart.

"My sister is an accomplished woman and well-educated," he said. "Though I don't see her much anymore."

"Why not?" Ashley offered him another cookie, which he refused.

"I only like them frozen." He shook his head. "Your tastes in food are wearing off on me."

"Try another cookie, anyway." With that, she plunked a cookie on his plate and asked again, "Why not?"

"Why not what?"

"Why aren't you in touch with your sister anymore?"

He waved an airy hand. "The artistic community is incredibly active in Manhattan, and obviously, I need a presence there because of my profession."

"Obviously."

He decided to follow Ashley's lead and dropped a sugar lump into his coffee. After stirring, he sipped and grimaced. Way ...too sweet. He set his spoon beside his napkin. "Quinn lives in Texas and is mostly married."

"Mostly?"

"She recently filed for a divorce from her current husband and tends to relocate often. She doesn't have children."

"Current husband?"

"Her third."

"Oh."

"Soon my sister will be footloose and fancy free. I love her, yet we fell out of step."

There was no better explanation. Quinn had never understood his art—had never understood *him*. She embraced traditional art, seeing no point in upside-down dogs and neon-green trees painted on the side of a building. Whenever the occasion arose, she told him as much.

"I'm sorry," Ashley whispered.

"I suppose it's my fault." He shrugged. "I tend to be cynical regarding relationships."

"Logical, considering your father's infidelity. Don't be hard on yourself and never forget how successful you are."

"Success is the part everyone remembers. However, failure defined my in-between years." He picked up the creamer. Perhaps his coffee needed cream to offset the sugary taste. "Enough about me. What about you?"

"My upbringing was the opposite of yours. Nothing rowdy. Mine was quiet because my household consisted of me and a parent."

He filled his cup to the brim with cream and tried it. Grimacing again, he decided black coffee was much better than the other options. "Your mother raised you?"

"My father. From when I was a toddler, he taught me all God's creatures are my friend."

"Where is he now?"

"Sadly, he died five years ago, and I never knew my mother. She abandoned us when I was a newborn. Years later, I learned she'd died in a car accident a few states away. She'd been speeding late at night and drinking heavily."

David kept his attention fixed on her. "She was an alcoholic?"

Ashley bobbed a yes.

"Why did you open an art studio for children with disabilities?"

"I had trouble reading when I was young. I assumed all the letters were supposed to be backward." Ashley ran a hand through her hair. "Turns out, they weren't."

"Did you attend college?"

"I attended a state school where I was a dual art education and disability studies major. I was a shy kid, and daydreaming became a favorite pastime. I always wanted to teach art to children with special needs, and thus my two passions merged."

David nodded. "And you're single."

"I'm thirty and definitely single."

"Then I shouldn't be looking over my shoulder for an irate boyfriend?"

"Hardly. I dated a guy for a couple years."

"What happened?"

"He dumped me."

Their gazes met. David refused to let go. "The guy is a fool."

Her cheeks colored. She looked away, focusing on the tiny pinpricks of candlelight flickering from each table.

They lingered over coffee, neither one willing to break the spell of attraction that drew them closer. David didn't want the night to end. He sensed she felt the same.

An hour later, in the nearly deserted dining room, their laughter still rang out. The waitstaff unobtrusively glanced at them and smiled as they cleared the other tables.

David peered at his watch. Nearly ten o'clock, and the restaurant was scheduled to close.

"Thank you, Ashley." He sought to remove himself from the magnetic spell they'd created by capping their evening with politeness. "Again, I apologize."

"You apologized already for not listening to me yesterday."

"Indeed, we established I *was* listening."

She propped her chin on her palms. "You thanked me for the peaches."

"Then thank you for the past few hours. Too few." His voice was hoarse, and he scarcely recognized it as his own. "After you left…"

Her eyebrows shot to her hairline. "You're referring to when I stormed off?"

"Yes." He laughed out loud. It felt freeing to laugh. "I like your honesty." He liked a lot more than that about her. He liked everything.

He fished in the pocket of his sport jacket. "May I show you a photograph I took?"

"The one of the tree?"

"And you."

She sat back. "Me?"

"You happened to be in several photos."

"*Happened*? How?"

"I didn't realize it." Or maybe he did. In any case, he'd blamed the mistake on his failing eyesight.

He slid the photo across the table. The tree and flowers were clear. However, Ashley, clad in shorts and a chambray top and sitting in the tree, took center focus. "I'd welcome your permission to paint you."

"Why?"

His gaze was steady. "Because you're beautiful."

"David, I'm definitely not—"

He pressed a finger to her lips, stopping her from protesting. "You really don't realize it? Your humbleness is disarming."

"Reality, you mean." Appreciation edged her self-conscious laughter. "But thank you."

He felt as if a warm hand had settled on his heart. This woman unearthed sentiments he'd buried long ago, bringing him a newfound excitement and pleasure. She was unpretentious, yet joyful. Kind and truthful.

Inwardly, his conscience chided him. A permanent relationship between them wasn't practical. Besides the fact she lived miles away, she was a people person.

Him? He preferred to sit back and observe the world.

Nonetheless, he captured her fingers. "Is that a yes? I can paint you?"

"You have my permission, but only if I can see the painting."

"After it's done, and not before."

That's it. Establish a practical boundary. Finish the evening with a kiss on her cheek and a "'Have a good life. I'll call you.'"

He did the opposite.

He came around the table to pull out her chair, then inched closer.

He scanned the dining room. Empty. Julian and the wait staff had disappeared. When had that happened? He had been so engrossed in everything about Ashley, he hadn't paid attention to his surroundings. Even the violins had been shut off.

He tipped up her chin. "How long will you be in Cherish?"

"I intend to travel back to my studio somewhat soon, because I miss my students. Thankfully, a couple volunteer instructors are filling in for me." Her gaze drifted to his. "Initially, I arranged to be here only for the weekend."

"You're extending your stay because…?"

"I like it here."

"I like it here too." He dipped his head and brushed his lips against hers in a tender kiss. "Especially because you're in town."

"Church service on Sunday was wonderful."

"An invitation?"

"Definitely."

"Church." He sighed. "I'll paint the outside. No reason for me to venture inside. Let's leave it at that."

Her fingers teased the soft hairs at his nape. "Perhaps—"

His arms wrapped around her, and he captured the rest of her words in a long kiss.

"Dining room is officially closed, folks." Julian's deep voice came from the doorway. "You can continue smooching in the hall." He flipped the light switch, and the room sank into darkness. "Our generous Lord will give each of us another day."

A minute later, Ashley and David reached the lobby, hand in hand.

"I'll settle up for tonight's meals," David said to a waiting Julian.

Julian winked. "I'm certain you'll be back and will keep a tab running."

"I'll walk you to the door." Ashley linked arms with David and led the way to the front entrance.

"Thanks." He grinned. "What are your plans for tomorrow?"

"I want to revisit Aaron's art shop."

"Aaron is a nice guy."

"Yes." Her tone was soft, her smile warm.

David pieced together her missing words. She hadn't extended her reservation in Cherish to purchase art supplies. She was staying in town because of him. He knew this as surely as his heart took a beat.

The upcoming days held infinite appeal, though his mind shouted a reminder. What could come of a serious relationship? Three months had always been his dating limit.

Luckily, it hadn't been three months yet.

And afterward? Was a long-distance relationship with Ashley possible?

He rubbed a hand over his chin.

In fairness to Ashley, he needed to attend to his vision problem first. There was no quick fix, and although his brain had adjusted, the disability was affecting his painting. He couldn't even paint a tree.

His art, his vision, his problem.

All well and good, although he clung to a decision he couldn't believe, considering there was no future with Ashley. Still, the idea took shape without warning.

"How about a tour of the town's main attraction tomorrow?" he asked.

"What is the main attraction?"

"A surprise."

Her hazel eyes widened. "You're still a newcomer here."

"Compared to your mere days, I'm a lifelong resident." He hesitated. "May I have your cellphone number?"

"Phone the reception desk and they'll transfer your call to my room."

"I'd prefer to text you directly."

One eyebrow cocked. "We hardly know each other."

"In case you haven't figured it out, I'm trying to change that."

She drew her cell phone from her purse and handed it to him. He texted himself and checked his phone. Then he texted her back. *Will you accompany me tomorrow?*

He handed the phone to her.

With a grin reaching her eyes, she replied, *Where?*

He pulled her into his arms, more than delighted she rewarded his kiss with gratifying acceptance. "A surprise, remember? I'll text you in the morning. I have somewhere special in mind."

For tomorrow. And the next day. And the day after that.

CHAPTER 9

It takes a long time to become young.
– Picasso

At daybreak, Ashley woke in her luxurious room at the inn. She drew back the snowy-white lace curtains framing the window and peered outside. The morning streets were quiet, and the whiff of buttery, yeasty biscuits from the kitchen wafted through the air. The sky was bathed in the rosy radiance of sunrise.

She debated about working out and rationalized that walking and hiking with David sufficed.

Excuses, excuses.

The bouquet of wildflowers the maître d' had sent to her room, vibrant and cheerful, held center stage in a gleaming crystal vase on a side table. She envisioned David revisiting the river, bending to choose the exact flowers she'd favored. He was a man capable of thoughtfulness and tenderness, and no one could fault her for being helplessly drawn to him.

She resolved to keep her wits about her. Attraction was fleeting. Promises of a commitment called for something else entirely. Honesty, integrity, and a long-lasting love.

As the morning hours passed and she waited for David's text, she felt increasingly guilty.

She'd sought him out over false pretenses, and it was wrong. She was a Christian woman. How could she explain to him that her car breaking down in front of his cabin hadn't been a coincidence?

She opened the pocket Bible she'd brought with her. Her father had taught her to study the verses and pray often. Today she began with Romans 8:31 and reflected on the message.

If God was for her, who could be against her? God's presence in her life didn't mean she'd never face sorrow. Instead, the words held the promise she'd never experience sorrow alone, for He was always with her.

"Dear Lord," she whispered. "Allow faith to remain my focus. I must do better. I can count on God. Can He count on me?"

Assuredly, she made excuses and there were things she should have done differently, but she vowed to learn from her missteps and apply them to her upcoming decisions. Today she had wisdom. Today she would tell David the truth of why she was in Cherish before courage abandoned her. A relationship depended on her coming clean with him.

He had trust issues and valued honesty. Had he truly believed she'd gotten lost on a one-way street in the middle of nowhere?

Don't shift the blame onto his shoulders, she scolded herself. This was all her doing. He had no reason not to accept her explanation when she'd landed on his doorstep, which only made matters worse.

In times of conflict, she prayed. She did so now in a

hushed whisper, without reservation. "Lord, in the midst of my uncertainty, I praise your glory and honor. I value your consistent presence in my life. Please do not give up on me. I appreciate that you are ever faithful."

David's text appeared on her phone screen just as a pleasant young waitress arrived with a continental breakfast tray. After Ashley positioned the tray on a table by the window, she clicked on the text.

Good morning, gorgeous, David began.

Top of the morning to you too.

Did you sleep well?

His question unsettled her, because all her dreams had been of him. She grasped the china coffeepot and poured steaming coffee into her cup.

Ashley?

I'm here. Yes, I slept well. You?

I painted until midnight. I was inspired. Pickle stayed up and kept me company.

Against her better judgment, she asked, *What did you paint?*

He didn't reply, but somehow, she already knew. He'd been painting her. As the image took hold, she hoped he hadn't sketched her with unruly blond hair and her cowlick sticking straight up. And what about her pointed chin?

Worse, had he attached her nose to her face? One never could be certain with avant-garde artists.

I kept wondering if you enjoyed yourself last night.

She reread his text. Now why would he wonder about that? His question sounded insecure, yet David was strong and confident. She could see it in his artwork, his paintings bold and emotional.

She nodded at the phone, then felt foolish because he couldn't see her. *I enjoyed myself very much. It was fun.*

It was magical, she thought.

I still feel your hand in mine.

Her heart quickened at his message. Had he really typed something that romantic?

I'll pick you up at eleven.

She paused in the act of stirring three sugar lumps into her coffee and typed, *Where are we going?*

We might go on a hike.

Might?

I'll pack everything we need.

Food?

Are cookies okay? Just kidding. He inserted a smiley emoji. *Wear comfortable shoes.*

TWO HOURS LATER, she waited in the inn's sunny, plant-filled lobby. She'd decided on lightweight jeans, a long-sleeved blouse, cotton socks, and serviceable hiking boots. She didn't intend to get bit up by mosquitoes. Also, she carried a tan leather tote bag.

A foray into her suitcase had yielded the boots she'd brought on a whim, and she was thankful. Surely God had a hand in this.

The inn provided miniature bottles of lemon and sage soap and shampoo, and the scent was heavenly. The discovery had delighted her. She was one of those women who dashed to the hotel bathroom first to check out the toiletries.

After her shower, she'd wrapped herself in a luxurious, blue-striped terry robe and applied a touch of blush and a rosy lip gloss.

She'd secured her freshly washed hair into a ponytail, then loaded her tote bag with essentials—sunscreen, a water bottle, and a thin cotton sweater in case the weather got cool.

Unlikely, though. Sunshine poured in the front window,

the blue sky speckled with clouds, and the weatherman predicted ninety-degree temperatures and the prerequisite humidity.

Julian strode over, displaying a smirk she could only describe as amused. "Greetings, Ashley. Are you sticking around for anyone in particular?"

"David suggested we see a little of Cherish today."

Julian wiped minuscule dust particles off the bannister with his fingers. "What a thoughtful guy. I give a fellow credit when he seizes a golden opportunity and runs with it."

She raised her chin. "He's showing me around because he's been in Cherish longer."

"A whole few months longer. Though it's a superb excuse for a date."

"This isn't a date."

"If you say so." He chuckled. "Where are you two exploring?"

"He mentioned a hike."

"Probably Juniper Mountain, the town's favorite."

"Sarah spoke about the Walnut Forest route. She claims the climb is easy." Ashley shoved her hair from her forehead. "I'll point that fact out to David."

"Don't forget bug spray."

"He's packing everything."

Julian laughed. "I applaud a guy who thinks ahead."

Before Ashley responded, David entered the lobby, clad in jean shorts and a gray T-shirt, and cradling Pickle under one arm. She considered that his tanned, strong-featured face belonged on the big screen of a Hollywood movie. Yet he preferred to live as a hermit and paint.

"I trust you don't mind I brought Pickle," David announced to Julian. "As you can see, I'm holding him."

"I do." Julian nodded. "As a reminder, Frank's Pizza allows dogs."

"Thanks for the tip."

Julian extended his hand to David and exchanged a friendly shake. "And I recognize Pickle from your painting that hangs in our dining room."

"You're very discerning."

"I try."

"Good morning, Ashley." David's admiring gaze fixed on her, moving gradually down her face, hair, and legs. He bent his head and their lips touched. "You are exquisite, as always."

His words caused her stomach to flutter with anticipation, and his fleeting kiss ignited a spark she hadn't felt in years. "You're not too shabby yourself."

A smile crept across his face. "And your hair smells like—"

"Lemons," she and Julian chorused.

Julian brightened. "The inn sourced our toiletries to a local woman who makes her own garden-inspired soaps and shampoos. She's experimenting with a variety of different perfumes."

"Tell her to stick with lemons," David replied.

Ashley patted the bag hoisted on her shoulders. "I'm ready for our surprise."

"Some surprise." He dropped his gaze to her hiking boots, muttering an effective analysis for their mutual foolishness to hike on such a hot day.

She burst out laughing. "We live in the South. Get used to scorching summer weather."

He joined in with a chuckle. Reaching for her hand, he led her to the front door.

"Bye, you two," Julian called out. "I'm clearly invisible because you only have eyes for, well, you two. Oh, and by the way, Tom, the previous owner of the inn, didn't allow dogs inside."

Ashley peeked over her shoulder. "We appreciate your flexibility, Julian."

He beamed. "Who am I to enforce the rules? I'm just the owner."

David proved a proper gentleman, exhibiting old-world manners. He insisted on opening the passenger door of his truck for her before dashing to the driver's side and buckling Pickle into a dog harness in the seat behind her. The truck's interior smelled of oil and canvas and paint. She recognized the scents from her art studio and recalled the same smells when she'd entered David's cabin.

After they buckled their seat belts, he switched on the radio, and while Tim McGraw sang, she stole a glance at David. He sat on the ripped leather seat beside her and stared straight ahead. She sensed his need to focus and surmised it was because of his failing eyesight.

He glanced sideways at her. "Before our hike, there are a couple places I'd like to show you."

"You're the tour guide and the driver. Will we stop at Aaron's Art Shop?"

"Let's save the art excursion for another day."

Another day. Her heart squeezed. Another day to spend with this compelling man.

Despite any misgivings, happiness drifted through her. They were two friends savoring a scenic day together. Indeed, she envisioned herself looking back someday and reliving her hours with David as summer memories to cherish.

As they passed the sign advertising the Renaissance Faire, she sighed. "If I had more time, I'd choose to spend a day at the Faire."

"You do now."

"Do what?"

He sent her a smile. "You're staying for the week instead of a few days."

"True." She relaxed in her seat. "Have you ever gone to a Faire?"

"Never. In fact, wild horses couldn't drag me there." He paused. "Unless it meant a lot to you."

She was not only speechless, but she was also unexpectedly touched. He was considering her happiness before his own. That particular trait had been noticeably absent in her past relationships.

"First stop is Canine Helpers." He slowed his truck. "The volunteers train dogs to assist veterans."

"Samantha mentioned that she and Julian volunteer here."

"Yes. Scarlett Slater will show us around."

"Who is she?"

"A woman with a heart of gold."

Ashley sighted the sign and turnoff ahead. "You donated a painting to benefit the Canine Helpers auction."

David darted her a glance. "Close-knit communities. Nothing stays hush-hush for long, and everyone knows everybody."

At the intersection, he flicked on his turn signal.

She flashed a glance behind her. Pickle was contentedly snoring in the back seat. "Is your generosity a secret?"

"I'm delighted to help." He parked and rounded the truck to open the door for her. He woke Pickle up, unbuckling and then leashing him. He steered them to the entrance, where a woman with flaming red hair and a generous smile greeted them.

"David Fodero. Such an honor to see you again." The woman showed them inside, and David placed a hand beneath Ashley's elbow.

"Scarlett Slater, please meet Ashley Madden, my special friend."

Ashley smiled at the introduction. She and David were friends. Special friends. Whether she was being naive or idealistic, her pulse quickened with the observation.

She glanced at him, surprised to find him intently watching her.

Scarlett beamed at Ashley. "Any friend of David's is a friend of mine. His painting commanded ten thousand dollars at our silent auction, and the money will go toward supplies for the vets. We are a Christian facility and welcome donations of any amount."

Ashley digested the mind-boggling sum a patron had paid for one of David's paintings while David explained, "Owning a dog is like having a child."

"Dogs give us absolute allegiance." Scarlett crouched to rub Pickle's head, then stood. "C'mon into the common room. We've done various improvements since you were last here, David, beginning with a new sink."

As they toured the facility, Ashley asked what type of services Canine Helpers offered.

"We specially train service dogs and match them with veterans who require emotional or physical support." Scarlett gestured to a row of leashes hanging on a wall. "Many of the men and women in our armed forces return home with PTSD or physical restrictions."

David's blue eyes lit with compassion. "Canine Helpers furnishes the animals and the assistance at no charge to the veterans."

"Our aim is to ensure our veterans lead healthy, positive lives again." Scarlett spoke with such earnestness; Ashley was taken aback by the woman's commitment. "Luckily, grants and generous donors like David's contribution to our auction help the organization remain viable."

"I wish there was a way I could help too." Ashley's gaze encompassed the clean dog dishes neatly lined up.

"Some elderly folks are donating dogs they expect will be of wonderful service." Scarlett stacked retrieval toys—discs and balls and rope tugs. "Are you available to foster a dog?"

Ashley shook her head. "My apartment is tiny."

Scarlett bent to tidy a group of empty water bowls, then stood to face Ashley. "You aren't required to train the dog, if that's the reason for your reluctance."

"I don't live in Cherish. I'm visiting. At home, I work twelve-hour days." She replied as if the reasons were clear. "It's unfair for a dog to be alone all day."

"If you're ever interested at a later time when you're not as busy, here's my cell phone number." Scarlett handed Ashley a business card.

Ashley dragged her gaze from the card to David's face. His features were undecipherable, though he hadn't lectured her about dog ownership. In fact, he hadn't uttered a word.

He gave her hand a reaffirming squeeze. "You'll recognize when the time is right."

"Eventually." Ashley placed the card in her pocket. "A dog is somewhere in my future."

"Hopefully sooner rather than later." David paid for a bone baked on the premises and gave it to Pickle. The dog whined, carried the bone in his mouth, then quickly consumed it. "Sooner is better. A dog offers devoted companionship and you're missing out."

"I've elected Frederick, my goldfish, as my only pet for the time being," she replied.

A few minutes later, Ashley, Pickle and David emerged from Canine Helpers. Scarlett had recommended they visit the music store, Musically Yours, located a few blocks away.

"My darling husband, Joseph, teaches guitar lessons there." Scarlett's green eyes had radiated with affection. "Currently, he's on a two-week tour of the eastern United States. Often, I accompany him. This time, I opted to stay in town to facilitate the training for some new dogs. However, Dorothy Edwards, the owner, will show you the music store."

"I've met her." Ashley tightened her ponytail. "I stopped in, and she told me all about Percy Grainger."

"Who is Percy Grainger?" David asked.

"He was born in Australia but is considered an American composer. Dorothy mentioned he had several peculiar obsessions."

David looked intrigued. "Spill the details."

"He gave up meat and ate mostly fruit pies."

"Better than copious amounts of sugar," he joked.

"David donated a painting to Dorothy's music shop," Scarlett said, steering the discussion back to Musically Yours. "I'm certain she'd love to see you both. I'll text her."

Agreeing, David and Ashley linked arms and exited. When all three were settled in his truck, he started the engine. There was minimal traffic on the short drive and they soon reached the corner of Myrtle and Magnolia, where the store was located.

"Scarlett's husband is a well-known contemporary worship musician." Ashley signaled to David to move closer to the curb as he parked. "I didn't put that together until you introduced her. Have you heard of Joseph Slater?"

"I don't listen to church music. Country is better."

"I disagree. Country music lyrics are all about cowboys and muddy trucks and—"

"Are you kidding? Every song tells a story. Though I recall 'worship music is your choice.'" He finger quoted with one hand, echoing the statement she, Julian, Nora, and Samantha had affirmed at dinner.

Ashley nudged his elbow. "God's grace is the best choice of all."

"Your words, not mine."

"What did you like most about church while you were growing up?"

"You don't want to hear my answer."

His confusing reply brought additional questions to mind. She sat up straighter. "Of course I do."

"To begin with, the pastor was kind."

"And the sermons?"

"I was a kid."

"Meaning you fell asleep?"

"Meaning I carried a small pad and pencil with me and sketched the pastor."

"Flattering renditions, I hope?"

"You can hope. However, on the bright side, I recall the message from one particular sermon that always stayed with me. 'The blessing ahead of you is bigger than any battle you left behind.'"

"Hallelujah, David. You had a wise pastor."

"Sometimes."

She ignored the amusement in his tone. "Go on."

"What I liked most were the refreshments served afterwards in the basement." He studied her in a beat of silence. "My mother used to bake a spicy cinnamon coffee cake with a streusel crumb topping."

"Nothing surpasses the food prepared in a church kitchen."

"Agreed. I'd sneak a cup of coffee, which was probably the beginning of my addiction to caffeine."

"You're blaming your caffeine addiction on church and your mother's coffee cake?"

Somehow, he managed to look innocent. "I told you that you wouldn't like my answer."

"Why did you stop attending?" She prayed David hadn't gotten involved in drugs or alcohol or the wrong crowd.

"Life got busy." His tone grew soft. "Life was good. I didn't need God."

The tension in the truck became smothering. She fixed him with a level stare that might have coerced a longer explanation from him had he glanced at her. However, he lowered his window and scanned the street.

A hot breeze blew inside the truck, along with the guarantee of heavy air awaiting their afternoon.

"Do you need God now?" she asked.

He met her stare, his features completely bland. "God and I don't have a running dialogue. At least, not anymore."

"One of the most profound blessings God offers is peace." She spurred herself to press onward. David harbored fears, as did everyone, but surely God would reveal Himself, allowing David to release his burdens. "He hears you," she added.

David tapped his fingers on the steering wheel. "If only He listened."

To inspire his observations, she presented a radiant smile. "You're not confident He listens, or you don't reach out to Him?"

"Both. Neither."

Silence followed his reply.

"I waited for God to communicate with me." He expelled a heavy sigh. "Nothing. Naught. Zilch. Now that I could use His guidance, He never answers."

"Why do you need His help?" She prayed David might confide to her about his vision. She wanted to comfort him, though she didn't wish to overstep her bounds.

"Because I'm human, although I like to believe I'm superhuman."

"Don't we all."

David didn't miss a beat. "I suppose you're going to lecture me on how I should pray regularly."

"I won't, then." Too tense to say more, she gazed out the passenger side at the scenic beauty of brick sidewalks, tidy shops, and window boxes overflowing with speckled petunias and dusty miller. Then she turned back to him. "Follow your heart."

"My heart is silent more often than not these days." His expression was laced with uncertainty. "Do you remember when I asked Sarah if her husband was a musician?"

"Are you changing the subject?"

"Religion is too deep a subject for such a fine summer day."

To him, maybe. Certainly not her.

Nonetheless, she'd spent enough time with David to detect his subtle nuances. Currently, his tone brought an end to their religious discourse.

"Besides," he went on. "I have something else in mind." He drew her close for a heady, unexpected kiss.

She pulled back a cautious distance. "We should go inside the store. Dorothy is expecting us."

"I'm looking forward to meeting her. Julian told me that Dorothy is a pianist, and her husband is an opera singer."

Ashley wondered if the conversation would proceed down the same path as when David compared his blindness to Beethoven's deafness.

Instead, he said, "I respect all musicians. I'm one myself."

"You are multi-talented?"

"I played the oboe in high school." He retrieved Pickle from his dog harness. "You?"

"I've never been able to sing on pitch. I took piano lessons for a couple years when I entered middle school, though I don't remember how to read a single note."

"My sister is taking piano lessons." David set Pickle on the ground and leashed the dog. "I hope Dorothy allows dogs."

"This entire community is dog-friendly."

"Another positive aspect of living in Cherish."

They lingered a half hour in the music store, chatting with Dorothy, favoring the harp earrings, and perusing stacks of sheet music.

After they left with an assortment of classical piano books for David's sister, he declared, "Now it's time for our hike."

"I don't expect you to devote your entire day to me," Ashley said as they walked hand in hand to his truck. "I'm assuming you should get back to your commissioned painting."

"I'm taking the day off."

"Are you making progress on the painting?"

A sardonic smile formed on his lips. "It's too soon to tell."

"Have you started it yet?"

"I'm waiting for inspiration to strike."

He picked up speed as they traveled on the two-lane road toward Juniper Mountain. She slanted glances at him when he wasn't looking. He had a magnificent profile, resembling a classical statue with his Roman nose and chiseled features.

During their drive, she determined he didn't have any peripheral vision to the right and could only see her if he turned his head or she sat forward. She did so, careful to make conversing as effortless as possible for him.

When they reached Juniper Mountain's parking area, he eased his truck into a space beside a vintage turquoise convertible with a "Just Married" banner draped over the rear bumper.

"How romantic." She glanced at David and was pleased he nodded in agreement. "The newlyweds must be camping to celebrate their marriage."

"Would you ever go camping on your honeymoon?"

"I'm more of a city girl." She hid her sentimentality behind a shrug. "You?"

"Whatever my future wife wanted, I'd comply without question. Her happiness would be my first priority."

"You don't seem the compliant type."

"Depends on the woman I marry. She may wind me around her little finger." He shut the ignition and covered her teasing lips with his.

Time dissolved.

The pad of his thumb smoothed her cheek. "Ashley Madden, you unbalance me," he murmured.

Her heart flipped over in her chest. His quiet utterance had a magical effect. She closed her eyes and savored his kisses. His male scent—woodsy and sandalwood—enveloped her, and she ran her fingers along his muscled forearms.

Sensing his gaze on her, she opened her eyes. She wondered what he'd say next and was surprised when he pulled back.

He blew out a breath. "Let's plan our hike for some other time."

"Why? We came all this way."

"In Cherish, everything is close. The middle of the afternoon isn't ideal for a sweltering trek up a mountain."

"What can we do instead?" Cautiously, she considered bringing up the idea of the Renaissance Faire but decided David's reaction wouldn't be positive.

His gaze rested on her lips, within inches of his. "I'll switch on the air conditioning, and we can continue kissing."

"Try another option."

He sighed. "Let's order a pizza, then enjoy a late lunch in my vintage kitchen."

"Your cabin is tastefully appointed, except for the absurd redwood chair."

"What's wrong with my chair?"

"No one in their right mind would ever sit in it."

"Why not?"

"It doesn't look at all comfortable."

"You haven't seen my kitchen yet." Absently, he fingered her renegade cowlick. "You're in for a treat."

She *had* seen his kitchen, but decided it was best not to share that knowledge with him.

CHAPTER 10

I paint objects as I think them, not as I see them.
– Picasso

A half hour later, David, Ashley and Pickle stood in Frank's Pizza, waiting for a pepperoni pizza. From what Ashley had learned from the residents, Frank's Pizza was not just the local pizzeria, it was the *only* pizzeria in town. The restaurant was empty except for a teen boy tossing pizza dough behind the counter, and David remarked that the air-conditioning was a welcome respite from the afternoon heat.

She stepped to the vending machine near the exit. "Do you want a candy bar to tide you over until we get back to your cabin? I need a sugar fix."

"I can wait another few minutes."

"I can't." With that declaration, she plunked three quarters into the machine. She waited for her choice to drop to the shelf at the bottom, but the candy bar kept dangling from the release mechanism. Muttering, she banged on the side. Nothing.

She began shaking the machine. "David?"

"Careful. It might topple, and the glass will break." He strode over, the pizza box balanced in one hand and Pickle's leash in the other.

"My candy bar is stuck, and I lost three quarters."

He sighed, set the box on an empty table, and secured Pickle's leash to a chair leg. "This can only happen to you."

"Help."

"Wait a couple seconds. Be patient. The machine might sense your candy bar hasn't dropped."

She tapped her foot. "Nothing is happening."

"Here." He dug into his pocket and handed her more quarters. "Try again and select the same candy bar. Maybe it will jerk yours loose."

She did as he suggested. Nothing changed.

She crouched to peer up into the machine. "The flap is stuck. Now you've lost your quarters too."

He cocked his head, considering the machine, then reached in his pocket. "This is the last of my quarters. Choose another candy bar from the row above."

"Grand idea." She inserted the quarters, made her selection, then exhaled. "Sadly, it isn't working."

"Right. Okay. Let's shake the machine. You take one side; I'll take the other."

No amount of jostling dislodged the candy bar.

"I wish I had those frozen chocolate cookies from the other day," he said, once they were back in his truck and following the road to his cabin. "They might alleviate your chocolate craving."

"Where are the cookies?"

He grinned. "I ate most of them. You're right, they're much better frozen. I refroze the rest."

"Frozen, thawed, and refrozen? David!" She sputtered in righteous exasperation.

After they parked in his driveway, he pressed a kiss on her forehead. "There are cookies left."

"You're trying to placate me."

"Maybe."

Before he opened her door, she jumped from his truck, the dog at her heels, and grabbed a Frisbee off the ground.

"Fetch, Pickle!" She threw the Frisbee across the lawn, and Pickle gleefully dashed after it. The sky was a dazzling blue, the sun blinding overhead. She enjoyed the radiant heat and had grown accustomed to it, though she would've welcomed a breeze. The air was motionless.

"Let's feast on pizza, then plan a walk after dinner," David said.

"Do you know what I have to say about that?" Amidst a cluster of buttery-yellow dandelions, she plucked a fluffy sphere and poised it before her lips.

"What?" He stepped closer and squinted at her, shading his eyes from the sun's glare.

She took a hearty lungful of air and puffed, sending delicate cottony seeds through the air.

He laughed and ducked. "What's that for?"

She blew again.

Another shout of his laughter almost drowned out her reply. "For making fun of me in the pizza parlor when I lost my quarters."

"You nearly broke the vending machine with your muscling."

"Muscling? Muscling?" Delighted she could make him laugh, she softened her voice and cooed, "The machine eats quarters and stole our money."

"We're the ones who put the money in to begin with." He set the pizza box on the ground and regarded Pickle, who had discovered a cool spot under the massive oak tree in the side yard. The dog's newfound Frisbee lay beside him. "Blame it on a machine malfunction."

"Sure, stick up for the vending machine instead of me."

David moved so swiftly she didn't have time to react, save for a surprised screech as he plucked a handful of fluffy dandelions.

"Now David, I assume you're not childish enough to retaliate."

"Do you recognize the foolishness of needling someone who is bigger and smarter than you?" he asked.

"Hah! You wish!" She hurled her hands to her hips. "Absolutely not."

He chased her to the oak tree, and she picked dandelions while she ran and flung them at him. Her shrieks of laughter sounded across his secluded acreage.

When he caught her, his boyish smile sent her pulse reeling. A bead of sweat trickled down his forehead, and she wiped it with her forefinger.

"You're a treasure, Ashley Madden." He brought her into his arms, and their laughter faded, replaced by a deep kiss.

She gazed past him, eyeing the oak tree. Somewhere overhead, a robin chirped. "David?"

"Hmm?"

"That tree is ideal for climbing. The branches are low-hanging and sturdy."

"Don't even think about it."

ONCE INSIDE THE CABIN, Ashley yanked off her boots and set her tote bag on the redwood chair. She filled Pickle's water bowl at the sink while David grabbed cold drinks, plates, and silverware from the kitchen cabinets. He excused himself to freshen up and reappeared minutes later, wearing denim shorts and pulling on a white T-shirt. Her breathing stopped as she stared at his bare chest and broad-shouldered physique. The magazine photos of him had pictured him unfairly. In person, he displayed a reserved strength and a strong allure that film couldn't capture.

He gave her one of his devastatingly lazy smiles, and she scolded herself for allowing her mind to wander where it had no business wandering.

I'm falling in love with him.

Panic bumped. What? No. Never.

David Fodero is infinitely appealing.

Yes, but…

David Fodero basked in a wealthy Manhattan lifestyle she could hardly fathom. He was unreachable, unattainable, and altogether out of her league.

"Quite the kitchen, David," she joked, clamping down her emotions. "Vintage is a suitable adjective." She adjusted the faucet and splashed cold water on her cheeks. She dried her face with a clean towel, then spun to arrange the place settings on the wooden table. A window overlooked the unaffected rural surroundings. A grassy meadow beyond evoked a scene from a different era.

"Everything here is marvelous," she added. Beyond marvelous. His park-like location brought to mind temperate summer days spent resting in a hammock and reading the Bible.

He stepped to her, pulling her close to his chest. "I can see the stars at night."

"It must be beautiful." She smiled, trying to contain her growing tenderness for him.

"So you like the kitchen?" A faint catch in his voice disarmed her. He was always so self-assured, yet he valued her opinion.

"Stone floors and blue cabinets." She twisted and discovered he was studying her. "What's not to like?"

"Nothing." He offered a self-indulgent grin. "My kitchen has periodic appeal."

"Perhaps an acquired taste, and it may lack a little… modernization. Let's begin with the yellow stove and blue oven."

"Yellow and blue don't match?" He reached for two green speckled ceramic cups from the cabinet, then opened the refrigerator for an energy drink and a sugary soda.

"Stainless steel appliances are in style." She teasingly smacked him with the towel. Then, sobering, she focused on a paint splatter on the floor. "David, I have a confession."

His hand stilled for a split second before he closed the refrigerator door. "Go on."

She lifted her gaze to meet his. "I've already seen your kitchen."

"When?"

"The day I dropped off the peaches. I couldn't resist a peek." She folded the towel on the counter. Silence reigned for too many seconds.

"I'm sorry."

He poured their beverages into the cups. "Please explain."

"I was curious."

"No." His jaw was tight. "Explain why you didn't tell me sooner."

She dug her nails into her palms. "I should have. I let you down. I let myself down. Please accept my apology."

"I'm not quick to point a finger. We've all made mistakes and I'm grateful for your honesty. It means a great deal to me."

She drew back slightly. "All is forgiven?"

"All is forgiven."

Because of the lump in her throat, she couldn't form any

words. She picked up Pickle's water dish and stepped into the living room.

"The stove is a cast iron antique," David said from the kitchen. "I'll grant the oven might require replacing, although it heats up to temperature."

"What temperature?"

"Two hundred degrees Fahrenheit."

"That's not hot." She set Pickle's dish down. "Do you bake?"

"Never. There's a tasty bakery in town, though."

She rolled her eyes in humorous exasperation. "Spoken like a true guy."

"I'm practical," he called out. "Why replace a working appliance?"

"I see. You're aiming for retro, whether the oven heats or not."

"I heard that. Two hundred degrees—"

"Isn't hot enough to bake a cupcake," she muttered.

She paused, noting the rusted coffee can by the fireplace. She cast a quick glance toward the kitchen, then grasped the can and peeked inside. Two dollar bills lay crumpled at the bottom.

David strode into the living room, sipping from his speckled cup. "Ashley, do you prefer your soft drink in here?"

"I'm fine for now. Thanks."

He stopped. Swallowed. Propped a shoulder against the doorjamb. "What are you doing?"

She held up the coffee can, regretting the timing of his entrance. "I'm sorry. I didn't mean to snoop—"

"You did, though." His face became expressionless, his voice sharp in contrast.

She set the can back down. Tears stung her eyes. "I said I was sorry."

"C'mere." He set his cup on the table and beckoned her to sit on the sofa.

"What about the pizza?"

"I prefer cold pizza. I hope you do too." He raked a hand through his hair. "I didn't intend to charge you with a crime for picking up a rusty old can."

She planned to answer when she was good and ready. She planned to sit when she was good and ready. But there was no contest when it came to David's quiet apology.

She perched on the edge of the sofa. "Sometimes, you are thoroughly impossible."

"Others have said the same. I'm working on becoming a better person. I make excuses, though I try to take full responsibility for my words and actions."

She had leftover anger to challenge him. Nevertheless, she wasn't *that* upset. Besides, she was a Christian and granted forgiveness graciously. Nor could she ignore the mindlessness of upsetting their precious minutes with a needless misunderstanding.

He settled on the sofa and requested she sit closer. Once she scooted near, he slung an arm around her shoulders. "We've spent hours together, yet we're virtual strangers in many respects."

After all their banter, an upscale dinner, and endless delightful kisses, they were still strangers?

Still, she bestowed her best smile. "More sharing? You go first."

"Why am I always first?"

"Because you owe me a candy bar, and the suggestion is yours."

He kept his gaze on the fireplace. "Are you ready for more accounts of my artistic struggle?"

Stunned and flattered because he'd relented so quickly, she nodded. He was a private man, yet he chose to share his personal stories with her. And she sensed that this story held special significance for him.

"Did you ever hold on to something that meant the world to you, even though it carried little monetary value?" He smiled, and the curious tug on her heart occurred again, that tender odd ache.

"A rusty coffee can?" she teased.

"The can is a symbol."

"For what?"

"Do you recall when I told you the road to success is built on hard work?" His tone was strangely hoarse.

"And you mentioned it takes years and years."

He stared at the can. Abundant silence. With David, she was learning patience.

"When I attended NYU…"

"You were awarded a full scholarship." She patted his forearm, a congratulatory pat he probably considered sophomoric. Still, their relationship was tentative, though for her, it was on the verge of becoming more serious with each of his tales. "Your family must've been proud and thrilled." She switched to an encouraging note.

His features remained somber, and she doubted his father had sent any gratifying "*Atta boys*" his way.

Every minute she spent with David, she understood him more. He was complex. He was smart and talented. And he'd been hurt. His recollections brought a broader comprehension of his nature. He was kind, yet vulnerable.

"A scholarship doesn't compensate for everything." His voice deepened. "Tuition and books, sure, though not the infinite art supplies."

She nodded in commiseration. "I can't operate without the countless paintbrushes and watercolors I resupply for my studio each month."

"Nor did my scholarship pay for meals and living costs."

She looked up at him. "Your parents didn't help you financially?"

"My father didn't want his son to become an artist, remember?" David reached for his cup and sipped. "He was pleased about the scholarship. Nonetheless, I was on my own."

She sat engrossed, listening to every sentence, every tenuous shade of David's voice. She had learned already that whenever he mentioned his father, aloofness laced his expression. In this case, she suspected his father's reaction had hurt David the most. She considered remarking that his father's disinterest was cruel, for it had deeply wounded his talented, impressionable son. However, she reserved judgment. "How did you earn money in college?"

"I staked out busy street corners and sketched people. I carried a stool, drawing paper, charcoal pencils, and a kneaded eraser."

"An artist's favorite friend," she agreed. "The eraser doesn't leave any heavy marks behind."

"Hurray. A woman who knows art." He kissed the top of her forehead. "I charged five dollars for each portrait."

A portrait that now commanded over a thousand dollars.

"The key to drawing a good portrait is shading and proper proportions." His smile quickened her heart. Art was, first and foremost, a passion for him. "The distance between the nose and mouth is important."

"You sketched in the middle of busy New York?" She visualized him as a young man, alone in a city of eight million people.

"At the intersection of Broadway and West Forty-First Street, just south of Times Square." His answer was matter of fact, though his arm tightened around her. "I displayed the coffee can in a conspicuous spot for tips. I was an emerging artist developing my craft while earning money at the same time."

"Very enterprising."

"The first two dollars I ever earned are in that coffee can." He ran his thumb around the rim of his cup. "A gray-haired grandmother came by on my first day and requested I sketch her granddaughter. When I finished, I thought the grand-daughter's teeth were too white of a contrast, though they seemed pleased. The can is a reminder to celebrate the triumphs, no matter how small."

He'd saved his first tip and carried the money with him all these years. Ashley wrestled with the explosive emotions welling in her chest.

She blinked back tears and searched his face. His expression was carefully aloof.

Be proud, she thought. *Embrace your God-given talent. Never second-guess yourself.*

Lightly, she touched his hand. "That grandmother must've recognized your tremendous ability."

"I doubt it, though I value your compliment." He set down his cup, lifted her hair and nuzzled her nape.

Ashley rested her head on his shoulder and propped her feet on the coffee table. He held her close.

She drew a fortifying breath, reluctant to shatter the inti-mate mood. Nevertheless, she plunged ahead. "I noticed your vision loss."

He shifted positions. "How can you tell?"

"When you look at me, you favor a certain side. Plus, your reference to a deaf Beethoven the first day we met, coupled with Cherish's rumor mill."

"Am I completely transparent?"

"In times of trouble, we all reach out, whether we realize it or not. You did when you alluded to Beethoven. What happened to you?"

He sighed. "More than enough questions about me."

She almost flinched at the brusqueness in his tone.

His unwarranted flippancy grated on her. How could they not discuss what was so significant to him? Wasn't he the person who had declared not ten minutes earlier that they were virtual strangers?

"Please don't brush off the topic," she replied. "I want to identify with what's important to you. Don't stop painting. You're too talented."

"Thanks for the encouragement." He shoved a throw pillow aside, stood, and reached for her hand. "Let's eat the pizza before it gets cold."

"I thought you preferred cold pizza."

"I changed my mind."

"You're dismissing me."

"I'm dismissing the subject because I refuse to allow an in-depth analysis of my vision loss. Not to anyone except my physician. Not even you." He succeeded in displaying a semblance of a smile. "Come into the kitchen. I prefer to dine with a lovely companion rather than eating alone."

Youth has no age.
– Picasso

As they ate their pizza, sitting across from each other at the kitchen table after she'd whispered a prayer of grace, David was courteous, yet pensive. When they finished, she cleared their dishes, stacked them in the sink, and discarded the paper napkins in the trash.

"No dishwasher?" She tried for an easy-going conversation, hoping he'd bounce back from his contemplative mood.

"I prefer to wash dishes by hand," he replied.

His profile was silhouetted in the glow of the afternoon sun gleaming through the window. His hands were jammed in his pockets, and Pickle relaxed by his feet. A jug of water still sat on the table. She'd sliced lime and lemon into the water for flavor, and two half-filled glasses of water remained.

She started for the living room, intending to pull on her

hiking boots, then ask him to drive her back to the inn. The walk he'd mentioned? Well, they wouldn't be taking a walk anytime soon.

He balled up a napkin she'd missed collecting. "A few months ago," he said softly, "I woke up and discovered I'd lost vision in one eye."

She stopped.

Ignoring the solid beating of her heart, she padded into the kitchen and seated herself at the table again. He sat across from her.

"This subject is difficult for me." He held out his hand. She grasped it and gave a supportive squeeze.

More than a little unnerved, her thoughts spun, one in particular. When she'd studied for her art degree, she happened upon a quote by Pablo Picasso, the renowned Spanish painter and sculptor.

"'Others have seen what is and asked why,'" she quoted. "'I have seen what could be and asked why not.'"

"Picasso," David replied.

With a vague sense of foreboding, she refilled their water glasses. "Maybe I can help you."

"I don't need anyone's help." His dark eyebrows snapped together. "I'm explaining because you pressed me for details."

She hadn't but didn't argue. Stiffening, she shoved her chair back.

Pickle came to his feet and stared up at her.

"Point taken, David," she said. "Loud and clear. I'm leaving and phoning an Uber."

Because the point *was* taken. Now she finally understood.

David enjoyed spending time with her, but she wasn't allowed any closer than a shared pizza. *Virtual strangers.* She'd been an amusing diversion when he was wearied, an excuse for procrastination when he was supposed to be working on a commissioned painting.

He stood, shadowing her. He placed his hands on her shoulders. "Please stay."

Her heartbeat doubled at the despair in his voice, though her tolerance and patience had worn thin. Only a fool would keep listening, conscious of being used as a sounding board because there was no one else.

She swiveled toward the living room.

"Ashley." His voice came from behind her. "Forgive my abruptness."

She whirled. "You drive me away when I want to support you." She seized her tote bag and fished for her cellphone. "I'm a silly art teacher and will never meet your lofty standards to—"

He reached her in two steps and gently caught her wrist. "Don't go."

She jerked from his grip.

"I've got cookies in the freezer." His pleading tone, his grasping for something to keep her near—cookies, of all things—demolished her anger. Undecided whether to laugh or cry, she did both.

He cradled her, kissed her neck, her lips, and wiped the tears from her cheeks. She didn't resist. She couldn't resist. She was falling in love with a man who was creative, enterprising, skeptical, and in many ways reminded her of the enchanting, vulnerable students she taught—all seeking support.

He rested his chin on the top of her head. "I don't deserve someone as sweet and caring as you in my life."

"I'm here," she whispered, and buried her face in his chest. His heart beat fast and solid against her cheek.

He led her into the living room, to the sofa, and circled his arm around her. She sank down beside him, picking up a throw pillow that had fallen to the floor. Pickle took up his usual spot by the fireplace.

"My condition is called NAION, an abbreviation for a lengthy description," David began. "Non-arteritic anterior ischemic optic neuropathy."

"You expect me to remember that?" She smiled, eager to ease a challenging conversation.

Her teasing did the trick, because he chuckled. "In summary, there's a loss of blood flow from my optic nerve leading to the brain."

"Were you in pain when it happened?"

"No. I'm not in pain now, either."

Her smile wavered. "What causes the condition?"

"My doctor in New York referred me to numerous studies citing high blood pressure and/or smoking. Neither applies to me."

"What is your doctor's treatment recommendation?"

"Nothing, except for daily aspirin and a healthy lifestyle. Usually, the condition doesn't get any worse."

She placed a hand on his forearm. "This is encouraging news."

"Nor does it get any better."

She winced. "Will wearing eyeglasses help?"

"No. Eyeglasses aid nearsightedness or farsightedness but won't restore a damaged optic nerve. The doctor assured me that my brain will adjust, and it has."

"Oh, David, I'm sincerely sorry." A thought arose, one she blurted before fully considering. "Is your other eye affected?"

"There's a 30 percent chance. Luckily, my vision is twenty-twenty in that eye."

Thrown off balance, she echoed half to herself, "A 30 percent chance."

"I'm absolutely fine." He gave her a cheerful smile she didn't believe for a minute.

"Really?"

"Really."

"Is your vision loss the reason you aren't painting?" She wavered to steady herself and pace her questions. "You're known for being prolific."

"I can still paint."

"But you're not."

He shrugged. "I'm a realist, and not a very productive one."

"Perhaps you've set impossibly high standards for yourself." *Much like what she'd been accused of doing with her ex-boyfriend.*

"Perhaps." David released a heavy sigh. "Time will tell, though I imagine my painting has changed."

"Change is good."

He rubbed a fist over his jaw. "Sometimes."

"Prayer is better." She kept her hand on his forearm. "Will you pray with me?"

"You pray. I'll listen."

She bowed her head, and David did the same.

"Dear Lord, David is becoming a new creation," she whispered. "Please make way in his mind for fresh prospects and habits. Some of your greatest miracles are created when people are in transition. Encourage David through this difficult period and grant him wisdom and peace. Give him faith to comprehend. Amen."

David lifted his head. "I admit I feel better."

"It's not me. It's God." She raised her palms to heaven. "He promised He will never leave us or forsake us. Take heart in His assurances."

"I'll try."

Unlike the past hour's ups and downs, the next few minutes passed serenely. She relaxed in the comfortable surroundings, a dog by the fireplace, the special man she'd fallen for holding her as if he'd never let go.

A sharp pang of longing went through her. This restful,

contented life was a life she'd never live. She wanted children someday. However, children necessitated marriage and a husband, and neither was part of her future.

David pressed a kiss to her temple. "Now I want to hear more about you."

"Me?" She leaned back.

"Why did Sarah call you Twinkle?"

Something about his engaging smile prodded her to answer. After all, he'd spoken with honesty and openness.

"I've always gotten excited about my students' drawings," she said.

He threw her a speculative grin. "Please continue."

"A few years ago, an adorable autistic boy remarked that my eyes twinkled like sparkly green stars after I'd praised him. He is wonderfully artistic."

"How old is he?"

"Ten." She crossed her feet. "These kids appreciate art. They're my type of people."

"I appreciate art."

She nudged his rib with her elbow. "Therefore, it goes without saying…"

"I'm your type of person. I'm flattered, Twinkle."

She grinned. "Are you making fun of me?"

"Never."

"In summary, the name stuck. My close friends use my nickname often."

"Twinkle, twinkle, you are my shining star."

Heat hastened her pulse at his tender words and heavy-lidded gaze. Surely a man capable of evoking such profound emotions through his paintings wasn't teasing any longer.

Regardless, she wouldn't be drawn in by an artist who was brilliant, funny, and so attractive that her temperature rose ten degrees the moment she set eyes on him.

No, no. Surely, she wouldn't be a pathetic fool a second

time—charmed by a man feigning interest, then dropping her when he found a more appealing woman.

That is, unless that particular man began kissing her with such abandon, cuddling her, his lips caressing hers so urgently her heart responded with intense longing.

Minutes after their kisses ended, he didn't take his gaze from her face as he invited her back into the kitchen.

She lifted a teasing eyebrow. "For cookies?"

"We could eat a box, although I want to paint you first."

"I thought you were using the photograph by the river to paint me."

"You're here in person. What could be better?"

They exchanged smiles.

"I'll take the dog out and grab some special paints I store in my truck," he said.

She perched on the edge of a kitchen chair and waited. He returned carrying an assortment of flamboyant shades of blue and red paint, gold glitter, a brush, and a sea sponge. An old T-shirt cut up as a rag was tucked into the waistband of his shorts.

Her gaze narrowed. "Where's your canvas?"

"Don't need one."

"Aren't you going to paint me?"

And then she realized it. He intended to literally paint *her*.

"Um, nope." She jumped up and backed away. "No dice." It hadn't occurred to her beforehand because the idea was absolutely, utterly insane. "Find someone else to paint."

He looked around. "Who?"

"Call one of your Hollywood models."

"None hold a candle to you." He approached her with the sponge and a pot of cobalt-blue paint. "This is water soluble and will wash off."

"Your assurances are supposed to appease me?" She gazed at the ceiling, searching for a guarantee somewhere, anywhere. "You lured me into the kitchen because I assumed we were eating cookies."

"We can. I have a half box left."

"That's all?"

"I'll spare you a couple."

She lunged for the freezer, pulling open the door, but he was faster. He set down the sponge and paint and snagged the box.

She peered into the freezer. "Where's your frozen pizzas and peanut butter ice cream?"

"I don't eat junk food."

"Yeah, right. What kind of guy doesn't eat Hungry-Man dinners?"

"Me." He held the cookie box over her head. "Shall we eat these now or later?"

She blew out the air stuck in her throat. "Let's wait."

"Wise choice. Body art is fascinating, and you're an inspiration, Ashley."

She cast a sideways glance toward the doorway. "I'll agree under one condition."

"Conditions, now?"

"Absolutely. You paint my face, and I'll paint yours."

"Agreed. Stand still." He tapped the sponge into the paint, then dabbed numerous drops on her cheeks. "Remember, don't sweat."

"On the hottest day of the year?"

"The air-conditioning is on."

"Great. Until I step outside into the eighty-degree heat and humidity."

She curved toward the window, eager to view her reflection in the glass. Her blue cheeks were muted, giving her the appearance of a lopsided clown.

"Ninety-nine percent of people who are body painted say they would do it again." David spoke calmly, his actions focused, as he guided her around to face him. He stood back, then applied a dab of gold glitter on her nose. "Excellent!"

"This calls for retaliation." She flipped him a smile, snatched the sponge, and aimed for his forehead. A blob of gold glitter dripped from his chin when she missed. "Sorry." She reached for the blue paint and knocked over the pot, splattering paint across the stone floor.

"I might need to renovate the kitchen after all." He drew her to him and kissed her. "It's also been noted that face painting unites people."

"Where did you read that?"

"Somewhere."

Yes, he was impossible.

In a lushly renovated cabin in the woods, their laughter rang out.

Pickle barked and raced around them. Frozen cookies were left to thaw.

And all was perfect in Ashley's world.

CHAPTER 12

The chief enemy of creativity is good sense.
- Picasso

The following two days passed in a blur. Ashley notified Nancy at the art gallery, reporting that she'd found David and he was all right. She didn't reveal his eyesight loss. The subject was personal and up to him to explain.

Ashley phoned the leader of the fellowship group at her church that evening. "I'll drive back to my apartment on Saturday, so I'm prepared to teach Sunday School," she told her.

Then she texted her substitute teachers and was assured her students were doing splendidly.

Taking maximum advantage of their days together, David invited her to peruse the boutiques in town, and dine with him at respective restaurants including The Garden Terrace, recognized for their mesquite barbecued ribs and sugar-free lemon cake, both of which delighted Ashley.

She wore light summer dresses, thankfully she'd packed several, as she had the tendency to over-pack. From Sarah, she borrowed flirty straw hats and applied black mascara to bring out her large hazel eyes. Friends had remarked that her eyes were her best feature, so why not accentuate them?

During a shopping trip to Aaron's Art Shop, David insisted on purchasing hundreds of dollars' worth of supplies for her studio. They left the shop with their arms laden with bags, and Pickle walked with them on a secure leash as they crossed the street to David's truck.

Ashley sighed. "I wanted to reach my exercise quota by working out at the inn's gym. Julian told me he recently updated with state-of-the-art equipment."

David deposited their bags into his trunk. "*Wanted* to reach your goals?"

"Yes, that's the key word. I haven't visited the gym once."

"At least your intentions are good." His eyes crinkled at the corners. "I owe you an excursion to Juniper Mountain and the hiking trip I promised the other day."

"You're referring to the day we ate pizza in your cabin?"

He shut the trunk and took hold of Pickle's leash. "The very same."

"And the day you painted me."

"Yup."

She accepted his outstretched hand. "Despite your assurances concerning water-soluble paint, Julian definitely gave me an odd look when I arrived back at the inn."

"You washed the paint off in my bathroom before I drove you to the inn."

She tilted her head. "Yes, I did. Lots of scrubbing and rubbing alcohol helped remove the paint, but the gold glitter insisted on sticking to my nose."

He kissed the tip of her nose. "Lucky for you, all the paint has worn off now."

"Lucky for *you,* or I would've cheerfully thrown you out of a tree."

"If you recall, I don't climb trees anymore."

"There's always a second time."

He chuckled and stopped in midstep. "That's something else I love about you. You always express exactly what's on your mind."

Something else he loved.

Her heart cartwheeled in her chest. David spoke about love.

She stared into his arresting gaze. For a number of seconds, she permitted herself to wonder what it would be like to be loved by this artistic, enigmatic man? They'd spend hours together, conversing about art, wisecracking, and relishing each other's company.

I'll help you confront your vision problem, she thought. *I'll lend support at every crossroad, and you can show my precious students your exquisite canvases and provide expert tips. We'll attend concerts—maybe the music of Percy Grainger. We'll serve in church. We'll pray.*

Where, exactly? In Cherish? In New York City? In Greenwood?

He cupped her chin, smoothing his thumb along her jawline. His woodsy, male scent floated to her nostrils, prompting an intense awareness of the vital man bending his head to kiss her.

Right there. In the middle of the main street.

From the first second she'd met him, her feelings had been overwhelming. No matter how light-hearted their conversations, a kiss invariably followed. Around David, she was comfortable, and everything seemed familiar. With him she felt cared for and safe.

"You're very special, Ashley." His voice lowered to a murmur. "Never forget that."

His deep tone blended with the hum of residents chatting among themselves. A mother chased after a toddler who lifted his shirt over his head as he ran across the sidewalk. On the grassy lawn of the park, children invented a game, legs churning as they ran in circles.

A life worth living. A life with David. A wonderful, fanciful dream.

She recalled the sting of heartbreak, the crushing, biting wound, and she determinedly shoved her dreams aside. She'd been hurt by a man once, her fantasies shattered, and she wouldn't risk it again. Besides, no one fell in love in mere days.

Did they?

They continued their wanderings to Whitney's, the local ice cream parlor. She ordered a chocolate sundae topped with hot fudge and a cherry, and David selected a triple decker coffee cone. Pet-friendly, the owners produced a natural frozen yogurt for dogs served in a bowl. Pickle's eyes grew round, and he lapped up the yogurt.

"We've gone to the dogs," the owner joked, which earned a burst of laughter.

Ashley and David assembled outside on sunny-yellow chairs, leaning their elbows on the wrought-iron table. When they couldn't eat another bite, David offered to walk her to the inn, assuring he'd double back to his truck and deliver her art supplies in the morning.

They resumed their pace, strolling hand in hand. The afternoon sun beat down on them, though a faint breeze stirred and ruffled her hair. Nevertheless, the minutes were sleepy and motionless, the air hot and aromatic. Songbirds chirped from the trees, and joggers passed them at a slow clip.

"About that invite…" David began.

"To Walnut Forest and Juniper Mountain?"

"You're a hiker. Here's your opportunity to show off your expertise." The sparkle in his gaze underscored his sheer enjoyment of joking with her.

"I hike a couple blocks around my apartment, which is on a flat sidewalk." She chuckled. "Primarily, I walk on a treadmill in my living room while I listen to audiobooks."

"What type of books?"

"I gravitate toward adventure thrillers."

They curved onto a quiet, residential lane. "We share many interests, Ashley, beginning with art and audiobooks."

She studied his face, his expressions of tenderness.

By silent agreement, they zeroed in on a park bench. "You're on a roll, David. Please continue."

"Continue what?"

"Listing our interests."

He pressed a kiss on her cheek. "Exercise is another."

She jabbed him with her elbow. "I haven't found the time because I'm spending every waking minute with you. Therefore, it's all your fault I've gained weight this week."

"My fault?" He held a hand over his heart. "I'll willingly accept the blame, honored you'd use me as an excuse."

His good humor erased any reservations for missing her workouts, and she couldn't contain her joking. "As well you should."

"Set aside an hour each day," he said. "Mornings work best for me."

"Your suggestion takes discipline, which I evidently lack."

"You're the most disciplined woman I've ever met. You operate your own studio, you're clearly excellent with children, and your inspirational words shine with conviction."

His observations floored her. She flipped back her thick hair that kept falling over her eyes and studied him. God's purpose was to redeem and rebuild. It wasn't too late for David's faith to be restored.

"The old has gone, the new is here." She referenced a passage from Corinthians.

David grinned. "Make way for the new." His grin widened, his eyes an electric, luminous blue. In its depths, she lost herself in her expectations, her imaginings, her emotions.

She recalled the first day they met at his cabin and formally shook hands. Every part of her senses had fixated on the touch of his calloused fingers linked with hers. He reminded her of the fictional heroes she adored, a resilient, charismatic male. A protagonist straight from a storybook, complete with a happily ever after. The more hours he occupied, the more her initial observations had proved correct. David Fodero could overcome any obstacle, if only his faith and optimism were reinforced.

She pondered a second possibility. Should anything happen and he lost eyesight in his good eye—Well, she couldn't permit her thoughts to go there.

An artist who couldn't see. An artist who couldn't paint.

No.

Nevertheless, uncertainties persisted.

What if?

Her internal response was immediate. *Trust God.*

David shouldn't allow his hardships to prevent him from appreciating what God had planted inside him. Every person was unique and special. Every person had something in them to help press through their adversities and reach the other side.

So deep in thought, she didn't hear David's question at first. "Have you ever gone camping?" he asked again.

She viewed the inn, visible up ahead. "When I was eight years old, I camped overnight with my father and an elderly couple from our church. They'd been married for decades and were schoolteachers. They were reaching retirement age and wanted to serve the Lord by volunteering."

"Did they retire?"

"Yes, and they were excited to offer their unique gifts of support and mentoring children in a remote country. They were Christians and believed giving their lives to God helped to change people."

David picked up his steps and steered her toward a park bench beneath a large magnolia tree. The shade from the fragrant pink blossoms offered a welcome respite from the heat, and Pickle chose a place in the cool grass.

"How did your camping expedition go?" David secured the dog's leash to a tree and grabbed Pickle's striped elephant from his pocket, tossing it to him.

"Camping was an adventure." Ashley settled on the bench, the cool iron pressing against her bare legs. She was grateful she'd worn a casual outfit—cotton shorts, a white eyelet blouse, and sandals. "My father and I prayed with our friends and asked God to mark their journey with safety."

"Sometimes, I miss church."

She touched his wrist, hearing the desire in his deep voice. "Church misses you."

"I'm struggling. You rely on God and never lose faith."

"I've lost faith more often than I can count, beginning with the camping trip."

"Hard to believe."

Seconds ticked.

She expelled a breath, knowing he waited for a reply.

"The married couple was scheduled to devote the upcoming six months to a mountain village overseas, though the wife expressed reservations. There had been recent news reports that the impoverished country was suffering an unanticipated upheaval. I talked them into traveling."

"You?"

"They planned to do so much good and spread the word of the Lord."

Happy remembrances of the tan canvas tents erected side by side, sitting around the campfire toasting marshmallows over a sizzling fire, brought fond memories.

At least initially.

"When did they return from their missionary trip?" David's question pulled her out of her musings and yanked her back to reality. "Are you still in touch with them?"

"No." She choked on the single word.

"Why? What happened?"

"They were killed. Guerillas attacked their village late at night and none of the townspeople and missionaries survived." She swiped at the tears forming at the corner of her eyes. "For months afterwards, I blamed myself."

The warmth of David's reassuring fingers lifted the weight off her chest. "An attack in a foreign country is hardly your fault."

Pickle inched toward them, and she picked him up, allowing him to lick her arms. "I was the person who encouraged them to go on the trip."

"You were eight years old. It's unlikely you influenced their decision."

"I still believed it was all my fault, and my convictions faltered. My father uplifted me, brought me to church, prayed with me at night." She sucked in a lungful of oxygen. "I remember the wife read stories from the Bible that night we were camping. They were righteous, kind Christians."

David leaned closer. "What kind of stories?"

"She spoke about Paul's thorn in the flesh from 2 Corinthians 12:7." While Ashley recited the verse, David trained his gaze on Pickle.

"When I was young, I studied the New Testament and memorized favorite passages," he replied.

"Do you remember the significance of Paul's story?"

"There are many theories." David repositioned himself and faced her. He was so close his legs brushed against hers. "Recollections of Paul's past, former temptations, or perhaps a physical ailment."

"Paul's eyesight, his difficulty seeing, is a possibility often examined." She adjusted Pickle so he wouldn't slide off her lap. "Sometimes God uses our physical weaknesses to humble us."

"I'm hardly a saint, Ashley. You're comparing my eyesight loss to Paul's thorn?"

His question hung in the silence between them. In his tone, she heard defensiveness and despair.

She instructed herself to breathe, and slanted a glance toward him. He didn't meet her gaze.

Who was she to judge him if he was bitter at God? Was she a better Christian?

The sun lowered behind a cloud and softened David's rigid features. She breathed in a bottomless breath, saturated with the scent of fragrant magnolias.

She took his hand. "I'm truly sorry about your vision loss, David."

Absently, he scratched Pickle's head and stared at the empty lot across the road. "I appreciate your concern."

"Remember God's grace and know it is enough. Walk through your season of uncertainty and praise Him. His power is made perfect through our weaknesses."

"Once, I believed. When adolescence kicked in, I questioned everything." He met her gaze for a split-second before refocusing on the lot. "Despite my mother's prodding, I never returned to church."

"How many years has it been?"

"Two decades."

Her lips parted in astonishment. "Yet you're commissioned to paint a church."

"The exterior." He shifted. "Not the interior."

She envisioned him as a young boy, as an adolescent, and her heart fluttered at the image. Fresh-faced, probably skinny with long arms and legs. He craved love and protection and assurance. Quiet and reserved, with a spark of creative mischief. Even when attending elementary school, his artistic ability must have spilled from every pore, although he had recognized his father's displeasure.

She formed her lips into a smile. "Are you sorry you accepted the commission?"

"It brought me to Cherish. It brought me to you."

Her movements never faltered as she placed the dog on the ground, though her emotions spun in a thousand directions. She stared up at David's face, felt the familiar strength of his strong arms as he cuddled her.

Her heart burst with something she could only identify as love.

She longed to vocalize her feelings because she agreed with him. Come what may, their meeting each other had been predestined.

Although no. It had been calculated. By her.

Her throat tightened, and her voice was snatched away.

"Your emotions are written all over your face, Ashley." David seemed unaware of the tears threatening to blur her own vision. "You're an open book."

"Am I?" She drove a hand through her hair, tempted to pat down her rambunctious cowlick, which surely must be sticking straight up in this humidity. She didn't, because David patted it down for her.

"I knew it the moment you showed up at my cabin wearing sandals, searching for a mountain located in another state." A grin tugged at his full mouth. "The expression on your face was a definite giveaway."

A giveaway for her stupidity, she chastised herself. Again, she sent a prayer to God to forgive her for deceiving David.

She shoved to her feet. "I should tell you something."

"No climbing trees, I hope." He stood and unleashed Pickle. "Although I'm accepting options for tomorrow's plans."

"It's not about tomorrow."

And just like that, she lost her nerve, refusing to deflate the shining admiration for her in his gaze.

"What is it?" he asked.

"I can't. I should spend the day packing since I'm planning to leave on Saturday."

His gaze narrowed. He grabbed her hand. "You're leaving so soon?"

"David, I've been in Cherish almost a week."

He stared down at their fingers, firmly entwined. "You can't stay any longer?"

"My students miss me, and I miss them. In addition, I'm in charge of a Sunday school class at my church. I love teaching five-year-old's about God. Besides, I imagine you've neglected your commission because you've invested all your hours with me."

"I've been painting."

"Great! The centennial portrait?"

He paused, forcing her to pause, too. "A subject far more important to me."

His heated gaze robbed her of any ability to form a coherent sentence. She yearned for more, a pledge that he'd phone, a promise to see her, although he hadn't offered any commitment. None at all. Nothing.

Did he even know where she lived? She riffled through their conversations. He'd never asked. She'd never told him.

She didn't press. She didn't wish to become another conquest. Yet the intensity of how much she cared for him already scared her.

She focused on the scattered sunlight dappling through the tree leaves. An artist's eye would be scrutinizing the sun's position, the contour of the spaces where the light shone through, the elevation of the tree canopy.

David looped an arm around her shoulders. "Instead of packing, will you go to the Renaissance Faire with me?"

Taken aback, she gaped. Had she imagined his invitation?

"I have it on excellent authority, specifically yours, that you're not a fan of Renaissance Faires," she said.

"You're a fan, which is all that matters."

"You're not exactly the most sociable guy on the planet."

"I like people."

"Who?"

"You. Very much. It's the silliness involved in dressing up as a character from the fourteenth century that I object to." He held up a hand. "Don't ask, because I won't be wearing any costume."

She eyed him from head to toe. "I envision you as a knight."

He gave a gallant bow. "And you're my lady. We'll eat, drink, and watch a jousting match."

A Renaissance Faire. At last. Her veins hummed with excitement. She steeled herself not to react, but wrapped her hands around his nape, anyway. "I'm so excited, David."

"My pleasure. Let's seal our date."

Happily, she obliged, a treasured kiss beneath a Carolina-blue sky.

Savor every minute, she told herself. Someday, she'd look back upon this wondrous week with joy. A summer to remember. A summer to cherish. Days filled with brilliance and wonder and David. This cynical, witty, artistic, generous man.

She'd miss him terribly after they parted. Nonetheless, she'd provide a clear and simple explanation for why she'd initially come to Cherish. Sure, it was easier to flee than cope with her wrongdoing, but their relationship insisted she push past her fear and risk seeing the disappointment on his face.

Her jaw set, her mind made up. Though her stomach pitched at the thought, she'd tell him the truth tomorrow, at day's end.

And then she would pray, intending to make peace with her failings.

CHAPTER 13

Colors, like features, follow the changes in emotions.
- Picasso

"I refuse to wear a metal helmet." David frowned at himself in the full-length mirror of the Renaissance Faire's costume shop. "What will people think?"

Ashley gazed at him with giggling delight. "They'll think you're ingenious and original."

Considering half the men at the Faire were also dressed as knights, David highly doubted it.

Ashley had dragged him into the first shop she'd spotted and talked him into renting a knight's costume. Of course, she hadn't literally talked him into it. The joy lighting her face was all the convincing he needed. Besides, the Faire was held in a neighboring town. They wouldn't bump into anyone they knew.

As soon as he and Ashley had stepped through the gate-opening, they were hailed by a court jester sporting a three-pointed hat and ringing a tiny bell while being serenaded by an animated group of musicians playing wooden flutes and tambourines.

She brushed a piece of lint off his polo shirt collar, which peeked through the cape. "What's the definition of a brave knight without armor protection?"

"A wise, practical man who can breathe."

There was something about a guy dressed in shorts—David had refused the woolen stockings and metal chest plate—and wearing a red cape that didn't quite match.

Ashley tightened the ties around his neck. "Despite you wearing sneakers instead of pointed boots, you're still the pluckiest, most dashing knight I've ever met."

He peered down at his shoes. "How many knights are plucky?"

"None until now."

She looked adorable, standing in front of him in an emerald-green velveteen gown that brought out the green hues in her hazel eyes. His gaze glided over her figure, lingering on her slim hips.

He placed a roundelet, a headpiece of padded round rings and braided trim, atop her glossy hair. The fake jewels, satin, and gold ribbons flowing from the raised bow enhanced her understated elegance. "You are a classic beauty, Lady Jane."

She grinned at the reference to her costume, fidgeted with the pearl beading along the gown's bodice, then twirled. "You're handsome indeed, Sir Galahad, especially wearing a surcoat."

He fingered the thin cotton fabric. "Surcoat? I thought it was a cape."

"You're confusing the Renaissance era with Batman."

He burst out laughing. "You expect me to walk in this getup? Or take in any air? I'll smother in this mesh metallic hood." He tapped on the hood to emphasize his point.

"Consider yourself lucky. At least the hem of your gown won't drag in the dirt."

He fanned himself before tugging the hood over his head. "I may sweat to death."

"You're wearing shorts. Be brave, Sir Tristan."

"I thought I was Sir Galahad."

"I'm naming all the knights at King Arthur's Round Table."

"There were hundreds of knights."

"I'll list the most memorable, Sir Lancelot."

He produced a gallant bow, then guided her out of the air-conditioned shop. Appetizing aromas of steak and mushroom pies, caramel apples, and roasted turkey legs made his mouth water. "I'm beginning to understand the attraction to these silly Faires."

"Silly?"

"Entertaining," he amended.

She grinned up at him. "Because of the noble knights and elegant ladies parading around?"

"No. Because of the delicious food."

A Renaissance Faire was an elaborate week-long affair, affording a schedule of daily events including royal jousting, comedy improvisation by a swashbuckling trio, and themed weekends such as a pirate invasion.

She tugged at his hand as they walked. "Let's order two glasses of orange soda."

"Does your sweet tooth have no bounds?"

"None at all."

"They didn't serve orange soda in the fourteen hundreds."

"Now you're a purist?" She drew herself up to her full height.

He purchased soda for her, and an iced coffee for himself. While she perused the handmade beeswax candles at an adjoining shop, he debated whether to order roasted almonds sprinkled with cinnamon, or jalapeno.

She skipped back to him. "I'd prefer chocolate-coated."

He ordered the almonds in a cone for each of them—chocolate-coated and cinnamon, respectively. As was her custom, she thanked him, bowed her head, and whispered a prayer of grace. Even here, in the middle of a noisy, bustling crowd, she openly expressed her faith because, as she informed him, "All the food we eat is a result of God's bounty."

He nodded. Her sincere conviction was beginning to rub off on him.

She fished for a handful of chocolate nuts and fed him a couple.

"These nuts are too sweet." He groaned in feigned dismay, smirked impenitently, and snatched another handful. "If I eat any more, I might be sick."

She pushed his hand safely away from her cone. "Uh, huh."

As the afternoon passed, they meandered around the open-air booths hawking items from cloth doll patterns to plush blue dragons, inhaled cheesy French fries and sausage on a stick, and joked about who was brave enough to ride the Whirl and Hurl.

He laughed more than he'd ever laughed in his lifetime.

The reason? He was with Ashley, and she had the ability to bring joy to everyday events.

Children gravitated to her. She applauded enthusiastically while little girls, muffling giggles during a ceremony, extended deep throne curtsies, then were elevated to become ladies of the realm. "By the queen herself," Ashley congratulated the girls, which earned her unreserved smiles. Their smiles included David, which brought an endearing clutch to his heart.

Ashley picked up a pamphlet and noted that the jousting match began at three o'clock. "Let's get there early so we can snag a good seat."

"Is the jousting held outside under the blazing hot sun?" He snatched a last handful of sticky almonds.

"Medieval England didn't offer indoor air-conditioned arenas." She grabbed a few nuts from his cone. "Are you expecting an indoor movie theater with reclining stadium seats?"

"Does that mean no?"

Her shoulders shook with mirth. "An unequivocal no."

As they wandered, munched, and sipped cold drinks, her gaze riveted to a display of handmade jewelry, and she lingered to rhapsodize over a cross pendant suspended from a gold chain. The artisan ran his fingers along the smokey quartz beads, zeroing in on the center green stone.

"Pearls and peridot." He brought the necklace closer so Ashley could examine the quality and craftsmanship. "These necklaces are one of a kind. A set of matching earrings is also available."

"The cross is gorgeous and the design so intricate." She turned it over to view the price tag and pushed it back toward him. "Unfortunately, it's way out of my price range."

David bent and kissed her cheek. "Do you like the necklace?"

"I love it."

"Then it's yours."

She placed her hand on his, her smile shy. "I could never accept such an expensive gift."

"You'd deprive me from buying a special necklace for my fairest lady?"

Before she objected further, he settled up with the vendor and hooked the fine gold chain around her neck. She fingered the cross and grinned into the hand mirror the vendor supplied.

"You're too generous." She kissed David with so much enthusiasm he considered purchasing the entire jewelry display.

"My pleasure." He tripped on the words, his throat welling with emotion.

He was starting to care for her more than he ever dreamed possible.

A rosy tint enhanced her fine cheekbones. "I realize a Renaissance Faire isn't your favorite way to spend the day."

He cradled her, kissed her again. "I'm enjoying every single minute more than I ever imagined." To his astonishment, this was the most pleasant afternoon he ever recalled.

She changed direction, evidently distracted by the scent of leather at a table touting handcrafted leather goods. He grabbed the opportunity to purchase the matching earrings to Ashley's necklace and slipped the gift bag into his shorts pocket.

He pointed to a ride, a swinging suspended barrel. Thrilled screams from the riders blasted whenever the barrel flew into the air. "Are you agreeable to riding the Barrel of Mayhem?"

"Absolutely. It looks a little tamer than the Whirl and Hurl." She set her hand on his outstretched palm. "Human-powered, naturally."

He had turned to a booth to purchase tickets for the ride when a vendor at Robin Hood Archery called out, "How are your abilities with a bow and arrow, sir? Step right up and win your lovely lady a simulated diamond ring. All you have to do is strike the tree stump. If you hit the target six times in a row, you'll win her a cuddly black bear."

David stepped to the booth and scrutinized the bows and arrows laid out on a table. He knew nothing about archery, but how hard could the sport be? No special equipment was required, and his one good eye boasted perfect vision.

Decisively, he dug in his pocket for loose dollar bills.

The vendor focused on David. "All it takes is a steady hand, flexible muscles, and a cool disposition."

Ashley giggled. "David, the man must know you."

He scanned the selection, the sleek curves of the bows, and decided on a recurved design.

Ashley tapped him on the shoulder. "I thought we were riding Mayhem?"

He steered her around and yanked off his metal mesh hood. "Not when I'm presented with the prospect of winning you a diamond ring. The opportunity is practically falling in my lap."

"Only takes one bulls-eye." The vendor's voice lowered as he peered at David. "Haven't I seen you somewhere? You look like that hermit artist guy. My wife showed me a picture in a magazine last year of a famous painting, *Lady by the River*. The article reported you were taking the art world by storm."

A sidelong grin accompanied David's attempt to correct the vendor. "*Woman by the River*."

"Huh?"

"*Woman by the River*," David repeated. "Not lady."

The vendor waved a hand. "Woman, lady, something like that."

Ashley met David's grin with a challenging smile. "You realize that no one can find the actual river in your painting."

"My wife said the same thing," the vendor agreed.

"You're kidding. The river is obvious." David shot a stunned look at them both, his eyes narrowing as he took in Ashley's vibrant expression.

Tension filled the air as David secured the arrow, stretched back the bow string, and took aim.

"Rembrandt!" Ashley shouted.

The arrow missed and landed in a mound of dirt.

He lowered the bow, tossed her an offended look, and picked another arrow.

"Not Rembrandt," the vendor corrected. "This hermit painter is supposed to be more avant-garde. My wife claims his paintings are fine art and innovative. Me? I'll take a Michelangelo any day."

While David pondered whether he'd just been complimented or insulted, he granted Ashley a self-assured smirk. He notched his arrow and tried again. On his last attempt, he'd finally gotten the hang of archery and hit the tree stump.

"Hurray! You've won your girlfriend a diamond ring." The vendor fumbled behind the display and planted a plastic case in David's outstretched palm.

David peeled off the cellophane and examined the cheap faux diamond.

"Will you wear my ring?" He gazed at Ashley, delighted by the brilliant smile crossing her face. "I'll buy you something better, something bigger. I promise."

"I don't need anything better." She extended her right hand. "The sentiment is what's meaningful."

He slipped the ring on her fourth finger. "Now it's official."

"What is?"

"We're formally dating." At the realization of how much the moment meant to him, he cleared his throat and noted a banner draped over a gigantic rocking horse. "Like the sign states, I'm a contented fairgoer. I hope you're contented too."

"I am. Thank you." She pressed the ring to her cheek as if it were the most precious item she'd ever worn. "David?"

"Hmm?"

Her lilting voice uttering his name had an odd effect. He felt alive and valued. He trusted her, trusted her enough to be his true self. He felt safe, encouraged by the knowledge he'd found the woman of his dreams.

Here. Not in Manhattan, not at a fancy art gallery in Los Angeles, or on a swanky island in the Caribbean. Here. In this tiny Southern community, that embraced their faith in God.

He smiled as he stuffed the knight's hood into a free pocket.

He was still smiling when they passed a line-up of food stands that led to the jousting arena. At the entrance, he deliberated about ordering an enormous turkey leg and muttered, "A carnivore's dream."

He scanned the gigantic field, humming with merchants, scampering youngsters, and a horde of men clothed in tunics, capes, and plumed feather hats.

Ashley gazed at the scene and sighed. "Sadly, there are no chocolate candy bars sold during the Renaissance, either."

"You eased your sugar fix when you devoured the chocolate-covered almonds."

A frown formed between her delicately arched eyebrows. "You ate half of them."

"Me? Two handfuls at the most."

Good-naturedly, she swatted his forearm. "Your handfuls were more like scoops. The jousting is starting. I don't want to miss it."

"David Fodero!" a familiar male voice called.

David and Ashley turned.

Julian Wilson and his wife, Nora, stood by the fish and chips stand. Julian sported a high-collared hourglass-fit jacket, white ruffled shirt, and matching breeches, every inch the country gentleman. Nora raised a monocle to her eye and waved. She wore a linen sheath and buttercups were braided in her hair.

David looked around. He and Ashley were hopelessly

trapped between a mob and a musician playing the hammered dulcimer.

In the spirit of friendship, Nora extended her hands as she and Julian approached. "How fun to see you two here."

David inclined his head. "What a coincidence."

Julian surveyed David's costume and chuckled. "You're a knight, I gather?"

"I'm a knight if you're a country gentleman."

"Touché."

"I hoped no one would see me except Ashley." David reached for her hand. "I have a reputation to preserve."

"Don't we all." Ever the diplomat, Julian sidetracked the exchange. "Before you ask, Pickle is safe with Samantha. Your dog and ours get along grand."

"Excellent." David had asked Samantha if she could watch his dog, and she'd cheerfully agreed.

"Pickle is so well-behaved, I'll dog-sit whenever I'm free, Mr. Fodero," she'd assured him.

"Did Samantha tell you where Ashley and I were headed?" David inquired.

Julian's smile was one of exaggerated innocence. "As a matter of fact, she did."

"Are you two planning to watch the jousting match?" Nora asked. "We can sit together." With an exclamation of delight, she stared at Ashley's necklace. "Oh my. How lovely!"

Ashley stole a glance at David beneath her long lashes. "David bought it for me at an artisan shop."

"Gorgeous. And your ring." Nora gazed meaningfully at Ashley's right hand. A slow, disbelieving smile bloomed. "Is it new also?"

"David won it for me at the archery game." Ashley tossed her shiny hair over her shoulders. "We're officially dating."

Nora's perceptive eyes met Ashley's. "Congratulations!"

"You're a lucky man." Julian offered his usual clap on David's back. "Aren't you going to kiss her?"

David appraised Ashley's exquisite features. "I believe another kiss is in order."

She displayed a jaunty smile. "Is it?"

"Absolutely." His husky voice betrayed his affection. His lips moved closer, and he kissed her long and thoroughly.

"Remember, our generous Lord will give each of us another day," Julian interrupted.

As the couples picked up their steps to stay with the crowd, Julian joked with David about whether the archery game was fixed, especially when Ashley recapped the vendor's announcement that David had six tries.

David tucked Ashley's fingers in the crook of his arm. "I made a bulls-eye on my last shot."

She flicked a glance at her right hand. "If you had hit the stump all six times, you would've won me a cuddly black bear."

"Which do you prefer? The ring or the bear?"

"The ring."

Her expressive eyes shone with a love he recognized because he felt it, too. The exhilarating promise of a future together beckoned. Ashley was faultless in every sense—goodness, generosity, and a devout faith he felt growing inside himself. A warmth of happiness flowed through him.

The foursome made their way into the arena. In seconds, the space was split with thunderous applause as a juggler appeared near the tent opening.

"It's a shame Ashley is leaving on Saturday." Nora started for a row of empty seats. "Luckily, Greenwood isn't that far away. A little less than two hours, right?"

David grasped Ashley's hand to help her climb the metal steps. "You live in Greenwood?"

She looked at him as if he were unjustly vilifying her. "Yes. Why?"

"We've seen each all week, and I never asked where you lived." His mind raced. "I'm familiar with the town. Do you know a woman named Nancy Trainor? She owns an art gallery there."

"My art studio is connected to her gallery, along with a café."

He stilled. Thoughts came rushing at him, too numerous to comprehend.

Ashley had looked familiar the first day they'd met at his cabin.

As the jousting commenced, the knights paraded out of the tent waving red and blue flags, their magnificent, broad-chested horses flaunting a bard, a glitzy cloth that displayed the knight's emblem. They were introduced and presented to the audience amidst good-natured cheers and boos. A drum roll began, and demonstrations of the knights' skills on horseback ensued as they knocked over progressively smaller targets with their wooden lances.

The announcer lauded unbridled participation, which prompted Julian and Nora to stand and clap. The crowd dissolved in laughter as a jester appeared and cartwheeled across the ground.

David became increasingly aware of the beautiful woman seated next to him, her posture rigid. She didn't stand. She didn't clap. She didn't move. The diamond captured the sun's rays and gleamed.

"Points are awarded for broken lances." Julian pointed to a knight standing by his horse. "No points awarded for broken shields."

What about a broken heart? Any points awarded for that?

Julian and Nora seemed completely unaware of David's

rising tension or Ashley's silence. The rallying roar increased as the knights charged and battled.

For the next fifteen minutes, Nora kept up an animated conversation with Ashley, while Ashley responded in mono-syllables.

David carefully considered Ashley's lovely profile. The beaded cross swayed when she shifted.

And during that time, he pondered.

Finally, it dawned on him. She knew he couldn't see out of his right eye and had purposefully moved to his left. In fact, she always did that.

In addition, whenever she rode in his truck, she always sat up straight and turned toward him when she spoke.

She was empathetic and cared about him. She was considerate, often reassuring and loving. *Yes, loving.*

Or so he imagined.

As the jousting continued, his speculations took him further, his recollections in turmoil.

When she'd shown up at his cabin, on a road with no outlet, she'd claimed her convertible had broken down. Once she stepped inside, she spent several minutes fawning over his canvas.

Her friend Sarah had come to the rescue and "fixed" her car.

On another day, Ashley had gifted him with a basket of peaches she'd placed in his cabin, admitting she'd snooped inside. Then she'd appeared at his favorite spot where he painted.

All these coincidences? Maybe. Maybe not.

He shook his head. An idiot could've figured it out sooner. Ashley's studio was linked to the art gallery carrying his paintings, which was the reason why she'd looked so familiar. When he'd visited Nancy several months ago to drop off a painting, he'd glimpsed Ashley on the floor of her studio with a student. She'd smiled and waved.

Nancy must have sent Ashley to Cherish to figure out why he hadn't responded to her messages.

He'd trusted that meeting Ashley in Cherish was circumstantial. Fate. In actuality, it had been planned and calculated. She'd come to Cherish to spy on him.

But why?

He gave a short, bitter laugh, and Ashley glanced at him. He looked away.

Because of money. The stream of revenue from his paintings was obviously an asset for Nancy and the other shop owners.

Ashley wasn't interested in him for himself.

With that knowledge, something inside him splintered apart.

What else had Ashley conveniently forgotten? The fact she was Nancy's spy? The fact she used him, his art, to fill her coffers? All three businesses—the gallery, the café, and Ashley's studio—relied on each other's sales to survive. Nancy had mentioned that to him when he'd commented on the businesses' adjoining doors. Customers walked from one shop to another.

He pondered all this, though, but said nothing. No matter how he tried, he couldn't focus on the match or Julian's jesting commentary.

When the joust finished after an endless sixty minutes, he curtly declined Julian's invitation to watch a glass blower, drawing the other man's piercing gaze. David used Pickle's long day with Samantha as an excuse.

After he and Ashley exchanged their costumes for street clothes, the drive to Cherish was hushed and oppressive.

Sitting in the passenger seat, Ashley tentatively asked, "Is anything wrong?"

"Wrong?" His knuckles tightened on the steering wheel.

She sat straighter. An eternity passed before he realized she was waiting for him to speak.

As they made the final turnoff, he followed the road up a hill, straight as an arrow. He pulled into a lookout point and shut off the engine.

"Ashley Madden." He stared out the window into the fog-shrouded valley. "Who are you?"

"I'm Ashley."

"We've concluded you're not a mountain climber."

"I confessed."

"And you poked around my cabin when you delivered the peaches."

"I confessed to that too."

"You're a Christian woman?"

Her gaze raised to his, glittering with tears. "I try my best."

He swallowed, tasting a heartbreaking defeat. "Maybe your best isn't good enough."

She groped for a handkerchief in her purse and dabbed at her eyes. "If you're concerned about my art studio being located in Greenwood—"

"This has nothing to do with Greenwood." Already, he felt himself separating from her. "I'm trying to deal with your deception."

"I'm not following."

"Aren't you?" A kaleidoscope of distrust emerged. "You should've been up front with me from the beginning. Told me why you landed in Cherish and what you expected to find out."

"David, I didn't intend to deceive you. It's just that you never responded to Nancy's emails and texts and—"

"Let me guess. She was worried."

Her lips trembled. "We all were."

"Worried about me? Or were you concerned about the

revenue loss if Nancy wasn't able to secure any more of my paintings? What am I to you, a dollar sign?"

"What am I to you, an excuse to procrastinate?"

"Don't be ridiculous."

A mix of distressing emotions crossed her face. "Likewise."

"You drove fifty miles to Cherish and planned on spending the weekend nosing around. How did you find me?"

"Sarah suggested I contact the state park ranger."

"She was in on this deception too."

"Yes, but—" Ashley tore her gaze from his. "The ranger gave me the name of your road. It was the easiest way to track you down."

"I assume you've reported the news of my eyesight loss to Nancy." David gathered steam to deliver his ace advantage. "Well, tell her this. I'll sell no more paintings in her gallery."

If he ever actually painted again.

Ashley didn't respond at first. Instead, she rested a hand on his arm. "I'm sorry. There were many instances when I—" Tears formed at the corner of her eyes. "I've loved every moment we're together and never wanted to spoil it."

Love. The word brought hope and sadness, snapping his self-control.

"No more of those, I assure you."

"No more of what?"

"We won't spend any more time together." He leaned his head against the seat. In the empty space between them, the distance grew wider. "I'm returning to New York."

"To paint?"

"I'm unsure of my abilities, my career." He rolled down the window. The wind carried the noise of the town below. Cherish. Once, he hoped to belong there. Not anymore.

"You're dealing with your loss the wrong way." Raggedly,

she inhaled. She still had her hand on his forearm. "Keep painting. You can overcome this, the way Sarah did when she confronted her deafness. Her life is full and happy. Rely on God's promise."

"Which is what?"

"God will walk with you through the storm."

He shrugged off her hand. He couldn't forgive deceit. He couldn't forgive God for placing an unfair hardship on him. He'd never forgiven his father. Ashley only proved what David already recognized. Few people could be trusted. Certainly not her.

His motions quick and jerky, he started the engine, rolled up the window, and switched on the air-conditioning. The truck idled. "You're attempting to convert me back to Christianity after learning my religious views?"

"I've always wanted to help you." The tension in her exquisite face gave way to pleading. "Through God's grace, my specialty is fixing problems."

"I'm not a broken car."

"So what if you have a handicap? Don't deny it. Embrace it. Never give up. You're commissioned to paint a portrait of a special church. Memorial Street Church is a building, but the real church is what happens on the inside."

"It's over Ashley." He couldn't trust his voice to say more. To consider the magnificent future he'd once envisioned for them.

"I understand." Ashley didn't falter for a beat. "Now understand this. God will always be there for you."

"What part of *church not being part of my life* don't you comprehend?"

"If there's anything I can do—"

"There isn't." He enunciated the words clearly.

"David, I'm sorry."

"We've already invested a conversation around your apologies. No need for another."

For the remainder of the drive to town, stillness reigned.

As they neared the inn, he slowed, then parked near the curb. "Go home, Ashley. Go back to Greenwood and take the art supplies I bought with you."

She raised her chin. Her face reddened. "You're joking, right? Keep your supplies." Her fingers fumbled with the chain as she unhooked the necklace. "Take this." She placed the necklace on the seat. Her hands shook as she removed the ring and flung it at him. "And don't forget this."

"Those were gifts." He ducked as the ring hit the window. "They're for you."

"I don't want them!" Her shoulders set. Her glorious eyes glittered with unshed tears. She shoved open the door before he could go around and open it.

She stomped from the truck and didn't turn around.

He watched her leave, fighting with himself, wanting to dash after her, but stopping himself from looking more like a fool than he already was. As she flew up the steps and entered the inn, his stomach sank. Somewhere inside, he knew his happiness was slipping away.

He should reach out and grab it. Take the initiative. Life is short.

No. Mission accomplished. He'd broken off their relationship.

It was for the best. They lived miles apart. Long-distance dating seldom worked.

Doubt simmered inside him as he picked up the ring and arranged the necklace with the earrings. He hesitated. He'd placed the ring on her finger. She'd pressed the ring to her cheek as if it were her most precious possession, then kissed him with unabandoned joy.

A faux diamond ring that meant so much.

He stared at the inn in silence. He needed to come to grips with his decision.

The day had held such promise. And just like that, happiness was gone.

Sighing, he briefly closed his eyes. No practical man heeded his heart first. And he was a practical man.

He debated one last time, facing the future without her in his life.

Then he shifted his truck into gear and headed for the Wilsons' home to pick up Pickle.

CHAPTER 14

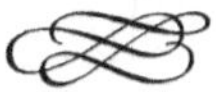

After a restless night, Ashley got out of bed, groggy from fragmentary dreams. She showered, phoned Sarah and left a voice message that she was leaving, then quickly packed her suitcase. The forecast predicted an unseasonably cool day, and she dressed in tan cotton slacks, a blue blouse, and a jeans jacket.

She descended the inn's broad staircase on rubbery legs and scanned the lobby. The pendulum clock rang out the early hour. The clink of silver coming from the solarium meant breakfast was ready to be served.

Julian stood at the reception desk and hailed her with a chipper "Greetings."

She approached with her suitcase in tow. "I'm checking out today."

He frowned. "I thought you were staying longer."

"No. I'm done here." She wiped an errant tear. "Naturally, I'm happy to pay for the extra nights I reserved."

"There are folks on a waiting list, and your room is easy to fill." As soon as he finished processing her refund, he said, "None of my business, but I assume things didn't work out with David?"

"That's a kind spin."

"You both fairly floated in and out of here. I remarked to Nora that you two have a chemistry people rarely share."

Ashley managed a wan smile. "Did we?"

"You're lucky."

"Coincidental. Circumstance." She shook her head in denial. "We had a falling out, and it was my fault. I apologized."

"Did he accept your apology?"

"Hardly." She pushed up the sleeves of her jacket. "Just the opposite."

"Hopefully you gave him something to think about."

Her face heated. *Yes, had she ever.*

On the mountainous return drive to Greenwood, Ashley blamed herself for handling things so badly. She had an explanation for David on the tip of her tongue more often than not, but in the end, she'd lacked courage. David clearly cared for her. He'd placed her on a pedestal she hadn't deserved.

"Your sincerity is disarming." He'd sealed his declaration with a kiss.

Stunned by her leaking tears, she pulled her convertible over to the side of the road. She'd been hurt before, her heart broken, but never like this.

She recalled his high-handed dismissal. David, the handsome, impossible artist with a sterling character. David, the man she'd come to love.

No. It wasn't possible to fall in love in only a few days. For a second time, she'd been charmed by a man who feigned interest. He probably had already found another woman more to his liking. Sophisticated and alluring and ravishing.

She forced herself to breathe while her heart hammered a heavy beat. There was no sense in denying her emotions. She missed his lazy smile, his wry humor.

She reached for her phone. Perhaps she could text him and apologize again. Her pride would be salvaged if he accepted her apology, even if he was coolly unenthusiastic.

Julian had offered insight into the chemistry between her and David, and she'd denied it. Sadly, her denial wasn't true.

There was interest and magic. Judging by his smiles, David had enjoyed being with her. The memory of his warm lips moving on hers, his murmurings. *"You're beautiful, Ashley."*

Her, the plainest of plain Janes.

Her heart swelled as other memories surfaced.

The first time they officially met at his cabin. Their pillow fight.

The afternoon he declared he was painting *her*, and how she imagined their laughter could be heard for miles.

He cared deeply, which was why he was so hurt by her deception. He'd assumed she cared for him, and then concluded she was after his money.

She slumped in her seat. If he only realized how much she *did* care.

However, he was gone now. Gone forever.

A lump of sadness swelled in her throat, but she vowed not to cry anymore. Unwanted tears trickled, and she brushed them away.

"Show me the way, Lord." She closed her eyes and prayed. "I'm your daughter. You are my friend. I'm sorry for hurting David. I can't control the guilt welling up inside me because of my wrongdoing. I'll rely on your healing grace."

She switched on the ignition and turned the radio to a contemporary Christian station. This drive would mark her last trip from Cherish.

A DAY LATER, in response to Nancy's queries, Ashley explained David's eyesight loss.

"Will he continue to paint?" Worried shadows under-scored Nancy's brown eyes when she'd swept into Ashley's studio and claimed the nearest chair. "I—we, all three of our businesses, need his pieces to survive."

"He refused. I pray he will concentrate on healing and taking care of himself."

Nancy took an overlong time, adjusting her flowing bohemian skirt. "Are you suggesting he can't paint?"

"He *won't* paint, at least not to sell any pieces in your gallery."

Ashley turned to the sound of commotion. Two children in wheelchairs argued over the same brush. She lifted one of the children's wrists, then the other, and clapped their hands together simultaneously. Once they giggled, she encouraged their friendship and asked them to share. Then she swiveled to Nancy.

"Honestly, David can see. For him, it's a struggle to accept his disability."

Nancy stood, staring critically at Ashley. "You look terri-ble, by the way."

Ashley was fully aware her complexion was pale, and that lines of sadness marked her mouth. Wryly, she replied, "Thanks."

"When you extended your stay in Cherish, I assumed you were having a blast."

"Cherish has a storybook quality, and the residents are right-minded and decent." Unwilling to show her regret and heartbreak, Ashley pleaded busyness and excused herself to tend to a curly-haired girl who demanded attention. "I'm grateful to be back."

"My relationships never go over three months," David had told her.

He'd certainly succeeded this time.

THE NEXT MONTH drifted by in a haze of desolation. Ashley continuously checked her phone, hoping to hear from David. Perhaps a text.

Nothing.

Too many times every day, she attempted to shake off the heartbreaking memories that haunted her.

David playing fetch with his dog.

David absorbed in taking photographs of a tree, of a river. David photographing her.

She immersed herself in teaching her precious pupils. When a David Fodero painting was alluded to during a meeting with students and their parents, Ashley couldn't respond. Hiding her face from her students' puzzled glances, she rushed from the studio and into Nancy's gallery, tears streaming down her cheeks.

"What happened?" Nancy grasped Ashley's cold hands.

"David and I were together every day. He was wonderful."

Nancy's fingers tightened. "Will you please tell me more?"

Ashley bent her head. "I deceived him, although it wasn't intentional. I was a coward and never explained my reason for being in Cherish. When he discovered my deception, he was angry."

"You're not deceitful, Ashley. Praying helps. God's got this."

Ashley stared at the blank wall where Nancy had repeatedly hung David's paintings. Once again, she was alone. Once again, she relied on herself and her faith in God.

WHEN THE CALENDAR neared the end of July, Nancy casually mentioned that David had moved back to his penthouse in Manhattan. He'd phoned to inform her he was selling his cabin, and felt he owed her some explanation for his whereabouts because they were old friends.

"If anyone wants to buy the cabin, direct them to my agent in New York," he'd instructed.

Ashley had been thanking a sturdy five-year-old who'd offered her a puffy white hydrangea flower.

Her head jerked up when Nancy relayed the news. She rubbed her palms on her plaid shorts and turned to the half-dozen children staring at her.

"What fun we're going to have today," she declared. "Has anyone ever painted a picture of a tree?"

Smiling at the children's eager, enthusiastic faces, she threw herself into their paint splattering and chortles, giving scrupulous attention to each and every brushstroke.

ON THE FIRST Saturday of August, David stood in the living room of his Manhattan apartment, scrutinizing the painting perched on his easel. He'd painted Ashley, sitting at the top of an oak tree, surrounded by wildflowers—fiery pinks, cardinal reds, and gray-purple violets.

His depiction of her was delicate, resembling a fairy—mischievous and kind, the size of a thumb. He'd captured her profile—small turned-up nose and rounded chin. The luxuriant mass of honey-blond hair, the full pink lips, the cream-colored complexion. He'd harbored the hope she'd someday see it.

Torn between his internal critic and the lovely portrait, he gave a grim laugh. He only needed to make a few additions beginning with a river … somewhere.

He'd arrived in Manhattan, believing the anonymity of the city would ease the sadness in his gut. He'd painted for hours with an uncontained fervor. Now he stood back and assessed the painting he'd begun in Cherish.

"What's your opinion, Pickle?" He observed his dog snoring by the window. "Ashley is beautiful, isn't she?"

Yes, she was. Only he hadn't captured her genuine beauty, the kindness radiating from her heart.

He stayed where he was, lost in thought.

When he'd retreated to his cabin the day of the Renaissance Faire, he'd devoted himself to his work for weeks. In all that time, he'd produced a few lithographs and sketches, and nearly completed the commissioned painting of Memorial Street Church.

He had never missed a deadline, and the painting was scheduled to be delivered to Marge Addyson by the final week in August. He'd left it in Cherish, assuming he'd add final touches when he returned to pack the last of his boxes.

He'd decided on a two-sided art, two renderings, past and present, of the same church. He'd sketched the older version in charcoal, as he'd mentioned to Ashley. He'd enhanced the painting of the present-day church with a sparkly purple star in the corner and his initials, *D.F.*

Beneath was one letter.

A.

The letter and the star were minuscule.

He hadn't been able to help himself. His dreams were of her. Always of her.

The expansive window of his penthouse faced Central

Park, and rain pounded on the glass. It had rained constantly. Incessant and never-ending, and he'd come to realize he vastly preferred sunshine.

He stared out at the relentless raindrops, the wet pavement far below, pedestrians walking swiftly and carrying umbrellas.

He caught his reflection. His forehead creased with fatigue, and he averted his gaze. He couldn't look at himself anymore. Self-doubt had become his foremost companion.

He sank down on the enormous leather sofa and placed his head in his hands. He hadn't trusted his father after learning of his unfaithfulness. He'd never forgiven him.

David opened the Bible he'd purchased when he'd landed in New York. He leafed to Psalms, reflecting on the passage about God's grace and forgiveness. His mercy was great.

He turned the Bible over, running his thumb along the edges of the sacred book.

David longed to put the past behind him and proceed. But how could he do that when his hopes had abandoned him? Or rather, he'd abandoned his dreams. If people realized his backstory, they'd sympathize. He'd never had any prior health problems. Why an eyesight loss?

Rewind. Remember the exhilarating days with Ashley. The happiest moments of his life had been the hours spent with her.

He'd convinced himself she'd played him for a fool. But hadn't she declared her love for him? Not outright, but in numerous instances.

He straddled two conflicting visions of his future. Him alone in his Manhattan studio, endless months painting in solitude. Or days in Cherish, accompanied by the gorgeous Ashley Madden. Her fresh scent of lemon and sage, wholesome and uplifting, so different from the expensive perfumes of the women he'd escorted to fancy parties.

He could still feel Ashley in his arms, her hand touching his heart. Her gaze had darkened with empathy when he talked about his father.

And there were other times. Pleasurable, joyous times.

Ashley, sitting in a tree:

"I'm an adult, but it doesn't mean I should give up everything I loved to do when I was young," she'd said. *"The view is different up here. Better."*

Better.

Ashley peering in his freezer.

"What kind of guy doesn't eat Hungry-Man dinners?"

Ashley jostling the vending machine:

"Grand idea," she'd said as she inserted his quarters. *"Sadly, it isn't working."*

She was right. Being apart wasn't the answer. He'd presumed self-worth came from his paintings, not himself. That his job defined his existence. The hardest lesson was facing his weakness. But weakness could be turned into strength.

He could paint. He could overcome his impairment by refusing to fixate on it. Instead, he could apply his efforts to helping others and truly appreciate the positive.

With Ashley.

Reach out. It was worth it.

They deserved to be happy.

He recalled the sermon he'd related to her, the sermon he'd heard as a child:

"The blessing ahead of you is bigger than any battle you left behind," the aged pastor had proclaimed.

Those words were appropriate for yesterday and today. David sent a belated acknowledgement to his long-ago pastor, and to his mother for dragging him to church.

"Lord, you must have a plan for me," he prayed. "Ashley

provided inspirational messages every time we were together, and I'm ready to connect the dots."

He came to his feet, his mind made up.

"I'm glad you're a top-notch passenger, Pickle." He scooped up his dog, already deciding to charter a plane to Atlanta, then a car to Cherish. "We're heading back to my cabin tomorrow. You'll sleep in the carry-on. Just think, you might soon get another belly rub from a certain beautiful woman you'll recognize."

David yanked out his phone, then paused. He tried to avoid thinking about his next obstacle, but here it was.

He didn't have the slightest inkling if Ashley would even speak to him. In all these weeks, he hadn't contacted her, hoping she'd contact him.

She hadn't. He hadn't. Two stubborn individuals.

All he knew was that he loved her, and he knew in his heart she loved him.

He wasn't certain of the reaction he'd receive or if she'd agree to his plan.

Never give up.

He was eager to see her. Eager to make things right.

He plugged in the number for an esteemed Manhattan jeweler and requested an early morning appointment. The business didn't open until ten, but for the exorbitant price David was willing to pay, he was confident the jeweler would meet him earlier.

"Tomorrow," David said to Pickle as he set him down in his doggie bed. "We're going home."

Action is the foundational key to all success.
- Picasso

"David Fodero." Nancy Trainor's eyes narrowed as David strode into the Greenwood art gallery carrying an art portfolio case. "I never expected to see you again."

He grinned. "Yet here I am."

"Is that a painting for my gallery?" She zeroed in on the case, and the withering look on her face died. "Can I sell whatever is in there?"

"Sorry." He broke off, nodding casually to the art patrons. "It's not for sale."

People gasped and discreetly gestured toward him. A noticeable silence ensued.

He heard his name whispered but didn't turn. Instead, he quickened his steps and followed the sounds of giggling children behind an adjoining closed door.

He spotted Ashley sitting cross-legged on her studio floor before the door fully shut. She wore a pair of jean shorts and a fitted purple T-shirt. Her hair was secured in a high ponytail.

The room was tidy, and white canvases lay in a pile, along with paper towels. A dizzying array of artwork hung on the wall. A handwashing station was tucked in one corner, and the smell of acrylic paint filled the air.

Surrounded by a group of children wearing imaginative orange smocks, she smiled at a slim little boy dipping his brush in a jar of water.

"Freddie, try to concentrate." Ashley snatched a clean brush from a metal bucket. "Trees aren't hard to draw."

David stepped nearer. His heart hammered in hope, in anticipation.

"Because anyone can paint a tree," he said softly.

Two boys in wheelchairs looked up at him and gaped.

Ashley jumped to her feet. Her fine, pale eyebrows drew together. Her hand touched her throat. "David?"

"Hey, I recognize you." One of the boys wheeled his chair protectively in front of Ashley. His thin shoulders squared. "You're the artist guy Miss Ashley cried about when my mother mentioned your name a few weeks ago."

"I'm here to tell her I'm sorry." David set down the case. His gaze remained on Ashley. Her face lost all color as she continued to stare at him. "I hope she'll forgive me for being a fool."

Tears poured down her cheeks as she picked her way between the children and flew into David's outstretched arms.

"She's crying again," the second boy in a wheelchair remarked accusingly.

"I'm fine." Ashley's shoulders shook with sobbing. "I'm crying tears of joy."

David framed her face and wiped her cheeks with his thumbs. He sheltered her from the children's gazes. "I missed you. I came to tell you I love you."

She slid her hands around his neck. "I love you too."

"Okay, you two." Nancy stepped into the room, unsuccessfully hiding her amusement behind a mask of genteel professionalism. She looked at the children. "Miss Ashley has a substitute teacher filling in for her."

"Who?" The boys chimed.

"Me."

David smiled his appreciation at the keenly perceptive Nancy. She diverted the children by debating color combinations and an abbreviated embellishment of the tree the one boy had begun to paint.

David steered Ashley to a secluded corner. "I couldn't stay away." He kissed her forehead, his fingers drifting up and down her spine. "Please forgive me."

"I'm the one who needs forgiving."

"No." He shook his head, his laugh bitter. "I focused on myself, my pride. In so doing, I overlooked what's most important."

"David, don't feel guilty."

"I have several reasons for being here, but guilt isn't primary."

"What is then?"

"I want to have sons and daughters with hazel eyes and a tender, giving heart. I want to give you my name and all that I have."

She bit back a smile.

He withdrew a jewelry case from his pocket and handed it to her. "Ashley Madden, will you marry me?"

Elation shimmered in her eyes as she opened the case. The ring was larger than the imitation ring he'd won at the Renaissance Faire. This diamond was four carats and exquisitely cut, reflecting the natural light of the sunshine streaming through the window.

"Yes. I'll marry you." Her gaze radiated with love. "Meeting you was a gift from God."

He had hoped she'd recognized the extraordinary hand of fate that had led them to each other. There were no coincidences. He'd met an angel who believed in him and loved him.

He slipped the ring onto the fourth finger of her left hand and kissed her palm. "We're officially engaged."

"You are?" Nancy peered up from the center of a circle surrounded by children. "I didn't mean to eavesdrop but—"

"What's that?" The slight boy named Freddie examined David's carry case. "Aren't you going to show us what's inside?" Freddie inched nearer as the other children gathered round.

"It's a special painting." David reached for Ashley's hand. Her smile radiated with love, and he was certain he'd gotten his first glimpse of heaven.

From the second she'd accepted his hand; he'd recognized the special bond between them. Carefully, because he didn't want to break their connection, he continued, "The decision is totally up to Miss Ashley."

"Why, Mr. Fodero? It's not her painting." Freddie waited for the other children to join him and echo his opinion. "The painting is yours."

"I painted the canvas, but the subject is essential." David focused on Ashley.

She smiled. "Go ahead."

"Yay!" For several seconds, the room filled with laughter from seven children and Nancy, all sharing a collective goal: discovering what was inside David's carrying case.

He pulled the canvas from the case amidst a variety of oohs and ahhs.

"That's Miss Ashley!" Freddie pointed to a whimsical woman sitting in an oak tree. "She's so pretty. Why is she up there?"

"She likes to climb trees," David replied.

Flowers of every color and type surrounded her—gold, silver, and dots of colorful wildflowers. Pickle snoozed beside the tree.

Ashley turned to him. "Where is Pickle today?"

"I left him with Samantha Wilson. When I arrived from New York, I rented a jeep, and drove several treacherous curves on the road connecting Greenwood to Cherish."

She laughed. "The route is challenging."

"Fortunately, it isn't as difficult as climbing Grandfather Mountain."

She took a step back. "Have you ever climbed—?

"Never."

"David, you titled your work," Nancy interrupted, examining the words written at the top of the painting.

Freddie tugged at the bell-shaped sleeve of Nancy's blouse. "What does it say?"

"Mr. Fordero's initials, the letter A, and a sparkly purple star. The painting is titled *My Wife by the River*. My *wife*." Nancy's thick black eyebrows lifted in surprise, though she quickly recovered her diplomatic self. "Congratulations. You took a chance, there, David, didn't you?"

"I prayed."

"Your painting is superb."

"Thank you." He considered the words he'd wanted to write on the canvas.

My dearest Ashley. I vow to fill our days with faith and laughter. Please love me as much as I love you.

He feasted his eyes on her exquisite face. She had the ability to enchant and charm him. "Do you like it, Twinkle?"

"I can't trust my voice." The love in her fathomless hazel

eyes warmed his heart. "Thankfully, you attached my nose to my face."

He laughed. "Where else would I put it?"

"On the tree, on a cloud, floating somewhere in the sky."

"Mr. Fodero?" Freddie was scrutinizing the painting.

"Hmm?"

"Where's the river?"

Stunned, David sobered. "Can't you find it?"

"No." Freddie, along with Nancy and Ashley, murmured agreement.

"Mr. Fodero?"

David shifted. "Yes, Freddie?"

"What's the pointy gold thing growing out of the grass?"

Unable to suppress his amusement, David pulled Ashley nearer and kissed her hair. "Miss Ashley's cowlick."

EPILOGUE

ne Year Later

"ASHLEY, we won't be able to do much more of this." David gazed at his beautiful wife, precariously balanced on a tree branch beside him.

"Why not?" Ashley popped a frozen chocolate cookie into her mouth and chewed. "The obstetrician advised sweets in moderation and claimed they're safe for the baby."

"I'm not referring to cookies." He gazed out at the lawn, the garden overflowing with zucchini. *What would they do with all that zucchini? Was there such a thing as zucchini bread?* "I'm discussing your penchant for climbing trees and dragging me up here alongside you."

"You won't let me climb alone anymore."

He patted her stomach. "With excellent reason, considering you're two months pregnant."

"Thank you for getting over your fear of tree climbing."

He chuckled. "I didn't have a choice. My heart was in my throat at the thought of you climbing up here alone."

She planted a sweet kiss on his lips, immediately appeasing him.

From below, Pickle romped across the lawn carrying a Frisbee, Ashley's mixed breed chihuahua racing at his heels. She'd adopted the five-pound dog with solid red fur and an angelic face from an animal rescue center in Greenwood, before relocating to Cherish. David affectionately named the puppy Dogzilla because of his feisty personality.

"Next month when I see the doctor, we should be able to hear the baby's heartbeat."

"I can't wait," he said in a husky voice he hardly recognized. "Together, my beautiful wife, we are complete."

He sipped his energy drink, then balanced it gingerly on a tray secured to a sturdy branch. He was trying to quit caffeine altogether and had weaned himself down to only one drink per day, which he savored.

He gazed at the Just Married sign they'd attached to his pickup a year earlier, for they'd gotten married not long after their engagement. He didn't own a vintage turquoise convertible. Instead, he'd opted for the sign embossed in bold turquoise letters. The sign now hung as a banner draped over the railing of his front porch. A reminder of a wonderful life, an exquisite marriage.

He'd wanted to give Ashley a lavish wedding in New York City with hundreds of guests, an orchestra providing entertainment, and a honeymoon in the Caribbean. She'd declined, requesting an intimate wedding and a quiet cabin in the Carolina mountains.

Two nights before their wedding, he'd sensed something was on her mind.

"I have one special request," she said, her smile dazzling.

She'd been typing last-minute notes on her laptop, and he adored her for handling all the pressure she'd been under so well—planning their wedding, moving to Cherish, and delivering a tearful goodbye to her students with a vow to visit often. Nancy had graciously offered to teach several classes, and Ashley's substitute teachers became full-time employees.

Before he had time to respond to her, a knock sounded on his cabin door. He opened it and stared at his two older brothers and his sister, Quinn. Ashley disappeared out the back door with Pickle and Dogzilla.

"Thanks for the piano books," Quinn began.

He hadn't heard from her since he'd sent the books, but Ashley had taught him about God's love and forgiveness. His doubts could die so that his faith could live.

"And congratulations on your wedding, David."

He shook hands with his brothers, embraced his sister, and invited them inside.

He hadn't imagined a way to forgive, especially when his eyesight loss still hung heavy on his mind. Ashley kept assuring him the hand of God was on his life.

On a sultry day at the end of August, he'd entered Memorial Street Church and presented Marge Addyson with the commissioned painting. Ashley had stood by his side. The first Sunday he'd attended church in over two decades, he had sung praises along to an amazing selection of worship music.

He had held Ashley's hand as they slid into a front pew and was encouraged by an inspiring sermon. All the while, he remembered her words: *Memorial Street Church is a building, but the real church is what happens on the inside.*

Since their engagement, and then marriage, he'd worked on a new collection of six avant-garde paintings, each with a theme centering on stars. The collection was scheduled to be exhibited at an exclusive auction house in New York. His return to the art world after nearly a year's absence assured widespread publicity and demand.

For now, he enveloped his wife in his arms.

"Thank you, David, for buying that empty lot in town," she said.

"It's not empty anymore. The art studio should be finished within the month."

"Special needs children and adults can enjoy the facilities." She smiled. "I love the name Starlight Vision."

He buried his face in her fragrant, lemon-scented hair. "Art should be nurtured. Creative expression and all that."

She laughed. "Typical artist."

"I hope every student, no matter their disability, will express themselves freely." He slid a hand around her waist, drawing her close. He kissed her stomach. "A miracle to cherish."

"Any plans after your art collection is sold?"

"I might consider purchasing a television for my study."

"You? The minimalist?" She didn't seem the least bit deceived by his nonchalance. "What will you watch? Another documentary?"

In between nuzzles, he murmured, "I'll begin with a certain black and white sitcom."

She began whistling the theme from *The Andy Griffith show*.

From high in a treetop, near a lushly designed cabin set in the woods, laughter rang out.

Pickle and Dogzilla barked and played tug-of-war with a plush striped elephant beneath a large oak tree.

Frozen cookies were left to thaw.

And all was right in a summer to cherish.

THE END

RECIPE FOR MELISSA'S SWEET & SOUR MEATBALLS

Ingredients:

1 lb ground beef

1 lb ground sausage

Spices such as pepper, salt, garlic powder, onion powder (whatever spices you enjoy in your meatballs)

1 bottle of chili sauce

1 large jar of orange marmalade

Directions:

Mix ground beef, sausage, and spices to taste. Form small meatballs, a little larger than a marble. Fry or bake meatballs until almost cooked through. Set aside and drain.

In a Crock-Pot or large saucepan, mix the bottle of chili sauce and jar of marmalade. Over medium heat on the stove or high heat in the Crock-Pot, let the chili sauce and marmalade melt together. Once mixed, lower the heat and add the meatballs.

Mix the meatballs into the sauce. Allow to simmer for about 30 minutes. Lower the heat to keep warm.

Serve with toothpicks for guests to pick them up.

Or serve with rice or on a bun if wanting more of a dinner item.

Enjoy!

A NOTE FROM JOSIE

Dear Reader,

Thank you for reading my sweet inspirational romance, A Summer To Cherish. I hope you enjoyed this heart-warming story, featuring Ashley and David. This is the sixth book in my contemporary "Cherish" series.

Faith is fragile. Faith takes time. And the best solutions are always painted with love.

This story is set in the charming fictional small town of Cherish. Here, I introduce two new characters to our beloved mix of familiar heroes and heroines. I loved writing the spunky, fun heroine, and David was a swoon-worthy hero.

I also researched the hero's profession—painting—and his heartbreaking eyesight loss.

If you loved this story as much as I loved writing it, please help other people find it by posting your review.

A Summer To Cherish is available in ebook, paperback, Large Print paperback, audiobook, and Hardcover.

I'd love to meet you in person someday, but in the meantime, all I can offer is a sincere and grateful thank you. Without your support, my books would not be possible.

As I write my next sweet or inspirational romance, remember this: Have you ever tried something you were afraid to try because it mattered so much to you? I did, when I started writing. Take the chance, and just do something you love.

Josie Riviera

Love music?

My Spotify List for A Summer To Cherish is here.

ABOUT THE AUTHOR

Josie Riviera is a *USA TODAY* bestselling author of contemporary, inspirational, and historical sweet romances that read like Hallmark movies. She lives in the Charlotte, NC, area with her wonderfully supportive husband. They share their home with an adorable shih tzu, who constantly needs grooming, and live in an old house forever needing renovations.

Become a member of my Read and Review VIP Facebook group for exclusive giveaways and ARCs.

To connect with Josie, visit her webpage and subscribe to her newsletter. As a thank-you, she'll send you a free sweet romance novella directly to your inbox.

Seeking Patience

Seeking Catherine (always Free!)

Seeking Fortune

Seeking Charity

Seeking Rachel

The Seeking Series

Oh Danny Boy

I Love You More

A Snowy White Christmas

A Portuguese Christmas

Holiday Hearts Book Bundle Volume One

Holiday Hearts Book Bundle Volume Two

Holiday Hearts Book Bundle Volume Three

Holiday Hearts Book Bundle Volume Four

Candleglow and Mistletoe

Maeve (Perfect Match)

A Christmas To Cherish

A Love Song To Cherish

A Valentine To Cherish

A Christmas Puppy To Cherish

A Homecoming To Cherish

Romance Stories To Cherish

Aloha to Love

Sweet Peppermint Kisses

Valentine Hearts Boxed Set

1-800-CUPID

1-800-CHRISTMAS

1-800-IRELAND

1-800-SUMMER

1-800-NEW YEAR

The 1-800-Series Sweet Contemporary Romance Bundle

Irish Hearts Sweet Romance Bundle

Holly's Gift

A Chocolate-Box Valentine

A Chocolate-Box Christmas

A Chocolate-Box New Years

A Chocolate-Box Summer Breeze

A Chocolate-Box Christmas Wish

A Chocolate-Box Irish Wedding

Chocolate-Box Hearts

Chocolate-Box Hearts Volume Two

Chocolate-Box Double Hearts

Recipes from the Heart

Leading Hearts

New Year Hearts

SENIOR HEARTS

A Summer To Cherish

Summer Hearts

Romance Stories To Cherish Volume Two

Cherished Hearts

Christmas in the Air

A Very Christian Christmas

Most books are available in ebook, audiobook, paperback, Large Print paperback and Hardcover.

Many are FREE on Kindle Unlimited!

www.ingramcontent.com/pod-product-compliance
Lightning Source LLC
Chambersburg PA
CBHW022013120726
47902CB00012B/7